THE WHITES

This Large Print Book carries the
Seal of Approval of N.A.V.H.

THE WHITES

RICHARD PRICE WRITING AS
HARRY BRANDT

THORNDIKE PRESS

A part of Gale, Cengage Learning

GALE
CENGAGE Learning·

Farmington Hills, Mich • San Francisco • New York • Waterville, Maine
Meriden, Conn • Mason, Ohio • Chicago

GALE
CENGAGE Learning·

LIBRARY OF CONGRESS CATALOGING-IN-PUBLICATION DATA

Brandt, Harry, 1949–
    The whites / by Richard Price (writing as Harry Brandt). — Large print edition.
        pages cm. — (Thorndike Press large print reviewers' choice)
    ISBN 978-1-4104-7968-6 (hardcover) — ISBN 1-4104-7968-4 (hardcover)
    1. Large type books. I. Title.
PS3566.R544W48 2015b
813'.54—dc23   2015004953

Published in 2015 by arrangement with Henry Holt and Company, LLC

Printed in Mexico
1 2 3 4 5 6 7 19 18 17 16 15

To my astonishing wife,
Lorraine Adams
On my block we still play . . .
On my block we still pray . . .

To my sublime daughters,
Annie and Genevieve

To my mother, Harriet, and
my brother, Randolph Scott

To the memory of Carl Brandt
(1935–2013)

And to the memory of my father,
Milton Price (1924–2008)

Who ever thought they
would not hear the dead?
Who ever thought that
they could quarantine
Those who are not,
who once had been?
— Stephan Edgar, "Nocturnal"

Death investigation constitutes a heavy responsibility, and as such, let no person deter you from the truth and your own personal commitment to see that justice is done. Not only for the deceased, but for the surviving family as well.
— Vernon Geberth,
Practical Homicide Investigation
(fourth edition)

CHAPTER 1

As Billy Graves drove down Second Avenue to work, the crowds worried him: a quarter past one in the morning and there were still far more people piling into the bars than leaving them, everyone coming and going having to muscle their way through the swaying clumps of half-hammered smokers standing directly outside the entrances. He hated the no smoking laws. They created nothing but problems — late-night noise for the neighbors, elbow room enough for the bar-cramped beefers to finally start swinging, and a plague of off-duty limos and radio cabs all tapping their horns to hustle fares.

It was the night of St. Patrick's, worst of the year for NYPD's Night Watch, the handful of detectives under Billy's command responsible for covering all of felony-weight Manhattan from Washington Heights to Wall Street between one a.m. and eight

9

a.m., when there were no active squads in any of the local precincts. There were other worst nights, Halloween and New Year's Eve for two, but St. Patrick's was the ugliest, the violence the most spontaneous and low-tech. Stompings, blunt objects, fists — more stitches than surgeries but some very malicious acting out.

One-fifteen in the a.m.: tonight, as always, the calls could come in at any time, but experience had taught him that the most fraught hours, especially on a drinking holiday, were between three a.m., when the bars and clubs started shutting down, everyone pouring out into the streets at once, and five a.m., when even the most hard-core animals were out of fuel and lurching off to oblivion. On the other hand, the city being the city, Billy never knew exactly when he'd see his pillow again. Eight a.m. could find him at a local precinct writing up bullets on an agg assault for the incoming day squad while the actor was either still in the wind or snoring in a holding cell; it could find him hanging around the ER at Harlem Hospital or Beth Israel or St. Luke's–Roosevelt interviewing family and/or witnesses while waiting for the victim to either go out of the picture or pull through; it could find him strolling around

10

an outdoor crime scene, hands in pockets, toe-searching through detritus for shell casings; or, or, or, if the Prince of Peace was afoot and Yonkers-bound traffic was light, he could actually be home in time to take his kids to school.

There were gung ho detectives out there, even on the lobster shift, but Billy was not one of them. Mainly he hoped each night that most of Manhattan's nocturnal mayhem was not worthy of his squad's attention, just petty shit that could be kicked back to patrol.

"Seoul man, how you be," he drawled, stepping into the 24/7 Korean's across Third Avenue from the office. Joon, the night clerk with his gaffer-taped horn-rims, automatically began gathering up his regular customer's nightly ration: three sixteen-ounce Rockstar energy drinks, two Shaolin power gel squibs, and a pack of Camel Lights.

Billy cracked a can of Go before it could be bagged.

"Too much of that shit make you even more tired," the Korean delivering his standard lecture. "Like a boomerang."

"No doubt."

As he reached for his Visa card, the security monitor next to the register caught Billy in all his glory: football burly but slump-shouldered, his pale face with its exhaustion-starred eyes topped with half a pitchfork's worth of prematurely graying hair. He was only forty-two, but that crushed-cellophane gaze of his combined with a world-class insomniac's posture had once gotten him into a movie at a senior citizen's discount. Man was not meant to start work after midnight — end of story, pay differential be damned.

The Night Watch office, on the second floor of the Fifteenth Precinct and time-shared with Manhattan South Homicide, which occupied it during the day, looked like a cross between a fun house and a morgue. It was a drear, fluorescently lit scrum of gun-metal-gray desks, separated by plastic partitions brightened with auto-graphed eight-by-tens of Derek Jeter, Samuel L. Jackson, Rex Ryan, and Harvey Keitel, along with mug shots, family snaps, and garish crime scene photos. An eight-foot glass tank filled with miniature sharklike catfish dominated one cinder-block wall, an embassy-sized American flag fronting the other.

None of his regular squad were in: Emmett Butter, a part-time actor, so fresh to the unit that Billy had yet to allow him to spearhead a run; Gene Feeley, who, back in the late '80s, was part of the team that broke up the Fat Cat Nichols crack empire, had thirty-two years on the Job, owned two bars in Queens, and was just there to max out his pension; Alice Stupak, who worked nights in order to be with her family during the day; and Roger Mayo, who worked nights in order to avoid being with his family during the day.

It wasn't unusual for the room to be deserted thirty minutes into the tour, given that Billy didn't care where his detectives spent the shift as long as they answered their phones when he needed them. He didn't see the point of making everyone sit at their desks all night like they were in detention. But in exchange for this freedom, if any one of them — with the exception of Feeley, who was so old-boy-wired into One PP that he could do or not do anything he wanted — if any one of them failed to pick up when he called, even once, they were gone from the squad, dead batteries, toilet drops, drop kicks, theft, Armageddon, the Rapture, or no.

Depositing the grocery bag in his minute windowless office, Billy walked out of the squad room and down a short hall to the dispatcher's desk, manned by Rollie Towers, a.k.a. the Wheel, a big Buddha boy in track pants and a John Jay college sweatshirt, ass ballooning off either side of his webbed Aeron chair as he fielded the incoming calls, taking all requests for Night Watch from the various crime sites and fending them off like a goalie.

"Well look, Sarge, my boss isn't in yet," Rollie nodding to Billy, "but my guess is here's what he's going to say. Nobody got hurt, guy can't even say for sure it was a gun. I'd just throw a good interview at him, wait for the Fifth Squad to come in tomorrow morning, see if it fits any kind of pattern they're working, all right? There's really not that much for us to do on this one. No problem . . . no problem . . . no problem."

Hanging up and swiveling to Billy: "No problem."

"Anything happening?" Billy reached for one of Rollie's Doritos, then changed his mind.

"Throwdown in the Three-two, both shooters female, one on the sidewalk, the other in the rear seat of a ghetto cab. They're like maybe a couple yards apart, six shots fired back and forth and get this: neither of them gets hit. How's that for sharpshootin'?"

"Was the cab moving?"

14

"It started out, one of the broads was chasing the other through the Eisenhowers, she jumps in the car, screams for the driver to haul ass, but the minute he sees the guns he jumps out and starts hoofing it back to Senegal, probably halfway there as we speak."

"Feets do yo' stuff."

"Butter and Mayo are up at the Three-two watching Annie Oakley and Calamity Jane sleep it off."

"And the driver? For real."

"They found him eight blocks away trying to climb a tree. They took him in for an interview, but he only speaks Wolof and French, so they're waiting on a translator."

"Anything else?"

"No sir."

"And who do I got." Billy dreaded the voluntary sign-ups, the ever-changing collection of overtime-hungry day-tour detectives who nightly padded out his paltry crew, the majority of them no good for anything after two a.m.

"There's three, supposedly, but one guy's kid got sick, another was last seen at a retirement racket down in the Ninth, so maybe you should find out if he's in any shape to come in at all, and you better check out what Central Park sent us."

15

"He's in? I didn't see anybody."

"Check under the rug."

Back in the squad room, the sign-up, Theodore Moretti, was hiding in plain sight, hunched over, elbows on knees, at the desk farthest from the door.

"I'm in the air," he hissed into his cell, "you're breathing me in right now, Jesse. I'm all around you . . ."

Short and squat, Moretti had straight black hair parted precisely down the middle of his skull and raccooned eyes that made Billy's seem limpid and tight.

"How you doing?" Billy stood over him, his hands in his pockets. But before he could introduce himself as the boss, Moretti just up and walked out of the office, coming back a moment later, still on the phone.

"You really think you can get rid of me that easy?" Moretti said to the lucky-in-love Jesse, Billy right then recognizing him for what he was and writing him off accordingly. Although money was the prime motivation for those signing up for a one-off tour with Night Watch, occasionally a detective volunteered not so much for the overtime but simply because it facilitated his stalking.

One forty-five a.m. . . . the sound of tires rolling over a side street full of shattered

16

light bulbs was like the sound of Jiffy Pop achieving climax, the aftermath of a set test between the Skrilla Hill Killaz from the Coolidge Houses and the Stack Money Goons from the Madisons, four kids sent to St. Luke's for stitches, one with a glass shard protruding from his cornea like a miniature sail. Where they got all the light bulbs was anyone's guess.

By the time Billy and Moretti stepped out of their sedan, the 2-9 Gang Unit, six young men in windbreakers and high tops, were already harvesting collars, plasti-cuffing belly-down bangers like bundling wheat. The battleground itself was lined with two layers of rubberneckers: on the sidewalk, dozens of locals, a few, despite the hour, with kids in tow; overhead, an equal number of people hanging out the windows of the exhausted-looking SROs that ran along both sides of the narrow street.

Sporting a shaved head and calf-length denim shorts like a superannuated playground bully, Eddie Lopez, the unit FIO, stepped to Billy, a dozen as yet unused plasti-cuffs running up his forearms like bangles.

"These two crews been trading smack on Facebook all week. We should have been here before they were."

17

Billy turned to Moretti. "The kids in the ER, go over with somebody from the Gang Unit, start taking interviews."

"Are you serious? They won't say shit."

"Nonetheless . . ." Billy waving him onward, thinking, One asspain down.

From the opposite end of the block, emerging out of the tree-lined darkness like a charging carnivore, came a battered livery cab, hitting its brakes nearly on top of the arrestfest, a fortyish woman in a bathrobe popping out of the rear seat before the car had even come to a full stop.

"They say my son could lose his eye!"

"Seven dollars," the driver said, extending his hand from the side window.

"Here we go," Lopez muttered to Billy before leaving his side. "Miss Carter, all due respect, we didn't tell Jermaine to be out here two in the morning hunting for Skrillas."

"How do you know what he was doing out here!" The streetlight turned her rimless glasses into disks of pale fire.

"Because I know him," Lopez said. "I've had dealings with him."

"He's going on a financial scholarship to Sullivan County Community College next year!"

"That's great, but it don't throw a blanket

18

over it."

"I'm sorry, Charlene," one of the women said, stepping off the sidewalk, "all due respect, but truth be known you're just as much to blame as the boy who threw that glass."

"*Excuse* me?" Miss Carter cocking her head like a pistol.

"Seven dollars?" the driver said again.

Billy slipped him five bucks, then told him to reverse out of the block.

"I hear you every community meeting," the woman said, "you keep saying, My boy's a good boy, he's not mobbing for real, it's the environment, it's the circumstances, but this here officer is right. Instead of confronting your child you keep making excuses for him, so what do you expect?"

The kid's mother became big-eyed and motionless; Billy, knowing what was coming, hooked her arm just as she threw a punch at the other woman's jaw.

The crowd rippled with clucks and murmurs. A spinning cigarette landed on Billy's shoulder, but in these close quarters no real telling who had been the intended target, so *c'est la guerre.*

As he stepped back to brush the ash off his sport jacket, his cell rang: Rollie the Wheel.

19

"Boss, you remember the '72 Olympics?"

"Not really."

"The Munich massacre?"

"OK . . ."

"We had a guy there, helped take the silver in the four-by-four relays, Horace Woody?"

"OK . . ."

"Lives in Terry Towers in Chelsea."

"OK . . ."

"Patrol just called in, somebody stole his medal. You want us to take it? Could wind up being a media thing, plus Mayo's just sitting at his desk talking to himself again."

"Then have him head over to the St. Luke's ER and babysit Moretti, make sure he isn't boosting scalpels or something."

"And the case of the purloined medallion?"

Lopez peered at him over the head of a thirteen-year-old manacled Money Stacker. "Hey, Sarge? No sweat, we can take it from here."

"Send Stupak to meet me," Billy said into the phone. "I'm heading over now."

It sounded like a whole lot of nothing, but he had never met an Olympian before.

Terry Towers was a twelve-story Mitchell-Lama semi-dump in the West Twenties, one step up from a housing project, which

20

meant a few less elevators chronically out of commission and hallway odors not quite as feral. Apartment 7G itself was small, stifling, and untidy, dinner dishes still on the dinette table at two forty-five in the morning. In the middle of the cramped living room, Horace Woody, deep into his sixties but DNA-blessed with the physique of a lanky teenager, stood hands on hips in his boxers, the taut skin across his flat chest the color of a good camel hair coat. But his eyes were maraschinos, and his liquored breath was sweet enough to curl Billy's teeth.

"It's not like I don't have my suspicions as to who took the damn thing," Woody slurred, glaring at his girlfriend, Carla Garrett, who leaned against an old TV console covered with esoterically molded liqueur bottles and dog-eared photos in Lucite frames. She was maybe half his age, on the heavy side, with steady, realistic eyes. The droll, resigned twist of her mouth confirmed Billy's hunch about this one being a dummy of a run, at worst a slow-motion domestic, but he didn't really mind, fascinated as he was by the older man's uncanny youthfulness.

"Some people," Woody said, "they just don't want you to have no life in your life."

There was a light rapping at the front

door; then Alice Stupak, five-four but built like a bus, eased into the apartment, her chronic rosacea and brassy short bangs forever putting Billy in mind of a battle-scarred, alcoholic Peter Pan.

"How's everybody doing tonight?" she blared with cheery authority. Then, zeroing in on the problem child: "How about you, sir? You having a good evening?"

Woody reared back with narrow-eyed disapproval, a look Billy had seen Alice get before, mainly, but not exclusively, from their suddenly off-balance male customers. But as fearsome as she was for some to behold, Billy knew her to be chronically lovelorn, forever pining after this detective or fireman, that bartender or doorman, endlessly driven to despair that all these potential boyfriends automatically assumed she was a dyke.

"Ma'am?" Stupak said, nodding to Woody's girlfriend. "Why are we here?"

Carla Garrett pushed off the console and started camel-walking toward the back of the apartment, curling her finger for Billy to follow.

The halo-lit bathroom was a little too close, uncapped bottles and tubes of skin- and hair-care products rimming both the sink and the tub, used towels drooping from every knob, rod, and rack, stray hairs in places that made Billy look away. As Woody's girlfriend began rooting around inside a full and ripe laundry hamper, Billy's cell rang: Stacey Taylor for the third time in two days, his stomach giving up a little whoop of alarm as he killed this call from her like all the others.

"You got it in there?" Woody barked from the hallway. "I know you got it in there."

"Just go back and watch your TV," Stupak's voice coming through the closed door.

When the girlfriend finally stood upright from the hamper, she held the silver medal in her hands, as big around as a coffee saucer.

"See, when he gets his drink on he wants to pawn it and start a new life. He did it already a few times, and how much you think he got for it?"

"A few grand?"

"A hundred and twenty-five dollars."

"Can I hold it?"

Billy was disappointed in how light it was, but he felt a little buzzed nonetheless.

"See, Horace's OK most of the time, I mean, I certainly been with worse, it's just when he gets his hands on that Cherry Heering, you know? The man has got a alcoholic sweet tooth like a infant. I mean, you could get a good bottle of fifty-dollar cognac or Johnnie Walker Black, leave it on the table, he won't even crack the seal. Something tastes like a purple candy bar? Watch out."

"I want my damn medal back!" Woody yelled from farther away in the apartment.

"Sir, what did I just say to you?" Stupak's voice flattening with anger.

"Start a new life . . ." the girlfriend muttered. "All the pawnshops around here got me on speed dial for when it comes in. Hell, he wants to take off? I'll loan him the money, but this here is a piece of American history."

Billy liked her, he just didn't understand why a woman this lucid didn't keep a cleaner house.

"So what do you want me to do?"

"Nothing. I'm sorry they sent you. Usually some uniform guys from the precinct come up, mainly just because he was a famous athlete, and we play Where'd she hide it this time, but you're a detective, and I'm embarrassed they bothered you."

When they opened the bathroom door, Woody was back in the living room, sprawled on the vinyl-covered couch watching MTV with the sound off, his jellied eyes

24

dimming into slits.

Billy dropped the medal on his chest. "Case solved."

Walking with Stupak to the elevators he checked the time: three-thirty. Ninety more minutes and the odds were he'd have gotten away with murder.

"What do you say?"

"You're the boss, boss."

"Finnerty's?" Billy thinking, What the hell, you cannot not celebrate, thinking, Just a taste.

"I always wanted to go to Ireland," Stupak shouted over the music to the dead-handsome young bartender. "Last year we had reservations and everything but, like, two days before the flight my girlfriend came down with appendicitis."

"You can always get on a plane by yourself, you know," he said politely enough, looking over her shoulder to wave at two women just coming through the door. "It's a very friendly country."

And that was that, the guy leaning across the wood to buss the new arrivals and leaving Stupak to blush into her beer.

"I've never been to Ireland myself," Billy said. "I mean, what for, I'm around Micks all day as it is."

"I never should've said 'girlfriend,' " Stupak said.

His cell rang, not the Wheel, thank God, but his wife, Billy racewalking out onto the street so she wouldn't hear the racket and start asking questions.

"Hey . . ." his voice downshifting as it always did when she rang him this deep into the night. "Can't sleep?"

"Nope."

"Did you take your Traz?"

"I think I forgot but I can't now, I have to get up in three hours."

"How about you take a half?"

"I can't."

"All right, just, you know, you've been here before, worse comes to worse, you'll have a tough day tomorrow but it won't kill you."

"When are you coming home?"

"I'll try and duck out early."

"I hate this, Billy."

"I know you do." His cell began to vibrate again; Rollie Towers on line two. "Hang on a sec."

"I really hate it."

"Just hang on . . ." Then, switching over: "Hey, what's up."

"Just when you thought it was safe to go back in the water."

26

"Fuck you, what do you got."

"Happy St. Patrick's Day," said the Wheel.

By the time Billy and most of his squad made it to Penn Station and then to the long, greasy, lower-level arcade that connected the Long Island–bound commuter trains to the subway platforms at the opposite end, the cops who were on the scene first, both Transit and LIRR undercovers, had taken control of the situation better than he would have expected. Not sure what to preserve of the one-hundred-yard blood trail, they had cordoned it all off with tape and garbage cans like a slalom run. They had also miraculously managed to round up most of the sodden homebound revelers who had been standing under the track information board when the assault occurred, corralling them into a harshly lit three-sided waiting room off the main concourse. Taking a quick peek into the room, Billy saw the majority of his potential witnesses sitting on hard wooden benches gape-mouthed and snoring, chins tilted to the ceiling like hungry baby birds.

"Looks like the guy got slashed under the board here, took off running, and ran out of gas by the subway," Gene Feeley announced, his tie unknotted and dangling like Sinatra at last call.

Billy was surprised to see Feeley there at all, let alone first detective on the scene. But then again, this was Feeley's thing, the old-timer usually disdaining any run unless there were at least three dead or a shot cop, front-page stuff.

"Where's the body?" Billy thinking he'd be lucky to see his kids by dinnertime.

"Just follow the yellow brick road," Feeley said, pointing to the red-brown sneaker prints that marked the way like bloody dance-step instructions. "It's one for the scrapbooks, I'll tell you that."

They arrived at the subway turnstiles just as a southbound express pulled into the station, more pie-eyed revelers disembarking onto the platform, ho-shitting, laughing, stumbling, blowing *vuvuzelas,* everyone assuming the wide-eyed stiff was just drunk except for the two middle-aged detectives from the Crime Scene Unit who had opted to take the subway to work, their forensics kits making them look like down-at-the-heels salesmen.

Billy snagged a wandering Transit detective. "Listen, we can't have trains stopping here right now. Can you call your boss?"

"Sarge, it's Penn Station."

"I know where we are, but I don't want a

fresh herd of drunks stomping all over my scene every five minutes."

The victim lay on his side, neck and torso compressed into a hunch, his left arm and leg thrust straight out before him as if he were trying to kick his own fingertips. It looked to Billy as if the guy had been trying to jump the turnstile, bled out mid-vault, then froze like that, dying in midair before dropping like a rock.

"Looks like a high hurdler just fell off the front of a Wheaties box," Feeley said, then wandered off.

As a CSU tech began teasing the wallet out of the victim's formerly sky-blue jeans, Billy stopped marveling at his live-action lava cast and took his first good look at his face. Mid-twenties, with wide open, startled blue eyes, arched pencil-thin eyebrows, milk-white skin, and jet-colored hair, femininely handsome to the point of perversity.

Billy stared and stared, thinking, Can't be. "Is his name Bannion?"

"Hold the phone," the tech said, pulling out the guy's driver's license. "Bannion it is, first name —"

"Jeffrey," Billy said, then: "Fuck me sideways."

"Why do I know that name?" the CSU

tech asked, not really interested in an answer.

Jeffrey Bannion . . . Billy immediately thought of calling John Pavlicek, then considered the hour and decided to wait at least until daybreak, although Big John might not mind being woken up for this one.

Eight years earlier, a twelve-year-old boy named Thomas Rivera had been found beneath a soiled mattress in the tree house of his City Island neighbors, the Bannions. He had been bludgeoned to death, the bedding atop his body spattered with semen. John Pavlicek, back in the late '90s Billy's partner in anti-crime but at the time of the murder a detective assigned to the Bronx Homicide Task Force, was called in when the body was found by a cadaver dog three days after the boy went missing.

Jeffrey Bannion's oversized, learning-disabled younger brother, Eugene, admitted to the jerking off — the tree house was where he always went for that — but said that when he discovered the boy, he was already dead. Nineteen-year-old Jeffrey told Pavlicek that he himself was sick in bed that day, said Eugene had already told him that he had done it. But when the cops turned the lights on the younger Bannion, Eugene not only stuck to his story but couldn't even begin to speculate on how Thomas Rivera had come to be in the tree house or talk about what kind of weapon had done the deed, no matter how much trickery or cajoling the Homicides employed, and it made no sense that a fifteen-year-old that dim could hold out on them.

Pavlicek liked the older Bannion for it from the jump, but they couldn't shake his sick-bed story, and so the younger brother went to the Robert N. Davoren juvenile center at Rikers, a Bloods, Ñetas, and MS-13 petri dish, where he was placed in Gen Pop without the requisite psych eval, a big oafy white kid who tended to throw indiscriminate punches when he was freaked, and his murder, only five days into his incarceration, racked up nearly as many headlines as that of the boy he had allegedly killed.

Within days, despite Pavlicek's full-bore campaigning, the Rivera homicide was marked "closed by arrest," formally shutting down any further investigative work. Shortly after that, Jeffrey Bannion packed his bags and moved in with various relatives out of state. At first, Pavlicek tried to swallow his frustration by burying himself in other jobs — although he never lost touch with Thomas Rivera's parents and he never lost track of Bannion's whereabouts — but when he learned, through connections, of two incidents of assault in which the vics were preadolescent males, one in each of the small towns Jeffrey was living in at the time, neither investigation leading to an arrest, his obsession with nailing this kid returned in raging full effect.

Eventually Bannion moved back to New York, sharing a house in Seaford, Long Island, with three friends. Pavlicek, still on him like Javert, reached out to both the Seventh Precinct in neighboring Wantagh and the Nassau County Detective Bureau, but either Jeffery had kept his nose clean or he had gotten even slicker with age. The last anyone had heard of him — and most galling of all — was that he had recently applied to the auxiliary PDs of a dozen Long Island townships and had been offered training by three.

"My supervisor wants to know how long we have to be shut down for," the returning Transit detective said.

"We'll be as fast as we can be," Billy said.

"He says we got to mop that blood up out there by five-thirty, same for removing the body. That's when the commuters start coming in earnest."

Clean it up or preserve it . . . Clean it up or preserve it . . . Somebody will complain; somebody always complains.

As another mob staggered off the latest 2 train into Penn Station, a teenage girl stared goggle-eyed at Bannion for a second, looked up searchingly into her boyfriend's eyes, then wheeled and puked onto the platform, adding her DNA to the mix.

"It's a bad night for this," the Transit cop said.

Stepping back into the seamy arcade, Billy stared down the length of the tape. Other than the still-congealing blood, the killing floor — a debris field of candy wrappers, Styrofoam cups, the odd article of clothing, a shattered liquor bottle barely held together by the adhesive on its label — gave up too much and nothing at all.

As CSU continued to bag and photo-graph, as the LIRR and Transit detectives and his own crew began to work the waiting room, wandering among the semiconscious potential wits like a squadron of visiting nurses, Billy noticed that one of the com-muters sleeping there had what appeared to be blood on his Rangers jersey.

He took a seat next to him on a wooden bench, the kid's head tilted back so far it looked as if someone had slit his throat.

"Hey you." Billy nudged him.

The kid came out of it, shaking his head like a cartoon animal just whacked with an anvil.

"What's your name."

"Mike."

"Mike what."

"What?"

"How'd you get the blood on you, Mike?"

"Me?" Still whipping his head from side to side.

"You."

"Where . . ." Looking at his jersey, then: "That's blood?"

"You know Jeffrey Bannion?"

"Do I know him?"

Billy waiting, One Mississippi, two . . .

"Where is he," the kid asked.

"So you know him? Jeffrey Bannion?"

"What if I do?"

"You see what happened?"

"What? What are you talking about, what happened?"

"He's been stabbed."

The kid shot to his feet. "What? I'll fucking kill them."

"Kill who."

"What?"

"Who do you want to kill."

34

"How the fuck should I know? Who did it. You leave them to me."

"Did you see it?"

"See what?"

"When was the last time you saw him? Where was he, who was he with."

"He's like a brother to me."

"Who was he with."

"How should I know. What am I, his bitch?"

"His what? Where do you live."

"Strong Island."

"More specifically."

"Seaford."

"Who else was with you, point out your posse."

"My posse?"

"Who, sitting here, in this waiting room, was with you tonight, everybody going home to Seaford."

"I'm no rat."

"I'm asking who are his friends."

Mike turned his head as if it were on a rusty turret, taking in half the dull-eyed commuters around him.

"*Ey*," he blared. "You hear what happened?"

No one even turned his way.

"Anybody carrying anything tonight?" Billy asked.

"Like weed?"

"Like a weapon."

"Everything's a weapon."

"How'd you get that blood on you, again?"

"What blood," the kid said, touching his face.

"Was anybody in your pos . . . was anybody beefing with anybody tonight?"

"Tonight?" The kid blinked. "Tonight we're going into the city."

Billy decided to send him and everybody else to Midtown South in order to sleep it off, then be reinterviewed. His guess was that these interviews would yield nothing. He was also pretty sure that with half the eastern seaboard stomping through the crime scene like migrating wildebeests, the forensics would be useless as well. His money was on the surveillance tape.

He called it in to his division captain, the guy instantly starting to quack like a duck as if Billy had killed Bannion himself, worked for a while with the Transit cops down by the subways and the LIRR detectives under the track information board, and then, praying for a money shot, climbed the stairs to the cramped room where the monitors were set up, only to be told by the tech on duty that the master hard drive that

36

uploaded all the security footage had been damaged by a coffee spill a few hours before and the only way to salvage the film at this point was to send it out for file retrieval, a process that could take days, if not weeks.

Back down on the floor, needing one of his squad to supervise the witness transport, Billy started to approach Feeley but balked when he saw him yakking it up with a white-haired deputy inspector, the two of them probably swapping memories of their time together chasing Pancho Villa. He went looking for Stupak instead and found her standing in front of a riot-gated calzone shop interviewing a maintenance worker.

As soon as he told Stupak what he wanted done, her glance reflexively went to Feeley. "What," she muttered, "General Grant too busy prepping for Gettysburg?"

No one liked having Feeley on the squad, but no one liked him less than Alice, a hater of both the old boy network and shirkers in general. It was personal, too: despite her sixteen years on the Job, including seven in Emergency Services and three with the Violent Fugitive Apprehension Team, the old bastard took way too much pleasure in addressing her now and then as Babydoll.

Once Stupak was on her way, Billy fielded another overwrought call from his division cap, followed by one from the squad commander of Midtown South. Then, at seven a.m., with the scene secured and none of the possible witnesses in any shape to talk, Billy decided to sneak back to Yonkers just long enough to take his kids to school.

At this hour the traffic on the northbound Henry Hudson Parkway was mercifully light, and by seven forty-five he was turning onto his street. As he pulled up to the house, he saw Carmen standing on a six-foot ladder in front of the carport, trying to extract the deflated basketball jammed between the portable hoop and the backboard, the thing having been stuck like that since January, when it became too cold for the kids to play.

"Just poke it, Carm."

"I tried. It's in too tight."

Sitting behind the wheel in a half-trance of exhaustion, Billy watched her try to muscle the ball free, the morning sun turning her polyester nurse's whites the color of ice.

She was his second wife. His first, Diane, an African-American art therapist, had left him in the wake of the highly publicized protests over his accidental and near-fatal shooting of a ten-year-old Hispanic boy in the Bronx. In all fairness, the bullet that hit the kid had first passed through its intended target, a Dusted giant armed with an already bloodied lead pipe. At first, Diane, only twenty-three at the time to his twenty-five, tried to hang fire with him, but after the papers picked it up and a Bronx reverend with a fat press book set up a month-long protest vigil around their Staten Island home, she gradually came apart and then bailed.

Billy had met Carmen when he was in the Identification Squad posted to the ME's office, having been sent there from anti-crime as a form of internal exile after the shooting. She had come in that day to identify Damian Robles, until his OD, thirty-six hours earlier, her living husband.

Despite being a heroin addict, Robles had been a mixed martial arts professional with a ridiculously chiseled physique, and it embarrassed Billy to admit that two days after death the guy still looked better than Billy did on the best day of his own life.

Dead was dead, however, and twenty minutes after first laying eyes on her, as they stood side by side staring at the corpse through a long rectangular window, he just came out and said it: "What were you doing married to a lowlife like that?"

But instead of going for his face or screaming bloody murder, she calmly answered, "I thought he was what I deserved."

Within a month they were leaving clothes in each other's apartments.

Within a year they were sending out save-the-dates.

Her initial attraction to him, or so he thought at the time, was a no-brainer: sudden widow looking about and glomming onto the protective policeman standing by her side. Billy had always been a sucker for any kind of My Hero vibes when they occasionally came his way, but in truth he had fallen in love purely because of her looks and the way she sounded: her huge, smudge-rimmed eyes in a heart-shaped face, her skin the color of light toast, and that voice — lazy and smoky when she felt that way and backed by a deep and easy laugh that made him drowsy with pleasure. Lust was there from the beginning, but every other long-playing thing — trust, tenderness, companionability, et cetera — had only come about with time.

Not that living with her was any walk in the park. Her mood swings were fierce, and she was prone to savage dreams, often waking him up with her sleep talk, semicoherent tear-choked pleas to be left alone. And what he at first thought was a temporary desire for a protector in her life had over the years morphed into a river of visceral, mostly inarticulate need for him, a neediness he never quite understood but responded to with everything he had. She could never wear him out with her demands; there was something about her that made him want to be the best possible version of himself. He loved her, loved to come through for her, loved that what he had always thought of with embarrassment as his flatline personality, his bland stolidness, could become the rock in the raging sea of another soul's life.

Still, there was something inside her he could never quite get at. Sometimes he felt like a knight assigned to protect a maiden from a dragon that only she could see, and so he paid attention to the words when she cried out in her sleep, when her half-panicked rants became less coherent and maybe closer to the bone, but he was not a particularly analytical individual, so all his secret studying came to nothing. And given that he had been raised in a home in which he'd been taught to take people as they were, no questions asked, a home in which the character trait prized above all else was an Apache level of forbearance, he would die before straight up asking his wife of twelve years, the mother of his two sons, Who Are You.

"Where are the survivalists?" he called from the car.

"You're taking them?" she asked.

"Yeah, but I left a body at Penn Station, so I got to go back right after."

"I can take them."

"No, just where are —"

"Declan!"

Billy's all-night eyelids butterflied in pain: Carmen's initial solution for finding anyone was to yell.

Stalling for a last heartbeat of inaction, he let his gaze stray to their front porch, where Carmen's green nylon St. Patrick's Day banner, all shamrocks and wee people, snapped in the wind, one day past its expiration date, although Billy knew that by dinnertime it would be replaced with the Easter banner, bunnies and parti-colored eggs on a backdrop of powder blue.

"I'll get them," he finally said, climbing out of the car like a man with prosthetic hips.

The interior of the house was a rambling, amiable mess — a war chest's worth of boys' toys and sports gear strewn around the living room, smothering the worn brocade couch and matching easy chairs; a big yellow eat-in kitchen with its painted-wood "country" table perpetually covered with bills, circulars, condiments, and the odd hat or glove; three thin-walled bedrooms all crying out for a fresh coat of paint; and a sunken den that for some reason always smelled like mushrooms. And wherever one looked was evidence of Carmen's obsession with country cornball: real, ceramic, or papier-mâché Indian corn and pumpkins resting on every available surface, homely homilies inscribed on chain-hung plaques, farm-stand-purchased whirligigs, milkmaids painted on wooden ovals, and enough framed sketches of barnyards, thatched cottages, and lonely rural lanes to fill a Hallmark museum.

All of this occasionally set Billy's teeth on edge, but given his wife's childhood and early adolescence in the cracked-out Bronx of the late 1980s, her later teen years in the notorious East Metro section of Atlanta, and her current job as a triage nurse in the St. Ann's knife-and-gun-club ER, he didn't have the heart to question her taste in decor. In fact, he couldn't care less what the house looked like, as long as it made her happy.

All he cared about was his books, the shelves in the den filled with crime novels written mainly by ex-cops, retirement for dummies self-help volumes, sports memoirs, and real estate study guides, these last foisted on him by John Pavlicek, who was hell-bent on hiring him to help run his empire of apartment buildings the moment Billy put in his papers.

Looking for the kids, Billy came upon his six-year-old, Carlos, sitting on the side of his bunk bed dressed in full camo, staring at his seventy-eight-year-old grandfather asleep under the kid's X-Men blanket. Billy's dad was a well-remembered city-wide Chief of Patrol who had first made his name as a foot soldier with the Tactical Patrol Force, a.k.a. Riot Squad, during the anti-war, let-it-burn days of the late '60s. These days, however, the old guy tended to go in and out of thinking that his grandsons were both Billy and that he was still living in his first home in Fordham Heights with his dead wife. Additionally, he often got up and crept into someone else's bed in the middle of the night, either one of the kids' or Billy and Carmen's, making pajamas mandatory sleepwear for one and all.

"Let's go, buddy."

"Is Grandpa gonna die?" Carlos asked

calmly. "Not today."

Eight-year-old Declan, also wearing camo from boots to forage cap, was on his knees in the living room, trying to get the pet rabbit out from under a couch with a hockey stick, the huddled, personality-less thing hissing and sneezing like a Komodo dragon.

"Dec, just leave him there."

"What if he bites an electric cord?"

"Then we'll have rabbit for dinner. Let's go."

Just as they finally left the house, Billy's cell rang, the division captain again, and he locked himself in the car before the kids could get inside and screw his play.

"Hey, boss."

"Where are you at?"

"Midtown South doing the bullets and waiting for some of the witnesses to revive."

"Why'd you let them clean up the scene?"

"Because it's Penn Station, you have fifty thousand people walking through."

"It's a crime scene."

"Again, it's Penn Station. It's the crossroads of the Western world."

"What are you, Radio Free America? Since when does Transit call the shots?"

"This time they were right." Then adding: "In my opinion."

"How about the security tapes."

"Computer glitch."

"Computer glitch."

"They sent them over to TARU."

"Dad!" Declan belted out, slapping the car window.

"Billy!" Carmen came over with the frozen basketball. "What the hell are you doing? They're going to be late!"

"Who was that?" the division cap asked.

"Boss, one of the wits just gave up a name. I'll call you back."

After dropping off the boys at their school, Billy headed back into the city, wrote up his bullets for the day-tour detectives in Midtown South — it was their headache now — debriefed a few bosses, fended off a police shack reporter, ducked a TV camera, and got back in the car. When he finally re-returned to the house at one p.m., Millie Singh, the alleged housekeeper, was watching *Mob Wives Chicago* with his father in the living room, neither of them acknowledging his presence.

Millie barely knew her way around a mop, prepared spicy Indo-Caribbean dishes that would tear your throat out, and tended to take naps on the job. But back in the day she had been the only one in their moonscape of a precinct with guts enough to take

46

the stand in a gang-related homicide, and as a result she'd had to sleep in her bathtub in order to protect herself from the nightly gunshots coming through her windows, until Billy and the others moved her into one of Pavlicek's newly renovated buildings. Ten years later, at roughly the same time that Billy's father had first been diagnosed with dementia, Millie's teenage daughter moved back to Trinidad to live with her father and she lost her job at Dunkin' Donuts. Hiring her as their housekeeper had seemed like a good idea at the time, and in all fairness to Millie, the kids loved her, she loved his dad, and she was in possession of a valid driver's license. Besides, Carmen liked to do her own housecleaning, if you could call it that.

Billy stepped into the kitchen, poured himself half a milk glass of vodka and cranberry juice — the only thing that could put him to sleep at this hour — and went into the bedroom. He stowed his Glock 9 on the top shelf of his closet behind a shoe box filled with old bank statements, and with a last burst of energy called Pavlicek to give him a heads-up about Bannion.

"Hey."

"I heard," Pavlicek said.

"What do you think," Billy said, crawling

into the cool swan boat of a bed.

"That there's a God after all."

"It was a freaky scene."

"I heard that too."

"Heard from who?"

"The drums."

"Do the Riveras know?"

"I called them this morning."

"How'd they take it?"

"The mister was cool, Mom not so good. I'm going out to City Island to see them later."

"Good." Billy's eyes felt like sandpits.

"I want you to come with me."

"John, I'm sleeping."

"You saw the dead fuck. They might need to ask you things."

"Come on, this is private with you and them."

"Billy, I'm asking you."

He gargled the last of his drink, crunched on a sliver of ice. "Make it about six, I just got into bed."

"Thank you."

"You owe me."

"Afterwards we can pick up Whelan, then head downtown to the restaurant."

"The dinner's tonight?"

"Yes sir."

"OK, let me sleep."

"Hey," Pavlicek held on, "what's the most bullshit word in the English language."

"Closure."

"Give that man a cigar," Pavlicek said, then hung up.

He had forgotten all about the dinner, the monthly steak house reunion of the self-christened Wild Geese, seven young cops averaging three years on the Job, fresh to anti-crime in the late '90s, a tight crew given a ticket to ride in one of the worst precincts of the East Bronx. Of the original seven, one had moved to Arizona after retirement, and one had died from a three-pack-a-day habit, leaving a hard-core five: Billy, Pavlicek, Jimmy Whelan, Yasmeen Assaf-Doyle, and Redman Brown.

They had been something else back then, preternaturally proactive, sometimes showing up at the trouble spots two steps ahead of the actors, and they were decathletes, chasing their prey through backyards and apartments, across rooftops, up and down fire escapes, and into bodies of water. Many cops administered beatdowns as a penalty for being made to run, but the WGs got high off the chase, often treating their collars post-arrest like members of a defeated softball team. They thought of themselves as a family, and family membership was extended automatically to those in the neighborhood they liked: the owners of bodegas, bars, barbershops, and take-out joints, but also the numbers runners — the numbers going back to the Bible as far as they were concerned — a few of the old school reefer men, and a handful of restaurateurs who had secret gaming rooms upstairs or in the basement where the WGs could throw some bones and drink for free.

As far as stolen goods went, fell-off-a-truck merchandisers oftentimes offered NYPD courtesy discounts on everything from kids' backpacks to designer pantsuits to power tools. A drink here, a standing hump there, a cut-rate cashmere pullover now and then — no one in the Wild Geese took money, demanded a sin tax, or even lost their civility. Although they were periodically called on to corral a few for the requisite trip to the Tombs, they generally tolerated whores who were reasonably discreet and, as an added bonus, funny. Nonviolent junkies were left on the street and used as informants. Their dealers, however, were fair game.

And if one of the family got hurt by a bad player — a street girl having her eye blackened or finger broken by her Slapaho Mac

Daddy, a Wild Geeser catching a paintball or pellet-gun round in the back, a casino operator or bodega owner taken off by the local mokes — then they would all descend as one, and the beatdowns and banishments would commence. It was all about family; they would do the job as required, but they would really step to the fore for those they deemed "worthy," given that some people in the East Bronx, as elsewhere, as everywhere, would always try to get high to escape, want a little extracurricular loving, chase a money dream scribbled in numbers across a crumple of paper. Not all cops were as laissez-faire in their attitude toward the outriders of the precinct, but the Wild Geese, in the eyes of the people they protected and occasionally avenged, walked the streets like gods.

The good news and the bad news was that their kind of high-yield police work was a fast track to a gold shield. Within five years, all the original WGs had moved on, the irony being that Billy, who was the youngest and least experienced, had been the first one to get the nod. After the double shooting, which earned him both a citation for bravery and a civilian review board hearing, the department, in its slap/caress way, decided to promote him in order to bury

51

him — in his case, to the basement of the morgue, since the Identification Squad, like any other, was composed primarily of detectives.

At the end of the day, some of the WGs became better detectives than street soldiers, others lesser cops behind their gold shields. Some discovered gifts never used before; others lost the opportunity to use the gifts they had had all along.

And it was also as detectives, dispersed to various squads across the boroughs, that, like Pavlicek coming up against a Jeffrey Bannion, they had all met their personal Whites, those who had committed criminal obscenities on their watch and then walked away untouched by justice, leaving their obsessed ex-WG hunters heading into retirement with pilfered case files to pore over in their offices and basements at night, still making the odd unsanctioned follow-up call: to the overlooked counterman in the deli where the killer had had a coffee the morning of the murder, to the cousin upstate who had never been properly interviewed about that last phone conversation he had with the victim, to the elderly next-door neighbor who left on a Greyhound to live with her grandchildren down in Virginia two days after the bloodbath on the other side of the shared living room wall — and always, always, calling the spouses, children, and parents of the murdered: on the anniversary of the crime, on the victims' birthdays, at Christmas, just to keep in touch, to remind those left behind that they had promised an arrest that bloody night so many years ago and were still on it.

No one asked for these crimes to set up house in their lives, no one asked for these murderers to constantly and arbitrarily lay siege to their psyches like bouts of malaria, no one asked to feel so helplessly in the grip of this nonstop black study that they had no choice but to pursue and pursue. But there they all were: Pavlicek forever stalking Jeffrey Bannion; Jimmy Whelan pursuing Brian Tomassi, the ringleader of a white street gang who, in the aftermath of 9/11, had chased a Pakistani kid into an oncoming car; Redman Brown stalking Sweetpea Harris, the murderer of a college-bound high school baller who had made him look bad in a playground pickup game; Yasmeen Assaf-Doyle forever tracking Eric Cortez, a twenty-eight-year-old small-time felon who had stabbed to death a reedy myopic ninth grader because the kid had talked to Cortez's fourteen-year-old girlfriend at their school.

And Billy himself, in his first year above-ground as a precinct detective after too many living below like a mushroom among the dead, shackled for all time to Curtis Taft, the killer of three females in one evening: Tonya Howard, a twenty-eight-year-old who had just dumped the man who would become her murderer; her fourteen-year-old niece, Memori Williams, who happened to be sleeping over the night Taft decided to get back at his ex; and Dreena Bailey, Tonya's four-year-old daughter by another man. Three shots, three dead, then right back to bed, Curtis Taft, as far as Billy was concerned, the most black-hearted of the Whites. But so were they all, if you asked each of their star-crossed hunters.

Twenty years after they had started out running the streets like high-topped commandos, almost all of them were living new lives. Redman got shot through the hips in a hostage situation, went out on a three-quarters medical, and took over his father's funeral parlor in Harlem. Fast-and-loose Jimmy Whelan put in his papers before he could be fired and became an itinerant building super, living from year to year in some of the finer basement apartments of the city. Yasmeen, who couldn't take the boss mentality, quit to become assistant head of crimes against students at a university in lower Manhattan and achieved a black belt in complaining about her new bosses over there. Pavlicek, already on the make while still in uniform, just got too busy being rich. Only Billy, the baby of the group, still hung in. He had no reason not to: as his father had declared over a raised glass on the night of Billy's graduation from the academy: "Here's to God, because the man had to be a natural-born genius to invent this job."

An hour after his phone call with Pavlicek, Billy was dreaming about Jeffrey Bannion — nude and adrift in an oversized bell jar filled with red punch — when one of the kids came home from school and slammed the front door as if he were being chased by wolves. A moment later he heard Carlos yelling at his brother, "You quit so I win!," followed by Carmen shouting, "What did I tell you about yelling in the house!"

Even so, Billy managed to fall back asleep for half an hour, until the sheets began to rustle and Carmen, naked, nuzzled into the small of his back, her left hand reaching around to burrow into his boxers. Billy was so tired he thought he would die, but her hand on his prick was her hand on his prick.

"We had three kids brought in with gunshot wounds three days in a row," she murmured in his ear. "Turns out the second kid shot the first for shooting someone in his crew, the third shot the second in retaliation, and the best friend of the second shot the third for the same reason. It was like the bonehead Olympics. Anything going on down there?"

"Give me a second, will you?"

After twelve years they were doing pretty good, he thought, hitting it twice a week more often than once, and they seemed to be putting on weight apace of each other, also not so bad, Carmen still able to pull off wearing a two-piece, although Billy kept his T-shirt on at the beach. In the beginning, there wasn't a physical position or a sexual fancy off-limits, but as they grew more comfortable with each other, it always seemed like straight-up missionary, after a little of this and a little of that, unfailingly ended with both of them afterward euphorically raiding the refrigerator in search of the next fun thing to do.

"So," she said.

And in a rush of bleary optimism Billy decided that maybe he didn't need to sleep this week after all.

MILTON RAMOS

The handcuffed drunk in the backseat had lost three thousand, dollars betting on the NCAA Final Four and decided that it was the fault of his wife's face, which he promptly set to rearranging.

"March Madness. I was you, that would be my defense," Milton's partner said without turning around.

"Fuck her, and fuck you."

"You know what? Stick with that attitude, because judges hate sincere remorse."

"And what are you?" the drunk said, squinting at Milton sitting silently behind the wheel.

"Excuse me?" Seeking the guy's eyes via the rearview mirror.

"You know what *SPIC* stands for?" The drunk leaned forward, his alcohol-fueled malice expanding, searching. "Spanish Indian Colored. Otherwise known as Greaser, Savage, Nigger. Put them all together you get one big fucking unibrow Monkey. You."

Milton pulled the car over alongside Roberto Clemente Park, then turned off the ignition. He sat there for a moment with his hands palms up in his lap.

"Can we not do this?" his partner asked with an air of resignation.

"Ook, ook," from the rear seat.

Milton popped the trunk via the lever beneath the steering wheel, got out, and walked to the back of the car.

"The fuck's he doing?" the drunk asked.

"Shut up," the partner said, sounding both angry and a little depressed.

The rear door opened abruptly and Milton lifted the prisoner out of the car by his elbow. In his free hand he carried a telescoping baton and a grease-smudged towel.

"The fuck are you doing?"

Without answering, Milton frog-walked his prisoner into the maw of the park until he found what he considered a suitable spot. Not too open, not too constricted, and branches low enough to grip.

"What are you doing?"

"Down, please?"

"What?"

Milton popped him in the chest and the drunk was suddenly lying faceup in the grass, his shoulders on fire from the impact of landing with his hands cuffed behind his back.

"Jesus, man, what are you doing?" Near-pleading now, his voice suddenly much closer to sober than a few minutes earlier.

Milton knew he should never have been given a gold shield. It was a misguided reward for being in the wrong place at the wrong time, a barbershop during a holdup in his own Bronx neighborhood when two assholes with .38s had come in while he was buried in aprons, towels, and shaving cream. The shop was a known numbers drop, easy pickings, and after they kneecapped one of the barbers, Milton kicked his chair around on its swivel and started shooting from beneath his polyester body bib, which promptly caught fire. By the time his barber whipped off the flaming sheet he had second-degree burns on his left arm and thigh.

Both perps, one shot in the throat, the other in the face, survived but went directly from Misericordia to the Tombs. The mayor and the police commissioner came to see Milton in the burn unit of that same hospital, the PC presenting him with his detective's shield in front of cameras.

The question put to him was "Where do you want to go."

Where. He wanted to go wherever he could hide.

Patrol had always been his thing, the street his wheelhouse — frontier justice, an eye for an eye, and the culling of information through extracurricular beatdowns. He would be a terrible detective, and he knew it: not too bright with paper trails, not particularly subtle or patient in an interview room, and possessed of a freakishly violent yet icy temper when provoked.

Since the shootout at the barbershop he'd been transferred to seven different precincts in five years. Truculent and inept, he was a burden to each squad, until he landed at the 4-6 in the Bronx. Even before Milton arrived, the lieutenant there got the message that he was doing a great job with Detective Ramos, we all appreciate it, no more hot potato. Milton's new boss made the savvy decision to stash him in the burglary squad, which averaged thirty-five cases a month, all difficult to solve. But even in that Eeyore world of low expectation he managed to go three years without a single arrest, at which point he became the supervisor of night complaints, his job to come in at eight a.m. and farm out the complaints that had accumulated since the previous midnight to the other incoming day-tour detectives — a housecat gig that reeked of dunce cap.

But after a long stretch in that purgatory, a new boss finally put him back in the regular squad, and six months after that there wasn't a known actor in the 4-6 who didn't come to dread hearing the phrase, usually spoken in a low-key, near-distracted monotone, "Get out of the car, please?"

Milton took the dirty towel and carefully folded it into a thick band. He then straddled the drunk and laid the towel across his throat. Snapping the telescoping baton out to its full length, he perched it lengthwise along the center of the towel. Carefully stepping on the narrow end with his right foot, he pressed the steel rod into one side of the guy's throat. Then, holding on to a branch in order to keep his balance and modulate the pressure, he placed his other foot on the handle end so that now his full weight was coming down on the Adam's apple, that weight fluctuating between 180 and 190 pounds, depending on the time of the year and what holidays had just passed.

The drunk's suddenly bulging eyes turned

a damp, golden red, and the only sound he was capable of making was a faint peeping like a newborn chick heard from one farm over.

After thirty seconds or so, Milton stepped off the baton one foot at a time, then squatted and lifted the thick towel beneath; the throat was unblemished. He replaced the towel on the guy's throat and once again balanced the baton across its center.

"One more time?"

The drunk shook his head, even the weak peeping sound gone.

"Come on . . ." Milton rose to his height, found his balance again at both ends of the rod, and started seesawing. "In case I never get to see you again."

CHAPTER 2

As they crossed the Triborough Bridge in Pavlicek's cream-colored elephant of a Lexus, Billy felt like he could stand up in the shotgun seat without grazing the ceiling. For its owner, though, the oversized SUV was a necessity. Pavlicek was nearly big enough to have his own zip code, six foot four, with a head as big around as a diving bell, the upper body of a power lifter, and hands that once, on a bet, had crushed a raw potato. Even with his face and frame somewhat softened by retirement and wealth, his presence still tended to make everyone around him, including Billy, behave. Big man, big car, big life.

In Billy's opinion, of all their original crew, Pavlicek had played the exit game most righteously. Any cop working a precinct could tell you where the money went, but Pavlicek's genius back in the '90s was to see where it wasn't: in the roofless brownstone shells that had become crack squats, the decimated walk-ups, the derelict working-class ghost palaces that had peaked in the 1940s, if they had ever peaked at all. He had bought them one at a time for a renegotiated accumulation of back taxes and liens, either from the city or the desperate owners themselves, paying an average of $7,500 in the beginning, never more than $50,000 later on, once other speculators started to get in the game. And after completing the purchase, Pavlicek was good at vacating buildings, offering first cash, then violence to the squatters and junkies still cooping after the sale.

In the early days, Pavlicek did all the dirty work himself, rarely needing to do more than show up unannounced at dawn and display his holstered service revolver or a baseball bat. As his holdings grew, he began contracting out these spontaneous evictions, as he called them, to others: mainly defrocked cops, guys who had gotten jammed up for taking money or beating a prisoner or worse, losing both their badges and their pensions in the aftermath and now desperate for even the shadiest of paydays.

Once the troublemakers and deadbeats were gone, he quickly rehabbed the properties and got decent people to move in —

there were always decent people — Pavlicek specifically courting the elderly on Social Security or other kinds of fixed income, as well as those who could arrange for the city or their bank to make direct rent payments to his corporation, the bottom line being that five years after retirement Pavlicek owned twenty-eight mostly beat-up but relatively violation-free properties in Washington Heights and the Bronx, had a house in Pelham Manor the length of a tanker and a personal worth of $30 million if a dime.

But if he had been blessed with wealth, he had been cursed with loss: after three years of reasonably happy marriage, his wife, Angela, had attempted to drown their then six-month-old son in the backyard wading pool. Four months later, on her first leave from the Payne-Whitney Psychiatric Clinic, she tried it again. Nineteen years later she was still institutionalized, most recently at a residential treatment facility in Michigan, not far from her parents' home in Wisconsin. Pavlicek still grieved for her and still hated himself for being so oblivious to her pain and madness back then. As far as Billy knew, they were still married.

"You ever been out of the country?" Pavlicek asked as they cruised past the Forensic Psychiatric Center, a.k.a. the Hat Factory, on Wards Island.

"Nope," Billy said, trying to peer through the barred windows to the Thorazine-infused prisoners within. "My dad was in England a bunch of times, did a tour in Vietnam."

"That's him. Plus, war doesn't count."

"Been to Puerto Rico with Carmen to see her grandmother once."

"Puerto Rico is part of the U.S. Plus, visiting family doesn't count."

"Then I guess I've been living in my ass for forty-two years. What's your point, big shot?"

"Did I ever tell you about the time I went to Amsterdam with John Junior?"

"You went to Amsterdam?"

"Four years ago I was invited to talk at an urban renewal conference there, and I wanted to bring him. He was sixteen, it's a cool city, sort of, so he says, 'I'll let you take me to Amsterdam . . .' "

"Let you."

" '. . . let you take me if you get stoned with me there. Nick Perlmutter went with his dad last year and told me they got wasted together.' Says to me, 'Hey, at least you'll know who I'm getting high with.' "

"You did not do that."

"I'm sorry, you never got high?"

"With my kids?"

"Your kids are little, Billy. It's different later, it's like trying to hold back water with your hands. Trust me."

"You still don't have to smoke up with them."

Pavlicek shrugged.

Feeling a little scandalized, Billy shut up.

"In any event, we got there, made a beeline to the nearest coffee bar, sat outside facing this plaza, platz, or whatever, Junior's all showing off how he can read a pot menu like a wine list, orders us something supposedly mild, a few hits and we're both zotzed. It was fun at first — we couldn't figure out how to take our picture, holding the camera every whichaway, laughing, you know, stupid stoned. Finally this Dutch lady inside the bar takes pity on us, comes out and does the honors. Two American morons getting high in Amsterdam, never seen that before. We're laughing our balls off for about a half hour, then the paranoia just shuts us down like, blam. I mean like a solid hour of Can't Talk, sitting there wondering how do we find the fucking hotel, Prinzengracht, Schminzenstrasse, where's the Anne Frank House and are we bad half-Jews if we blow it off, how do we even just, like, stand up. Hours like that, then Johnnie finally turns to me, says, 'Well, this wasn't one of my better ideas, was it.' He flies home the next day, it's really a nothing city, but I'm stuck doing the panels. I felt horrible . . . I mean, OK, you're right, what kind of pandering asshole has to curry favor with his kid like that. But you know what? A week later I finally come home and I see that on his bedroom door Johnnie had taped blowups of all the photos of us that the Dutch lady took, and goddamn didn't it look like we had a blast. And now when we . . . It always plays for a laugh when it comes up in conversation, between the pictures and the way we tell it to people. It's like, after a while, the two of you are like a comedy team. And you forget, I forgot, how bad it felt, I just . . ."

Billy heard a sudden rasp of tears in Pavlicek's voice that he had no idea how to interpret and so he held his peace until they got where they were going, twenty strained minutes later.

The Riveras, like everyone else on City Island, lived on one of the short streets branching off the sole avenue that ran like a spine for two miles from the land bridge to the Long Island Sound. Their house, a rundown Victorian gingerbread, was at the

68

tail end of Fordham Street, the lapping waves audible from every room. The family had two views: the Sound at a point where New York and Connecticut met underwater, and the ruins of the house directly across the way, not a hundred feet opposite, behind which the body of their son Thomas was found five years earlier, discarded and torn. The house was now in the midst of being demolished by the new owners, the walls collapsed in a violent heap, jagged spears of lumber shooting out in all directions like an abstract expression of its own notoriety.

Ray Rivera, now sixty pounds heavier than the night his son was discovered, stood on his lawn with Billy and Pavlicek, chain-smoking and staring at the wreckage across the way. His wife, Nora, was somewhere inside their house, undoubtedly aware of the visit but declining to come out. To Billy most of Rivera's new obesity seemed to be in his upper body and face rather than his gut, in the multi-tiered pouches under the eyes, the softening flesh of his broad chest, and the forward slump of his thick shoulders. Billy had seen this transformation before in parents who struggled daily with the violent death of a child. After a few years that emotional heaviness could visually de-sex a couple, leave them looking more like each other than if they'd lived into their nineties together.

"You know, I have real mixed feelings about that shit pile coming down." Rivera coughed wetly into the side of his hammy fist, took another drag. "I keep thinking, Maybe they're destroying evidence, or maybe a shred of his soul is still in there."

"He's not there anymore, Ray," Pavlicek said. "I know you know that."

Billy saw movement behind a second-floor window in the Rivera house: Nora up there, hours every day looking across the street.

"People asked us why we didn't move away, but it would have been like abandoning him, you know?"

Suddenly the window opened and Nora Rivera leaned out, red-faced, cawing: "Why didn't *they* move away!"

Pavlicek raised a hand in greeting. "Hey, Nora."

The window slammed like a gunshot.

"You know, I know people, and I could've made some calls, anytime I wanted. Once a guy called me. But if I wanted that Jeffrey kid dead, I would have done it myself."

"That's not you, Ray."

"I mean, do you have any idea how many times I sat on that porch with a piece of steel in my hand? I always drank my way out of it."

"Is there anything you want to ask me about Jeffrey Bannion?" Billy offered.

Rivera ignored the question. "Last year we went to the national Memory Keepers convention, Johnny here came with us," nodding to Pavlicek. "They had a bunch of workshops and seminars, and I sat in on a support group for fathers with murdered kids." Rivera took another moist drag on his cigarette. "And this guy, some old biker from Texas, he said he sat in on the execution of his son's murderer in Huntsville. Said it didn't make a difference. Called it a letdown. But I'm not so sure that would've been the case with me."

"Ray," Pavlicek said gently, "we have to go."

"Our pastor says Jesus wants us to try and forgive, but I'll tell you, these last few years? I'm all about the God of the Jews."

They came upon Jimmy Whelan in the lobby of the apartment house where he lived and worked as the super, a run-down prewar with a deep H-block courtyard on Fort Washington Avenue. At this hour the food odors of three continents crept down the elevator shaft like fog.

Whelan looked good for forty-six, a lean,

71

sometime weight lifter with a full head of brown hair, a big nose, and the exaggerated mustache of a gunslinger. Which wasn't too far off: by the time he'd retired he held the record for justifiable shots-fired incidents of any active police officer in the NYPD. Toward the end of his career, he was transferred to the Crime Scene Unit, one of the least likely places where a detective could find a reason to pull his weapon, but even with that squad he managed to get into a shootout, having wandered into a three a.m. bodega robbery while on a coffee run two blocks away from an indoor doubleheader being processed by his CSU team in the New Lots section of Brooklyn.

Dressed tonight in a dagger-collared cherry leather car coat and flare-bottom jeans, he was standing in front of the geriatric twin elevators, barking at a toffee-colored tenant with vaguely Asiatic eyes and a whippet mustache, the guy shoulder-toting a duffel bag as if on shore leave.

"What are you doing?" Whelan snapped.

"Spreading the joy!" His whiskey-hoarse voice just shy of a shout.

"The joy? Are you crazy? Get your ass back upstairs."

"How you doing, sirs!" the guy said, turning to Billy and Pavlicek and extending his free hand. "Esteban Appleyard."

Whelan abruptly walked away, shaking his head as if he had just about had it with this idiot.

"What you got in there?" Billy asked.

Appleyard opened his duffel to display mini-bottles of Rihanna Rebelle perfume, half-pints of Alizé VS cognac, and cellophane-wrapped packs of White Owl cigarillos.

"Have a cigar." Appleyard beamed.

"I don't smoke," Billy lied.

"I'll be in the car," Pavlicek muttered, wheeling so abruptly that he nearly collided with Whelan, who was steaming back for more Appleyard.

"Where's the money?"

"They gonna wire it to my bank."

"When."

"I don't know."

Whelan turned to Billy. "This guy just won ten million playing the lottery, can you believe that?"

"For real?"

Billy knew Whelan's irritation had nothing to do with envy. Taking his super's job to heart despite his run-and-gun résumé, Jimmy always projected this scolding vibe toward the more obliviously self-destructive members of what he considered his flock.

One of the elevators groaned open and a woman sporting an African head wrap stepped out, her arms filled with folded laundry.

Appleyard dug in his duffel and pulled out a bottle of perfume. "For you, *Chiqui*."

"I don't wear that," she said sharply, as angry at him as Whelan.

"Give me a kiss."

"You should move out of here," rearing back from his ninety-proof breath. "Everybody knows."

Looking to the lobby, now stripped of nearly all of its original 1920s furniture and mirrors, Billy was surprised to see Pavlicek still in the house, slumped over on the lone couch, his head sunk into his hands as if he were too exhausted to make it back out to the street.

"You got a car?" Whelan asked Appleyard.

"Buyin' one. I like that Maybach, like Diddy got. A nice chocolate brown."

"Can you even drive?"

"Drove a truck out of the poultry terminal for fourteen years before I got shot that one time," yanking down his sweater collar to show the skid-mark scar on his collarbone.

Whelan pulled out a set of keys, stuffed them in Appleyard's pocket. "You know my car?"

"The Elantra?" Appleyard sniffed. "I wouldn't be caught dead in that."

"You go upstairs and pack. You take my car and go up to my cabin in Monticello for a week. Figure out where you want to live, what you're gonna do with yourself, because around here, they're gonna eat you alive."

The woman nodded in agreement.

"Naw, man." Appleyard waved him off. "People know me."

"Exactly. Somebody comes to my door three days from now, says there's a smell from 5D? I don't want to find you, see some three-legged alligator tortured you for your ATM code, left you with a screwdriver in your ear."

"Yeah, well." Appleyard's duffel slipped from his grip, the perfume and cognac bottles clinking on the smooth stone floor. "I can't see that."

The African tenant finally took off, crossing the lobby on her way to the front door, Pavlicek not even raising his eyes to her as she glided past the couch, her voluminous housecoat brushing his knees.

"And stop handing that shit out or you won't even make it to two days. What's wrong with you?"

"How much you want for the cabin and the car," Appleyard asked, peeking into the duffel for spillage. "Because I know you want something."

"For a week?" Whelan said, squinting at the ceiling. "Fifteen hundred."

"And I'm supposed to worry about everybody else takin' me off, huh?"

"Make it two thousand and I'll come with you."

"Charge me for you to come to your own house? You got a TV up there?"

"Of course."

"They sell groceries up there?"

"No, everyone crawls around eating grass."

"Bars?"

"You stay out of bars."

"Naw, I'm gonna stay right here," handing Whelan back his keys. "This is my block."

"I tell you what," Whelan said. "I'll sell you the car for twelve grand."

"I don't think so." Appleyard laughed, then hauled the duffel back up on his shoulder and took off down the hall to knock on doors.

As they finally headed out to the street, Pavlicek falling in with them silently, Billy's cell rang, Stacey Taylor again, Billy killing this call from her too.

Collin's Steak House was situated in the financial district on a small cobblestoned lane lined with landmark nineteenth-century merchants' homes and low she-beens named after Irish poets, the whole plunked down like an antique snow globe dwarfed and surrounded by a futuristic ring of office towers. They were the first to arrive, and the publican Stephan Cunliffe, a Belfast transplant who by blood mandate loved cops and writers, brought over a tray of Midleton shots before they had even taken their seats.

"Sláinte," Cunliffe said, hoisting his own.

Although Irish himself, Billy could live the rest of his life without hearing that particular toast again.

"Is Mr. Brown coming?"

"Redman's got a funeral service uptown," Billy said.

"And the lovely Ms. Assaf-Doyle?"

"As per usual, she'll be coming when she comes."

Which was twenty minutes later, swooping to the table like a rush breath, her enormous dark eyes beneath blue-black hair, wet and combed straight back as if she had just come from a workout, and wearing, as always, her trademark hippie coat, calfskin shearling trimmed with vaguely Tibetan embroidery and frogged buttons.

"Where's mine?" Yasmeen said, looking at the empty glasses.

Cunliffe snapped his fingers, and a fresh round appeared as if the waiter had it behind his back all along.

"My job this week?" Shrugging off her coat. "I had a girl in the dorms from India, lost her virginity to some douchebag in the Village, the guy made a tape and now he's threatening to send it to her parents if she stops putting out, so I had to go up to his skank-ass crib and scare the piss out of him, like, call out the dogs of war, right? Oh, and today? They had me investigating a missing sweater, anyways, *besahah'*," draining her shot. Then: "So, Billy, you caught the Bannion job?"

"Four in the morning."

"Penn Station, a real clusterfuck, right? Any leads?"

"At this point, ask Midtown South. I'm just the night porter."

"You ever see that movie? I almost asked for my money back."

"What movie," Whelan said.

"Anyways, here's to Bannion," hoisting

her second glass. "When bad things happen to bad people."

"Hear, hear."

"First Tomassi, then Bannion," she said. "It's like justice started peeking under the blinds."

"When people say 'hear, hear' like that," Whelan said, "do they mean 'hear' like to hear something? Or like, 'Hey, over here.' "

"Whoa, wait." Billy held up his hand. "Brian Tomassi? What happened to him?"

"Are you serious?" Whelan said. "Do you not read the papers?"

"Just say."

"You know that stretch of Pelham Parkway by Bronx House where him and his crew chased Yusuf Khan in front of the cab?"

"Yeah, and . . ."

"Take two giant and one umbrella step south of there, Tomassi, two a.m. in the morning, tweakin' like a beacon, steps off the curb and becomes one with the 12 bus."

"When was this?"

"Last month."

"Just like that?"

"Just like that."

Laughing, Billy nodded to Whelan. "You push him?"

"I would've, you better believe that."

Billy remembered, the day after it happened, Whelan telling him that when the panic-stricken Khan, running blindly across the four-lane northbound parkway, had been struck by a muscle car doing sixty-five, the sound of the impact had been loud enough to set off car alarms for blocks around.

"Hey, what's the last thing that passed through Tomassi's mind after he got creamed by that bus?" Yasmeen asked.

"His ass," Pavlicek grunted, his first words since they had all sat down. "Christ, if you're going to tell stupid fucking jokes . . ."

Once again Billy noticed that he seemed on the verge of tears. "You OK, big guy?"

"Me?" Pavlicek brightened a shade too fast. "You know what I was doing today when I called you? Going through one of my buildings with an exorcist. I got a Chinese contractor to gut the place, his people go in, they come right back out fifteen minutes later saying it's haunted, no way they're going back in. So I went and hired an exorcist."

"The Chinese are the worst," Yasmeen said, "they're so superstitious."

"You ever see a Chinaman commit suicide?" Whelan added. "They don't believe in quick and painless."

"Where'd you get the exorcist?" Billy asked.

"This lady runs a smoke shop near my house. She's some kind of Wiccan with a sideline in ghostbusting."

"She's for real?"

"She knows what's expected of her, puts on a good show. Comes with flashlights, humidifiers, wind chimes, Enya tapes . . ."

"Who you gonna call . . ."

"Only thing is, they have their gods and we have ours."

"We have gods?"

They waited for Pavlicek to continue, but he seemed to have lost interest in his own story.

"So did it work or not?" Billy asked.

"What."

"The exorcism."

"It's ongoing," Pavlicek said, looking off.

"So, Billy, how's your family?" Yasmeen catching his eye — Let it be — then downing her third or maybe fourth shot.

"Good, you know, I mean my father's not getting any better, but . . ."

"My dad once tried to talk me into letting him come to live with us? I had his ass in a home before he got the first sentence out."

"You're all heart there, Yazzie," Whelan said.

"What do you mean, I'm all heart? The guy was a psycho. He used to get drunk and burn us with cigarettes. I got a heart. Why do you always want to make me feel so bad?"

"Yasmeen, I'm kidding."

"No, you're not," she slurred. Then, after a too-long beat: "Fucking Whelan. You always make me feel bad. What did I ever do to you?"

She then proceeded to descend into one of her legendary sulks, Billy knowing from experience that there was a good chance they wouldn't hear from her for the rest of the evening.

Yasmeen was the only woman Billy knew who could match his wife mood swing for mood swing. They even looked alike, although Yasmeen's coloration came from her Syrian father and Turkish mother, which had made being constantly addressed as *mami* and automatically spoken to in Spanish out on the street agitating enough for her to more than once ask for a transfer to a more upscale precinct. But she was a fierce friend, dressing down his first wife in the street directly in front of the demonstrators who had driven her to leave him after his shooting — well, that wasn't such a hot idea — then, years later, when Carmen was going through a particularly black spell, taking in their kids for an entire summer until his wife was back on her feet.

So Billy would put up with any kind of stormy behavior that came his way, but with Yasmeen now brooding in her tent and Pavlicek halfway to a morose coma of his own, the table suddenly had the energy of a brownout.

"Can I tell you something?" Billy began, trying to plug the gap. "You talk about exorcisms, I never told this to anybody before because it embarrassed me, but about six months into trying to nail Curtis Taft? Carmen convinced me to consult a psychic."

"Get out," Whelan stepping in like a straight man.

"Some old Italian lady up in Brewster, I mean, I was so desperate at that point . . . So I call her up, go to her house, I swear she looked just like Casey Stengel. Hey, how you doing, thanks for seeing me, and I walk into the living room, the walls are covered with appreciation letters from different police departments around the country, maybe a few from Canada, another from some town in Germany. It was pretty impressive until you go up close and read one: 'It has come to my attention that you might possibly have been of some assistance in the as yet unsolved homicide death of fill-in-the-blank. Thank you for your time and enthusiasm. Sincerely, Elmo Butkus, Chief of Police, French Kiss, Idaho.' But whatever, I'm there. I sit on the couch, she's in a rocking chair, I was told to bring some objects belonging to the vics, so I hand over a barrette belonging to the four-year-old, Dreena Bailey, Memori Williams's iPod, and Tonya Howard's Bible. I tell her what we think happened, Taft coming in there around sunrise, three shots and just walking out, going home, getting back in bed with his still-asleep girlfriend.

"She says to me, 'OK, here's how it works. I'm gonna sit here and think about what you just told me, and I'm gonna get a little worked up and I'll say things, a word, a phrase, and you write everything down. Whatever I say.' And then she says, 'Now, the things I'll be saying? I don't know what any of it means, they're like pieces of a puzzle that you got to put together, OK? You're the detective, not me, OK?'

"I say OK.

" 'And oh, wait,' she says, 'by the way, I never charge cops for helping them, that's my civic duty, all I ask in return is a letter from you on your police department stationery thanking me for my assistance.' I say,

'Yeah sure no problem, let's go, let's go.' And then she starts rocking in the chair, rubbing Dreena's barrette, and lets it rip. 'Four years old, that poor little kid, she never had a chance, she'll never see her mother again, or play jump rope, that evil cocksucker, that fucking . . . BUTTER!'

"I almost jumped out the window she shouted it so loud, but I write down 'Butter,' then she's off again. 'What kind of cold-blooded scumbag would take the life of . . . RUNNING WATER!' OK, writing it down, 'Running water.' I mean, everything in the world is near running water, a river, a sink, a sewer, I mean, are you serious? Then she starts going on about Memori. 'Fourteen-year-old girl, her whole fucking life in front of her, this vicious pig, this miserable piece of shit, this . . . TIRES!'

"OK, 'Tires.'

" 'He snuffs the life out of three young ladies and then what does he do? He goes home and crawls back in bed with his new girlfriend, like he just got up to take a piss, and can you imagine what a piece of work that stupid bitch . . . BROKEN TOILET!'

"And, I swear on my children, when she said that, 'Broken toilet,' I just about pissed myself."

"Yeah?" Whelan apparently his only listener.

"Listen to me," Billy said, leaning forward. "The bodies were discovered by Tonya Howard's new boyfriend when he came to the house about five, six hours later, and by the time we got there, rigor was going pretty good. We found Memori and Tonya in the living room and we thought that was it, but when I opened the bathroom door . . ." Billy wiped his dry mouth. "See, when Taft lived with Tonya, whenever he would discipline the little one he'd always take her into the bathroom, and that's where he took her to shoot her that morning, and after he shot her he stuck her head and shoulders in the toilet. Like I said, rigor had set in and we couldn't get her out, so we had to use a sledgehammer to shatter the porcelain. So, 'Broken toilet,' the lady said. Don't ask me how."

"Then what happened."

"I brought her back to the projects and let her into the apartment, see if she could maybe pick something up in the air."

"Did she?"

"Nope."

"What did she say when she saw the broken toilet?"

"Just nodded, like, 'I told you so.' "

"She got you on the running water, too," Whelan said, "if you want to be technical about it."

"That too, I guess."

"You write her that letter?"

"I'm working on it."

"The thing about the younger brother," Pavlicek suddenly said, addressing his clasped hands. "The one who went away for it? Truly stupid people are the toughest to interview because they can't tell when you've talked them into a corner. 'Forensics says he was killed with a golf club, Eugene. Is there a golf club in the house?'

" 'I don't know.'

" 'Well, we found one.'

" 'OK.'

" 'We found your fingerprints on it.'

" 'OK.'

" 'So how could you not know there was a golf club in the house?'

" 'I don't know.'

" 'Do you like to play golf?'

" 'No.'

" 'So then, once again, I have to ask, how'd your fingerprints come to be on the shaft?'

" 'I don't know . . .' "

Pavlicek took a breath, his gaze going from his hands to his untouched shot glass. "I remember, I tried to get Jeffrey's goat, so I ask him, 'It can't be easy living with a retard for a brother.' You know what he says to me? 'You should try it.' "

He reached for his Midleton's, threw it back.

"A real sweetheart," he muttered, then shut himself down, not once in his story having raised his eyes to his friends, leaving Billy to wonder whether maybe Bannion's murder had him deeply crashing, like a postpartum Ahab if the author had allowed him to kill the whale and go home to his family.

"Fuck you, with your 'I'm all heart,' " Yasmeen bawled, suddenly deeply drunk and in tears. "Why do you always have to make me feel so bad?"

Before Whelan could respond, she tilted into Billy, slurred in his ear, "Sometimes I can still taste you," then lowered her forehead to the table and went to sleep.

"I think for Jeffrey," Pavlicek said to no one, "Thomas Rivera, his brother Eugene, the whole thing was like snapping a table-cloth." Then, thickly, "If anybody had it coming, right?"

Billy and Whelan looked at each other blankly before raising their eyes to the waiter, who had finally come by to pass out

88

menus and announce the specials.

Billy's first run of the night didn't come in until just before dawn, an assault in a flower shop on a beat-up stretch of upper Broadway where Harlem became Hamilton Heights, the roughness of the neighborhood offset by its heart-stoppingly abrupt view of the Hudson River, which seemed to leap up to meet the cresting avenue. Given the limbo hour, Billy's partner of choice was Roger Mayo, a hollow-eyed, scoop-chested chain-smoker in his eighth year on Night Watch, a borderline mute, a mystery, no one in the squad having any idea where he came from or where he went afterward. But Mayo was also a natural nocturnal, someone Billy could count on not to fall face-first into the lap of a suspect halfway through an interview at six in the morning, which was not nothing.

Wading to the sidewalk through double- and triple-parked cruisers, they passed the open back doors of an ambulance and saw a young chunky Latina sitting inside, a sepia necklace of fingerprints around her throat.

"How she doing?" Mayo asked an EMT.

"She's pissed."

Leaving Mayo to take her statement, Billy headed to the scene of the crime, the florist shop a cramped, ramshackle affair with wind-riddled, rotten wooden moldings around the door frame and the sole display window. The low-ceilinged selling floor was covered with cracked linoleum, and the near-empty flower refrigerator was overhung by a roughly built half-loft, the squeak and groan of shifting feet up there nearly drowning out the soft jazz playing somewhere behind a battery of poinsettias and greeting card spin racks down below.

.Climbing a short flight of raw pine stairs, Billy found himself in a cell-like, three-walled bedroom, cops and medics obscuring his view of the perp, Wallice Oliver. The guy was a frail, bare-chested seventy-year-old with a pharaonic goatee, wheezing asthmatically as he sat slumped on the side of a narrow bed. The towel draped around his neck made him look like a geriatric boxer.

As an EMT inserted a spirometer in Oliver's mouth to gauge his lung capacity, Billy took inventory of his surroundings. In one corner a gold saxophone perched upright in its stand; in another stood a spindly desk, its blotter covered with a scatter of prescription bottles, a jar of olive oil, an ankh, a crucifix, and a Star of David. Scotch-taped to the walls were two photographs of Oliver as a younger man, one of him onstage with Rahsaan Roland Kirk, the other of him performing in Sun Ra's Arkestra.

Billy made his way through the milling uniforms to the bed.

"You want to tell me what happened?"

"I already said all that." Oliver reared back to peer up at him.

"Just one more time."

"She come in once, like around Valentine's Day," pausing to take a hit of Primatene Mist, "says she was looking to buy a plant for her mother, young girl, looked around, didn't buy nothing though, walked out, then came back a hour later, asked if I needed any help in here, and to tell you the truth I just barely support myself with this, you know? So she leaves again, then comes back a third time that night, knocks on the door right as I'm turning out the lights, steps inside, drops to her knees, puts me in her mouth, says, 'Daddy, you let me live up there, you can have me anytime you want.' Next thing I know I'm a man again, but she's Satan and everything in my life's all fucked up. I had a wife was a schoolteacher, a nice crib, moved out on them both to be up here under a seven-foot ceiling with her. I can't even straighten my back no more, and I tell you I will put up with a lot of meanness just to have a hard dick again, but the things she said to me tonight?" Oliver bowed his head, kneaded his waxy, amber fingers. "I have never been hurt by words like that in my life."

Leaving the scene an hour later, the rising sun accentuating the emptiness of the street, Billy heard his cell go off, Stacey Taylor again, this time a text:

i know u r screening my calls dont

MILTON RAMOS

"I'm not even going to ask you who threw the shot, because I know you didn't see, right?"

Milton was talking to the head-bandaged Shakespeare Avenue banger, who was sitting up on his wheel-locked gurney in the trauma room of the St. Ann's ER.

"Where my clothes at," the victim ducking and weaving in an effort to look past Milton, standing less than a foot away from him in the curtained-off space. "Call the damn nurse."

Milton gave it a beat, watching dispassionately as the traumatized tissue around Carlos Hernandez's bullet-creased temple finally began to balloon in earnest, forcing the thick gauze dressing to slowly rise like a bloody soufflé.

"You know what?" he finally said. "Don't tell me. Take care of it yourself, or at least let him get another crack at you and finish what he started, because God's truth?" Milton shut his notepad. "I don't give a shit."

"Yeah, see? You going psychological on me."

"Really, I'm not. I mean this from the bottom of my heart, soldier boy, I don't give a shit. Just try not to let it go down near a playground or on a basketball court, that's all I ask."

Milton never saw the point of the detective squad getting involved in a gang shooting so early in the game like this, knowing that the 4-6 Street Intel Unit, on a first-name basis with every young Morlock out there, had probably already hauled in their informants. By this afternoon they would be not only smart-bombing the streets looking for the shooter but scarecrowing the two beefing crews — Shakespeare Over All and Creston On Top — from any planned retaliation and/or re-retaliation. The fact of the matter was, only two hours after getting creased, Carlos here was already old news, the only thing anybody cared about right now was minimizing the inevitable mayhem to come.

"I tell you what," Milton said, leaning in and putting a hand on Carlos's bare knee. "Give me a name and you get one free get-out-of-jail card, on me."

"I ain't in jail."

"Not today."

"You like putting your hand there?"

"I'd rather put it around your throat."

Milton turned to leave.

"You supposed to give me your card," Carlos said.

"I would, but I'm running kind of low."

Psychology, my balls.

Coming back out into the main reception area, Milton walked past the Latina nurse manning the triage desk and up the center aisle of the waiting area, the benches eerily silent despite a full house. Reaching for the wall-mounted remote button that opened the door to the street, he hesitated, abruptly overcome with a powerful sense of having forgotten something important, the sensation like waking from an intense dream and trying to remember the fading details. He patted himself down — sidearm, notepad, wallet, keys, all there — then turned and started to retrace his steps, walking back past the triage station, getting as far as the door to the trauma room before stopping in his tracks and once again reversing his steps, this time coming back at an angle so that he could take a good look at that nurse without her noticing.

Standing in the near shadows, he stared at her, then stared some more, only snapping out of it when he felt her starting to sense his presence, at which point he put his head down and took off, not looking up until he was back out on the street, the sudden sunlight adding to his hyped sense of disorientation.

It wasn't until a few hours later, still in a daze as he typed up the Fives on Carlos Hernandez, that he belatedly registered the name tag that had been affixed to her whites, Milton reaching for a pad and writing it down in a chittery hand:

C GRAVES

Wanting to be alone with this, he slipped into the windowless bunk room. Ignoring the two detectives lying belly-up and near lifeless in opposite corners of the fetid cell, he perched himself on the edge of an unmade bed and tried to think it through.

C Graves. The *C* he got. The *Graves,* he assumed, was her husband.

"Carmen Graves," he said, trying it on for size.

So. Married, moved on, a few kids most likely, and a career.

Moved on.
It was enough to snatch your breath.

CHAPTER 3

Stepping into the house at eight in the morning, Billy came across his father and his two sons seated at the dining table eating Eggos, Billy Senior in his pajamas, the boys, as usual, in full Enduring Freedom gear from dog tags to child-sized paratrooper boots.

"See, at the college, the students, they took over two buildings, one by the blacks, you know, the Afro-Americans, the other the white radicals, the Suburbans we called them," his father said. "I don't think they trusted each other, or at least the blacks didn't trust the whites. And Charley Weiss, my boss in the TPF, after two days standing around waiting for the go-ahead, he finally gets on the bullhorn, says, 'You have fifteen minutes to vacate the building or we're coming in after you.' "

"Dad," Billy said.

"Now, the, the Afro-Americans, they been

around the block a little more, and they know we mean what we say, so after a little trash talk from the classroom windows, they pretty much come right out. But the Suburbans? They never had any dealings with the police before, so it's all a big adventure for them: 'Come and get us, pigs.' "

"Pigs?" Carlos looked up from his waffle.

"Dad."

"And whenever we had to go in someplace, Charley Weiss always put me in the first wave, 'Send in the Big Guy,' he used to say. Riots, blackouts, demonstrations — 'Send in the Big Guy.' "

"The Big Guy," Declan whispered, his face shining.

"And so we went in, and we went in swinging. It was ugly, and some of us were sick about it after, but we cracked some heads that day . . ."

"Dad . . ."

"Some of those kids were crying and begging us to stop, but you get to this place in yourself, you're so pent up with all the damn waiting, your heart's pumping so hard . . ."

"Hey, guys . . ."

"I put one kid down who tried to snatch my radio, rammed him in the ribs with my baton like they taught us, it hurts like hell, let me tell you, he's laying on the ground, looks up at me, says, 'Mr. Graves, stop, please stop . . .' I take a good look at this kid, I'm . . . You got to be kidding me. Turns out he was the son of the people who we bought our house from when we moved out to the Island. Nice couple. Nice kid, too. Last time I'd seen him was about four years earlier, he must've been fourteen, fifteen, but we recognized each other that day, we surely did."

"Did you feel bad, Grandpa?" Declan again, the story a little over Carlos's head.

"Yeah, I did. I started yelling at him, 'What the hell did you grab my radio for?' He says, 'I don't know! I don't know!' I get him up, march him out of the building, take him around the corner to Amsterdam Avenue, and I tell him to go over to the St. Luke's ER, just get lost."

"My mom works at the ER," Carlos said brightly.

"I tried to tell myself that these kids had it coming, that they were trying to bring us down as a great nation, but yeah, I felt bad. That day I felt bad."

Knowing the worst was over, Billy finally retreated into his coffee, marveling, as always when he heard this story, that when his father finally retired, twenty years after

100

those bloody sit-ins, his first job as a civilian was director of student safety at the same university.

"Anyways," Billy Senior rising, "I have to go pick up your grandmother at the bank."

Declan looked to Billy, then back to his grandfather. "Grandpa," he said not unkindly, "Gramma's dead."

Billy Senior stopped at the door, turned to the table. "That's not a very nice thing to say, Declan."

Billy watched his father go out to the driveway and get in the keyless sedan, knowing he'd sit there until he forgot why he was sitting there, then come back inside.

Up in the bedroom, Billy stashed his Glock, stripped down to his boxers, and fell into bed. Fighting off sleep, he stared at the ceiling until he could hear Millie's muffler-shot old beater coming down the street, signaling the start of her workday, which consisted of impersonating a housekeeper and, more importantly, watching daytime TV with his father. She would sit as close to Billy Senior as she could without jumping on his lap, while constantly touching his arm and commenting on the screen action, all in an effort to keep him in the here and now, which was becoming an increasingly demanding job.

In the way of these things, Billy's father had become his child, and he was determined to parent him in the manner in which he had been parented himself — with patience, amusement when he could manage it, and an infinite tolerance for the weakness of his mind. Growing up, Billy's mother had been just his mother, doing her duty as required, not exactly indifferent to him but more focused on raising and training his sisters, two out of three children, in her eyes, job enough. As a father, Billy Senior had been low-key but there, not much more demonstrative than his wife but a powerfully comforting presence in his son's life nonetheless. When he was home, he was home all the way — a skill Billy had yet to master with his own family — and no fool when it came to wading through his son's alibis regarding everything from flunking Spanish and Biology, to adolescent beer benders, to a brawl in a White Castle parking lot. He rarely punished and, in a neighborhood where half the parents seemed to treat their screw-up sons like piñatas, never with his hands. But most important to Billy, his father attended all his football games, from peewee and sandlot through varsity, without ever once shouting red-faced from the sidelines or criticizing his son's play. In the Nassau County Youth League, when Billy had quarterbacked his team to a 3–0 midseason mark only to have his coach replace him with his own athletically inferior son, he remembered his father that Saturday morning trying to reason with the guy, but when he realized that the conversation was futile, he just shrugged and walked away, his eyes shining, on the edge of tears.

At Hofstra, which Billy attended for two years on a football scholarship, his father continued to show up in the stands, making it to the majority of the Pride's away games, including overnight trips to Orono, Maine, and Burlington, Vermont, until it all came to an end in the spring of his sophomore year, when Billy was busted for selling weed in the dorms. His father used whatever connections he had with the Hempstead PD to prevent Billy from being formally arrested, but he made no effort to intervene when Hofstra booted him off the campus. And when Billy came home the day of his expulsion, crushed and too ashamed to ask for his parents' forgiveness, his father, deciding that his kid's self-laceration was punishment enough, simply asked him what he intended to do with his life. When Billy couldn't come up with an answer, either that first night or the next, then and only then did he suggest the police academy.

When Billy came back downstairs at three in the afternoon, he was surprised to find Carmen's younger brother, Victor Acosta, and Victor's husband, Richard Kubin, standing together in a corner of the kitchen. Only two years younger than his sister, Victor looked barely old enough to vote, an effect, Billy thought, that had less to do with his short stature or his absurdly buffed physique than with his permanent expression of readiness — wide, alert eyes beneath arched, nearly triangular brows, lips slightly parted — making him appear as if he were perpetually attempting to pick up a distant voice bearing important news.

"Hey, what's up," Billy mumbled, embarrassed to still be in his pajamas.

"Hey," Victor said flatly, shaking his hand without meeting his eyes.

"You all right?" Billy asked, his brother-in-law coming off uncharacteristically grim, a photo negative of himself.

"Fine."

"Hey, how are you?" Billy extending his hand now to Richard, older, less eager-eyed, an easygoing enough guy — no gym for him — who tended to fade into the background when it came to Victor's family.

"I'm good," Richard saying it like he wanted to leave but didn't want to offend anyone.

"Where's Carmen?"

"Here." A third flatliner heard from, his wife standing behind his back in the opposite corner of the room, her arms crossed over her chest, her eyes fixed on the floor.

"What happened?"

"Nothing," Carmen said without looking up.

"Nothing?" Victor said sharply.

"What happened," Billy addressing the men now.

"We're adopting," Victor said. "That's all."

Carmen exhaled through her nose, studied the tilework.

"We just came by to share the good news," Richard added, his voice so even-keeled that Billy couldn't tell if he was being sarcastic.

"No, I'm happy for you," Carmen said, her gaze shifting to the backyard. "I am."

Billy followed the men out to their ancient Range Rover in the driveway.

"So wow, adopting," he scrambled. "Where from?"

"Brazil," Victor said.

"Brazil, huh. Boy? Girl?"

"One of each."

"Twins?"

"Can't break up a set," Richard said, unlocking the driver's-side door.

My husband . . . Billy had never thought of himself as having a problem with gay marriage, but he still couldn't quite wrap his head around another man uttering those two words.

"Did you tell your sister it's two?"

"I would've," Victor said, "but I was afraid her heart couldn't handle the joy."

"Anyways, that's terrific, really great," Billy said, then added by way of apology: "You want us to throw you a baby shower or something?"

At least that got them smiling.

When he returned to the house, Carmen was still standing wedged into her corner of the kitchen.

"What the hell's wrong with you?"

"Heather has two daddies," she muttered, looking away.

"I don't get it, your brother comes over with such big news, you couldn't even give him a hug or something?"

"Guess not," she said defiantly but starting to tear up a little.

"Just tell me what's going on."

"Why does something always have to be going on with you?" she snapped, then walked out of the kitchen, up the stairs, and into the bedroom, closing the door behind her.

And that's where they left it. That's where they always left it when it came to Victor and, if he thought about it, so much else.

At five in the evening, Billy walked into Brown's Family Funeral Home, on Adam Clayton Powell Boulevard. The chapel, a glorified living room, fluorescently lit and lined with folding chairs, was standing room only and awaft in dope smoke. A twenty-two-year-old banger tagged Hi-Life, who had been shot dead in retaliation for an earlier retaliation, lay in his coffin in a front corner of the chapel facing his people, most of whom were wearing oversized rest-in-peace T-shirts silk-screened with a photo of Hi-Life sitting on a stoop. A second laminated RIP snapshot on a bead chain hung off their necks like a backstage pass.

Walking down the room-length particle-board partition that divided the chapel from a line of office cubicles, Billy passed Redman's elderly father in the first cubicle, Redman Senior leaning back in his chair playing computer poker. In the second cubicle, Redman's twenty-three-year-old fifth wife, Nola, was lying on a daybed reading a book in her Côte d'Ivoirian accent to Redman's seventh or eighth son, Rafer, a toddler with a gastrointestinal feeding tube inserted into his stomach. And then finally, in the last cubicle, was the man himself, all six foot five of him, hunched over his desk slurping lo mein from a take-out carton, the spindly wire bookcase behind his back filled with unclaimed cremains in cardboard urns going back to the 1990s.

"There he is," Redman said, extending an absurdly long-fingered hand but remaining in his chair due to the bullet that had drilled him through both hips five years earlier.

"Christ," Billy said, waving away the chronic in the air.

"They pay like everybody else."

"You ever hear of secondhand smoke?"

"That's just a story they tell you."

"A conspiracy, you mean."

"You said it, not me."

"Like seat belts?"

"Government can't tell me to buckle up. I break some bones, that's my problem."

"Don't tread on me."

A toddler wearing a Hi-Life T-shirt down to her sneakers wandered in, then wandered back out unattended.

"How was dinner last night?"

"Not to be funny," Billy said, "but it was like a funeral."

"Not over Bannion, I hope. You all should have been Riverdancing up and down the block."

"What can I say, the whole thing was just off."

"I heard he was exsanguinated?"

"Never seen anything like it. Apparently he just bled out in midflight, came down like a shop sign."

"Exsanguinated . . . Makes my job easier."

"Not mine. I had me a blood trail long as a Nantucket sleigh ride."

An elderly woman, also in a Hi-Life tee, wandered the hall while coughing up her lungs. They both watched as she pulled back a heavy curtain drawn across the end of the corridor and found herself staring at a leg-less body lying on a prep table like a three-hundred-pound mound of pancake batter, a nine-inch steel syringe jammed into the jawbone through the side of the gape-locked mouth.

"Oh."

"Bathroom's near the front," Redman said. "The other way."

"Oh." She turned and wandered off without looking at them.

"Got to get a door put up," Redman said, resuming his dinner.

Rafer, now in a wheeled Elmo activity

baby walker, came flying into his father's cubicle and had to be intercepted before he crashed into the cremains stand.

"Slow your roll there, Little Man," Redman said, wincing from the sudden movement.

It pained Billy to see him so fragile; back in the early days, Redman had once saved his life by catching him one-handed after he fell from a corroded fifth-floor fire escape while they were trying to hit a dope apartment through a bedroom window. Redman, coming up behind him, had been one story below, and he had snagged one of Billy's arms on his way down and held him like that, Billy's feet pinwheeling forty feet above the sidewalk, until he could grab onto something with his other hand. The memory of that aborted plummet could still make him shoot up in bed at four in the morning.

"Is he getting any better?" Billy asked, nodding to Rafer and unconsciously touching his own gut.

"No."

Redman had never been one to countenance blather, so Billy was at a loss for something else to say on the subject.

"See that shine-head nigger in there?" Redman pointed out a trimly built middle-aged man seated in the chapel sporting a

110

bow tie and an inexpensive but impeccable white suit, his shaved scalp gleaming under the cheap chandelier as if Turtle Waxed. "Antoine Davis-Bey. That's the eel that got Sweetpea Harris out from under the rock."

"I fought the law and the law lost," Billy said, bracing for another Sweetpea diatribe.

"You know, I saw him last week, Harris. Came right in here for a friend's funeral, had the gall to come up to me at my desk and ask me how I've been, you believe that? 'Detective Brown! That leg still hurting you?' " Redman rearing back from his dinner in disgust. "He's been locked up a few times since killing Salaam, but I heard the last time he was smart enough to claim he had a drug problem, avoided jail for rehab, although some people would say sitting in a group circle eight hours a day and getting yelled at by every idiot and their cousin is worse than six months on a prison barge."

In Billy's estimation, Redman, for all his unrelenting focus on bringing Sweetpea Harris to justice, was less obsessed with his homicidally peevish White than he was with the victim, Salaam Pridgen. Like Redman himself way back when, Salaam had been a fifteen-year-old high school phenom already being courted by college scouts, a too-skinny kid with cheetah speed who, as Redman would tell anyone who would listen, owned the most explosive first step to the basket he'd ever seen. A detective in Harlem at the time of the murder eight years earlier, Redman had been watching the boy play since ninth grade, for Rice, for the Gauchos, and even, now and then, in pickup games, anywhere from Marcus Garvey Park to some random one-hoop half-court attached to the ass end of an elementary school.

Redman had no trouble talking about these things to one and all, including the mute bodies he daily prepped for Homecoming, but only Billy and a few others knew that in addition to his interest in the kid, he had been sweet on Salaam's mother. In between wives at that time of his life, Redman had struck up a casual friendship with her while going to her son's games. For a while it looked like the friendship would lead to something more, but then her son's death turned her from a smart and vigorous woman with an appetite for the world into a dead-eyed stutterer who took forever to turn to the sound of her own name.

"You repped this piece of shit too?" Redman grunted to Antoine Davis-Bey, who had materialized in the doorway of the cubicle.

"Black and poor," Davis-Bey said, winking at Billy.

"Black and poor, huh? That's a eight-thousand-dollar casket, and his people paid in cash."

"You're up, you're down. See how they're doing six months from now," tossing Billy a second wink, as if getting Redman's goat was everyone's idea of fun.

"You know what they call four hundred lawyers chained up and thrown into a volcano?" Redman said.

"Hey, guys," Billy said.

"And let me just ask," the lawyer checking the time on his oversized watch, "that eight thousand dollars, whose pocket is it in now?"

"How about I take that bow tie, twist it around your neck a few times, let go, and see if you spin around the room."

"Oh, for Christ's sake," Billy said, "you're like my kids."

"He started," Bey winking at him one last time and then heading out.

Watching him go, Billy looked toward the chapel and saw one of the eulogizers take the pulpit, three gold teeth and a blue Giants cap.

"Hi-Life, one thing about Hi-Life, he had jokes, man, he always had jokes. Like, he

113

was always complainin' how his teeth was cold, right?"

"Fucking Sweetpea," Redman said, offering a strand of lo mein to his g-tubed toddler. "I keep waiting for someone to cap his ass."

"He's still living in the neighborhood?"

"122 West 118th, third floor rear, but I hear he spends most of his time with his quote unquote fiancée up in the Bronx."

"Well, if the Bronx is good at one thing, it's hurting people," Billy said. "He'll get his."

Billy's cell rang halfway between the funeral home and his car.

"I got your shield here," Yasmeen's husband, Dennis Doyle, said. "It was under our bed, you must've dropped it last night when you brought her home. You want to come get it?"

Before answering, Billy took a second to minutely analyze every dip and rise in Dennis's voice, searching, as always, for the slightest hint of anger.

"Hello?" Dennis said.

There was no edge that Billy could detect. There never was, and it drove him crazy.

"I'll come right now."

Sometimes I can still taste you . . . . Yas-

114

meen's last words to him in the steak house, and then whispered again into his ear right before she passed out for good, her arms around his neck as he lowered her fully clothed into bed. She had been way too drunk to drive after last night's catastrophe of a reunion, and with Dennis stuck working four to midnights as a robbery sergeant in the 4-6, Billy took it upon himself to drive her home, half-carry her up to the apartment, and lay her out for the night — completely on the up-and-up, as if Dennis had been watching on a hidden monitor.

All three had known each other since their academy days when, unwittingly, both Dennis and Billy were going out with her. Dennis was in love, Billy was not. It went on for five months like that, both boys in the dark until New Year's Eve 1994, when Yasmeen had walked into Gordon's, a cop bar near the academy, and both he and Dennis simultaneously moved to her. Billy got it instantly, the whole picture, and quickly, quietly stepped back, letting Dennis obliviously go forward into her arms, Yasmeen's sad and knowing eyes staring into his over Dennis's shoulder. And that was the end of that: No hard feelings, it was fun, you deserve the best.

Dennis proposed to her at the bar that

115

night when they were both blasted, the barmaids sailing unsteadily about the dim, damp room with plastic crates of free beer. At first she said no, said, Who the fuck proposes to any kind of respectable girl at some shit-face, after-hours cop bar at five in the morning? Dennis felt so bad about his terrible timing that he started to cry, and it was those idiotic tears, to Billy's astonishment, that did it. OK, Yasmeen finally said while stroking Dennis's hair. Sure, let's get married. Billy saw the whole thing from the short end of the bar, and he thought it was the most pathetic proposal he'd ever witnessed — Dennis never even got off his stool.

He thought it wouldn't last a year, but it was going on twenty and counting: two girls, a three-bedroom terraced co-op overlooking the Hudson in Riverdale, and a summer place upstate in Greenwood Lake.

"So how's she feeling?" Billy asked Dennis, sitting across from him in the living room.

"You're looking at it," Dennis answered, tilting his chin toward the closed bedroom door at the end of the hall, Yasmeen's shucked-off Tibetan hippie coat still lying in front of the door like a shaggy guard dog eighteen hours after Billy had carried her inside.

"So listen," Dennis said, tilting forward from the edge of his couch, "I'm sorry about last night, and I thank you for bringing her home, but help me out here: what the hell happened?"

"Hey, all I can tell you was that she was two-fisted throwing them back from the door on in. I don't know, maybe the news about Bannion got her all agitated about Cortez again."

"Christ, I hope not. I swear to you, living with her when she's on a Cortez tear? It's like a reign of terror around here, yelling at the kids, at me, first she can't go to sleep, then she can't wake up, first she can't eat, then she can't stop. I try to get her to smoke a little weed, but even that doesn't help."

"And she's drinking like this now?"

"She's been going through a patch."

"What's a patch."

"Two months, maybe?"

"Every night?"

Dennis opened his hands and closed them.

"That's not a patch, that's forty acres and a mule."

"I'm talking to some people about it," he said.

"But she's off Cortez?"

117

Yasmeen's White, Eric Cortez, had been — and as far as Billy knew still was — a real honey, a fully grown man who, five years earlier, had plunged a knife into the heart of thirteen-year-old Raymond Del Pino, ostensibly for talking to Cortez's fourteen-year-old girlfriend in the junior high school cafeteria.

That alone would have been horrific enough, but Cortez had also called his young vic twenty-four hours before the deed, just to tell him what he was going to do. Yasmeen's squad quickly learned about the call and the caller from the victim's friends, and in order to start building their no-witness case against Cortez they needed to get their hands on his cell. But when they showed up at the murderer's apartment with a warrant for his phone, Cortez, sprawled on his couch with his half-wit girlfriend, glanced at the writ, laughed, and said, "That's not my number." And it wasn't: in her rush to get the judge to sign off on the warrant Yasmeen had accidentally transposed two of the digits. They were back in his apartment within two hours with the proper paper, but by then Cortez had ditched the object of their desire and that was the end of that, Cortez still out there doing his thing while Yasmeen, curdled with guilt, had spent the past five years banging her head against the wall searching for new ways to bring him in.

Dennis got up from the couch and pulled two legal boxes from under a small desk. The last time Billy had seen the Raymond Del Pino homicide cartons they were stuffed with case files, court docs, and note pads, just as they had been on the day she retired and finally snuck them out of the precinct, her overjoyed squad holding the doors for her all the way to the street. But now all they held were invoices, checkbooks, stationery, and stamps.

"Do you have any idea how elated I was when I saw her dump all that shit?"

"When was this?"

"A few months ago, I come out of the elevator and there she is, throwing everything down the incinerator chute. I couldn't believe my eyes." Dennis glanced toward the heaped coat by the door. "I was hoping that would be that."

"Look, if it's any consolation, she wasn't the only freak show last night."

"Billy, she's not a freak."

"No, hey, look, you know I didn't mean . . . But I have to tell you, Pavlicek? It was like somebody was walking around inside his head with a flashlight."

"Well, that's understandable, given the thing with Bannion."

"You think? Let me tell you something, if it was Curtis Taft who bought the farm instead? Are you kidding me?"

"Well, Pavlicek's a different animal."

"The hell he is. Did Yasmeen ever tell you about the day we came on three Ñeta Juniors tied up and head-shot in an apartment on Southern Boulevard? Scumbags, but still, they were kids. You know what Pavlicek did? He took us all out to Jimmy's Bronx River Cafe."

"People change."

"If you say so."

Behind the bedroom door, a broken-voiced Yasmeen called for her husband.

"So how's Night Watch?" Dennis asked, trying to ignore the softly cracked wails.

"You know, quiet, busy, quiet, busy. How's the kids?"

"Good, yours?"

"Everything's a weapon," Billy said as Yasmeen's cries became more full-throated.

"Got to have girls," Dennis grunted as he finally, reluctantly, rose for the bedroom. "The worst thing they do is exclude each other."

Alone now, staring out the window at New Jersey across the river, Billy afforded himself the luxury of remembering Yasmeen in the days before that night in Gordon's when Dennis had inadvertently pulled the plug on all their fun. They got along well enough over the months they were together, doing all the usual out-of-the-house dating stuff, but basically it was about the sex. They both swore to each other that they were the best fucks they'd ever been with, which wasn't saying much when you're both working-class Catholics in your early twenties, and Billy's entire erotic repertoire consisted of sticking it in as fast as he could, withdrawing partially as fast as he could, and repeating if necessary. At the time, Dennis was even more of a sexual bumpkin than either one of them; at his bachelor party he confessed to Billy, his best man, that he knew Yasmeen was no virgin when he proposed, but he loved her too much not to forgive her.

Dennis came out of the bedroom looking like a surgeon with bad news. For the thousandth time in the last twenty years, Billy wondered if he knew about them and just wasn't saying.

"Anyways . . ." Billy slowly rose and reached for his jacket.

"You sure you don't want some coffee, a shot of something?" Dennis stood there, tilting toward the kitchen.

"I'm good."

"You sure?"

"Seriously, I got to book."

Giving up, Dennis finally sat back on the couch. "I should have brought your shield down to you, you know?"

"No problem," Billy said, backing toward the front door.

"I just didn't want to leave her alone like this, you know?"

"Totally understood."

"I just hope she doesn't start getting crazy about Cortez all over again, you know what I'm saying?" Dennis staring right through Billy. "I just could not live with that."

The night was nothing but softballs, the highlight being a report of two women hacking away at each other with hatchets or swords in front of an NYU dorm, which in the end turned out to be just a drunken fight between two Xenas coming out of a costume party and throwing down with their foam axes. By seven-thirty in the morning Billy was on his way home, making it nearly to his exit before he remembered the date and, with a dulling heart, dutifully hit the turnaround and headed back toward the city.

Carmen saw two therapists, one of them a stocky ex-nun who, sponsored by Local 1146 of the Home and Health Care Workers, bounced around from hospital to hospital in the Bronx like a circuit court judge. She had a makeshift office in the basement of St. Ann's that faintly reeked of the morgue at the opposite end of the hall, an all-too-familiar odor that seemed to underscore Billy's attitude toward his bimonthly shared sessions, especially when they were scheduled so early in the morning.

"You have to understand," Carmen said. "Victor, when he was a kid, he couldn't even keep his sea monkeys wet, and now he's going to have a child? It'll be dead in a month."

"Jesus," Billy said. "Are you hearing yourself? That doesn't even sound like you."

"Can you elaborate on that, Billy?" the therapist said, her tone mildly sedating.

"Yeah, Billy, can you elaborate on that?"

"Carm, he's your brother, why are you always so mad at him?"

"Why is he always so mad at me?"

Billy gave up.

"OK," the therapist said, "let's take your question first, Carmen. Why is your brother always so mad at you?"

"He isn't," Billy said.

"Let her talk now."

"We went over this a million times," Carmen said. "When he was twelve, I had to go live with my father in Atlanta and he felt like I abandoned him. One million times I have said this to you."

" 'Had to' implies no choice."

"My father was *sick*."

"He was remarried. He had a wife," Billy said, expecting, then receiving, a warning finger from the therapist.

"His wife was borderline retarded," Carmen said, "just like him."

"So a fifteen-year-old girl 'had to' uproot her entire young life in the Bronx — mother, brother, school, friends . . ."

"I didn't *have* any friends."

Except Victor, Billy knew, Carmen always telling him that her younger brother back then was her only friend in the world, "like two nerds in a pod," she called them.

". . . and leave all those she loved in order to be with a man who walked out on her and her family so early in her childhood that she had no memory of what he even looked like?"

"There were other things going on," Carmen said. "I told you that, too."

"Yes, you did, but I think maybe the time has come to finally start exploring a few of those 'other things.' "

The room descended into a tense silence, Billy avoiding his wife's eyes, hoping that she would finally say something, anything, about what he had come to regard as the Flight to Atlanta.

"Would you feel more comfortable if your husband left the room?"

Carmen shrugged.

And so they all sat there, listening to the squeal of gurneys out in the hall for a full minute or more, until Carmen finally opened her mouth.

"I don't like the Cymbalta you have me on. It makes me too manic, plus I think it stops me from having orgasms."

"Jesus, Carmen." Billy blushed, not so much embarrassed for himself as pained for his wife.

Afterward, as they walked to the St. Ann's parking lot in silence, each to their own car, Billy remembered asking Carmen once why she hadn't spoken to her therapist about a serious issue involving their kids. Her answer — *"Because that's personal"* — had made him laugh so hard his eyes filled with tears.

MILTON RAMOS

Rose of Lima.

Daughters of Jacob.

Ten minutes in either institution made him feel like he was breathing air through a pinched straw. Visiting both in the same day left him feeling like a clubbed seal.

First that fucking school: some kind of parent/career-day event that had him standing there rocking from foot to foot like a beetle-browed dummy in front of two dozen third graders, the good-looking lay teacher in the back of the room nose-down in paperwork, not even listening or raising her eyes to him as he mumbled his way through the joys of the Job.

And those questions . . .

Did you ever kill anybody?

No.

(One, but he had it coming.)

Can I see your gun?

I'm not carrying one.

126

(No, you can't see my goddamn gun.)

Did you ever come to my *tío*'s house?

Who's your *tío*?

Reuben Matos. He lives on Sherman Avenue.

Yeah, once.

(At least.)

How much money do you make?

Enough to pay tuition here.

Do you ever get mad at Sofia?

Never.

(Never.)

How come she's so fat?

Milton looking to his daughter seated front and center, staring at him with resigned eyes, then back at the kid who asked the question.

How come you're so ugly?

Is her mommy really dead?

Yes.

How did she die?

Hello? This to the head-down half-a-nun in the rear of the room. What are you doing back there, smoking crack?

That's not a nice question, Anthony, she said, still not looking up.

What's your favorite team?

The Red Sox.

Boooo . . .

Do you like Big Papi?

I am Big Papi.
And again: Did you ever kill anybody?
I said no.
(Two, but they had it coming. Three.)

And now this here, the Daughters of Jacob
Assisted Living Center, the air redolent of
boiled hot dogs and Lysol, Mantovani
strings drifting through the halls like musical Haldol, old folks sitting alone in the
lobby just staring at air, filling him with
anger at their AWOL kids. Before he could
even make his way to the elevator banks,
and not for the first time, one old lady,
confusing him with some José from building services, asked him when he was coming to fix her radiator.

His aunt Pauline had her own small suite
— at least he had been able to swing that
for her — and as she went on and on about
a gluey Hawaiian salad she had been served
the week before, he sat on her living room
couch and took in the art on display: a bowl
of silver and gold papier-mâché fruit, a
plaster pair of life-sized praying hands, two
— count 'em — two ceramic menorahs, a
glazed and mounted ram's horn, and a
framed print of a fiddler floating sideways
above an off-balance ghetto. Aunt, excuse,
Tante Pauline had stayed in the faith, if only

128

sentimentally, unlike her sister, Milton's mother, who married a PR to spite her parents. On the other hand, his father had married his mother to spite her parents, too. It was a match made in hell, and if his old man's this-time-for-good disappearance when Milton was ten was not exactly a cause for celebration, it wasn't nearly enough of a blow to throw anyone off their feed.

"So, you didn't bring Sofie?" Pauline asked.

"Sofia. She has school. I'll bring her on the weekend."

Seated across from him on an oversized throne chair, her hands clasped atop her kettle-drum midriff, his aunt tracked his gaze to the framed photos of his, and her, dead family members, the images scattered across the side tables and windowsills.

"I talk to them all the time," she said.

"Me too."

"In the middle of the night, sometimes I wake up and see my sister standing in a corner of the room."

"I see all of them."

"Your brother was such a sweetheart."

"Which one," although he knew. Little Man had been everybody's favorite.

"That day killed your mother."

"Killed my other brother too."

"Who, Edgar?"

"Yes," he said slowly, "your oldest nephew."

"Edgar was always so surly."

Milton stood up, took a little walk around the coffee table to settle himself.

"He took care of us, Aunt Pauline. My mom with her circulation, half the time she couldn't even make it out of the house."

"You were pretty surly back then, too. The both of you. But look at you now, a real man who doesn't forget his family."

"Family's everything."

"I can't even get my own children to visit me, but you come by like clockwork."

Of course he did. Pauline had taken him in for three years, right after the slow-motion massacre had come to an end, the move from the Bronx to her home in Brooklyn most likely saving his life.

He drew a breath before shifting gears. "Aunt Pauline, when you would come and visit us back then, do you remember a girl in our building, Carmen? Puerto Rican, about fifteen years old?"

"Carmen?"

"Maybe spent time with Little — with Rudy?"

"Carmen . . ."

"Skinny, big eyes, long hair."

"Wait, Carmen. From downstairs. Her mother was Dolores."

"Right. Did you ever see her with Rudy?"

"Dolores?"

"Carmen."

"What, like together?"

"Like anything, holding hands, making out, arguing maybe."

"Dolores had a son too, Willy? William?"

"Victor. But let's stick with Carmen."

"He was supposed to be a little, you know, that way, the boy, not that it bothered me."

"Aunt Pauline," Milton said, waving his hand. "Carmen. Did you ever see her with Rudy."

"I can't remember."

"Think hard."

"I wish I could."

"No problem." It was a long shot anyhow.

"Why are you asking about Carmen all of a sudden?"

"Nothing." Milton shrugged, trying to keep his voice as casual as he could. "I thought I maybe saw her. It was probably somebody else."

But was it really her? Oh yeah, you bet. How could he ever forget those tea-stained big eyes, pulled down sad at the corners like the eyes of the lost and burning girls on the *Anima Sola* postcards that used to turn him on when he was a kid. He'd even had a crush on her for a hot minute when her family had first moved into the building, a sense memory so galling and torturous to him now that it made him want to rip out his brain.

He glanced at the sunburst clock over Pauline's head: two-thirty, tea-time. He went to the refrigerator and poured her a brimming glass from the half gallon of Gallo Family Zinfandel she kept in there.

"Seventy-four years old, I'm finally an alkie," she said, her standard line whenever he did the honors.

"You'll live."

"Why did you and your brother always call Rudy Little Man?"

"Because everybody else in the family topped out at five-eight, then Rudy gets born and he's all of a sudden six-three."

"I don't get it."

His eyes turned dull as nickels.

"Whatever happened to Dolores?" Pauline asked.

"I heard she got cancer," Milton said, "about two years after the . . ."

After the what: tragedy? He hated that word, it reeked of, what . . . Fate? Inevitability? Bullshit. Tears and a turn for home?

Fuck you. Surrender to the mysteriousness of the Great Mysterian?

Surrender; what can ya do.

Plenty.

"And they never found those bastards who killed him," she said.

"No, they didn't, Tante Pauline." Milton rising, this time to leave. "And they never will."

CHAPTER 4

By the time Billy arrived at the scene of a double shooting on the Lower East Side directly across the street from the Alfred E. Smith Houses, both victims, conscious and looking more pissed than traumatized, were being gurneyed into separate ambos as a mixed crowd of club kids and born-heres took snaps with their iPhones.

"Anybody looking to go out of the picture?" he asked Stupak.

"Doubt it. They were both howling pretty good before you got here."

"Anything on the shooter?"

"You're looking at them," Mayo said.

"Which?"

"Both."

"Yeah?"

"It looks like they were walking from opposite ends of Oliver," Stupak said, "and decided to jack each other at the same time.

It's all on camera and we recovered the guns."

"Spy versus Spy, except they're both black," Mayo said, then, having filled his word quota for the night, stepping to the corner for a smoke.

"So my question to you, boss," Stupak said, "are they perps or victims?"

Billy thought about it a moment. "They're perptims."

"You think this is funny?" a young Hispanic woman snapped, her eyes shimmering with anger.

"Hey, how're you doing, did you know either of these guys?" Stupak asked easily, making her disappear into the Smiths. "Can you bring her back here please?" she asked a uniform.

Billy's cell thrummed inside his sport jacket, a fresh text from Stacey:

can you please answer my calls please thats the only way to get me to stop

He knew her enough to know that this was true and it was time to get it over with. To brace himself he went into an all-night bodega and came out chugging a Turbo Tea.

"Hey, it's me."

"Jesus, he lives."

135

"Sorry, my phone's been . . ."

"Don't, don't, don't."

Was it the energy drink that made the cigarette taste so good or the other way around? "So what's up. You OK?"

As usual after building up a case against returning Stacey's calls, now that he was actually talking to her, he couldn't remember what the big deal was.

"Yeah, but I need to tell you something," she said.

"What's that."

"Have breakfast with me. It's a long story."

"Give me the headline."

"Just have breakfast with me."

"Stacey . . ."

"You'll be glad you did. Well, maybe 'glad' isn't the right word."

That right there was the big deal.

Five hours later, Billy sat in his parked car outside the tin can of a diner in Mount Vernon where he was to break bread with Stacey Taylor. He smoked one cigarette, then another, delaying as long as possible the sit-down to come. Seeing her was always a wrenching experience, the psychic equivalent of returning to a battlefield with your former enemy years after the bloodbath that had scarred you both, eager to reach out

136

but unable to rid yourself of the lingering acid that still bit at the back of the throat.

In 1997 Stacey had been a young reporter for the *New York Post,* an aggressive up-and-comer who glommed onto Billy's notorious double shooting in the Bronx, attempting to make her journalistic bones by investigating the rumor that he'd been high when he pulled the trigger. Backed by two independent eyewitnesses, both willing to go public, both claiming to have seen him doing blow in the rear of an Intervale Avenue bar an hour before the shooting, as well as two more witnesses who wouldn't go on record but corroborated the statements of the two who would, Stacey went in and made a hard pitch to her editors, touting the thoroughness of her background checks on her sources, then bombarding them with reports about police abuse in the area, anecdotal evidence that was as easy for her to gather out on the street as picking daisies.

In the end, she needn't have tried so hard. One week earlier, the *Post* had lost out to the *Daily News* on the suicide of a retired police lieutenant in a Queens dope motel, and her editors were hot to get back on top. The story was page one for two days running, so when it all fell apart shortly after, everyone involved got scorched, but no one as badly as Stacey. In the end it came down to those background checks: in her anxiety about losing her scoop to the time-sucking demands of a thorough vetting of her sources, she hadn't done them at all.

The real background checks — conducted, embarrassingly enough, by the *Daily News* — revealed that one of the on-record eyewits was the brother of a heroin dealer Billy had sent upstate, while the other had twice before born false witness against cops as payback for his own slew of arrests in that precinct. As for the two others who would only talk off the record, no one had seen them since the article hit the stands.

With Stacey caught flat-footed in her lie, and with no hard evidence to back up her account, the story was quickly buried, although never retracted. Within the week she was out the door, the story behind her story having become its own newsworthy story, the subject of self-examining op-ed pieces across the country and not a few panel discussions.

Excoriated for unhesitatingly scuttling a good cop's reputation to further her own, emotionally whittled to a nub by her disgrace, and unable to support herself even if she chose to make a stand, Stacey moved back in with her parents in Rochester. With her father's help, she became a part owner of a food truck christened My Hero, which was more or less permanently stationed across the street from the SUNY Brockport dormitory complex. After two years of full-time sandwich making in this drizzly exile, she endured another blow when both her parents died in a collision with an ambulance at an intersection three blocks from home. She spent the first two weeks after the funeral living alone in their house hoping for a visitation, then put it on the market. A few months later, temporarily flush with the proceeds of the sale, a small inheritance, and the buyout money she received from selling her share of My Hero, she quietly returned to the city.

Unable to find work as a reporter but banking on the skills she had developed as one, she reinvented herself as a private investigator, earning just enough to take a lease on a one-bedroom walk-up near Columbia University. For a while she held on to the hope of finding her way back into the newspaper business, but that pipe dream came to an end the day she accepted an invitation to address an Ethics and Ambition seminar in the university's J-school, the experience leaving her feeling like a stillsentient cadaver picked over by medical students in an anatomy class.

Rather than enjoying the poetic justice of Stacey's downfall, Billy felt torn — no, actually sorry for her, mostly ignoring the fact that she had tried to advance her career on his broken back. In fact, he had been the one to make the first move, reaching out to her with an e-mail a year after she returned to the city, and since then they had gradually, cautiously become friends. For her part, Stacey had been both astonished and humbled by his lack of vindictiveness, never once imagining that his gentle overture was motivated by anything other than old-time Christian compassion.

When Billy finally got it up to enter the diner, he spotted her at once, sitting at a booth in the back — north of forty now, too thin, too much wine, too much late-night TV — paradiddling an unlit cigarette against the Formica and reading the paper that had shit-canned her eighteen years ago for getting it all wrong about Billy and the shooting. She was wearing a ribbed turtleneck that made her look even bonier than she was and accentuated her slightly scoliotic posture. Her hair, a blond so ashy that it was impossible to tell how gray it might be turning, was pulled back in a short, rubber band–bound ponytail, and her watchful eyes were, as always, a little too quick, as if she were jonesing for something she couldn't have. She'd been a golden girl once, and she took her tumble hard.

"Hey, how's it going," Billy said as he took a seat.

"The meat's so tough that it got up off the plate and beat the shit out of the coffee, which was too weak to defend itself."

"No kidding."

"The PI business sucks. I hate the people who hire me, and I hate the people they want found."

"I hear you."

"Never serve a subpoena on a guy holding a pan of bacon. I put up my arm to protect my face and ruined a perfectly good North Face coat."

"Good thing it was a cold day," he said mildly, then, wanting her to get to it: "So . . ."

"I'm back to writing."

"For money?"

"Not much, but you bet."

"Good for you." This could take a while.

"I'm writing an online sex column."

"A what?"

"For this e-zine, *Matterhorn*."

"What's an e-zine?"

"Don't worry about it — my nom de plume is Lance Driver."

"A guy?"

"A guy advising other guys."

"Wow, that's . . ."

"Yesterday I advised some moke that if your girlfriend wants to stick a finger up your ass it doesn't mean she thinks you're a fag."

"No?"

"It means she's curious, she wants to know your body."

"OK," Billy said. "How far up?"

Stacey finally lit her cigarette, took a quick drag, and then put it out before they could arrest her.

"I draw the line at the first knuckle."

"OK," shifting in his seat. "So what did you want to talk to me about?"

"I have a new boyfriend."

"Oh yeah?"

"I'm forty-five and I have a boyfriend, he's fifty-seven and he has a girlfriend. I mean, what the fuck, right?"

Whatever it was that she had to share, it was making her very nervous, although calling Stacey nervous was like calling water wet. When she was in a state like this it was cruel to rush her.

142

"The boyfriend, what's he do?"

"He edits *Matterhorn.*"

"He's good to you?"

"That's a very considerate question."

"Yes? No?"

Stacey looked off. "He's no stranger to the vine."

"How much?"

"Two bottles, maybe a little more. He's a sweet drunk, but it's like talking to a small child towards the end of the evening."

"Did you try AA?"

"I can't even get him to Triple A."

"He'll lose you."

"He'll die is what he'll do."

"Threaten to walk out."

"I don't want to."

"Threaten?"

"Walk out. I haven't had a boyfriend in eight years. I like caring about what I look like again. I like being spooned."

"Sounds like a problem there, Stace."

The waiter finally came over, the guy sporting a reddish-gray comb-over and an apron up to his sternum.

"Try the grape jelly omelet." Stacey coughed. "It's excellent."

"Just coffee." Then, turning back to her: "Not that I don't enjoy seeing you, but why am I here?"

143

"Are you ready for this?"

Billy waited.

"You remember Memori Williams had this twin sister?"

"Shakira, right?" Billy took one of Stacey's cigarettes; this couldn't be good.

"Shakira Barker. How twins can have different last names I'll never understand."

Billy envisioned that couch in the living room again, Memori's head in Tonya Howard's lap, the entry wound above her right eye like an erupted raspberry.

"Last I heard, Shakira was doing better," he said hopelessly, "taking one of those mothering classes from the Children's Initiative."

"Yeah, well." Stacey took a breath. "Not no more."

Billy just stared at her: This is why I screen your calls, this is why I . . .

"What happened."

At the end of Stacey's tale, Billy was staring at his ashy coffee, his jaw askew with fury.

"I need you to find someone for me," he said.

"I thought you would," Stacey sliding a single sheet of paper across the table. "Got the horse right here."

Billy speed-scanned the document and

learned that Curtis Taft was still working for the same security outfit that had employed him at the time of the triple homicide and was now living in Co-op City in the Bronx, although the place to find him this week was neither work nor home but at Columbia Presbyterian, where he was recovering from surgery on a perforated ulcer.

"I thank you for this," holding up the sheet.

Stacey shrugged and then looked away, Billy sensing the mortification that still coursed through her veins over the long-ago debacle that had ended her career.

"Seriously," Billy said, his own mortification equal to hers, given that she'd been right about him all along: when he had fired the shot that killed a man and then entered the groin of the ten-year-old boy who had been standing behind him, he was coked to the gills. All the WGs were that night, a fact they would keep to themselves until the day they died.

"So, Mr. Taft, how are we feeling today?" Billy's voice burbling with rage-induced pep as he whipped back the curtain that curved around the hospital bed. The sight of his White made Billy tingle with a rush of dazed energy, made his eyes brim with light.

"Aw, you again," Curtis Taft moaned, rolling his fleshy head away.

Billy couldn't believe it: the guy had nearly doubled in size since the murders, his torso so inflated that his arms looked like flippers.

Taft attempted to reach across himself in order to press his call button, but Billy grabbed his wrist.

"Perforated ulcer, huh? Goddamn, from what I hear you can get that from smoking, but you smoking? Shit, you don't even eat off plastic as far as I remember, right? Everything had to be in stone bowls, incense all over the place, a real my-body-is-my-temple-type individual. So, my theory is," poking the soft mound of dressing across Taft's belly, "this right here? I think it's just Tonya and those kids in there getting to work on you."

"I don't know what you're talking about, Graves, get the fuck out of here." He reached for the call button again, Billy this time yanking it out of the wall.

"What's going on over there," the old guy on the other side of the curtain called out.

Billy stepped over and raised the volume on his ceiling-suspended TV.

"So," flopping down on the side of Taft's bed, "you hear what happened to Memori

146

Williams's twin sister, Shakira?"

"Who's Memori," Taft said, then, barking to his roommate: "Yo, call the nurse station."

"Oh c'mon, you got to remember Shakira, real wallflower type? Well, that wallflower just killed a sixteen-year-old girl last week, stabbed her through the lungs with a bread knife over in Jersey City, can you believe that? She's in Hudson County CC right now, but she'll wind up in Clinton Correctional Institute for Child-Eating Psycho Bitches — that is, if they aren't full up, in which case they'll put her in Bellehaven, that temporary women's wing they got out there in Sparta, but the ACLU is trying to get that shut down because of the rapes. We'll see."

"I don't know no Shakira nobody." Then, attempting to sit up, barking: "I told you call the fucking nurse."

Billy shoved him back down, Taft grimacing through his close-cropped beard. "Now, Memori was a handful, no doubt, fighting in the cafeteria, cutting school, running away from home, always with a boy, but Shakira, she was no trouble to anybody, fourteen years old and never been kissed, had all the answers in class but too shy to raise her hand. But soon as you killed her sister . . ."

"I din't kill nobody, and you know it."

". . . as soon as you killed her sister, all of a sudden she starts banging with the Black Barbies, gets caught with a razor in her mouth going through the metal detectors, threw a chair at a teacher, they finally sent her to a social worker, the lady says to her, 'Kira, what happened to you?' You know what she said back? 'Well, somebody's got to be my sister.' "

"Graves, you just pissed off because you ain't police enough to catch a fuckin' cold. Cops like you, you just grab the first nigger you see and hope for the best. Well, it didn't work out so well, did it."

"Anyways, Curtis, that was five years ago and now the kid's a nineteen-year-old murderer with two babies of her own, and she is as fucked as fucked gets. It would probably have been better if she was in the apartment that morning and you put a bullet in her head too, because this, this is gonna be one slow-motion death she's facing in there. So, as far as I'm concerned, they are *all* in there," poking his sutured gut again, "all those angry females chewing you up from the inside out. And when they finally cut you open to see what killed your ass, you know what they're going to find?

148

Teeth marks, motherfucker, nothing but teeth marks."

"You stop that bullshit right now," Taft said more quietly, his eyes going a little bit wide.

"Tell me you don't feel them," Billy pressed. "Look at me and tell me you don't feel them."

Gingerly touching his gut as if something might pop out, he looked at Billy full-on, no resistance, after all these years, no resistance, Billy's heart slamming as he scrambled to seize the moment.

"You were raised in the church, right? I remember interviewing your sister, she said you all were."

"So," Taft said carefully.

"So you believe in God?"

"Who don't believe in God."

"Know your Bible?"

"Some," Taft said, still palming himself.

"Remember your Luke? Jesus coming on a man had so many demons inside of him that when He asked for his name . . . You remember what the man answered?"

"Legion," Taft said, his eyes unblinking.

"Legion, that's right. Legion. A whole fuckin' battalion. And that's what you're dealing with too."

Taft removed his hand from his belly,

149

placed it flat on the bed, then went still.

"Now, you know and I know that the only way to get those angry bitches out of you before they can finish what they started is for you to make a clean breast of it and say what happened that day. Say it right now, say it to me, and they will be gone before you know it."

Taft kept staring at him, his mouth slowly going as round as a doughnut, just staring and staring until he apparently saw what he wanted to see in Billy's eyes, that small quivering . . .

"Graves," his voice abruptly all the way back, "I got a better chance of cleaning you out in court for harassment than you got of giving me a motherfucking parking ticket. Where's the goddamn nurse."

Billy yanked the pillow from under Taft's head and held it an inch from his face. "You know how easy it would be to punch your ticket right now?"

"But they know you're here," he said, shoving the pillow away with surprising strength for a man fresh out of surgery. "So what are you gonna do, huh? This a public building, you gonna kill me? Kill that man in the other bed, too? What are you gonna do. *Fuck* you."

"Hi there, everything OK?" The nurse in

150

the doorway sounded cheerful but in charge.

"Nah, he's just upset over me being like this," Taft said.

"You'll be fine," she said, no one's fool. "Are you just about done in here, sir? I think your friend —"

"Needs his rest," Billy finished for her, then, leaning over Taft as if to say goodbye, whispered, "You will never get rid of me," and walked out of the room.

Unable to leave the hospital, Billy paced the main hall atrium, now and then charging halfway back to Taft's room, then reining himself in until a security guard finally approached him to see what was up. Flashing his ID, Billy muttered something about a sick cop, the square badge at first backing off leery, then quickly losing interest.

And then Billy saw her, Taft's wife, tall and gracefully obese, pushing a two-year-old in a stroller across the sun-dappled floor. He reflexively moved to her, then blocked her way.

"Hey, Patricia, right?"

She stopped and stared, not able to place him.

"Bill Graves, I was at your wedding."

She reared back, got taller, gave him a face like a fortress. "I remember you."

As well she should. When he had heard that Taft, less than a year after the murders, was getting married, Billy and Whelan, who was about to retire in any event, put on suits and crashed the wedding. Right after the minister asked if anyone objected, Billy sang out, "Right over here, because that bastard is a baby-killing triple murderer. He did it once, he'll do it again."

They got their asses good and kicked that day; half the wedding party, both male and female, were correction officers related by blood to Taft. But it was worth it just to ruin the ceremony — or maybe not, given that the incident led to his being transferred to Night Watch, his second banishment to the underworld, most bosses believing that working any kind of steady midnights was just this side of a firing squad.

"So," Billy said amiably, "I just want to know, how's it working out for you two, everybody happy?"

"You have no right to be accosting me," her voice as stiff as her posture.

"I just want to ask you, does he ever wake up in the middle of the night all covered in sweat and screaming his head off? You know what I'm talking about, right?"

She waved to the same security guard across the floor, but Billy retinned him without even looking in his direction, the man once again backstepping to his post.

Billy felt light as a feather, out-of-his-mind spontaneous. "How's he as a dad?" nodding to the stroller, kid number three from what he'd heard. "A real disciplinarian I'll bet."

She attempted to walk away, but Billy, astonishing himself, blocked her escape.

"One last bed question: does he ever get up, say, about six in the morning, come back about an hour later, a little winded, maybe a little bloody? I'm just curious."

"I work for Christian Outreach," her voice suddenly a hoarse, teary mess, "I *help* people, and you have no right to talk to me like this."

No, he didn't; suddenly red-faced, Billy turned from her without another word and walked away.

Finally striding across the central atrium toward the exit, Billy was startled to see Pavlicek coming in through the revolving doors, moving like a sleepwalker, his eyes off-center and shining as he made his way through the slanting beams of captured sunlight to the elevator banks.

"John!"

"Hey," Pavlicek said flatly, turning to Billy

as if they had just seen each other an hour ago.

"What are you doing here?" Billy's voice still burbling with adrenaline.

"My doctor's here."

"You OK?"

"Yeah, just some tests."

"Tests for what?"

"Cholesterol's through the roof."

"Yeah? What's he got you on, Lipitor? Crestor?"

"Vytorin."

"Jimmy Daly takes that. He says it's a lifesaver."

"Tell me about it."

"You're not here to see Curtis Taft by any chance," Billy asked, his voice sly-dog low.

"Curtis Taft works here?" Pavlicek blinked.

Billy took a moment, then: "He's a patient. I just about put my hands around his throat."

"Still fucking with him, huh?" Pavlicek sounded elsewhere, his eyes over Billy's shoulder as if there was bigger game to be had.

"You all right?"

"I just told you."

"I mean otherwise."

"It's a funny day. I'm late for a meeting."

"A meeting here?" Billy not sure whether

he was still too jacked to keep track of the conversation or it was just careening off point on its own.

The elevator arrived, Pavlicek silently giving him his back as he stepped inside.

"Hey, what's your doctor's name?"

"What for?" Pavlicek towering over everyone else in the car.

Billy tapped his own heart. "You're not the only one."

"Go to someone up by you," Pavlicek said as the door began to close. "My guy's not all that."

The sixteen-year-old Yemeni kid lay flat on his back, arms flung wide, staring up with his one unexploded eye at a cardboard placard taped to the ceiling: "SCREW THE DOG — BEWARE OF OWNER." Above the words was a caricature of a stubble-jawed bruiser aiming a hand cannon at the viewer, the circumference of the muzzle almost as big around as the guy's head. The real shooter — who had accidentally killed his best friend while showing off his father's gun, which had been hidden beneath the cash register — was on the floor too, sitting at the end of a food aisle. Glaze-faced and weeping, he was being interviewed by Alice Stupak, squatting on her hams as she attempted to gently tweeze out his version of events.

As Billy stood by the front window debriefing the first uniform on the scene, Gene Feeley came into the store with a young man, not a cop, the kid involuntarily inhaling when he first saw the body.

"Back in the day the homicide rate around here was so high, Jackie, that the precinct had to split in two just to keep pace with the bodies," Feeley explained. "But those days are dead and gone, so they say, although I would no sooner walk down the street unarmed around here than I would if I was living in Iraq."

"What's going on, Gene?" As far as Billy knew, Feeley had the night off.

"My sister's kid, he's doing a paper for his journalism class, I thought I'd help out."

"No kidding," Billy said, thinking, The guy never shows up when he's supposed to, now he starts showing up when he isn't.

"Uncle Gene," the kid said, taking in the gun cartoon directly over the body. "Look at that."

"Go on over there," Feeley said, taking his nephew's iPad. "I'll take your picture, you can tweet it on Facebook."

"Maybe you should wait until they finish," Billy said.

156

"No problem, Billy," one of the CSUs said, raising up from the body and taking the iPad from Feeley. "Go ahead, Gene, get in with the kid."

A moment later, the store owner, the hem of his pajama bottoms peeking out from beneath his trouser cuffs, finally stumbled into the store, his gun permit held out before him like a magic charm. Avoiding looking at either the dead kid or his son, he walked right past Billy to Feeley, the most senior-looking cop on the set.

"Talk to her," Feeley said, chucking a thumb at Stupak, who was coming back up to the front.

"Talk to me? What's wrong with you?" she snapped. "Your hearing aid on the fritz?"

"Watch your mouth," Feeley said, heading for the door.

"Where are you going?" she squawked, her arms outstretched in mock bewilderment.

"I got to be somewhere."

"Somewhere *where*," she blew. "You're *here, here's* where you got to be, so how about you stun the shit out of everybody and do your fucking job for a change."

"Alice," Billy pulling her back.

"You better talk to her," Feeley said to Billy.

"Talk to me?" The front door shut with a jingle.

"Alice . . ."

"Talk to *me*?"

"Take it easy, he's off tonight."

"Oh yeah?" she said, grabbing the store owner by the arm and steering him off to a neutral corner. "How can you tell?"

MILTON RAMOS

He sat in his den. He had a den now, damp-smelling in a way he couldn't eradicate but a den nonetheless. He didn't even know what a den was when he was a kid. And not just a den: he had a house, a goddamn house, was the unencumbered owner of a two-story, three-bedroom, mock mock-Tudor. Of course, the neighborhood was so shitty that he had to enclose the entire exterior in decorative iron security grilles, which made it look like a birdcage for a pterodactyl, but it was his, earned and paid for. And he had Sofia, sitting next to him now, watching, for the second evening in a row, *Pocahontas.* He must have seen that thing seventy-five times, *Snow White, Little Mermaid, Sleeping Beauty, Mulan,* and all the others at least as many times as that. But he never grew bored, because what he was really doing was watching her watch the movie.

She was built like him, like her late mother, and she came in for her share of schoolyard torture. When he had been the porker back then, the teasing had quickly ended after the ringleader lost two of his brand-new front teeth to a cross pipe on the monkey bars. But she was a girl, and he had no idea how girls were supposed to deal with that kind of cruelty and so he let her watch slim pretty young females being rescued from their tormentors by handsome boys, night after night after night. A real father of the year.

Big, fast, and devoid of mercy — ever since he was a kid, that had been the rap on him. Everyone outside his family had always been afraid of him — in school, then later on the street, then later on the Job, even though he had never provoked a fight in his life. Devoid of mercy, devoid of humor, devoid of personality. But he loved deep if not demonstrably: his mother, his two brothers, and his wife, all gone now. And this kid right here, who — fortunately, he guessed — had been an infant when her mother passed.

"Give me a sip," she said, nodding to the glass of Yellow Chartreuse in his hand.

"Cut it out."

"I want some," she wheedled in a high

teasing voice, the same ritual every night.

"It's medicine, I told you that."

"I'm sick," dropping her forehead to his arm. "Please?"

He dipped a finger in the glass and touched it to her tongue. "It's bedtime, go upstairs."

"Carry me."

"I can't, my back hurts," he said, wincing.

"Maybe you had too much medicine."

Milton winced again, this time for real. "Go ahead, Marilys is waiting, I'll come up later."

Moving like Creeping Jesus, Sofia reluctantly headed for the stairs, placing one foot then the other on each riser, groaning like an old lady before stepping up to the next. One foot then the other, her nightly protest march.

"Go ahead now."

Milton switched to ESPN, then reached for the lined sheet of yellow paper on the coffee table, so obsessively handled today that it was starting to blacken along the folds. He left it unopened in his lap.

He tried to concentrate on the last five minutes of the Nets-Thunder game, but his thoughts drifted, as they often did after a few shots, to Sofia's mother, Sylvia, seven years earlier the victim of a hit-and-run driver on Bronx Park East, directly in front of the geriatric hospital where she had worked for a radiologist.

If he had to describe their eight-year marriage in two words, if he was allowed to go back in time and rescript their wedding cake, he would choose, in sky-blue icing, *Good Enough,* as in good enough companions, good enough lovers, good enough parents. *Good Enough,* as in if God or some fortune-teller had told him, early on in their relationship, that Sylvia was to be his mate until the end of his days, he wouldn't have complained. Except the end of her days came first.

Marilys Irrizary, Milton's housekeeper and Sofia's five-days-a-week stand-in mother, had a distinct tread: halting and striving for cat-burglar light, as if just leaving the bedroom of a colicky baby. But she was a short, solid, broad-foot Guatemalan, and he could always hear her on the move from anywhere in the house.

She came into the den and stood directly behind where he sat on the couch.

"She's waiting for you."

"I'll be up," draining his 'Treuse without turning to look at her.

"I finished everything I could, but there's

still stuff in the dryer."

"You're going home?"

She leaned over his shoulder for the empty glass on the coffee table, the sweetish tang still hanging in the air.

"I could stay."

Most witnesses at the scene of the accident, the vehicular homicide, disagreed on the make and model, let alone the color, of the car. One old guy was able to come up with a description of the plate, which he said was out of state, had a tree splitting the numbers against a blue-orange sunset.

"Or I could go."

Visiting that half-cocked witness on the sly two days later, Milton asked him how he could possibly remember the tree splitting the digits against a blue-orange sunset yet not recall any numbers or letters off the same.

3-T-R, left side of the tree, the old man said. It had come back to him that very morning on the toilet.

Make and model?

Black maybe gray Accord or Camry, those cars to him like two peas in a pod.

The case wasn't Milton's, of course, the visit enough to get him suspended for hindering the investigation of the local squad, although probably not really, given the mitigating circumstances, emotional duress, extreme grief, et cetera. Nonetheless, he kept the news of the partial plate to himself.

From one flight above, the front door opened, then closed, followed by the jingle of keys in the lock, Marilys heading for home.

Three weeks after Milton's talk with the eyewitness, a middle-aged male with a suspended driver's license lay on his deathbed in Cherokee County Memorial Hospital after suffering grievous wounds in a car accident. Aaron Artest, an individual who lived in Queens but had unexpectedly returned to his hometown of Union, South Carolina, about the same time as Sylvia's funeral, told investigators that an old rust-bodied sedan with heavily tinted side windows had pulled up next to his gray Accord — plate 3TR-AM7 — as he was driving alone on Highway 150. The unseen driver kept apace for a minute or so, as if to make sure he had Artest's attention, before poking a shotgun out of the passenger window, which, naturally, inspired Artest to haul ass. Then his brakes, which had been serviced not even a month before, on the day he left New York, must've somehow given out.

"No, he didn't fire at me," Artest said to

the cops. Then: "It looked to be a Nova, no wait, a Caprice, hang on, hold on." Then his dying words: "Just give me a minute."

Milton clicked off the TV without registering the outcome, retrieved his glass, poured himself another Chartreuse, then finally unfolded the paper in his lap, the names and addresses written there writhing like eels.

Carmen Graves. RN, St. Ann's Hospital.
Det. Sgt. William Graves, Manhattan Night Watch.
684 Tuckahoe Road, Yonkers.
Declan Ramon, 8. Carlos Eammon, 6.
Immaculate Conception Day, 24 Van der Donck Street, Yonkers.

Big, fast, and devoid of mercy.

All he could say in his defense was that his older brother had been worse.

From two floors above he finally began to hear his daughter plaintively calling out for him. He had no idea how long she'd been at it, the sleepy but insistent oscillations of her voice coming down on his ears like the offbeat siren of some alien ambulance.

CHAPTER 5

It was one of those fortuitous early mornings when Billy was able to crawl into bed a half hour before Carmen had to get up, the bakery warmth of her body coming at him as he raised the quilt, making him both alert and drowsy. Still asleep, she rolled into him, a heat-radiant breast fanning flat against his ribs, an equally hotted-up thigh carelessly flung over the front of his suddenly ridiculous boxers. But she was still lightly snoring, and with the kids about to overrun the base camp it was better for him to concentrate on the stray curls of her hair that had managed to find their way up into his nose. It was all he could do not to sneeze.

"So you're calmed down about Taft now?" she asked him thirty minutes later.

"Yeah, but I think I want to do this thing," Billy watching her from the bed as she slipped into her whites.

"You should," turning away from him to

brush her hair.

He could hear both boys flying out of their bedroom as if someone had shouted, "Incoming."

"But why should I?"

She took a breath. "Because you want to. Because it would make you feel better. Because it's good karma."

"It's not like we're rolling in dough."

"Well," applying mascara now, which as far as he was concerned was like applying black paint to coal, "we're not exactly on the street either."

Something containing liquid shattered in the kitchen, neither of them reacting.

"So you really think I should?"

"I think you want my permission or something."

"I don't need your permission."

"I agree."

"So I should do it, right?"

"Who."

"Billy Graves, looking for Miss Worthy."

Hearing his flat Irish municipal accent from the other side of her door, and most likely assuming he was just another Hudson County homicide detective, Edna Worthy — the grandmother of Martha Timberwolf, the girl murdered by Memori Williams's

167

twin sister, but really by Curtis Taft, if you wanted Billy's opinion — called out, "It's open," letting him into her Jersey City apartment without so much as looking away from the TV.

She apparently made ends meet as a baby farmer, three subsidized foster kids roaming her overheated living room like cats, although as old and heavy as she was, she could barely rise off the couch.

"Can I sit?" Billy asked.

She gestured vaguely to the left side of the room, nothing there like a chair.

At first glance, Miss Worthy, a TV remote in one hand, a cell phone in the other, seemed unaffected by the catastrophic loss that had been visited on her only two days earlier, Billy chalking up her indifferent demeanor to a long, tragedy-packed life; it wasn't as if he hadn't witnessed this kind of non-reaction in people before. But then he noticed the carefully arranged semicircle of plastic-framed photos on the Cheerios-littered coffee table in front of her, the murdered girl staring back at her grandmother from all of her ages, toddler to confirmation to junior high school cap and gown, the face consistently heavy and glum, as if she had known her fate from the day she was born.

"Martha was the only blood to me left," Miss Worthy eventually said, reaching across herself to pick up a toddler who came close enough for her to grab. "Now she's gone, too."

"I'm sorry about that," Billy said.

"She helped me take care of these kids, and so how am I supposed to do that now. This ain't a hotel, but you should have seen where they was before."

"I'm sorry," he said again, glancing at a card table strewn with the silver-foiled leftovers of a half dozen condolence casseroles.

"Well, they all going back now. Except maybe this one here," lifting up the kid in her lap like a kitten. "She looks like Martha a little, maybe she can grow up to be some kind of conversation to me, but it's gonna be a race between her growing up and me growing down."

"I hear you."

"So what do you want to know I ain't already said ten times to the other detectives?" Miss Worthy asked, palming crumbs off the girl.

"Nothing, really. I just came by to offer to help you with the burial, you know, if you need it."

Miss Worthy finally looked at him straight

on, her cat's-eye glasses catching the light. "You police or not? 'Cause if you're not, I'm calling them right now," holding up the business card of the last sport-jacketed individual before Billy to come into her home.

When Billy entered Brown's Family Funeral Home, Redman, draped in his work apron, was displaying, from the breastbone up, a man in his fifties to two of his younger relations in the middle of his living-room-turned-chapel. Not ten feet away, Redman's son, velcroed into his activity walker, watched SpongeBob on a fifty-four-inch flat-screen, the volume insanely high, although no one seemed to be bothered by it.

"That don't look like him," the male of the two said.

"Did you see him when they brought him in here?" Redman asked.

"I'm just saying . . ."

"If you want, I can try to put him back the way he was," winking at Billy.

Billy sidled up to the TV and turned down the volume. A few minutes later, unhappy but not sure what to do about it, the relations left the building without saying good-bye.

"So what's up?" Redman asked, whipping

the sheet off the lower half of the body, revealing a makeshift diaper fashioned from a tall kitchen Glad bag in order to capture any post-embalming leakage.

"I want you to bury someone for me."

"Who."

"A murder vic, sixteen years old, her people don't have dime one."

Redman's wife, Nola, came in with a shopping bag of clothes: brown suit, white shirt, a tie, socks, and shoes, the suit and socks still bearing their price tags from Theo's Discount House of Men.

"Where is she now?"

"Well, she lived in Jersey City."

"So, Essex County morgue?" Redman began muscling the pants up over the Glad-bag diaper, the effort making his face bead with sweat.

"I assume."

"That's out of state."

"So?"

"That's extra."

"You want my E-ZPass?"

Redman propped the body into a sitting position so that Nola could get its arms into the shirt, their son now rolling across the room while chewing on a take-out menu.

"How much do you want to spend?"

"How do I know?" Billy said. "How much

171

does it cost?"

"Depends on the casket, the wood, the lining, the vault, the service, I assume you want a minister, some kind of celebrant, pallbearers, limo and a hearse out to the cemetery, do you have a cemetery lined up?" waiting on his wife to finish the buttoning. "Then there's the pickup, the body prep, burial clothes if you need them, flowers, printed programs, you want those memorial T-shirts? I have a guy for that, then there's the grave marker, the plot, the opening, the closing, the death certificate . . ."

"Just help me out here, OK?"

Redman wrestled the shirt tails into the pants, lifting the body off the gurney with one hand in order to do it, then stepped away to mop his brow while his wife threaded and then knotted the tie.

"Who's this kid to you?" he asked.

"Collateral damage from Curtis Taft. It's a long story."

Redman looked at his wife for a nonverbal business discussion, which ended when she abruptly took off to corral her son as he threatened to topple the cosmetics cart, a rolling jungle of wigs, makeup jars, brushes, palette knives, and cotton swabs.

"I can put something together for seven

K," he finally said.

"Seven. Are you high?"

"You want to take your business up the street? There's four parlors in the next two blocks, anyone offers you under that they're going to put her in a cereal box, take her out to the cemetery on the bus."

"I don't have seven K."

"I'll ask you again, who is she to you."

While Redman and Nola began dealing with the dead man's socks and shoes, Billy told them the whole story, from the death of Shakira Barker's twin sister five years earlier through her long slow nightmare transformation into a murderer herself, the victim, Martha Timberwolf, lying on a slab across the Hudson with no one to send her Home.

"I'll do it for six," Redman said, "and that's costing me."

Nola stiffened a little but said nothing.

"Thank you, I appreciate it."

"Can you pay up front?"

"No problem."

"Can you do cash?" Redman rolling his prep cart close and pulling a chair up to the body.

"If that's how you want it."

"Because that would help me."

"Help me help you," Billy said, watching

173

as Redman slipped on a pair of rubber gloves, then reached into the chaos of the cosmetics cart and extracted a tube of Krazy Glue. After squeezing out thin lines of the gunk on the lacerated palms of the dead man, he used his finger to carefully coat the skin.

"What are you doing?" Billy asked.

"What, this? If I don't put some kind of adhesive on these defensive wounds here and people start stroking this guy's hands at the service? They could walk away with a souvenir."

Billy took a moment, then shifted gears. "You see Pavlicek recently?"

"He came in here a few weeks ago to see how my son was doing."

"How was he?"

"My son?"

"Pavlicek."

"What do you mean?"

"I'm not sure, I ran into him at Columbia Pres today."

"Oh yeah? What was he doing there?"

"He said he was seeing someone for his cholesterol."

"I'm not surprised, are you?"

"He looked like a zombie. I swear to God, every time I see him these days, it's like he's on a different drug. Tell me that's high

174

cholesterol."

"All I know is," Redman carefully recapping the Krazy Glue, "men that big can't just eat whatever they want."

"So, this witness, so-called witness, Michael Reidy, that you interviewed — remember him?"

Sitting across the desk from Elvis Perez, a tall, vulture-necked detective working the Bannion homicide in Midtown South, Billy tried to recall the face of the blood- or ketchup-stained drunk in the Penn Station waiting room. "Sort of," he said.

"Well, we lost him."

"Lost him."

"We have his address from your Fives, but he's not there, and he's not answering his cell, so I was wondering if you remember anything he might of said to you or you overheard that maybe didn't make it into your notes."

"Do you know how many people we interviewed that night?"

Perez tossed a pencil on his desk and stifled a yawn. He had the kind of droopy eyes that suggested he had never recovered from the exhausting experience of being born.

"So where are you at on this?" Billy asked.

"Nowhere, really."

Billy gestured to the manila folder on Perez's desk next to a small plaster statue of San Lazaro.

"May I?"

Even in the bloodiest CSU photos, Bannion retained his startling Black Irish handsomeness, the best-looking corpse Billy had seen since Carmen's first husband.

"The ME said the wound was jagged," Perez said, rolling his chair away from the desk and then running the flat of his hand along the inside of his thigh. "The actor was no surgeon but he knew where to cut."

"And nothing on the perp?"

"Plenty. He was short tall black white heavy slim, came flying in on a skateboard, rolled away in a wheelchair. Are you kidding me? The guy could've been seven feet tall with a turban, a beard, and an AK, screaming, 'Death to America,' and everybody there would've chalked it up to the DTs."

"How about the tapes?"

"We finally got the south plaza footage back, but all it shows is Bannion running to the subways after the fact. The tape we really need, from over by the LIRR information board, we're still waiting on. TARU says it could take a few days, a few weeks, or never. All that state-of-the-art equipment and some asshole spills a cup of coffee. How's that for bang versus whimper."

"For what?"

"Forget it. You want to see what we got?"

Perez slid the disc into his desk monitor, Billy standing behind him, ignoring the buzzing of his cell.

The captured stretch of arcade between the Long Island commuter trains and the subway entrance at first appeared deserted, all the action having taken place out of the camera's range, the grainy footage of nothing and no one evoking the bleariness of the hour. But then here came Bannion running loopily into the picture, his light blue jeans turning purple with blood, his dripping shoes leaving those dark liquid footprints until he came to a baffled stop in front of the turnstiles and started fishing through his wallet for what — his MetroCard? — fishing and fumbling, and then, just as Billy had speculated at the scene, abruptly attempting to hurdle the low barrier but suddenly locking up in midair as if flash-frozen and dropping directly on top of the turnstile before falling to the ground.

"It's not like it's without entertainment value," Perez said, "but it all happened on the other end."

"And how long for that tape again?"

Perez shrugged.

Night Watch was strictly one and done; set up the morning man and move on to the next post-midnight felony. There were simply too many runs in a night, a week, a month to keep tabs, or even remain curious, about past crimes and still have the wherewithal to focus on the next one coming down the pike. Night Watch jobs, an old boss once told Billy, were like individual tears in a crying jag.

Still . . .

"Do me a favor?" Billy asked. "Can you let me know when it comes in?"

That night he was saddled with another strange player doing a Night Watch one-off, Stanley Treester from the DNA Liaison Unit, and when Billy entered the Metropolitan Hospital's trauma ER to oversee a run-of-the-mill stabbing, he found him sitting on the edge of a gurney staring intently at a damp-eyed elderly man under a blanket. The old guy, oblivious to Treester's presence, stared off into the middle distance as if into the void.

"I messed up," the patient said to no one.

"Who's this?"

"I thought I knew him from when I was a

kid," Treester said, his eyes never leaving the other man's face.

"Do you?"

"No."

"I messed up," the man said again.

"Does he have anything to do with the run?"

"No."

"Then . . ." Billy about to tell him to get in the game, then thought better of it.

"And I'm going to hell."

"I'll sell you my ticket," Billy said, before walking off to find the crime. The actual investigation into the stabbing took about five minutes, the Samaritan who had brought the victim to the hospital confessing the moment Mayo flashed his ID, the story behind the story being two brothers, a fifth of Herradura, dominoes, and a knife.

Stacey Taylor's call came through while the doer was being cuffed. Billy, grateful that it wasn't the Wheel with another run, answered right away.

"It's four in the morning, you know that, right?"

"I'm sorry, did I wake you?" she said.

"What's up?"

"Nothing. I just wanted to see how it went today with Taft."

"I messed up, just went in there with no

179

game plan and messed up."

"Yeah, well, you're only human."

"But I want to thank you for your help."

"Hey, that's how we do."

Still on the phone, Billy momentarily went south, thinking about the last few days: Bannion, Taft, Miss Worthy, but mostly John Pavlicek, wandering into Columbia Pres like someone had hit him on the back of the head with a bag of nickels.

"Hello?" she said.

"Hey. Sorry," Billy coming all the way back, then: "Let me just ask, how good are you with hospital records?"

"Which hospital?"

"Columbia Pres."

"I know a guy there."

"Yeah? Who?"

"Then you'd know him too."

"I need you to look up an outpatient for me."

"Who."

He hesitated. "John Pavlicek."

"Your guy from the Geese? What's wrong with him?"

"That's what I'd like to know."

"Do you know who he sees there?"

"Somebody for his cholesterol. Or so he says."

He heard her light up, then expel that first

buzzy lungful. "All right."

"What do you charge for something like this?"

"When have I ever taken your money?"

Billy's guilt made him wince.

"Maybe you should start."

Thirty minutes later, as he was leaving the hospital, his cell rang again: Yasmeen on the downside of a wee-hours drunk, her voice like wet flannel.

"I'm just calling you to say I'm really sorry."

"About . . ."

"The other night, I got so drunk, you know? I didn't even know you drove me home until Dennis told me in the morning."

"Oh c'mon, how many times . . ."

"Denny's a good guy, you know? He really is."

"Well, being he's your husband and all . . ."

The silence on the other end reeked of wrong answer.

"Anyways, it's four-thirty in the morning, don't you think you should . . ."

"You want to hear something?" she cut in. "Raymond Del Pino's older sister just had her second kid, you know what she called her? Yasmeen Rose. She told me it's because I was the only one who never gave up trying to get Eric Cortez."

"Well good for her," Billy said, fishing for his car keys. "And good for you."

"Good for me," she slurred. "I'm telling you, that baby is cursed."

MILTON RAMOS

2130 Longfellow Avenue, a six-story walk-up in the still semi-shitty East Bronx, was over a hundred years old but it had been built by fresh-off-the-boat artisans, and despite the fact that by the time Milton came to be born here it was a dump — its gappy mosaic tile floor like a piss-bum's smile, its walls festooned with wilting poker chips of plaster, and its glassed-in apartment directory listing long-dead Jewish and Puerto Rican tenants like a roll call of ghosts — it still had its touches of old-world flair. But now, as he stood in the vestibule more than twenty years after he had fled for the safety of his aunt Pauline's apartment in Brooklyn, he was shocked by what had become of his earliest home on earth, gutted and rehabbed in the cheapest possible way, the old crowned lathe-and-plaster brown-coat walls replaced by featureless plywood, the multicolored stone floors by prefab squares of ceramic, the ancient swaybacked marble risers by painted pine, and the amber-glassed hallway sconces by overhead halos of sputtering fluorescence.

"It stinks in here," Sofia said, standing alongside him beneath the dented aluminum mailboxes.

"Don't say stinks, say smells," he said, then, gesturing to the stairs with the head of his 34-inch Rawlings Pro Maple (because you never knew): "Beauty before age."

A baseball bat is a versatile thing. As Milton learned while still a teenager, a moderate swing across the shins will get a piece-of-shit dope slinger to share with you his strategy for keeping financially afloat, which basically comes down to stiffing Peter in order to pay Paul, then stiffing Paul and finding new suppliers. Another rap will get the slinger to tell you who the most recent Peter is, who the most recent Paul. And if, a day later, you bring the butt of the bat down reasonably hard on the splayed knuckles of either Peter or Paul, both of whom wanted to kill that little rip-off artist, you will find out the names of the hitters who were sent out to consummate the deed. Now, once you get the actual hitters in an unoccupied apartment, bound hand and foot with gaffer's tape — you won't put another piece of tape across their mouths until they try to talk their way out of dying by telling you everything, including the truth — you can just go ahead and play home-run derby until the walls, the ceiling, and your clothes are streaked with red.

Sofia had a hard time climbing — "I like to go as high as I can," she had once explained to him, "because then all I have left is to go down" — and by the third floor she was struggling. But he was as patient with her as he had been when climbing these same steps all through childhood with his morbidly obese mother, her trudge-mantra back then, "What a world Milton, what a world," thrilling him with terror.

4B, Sofia announced. Who lived here?

Mrs. Sanchez, she was a very nice lady.

She was nice?

Yes.

4C. Who lived here.

The Kleins.

Were they nice?

They were old.

The apartment doors, once oak, were now all single slabs of siege-mentality sheet metal, their numbers, in his time screwed-in brass, nothing more than hardware-store decals. But he couldn't care less about these particular outrages against memory, because in the end the information they provided was the same information as twenty years ago, and any way you cut it the doors and their numbers would always tell the same story.

4D. Who lived here?

If he let her, she would announce every apartment in the building. But in a way, that was what they were here for, Milton taking his daughter on this stations-of-the-cross pilgrimage as an inoculation against the worst parts of himself, as a living, breathing reminder of what he had to lose if he allowed himself, at this moment in time, to follow his nature.

4D. Who . . .

The Carters.

Were they nice?

They were OK. They had a son who was retarded.

What's retarded?

Not right in the head.

What?

Stupid but not his fault.

Sofia rolled that around for a bit, then: What was his name?

Michael.

Did the kids make fun of him?

Some.

Did you?

No.

How about Uncle Edgar?

No.

How about Uncle Rudy?

He could be kind of mean, but he was a kid.

Did you and Uncle Edgar get mad at him when he did that?

He was just a kid.

Did Grandma Rose get mad at him?

She didn't get mad at anybody.

Were there other retarded kids in the building?

No, but one boy was gay.

He kissed other boys?

I guess.

What was his name?

Victor.

Did the kids make fun of him?

Oh yeah.

Did you?

No. Actually, one time when some older guys were pushing him around outside on the street, I made sure they never did that again.

How did you do that?

Don't worry about it.

4E. Who lived here?

Some girl, Inez. I can't remember her last name.

Was she nice?

I guess.

Did you like her?

I didn't hate her.

Did you want to marry her?

No.

4F. Who lived here?

Guess.

You.

And Grandma Rose and Edgar and Rudy.

Can we go inside?

There's other people in there now.

No matter how many families had lived behind that door since the Ramos family ceased to be, no matter how often the rooms and walls had been torn up and rebuilt in the name of affordable housing, 4F would always be haunted, and he could easily imagine some of those that moved in here afterward waking up and weeping in the middle of the night for no reason they could understand.

Little Man's death, if you wanted to look at it that way, was nothing more than a gruesome case of mistaken identity. The targeted dealer, as anyone in the building could have told the men sent to lay him out, lived in 5C.

So why, Milton just had to ask his killers that day in the empty apartment, did you go to 4F?

That's when they talked about the sulky girl on the stoop, Miss Information.

Describe her, Edgar said.

And they did, after which the Ramos brothers stared at each other in astonishment.

That girl on three? Milton said to Edgar. Then, turning to their prisoners, hog-tied and belly-down on the floor, She said your guy lived in 4F? You're sure?

Arching up to offer their gleaming faces, backs bowed, they swore to all the angels in heaven. How were they to know? They were sent out without the apartment.

And you told her the dealer's name? He still couldn't believe it.

We swear on our mothers' eyes . . .

And she said 4F . . .

Yes. Yes. Yes.

Now they're crying, Edgar grunted, tapping his bat against his calf.

Well, you know who else lives in 4F? Milton asked, lifting his own bat from behind his ear, the tip making small, not quite lazy circles. Us. His brothers.

189

■ ■ ■ ■

Sofia walked down to the third-floor landing, Milton behind her, absently rapping
the walls on his way down.

3D. Who lived here.

I don't know.

3E. Who lived here.

I don't know.

3F. Who lived here.

Breathe . . .

The gay kid.

Victor? Who else.

His mother.

What was her name.

Dolores.

Who else.

Breathe . . .

His sister.

What was her name.

I can't remember.

Did you like her?

Later, after long showers, he and Edgar
knocked on 3F and came face-to-face with
Carmen's mother.

Where's she at.

The answer — Atlanta — put Milton off
his game for twenty-three years. The same

might have been true for Edgar, but the dead hitters had friends and his big brother lived only another week.

His mother, heart-stunned, only a week after that.

Did you want to marry her?

Unconsciously humming, Milton rested the knob of the bat against the 3F peephole: Guess who.

Dad!

What.

Did you want to marry her.

Marry who. Then: I don't remember. Then: You know what? You're right, it stinks in here, let's go home.

As they started back down to the vestibule, Milton imagined his immense, huffing mother passing Carmen on the stairs at some point back then, the skinny girl with the martyred eyes most likely having to backtrack to the nearest landing in order for Mrs. Ramos to have enough room to pass, the two of them with self-conscious smiles, his mother's tinged with humiliation.

"What's with calling me 'Dad,' " Milton asked as he unlocked the car door. "What happened to 'Daddy'?"

"It's a baby word. The kids make fun of you if you say it."

"You got to learn to stand up for yourself, Sofia," he snapped, "otherwise those kids are never going to stop, and that kick-me kind of mentality of yours is going to make you miserable until the day you die, you understand me?"

No response — well, what the hell was she supposed to say?

"I'm sorry, I didn't mean to yell."

"It's OK," Sofia saying it in that resigned way of hers that made him feel like tearing out his heart and feeding it to the birds.

An hour later, after dropping his kid off at her school, he sat in his car halfway down the block from the house in Yonkers, far enough away not to draw anyone's attention but close enough to observe.

They had a house; he had a house. They had kids; he had a kid. Graves had a gold shield; well, so did he.

He was a widower, but no one here had any hand in that. So why on top of everything else, everything he had a right to feel, did he also feel, in this moment, envious? Where the hell did she get off having a normal life. What kind of ice-cold freak was she to just sail on like this, to make a go of it like anyone else.

Even before he and his brother had beaten two men to death at an age when all they should have been thinking about was sports, music, and ass, his sense of being "normal" was a tough sell in the mirror. He had always felt himself to be something of a miracle beast, trained to walk upright and mimic human speech. But after that day, a day launched by her, he never gave a moment's thought about belonging to any species but his own.

He saw the old man come out and slowly bend to retrieve a rolled-up newspaper from the lawn, Milton gut-reading him, despite his frailty, as an old school boss, still carrying an air of sober authority. Then, an hour later, a middle-aged Indian woman, most likely his caregiver, stepped out on the porch to have a smoke. There was no sign of Carmen (probably at work), the kids (probably at school), or her husband. Knowing Graves to be in Night Watch, Milton assumed he was either in the house catching up on his sleep or — more likely, given that the sole car in the driveway was a piece-of-shit Civic definitely belonging to the caregiver — he'd gotten stuck with an early morning run.

The thing was, now that he'd finally found

her after all these years, found her as sure as he'd found that Palmetto State cracker that snatched away his wife, where did he, where did they, go from here. In the past, no matter what actions he had taken on behalf of his dead, the suffering he had inflicted in return had always been of limited duration, whereas his suffering only intensified, leaving him afterward feeling more alone, more heartbroken, more subhuman than ever. For him, balancing the books had always been like bare-handedly punching to death a man whose face and body were studded with nails. And right now, at this point in his life, the thought of going through that again was unbearable, the cost, mentally if not physically, unsurvivable.

So let it go.
Can't.
Then find another way.
Find another way.

CHAPTER 6

It should have been funny, Billy thought, but it wasn't. Anytime you get called in to see the school therapist about your child, funny is the last thing on your mind. But still . . .

The day before, Declan had apparently pushed a kid who had been taunting him, knocking him face-first into the edge of an open locker door. The injury was minimal — they were eight-year-olds, after all — but there was a little blood and a broken pair of glasses. And so now, he and Carmen were seated in an empty classroom talking to a young man who couldn't have been more than a year or two out of school himself, asking whether Declan's birth had been a difficult one, whether they "employed" any physical form of discipline at home, whether there was any history, on either side of the family, of . . .

"How about we just get Declan to apologize to the kid and we pay for the glasses?" Billy amiably cutting him off.

"Those would be appropriate gestures, no doubt, but I think . . ."

"No!" the word flying out of Carmen's mouth like a command to a wolf as she thrust herself forward in her chair. "Where the hell do you get off asking me about giving birth to him, and how dare you ask us if we smack our kids around, if we have crazies in our family. I am a nurse, I am a *healer;* my husband is a New York City detective, he *protects* people. This is who we are and this is what we can't *do* today, because were stuck having this time suck of a talk with *you.*"

"Carm," Billy said uselessly.

"And no, my son isn't going to apologize to that little shit, and no, we're not going pay for those glasses. But you know who should? You and this whole goddamn school, because what happened yesterday is all your fault. You put on this stupid, boring show about the planets, all these poor kids dressed up like silver-foil meatballs, 'Hello! I am Mercury! Hello! I am Saturn!' And you know, *you know,* one poor kid has to come out and say, 'Hello! I am Uranus!' Jesus Christ, you're a shrink, do you know how humiliating that is? And of *course* he's

196

going to get teased and teased, and if he's got any heart to him, like my son has, at some point he is going to push back."

The therapist, more bemused than intimidated, looked down at his notepad, reached for his pen, then thought better of it.

"And if you people try to suspend him? Or even so much as lift a finger to discipline him? We're going to go first to our lawyer and then to the papers. And how stupid will your science teachers look when the story gets out. Don't they watch the news? Uranus isn't even a planet anymore."

With that she got up and walked out, leaving Billy to placate.

"I didn't actually see the play?" he said mildly. "But she's kind of got a point."

When Billy caught up to her in the school lot, he expected her to still be steaming, but instead she was close to tears.

"Tell me I didn't just fuck up," she pleaded, grabbing his hand. "I just get so scared for them, you know? Tell me I didn't fuck up."

When Billy woke up at four, the backyard was a beehive, Declan and Carlos dueling with Wiffle bats, Millie smoking up a storm behind their one tree, and his father, oblivious to the action around him, reading a book while lounging in one of their vinyl-weave lawn chairs. After returning to his bedroom for his slippers, Billy called Carmen at the hospital to see how she was holding up, made himself coffee, threw on last night's dress shirt against the chill, and stepped outside.

In the time it took him to prep, the boys had switched from fencing to tossing a football, each Mighty Mouse sidearm heave ending with the passer collapsed on the ground, and each reception, no matter how high the ball, willed into a diving catch, Dec and Carlos apparently more interested in flinging themselves into the earth than making it to the NFL. And although his own young quarterbacking chops had not only afforded him a halfway decent adolescence but a free ride to a Division I school, Billy couldn't care less if his kids became all-stars or ballerinas or computer geeks, as long as they learned the importance of never panicking when they got punched in the face.

Setting his mug on the backyard steps, he pulled up the waist of his pajama bottoms, dragged over one of the other aluminum-framed chairs, and took a seat by his father. The old man was half-dozing now, a creased paperback of *The War Poems of Thomas Hardy* sliding off his lap. A number of other well-worn paperbacks were piled in the grass at his feet, Billy not even having to look at them to know what some of them were: the collected poems of Rupert Brooke, of Wilfred Owen, of W. B. Yeats, Alan Seeger, Robert Graves, and Siegfried Sassoon. Maybe Walter de la Mare.

Billy Senior's grandfather, a Marine, had been fatally gassed in the Battle of the Argonne Forest in 1918; for his daughter, Billy Senior's mother, who had been nine at the time, her father's martyred absence became a permanent, supernatural presence. As a result, for as long as Billy could remember, his own father, brought up haunted by a man he never knew, had been obsessed with the Great War, especially the literature that it produced.

When he became head of student safety at Columbia University at the age of fifty-eight, Billy Senior, exploiting one of his job perks, immediately began to audit classes. He took basic 101s his first year, intermediate-level courses his second, advanced his third. He never participated in discussions or took exams, but he did all the required reading on his own, keeping a low profile year in, year out. Then, wanting to test himself in his fourth year, he wrote a paper on the work of soldier-poet Isaac

Rosenberg and handed it in, never expecting the teacher to read it, let alone to raise it above his head in the auditorium the following week and ask, "Who's William Graves?"

The same professor, using his connections abroad, secured a scholarship for him to the annual three-week summer seminar on Literature and the Great War, in either Oxford or Cambridge, Billy could never remember which. That July, Billy Senior attended classes while Billy's mother either tooled around town or took day trips to the south of England, the only time his parents had ever traveled together outside of the U.S. The summer after his mother died, his father went back to England on his own, the first of eleven solo summer pilgrimages until the time came when he was no longer able to travel by himself.

Of all his father had accomplished after retirement from the NYPD — heading up campus security for a major university, doing the same work for Mount Sinai Hospital and for the New-York Historical Society — nothing had impressed Billy as much as watching this high-school-educated man in his fifties slip into those high-wire Ivy League classes to shadow-educate himself, Billy Senior taking to scholarship the same

200

way many other men his age and station in life took to grandparenting and TV.

Tossing the remainder of his coffee onto the grass, Billy leaned over and picked up the collected Yeats, slowly flipped through the book, and saw his father's exquisite but strangely unreadable handwriting on nearly every page.

"What you got there?" Billy Senior asked, rising up from the tar pit.

"You used to read to me from this when I was a kid, you remember? 'The Second Coming,' it scared the crap out of me."

"How about returning the favor."

"Read to you?" Billy looked around the yard. "With my delivery? You might as well ask me to break-dance."

Billy Senior sat up a little, opened his eyes. "I remember working the Bronx for a while back in the late seventies when they started having those block parties with turntables and the disc jockeys scratching up the records, everybody spinning around on cardboard flats, spouting out these bragging rhymes . . ."

"You should hear some of your grandson's stylings," Billy said.

". . . next thing you know every kid with a portable tape recorder's marching up and down the streets belting out bad poetry."

"It's still kind of like that out there."

"Look, I don't mean to sound like some cranky old white guy and it's not like I didn't appreciate what that stuff was doing on the positive side in those neighborhoods, it was just, aesthetically? I hated it."

"Well, they can't all be Sam Cooke."

"Nothing wrong with rhythm and blues, my friend. Some of those singers were true bards."

Billy had to smile. The designation "bard" had always been his father's highest form of praise, synonymous with "sublime" and just a shade under "godlike."

"Dad, do you remember my friend Jerry Hart? After his freshman year at Fordham he came home and told his father that he wanted to be a poet. You know what Mr. Hart said to him? 'Anybody'd write a poem would suck a dick.' Excuse my French."

"Cocksucker," Senior said without heat.

"What?" Billy had never heard his father say anything worse than "shit," and rarely that.

"Cunt licker."

The boys stopped playing.

"Cocksucking motherfucking kike-faced little nigger boy." Another bland delivery.

Billy signaled for Millie to bring the kids into the house.

"Dad, what's happening."

"Are you going to read to me?" his father said.

"What?"

"You said you'd read me something," gesturing to the Yeats still in Billy's hands.

"What just happened."

"Happened with what?" Senior's eyes remained clear and untroubled.

Billy took a moment. "All right," he finally said. "Hold on."

Flipping through the Yeats, nervously rejecting poem after poem as being either too long, too beyond his understanding, or having too much unpronounceable Gaelic, he defaulted to the horror poem of his youth. But after quickly scanning the first few lines — the wildly spiraling falcon, the blood-dimmed tide, each image troubling him more than they ever had before, and then returning to "things fall apart, the centre cannot hold" — he closed the book.

"I tell you what," he said, rising to his feet. "How about I recite 'The Face on the Barroom Floor.' That one I can do from memory."

Somebody had angrily scrawled "dope house" with a broad Sharpie above the apartment 6G peephole in the Truman

Houses.

"The quality goes in before the name goes on," the CSU tech standing next to Billy said before entering the scene.

The living room was devoid of furniture, empty save for a few scattered, overfull ashtrays and some still-burning candles set in juice glasses here and there. An emaciated blond woman, looking sixty but most likely around thirty, lay star-fished face-up on the linoleum, a welt of gunpowder-stippled flesh beneath her left collarbone the only sign of violence done to her that was not self-inflicted. Another CSU tech, squatting by the body, gripped her by the jaw and rolled her head from side to side, ran his rubber-gloved fingers roughly through her lank hair, and then unbuttoned her blouse, all in search of other entry wounds.

Before anyone thought to stop her, another young mummy, her eyes looking awl-punched into her head, wandered in through the partly open front door, said, "I forgot my purse," laid eyes on the dead girl, "Oh, April, you still here? I thought . . ." then swirled to the floor.

"We was just sitting around passing the peace pipe, that's all, nobody hurting nobody," the revived woman, Patricia Jenkins, said through a billow of exhaled smoke to Billy and Alice Stupak as they all sat in a stairwell down the hall from the dead girl in 6G.

"All of a sudden this boy comes in with a rifle, says for everybody to give it up, but we're all skyin' so nobody wanted to do that. Donna asked him if he maybe just wants to party with us instead, and he says, 'You disease-drippin' bitches?' He takes all the rock we got left, then goes through everybody's shit for money, cell phones, and whatnot."

She paused for another lungful of smoke, ran a shaky finger across her brow. "He already turned to go, got a hand on the damn doorknob, April says, 'Shit, I bet that ain't even loaded,' and I'm like, 'Oh God . . .' "

Billy glanced at Stupak, neither of them wanting to distract her yet by taking notes.

"That boy, he hears that, he just turns around slow, sticks out that rifle like stickin' out a arm, got the bullet end almost right on her, and bang. Then he leaves like he should of done if April had kept her mouth shut. Then we all like froze until he's gone, then we go too."

Still smoking, she lowered her forehead

onto the heel of her palm, closed her eyes, and wept a little.

"All right, Patricia," Stupak began, easing out her pad, "I know you want to get this guy as badly as we do, so help us out here. The shooter, was he white, black, Hispanic . . ."

"Lightish Dominican."

"Dominican. Not, say, Puerto Rican, or . . ."

"Dominican."

"And when you say a kid . . ."

"Like, high-school-dropout age."

The fire door to the stairwell opened, all three turning to see Gene Feeley, the elusive war horse, size up the party and then, hands in pockets, lean against a cinder-block wall directly behind Stupak's back.

Alice took a moment, her temples pulsing with anger. "This guy, do you remember what he was wearing?"

"A orange sweat suit, tops and bottoms."

"Any words or images?"

"Said 'Syracuse' up the leg and across the chest."

Feeley coughed, shifted his feet, Billy watching him like a hawk.

"How about hair? Long, short . . ."

"Had, like, a short crop brushed forward like a Caesar cut, and those devil sideburns, you know, like a pencil line going down his jaw from each side then meet up under his chin, and he had a little mascara on his eyebrows like the boys now do to make them darker."

"Beautiful. And, other than what you told us already, can you think of anything else he said?"

"Not really."

"OK, Patricia," Stupak's eyes bright with the hunt. "How about you come with us to the precinct so we can show you some photo arrays?"

"Can I smoke there?" she asked. "Last time I couldn't smoke."

"No problem," Alice said, rising and reaching out to help the woman to her feet.

"Hey, Patricia," Feeley said, still leaning against his wall. "Before you go, you don't happen to know this kid's name, do you?"

"Oh yeah," she said. "Eric Cienfuegos, he lives upstairs in apartment 11C."

"There you go," he said to Stupak, then sauntered back out to the hallway.

"I want a transfer," she announced to Billy the moment Feeley was gone.

"I'll handle it," Billy said, wondering how.

"That's what you always say."

"Just let me make some calls."

"You always say that, too."

Burning with embarrassment, he jerked his head toward Patricia Jenkins, standing there like a scarecrow draped in laundry. "Just take her to the house."

He found Feeley as he was getting into his car, a restored '73 Dodge Polara, double-parked across from the scene.

"What," Feeley looking up at him through the rolled down driver's window.

Billy, hunched over to be on eye level, just stared.

"She had some goddamn mouth on her the other night," Feeley said. "Embarrassing me in front of my nephew like that."

"Gene," Billy began, his back killing him already, "I asked the Chief of D's last week to take you off my hands, I told him how unreliable you are, how you undermine me and everybody else in the squad. You know what he said? He said, Just do me a favor and keep him with you, I'll throw you another detective to pick up the slack."

"Where the hell do you get off . . . Do you know what I've done on this job?"

Billy stood up to stretch, then stooped to the window again. "Actually, I do. In fact, when I first came up, my loo once pointed you out to me, said if he ever got murdered he hoped they'd throw you the case, this way, the actor'd be on death row by the end of the year."

"Who was the loo."

"Mike Kelley, retired from the Five-two about three years ago."

"Kelley," Feeley grunted. "He put in some good work there."

Billy stood up again, took a breath, came back down. "Look, Gene, I can't do anything about you, we both know that, but here's what I propose. Don't show up anymore. I'll cover for you, sign you in, sign you out, this way you can max out your pension without wasting your time going through the motions and I can get my squad back to the way I want. What do you say."

Feeley sat flustered for a moment, then looked at Billy with a face like a fist. "Nobody tells me what to do."

MILTON RAMOS

The sisters — they had to be sisters, check out the mouths — came into the 4-6 precinct house just as Milton walked out of the vending machine room with a bag of Fritos and a can of Hawaiian Punch.

"My fiancé's missing," the less-big woman announced to Maldonado, the desk sergeant.

"How long," he asked without raising his eyes from his paperwork.

"Yesterday, day before."

"What's his name," still not looking up.

"Cornell Harris."

Thinking about where he was headed shortly and what he planned to do when he got there, Milton lost his appetite and tossed the chips without opening the bag.

"Got a picture?" Maldonado blindly put out his hand.

"No," the girlfriend said.

"Here," her sister said, digging into her

bag and taking out a snap.

The girlfriend looked at her. "Why'd you take his picture?"

" 'Cause I did. So what."

"So what?"

"This guy?" Maldonado finally looked at them. "That's Sweetpea Harris."

"I know."

Milton checked the time, then took a sip of punch.

"He's missing?" Maldonado said. "Like that's a bad thing?"

"He ain't like that no more," the girlfriend said.

"He turned himself around," her sister said.

"Like this?" Maldonado stood up, curled a hand over his head like an umbrella handle, and pirouetted.

"See, that's why people hate on you around here."

"Actually, they don't," Maldonado said, returning to his reports.

"You should ask harder about that."

"In any event, it's got to be forty-eight hours before someone can be considered missing."

"That's what it is, forty-eight hours," the girlfriend said.

"You said yesterday," he said.

211

"She meant the yesterday before yesterday," her sister said. "That's forty-eight
hours."

"Oh. OK."

"Yeah, he was, we were fighting on the
phone, then I heard some other guy say,
'Hey Sweetpea, come over here.' "

"Oh yeah? Then what happened."

"Sweetpea said, 'Oh shit,' and hung up."

"This is getting to be a real mystery," Maldonado said, again without looking at them.
"Where was this?"

"I don't know. Concord Avenue maybe?"

"Maybe?"

"I was on the phone, how do I know."

"When."

"Around three."

"Last night?"

"Yeah."

"Gotcha!" Maldonado lightly slapping his
desk. "See? That's not forty-eight hours."

"Fuck him," the girlfriend said. "Let's go
to Missing Persons direct."

"They'll tell you the same."

As they turned to leave, raised middle
fingers over their heads like pennants, Maldonado called out to them, the snapshot of
Sweetpea Harris in his extended hand.
"Keep it," he said. "We already have one."

Once the two women finally made it out

212

the door, the desk sergeant looked over to Milton. "Thoughts? Comments? Suggestions?"

Milton glanced at the wall clock again and drew a deep, shaky breath. "I got to be somewheres."

He sat alongside her desk as she listened to his heart, a stray fingertip brushing his chest.

He thought just the boom of it would knock her off her chair.

All she had to do was recognize him and it was game over.

What could he possibly do after that?

"Turn, please?" The cold disk now pressing into his lower back.

"Sounds pretty clear," she murmured, making a notation on his emergency room form.

"Maybe now they do."

"Any history of bronchitis, asthma . . ."

"No."

"Any recent injuries?"

"No."

"Been under any stress?"

"Everybody's under stress."

"I'm asking about you," finally looking up from her notes, her Pietà eyes blind in her head.

"Tell the truth, I'm feeling a little stressed right now."

"Well sure, you're in a hospital," she said, looking over his shoulder to a small ruckus in the waiting room.

How about you on that front? Milton thought. *Any stress on your end?*

"How about allergies, any allergies?"

"Could be."

"What's 'could be,' " looking at him again.

"I just got back from visiting my brother in Atlanta." He almost said "my brother Rudy," but that would make it too easy. "He bought his kid a cat since the last time and I got a little cloudy in the chest."

"That's no good," writing again.

"You ever been to Atlanta?" he asked.

Since taking a seat next to her, the tension he felt had him speaking in a near mumble, and either she didn't hear the question or she was just off somewhere in her head. Either way he didn't want to ask again, didn't want to lead her any more than that. It would be too much like begging.

Just recognize me. Stop me in my tracks by saying my name, then drop to your knees to ask my forgiveness and explain to me through your tears why you did it. Then maybe, just maybe, we can both survive this.

Last chance for us both.

When he next looked at her, she was staring back at him as if he had spoken aloud, her eyes fixed with a look of unguarded intensity.

His shortness-of-breath gambit was no longer a joke.

"Are you on the Job?" she finally said.

"I work for FedEx, it's right on the form there."

"Huh. My husband's a cop and I could have sworn . . ."

"I get that a lot."

Recognize me, just let me see you tremble with memory, I'll settle for that . . .

But the moment passed. She went into her desk, brought out a blood pressure cuff, and gestured for his arm.

Seated as close as they were, he could reach out and grip her by the throat so fast she couldn't make a sound, couldn't signal or even move. He could choke the life out of her before anyone even knew what had happened.

"Your BP's through the roof."

"Must be the cats," he said hoarsely, Milton near livid with despair.

CHAPTER 7

When Billy got home the next morning, he was relieved to discover that Carmen was at work and the boys at school. He went directly to the refrigerator, made himself his double usual, and was asleep within the hour.

He awoke at three-thirty to find himself back-to-back in bed with his father, who was chatting up a storm with his dead wife. The boys were somewhere in the house killing each other.

Billy got out of bed, put on his bathrobe, and went back into the kitchen. As he shambled to the coffeemaker, he nearly tripped over Carlos's camo jacket, which lay in a heap on the floor. When he picked it up, the jacket was tacky to the touch and smelled of paint. Holding it in front of himself by the epaulets, he discovered what he at first took to be a red five-pointed star, still in the process of drying, planted between the shoulders.

No, not a star. The bulk of the image was more fan-shaped than round, and the five points were actually all emanating in a curved line from the top of that fan, the thing now looking more like a handprint — was a handprint, a big one.

"Carlos!"

The kid came up from the basement wearing nothing but his underpants.

"What happened to your jacket?" Showing him the damage.

"I don't know."

The outline of the hand was crudely precise. Not casual. Not accidental.

"Did anyone touch you today?"

"Touch?"

"Put their hand on you." Then: "A grown-up?"

"I don't know."

"You don't know," Billy starting to pace a little. "How about did anybody talk to you today. Other than your teachers."

"My friends?"

"Not your friends, grown-ups."

"No."

"Are you sure?"

"I don't know." Carlos shrugged, bored by the whole thing.

Billy took a breath; was he making something out of nothing?

As if reading his father's mind, Carlos wheeled toward the basement, Billy half-relieved to see him go. But then he stopped at the head of the stairs and turned back around.

"Oh, wait. A man came up to me and said, 'Say hello to your parents.' "

"What? Whoa, whoa . . ." Billy felt a sprung dampness on the back of his neck. "What man?"

"By my school, he came up to me."

"And said what."

"I said already."

Once again, Carlos tried to make a run for the basement, this time Billy having to grab his arm.

"Carlos!" his older brother shouted from down in the dark.

"What do you mean 'by' the school," Billy said. "In the school? Outside? Before school, after . . ."

"When I was going to the bus home, he came up to me and said say hello to your parents but I didn't talk to him, I swear."

"What else did he say."

"Nothing, he just left."

"Did he say . . . Did anybody else see him?"

"I don't know."

"What did he look like?"

"I don't know."

Billy's bathrobe felt like an oven.

Declan, bored with waiting for his brother to return to the basement, came upstairs. He, too, was stripped to his underpants.

"Did you see the man who talked to your brother?"

"Yeah."

"Did he talk to you?"

"No."

"What did he look like?"

Declan extended his arms sideways and puffed up his cheeks.

"Fat?"

"Biggish."

"What else."

"He was, he had a mustache."

"What else."

"He had a big head, bigger than yours. But less hair in the front of it."

"Good. What color was he?" Billy couldn't imagine anything in the refrigerator that wouldn't make him vomit.

"Kind of brown."

"Brown like Mommy or brown like Uncle Redman?"

"White-brown, like Mom. I don't call her Mommy anymore, it's babyish."

"No it's not," Carlos said.

"OK, OK, what was he wearing?"

"A jacket."

"And a tie," Carlos added, pulling on his balls.

"A jacket and a tie. What else."

"Pants," Carlos said.

"And he had a lump," Declan said.

"What do you mean?"

"A lump," Declan touching his left hip where Billy carried his gun. "Like yours."

When Carmen came home from the hospital at eight that evening, Billy was still in his bathrobe. An hour earlier it had been all he could do to feed the boys and his father their cut cantaloupe and Stouffer's microwaved dinners.

"Are you kidding me?" she shouted from the living room, then marched into the kitchen. "This is a hundred-and-twenty-dollar jacket. Carlos!"

"Easy, it's not his fault," Billy said. Going on three hours of sleep, his head was a boiled egg. "Some guy came up to him in the school parking lot, said, 'Say hello to your parents,' and, I'm guessing, did this to the jacket."

"What do you mean, some guy. What guy?"

"That's what I'd like to know."

"Nobody knew him?"

"I'll have to ask tomorrow."

"Why tomorrow?"

"The kids don't know. It's better to go back there at the same time, see who's around."

"What did he look like?"

"From what I could get out of them, he sounds some kind of Latin, heavyset, maybe a cop."

"A cop?"

Billy hesitated, then: "He could have been carrying," wincing the second it came out of his mouth.

"A gun?" Her eyes as big as dishes.

"Possibly, but maybe I'm just . . ."

"Jesus God," putting her fingertips to her mouth. "You sure he was a cop?"

"I'm not sure of anything. Like I just said . . ."

"Well, how old was he?"

He couldn't believe he hadn't asked that earlier, though it probably wouldn't tell him anything about the guy's profession.

"Hey, Carlos!" he shouted up the stairs.

The kid came down wearing a Knicks jersey over pajama bottoms.

"The man who talked to you, was he older than me, younger than me, the same age . . ."

"I don't know."

"Declan!"

Carlos's older brother came down wearing a *Scream* mask, just what Billy needed.

"How old was the man you saw."

"I don't know."

"Guess."

"Your age? Mommy's, Mom's age?"

Billy turned to his wife. "Anything else?"

Carmen didn't answer.

"All right, guys, go back upstairs," he said, not wanting them to get infected.

He moved to the sink and ran some water over his face. When he turned back around Carmen was robotically setting the table for breakfast.

"What are you thinking?" he asked.

"Look," she said, straightening up, a stack of plates tucked into her ribs like a football. "He said, 'your parents,' he didn't say our names."

"So?"

"So maybe he doesn't even know us. Maybe he's just some random whack who wandered into the parking lot. Or a parent the kids don't know. Or it wasn't him."

"Wasn't who."

"The guy who put the paint there. Maybe it was an accident. Maybe Carlos just backed up . . ."

"Into what, a wide-open adult hand covered in red paint?"

"How about the father of that kid Declan punched?"

"The guy's in a wheelchair."

"How do you know?"

He knew because he had gone over to their house on the sly to pay for a new pair of glasses. "I just heard."

"Then how about you?" she asked, dealing out the plates.

"How about me what?"

"Is there anybody on the Job . . ."

"I thought about it. There's nobody."

Carmen dropped a juice glass with her right hand, caught it six inches from the floor with her left.

"And you?" he said as lightly as he could. "Anyone giving you a hard time? Maybe at work?"

"Everybody gives me a hard time at work."

"How about a cop. They're in and out of that ER all day. Any of them hit on you?"

"Constantly." Then, clutching her stomach: "Should we call the police?"

Billy took a breath. "I am the police."

"May I wake thee?" the Wheel inquired, darkening Billy's doorway at two in the morning.

223

"This better be good," Billy said, a pillow over his head as he lay in a fetal curl on his joke of an office couch. He had never been this tired so early in the tour.

"We got a guy just brought his kid into Metropolitan, says he accidentally dropped her."

"What's a kid," still not moving.

"Four months."

The young, disheveled-looking father of the injured infant, still in his bedclothes, was slim and tall, six-three, four, maybe more, although the anxious crook of his neck on this night seemed to shave a few inches off him as he paced the littered floor of the Metropolitan Hospital ER.

"He said the wife had a family emergency in Buffalo," the patrol sergeant told Billy. "Left him with the kid for a few days."

Billy's jacket buzzed, a text from Carmen at two-thirty in the morning:

can i burn the coat

"You know who that is, right?" the sergeant said, gesturing to the agitated pacer as Billy texted back.

absolutely not

"What? No, why?"

"You follow high school hoops?"

"It's all I can do to follow the pros."

"Aaron Jeter, played power forward for DeWitt Clinton about four years ago, took them to two state AA championships. You couldn't open the sports pages back then without there's a picture of him banging under the boards."

Billy took another look at the guy, this time noticing the outsized shoulder caps that topped his lean frame.

"Huh. And so where's he at now?"

"Now?" the sergeant shrugged. "Now he's here."

Alice Stupak, who put out a sympathetic, feminine vibe that she could turn on and off like a faucet, was usually the go-to detective for interviews of this kind, and she waited for the high sign to start working the guy. But Billy, after all that had happened today, wanted this one for himself.

"How are you doing, I'm Detective Graves," Billy having to look up as he introduced himself. The hand that enveloped his was as big as a first baseman's mitt. "You're Aaron Jeter, right?"

"What? Yeah," he said, staring anxiously over Billy's head to the closed-off rooms beyond the nurses' station.

"See, I'd be lying to you," Billy said, "if I pretended like I didn't know it already."

Jeter seemed deaf to the flattery, still riveted by whatever was happening beyond the screens.

"And your daughter?" Billy asked, as he gripped him lightly by a long, fluttering bicep.

"My daughter what," Jeter said, as Billy began walking him across the floor.

"Her name."

"Nuance."

His cell began to tremble again, Billy quick-checking Carmen's latest:

why not

Well, there was no answering her now.

"Nuance," he repeated automatically, then, reengaging: "That's a beautiful name."

Billy steered Jeter into a small, claustrophobic examination room that most detectives favored when responding to calls here — even the hospital staff referred to it as the Box — then took a seat on a backless rolling chair, the only place to park other than the examination table.

"So how are you holding up?" Billy asked, sliding his chair to the center of the room,

226

effectively cutting it in half.

"Holding up?" Jeter's eyes moist and wandering. "I'm holding up bad."

"Of course you are," Billy said. "You're her dad."

"Is she going to be OK?" Staring at the shut door. "I mean, what are they saying?"

Billy had no idea. The CAT scan machine was down, and the radiologist hadn't gotten around to looking at the X-rays yet.

"All I can tell you is they're going to do everything they can."

"Good, that's good."

As Jeter tried to figure out where to situate himself, Billy gave him the once-over again, taking in the wrinkled pajama bottoms and T-shirt, the slippers, his uncombed hair sticking up like a frozen splash of tar.

"Look, I know this isn't the greatest of circumstances," Billy said easily, "but I just have to tell you, you had to be the best high school forward I have ever seen."

"That was a long time ago," Jeter perching tentatively on the edge of the table, then popping right up. "Can we go back outside?" Nearly begging him. "They're supposed to tell me how she's doing."

Billy's jacket buzzed with another text.

"Hey, listen, do you by any chance remember a kid played for Truman, Gerry Reagan?" Truman, Reagan, Billy's imagination leaning toward the presidential tonight. "He was my nephew. I mean, he still is."

"Who?" Jeter spinning like a top. "Can they find me in here? I have to know what's happening."

"He hated covering you, said it was the most humiliating experience of his life."

"Jimmy who?"

"So did you get to play after Clinton?"

"Huh? Yeah, just a year in Belgium."

"Still, better than most, right?"

"Hey, look . . ."

"So what are you doing with yourself these days. You working?"

"Working?"

"Are you employed."

Jeter stared at him like he thought he was nuts. "I'm a warehouse man at Trumbo Storage." Then: "Why are you asking . . ."

"Trumbo Storage, the big red brick building with the clock tower, right? Where's that, Bushwick?"

"Sunset Park. Listen . . ."

"Sunset Park, I remember when that area was nothing but gangs and strip clubs. But not so much now, right?"

"I don't . . ."

"Can I ask you what time you usually punch in?"

"Do I what? I don't know, seven, look I'm worried about my daughter, could we please . . ."

"Yeah, no, of course," Billy easing out his notepad. "So tell me what happened tonight."

Jeter exhaled. "Like I told already, we were playing, you know, like I was tossing her up a little, just a tiny bit, catch her, toss her. She loves that, makes her laugh every time."

"And . . ."

"And my cell rang and so I turned my head for a second, you know, thinking it was my wife . . . and she just slipped through my hands. I just turned for a second, not even that."

"And when was this, timewise . . ."

"I don't know, about an hour, hour and a half ago? Nobody's telling me nothing in here, is that bad?"

"They're just busy. So an hour and a half ago, say about one a.m.?"

"I brought her right in, I mean, look at me," grabbing the thighs of his pajama bottoms.

"No, you did the right thing, absolutely."

Again his phone began to tremble with a text, Billy afraid to look at it, afraid to turn it off.

"So I take it you live in the neighborhood?"

"Hundred and Fourteenth and Madison, the Tubman Houses."

"And you punch in at seven, so, East Harlem to Sunset Park, you need to wake up around, what, five? Five-thirty?"

Jeter hesitated, then quietly said, "I don't need that much sleep."

"But still, what were you doing up with her at one in the morning?"

"She's a little colicky, you know?"

"Yeah, no, I had that with both my kids, it's like a nightmare, right?"

"It's not their fault," he said, the corners of his eyes starting to bead.

"Of course, it's heartbreaking, those little things suffering like that."

As Jeter's tears continued to collect, Billy gave him a moment to live with his thoughts, to go to town on himself.

"You know what my nephew always said about you?" Billy asked softly. "He said you were the best natural ball handler he ever saw. Said it was like you had that rock on a string."

"Made all-city three years running," Jeter's tears coming freely now.

"I can believe it. But then, Aaron," Billy rising from his chair, putting his hand on

230

Jeter's shoulder, "I just have to ask . . . How can an elite athlete like you, a master baller good enough to play pro in Europe, how the fuck can a guy with hands like yours drop his own four-month-old baby . . ."

"I told you, the phone rang . . ."

"And she's colicky, crying all night."

"She's colicky."

"One in the morning, you have to get up, what time did we say? Five? Five-thirty?"

"Is she gonna be OK?"

Billy moved in close. "Aaron, look at me."

Can't.

"Aaron, if I were to scroll down the incoming calls on your cell right now, am I going to find your wife or anybody else trying to ring you at one in the morning?"

"I don't know it was one exactly," his voice broken and hushed.

"Aaron. Can't you look at me?"

Jeter dropped his chin to his chest, then covered his eyes.

"Aaron . . ."

Again, Billy let a silence come down, the room a tomb.

"This is not me," Jeter finally whispered. "This is definitely not me."

"I know," Billy said softly, the next step to somehow get Jeter's statement on record before he could pull his head out of his ass

231

and start wondering out loud about his rights.

As Jeter turned away and wept into the wall, Billy, unable to help himself, quickly glanced at Carmen's last three texts:

can i wash it
can i wash it or is it evidence
wtf answer me

Milton Ramos

Milton rolled off Marilys, sat up, grabbed a washcloth and attended to himself, averting his eyes as she rose from the towel-draped couch and walked to the bathroom in order to do her thing.

Widow and widower, both on the north side of forty with three kids between them, over the last year they had become occasional humps of convenience, a casual pressure-relieving arrangement without the mess of a real relationship. Sometimes she wasn't in the mood and sometimes he wasn't, but nobody ever got their noses out of joint about it one way or the other. Besides, he was never much for kissing.

As he heard the shower begin to run behind the bathroom door, he lay back down and thought of Carmen's boys in the school parking lot today, bright-eyed and wild as chimpanzees, seemingly happy in their world and, as an added bonus, respectful to adults. Nice kids most likely, but when he was sizing up any child hc came across for the first time there was only one question on the assessment test and one question only: were they the type who would get off on taunting Sofia?

All he had known this morning was that he wanted Carmen to feel things, to experience things, give her a taste of what it feels like to have the most precious people in your life snatched away from you, to feel without any warning the ground buckle and split beneath your feet. But now that he had set things in motion, he realized that today was nothing, an unnerving incident that would be forgotten in a week or two. What was required here was evidence of a pattern, of an intelligent presence, an unseen wolf lurking just outside the perimeter of her life until . . . Until what?

He had no idea how or when it should end. But he did know this: if his campaign went on long enough, he would eventually get caught and that would be the end of him. And the end of them.

He would lose her.

So let it go.

Can't.

You will lose her.

And then an exhilaratingly anarchic no-tion:

She'll go to better people.

He had a half-a-half-sister in Pennsylvania who was pretty decent, and a childless cousin in Staten Island, Anita, who he liked and liked him in return. Better that Sofia go to her, but what the hell was he thinking . . .

Marilys came back into the den, squat and stone-faced, her torso un-indented from shoulder to hip. When the two of them stood side by side they looked like matching salt and pepper shakers.

As she slipped into her jeans, he dug four hundred dollars out of his heaped pants and passed it along to her in a tight roll. He knew four hundred was shit pay for the days and hours she put in, but she needed to be off the books, and that was all he could afford if he couldn't deduct her come April 15.

"The toilet's backed up on the top floor, you need to call a plumber."

"All right," shrugging into his own pants. "So what did she eat today?"

"Carrots, like you said," stooping to pick up his discarded washcloth.

"Oh yeah? What else."

"A turkey burger without the bread."

"Uh-huh. What else."

Marilys peeled the bath towel from the couch and replaced the pillows.

"What else."

"She was crying for a treat."

"What's a treat."

"A couple of Mint Milanos."

"What did I tell you about that?"

"Let me ask you," she said, "what did *you* eat today?"

And there was Marilys, who knew Sofia better than anyone, maybe even himself. But she was an employee with a family and problems of her own. Sofia was just her job.

Nothing you did so far was even illegal.

Milton watched Marilys stuff her pay in her purse, then get down on her knees to retrieve her sneakers from under the coffee table.

Housekeeper, stand-in mother, semigirlfriend. If he went then she went away, and Sofia would be up for grabs.

Nothing you did so far was even illegal.

Chapter 8

The next day Billy made sure he was back home in time to drive the kids to school, then sat in the parking lot to survey the terrain as they charged toward the building.

Nothing but the same teachers, parents, and nannies he saw every morning on the days when he dropped them off. No one even vaguely resembling the rough description given to him by the boys.

Once the lot was empty of all souls, he continued to sit for another hour before taking off for a meeting with Stacey Taylor in the city.

Release time would be better.

They met in a beer-damp neighborhood joint around the corner from Stacey's walk-up a few blocks south of Columbia University. At nine in the morning she was sitting at the not-quite-deserted bar reading the *Post* and eating a hamburger.

"Hey," Billy said, taking the neighboring stool and gesturing for a coffee. "How's it going."

"How's what going."

"I don't know, life, the boyfriend."

"The boyfriend's asleep," she said. "He gets up at three in the morning, has a cocktail or two, works on the magazine, and crawls back into bed at five. I could throw a flash grenade in there now, all it would do is scare the cats."

Billy took one look at the coffee set before him and knew it would taste like muddled cigarette butts.

"So, Pavlicek . . ." sliding the cup to the side.

"Pavlicek sees a doctor there, Jacob Wells, but he's not a cholesterol man, he's a hematologist. Been seeing him since August."

"Seeing him for what?"

"That I couldn't find out," she said. "Can't be anything good."

A too-tall, gaunt, middle-aged man sporting an old but expensive raincoat over pajamas came sauntering into the bar as if into the dayroom of a nuthouse. He had a long narrow face, nose big and sharp as a tomahawk, one eye brighter than the other. He could have run a brush through his tangled gray-brown hair a few times, Billy thought; that wouldn't have hurt.

He kissed Stacey's hair without looking at her and signaled for a beer.

"What are you doing up?" she asked.

"I have no idea." He extended a hand to Billy, again without making eye contact. "Phil Lasker."

"Billy Graves."

"What would someone see a hematologist for?" Stacey asked her boyfriend.

"A million things."

"Besides sickle-cell anemia."

"All kinds of vitamin deficiency, B12, folic acid, iron, et cetera, thrombocytosis, that's excess platelets, thrombocytopenia, that's low platelets, polycythemia, excess red blood cells, anemia, pernicious or otherwise, which is low red blood cells, leukocytosis, excess white blood cells, neutropenia, low white blood cells, all kinds of coagulation disorders, blood vessel abnormalities, hemophilia, scurvy, leukemia, acute and chronic, an encyclopedia of various syndromes, genetic or otherwise . . ."

Billy stared at him, then looked to Stacey.

"He's just a really good hypochondriac," she said.

"That means I'll live into my nineties," he said, sipping his nine a.m. Heineken.

Stacey looked away.

Billy left a few minutes later, drove home, and called Immaculate Conception. He left a message for the school security officer, asking for a meeting to review yesterday's footage of the parking lot, then fixed himself his usual Cape Codder, got into bed, and stared at the ceiling, his head a blender.

Early afternoon found him in a small physi cal therapy clinic on the banks of the Cross County Parkway, thumbing through a two-month-old *People* magazine as his father worked on his core strength with a young Serbian physical therapist on the other side of the mirrored room. Ferrying the old man here twice weekly for his sessions was the most stultifying chore in the world, but Billy insisted on doing it himself.

"Milan, are you old enough to remember Marshal Tito?" Billy Senior asked the therapist.

"He died when I was very young," the kid said. "Try not to tense your neck."

"His real name was Josip Broz."

"Really."

Billy stopped reading.

"I was assigned to his security detail in sixty-three when he came to the United Nations."

"You're still straining, Mr. Graves."

"He was a very short guy, you know."

"Better. Keep your shoulders back."

"Loved the ladies, that was the biggest headache with him."

"Dad, are you kidding me?"

"I had dealings with Khrushchev back then, too. I was on the Manhattan Bridge surveillance detail in sixty-one when he came up the East River on the SS *Baltika,* into, I believe, Pier 71."

Dates names numbers, Billy's heart rising.

"They had a floating high school docked next door at Pier 73, Food and Maritime Trades, and I had to go over and tell the principal that with the big Commie coming, he had to shut down classes for a few days and, brother, he was not too happy to hear that, but the students took it like Christmas in July."

"Keep your shoulder blades back, imagine they're trying to shake hands across your spine."

"Do you remember the name of that principal?" Billy just testing.

"Frank Stevenson, a real no-nonsense guy, but you had to be, with some of those kids he had."

"How about the boat."

"What boat?"

"That housed the school."

"It was a ship, not a boat. A mothballed Liberty, the *John W. Brown*. The navy donated it to the city in 1946."

"Dad, you never told me any of this," Billy grinning and grinning. "This is history."

"You want history? How about Fidel Castro staying at the Hotel Theresa up on a Hundred and Twenty-fifth Street? Do you know those Cubans were smuggling live poultry into the top-floor suites? Did you ever try to catch a chicken with your bare hands? It can't be done. Your mother had to give me rubdowns for a week."

"You're killing me," Billy still grinning like a mule.

"Don't forget to breathe, Mr. Graves."

"So, Charlie, how's my little sister doing these days?" he asked Milan.

"Your sister?"

"She says you're off the sauce for good. Is that true?"

"Sauce?" Milan looking to Billy.

"Just roll with it," Billy muttered, going back to his mindless magazine.

"Yes, I'm off the sauce."

"Well, you better be, because if I have to come up there and get her again, this time there's going to be some laying on of the hands, my friend, that I can promise you."

■ ■ ■

As he was adjusting his father's seat belt in the parking lot behind the rehab center, Jimmy Whelan called, Billy stepping away from the car to talk.

"What are you doing right now."

"Driving my father."

"Oh yeah? How's he doing?"

"The same."

"Same is better than worse. Listen." Whelan's voice dropped. "I need to talk to you about something."

"About Pavlicek?" the question just popping out of Billy without cerebral clearance.

"Pavlicek?" Jimmy sounding caught up short. "What about him?"

"Nothing," Billy said, burning to bring up the blood specialist but afraid of being asked how he had come across the information. "What did you want to talk about."

"Remember that movie *Fort Apache*?"

"With John Wayne, right?"

"What John Wayne. *Fort Apache, The Bronx*. They're doing a remake. Billy Heffernan's got an in with the people involved, and he asked me if I was interested in working on it."

"As what?"

"Some kind of consultant. You know, because of what we were doing around there back then."

"Sounds good to me."

"Money for nothing and chicks for free, right?"

"Could be."

"Why'd you mention Pavlicek?" Whelan asked, but Immaculate Conception was trying to ring through and Billy had to end the call.

After arranging a time to review the parking lot tapes with the head of school security, then taking a few minutes to calm himself down, Billy called Whelan back from a traffic jam on the Saw Mill River Parkway.

"Something going on with Pavlicek?" the first thing out of Jimmy's mouth. "I need to know."

"Forget it," Billy said, Pavlicek now the last thing on his mind.

"You all right? You sound off."

"I'm trying to drive here."

"Don't bullshit me."

"Something happened with my kid," this too coming out of him without any mental vetting.

"What happened with your kid?"

Billy didn't want to talk about it in front of his father, but the old man was down for the count.

"Jimmy," Billy keeping his voice low, "I'm freaking six ways to Sunday."

Although his meeting with security wasn't until four, Billy was back at Immaculate Conception at two-thirty, the first of the parents to arrive for the pickups. For the next forty-five minutes, he studied every car coming into the lot until a side door of the building opened and the students began to exit, the youngest first, those not bus-bound lined up against the side of the building until each was retrieved by a minder.

Billy hadn't told his kids he was coming, and he watched as Carlos ran to his designated bus unaccosted, no one taking the slightest interest in him, least of all some wide-bodied, red-handed possible cop. The person who did catch his eye, though, was the teacher with a clipboard posted by the bus's folding yellow doors, the guy chanting, "No pushing, no pushing," as the kids scrambled up the short stairs to their seats.

The bus monitor turned out to be the school's remedial reading specialist, Albert Lazar, a short, erectly trim middle-aged man who projected an air of constant alertness, although that just could have been his slightly hyperthyroidic eyes.

"Like I said, I wasn't on bus detail yesterday, we're on a rotating schedule for that."

"I understand," Billy said, "but were you in the parking lot at all?"

"We all are at release time, it's required."

"OK, how about this: just looking around yesterday, did you happen to notice anyone that struck you as unusual?"

"Unusual meaning . . ."

"Maybe someone who looked a little out of place."

"Like what, a homeless person?"

"Like anybody," Billy not wanting to lead with a more specific description.

"Well, there were some nuns from the Poor Clares down from Poughkeepsie."

"Who else."

"A boy's divorced parents apparently got their signals crossed and showed up for him at the same time. They started arguing in the lot, then they both left without him. That turned a few heads."

"Who else."

"That's about it."

"Any men?"

"Men?"

"Man. Maybe some guy, walking around, you're thinking . . ."

"You know . . ." Lazar hesitated.

"Just say."

"There was someone I hadn't seen before, could've been some kid's father, but I don't think so."

Billy took a breath and asked for a description.

"I'd say a little taller than me, but not much, heavyset, dark, Hispanic, Italian maybe."

Billy felt a surge, his exhausted body having trouble handling it. "What was he wearing?"

"A dark suit, nothing fancy, shirt and tie."

"How about his hair? Curly, straight, dark . . ."

"Dark, I guess," then: "He could've had a mustache, but he looked so Mediterranean I might be putting it on him."

"Did he speak to anyone?"

"Not that I noticed."

"Why don't you think he was a parent coming to pick up his kid?"

"There's not that many fathers doing the afternoon pickups and I pretty much know them all, at least by sight."

"All right," Billy winding down, pulling his card out of his wallet. "Anything else you can tell me about him? Just off the top of your head. Anything . . ."

"Yeah, actually, there is," Lazar said, taking the offered card but not looking at it. "He struck me like someone in the security business."

"Meaning?"

"You know, the way he carried himself, very alert and no-nonsense. It's hard to explain."

"You just did," Billy said woodenly. He tapped his card. "Anything else you can remember, night or day."

He hadn't identified himself as an NYPD detective, just as a concerned parent whose son might have been approached by a stranger on school grounds, and he saw the teacher's face darken as he read the new information.

For an instant Lazar looked at Billy searchingly, then shut himself down.

"Something else?" Billy asked mildly.

"No," his eyes reading, Yes.

Billy lingered, giving Lazar a moment to say what was suddenly so troubling to him, but the teacher stepped into the bus to handle some rowdiness and that was that.

And then the older boys came charging out of the building like their hair was on fire. He refrained from calling out to Declan, allowing him to board with his brother. Not that he didn't want to take them home, want to keep them close right now, but he was desperate to see the tape, the security officer waiting for Billy in his office.

The system was badly in need of an upgrade, the retrieved footage from the parking lot as grainy as an evaporating dream. Billy was unable to make out anyone's face, although he could track the progress of bodies across the lot.

"Are you kidding me?" Billy turned to the security man, Wayne Connors, a retired Westchester County state trooper.

"Hey, I tell them every week, I know Chinese take-outs with better surveillance equipment than us. You know what they say to me? We don't have the money. I say, What if something was to happen out there."

"Something did happen out there," Billy said.

On the third viewing he found who he was looking for, the guy built square and low to the ground, his back to the camera as he walked in front of the buses before stopping and bending briefly next to a kid — was it Carlos? who could tell? — so briefly that he could have simply been picking something off the asphalt or tightening a shoelace. Then, as he began to rise, he casually reached out to that kid's back or shoulder as if for support and calmly walked out of the frame.

"Look," Connors said after Billy had filled him in, "with the description you gave me plus what I saw just now, I think I have pretty good eyes on this guy. I'll post one of my people out there starting tomorrow."

"Great," Billy said, turning to leave.

Connors could post an army out there, this guy wasn't coming back. He'd done what he'd done knowing that Carlos's parents would see it and react, so no way he'd risk a return visit.

The question was, Where would he show up next.

At ten in the evening, Billy entered Whelan's apartment building and went down to the endless basement, its roughly plastered walls painted the color of dried blood. He walked past the pungent laundry room, past the caged storage bins filled with broken furniture and bust-ass suitcases, past the chained-up snow blowers and shovels and swapped-out radiators, until he reached the super's apartment, the peephole on its scuffed door dangling by one screw like a gouged eye.

"Who."

"It's me, don't shoot."

Whelan opened up wearing a towel around

his waist and holding a Walther PPK.

His apartment, if you could call it that, was a converted utility room infused with that down-the-hall detergent smell and consisting, at the moment, of a single unmade bed, a mini-fridge, and a two-burner stove. The only other article of furniture was a padded workout bench, the floor around it littered with free weights and a pair of work boots. A clothesline ran on a diagonal from one corner of the room to the sole window, and the walls were bare of decoration except for a framed certificate announcing Whelan's induction into the NYPD Honor Legion. For a fully functional middle-aged adult, the place was utterly devoid of dignity, yet Jimmy Whelan was the most unconflicted, reasonably happy individual Billy had ever known.

"So what's going on?" Whelan asked, stuffing the Walther under his mattress and taking a pair of jeans from the clothesline.

"What I told you on the phone," Billy said, offering him Carlos's coat, the painted handprint now starting to flake.

"The mark of the Beast," Whelan said.

The toilet flushed, and a moment later one of the women from the upper apartments came out of the bathroom in her underwear.

On seeing Billy she yipped and retreated, but not before he caught an eyeful of caramel-tinted mommy fat and a generous behind.

"I'll come back."

Whelan waved him off, fished her clothes out of the rumple of sheets, and passed them to her through the bathroom door.

"So did you talk to the cops up there?"

"And tell them what, a guy came up to my kid, said, 'Say hello to your parents,' and maybe, I can't swear to it, maybe did this to his jacket?"

"Guy with a gun."

"I don't know that for sure."

"Or better yet, reach out to the Chief of D's, let him bring in a Threat Assessment Team."

"Again, based on what."

"Then I don't know what to tell you."

"I know."

Whelan lit a cigarette and halfheartedly attempted to make the bed with his free hand. "I mean, obviously, if there's anything I can do personally . . ."

"I appreciate it."

"If you ever need me to, I can stay with your family," he said, giving up on the bed.

"Let's hope it never comes to that, but thank you."

"Be like old times," Jimmy said, opening the window and flicking his cigarette upward onto the sidewalk.

Back in '97, when the news of the double shooting hit the papers and Reverend Hustle from two boroughs to the north took the ferry and set up his camp of demonstrators around Billy's Staten Island home, Whelan, like all the other WGs, volunteered on a rotating basis to stay with him and his soon-to-be ex-wife every night, until negotiations with the mayor's office brought the protests to an end, a full month after they had begun.

"So what do you think?" Whelan asked.

"About the guy?"

"About *Fort Apache.*"

Billy paused, a beat behind the shift in topic. "When Brian Roe was the consultant on *Missing Persons NYC* they threw him four hundred dollars."

"A day?"

"That's what he said."

"I could live with that."

"He also said as long as you keep your thoughts to yourself and don't talk to the actors, they'll keep you on forever."

"As a consultant."

"I'm just telling you what he told me."

The tenant in the bathroom came out wearing tinted cat's-eye glasses, jeans, and a blouse, her hair swirled up in a damp white towel like a Mister Softee cone. Whelan walked her the fifteen feet to his door, then kissed her hard on the mouth, her knee reflexively coming up like a quarterback waiting for the snap. She left still wearing the towel.

"I have to be careful," Jimmy said. "Her husband just got out of Comstock, but I'm pretty sure he's staying with his other wife."

Gearing up to leave, Billy took back his son's jacket. "So how's your millionaire?"

"Who, Appleyard? All of a sudden he's got three new girlfriends, two crack hos and a trannie. I'm starting a dead pool: five dollars wins you a hundred if you pick the exact day, fifty if you pick the week."

"How about the month?"

"He won't make it a month."

"Do they even make crack hos anymore?"

"You should get out more."

"All right, brother," Billy said, stepping to the door himself.

"Why'd you mention Pavlicek today," Whelan asked abruptly.

"I told you, it was nothing," Billy said, turning back to the room. "Why are you so worried about Pavlicek?"

"I'm not." Whelan lit another cigarette.

Billy took a breath, then: "You said to me,

'Is there something going on with Pavlicek.' You said, 'I need to know.' "

"I said that? I never said that. You were the one that brought him up."

Billy pondered mentioning Pavlicek's lying about the hematologist again, then decided against it.

"So everything's good with him?" he settled for asking.

"Why wouldn't it be?"

When he was once again passing the laundry room on his way up to the ground floor, Whelan threw open his apartment door. "Hey, I forgot to tell you . . ."

Billy turned.

"This *Fort Apache* remake? It's in three-D."

MILTON RAMOS

His aunt Pauline, eight hours after an obliterating cerebral hemorrhage, lay on life support in the Jacobi Hospital ICU, flanked by her two speechless sons, Herbert and Stan. Out of blood deference, Milton stood at the foot of the bed, his hands resting on the guard rail. She was now a machine-breathing vegetable, and over the past few hours three separate nurses had dropped by to gently campaign for pulling the plug so that they could commence the harvesting, but neither of his guilt-ridden cousins could even bring themselves to hold their mother's hand, let alone respond to the request.

So when a fourth nurse came by to make the pitch, Milton cut her off before word one.

"She's ready," he said.

Neither son protested or even looked his way.

So fucking like them . . .

After his mother and brothers died and Pauline had brought him into her home, he had shared a bedroom with these two for years, but despite his status as a first cousin, they couldn't get past the tragedy he brought into the house with him, or maybe it was just his mixed-race jungle face, or maybe like most everyone else he knew they were intuitively scared of him. Whatever the reason, they had never accepted him as anything but a nerve-racking boarder, as welcome into their lives as an untethered bear.

At least Pauline had taken him in with an open heart; her only bone of contention, then and always, was his sullen demeanor. Not that she didn't understand.

After the nurse left, a volunteer grief counselor came by and touched his arm. "It's so hard to let a loved one go. But you have to take comfort in the fact that even though she might be leaving you physically . . ."

"Talk to them," chucking a thumb toward his cousins, then leaving for the street.

He wouldn't attend or even help with the funeral; they could at least handle that. He had pulled the plug, and that was enough.

Herbert and Stan: if they weren't dead to him before, they sure as hell were now, letting him call down the Reaper on their own mother like that . . .

Loss and loss and loss, each one unasked for, each one, come the end of the story, concluding with his hands gripping a scythe.

"Hey, stranger!" his cousin Anita, like his aunt, one of the decent ones, instantly recognizing his voice on the horn after a year without contact. "What's going on?"

"Nothing," he said. "I haven't talked to you in a while."

"I know! How's Sofia?"

"You should see her."

"I'd love to."

"How about we come visit sometime."

"Say when."

She'll go to better people.

"Soon."

Loss and loss and loss, Milton seeing that house in Yonkers again, that smooth-sailing home.

Why should they be happy.

CHAPTER 9

Billy didn't find out about Sweetpea Harris having gone missing until a two a.m. playground shooting of a sixteen-year-old in Fort Tryon Park took him and Mayo over the Macombs Dam Bridge to Lincoln Hospital in the Bronx.

The victim's brothers were sitting in a small, dreary waiting room, three of them, mute and seething, visions of payback already playing in their eyes. They knew everything there was to know about what had gone down but he would have had better luck interviewing statues, and after twenty minutes of listening to himself talk, Billy got up from a coffee-stained couch with a blank notepad, just hoping that the aforementioned payback would occur after eight in the morning when he was heading up to Yonkers.

It was on his way back to the nurses' station that he first caught sight of the two homemade Missing posters push-pinned into the community announcements board, each featuring a low-resolution photo of Sweetpea Harris on purple printer paper that was bottom-fringed with tear-away phone number tabs, as if announcing the availability of a dog walker. Billy took one of the posters, stuffed it into his coat pocket, and moved on down the line.

An hour later, after one of the doctors came out of the OR and told Billy that the vic would pull through, he returned to the visitors' room to see if the good news would maybe, just maybe, get the brothers talking. But they were already gone, Billy once again praying that the drama to come wouldn't play out until he was safely back in his own bed.

As he was leaving the hospital, intending to head back to Manhattan and monitor the canvass around the crime scene, he nearly ran into an army of the victim's other relatives bursting through the front door, those in front half-carrying the overcome grandmother as if she were their flagship. Billy was there for three additional hours, none of these further interviews yielding anything more than vaguely ominous variations on "They know who they are" and "I warned him" type pronouncements. Finally, the vic's fourteen-year-old stone-faced sister chin-signaled for him to follow her into the ladies' room, where she locked herself in a stall for a few minutes, flushed, and then left without ever saying word one.

The folded Post-it was perched on top of the toilet paper dispenser, the name and address of the shooter written in strawberry-scented neon pink with a swannish hand. Two hours later, armed with a search warrant, Billy followed six Bronx ESU cops into a Valentine Avenue apartment, catching the fifteen-year-old actor already dressed for school, his mouth filled with Franken Berries, his gun in an Angry Birds book bag.

Taking the kid to the nearest precinct, the 4-6, Billy handed him over for processing, then dragged himself upstairs to the empty predawn squad room in order to start banging out the requisite blizzard of paper. And when the day tour started rolling in at eight, he was still at it, blinking violently into the computer screen, his fingertips fluttering with the hour.

"What are you doing here?"

Billy looked up from his commandeered desk to see Dennis Doyle, a take-out coffee in one hand, a folded *Daily News* tucked up next to his ribs.

"What's it look like," he said, flicking a

finger against the screen.

"Come take a break," Dennis said, walking to his office.

Billy followed him inside, planting himself next to a stack of manila folders on the lone couch.

"So how's she doing?"

"Not great," Dennis said, opening his paper.

"The drinking?"

"Everything."

A burly, expressionless detective came into the office without knocking, dropped a new folder on Dennis's desk, and left the room.

"You know, she called me the other day, told me Raymond Del Pino's sister named her baby after her," Billy said.

"I know, Rose Yasmeen."

"She told me Yasmeen Rose."

"I'm sure she did," Dennis said, glancing at the fresh reports.

"Still, no one ever middle-named a kid after me, you know?"

"It's the least they could do, after all she's been through."

"Listen, while I'm here . . ." Billy took Sweetpea's Missing poster out of the side pocket of his sport jacket and handed it over. "You know anything about this?"

Dennis read it and shrugged.

"Look at the guy," Billy said.

"Cornell Harris?"

"Sweetpea Harris."

"Redman's Sweetpea?"

"He told me Harris was half-living with his girlfriend on Concord Avenue. That's you, so I'm thinking maybe she came in here to file a report."

"Hey, Milton," Dennis called out.

The detective came back in the room.

"Can you check the 494s for this guy?"

"Nothing there."

"Don't you want to check?"

"I was here when his sisters or whoever came in to file on him, but it was only twenty-four hours and they never came back, so . . ."

"His sisters?" Billy asked.

"Sisters, girlfriends," the detective said. "You should ask Maldonado, he's the one sent them away."

"Just do me a favor and check the 494s," Dennis said. "Maybe they snuck back in when you were off. If there's something there, don't be a stranger. Otherwise . . ."

When the detective left the room again, Dennis opened his newspaper and spoke in a low voice. " 'Sisters, girlfriends,' " shaking his head, "a real bloodhound."

"Maybe you shouldn't tell Yasmeen about

this," Billy said, reaching for the poster. "It could jack her up about Cortez again."

"Are you kidding me?" Dennis said. "In fact, take it the fuck out of here when you go."

After a few minutes of small talk, Billy went back out into the general squad room to finish his reports, then thought about checking to see if Sweetpea Harris was in the system somewhere. At first he balked, not wanting to leave an electronic trail and risk having to answer anyone's questions, but then he did it anyway, masking his search with a half dozen other names, including Eric Cortez, only to discover that neither were incarcerated or had any warrants hanging over their heads. Which told him, after all was said and done, nothing.

Realizing that he was in no shape to drive, Billy turned off his phone and crashed in the 4-6 bunk room, as fetid and rank as any he had ever known.

When he finally made it home a few hours later, the TV was off. Eleven a.m. on a Saturday morning and no one was watching cartoons, the house as quiet as a monastery. Given that Carmen's car wasn't in the driveway, he assumed that she had taken the boys somewhere, which was A-OK with him.

Then Declan, still in his pajamas, came out of the kitchen.

"Dad?" His voice high and tentative. "We lost Grandpa."

"What do you mean?"

"He's not here."

"What do you mean he's not here. Did you check all the beds?"

"He's not here."

"The basement?"

"He's not here," the kid's voice starting to quiver.

Millie walked into the room, Declan turning to her for help.

"What's he talking about?" Billy said.

"He's not here," she said.

"Explain that."

"I come in this morning, the front door was open and he's . . ."

"Why didn't you call me?"

"We did," Millie said. "Your phone was off."

Carlos joined them in the hallway, the anxiety in the air inspiring him to hit his brother, who was too freaked by now to hit him back.

"Where's Carmen?"

"She's out looking for him."

"All right," Billy said, the heel of his hand pressed into his forehead. "All right . . ."

His first call was to his wife, but she had left without her phone, her "Killing Me Softly" ringtone playing in the kitchen, which made Carlos cry out, "Is Mommy lost too?"

His second call was to the Yonkers PD, the desk sergeant on duty informing him that Carmen had already given them a heads-up over an hour ago.

"All right, why don't you get them dressed," Billy said automatically, already roaming the neighborhood in his head.

He began by driving the residential streets nearest to home, knocking on doors and asking his neighbors to take a peek into their backyards, many of them saying that Carmen had already been there, then branched farther out, hitting the nearest commercial strips, poking his head into every supermarket, bar, and pizza place within walking distance.

At the corner of Mohawk and Seneca he ran into a trolling squad car — the only one assigned to the search, which infuriated him — the cops having no luck either. Then, fifteen minutes later, on a street of imposing Tudors and haciendas, he passed Carmen driving the other way, both cars hitting the brakes and nearly rear-ending each other as they simultaneously backed up at speed.

"I was taking a shower, I came down, Millie's cooking breakfast, she asked me if he was still sleeping upstairs," Carmen blurted, her eyes wild in her head. "Nobody saw him leave."

"All right, just calm down, we'll find him."

"It's my fault," yanking on her hair and then taking off again.

"It's nobody's fault," he said to the air.

Forty-five minutes later, Billy pulled over alongside a junior high school ball field and forced himself to be still.

OK, you're him . . .

There were dozens of mysteries to be solved. For starters, how does a man who can barely find his way around a reasonably small house, who has neither access to a car nor the wherewithal to drive one, make it from Yonkers, land of zero subways, to Harlem USA on his own. But there he was, Billy's hunch playing out like a Powerball winner, his father, walking up and down Lenox Avenue between 118th and 116th Streets like he owned the sidewalk.

For late March, the weather was downright balmy, the people mellow, and he had his father in his sights, so Billy remained in the car and watched the old man do his thing. He stopped and jawed with some old-timers who were sitting on the stoop of an abandoned brownstone cheek by jowl to a latteria on 118th. He bummed a cigarette from one of them, thumb-flicking a bent match against the friction strip of the matchbook with a practiced hand, even though, to Billy's knowledge, his father hadn't had a smoke since 1988, the year his wife had been diagnosed with lung cancer. Then, taking his leave of this crew, he shook hands all around before moving on down the block.

On 117th, he helped a young Asian woman disentangle her Maclaren double stroller from a narrow doorway. On 116th, he told three kids racing scooters through a crowd in front of a ShopRite to put on the brakes. He made eye contact with everyone who crossed his path, but not in such a way as to give offense; he just wanted to let them know that he was back and that nothing escaped his notice. Lenox between 116th and 118th — in 1959, it had been his first foot post out of the academy.

Billy finally stepped out of the car.

"Hey, Officer," calling to his father over

the roof, then coming around to open the passenger door.

"Dad, how'd you get here?" he asked as casually as he could.

"My driver."

"What driver was that?"

"Frank Campbell."

Billy took a breath. "Frank Campbell is off today, Dad," afraid to remind him that his personal driver for his last three years on the Job had been dead for a decade.

"Well, then whoever was covering for him."

Breathe . . .

"Do you remember his name?"

"Didn't catch it."

"Was he in the bag or plainclothes."

"Plainclothes."

Another old-timer, this one a handball-gloved double amputee in a wheelchair, rolled past the passenger window at eye level, caught sight of Billy Senior, and reversed his ride until they were face-to-face. Then, winking against the smoke streaming up from his lip-locked cigarette, the guy crisply, sarcastically saluted, before resuming his journey.

His father was not amused. "How the hell did he make bail?"

"Dad," Billy tried again. "Your driver, what did he look like?"

"Beefy, Hispanic, on the quiet side."

Billy stared out his window until the numbness passed. "Did he say anything to you?"

"He said, 'Where to, boss?' I said, 'Where do you think?' But I had to tell him, so yeah, it couldn't have been Frank."

"And where did he pick you up?"

"Right in front of the house. Caught me by surprise when I went out to get the paper."

Think . . .

"What kind of car was he driving?"

"The usual."

"What's the usual, Dad?" The stress of keeping it light starting to make his voice climb.

The old man went off somewhere.

"A Crown Vic?" Billy leading the witness, but Frank Campbell always drove him around in a Crown Vic.

"A Crown Vic," Billy Senior laughed. "Boy, that takes me back."

"Dad," he begged.

"And by the way, somebody's got to tell that kid to make sure the paper lands on the porch. It goes on the grass and the dew just soaks right through."

■ ■ ■ ■

Billy's father was a big hit at the 2-8, two blocks west of Lenox, the commanding officer remembering him from 1985, when he was a rookie up here and Billy Senior was the West Harlem division captain, and happily giving him a house tour while Billy, waiting for the relevant street camera uploads, made his calls. First to home, Carmen crying with relief and maybe something a little edgier, then to the WGs, seeing if anyone could help him find a safe house for his family until this psycho was caught.

At one point or another over the past twenty years, they had all given temporary shelter to each other, Billy moving in with Pavlicek and his young wife when he lost the house in Staten Island to his ex, Yasmeen moving to Pelham to help Pavlicek take care of his young son after his wife's collapse and institutionalization, Pavlicek sending the adolescent John Junior to live with Billy and Carmen when he and the kid needed a time-out from each other. Later, Jimmy Whelan had stayed with Yasmeen and then Redman when one of his endless string of basement super's apartments had flooded, although no one ever wanted to

move in with Whelan. Then there was Redman staying with Billy and Carmen after
his second or third wife had caught him
with his third or fourth wife and set the
funeral parlor on fire, and Yasmeen again,
taking Carlos and Declan in that long-ago
black summer when Carmen was unable to
leave the bedroom and Billy had his hands
full simply coaxing her down the stairs.

And now, once again, every one of them
coming through: Jimmy offering his cabin
in Monticello, Yasmeen the summerhouse
in Greenwood Lake, Redman a two-room
apartment directly above the funeral parlor
— although he advised Billy to "think
before you say yes" — and Pavlicek, the
grand prize winner, offering them their
choice of twelve newly renovated flats in
buildings spread out over the Bronx and
upper Manhattan, as long as they didn't
mind the constant racket made by his
nonstop work crews.

The uploads from the street cameras,
when they finally came in, just added to the
mystery, the Lenox Avenue tape showing
Billy Senior arriving there on foot after having turned the corner from West 115th, the
tape trained on 115th showing him once
again on foot after having turned the corner
from Adam Clayton Powell, which he en-

tered from 113th, and so on, the precinct tech tracking his progress in reverse until an out-of-commission camera on 111th and Frederick Douglass Boulevard ended the trail with no sign of the car that had dropped him off somewhere south and west of where Billy had found him.

"The hell with that and the hell with that," Carmen clutching her head. "I'm supposed to take the kids and live where, upstate New York? On top of some dead bodies in Harlem?"

"Harlem's totally different now."

"I don't give a shit if it's the new Paris. I'm just not taking my kids to live in a funeral home. Where's your head at, Billy?"

They were standing face-to-face in the toy-strewn living room, each of them alternately crouching and then shooting upright to body-English their arguments, raising and then lowering their voices as the awareness of the two freaked-out kids in the house went in and out of their consciousness.

"Pavlicek has a dozen clean apartments all over the Bronx," Billy pleaded.

"Clean as in vacant, as in no furniture, no bedding, as in no anything." She straightened up and took a breath. "The point is,

Billy, I have a job, they have school, and we're not having our lives uprooted by some sociopath. But do you want to do something for me?"

"Carmen, you're here at night by yourself with the kids. What am I supposed to do, stay home from work and sit in a corner with a shotgun?"

"I asked," she said slowly, "do you want to *do* something for me." Then, lowering her voice: "Your father? Today? He needs to be somewheres else."

"Like where," Billy on full alert.

"I don't know, maybe it's time for him . . ."

"Don't even say it."

"Billy, he doesn't know where he is, he doesn't know *who* he is. This maniac comes along . . . You want to talk about who's vulnerable around here? You want to talk about the one person, the, the straw that's going to break the camel's back? Look, you said it yourself, you're either working or you're sleeping. One way or another you're never here, and I can't worry about him day in and day out, and frankly, with everything that's going on?" again dropping into that heated whisper. "I can't bear him right now. I'm sorry to be so . . . to be like this."

"What happened today, it wasn't his fault."

"Exactly."

"You want to kill him?" Billy's turn to start tearing up. "I put him in a home he'll be dead in a week."

"It's called assisted living."

"No fucking way."

"Then let your sister take him."

"She hates him."

"Too bad."

"She's got her hands full with her own mother-in-law." Billy back to pleading.

"She's got her hands full, huh? Not us, though, we're sailing to Tahiti next week."

"Jesus Christ, what the hell's gotten into you?"

"Get it through your *head,* Billy, we're not going anywhere. You don't want to put him in a, a, a place? Then you call your sister. She's his child too."

"Sometimes you can be a stone bitch, you know that?" Billy instantly ashamed to have said it.

Carmen at first looked struck, then furious, then left the room without another word, leaving Billy standing there, thinking, Why is he doing this to us?

From the kitchen, Carlos started howling in fury, his older brother having just punched him in the stomach.

Brenda Sousa, Billy's oldest sister, showed up three hours later dressed in a snowflake-patterned ski sweater and stirrup pants, her face a moon of aggrievement. Her husband, Charley, a private investigator specializing in insurance fraud, a small quiet man who always seemed to be embarrassed about something, brought up the rear.

Brenda marched up to her father in the kitchen without saying hello to anyone else, wrapped him in a brusque hug. "Hi, Pa," kissing him hard on the cheek, then turning to Billy. "For how long is this."

"Jesus, Brenda, he's right here."

"For how long."

"He's your father, too."

"Did I say he's not?" His sister always so angry.

"Not long."

"How long is not long."

Carmen, having no belly for her sister-in-law, left the room.

"I don't know, Brenda, there was a guy out there who picked him up today, drove him into the city, and just dumped him on the street."

"What? Why?"

"I don't know, but he's not safe here."

"So how is he supposed to be safer by me?"

"Because," Billy took a breath, "whoever took him is after our family."

There, he'd said it.

The NYPD Threat Assessment Team, two detectives named Amato and Lemon, arrived at the house two hours later. Carmen made coffee, then all four of them took seats in the living room, Billy and his wife on the brocade sofa, the detectives facing them in the matching chairs.

"Who should we be talking to here," Amato asked Billy. "You or your father?"

"In terms of what."

"In terms of who might be out there with some kind of personal hard-on," Lemon said.

"You're talking about previous collars?"

"That or anything."

"Well, my dad's retired twenty years, so whoever had a hard-on for him is mostly likely dead or bedridden."

The detectives stared at him, said nothing.

"As for me, I mean, I put away my share of actors, but except for a few years in the Four-nine, I've either been with the ID Squad or in Night Watch, so . . ."

"Any run-ins?"

"With other cops?" Billy shrugged. "There's guys I didn't get along with, but never anything heavy."

"Can you give us some names?"

"Honestly? I'd rather not. We all shook hands in the end."

"What's wrong with giving them names?" Carmen asked, her arms crossed tightly over her chest.

"Because there's not one of them I can't pick up the phone and call myself," he said. "Because there's no need to bring up dead and buried beefs from back in the stone age."

"Then what's the point of them being here?" she muttered.

"How about off the Job," Lemon asked.

"I have no idea," Billy still arguing with Carmen in his head.

"Curtis Taft?" Amato's turn.

"What about Curtis Taft."

"You assaulted him in his hospital bed," Amato said.

"I'd say assault is a little overdramatic."

They resorted to staring at him again.

"I don't think he's so stupid as to come after me or my family, but by all means, do what you have to do."

There was a pause as both cops went into

their notes.

"How about that shooting back when you were in anti-crime?" Lemon asked, still looking down at his pad.

"What about it?"

"There was a lot of press, a lot of angry people."

"It's been over fifteen years, you'd think they'd have plenty to be angry about since."

Carmen, still looking away, shook her head in exasperation, Billy having to restrain himself from getting into another fight with her, this one in front of their Threat Assessment Team.

"All right," Amato said, rising. "We'll put in a request for TARU to come out, mount a few cameras, and ask for the Yonkers PD to start running directed patrols."

"How soon for the cameras?" Billy asked.

"Hopefully right away," Lemon said.

"What do you mean, 'hopefully'?"

"All we can do is put in the request."

An hour later Billy and Carmen were sitting on the couch, each with their arms crossed tightly over their chests as they pretended to watch something or other on TV.

This was how the slow process of ending a fight always began for them, with a sullen agreement to tolerate each other's presence while engaged in a nonverbal activity, during which, at some point, one of them would make a not-quite-spontaneous comment about something unrelated to the argument, something safe, delivered in an offhand monotone, that didn't require a response but usually got one, also to be delivered in the same flatline tone. From there, the exchanges, always off the subject of the fight, would gradually begin to pick up speed until they were actually talking and that monotone was replaced by the natural oscilloscope of unself-conscious human speech. Formal apologies, if the situation really demanded it, usually came later in another room or, if they could get away with it, never, neither of them wanting to risk another potentially volatile encounter if it wasn't necessary. But at the moment they were still in Stage One, the accumulation of stressed silence such that when the phone rang they both nearly levitated off the couch.

It was Billy's sister calling to complain that Billy Senior had no change of underwear in his overnight bag. That call was followed a minute later by another, this one to announce that he had no toothpaste, then another to bitch that he had no pajama bottoms, each "had no" apparently deserving its own individual call.

"What the fuck is wrong with her all the time?" Carmen said when Billy returned to the couch.

"She thinks he didn't like her when she was a kid."

"Only him?"

The next time the phone rang Carmen leapt to pick it up. "I swear to Christ, Brenda, why do you always have to be such a pissed-off bitch . . ." Then: "Oh," her tone downshifting. "I'm so sorry, I thought . . . Sure, he's right here, right here."

Carmen extended the phone to Billy. "It's somebody from Immaculate, Albert Lazar?"

"Like I told you when I called, I would have been perfectly happy to come to you."

"No problem," Billy said.

Lazar had sounded like a wreck on the phone, like he needed to unburden himself, and Billy didn't want him coming to the house and being subjected to the double-team tension of two freaked-out parents. He needed this guy to feel free to talk, and so he found himself in Lazar's tiny home office in Sleepy Hollow, formerly the bedroom of his college-age daughter, the left-over floral-patterned wallpaper combining with the teacher's visceral anxiety to shrink

281

the already claustrophobic space to the size and feel of a sweatbox.

"So," Billy willing himself to be cool, "now that I'm here . . ."

"Understand, I had no idea that you were a detective until you handed me your card yesterday."

"No reason you should have."

"This is kind of a long story."

"How about we start with the punch line and work backwards?"

"Please, I need to tell it the way I need to tell it." They were alone, Lazar's wife and son watching TV one floor below, but he still seemed to feel the need to whisper. "Otherwise you'll never understand."

"Any way you want."

Lazar stared at his hands, his kneecaps motoring.

"So," Billy said.

"All right," Lazar said, dropping his elbows to his knees. "All right . . . Last week?"

Lazar's wife came into the room with a bowl of freshly made kale chips, her husband smiling at her with get-lost eyes. He waited for the sound of her retreating footsteps to fade before starting again.

"Last week? I had a few work meetings in Beacon, and I'm not really familiar with the town, but I was stuck there overnight and so purely out of boredom I took a walk and wound up wandering into a bar. Believe me, I hardly indulge, but I had a gin and tonic, and . . ."

"And . . ."

"Well, call me blind as a bat but I didn't realize it was a gay bar until I ordered drink number two."

"OK . . ."

"And I was so embarrassed that I just tabbed out and left." Tabbed out, Billy thinking, not the expression of a fair-weather tippler.

"It's just that when I was going out the door, I ran into my neighbor, one of my neighbors, Eric, from right up the block here, and when I saw him I was so flustered about coming out of that kind of place all I said was 'Be careful in there, I think something fishy's going on.' And he said, 'Thanks for the warning, I'll stay on my toes.' "

"So this Eric . . ."

"Eric Salley. Understand, I'm a very tolerant individual. I have no problem with him or anyone else being gay."

"Understood. So, this Eric Salley . . ."

"Is trouble."

"What kind of trouble?" When Lazar had difficulty answering, Billy added, "Is he making trouble for you?"

"No, not yet."

"Maybe he's tolerant, too."

"There's nothing for him to be tolerant about."

"Understood."

"Look, I teach at a Catholic school in a working-class city."

"Right."

"A rumor gets started . . . Those kids are my life."

"You're very popular, I know. But you're having a hard time telling me what it is you want me to know, so let me just ask, is this Eric Salley the one I'm looking for?"

"Looking for?" Lazar blinking in confusion.

Billy looked off, trying to control his temper. The guy was in the closet and he was scared of being dragged out. And that was all that this was about.

"So why am I here," he said. "He's trying to blackmail you?"

"No, but to be honest I never felt comfortable around him, and now every time I see him he smiles at me like he knows me. From what I understand he's lost his job and he's this close to losing his condo. And I don't want to go to the local police here, it would only make matters worse. So, I was wondering . . . is there any way, in your capacity as a New York City detective and the parent of one of our students, could you maybe have a talk with him before he does anything we'll both regret?"

"So Eric Salley was not the guy who approached my son."

"No, believe me, I would have recognized him from a mile away."

"How about you, are you the one?"

"Am I the one, what . . ."

Billy got up to leave.

"So, can you help me?" Lazar asked.

"I'll make some calls," he muttered, Billy-speak for Go fuck yourself, and then he was gone.

Leaving everybody home alone like that . . .

As Billy made his way back to Yonkers his anger toward Lazar started to fade. The guy had been terrified, had been carrying the burden of being who he was all his life and just couldn't imagine surviving the exposure. But gay, not gay, or whatever else, Billy couldn't imagine living his day-in, day-out life with a secret so heavy on his heart that the only viable alternative was some kind of oblivion.

Sometimes he worried about Carmen having that kind of weight on her, some specific interior thing that made her so anxiously alert during the days and such a tormented thrasher at night, that made every therapy session he had ever attended with her feel like a complete waste of time, filled with sulky bluster and air-ball bullshit, that periodically and without warning dropped a black-dog mantle over her so profound that it might be days before she could bring herself to open the bedroom door.

There were times when he wondered whether she had been sexually abused as a child and never told anyone or as a frightened teenager had abandoned an unwanted baby — that's where his worst-case imagination came to an end — but one thing he knew for sure: if she could ever find it in herself to finally speak the name of her demon, she would most definitely survive. Her husband would make sure of it.

Pulling into his driveway, Billy saw the silhouette of a stocky male prowling the lawn.

At first he was too startled to move, then moved without thinking, bolting from the car to bull-rush the intruder from behind. As soon as he brought him to ground, landing on top of the guy in a way that forced the air out of both of them, a second figure came running from around the back of the house and bellowed, "Freeze!" while simultaneously blinding Billy with a fierce beam of light. At which point the first cop got up, turned to Billy, and punched him in the head.

And so he was introduced to 24/7 direct patrol coverage, Billy talking as fast as he could to avoid being cuffed and thrown into the back of the Yonkers PD cruiser sent to protect his home and family.

At three in the morning, when Billy entered the sickly bright all-night gas station mini-mart off Frederick Douglass Boulevard, the young kufied African cashier was standing behind the counter, a half-smile on his face as he posed with cops, the majority of whom were holding out beers or candy bars for him to ring up while their partners snapped away with iPhones. The Wheel had said robbery-homicide, body on the scene, but all Billy saw was the cashier, the clowning uniforms, and Stupak.

"Where's the body?"

"Are you blind?" Stupak answered.

Wading through the posing cops, he took a closer look at the cashier: the smiling kid was stone-dead on his feet, a dime-sized bloodstain barely discernible on the chest pocket of his thick burgundy shirt. On the counter to his right sat a half-eaten Hot Pocket, still steaming from the microwave; to his left was a coiled nest of wooden prayer beads and an accounting textbook.

"Are you fucking kidding me?" Billy bellowed at the uniforms. "Everybody out."

Once they were gone, Billy took an extra moment to contemplate his upright victim, then had to turn away; staring into those unblinking yet still expressive eyes felt almost rude.

"It's like Madame Tussauds," Stupak said.

"You pull the store cameras?"

"Of course."

"Did you . . ."

"Of course."

"Any wits?"

"Feeley's in the back room interviewing the cabbie that called it in."

"Feeley's here?" Billy surprised but not really, having figured that after their car talk, Gene would either start showing up like clockwork just to spite him, or he'd take to heart Billy's suggestion to become a full-time no-show and never be seen again, a winning outcome either way.

"Is Butter here?"

"Give him a break, he just blew a big audi-

288

tion today."

"Playing what?"

"Are you going to make me say it?' "

"A detective, right?"

Stupak walked away.

"Hey, Sarge?" a uniform called out from the open door. "There's a guy out here."

Billy stepped out to see a plainclothes detective in jeans and a hoodie leaning against the door of what he guessed was a dope-confiscated vintage Firebird. Behind the narc, two uniforms posted at the pumps were waving off all cars, at this hour mostly taxis pulling in to gas up.

"Sorry to pull you out. I didn't want to contaminate your scene in there."

"Too late for that."

"John MacCormack," offering his hand, "Brooklyn North Narcotics."

"Excuse me," Billy said, walking over to the uniforms at the pumps. "These cars pulling in?" he said. "They're probably habituals, so start taking their vitals before you cut them loose, especially the hacks."

Moving back to MacCormack, Billy finally shook his hand. "So, John, what can I do for you?"

"I need to know your interest in Eric Cortez."

"Come again?"

"You ran his name yesterday? It raised a flag."

"Yeah, I did, him and a few others."

"Can I ask why?"

Billy knew the worst thing he could do was lie. "I was over at the Four-six wrapping up my Fives on a shooting. I had some time to kill, so I looked up a few bad guys from back in the day."

MacCormack looked off, smiling in temporary retreat.

"Like Facebooking old girlfriends," Billy said. "Why do you want to know?"

MacCormack let the question hang in the air, Billy not liking that at all.

"OK," Billy said, suddenly too nervous to wait him out, "I'm guessing that since Cortez is too stupid to be running any kind of crew or moving enough weight to be worth your while otherwise, he's your CI, most likely in deep for you with some bigger fish, and right now you're coming up here to see if he's into some of kind of outside jackpot that he neglected to tell you about. But I'm just guessing."

"Hang on a sec," MacCormack said, then walked away to make a brief phone call.

The CSU van finally rolled up, the emerging detectives heading to the mini-mart with their kits and cameras, probably unaware

290

that the tall young man visible through the plate-glass window and looking as if he were ready to ring up a beer was their body.

"Look," Billy said when MacCormack came back, "it was just curiosity on my part. I probably shouldn't have run him and I'm sorry I did, but number one, I'm not looking to fuck anybody's play here, and two, you're coming to me at three in the morning about this and not answering any of my questions, so maybe you can just tell me this . . . Am I in some kind of jam here?"

MacCormack hesitated, looking at Billy as if sizing him up. "He just needs to be protected right now."

Billy nodded, masking his relief, then became angry with himself for showing his ass like that.

"Protected," he said. "You know what this guy did, don't you?"

"You mean the Del Pino homicide?" MacCormack pulled out a pack of Winstons.

"All I can think, he must be one hell of a snitch."

MacCormack stared at Billy for a moment longer in that assessing way, then just shrugged, game over.

"I tell you, with CIs?" he said, offering Billy a cigarette. "I try to think of it like this: all those Nazi scientists working on the

291

V-2 rocket, we snatched them up like draft picks, us or the Reds, freedom or world enslavement. That was the stakes, so all is forgiven, welcome to Texas. I mean, Christ, some of those krauts wound up on postage stamps."

"Eric Cortez as Wernher von Braun," Billy said. "That there's a keeper."

MacCormack semi-laughed, then slipped back into the Firebird.

Billy stared at the Phoenix decal on the trembling hood for a moment, then just said it: "He's not dead, is he?"

"Cortez? No," MacCormack said, giving Billy a look that made him wish he'd kept his mouth shut.

MILTON RAMOS

She was throwing him all night.

First she wanted to do something in bed that they never did before and that made him blow his top in about two minutes flat.

Then, still turned on by what they'd just done, they went at it again — they were strictly one-shot lovers, and so that was a second first — Marilys moaning all the way through. Normally they were so silent that you could be sleeping in the same room with them and not wake up, so that right there was a third first, all three ground-breakers coming to pass in about twenty-five minutes.

They were both by nature physically modest people, so even though they had just fucked like banshees, when she finally came out of the bathroom still naked, Milton had no idea where to rest his eyes. And instead of immediately getting dressed like she always did, Marilys just sat on the edge of the bed without making any move for her clothes.

"Hey, Milton."

He had never heard her say his name out loud; somehow they managed to live amicably under the same roof for forty to fifty hours a week without ever saying each other's names, and he'd be lying if he said her doing so now didn't make him feel uncomfortable.

"What's up," still looking away from her water-dappled skin.

"I'm pregnant."

His first reaction was that she had just become pregnant in the last half hour, which was maybe why she had taken so long in the bathroom.

"What do you mean?" The question sounded stupid, he knew, but still.

She didn't answer.

Even in his state of low shock, he would not insult her by asking if she was sure it was his.

"OK," he said carefully, then: "What are you thinking?"

Her blue-black Indio hair, instead of being brushed straight back from her face as usual, had been carefully combed into long wet bangs that made her look a few pounds lighter, a few years younger.

"Because whatever you're thinking, I'll help you out."

"Thanks," still making no move to cover herself.

"I mean, now is not a good time for me, but anything I can do."

Much to his relief, she finally began reaching for her clothes.

"But so just tell me, what are you thinking?"

"I'm thinking it's a boy."

"You can tell, huh?"

"I have two sons, seven brothers, and seven uncles. It's a boy."

"OK."

He felt stoned, but not so badly that he couldn't deal.

She stopped reaching for her clothes and looked at him full-on. "Look, I don't want nothing from you and I'm OK raising him on my own, but that means I got to go back to Guatemala to be with my family, so pretty soon I can't take care of Sofia anymore, and I can't take care of you, that's all I'm saying."

"That's too bad," he said, both saddened and relieved.

A few hours later, a thermos of iced Yellow Chartreuse nesting in his cup caddie, Milton sat in the rear parking lot of the Bryant Motor Lodge and watched as Carmen's brother, Victor, pulled up in an old Range Rover, stepped out, and walked across the lot to the rear entrance, just like dozens of junkies, crackistanis, and pross-escorted johns had done since he had set up camp ninety minutes earlicr. Milton had nothing against Carmen's brother personally; in fact, in some detached way he was happy to see him, the sad undergrown gay kid he remembered from Longfellow Avenue having grown into a fairly squared-away-looking man with clear eyes and a forthright stride even at this ass-of-night hour.

Victor had been easy to find — Milton just hadn't ever thought of finding him before. A sociology instructor at City College, he had a website that described the paper he was working on, calling it a study of the "quasi-family dynamics" that developed over time among the drug dealers and sex workers whose base of operations was an unnamed hot-sheet motel in the Bronx. Which wasn't hard to find either, since there was a notorious cluster directly across the New England Thruway from Coop City, and talking to a few of the regulars along that stretch yielded not only the Bryant but Victor's working hours, which made sense, he guessed, given what the guy was going after.

Propping his bat in the passenger-side foot well, he slid his seat back as far as it would go, reached for the thermos, and drifted off, thinking about having unexpectedly run into Billy Graves in Dennis Doyle's office first thing this morning. After the fight-or-flight thing passed, Milton had instinctively sized him up physically, in case it ever came to that, then calmed down enough to get a rush off Billy's cluelessness. And then seeing him again later in the afternoon, this time gray-faced and shaking when he finally found his father, still half in his pajamas, walking his old post on Lenox Avenue like a living time capsule.

But Milton knew that what he had committed by taking Bill Graves Sr. from the house in Yonkers, given the man's deteriorating mental state, was both a felony and an escalation.

And now he was here.

Another escalation.

In the past, his rage, his satisfaction, climaxed in one act, one deed. But because of his desire this time around to keep his own life intact, he had decided on a strategy of long-term indirect payback, and in a way this was much harder on him, leaving too much time for thinking, for agonizing, for mulling over worst-case outcomes, for justifying and then retreating, retreating and then reversing.

Even worse, Milton was coming to discover, each act of carefully doled-out chaos set up a craving in him to get to the next one. He felt a burning urge to keep jacking up the stakes, intensify the act itself, until he could achieve something akin to that sensation of finality he had always experienced, for better or worse, in the past. But he was losing faith in his ability to rein himself in before the tale told out — if he had ever had that faith in himself to begin with.

When he'd taken Sofia to Longfellow Avenue he had thought it was to immunize himself from himself. But now, sitting here in the parking lot of Motel Hell, he realized that it had been more of a farewell tour. If things went out of control — *when* things went out of control, as he had always known they would — she would at least have some sense memory of the haunted house that, after twenty-three years, had finally claimed her father.

A son. Or so she claims. Well, it was hers. And his, scientifically speaking, but mostly hers, and he wouldn't interfere with her plans.

As two of the motel guests came out into the parking lot to swap powder for head, he thought about how Marilys had sat on the edge of the bed tonight, her hair combed straight down like a squaw, then thought about that thing they did the first time, the noises she made that second time.

He took another sip of Chartreuse.

But even if he was otherwise inclined about the baby, the way things were going he wouldn't be around to enjoy him in any event, and the kid would just become another log on the bonfire of loss.

Somewhere near a shot went off, a car peeled out, and a man lay on his back by the dumpsters, his legs slow-peddling the air. After a long moment he managed to flip himself over, raise up on all fours, and crawl back inside the motel.

They had always understood each other, he and Marilys, their silences pretty companionable, neither one ever a trouble to the other, although he always felt bad about not paying her more money.

The next thought that came to Milton was so major that after reflexively grabbing for his bat, he had to step out of the car in order to clear his head.

To avenge his family, he would be destroying what was left of it. The Ramos family would go from two here to two gone, which is to say no one left. But what if instead of Ramos obliteration they — he — went the other way and doubled their number?

He couldn't imagine what Edgar would say about this new way of thinking — his older brother was the only person he'd ever known whose darkness was blacker than his own, the only person who Milton had ever come close to fearing — but he was pretty sure that his mother would be weeping with relief.

He was still standing outside his car, bat in hand, when Carmen's brother suddenly came out of the motel, trotted to the Range Rover, and opened the passenger door. Victor grabbed a mini-recorder from the glove box, then dropped his car keys and accidentally kicked them into the night. Using the light on his cell phone, he sank into a hunch and began duck-walking all over the lot in an effort to find them, Milton watching as Victor unwittingly came in his direction, his bowed head like an offering.

After he'd identified himself half a dozen times through the steel door of her East Harlem SRO, Marilys, wearing a polyester nightgown, cautiously opened up, the scent of her skin lotion pleasantly knocking him on his ass.

"I should have called," he said, eyeing the steak knife in her left hand.

"What's wrong?" she whispered, her eyes wide with alarm.

"Nothing, can I come in?"

He had never been here before, and he was surprised by the number of plants she kept, both hanging and potted, and not so surprised by the army of religious tokens: the medallions and silver icons that festooned her walls, the plaster saints that stood on her dresser and night table, Marilys's minuscule home like Guatemala in a box.

There was nowhere to sit but the bed.

He took the time he needed to compose what he wanted to say, but once he got good and going he doubted he had ever uttered so many continuous words in his life.

"So, after my, what happened to my family, I lived with my aunt Pauline for a few years, she got me to finish high school out by her, I can't hardly remember any of my classes or teachers but I played a little football and I enjoyed that . . . Then after graduation, I worked construction off and on, was a bouncer in a few titty bars in

Williamsburg when it was still like that, got hired as a bodyguard for Fat Assassin, which was a good gig until he wanted me to start lining up girls for him this one night in some club like I was his fucking sex gofer . . . I mean, as I look back on it, me swinging on him in front of his people wasn't the smartest thing to do, but . . . And then so of course we wound up taking it out back, which turned out very bad for the both of us, you know, in our respective ways . . . After that I kind of lost myself for a year or two, the less said about that the better, until a girl in the neighborhood that I liked who was a police cadet started talking that up, and, at the time I figured, Well, that's one way to keep myself out of trouble, but they rejected my application because I didn't have any college. So I went to Medgar Evers in Brooklyn, but only for a year, reapplied, got in, graduated, got my shield, got married, had Sofia, as you know, lost my wife, as you know . . ." taking a breather, thinking, What else, what else . . .

"With women? There was a girl, Norma, in, I think, tenth grade, that was the first time, a few one-time things, some girlfriends, but nobody for long, my wife of course, plus I wasn't above paying for it now and then, especially at first after she died, then you, of course, you know, the way we do."

What else . . .

"I drink too much, as you know, and . . . I guess that's it."

Of course that wasn't it, but there would be time for telling the rest later.

"So," looking at her perched on the foot of her own bed, the hanging plants behind her head making him think of a jungle cat emerging into a clearing, "what do you think?"

When he left forty-five minutes later, she kissed him on the mouth, which made him jerk back with surprise, then avidly lean in for more.

All these firsts . . .

CHAPTER 10

There's something terrible going on the bathroom, he can hear Carmen moaning from behind the half-open door, a low animal keen, and then he hears a frantic scrabbling on the tiles as if she's desperately trying to get away from someone. He needs to get out of bed but he's physically paralyzed, not even able to brush away the pillow that has slipped over his face and is preventing him from drawing breath. She calls out his name in a hopeless sob, more like a farewell than a cry for help, and it's only with the greatest effort that he can even make a responding noise, a kind of high-pitched strangled mooing that actually, finally wakes him up. But though he is wide awake now, he still can't move or draw breath, and Carmen is still in that small room with him, and he's killing her, and Billy just cannot breathe or move, until suddenly he can, wrenching himself free from the bedsheets and stumbling into the bath-room, but of course there's no one there.

Sitting slumped and shaken on the edge of the bathtub, Billy wished — for the first time in nearly two decades — he desperately wished for a fat line of coke, the only thing he could think of to speed-vacuum his muzzy, terror-stricken skull.

When he finally made it downstairs, the first person he saw was his father, reading the paper in the kitchen, which was as per usual until he remembered that the old guy was supposed to be at his daughter's house.

The slam of a car door drew Billy to the window, his sister about to back out of his driveway.

"What are you doing, Brenda?" Wearing a T-shirt, jeans, and sneakers, he stood by her car door in the early morning chill.

His sister, having no intention of getting out of the car, or even turning off the engine, rolled down the driver-side window.

"I wake up this morning, I think it's Charley laying next to me, but guess who."

"I should have warned you about that."

"Oh. And let me tell you about breakfast," she said, lighting a cigarette. "We're all sit-ting there, me, Dad, Charley, and my head-case mother-in-law, Rita, and all of a sudden Rita says to Dad, 'So, Jeff, are we going to have relations tonight?' You know what our father says? 'Depends what time I get off.' And Rita says back, 'Well, call me when you know so I can cancel my game.' "

Billy took a light off Brenda's cigarette. "OK, so he thought she was Mom."

"Actually, he called her Irena."

"Who's Irena?"

Brenda put her car in gear. "Do you really want to know?" Then, reversing out of the driveway, "I can't do it, Billy, I'm sorry."

On his way back up to the house, Dennis Doyle called, Billy listening to him for less than a minute before jumping into his own car and taking off for the Bronx.

The first thing he noticed when he raced into the St. Ann's ER was Carmen's workstation chair upside down a good fifteen feet from her desk; the second was the bright red spatter of drops leading to the curtained cubicle.

At the sight of him Carmen started yelling at the Indo-Afro-Asian interns that ringed her gurney. "Jesus Christ! I specifically said do not call my husband, as in, *do not.*"

From what he could see of her partially averted face, there was a two-inch cut beneath her eye and the beginnings of a nasty shiner.

"They didn't call him, Carm," Dennis said. "I did."

"What happened." Billy wasn't sure who he was addressing.

"I think this might require some stitches," one of the interns said.

"What happened," he repeated.

"Oh for Christ's sake, it's a goddamn black eye!" Carmen back to barking. "Ice the goddamn thing, then let me go pick up my chair and get back to work. Jesus!"

Despite her fireballing, Billy saw that she was trembling. As was he.

"You caught the guy?" he asked Dennis.

"I told you three times, yes."

"In fact, you know what?" Carmen again. "I don't want you to go near my face at all. Go page Kantor."

"Where is he," Billy asked Dennis.

"Forget it, Billy."

"Is he still here? Where is he?"

"You know what?" Carmen said. "Screw it. Hold up a mirror for me, I'll do it myself."

"You have no idea what this whack's been putting us through," Billy said.

"What whack?" Dennis losing track.

"Dennis, I just want to lay eyes on him, I

won't even go in the room."

"I don't think so."

"How about this. You don't let me see him, I'll walk out of here and pistol-whip the first fat-assed, do-nothing hospital guard I see."

"Gentlemen," an older doctor murmured as he slid past them and into the cubicle. "So, Carmen," he said breezily, "when can we expect the lawsuit?"

"Pretend it's my collar," Billy pleaded, "and that's Yasmeen on that table getting worked on."

Dennis did a quick 360 around himself. "You are not to talk to him."

"You got it."

"Not a fucking word, you hear me?"

As they walked to the impromptu holding cell, an empty storage room down a long corridor, Dennis held firmly to Billy's arm, his tense mantra every few steps "Remember what you promised me."

"Did he say anything?"

"Who. This guy? Not that I know of."

"Really," Billy said lightly. "Not before, not during, not after?" Then, when Dennis tightened his grip: "I'm just curious."

"Just remember what you promised."

"You!" Billy shouted as he tried to leap over

308

Dennis's back and get to Carmen's attacker, who, guarded by a uniform, was cuffed to a chair at the far end of the room. The grimy, blaze-eyed stick figure in scavenged clothing looked at Billy with calm eyes and total incomprehension.

"What do you want from us!" Billy railed, this time with less heat. The guy was obviously a homeless nutter off his meds, if he'd ever been prescribed them in the first place.

"You promised me," Dennis said, his arms spread wide as he began chest-bumping Billy backward toward the door.

"Forget it," Billy said, lightly pushing him off before turning to leave under his own steam.

"I am John," the cuffed man abruptly announced in a voice so deep and booming they both jumped. "And I bring news of he who is to come."

The best of Pavlicek's offered apartments was, as Carmen had predicted, a furniture-free one-bedroom in a shittier-than-usual part of the Bronx, but Billy didn't care. This morning's assault had thrown him into a state of shameless hyperprotectiveness, and until their stalker was caught, they were leaving Yonkers, the hell with the goddamn designated patrols, which had done nothing last night but freak out his wife, the low voices and roving flashlight beams coming through the bedroom window at all hours making her feel like a hunted animal — which, if you thought about it, was what she felt like most of the time without any help from them.

"I was hoping so bad that was him, you know?" Billy said, perching himself on a living room windowsill that afforded him a partial view of the outfield in Yankee Stadium, one block west of the apartment. "At least it would all have been over."

"They'll catch him," Pavlicek said restlessly. "She's home now?"

"I had to drag her out of there, but yeah, she's home."

"Doctors and nurses, they always make the worst patients, right? They think they know everything, then when something happens to them they get all pissy and embarrassed. They're like two-year-olds, tell me I'm wrong."

For a man seeing a hematologist he seemed to be moving pretty good today, Billy thought, the guy roaming in a tight, repetitive circuit like a big cat in a small cage.

"All right, look, I'll get my guys to bring some furniture in from the warehouse, but it might take a day or two. Meanwhile, I'm having my security guy come up to the house and hook you up with a CCTV."

"John . . ."

"I can't believe you don't have one. In fact, it boggles my mind. First thing I did when I bought my pile was put in a system. I wouldn't have my family set foot in there until it was wired like the Pentagon, are you kidding me? Christ, Billy, you haven't seen enough shit in the last twenty years? You think you're immune? No one's immune. None of us."

"When you're right, you're right," Billy said, just trying to calm him down. "Thank you."

Pavlicek took a seat on one of the radiators, dropped his head, and ran his hands through his hair. When he looked up again it was like a sleight of hand, his expression having morphed from fiercely agitated to helplessly bewildered.

"How are you feeling these days?" Billy asked.

"What do you mean?"

"You know, your cholesterol."

"My what? I'm good."

"Good. Glad to hear it."

"So, how are the boys," Pavlicek said, just to say something.

"They're boys," Billy answered in kind.

"Kids. All we want in life is for them to be happy, right?"

"Sure."

"I mean, what are we asking."

"I know."

"John Junior, do you remember all the grief he put me through? With the rehabs, the dealing, the graffiti collars, dropping out of school . . . And that fucking room of his, I'd walk in, him and all his friends reeking of skunk, looking like red-eyed morons, 'Hey Mister P,' sitting there with the sideways hats over their ears. 'Hey, kids! Who knows what century it is? A hundred bucks to whoever can tell me what fucking century we're in or even just what planet we're on,' they're like, 'Uh, duh, uh . . .' "

"I remember," Billy said, recalling John Junior in his teens, an oversized bruiser like his father but in reality a sweet-tempered con artist who'd rather munch than punch.

"But I tell you, last year?" Pavlicek back to pacing. "I come home one day, he's there, says to me, Read this, and it's an acceptance letter from Westchester Community College. I didn't even know he applied. He says he wants to take some business classes, then get something going for himself. I tell him, Come work for me, you'll learn more about starting your own business than ten colleges, he says no, he wants to do it on his own. I say, If you work for me you'll earn enough money to hit the ground running, he says, Dad, all due respect? It's important for me to do this without help from you. Can you believe that? I was so proud of him I wanted to bust."

"Hey, it was his time and he recognized it," Billy said. "Many don't."

"What's that?" Pavlicek tilted his chin to the side pocket of Billy's sport jacket, Sweetpea's purple Missing poster still peeking out like gaudy origami.

Billy passed it over.

"Cornell Harris," Pavlicek read, then: "That's Sweetpea, right?"

"Looks like he pulled a Houdini," Billy said. "Or got Houdinied, more likely."

"What the hell do you care?"

"I'm not saying I do."

"Worry about your family."

"What do you think I'm doing here?"

"Worry about your kids." Pavlicek started to balloon again, his voice bouncing off the bare walls.

Billy stopped answering, refusing to engage.

"This fuck? Are you kidding me?" Pavlicek crumpled the poster, then tossed it backhand into a corner. "Piece of shit . . ."

Hoping he would storm himself out, Billy remained seated and watchfully silent until Pavlicek suddenly made his move, coming toward him so fast that he didn't even have time to raise his hands. But instead of throwing a punch, the big man blew right past him and without another word stormed out of the apartment, the flung-open door pockmarking the plaster of the tiny vestibule before slamming back into its frame on the rebound.

Trying to calm himself, Billy gazed out the window at the clean geometry of the distant stadium grass for a moment, then, turning away, picked Sweetpea's poster up off the floor and dialed the number that hung in multiples from the bottom.

Donna Barkley was a short, thick, snub-faced woman to begin with, and her company-issued maroon blazer did her no favors, her fingers barely peeking out of the too-long sleeves, the jacket's center back vent angling out over her high and wide butt like an awning.

"Hey, how are you," Billy said, rising from his white plastic chair in the cement pocket park alongside the office building where she

314

worked as a security guard.

She took a seat, reached into her bag for a Newport, fired up, and then turned her head away to exhale, exposing the cursive *Sweetpea* inked across her left carotid.

"Arista," Billy said, reading the insignia on her jacket. "They take care of you over there?"

"It's a job for pay," still not looking at him. "I got two kids and a grandmother."

"I hear you," he said, removing the crumpled Missing poster from his jacket and flattening it against the tabletop.

"You were only supposed to tear off the phone number on the bottom," she said, "not take the whole damn thing."

Billy gave it a beat, vigorously scratching his up-tilted throat. "So, let me just start by asking you a few questions, see where that takes us."

"Who are you with again?"

"Like I said to you on the phone, I'm an independent investigator."

She gave him a look. "You got an ID?"

He handed over his driver's license.

"Something with your business on it."

Digging into his wallet, he pulled out a card for Sousa Security, his brother-in-law's outfit, which listed him as the assistant head of investigations, even though he never did

315

a thing or took a dime.

"And this is for free?"

"I said that."

"Why is it free."

"Because," Billy looking her in the eye, "like I also mentioned to you on the phone, we're opening an office near Lincoln Hospital and if I can find him for you, word'll get around and hopefully it'll bring us clients."

A pigeon landed on their table, Sweetpea's fiancée glaring at the filthy thing but making no move to shoo it away.

"Has he ever been gone this long before?"

Taking her cell phone out of her purse, she responded to one text, then another, Billy torn between repeating the question and just packing it in.

"Outside of incarceration?" she finally said, still texting. "Now and then."

"So what made you so concerned this time?"

"Because," she said, stuffing her cell back into her purse, "we were talking on the phone, then some white guy called his name, and all of a sudden Sweetpea hangs up and where is he."

"OK, this guy . . ." he said, opening a steno pad.

"White guy."

"This white guy who called his name, did

he say anything else?"

"He just said, 'Hey Sweetpea, come over here.'"

"Then what."

"Then Sweetpea said, 'The fuck you want.' Then the guy said, 'Seriously, Pea, no kidding, come over here.'"

Billy looked up from his notes. "And you're sure the guy was white?"

"My phone doesn't come with eyes, but I know white when I hear it and that guy was white all day long."

"OK," Billy said. "Then what."

"What?"

"What did you hear next."

"Click."

"And roughly what time was this?"

"It was three-fifteen exact, you know how I know? Because he kept yelling at me. 'It's three-fifteen, bitch! Where the fuck are you?'"

"Good," Billy back to writing.

"Good?"

"Do you have any idea where he was when he called you?"

"I know that exact, too. He was just leaving my building to come get me, yelling, 'I'm walking out right now, I'm walking out right now.'"

"Walking out of . . ."

"502 Concord Avenue."

"502," writing, then: "This white guy, any ideas?"

"Not per se."

"What do you mean, 'not per se.' "

She shrugged as if the question wasn't worth answering.

Billy hesitated, then, chalking up her truculent vagueness to a general case of whitey hatin', moved on.

"Was he having any problems with anyone recently?"

"Well, he's a talent promoter, you know?" Her voice softened for the first time. "Trying to help the community, but these kids he takes under his wing, they expect miracles."

"Any kids in particular?"

"I'm just saying" — looking away — "in general."

"All right." He put down his pen. "I did a little research on your fiancé before I came here, it's a crucial part of a job like this, and I need to ask you . . ." Billy back in her eyes. "Is he still slinging?"

She stared at him as if he were too thick to live. "I don't want to talk out of my area of expertise."

"Do you want me to find him or not?"

She continued to stare, Billy once again

ready to call it a day.

"One last . . . I asked you before if you had any idea who this white guy was and you said, 'Not per se.' I need for you to elaborate on that 'not per se.' "

"Not per se meaning, like, I don't know who he is, per se."

"But you know . . . what, his type?"

"Oh yeah."

"From what, his tone of voice?"

"Uh-huh."

"And what type would that be."

"Your type."

"My type . . ."

She fired up another Newport, took a drag, then exhaled in a slow steady stream.

"You know what Sweetpea always used to say NYPD stands for?" she said, tossing Billy's bullshit business card on the table as she rose to her feet. " 'Not Your People, Dawg,' " having read him like a comic book from the door on in.

He was still sitting at the table when he got a call from home, the unexpected sound of his younger son's plaintive voice making him knotty.

"Hey, buddy, what's up?"

"I didn't even do anything and Mom started yelling at me like I did," Carlos said.

Billy exhaled with relief. "Well, she had an upsetting experience this morning, so don't take it personal and just extra-behave today, all right? You and your brother both."

"But I didn't do anything."

"Carlos, just do me a favor, OK?"

"OK."

Another incoming call flashed Pavlicek's name across his screen, Billy ignoring it. "Everything else all right?"

"Yeah."

"You sure?"

"Yeah."

"What are you doing right now?"

"Talking to you."

"All right, I'll be home for dinner, OK?"

"OK."

"And everything's OK?"

"Yeah."

"Your brother's OK?"

"Yeah."

"Grandpa?"

"Yeah."

"All right, buddy," he said, as Pavlicek attempted to ring through again. "I'll see you at home, OK?"

"You didn't ask about Mom."

"I'll see her back home too."

"Do you want to talk to her?"

"I'll talk to her at home," Billy said, knowing all too well that when things were tense between them the phone was not their friend.

He started to call Pavlicek back, hesitated, and instead called Elvis Perez at Midtown South to see if there was any kind of progress on the Bannion homicide. Perez was out, so Billy settled for leaving a message.

He sat there for a moment, thinking about Pavlicek's afternoon flip-out over the Sweetpea poster, then looked over his interview notes, which yielded only two pieces of hard information: 502 Concord, three-fifteen a.m.

If he were so inclined he could do a canvass for possible witnesses. But it probably wouldn't be too smart: a detective from outside the local precinct, on his own, knocking on doors in the middle of the night to ask about Sweetpea Harris, especially if Sweetpea turned out to be dead, Billy imagining the barrage of questions that would then come his way, none of which, at this point, he would be prepared to answer, especially after having come so close to stepping in it simply by entering Eric Cortez's name into the system.

So, it had to be someone else, and not a cop. For a hot second he thought about hiring Sousa Security but then bagged the idea; there was something about his brother-in-law he didn't quite trust. It wasn't that he was a liar exactly — more like an omitter, as if the answers he gave you had to hold up in court.

So.

"Hey, it's me."

"Hey," Stacey's voice high and on the shaky side.

"I have some work for you this week if you're up for it."

"Yeah, sure, absolutely," once again sounding sunny but strained, as if someone was standing behind her with a knife.

"Are you OK?"

"Sure."

Billy hesitated, then: "Where do you want to meet?"

"Can you come to my place?"

In all the years they had known each other, she had never invited him to her home.

"Yeah, no problem, what's a good time?"

"Now."

He began to smell the stale waft of old cigarette smoke coming from Stacey's apartment midway in his wheezing climb to her floor. When he finally reached her landing, Billy took a moment to catch his breath, then followed his nose down the long hallway to 6B, where she greeted him in the open doorway with a smile so tense he thought her face would crack.

With its dim corridors, greasy slit of a kitchen, and small living room filled with indifferent furniture and overflowing ashtrays, the apartment reeked of resignation, and it made Billy ache to think what life could have been like for her right now if she had only looked elsewhere to make her journalistic bones.

Her boyfriend's plaid bathrobe matched the fabric of the couch so well that Billy didn't even realize the guy was in the room until he reached for his beer.

"Hey, how are you." Billy couldn't remember his name.

Lying flat on his back, the boyfriend made no effort to sit up or even turn to face him. "Superb."

Stacey stood mutely between them, looking first at Billy, then her boyfriend, then back to Billy, her face still tense and expectant.

It was the collection of amber prescription bottles on the coffee table that first caught his eye. Then the edge of the butterfly bandage on the ridge above the boyfriend's averted brow. Then the face full-on, as lumpy as a thumbed hunk of clay, his skin the color of overripe bananas, the sclera of one eye hemorrhaged to a neon red.

"Did you call the cops?" he asked Stacey.

"Of course."

"And?"

"They came."

"And?"

"And nothing."

"What happened," he asked the boyfriend.

"Some gentleman must have come into the vestibule right behind me last night and . . ." He shrugged.

"What did he look like, this gentleman."

"He was behind me."

"Did he say anything?"

"Nothing."

"Race, hair, clothes . . ."

"Nothing." Then: "It's my own fault."

"Why do you say that?"

The boyfriend turned his face away again.

"Why do you say that?" Billy's voice sharper now.

Stacey touched Billy's arm.

"What time was this," asking both of them.

"About one in the morning," the boyfriend answered.

"And where were you coming from."

"The Jaunting Car."

"What's that."

"The bar where he first met you," she said.

"Were you there too?"

"I left about an hour and a half before he did," sounding embarrassed about it. No, not embarrassed, he thought, more like defeated.

"Did anybody in there talk to you? Either of you?"

"People in there tend to talk to themselves," the boyfriend said.

"Anybody giving you a hard time?"

"Not really."

"What's 'not really' mean?" Billy getting hot again.

"A seventy-five-year-old cirrhotic called me an asshole."

"Anybody else?"

"Call me an asshole?"

"I'm trying to *help* you here."

"I appreciate it," the boyfriend said carefully.

"All right, let me make a call," Billy said, this time by way of an apology. Gesturing to the opened beer, he said, "You have an extra one of those?"

As Stacey headed to the kitchen, Billy retreated to a corridor off the living room and worked to get a handle on his rage.

He tried to picture it: this guy stays to

325

drink after Stacey — and not for the first time — is unable to coax him out of the bar and so just gives up and leaves. He continues to drink alone for another ninety minutes, waiting for happy, or bright, or successful to kick in, before finally giving up and herky-jerking his way home. And at one in the morning, he couldn't have been more of a staked lamb out there, a street-dumb, self-hating smart-ass reeking of death wish, probably not even caring, once he got his load on, whether he was heading home or straight off a cliff.

Fuck the mugger: what detective worth his salt wouldn't want to strangle a guy like that himself? Victims like Stacey's boyfriend made you feel like a nameless bit player in some narcissistic melodrama performed before an audience of one.

Made you feel demeaned.

Billy paced the short corridor, hating on the victim while trying not to give a thought to the person who had battered his face into a bloody stew.

It couldn't be him.

Coming back into the living room, he ignored Stacey's offered beer and went right at the boyfriend.

"The guy who beat you, what did he take?"

"My dignity."

Billy threw him a look.

"And my wallet," he quickly added.

Then not him — unless he took the wallet to throw Billy off. But that would defeat the purpose, would obscure the message, and the message was the point, unless, unless . . .

"All right, let me make a call," he repeated.

Before leaving, Billy looked around the apartment one last time; then, thinking once again how Stacey's life might have turned out if she'd been a little less reckless with him, he added, "I'm sorry."

"For what?" she asked brightly, but she knew.

Heading to his car, Billy called home and got no answer, not even the answering machine. He called again and got the same, which made him break into a trot.

What was he up to.

Billy had been expecting him to keep moving in deeper on his family, but attacking Stacey's boyfriend — *if* he had attacked Stacey's boyfriend — seemed to be about going outward, maybe going so far outward that he and everyone else would be going crazy wondering if it was still him, and if that, in fact, who the fuck knew, was his game plan, then who would be next? Millie Singh? His sister? Maybe one of Billy's friends, or one of his friends' spouses or kids, then after that, maybe going in deep again, and the next time he came after Carmen or the kids or his father — Billy flashing on the boyfriend's bashed-in face — the outcome would be a lot more catastrophic than a vandalized jacket or a free ride to Harlem.

Was this guy a genius?

Or had Stacey's boyfriend just straight-up gotten mugged . . .

Either way he had Billy by the balls.

A third fruitless call home while driving north on the Henry Hudson had him pushing eighty-five.

Stacey called as he was flying past the Roosevelt Raceway. "Hey, you walked out so fast you forgot to tell me about the job."

"Turns out it's not happening for a while," he said, wanting to keep her and hers out of the line of fire.

Pulling onto his street in the early dark of the evening, Billy saw a figure sitting motionless on the front porch of his house. Knowing that no cop patrolling the grounds would just take a breather like that, he glided to a stop a few driveways down, got out of the car, and began to cautiously make the rest of his way on foot. But apparently his tread was heavier than he imagined; sensing Billy's approach, the figure slowly rose and then eased into a shooter's stance. Pulling his own weapon, Billy carefully stepped back into the shadowed shrubbery, the numbing notion abruptly rising in him that it was too late, *he* was too late, and that everyone inside was gone. In sudden free fall, Billy mindlessly recited the roll call of his dead as he sighted his Glock, center mass, center mass, and was about to squeeze one off when Carmen opened the door behind the shooter's back.

"Dad, come inside, you're going to get sick out here." Then: "What the hell are you doing? Give me that."

"There's someone out there," Billy Senior said tentatively, allowing his daughter-in-law to bring him back into the house.

Two hours later, Jimmy Whelan, accompanied by a small, nervous, near-mute woman, most likely another of his vertical harem of tenants, entered the house without knocking.

"Jimmy!" Carmen kissing him while shielding the shiner side of her face. "I'm sorry, this is a total waste of your time."

"Don't worry about it," Whelan said. "This is Mercedes."

The woman eyed the dinner dishes as if all she wanted in life was to clear the table.

"What's the matter with you," Billy nodding to the grip of the Walther sticking straight up from behind Whelan's belt buckle. "You never heard of a holster?"

"If you conceal it, then no one knows you're carrying and it defeats its own purpose. Hey! Chief Graves . . ." Whelan saluting as Billy Senior came into the living room. "Remember me?"

"You're that kid from Billy's street team."

"I am that kid."

"You make detective yet?"

"You bet."

"Where are you posted?"

"Fort Surrender," winking to Billy.

"I never liked that moniker, it's too cynical for my taste."

"Well, sir, we live in cynical times."

"What's a rook to think?" Senior said. " 'Congratulations, son, you've been assigned to Fort Surrender.' "

"You got a point there, boss."

"Well, keep up the good work," the old man said, turning to the TV.

Billy nodded toward the porch, and Whelan followed him out.

"The gun was his?" Whelan asked after getting the update.

"It's his old service piece, I had it spiked the day he moved in."

Whelan briefly stepped over to the window. Peering into the house, he tried to catch the eye of his sleepover date, sitting on the couch next to Billy Senior.

"Not for nothing and thanks for coming, but did you really need to bring the girl?"

"She's never been out to the country."

"You're being funny, right?"

"About what?"

"All we have for you is a bunk bed."

"We'll make do. So what else is going on."

Billy thought about bringing up Sweetpea, bringing up Pavlicek, then let it pass.

"All right, my brother," Billy wrapping him in a brief hug. "Gotta go."

Halfway to his car he stopped and turned. "Hey, let me ask you, Tomassi . . . Are you sure he was hit by a bus?"

"Am I sure?"

Pulling out his wallet, Whelan gestured for Billy to come back to the porch. "The American Express card," he intoned, handing over a crime scene photo of his White, chest-crushed and staring up at the stars from beneath the front wheels of a Pelham Bay–bound number 12 bus. "Don't leave home without it."

"Well, the other tape came in," Elvis Perez's voice in his ear, the Midtown South detective catching Billy on his cell as he was paying for his nightly speed bag at the Korean's. "From the LIRR end?"

"And?" Billy saluting Joon on the way out.

"And it doesn't really help us."

"Why not."

"There's too much of a mob under the track information board. It's like watching worms in a bucket. We can't even ID Bannion until he separates out from the crowd, and by then he's already spurting."

"You can't track him in reverse and blow up the frames?"

"Worms in a bucket."

Back at the office, the headline was that Feeley had reverted to being a no-show. Otherwise it was a next-to-nothing tour: a push-in robbery in Sugar Hill, a cabbie in the Meatpacking District getting beat on by two men after he had refused to take them to Brownsville. Neither required his personal attendance, so after sitting there in his office for a few hours listening to the Wheel effortlessly repel three more requests for the squad, Billy put Mayo in charge and headed up to the Bronx.

502 Concord Avenue was an eroding brick single-family Victorian chopped up into multiple SROs, and at three-fifteen in the morning there were no lights on in any of the six windows that overlooked the lifeless street. But 505, directly across the way, was a six-story walk-up, and Billy counted three lighted apartment windows on the second, third, and top floors, meaning three possible habitual night owls, three possible witnesses to the possible abduction of Sweetpea Harris.

Billy woke up the tenants on the second floor, an ashy-skinned middle-aged man, dumb with sleep, coming to the door in his boxers as a woman in the back of the apartment screamed like hell about having to get up for work in a few hours. On the third floor, the door was answered after five minutes of pounding by a moon-faced African in a wrinkled caftan, kufi, and busted slippers, this guy having no English to him, but the TV in his otherwise furniture-less living room was playing so loud that Billy couldn't imagine him hearing anything out on the street short of an explosion.

The sixth floor was the charm, the tenant, Ramlear Castro, a young, heavily inked Latino, his eyes pink with dope, coming to the door in sweatpants and a hairnet. Billy flashed his ID and Castro gave him his back, retreating into the apartment but leaving the door open for Billy to follow him inside.

"May I?" Castro held up a blunt.

Billy shrugged and a moment later the punky tang coming across the wobbly-legged kitchen table thrust him back into high school.

"Yeah, so yeah," Castro began, "I was up that night you said, and I was sitting right here, I like to write poetry here, and I heard like this *pop pop pop,* which around here don't mean firecrackers, and I thought it was Timpson GCG throwing down with Betances Crew again. But when I looked out the window all I saw was this guy getting out of his car and walking to the back like he was going to open the trunk, you know, but he was coming up on it sideways, you know, careful, then *pop pop pop* again, the driver like jumping to the side, but I didn't see no one shooting at him, I just heard the shots. And then after those shots went off, the driver just shoots his own damned trunk like he was putting down a horse, emptied the whole clip or whatever."

"Wait, this is after you first heard the *pop pop pop*?"

"Yeah."

"So the *pop pop pop* was someone else?"

"Which *pop pop pop*."

"The first. The one that made you go to the window."

"Yeah."

"Then the guy got out of his car and shot his trunk."

"No, then the second *pop pop pop*. I didn't see no one shooting, but the driver like jumped to the side of the trunk when the shots went off, and then the third *pop pop pop* was the driver shooting back."

"Into his trunk."

"Yeah."

"Like what, returning fire?"

"Returning fire, yeah."

"So like somebody was shooting at him from inside the trunk?"

"Could be," offering the blunt across the oilcloth-topped table, Billy demurely passing. "Then he shot back."

"So the driver came out of the car with a gun."

"Didn't I say that?"

"It was already in his hand?"

"I guess so."

"What did he look like?"

"Who, the driver?"

Billy waited.

"I couldn't say."

"First thing that comes to your mind."

Castro closed his eyes. "He had white hair."

"An old guy?"

"No, he had white hair, you know, straight hair."

"So a white guy?"

"Could have been."

"Not Latino."

"Could've been."

"Black?"

"I don't think so, but could've been."

"So you didn't get a look at his face?"

"Couldn't see it, because it's like a straight-down view from up here, that's how I know about the hair."

"Clothes?"

"Some kind of coat, I don't know. Shoes."

"How about the gun."

"From the sound of it, I'd say a single-action .38 'cause of the rhythm of the shots, you know, *pop pop pop.*"

"You know your firearms?"

Castro inhaled again, blew out enough smoke to announce a pope.

"Not really."

"Tell me about the car."

"Had a trunk, that's all I remember."

"So . . ." Billy hesitated, then: "No chance it could have been an SUV?"

"Could have been."

"You know," Billy leaned forward across the small table, "I asked you maybe ten questions, all I'm getting back from you is 'could've been's.'"

"Hey, Officer," Castro leaning forward right back at him, "I'm looking down six stories, three in the morning, high as a fuckin' kite. I think I did pretty good here, wouldn't you say?"

MILTON RAMOS

"Marilys, watch!" Sofia shouted, blow-darting the torn wrapper hanging from her straw across the small table into her father's chest.

"Don't call her Marilys anymore," Milton said.

"Why not?"

Marilys caught his eye: Go slow.

They had never gone out of the house as a threesome before, and this dinner at Applebee's was something of a test drive. The waitress arrived with their dinner orders, Double Barrel Whisky Sirloin for him, Double Crunch Shrimp for the lady, and a Fiesta-Chopped Chicken and Spinach Salad for Sofia, who immediately went into a jaw-quivering sulk.

"How would you like Marilys to come live with us?" he said.

"Yah! Yah! Yah!" His daughter shouting up a storm again.

"Easy, easy," he winced, although the din level of the room approached that of a machine shop.

"Can she sleep with me?"

Milton looked at his fiancée, a half-smile threatening to break across his face.

Scraping off the breading, Marilys put one of her deep-fried shrimps on Sofia's plate. "So this is it, I'm not working for you anymore?" she said.

"Of course not."

"But we're not getting married until next month, you said."

"So?"

"So I can work for you until then."

"Are you serious? I want you to go home and pack your stuff. I'll come by tomorrow with a van and move you in."

"I have a lease."

"Don't worry about your lease."

"So what do I do then?"

"What do you mean?"

"What do I do once I move in?"

"Nothing. You know, just be with me, take care of Sofia and the house."

"Sounds like my job but without pay."

Milton blushed. "If you want I'll get you a housekeeper, how's that."

"Don't be ridiculous."

"All I'm trying to say is, you'll never have

to worry about money again."

"I don't want anybody working for me," she said. "That's crazy."

"It's up to you."

Marilys stopped eating, stared at her plate. "I got a better idea."

"What's that."

"Can I say?"

Milton waited.

"My mother."

"Your mother."

"If she comes to live with us, she can help me with Sofia and the baby. And she loves to clean."

"Your mother . . ."

"All I have to do is go back and get her."

"To Guatemala?"

"She's never been on a plane before."

Sofia quietly took a shrimp off Marilys's plate, dipped it in the ketchup atop her father's fries, neither of them reacting.

"You don't want her to?" Marilys said. "It's your house."

"Our house."

"Well, you're the man of it, so whatever you say goes."

Sofia took another shrimp, a handful of fries.

"Excuse me for a minute," Milton said, then rose from the table, Marilys tracking him with anxious eyes as he made his way to the front door.

A wife and two kids, OK, Milton mulling it over as he paced the empty parking lot.

But the mother-in-law . . .

Then: *Think of it like this: drop the "in-law" part and that leaves you with "mother."*

Which, given that he had just lost his aunt Pauline, the closest thing he'd had to one, was not so bad.

When he returned to the table, he found Marilys, apparently having lost her appetite, feeding the rest of her breaded dinner to Sofia piece by piece.

"She's good with kids?" Milton asked.

"She raised me. Raised my sons too."

"How about otherwise."

"Not great."

"Pain in the ass?"

"Kind of."

Sofia had become way too quiet, Milton wondering if it was ever possible to truly talk over a kid's head.

To repeat . . . New mother, new wife, new son, all in one swoop.

Then, studying his already-child, working her way through the rest of his untouched fries: *New grandmother, too.*

"All right," he said, lightly slapping the table, "go get her."

Marilys put a hand to her heart, huffed in relief. "When should I go?"

"How about tomorrow? I'll cover the airfare."

"I swear to God" — touching his hand — "if you don't like her she can go right back, it's not like she doesn't have family."

"Just go get her."

"I can save you money on the tickets," she said excitedly, "my cousin's a travel agent."

"Well, there you go," wishing she'd gone and come back already.

Marilys leaned across the table and kissed him on the mouth again, which this time made him tense up given that his daughter was right there.

"Oh, Milton," Marilys saying his name for the second time in his life.

"Oh, Milton," Sofia aped, her eyes as lightless as pebbles.

Later that night it took him most of a bottle of Chartreuse to work up the resolve to quit drinking. He had never been anybody's idea of a light drinker, but since the day he first saw the adult Carmen in St. Ann's, he'd gone completely off the rails, each night worse than the last, waking up every morning on the couch wondering how the one

342

a.m. sports recap had morphed into cartoons.

Well, no excuse for that now, Milton pouring what remained of the bottle into the sink.

Still drunk on the liquor that hadn't gone down the drain, he took to wandering the house in order to start reassigning rooms: his first wife's sewing nook now a nursery for his son, the sometime fuck-pad guest room — no need for that anymore — going to his mother-in-law, as well as the nearest of the three bathrooms, hers alone. What else. Divide the den and make a playroom. All the hallway closets going to all the ladies. Then, running out of steam, he finally headed off for his own bedroom, walking in and seeing it for the first time as the gray cell it had become.

CHAPTER 11

A five a.m. after-hours bar shooting in In-
wood kept Billy on the job until ten in the
morning, and when he finally made it home
at eleven, still pondering his interview with
Ramlear Castro, he was startled to see
TARU techs everywhere. To cover the block
from intersection to intersection, they were
mounting Argus cameras on telephone
poles, as well as on the house itself, the buzz
and whine of all this work chasing away any
hope he had of immediate sleep.

Thirty minutes later, as he was standing
at the kitchen counter flipping through the
New York Post and sipping his morning
Cape Codder, Pavlicek called. This time
Billy picked up.

"You're screening my calls?"

"What?" Billy too tired to come up with
any coherent excuse.

"Look, I was just trying to reach out to
apologize for getting so crazed on you

yesterday. It's just that I have so much shit raining down on my head right now I might wind up moving in there with you."

"In where with me." Looking out the kitchen window, Billy spotted Whelan and his sleepover date making out on the kids' trampoline.

"Are you serious?" Pavlicek said quietly.

Christ, Billy recalling that barren, echo chamber of an apartment with the stadium view.

"Speaking of which, I talked to my guys and I can have it ready for you day after tomorrow. All you'll need are towels and sheets."

" 'My guys.' You're always talking about your guys," Billy stalled. "The only guys I have are my kids."

"Yeah well, you have your squad, too."

Billy put the phone to his chest. Just say it.

"Hey, John, I'm sorry to put you through all that trouble, but I talked it over with Carmen, and we're going to make a home stand."

Silence on the other end, then: "Are you sure?"

"Yeah, yeah, Intel sent over a Threat Assessment Team, TARU's out there right now putting up cameras, Yonkers PD is running directed patrols, it's like the fortress of solitude over here. It's nuts to pull up stakes."

Another bloated pause. "Are you OK?"

"Yeah," Billy said. "I mean, given the circumstances."

"Because you don't sound like you."

"Yeah? Who do I sound like?" Then telling himself, Don't strain for jokes.

"You're not ticked because I lost it over Sweetpea, are you?"

"Absolutely not."

"Is that why you weren't taking my calls?"

"I don't know what you're talking about," Billy said.

Whelan and his tenant, still in a kissing clinch, came into the kitchen through the rear door.

"I mean, how hung up are you over that skell?"

"John, I'm not hung up on him, I was just curious," Billy said carefully. "And now I'm not. Listen, I got to go feed the kids, I'll call you later."

"Just another Smirnoff morning," Whelan announced, nodding to the bottle.

"It's either that or chloroform," Billy said.

The tenant went silently to the refrigerator, took out the milk, and poured some into a saucepan that was already sitting on a back burner.

"Hung up on who," Whelan asked.

"What?" Billy stalling once again.

"You said, 'I'm not hung up on him.' "

"Sweetpea Harris," Billy said. "He's gone AWOL, and I think he bought the farm."

"No shit," Whelan pouring himself a coffee. "And John's giving you grief over that? What for?"

Billy took another sip of his drink.

"Do me a favor and tell me something," he said. "The other day, when I asked you why you were so hung up on Pavlicek . . ."

"Me?" Whelan reared back.

"You never answered my question."

"What question."

"Why you were all over me about Pavlicek."

"How was I all over you?"

Billy stared at him. "Jimmy, do you know something I don't?"

"Like what?"

"Jesus Christ, look out that window," Billy exploded, pointing to the TARUs crawling all over the front yard. "And that window, and that one," Billy spinning like a bottle. "I'm getting shredded here, I'm juggling chain saws, so if I ask you for a straight answer on something and you start playing me like I'm some idiot?"

Whelan held up a hand. "If I tell you this, you cannot tell anyone, you understand?"

"Is it his health?"

Whelan blinked at him. "What's wrong with his health?"

"Then just say."

Whelan took a long pull off his coffee. "He's trying to buy my building from the owner. But it's kind of very delicate right now, very touch and go, and I just thought maybe he said something to you about it."

Billy stared at him. "That's it?"

"What do you mean, 'That's it.' Are you kidding me? He swings this deal, I go from super to building manager at twice the pay. And if that works out, he's going to throw me more buildings. I mean, you know me, I don't need much, but I would like a little more than I got."

One of the security cameras fell out of a tree, nearly braining a passing TARU before smashing against a lawn chair.

"Anyways, this thing with Sweetpea going off the grid?" Whelan rinsed out his cup. "You should tell Redman when you see him today."

"Why am I seeing Redman today?"

"The funeral."

"What funeral?"

"For your kid."

Billy went white.

"I would go," Whelan said, reaching for his jacket, "but I have a guy coming for the boiler."

The tenant poured the heated milk into a glass and handed it to Billy. *"Para dormir,"* she said, laying her cheek on her palm and closing her eyes.

Edna Worthy was the only mourner to show up for her granddaughter Martha's funeral service that afternoon, so the folding chairs that lined Redman's living room–chapel were populated by a handful of last-minute stand-ins: Redman, his father, his wife, Nola, holding their son, Rafer, four of the old men who hung out every day in the windowless reception area of the parlor like it was their old-man clubhouse, two dragooned cops from the Twenty-eighth Precinct Community Affairs Unit, and Billy, who was paying for the whole thing.

"But Jesus said, 'Suffer the little children, and forbid them not, to come unto me: for of such is the kingdom of heaven,' " the four-hundred-pound minister intoned from the pulpit before pausing to take a hit of asthma spray.

"Suffer, you see, in the, the parlance of those times, did not mean to endure pain, it did not mean to put up with mistreatment. What it meant was to permit, to allow," pausing again, this time to reach for the diaper cloth draped over the shoulder of his three-piece box-plaid suit and swipe at his face. "You see, in those days children were not allowed to address adults directly, not allowed to speak up without the permission of another adult. Seen but not heard, I know you know that saying, and not just from olden times, I'm sure many of you heard it growing up — when Daddy is talking to Uncle at the dinner table, when Momma is talking to Auntie, you sat there, ate your peas, and maybe raised your hand for permission. But Jesus was saying, 'I don't want no middleman between me and these kids, I don't stand on manners, I don't need no hand raising, no permission slips, no velvet-rope doorman, just let them kids in, and today, today, Marrisa has come into the club direct . . ."

"Martha," her grandmother muttered, but loud enough.

"She has come into the club direct, has gone, in fact, straight to the VIP room, where He is waiting for her with two chilled magnums of Holy Ghost love."

"Are you kidding me?" Billy whispered.

"You said a hundred dollars for the celebrant," Redman whispered back. "That's what you get for a hundred dollars."

"So what's going on," Billy asked, as a prelude to bringing up Sweetpea.

"Later," Redman said.

" 'Blessed are the gentle,' " the celebrant crooned, " 'they shall have the earth as their heritage. Blessed are those who mourn; they shall be comforted . . .' "

"Her name is *Martha*," the grandmother low-blared again, staring at the floor.

Nola passed her son to Redman, got up, and took a seat next to the old woman, putting an arm around her shoulders and staring without expression at the casket.

After a few minutes of fussing in his father's lap, Rafer started to cry, and Redman, needing both hands to rise from his chair so he could leave the room, briefly passed him on to Billy. Trying to stabilize the boy, Billy advertently pressed the feeding tube protruding from the kid's stomach, then jerked his hand away as if he had touched a snake. Embarrassed by his reaction, he reflexively looked to Redman, now waiting for them in the doorway, the grimly knowing look on his face burning Billy to the core.

"So what's going on?" Billy repeated, once

they were settled in Redman's cubicle.

"There's some big-foot kid going around the neighborhood," Redman said, dropping Rafer into his activity walker, then locking the wheels. "Says he's working for a charity, selling boxes of candy bars to the store owners, fifty dollars a box, the implication being that if they say no they're gonna get their ass beat or something thrown through the window. Half the damn neighborhood's got those things by the cash register."

"For real?"

"Everybody say he's all soft-spoken about it, but it's like, Make no mistake."

"You want me to do something?"

"*I* want to do something," Redman said.

"Did he try it on you?"

"Hell no. People are too scared of this place. It's like, muscle an undertaker? Who's going to take on that kind of karma."

Enough.

"Can I tell you something?"

Redman waited.

"I think Sweetpea Harris was murdered."

"Did somebody tell you it was my birthday? Because it is."

"Well, many happy returns."

"Who did the honors?"

"I was hoping you could tell me."

"Me?"

"He was your guy."

"My guy, huh?" Redman said. "How'd you come to know about this."

Billy hesitated, then thinking, In for a penny, he began running down his interviews with Donna Barkley and Ramlear Castro, all the while bracing for another Pavlicek-style outburst about keeping his priorities straight.

"So the window witness tells me that this guy gets out of his car, walks to the back, ducks some shots, and then empties a clip into the trunk. Which to me sounds like maybe, probably, there was someone in there with a gun, like maybe the driver forgot to pat him down before he stuffed his ass inside."

"Did he give a description of the shooter?"

"Not really." Then: "He said he had straight hair, like a white guy, maybe a Latino."

"He saw that from the sixth floor but nothing else?"

"Apparently."

"Well then," Redman rubbed what was left of his receding corkscrew crop, "include me out."

"Done."

"So I hear you're moving into one of Pavlicek's apartments," Redman said.

"Actually, we're not."

"Just as well."

"Me and him, he and I, we're not getting on right now," Billy said, testing the waters to gauge how far he could take this. There would be no coming back from saying too much — that he knew for sure.

From the chapel they could hear Redman's father up on the podium singing "He's Prepared a Place for Me" in a high and furry voice.

How far . . .

"He's seeing a hematologist, did you know that?" Billy said.

"Who is, John?"

Billy didn't answer.

"Man, you're all full of news today."

"I'm just telling you."

"The hell he is," Redman said, sounding annoyed.

How far . . .

"I hired someone to find out."

Redman's stare could have stopped a train.

"I know," Billy said, "but I was worried about him. I *am* worried about him."

"I don't understand why you couldn't just straight out ask him yourself."

"I did," Billy said. "He lied to me."

A dapperly dressed funeral cosmetics

354

salesman, pulling a sample case on rollers, poked his head into the cubicle.

"Let me ask you something," Redman said, gesturing for the salesman to step off for a minute. "And I'm not even talking about any shit in the past, but do you have anything going on in your life right now that you don't want anybody knowing about?"

Billy didn't answer.

"Exactly. So whatever the hell is going on with Pavlicek these days?" Redman reached down to lift his crying son out of the walker. "If he wants to tell people, he'll tell people. Meanwhile, why don't you just respect the man's privacy and leave him be."

Too far.

Coming home at two in the afternoon, Billy walked in on Carmen and her brother weeping up a storm on the living room couch.

"What happened," Billy said.

"Nothing," Victor said, wiping his eyes. "It's all good."

"He's freaking out about being a parent," Carmen announced with unnerving happiness. "And he didn't know where else to come."

"I feel like an ass," Victor said.

"You and Richard are going to be the best parents," she gushed.

"I kill aspidistras," Victor trying to laugh at himself.

"Hey, you have that dog, right?" Billy just wanting to keep this good thing going.

"It's Richard's dog."

"I was just telling him," Carmen said, "no one was more freaked about having children than me. The dreams I had before Dec was born?"

Billy nodded, thinking, You still have them.

"I swear, Victor, I'm going to help you every step of the way," Carmen tearing up again. "Those babies are going to love you."

"Thank you," Victor whispered huskily, holding her close.

"Think of it like this," Billy said to his brother-in-law out in the driveway. "Cavemen had kids, so can you."

"And the average life expectancy was what?"

"That's not the point."

"Billy, I'm playing with you," he said, waving to Carmen, who was watching them from the living room window.

"You know, Victor, your sister, she's a real high-wire act but she's got heart by the mile."

"I know."

Billy lit a cigarette, inhaled, then twisted

his mouth to divert the smoke.

"So why is she always so tough on you?"

"She's ashamed."

"Of you?"

"Of herself, don't ask me why. Because she left me to take care of our so-called father down south? I was thirteen. And now I'm thirty-six, you know?" Shrugging the whole thing off. "But I do know this. Whenever she acts like she's trying to push me away? She's in a lot more pain than I am."

Billy felt like crying.

"I don't know," Victor said, taking his car keys out of his jacket, "with the twins on the way? I find myself thinking about family all the time, and I just want her to feel good about being my big sister. Even for a minute."

Billy nodded, then leaned in close as if Carmen could hear him through the living room glass. "Can I ask you something? How freaked are you really about these new kids of yours?"

"Not too," Victor said, waving goodbye to his sister in the window.

Tomika Washington, a tall, slender, light-skinned woman looking to be in her fifties, was stretched out in her bathrobe on the carpetless floor of her railroad-flat living room, the rawhide bootlace that had done the deed still around her neck. A rolled towel was propped under her head, as if to make her comfortable, and a washcloth was carefully draped like a veil over her face, as if to prevent her from staring at her killer — both gestures, Billy knew, textbook signatures of remorse.

With Butter and Mayo canvassing the neighbors and the Crime Scene Unit stuck in traffic, Billy was alone with the body when he heard a knock at the door. On the off chance that the actor had slipped the barricade in order to come back and apologize to his victim, Billy drew his gun before opening up and was surprised to see Gene Feeley, his elusive butterfly of love, standing there in what had to be the last Botany 500 three-piece suit in existence.

"You have Tomika Washington in there?" Feeley asked. Then, sliding past Billy: "I just want to see her."

"You know her?"

Ignoring the question, Feeley stood motionless over the body for a moment as if paying his respects, then dropped into a squat and delicately parted the lower half of her bathrobe.

"You looking for something, Gene?"

"That right there," pointing to a fading tattoo of a bird high up on her thigh. "You see that? That was his brand."

"Whose brand?"

"Frank Baltimore," he said, closing her robe as carefully as he had opened it. "He was kind of a player around here for a few years in the eighties, used to stamp his bags with a blackbird, same for a girl or two like Tomika here."

"She was hooking for him?"

"Never. Well, not for him — I mean, yeah, on her own, later, but she was strictly his girl before that. He found her down in Newport News on one of his dope runs when she was seventeen, beautiful kid, brought her back up and threw her a crib in Lenox Terrace. She told me she thought she was living in a fairy tale."

"She told you."

"Before I was transferred to the Queens Task Force after Eddie Byrnes got shot, I was in Narcotics up here and I had occasion to bring her in a couple of times, see if there was any kind of conversation we could have about Frank. She didn't know shit, but she never gave me grief about getting picked up, had these country manners, didn't know how not to be friendly, just never really got the hang of this place, you know? And when

359

Frank finally went upstate she got tossed out on her ass, a down-home kid ashamed to go home. Oh, it was a bad time for her, first she got dope sick, which is when she started turning tricks, and then when rock came on the scene? I would see her on the street, down to about ninety pounds . . . But even then she always had that smile for me, always that well-brought-up-southern-girl thing going on, and when she'd get picked up by the cops she had my number and I'd try to get her out of whatever jam she was in, but it was hopeless. Anyways," kneecaps popping, Feeley rose to his feet, his eyes still saying goodbye, "I heard she finally got herself clean a few years ago through some church program, so good for her."

"That blackbird tat?" Billy just had to say it. "It's kind of in a hard-to-know-about place, Gene."

At first Feeley threw him a hard look, then shrugged. "If I wasn't so afraid of catching the Package in those days? Me and her, we could of had a little something. We came pretty close once or twice, but . . . you know, what can I tell you, it wasn't to be."

"Any ideas about the actor?"

"With the towel, the washcloth, I'm think-ing it's someone close, a relative maybe. She has a nephew in the halfway house on a Hundred and Tenth and Lenox, Doobie Carver, a real nutcase. If you'll allow me, I can take it from here."

"All yours," Billy said, happy to see him seize the initiative on any run, for any reason.

Feeley stepped to the door, hesitated for a beat, then turned back to the room.

"I have to tell you," gazing down at Tomika Washington so intently that Billy wasn't quite sure who he was addressing, "I know I can be a real hard-on, and you don't have the juice to tell me to do shit, but you're a good boss, you respect your people, you don't have a political bone in your body, and you don't ever pass the buck. So," finally meeting Billy's eye, "after tonight? If you want me gone, I'll put in the call myself."

"How about you stay," Billy heard himself say.

"I would appreciate that," Feeley said solemnly, offering his hand.

"Does this mean you're going to start showing up when you're supposed to?"

Feeley threw him another look — *Don't press your luck* — then bent down one last time to Tomika Washington. "Take care, honey," he said.

MILTON RAMOS

She was supposed to come over at nine the next morning for the money to cover her airfare, but instead Marilys showed up at seven-thirty, Milton opening his eyes to see her standing red-faced and trembling at the side of his bed.

"What's wrong?"

"I'm so stupid," she whispered, her voice clotted with tears. "She doesn't have a passport. She doesn't have anything."

"Who's she."

More drunk than hungover, Milton sat up, stood up, and then had to sit back down as the Chartreuse rebooted.

"My mother, why am I so stupid."

"OK, all right," grinding the heels of his palms into eyes. "What time is it?"

Marilys dropped down alongside him, her shoulders as slumped as his own. "This was a bad idea."

"OK, so you'll go get her when she gets one."

"No. I mean getting married."

"Getting married is a bad idea? Since when?"

"Last night I dreamed the priest was blessing us and my mother just crushed."

"Crushed?"

"Like a flower, when they speed up the movie and you see it bloom then dry up then crush down to nothing. To dust, because she wasn't there."

"Wasn't where," his skull like a soft-boiled egg.

"There when we got married. She died in her house because she wasn't with us."

He took a deep breath, and his back teeth tasted bile. "Listen to me" — taking her hand — "you had a dream. It's a dream."

"No."

"Everybody has bad dreams. You should see some of mine."

"Mine always come true. Always. When I was a girl, I dreamed one of my brothers was in the hospital, and the next day he broke his back. When I was married the first time, I dreamed my husband got cancer, and I buried him in a year."

"Then whatever you do, don't ever dream about me," Milton joking to smother his growing panic.

Leaning into him, Marilys broke down, her boiling tears searing his skin.

"OK. How about this: we work on getting your mother a green card, a passport, or whatever. Meanwhile you come live with me, have the baby, but we wait to get married until you can bring her over."

"No."

"Jesus Christ," Milton starting to sweat. "Why not."

"We live like a man and a woman, maybe the same thing happens to her."

"I feel like a prisoner of your brain right now, you know that?" Despite the sharpness of his tone, he meant it more as a plea than a rebuke, though she seemed not to have heard him at all.

"We can't do it." Then, looking up at him like Our Lady of Sorrows: "Maybe I should just go back to work for you, live by myself."

"You're killing me."

"Maybe I should just go back to live with her."

"In Guatemala? Are you crazy?"

"I don't know what to do."

Milton shot to his feet, then immediately sat back down. "What about the baby?"

"It's still our baby."

"I know that," he snapped, then, casting

364

about for the next anchor: "What about Sofia?"

She put her head in his lap, her hand clutching his hip.

"Jesus Christ, what about *me*?"

She began to cry, her hot tears this time turning him on, which only increased his panic.

"OK," he said, not raising her head. "Let's think this through. Who do you know in Guatemala."

"My family," she said, then: "What do you mean?"

"All right, your cousin the travel agent, who does he know?"

"I don't know who he knows."

"You know what I mean by 'knows'?"

"I think so," she said, then: "Yeah, I do."

"How about you call him."

"He doesn't open up until ten."

"Then call him at ten."

But it was only eight, and they sat in coiled silence on the bed until nine. Then, without any preliminary communication, they began to go at it — and whether it was the overlay of doom in the air or just the emotional rawness of the last ninety minutes, when he finally rolled off her they were both crying like babies.

At ten, she went down into the den to

make the call, leaving him damp-skinned in his bed. He loved the idea of making a family with her, yet until now he had never thought he actually loved her. But something had changed this morning. Milton Ramos was officially in love with Marilys Irrizary. If he had a pocket knife he would carve it into a tree.

Forty-five minutes passed before he heard her coming back up to the bedroom door, forty-five minutes during which he had been afraid to so much as blink. But when she appeared in the doorway her relieved laughter came to his ears like a flock of butterflies.

"He said he has a friend."

"Dreams," Milton said. "You're crazy, you know that?"

"Maybe," she answered, her face near radioactive with joy.

Her travel agent cousin on Fordham Road in the Bronx had told her that he would be able to swing a round-trip ticket for her, Newark to Guatemala City and back, and a one-way ticket for her mother, all for fifteen hundred dollars, which was a good deal compared to the prices posted online. But in exchange for the deep discount, he wanted to be paid in cash.

Whatever.

The wincer came later in the day when Marilys called him at work to say that her cousin had made some calls to a law firm in Guatemala City with embassy connections and found out that the package price for getting her mother a passport and a U.S. work visa, both delivered within forty-eight hours of payment, would be eighty-five hundred American dollars.

Milton's first reaction was to balk altogether, his second to negotiate the fee. Unable to do that, and fearful of losing his crazy, superstitious *amorcita* forever over a few thousand bucks, he bit the bullet, went down to his union's pension loan unit, and withdrew the money.

Whatever whatever whatever.

At seven in the evening the line for the JFK express bus, which began across the street from Grand Central Station, was nearly two blocks long, the waiting travelers looking antsy and drawn in the early twilight gloom.

"It would have been easy for me to drive you," Milton said for the sixth time.

"I like the bus," Marilys said, leaning into him for warmth. "The bus always gives me good luck."

Fifteen minutes behind schedule, the

367

sleek, oversized carrier appeared at the crest of Thirty-ninth Street and Park, and then just sat there through three green lights, torturing the people waiting two blocks below on Forty-first.

"Anyways" — handing her a gift-wrapped package — "it's for your mother, from me and Sofia."

Instead of stashing the present in her bag, which would have frustrated him, she opened it on the spot, flapping out the hemp-colored serape he had bought from a Guatemalan street vendor in the West Village.

"Milton, it's beautiful."

"I didn't know her size, but it's basically a bath towel with a neckhole so . . ."

Marilys put her hands to the sides of his face and kissed him in front of everybody, Milton still a little awkward with her new full-frontal affection but starting to get used to it just fine.

The bus began to roll downhill to the waiting crowd, but so slowly that it caught a red light while still a block away, some people around them audibly groaning in frustration.

When the doors sighed open a few moments later and the passengers began to get on, Marilys continued to linger with him, until, worried about her missing the flight, he hustled her onto the bus himself.

It wasn't until she was well on her way out to the airport and he was most of the way back to the Bronx that Milton realized what an idiot he'd been.

Who the hell sends a gift of Guatemalan clothing to a person already living in Guatemala?

CHAPTER 12

Having caught yet another pain-in-the-ass, last-minute run, this one a nonfatal stabbing in an East Village halfway house, Billy finally walked through his front door at ten the next morning to find John MacCormack from Brooklyn Narcotics sitting across from Carmen in the living room, two untouched coffees between them.

"I thought I saw a Firebird up the street," Billy looking to his wife, who imperceptibly shook her head in warning, as if he needed any kind of high sign here.

"My supervisor says I should have pushed you harder the other night," MacCormack said.

"Pushed me harder about what."

"He was talking about collecting your guns, but I told him that was probably an overreaction."

"An overreaction to what."

MacCormack slowly got to his feet. "I

need to ask you again," going into Billy's eyes. "What's your interest in finding Eric Cortez."

The only one seated now, Carmen repeatedly ran her palms down the thighs of her jeans, her face quizzical and tense.

"You know what?" Billy's all-night exhaustion helped keep him calm. "I told you that the first time you asked me. What I also told you was that I had, I have, no intention to mess with anybody's play. So. You want to collect my guns? I don't know what the fuck for, but bring in your people and go at it."

"Is he dead?" MacCormack asked.

"What?"

"You asked me the other night if Cortez was dead. Why."

"Carm, let me talk to him in private."

"I'm not going anywhere," she said.

"Why," MacCormack said again.

"Because animals like him tend not to have long lives and I hoped he was. But if I thought asking you would put me in any kind of jackpot, I would've kept my mouth shut. I'm twenty years on the Job, how stupid do you think I am?"

MacCormack stood there scanning him for tells.

"So he is dead?" Billy asked, an honest question.

"No."

"Then I don't get it."

"Billy, what's going on."

"Carmen, just . . ."

"Hey, look who's here!" Billy Senior nearly shouted as he walked into the room and slapped MacCormack on the back. "Jackie MacCormack! I thought you were in Florida!"

Billy watched as MacCormack went into his internal face file for a moment, then shook his father's hand.

"Billy Graves, how the hell are you?"

"Never been worse," the old man said, then wandered into the kitchen, where Millie was making his breakfast.

"What was that about?" Billy asked.

"He's your father?" MacCormack seemed a little dazed.

"Yeah, how does he know you?"

"He doesn't. He was with my old man in the TPF for a few years back in the sixties. I wasn't even born yet. I just recognized him from pictures my mother keeps around."

Billy peered into the kitchen, his father sitting there now, eating dry cereal and watching a talk show on the miniature TV that sat next to the microwave.

"He's pretty much shot," Billy said.

"Are you sure about that?" MacCormack

still coming off slightly stunned. "Because I have to tell you, I look nothing like my dad."

Billy experienced an all-too-familiar surge of optimism, then shut it down, the rhythm of his father's inexorable deterioration always spiked with these cruel upticks of startling keenness that raised his hopes for a moment before dashing them with the next time-warp slippage into dementia, Billy suddenly desperate to get away from his father before the next inevitable reminder came about of what a fool he was, is, always will be around the old man, until death took him away.

Snapping back into the here and now, Billy first looked to his wife, then to MacCormack, both staring at him as if they had been following his thoughts.

"You want to collect my guns?" he said, ejecting the clip, then handing MacCormack the grip end of his Glock. "I have a Ruger in a lockbox in the basement, and my father's old hand cannon is in his room. My wife can take you, have a blast."

Billy walked into the kitchen to fix himself a double double, praying that his father would just keep his mouth shut and not make him weep. He didn't return to the living room until he heard the front door close; when he did, the sight of his Glock sitting on the coffee table in front of Carmen pulled him up short.

"Where'd he go?"

"Outside."

"What do you mean, outside. He left?"

"He's waiting for you."

Billy looked out the window and saw the dope-confiscated Firebird gurgling at the foot of the driveway, MacCormack behind the wheel and the passenger door open.

"Are you going to tell me what's going on?" she asked.

"I have no idea," he said, walking out of the house.

The state-run nursing home in Ozone Park smelled like cooking diapers. Eric Cortez was in the dayroom, Velcroed into a wheelchair, his face a soft balloon over his withering torso, his eyes, beneath a strapped-on hockey helmet, the popped silver of a gaffed fish.

"For the seizures," MacCormack said, nodding to the helmet.

"What happened?"

"He was shot in the head about three months ago and left for dead. A kid, actually the kid's dog, found him in a trash bag behind a housing project up in Dutchess County."

"When I ran him I didn't see anything about this."

"It's not our investigation, plus we weren't too eager to post it in case someone was interested in finishing the job."

"What kind of hitter's going to have access to the system?"

MacCormack stared at him.

"Are you serious?"

"The bullet was a 135 grain Speer Gold Dot from a Smith and Wesson .38, standard police issue."

"So what? We don't have a monopoly on that. Plus he was a snitch."

"What do you think, he was the only one we were running? And when he stopped showing up for our meets, none of the others knew shit. Then we got the call from Dutchess. So when you went online looking for him . . ."

"So you're looking at cops?"

Neither of them was looking at Cortez anymore.

"One of the people we interviewed said that he overheard our friend bragging on knowing about a protection-for-pay racket coming out of a Brooklyn precinct about two weeks before he caught a bullet. Maybe he wasn't just bragging."

"So you're looking at cops?" Billy having

no memory of just saying this.

"We're vetting a few."

"Anybody looking good for it?"

MacCormack didn't answer.

"But that's where you're looking . . ."

MacCormack cocked his head. "Why, you think we should be looking somewheres else?"

"Do I? No, I'm just curious." Then: "I wish I could call this a tragedy."

Taking Billy by the elbow, MacCormack led him to the lobby. "It's most likely one of the crew he was ratting on, but if it wasn't, if there's something to this protection ring, I mean, that trumps anything else going and we want to cover our bases."

When they got back to Yonkers thirty minutes later, Billy's father was sitting on the porch reading the newspaper, his mouth hanging open in concentration.

From the driver's seat, MacCormack ducked his head to take in all the TARU cameras trained on the house and the street.

"Something tells me the worst thing I could've done today was take away your guns."

The girl sat on her narrow bed in the sour-smelling suite, grinding her knuckles into bonemeal. A shoe box filled with Saran

376

Wrapped twists of coke and Ziplocs of pot sat on her desk, and a hollowed-out copy of *Gravity's Rainbow* packed with tens, twenties, and hundreds lay open on her dresser.

"*Gravity's Rainbow,* I never heard of that," Yasmeen said as she photographed the cash. "Is that a good book?"

"I never read it." The girl's numb gaze was locked onto the wedge of the Brooklyn Bridge visible from the dormitory window. "It's my dad's favorite."

Yasmeen silently hip-bumped Billy out of the way as she photographed the shoe box. He was there but not there, NYPD not allowed anywhere on campus without the permission of the university.

"Can I call my dad?"

"Absolutely."

Billy caught the eye of the roommate, who had started the ball rolling with a complaint to her therapist in the school's Wellness Center.

"Don't look at me," she said in a clipped Punjabi trill. "She's the drug dealer."

Two more school security officers, both retired detectives like Yasmeen, sauntered into the room, their faces immobile with boredom.

"So Redman said you found out Pavlicek's

seeing a hematologist?" Yasmeen asked, shrugging her Tibetan hippie coat onto the back of her chair.

"I did," Billy said, unable to read her tone.

They were seated at the window table of a hummus café directly across the street from the dormitory.

"Is it serious?"

"I have no idea."

A waiter came out with their orders, a bottled beer for Billy, a mug of herbal tea for Yasmeen.

"I've been on the wagon all week," she said. "It's incredible how fast your body forgives you."

"So you don't know anything about this?"

"About what?"

"About John."

"I think somebody said he was having headaches."

"What do you mean headaches, like migraines?"

"That's all I know, and I don't even know if I know that."

They watched through the window as the girl was finally escorted out of the dorm by the two other school security officers and handed over to city detectives, the kid's college career at an end barely into the second semester of her freshman year.

"This job is such bullshit, I swear to God," Yasmeen said.

Billy took a sip of beer, brushed someone else's crumbs from the tabletop. "And what do you hear about Eric Cortez these days?" he asked.

"Cortez? I haven't checked on him since forever."

"No?" Looking out the window.

"But I still see Raymond Del Pino's family a few times a year. It's so hard for them to get over losing him, you know?"

"So you don't know he's in a nursing home out in Queens."

"Cortez is?" Yasmeen perked up. "Really? Why?"

"He was shot in the head and stuffed into a garbage bag upstate."

"That's . . . Are you shitting me? Wow."

"His brain's a bucket of mush, and the only time he can move is when he has a seizure."

"If I go visit him, can I bring my camera?"

"You know how I know? They investigated me to see if I was the actor. They wanted to collect my guns."

"You?" dumping a ton of Splenda in her mug. "Why you?"

"They thought the shooter might be a cop. So when I ran his name, they thought I might be trying to track him down to finish what I started."

"You ran his name? Why'd you run his name?"

"You know what they asked me? If I had any leads for them."

"And you said . . ."

"That I didn't."

"But why the fuck did you run his name to begin with?"

"Because this is freaking me out."

"What is?"

Billy took her napkin and wrote:

Tomassi Bannion SweetP Cortez

Yasmeen's phone rang. "Excuse me," she said, pulling it out of her coat pocket, then half-turning away.

Even with the cell pressed to her ear Billy could make out the tinny wail of her younger daughter's voice.

"What's wrong," Yasmeen asked wearily, massaging her temple. "OK, whoa, who's pinching you . . . Jacob. Fat Jacob or Black Jacob . . . Is he there? Put him on the phone . . . Just, Simone, if you don't put him on the phone right this second," rolling her eyes at Billy. "Is this Jacob? This is Simone's mommy. Listen to me, you know that monster that lives under your bed? Your parents tell you he's not real, but they're lying to you. Not only is he real but he's a friend of mine, and if you lay one more finger on my daughter I will make sure he comes out from under there when you're asleep tonight and sucks your eyes right out of your head, you hear me? Yes? Good. Now give the phone back to Simone . . . Stop crying and give the phone back to Simone."

Yasmeen hung up. "I hate bullies."

"Is he dying?" Billy asked.

"Is who dying."

"Pavlicek."

"Is Pavlicek dying? Is that what you just asked me?"

"He's my friend, if you know something I don't know just say."

"Huh," Yasmeen starting to flush as she snatched up Billy's list of Whites. "So, what are you asking, do I know if he's got some kind of fatal sickness that made him lose his rudder and go rogue on all these scumbags?"

"I didn't say that." Billy's turn to flush. "I just want to know how sick he is."

"The guy's healthy as a horse, he's worth something like thirty million dollars, and he lives like a king."

"That's good," he said. "That's what I

381

want to hear."

"So what else, you think he misses the good old action-packed days of yesteryear? He's bored? The fuck is wrong with you, Billy."

"I don't know where you're going with this."

"Where *I'm* going with this?"

"I just asked about his health."

"And why the hell were you running Cortez to begin with. Who told you to do that. And Sweetpea? Denny said you were walking around with some fucking Missing poster for Sweetpea Harris. And yeah, I was being nice about it before, but you hired some PI to investigate John's medical records, didn't you."

Having fucked everything up now, elephant-stomped across every line, Billy belatedly opted for silence.

"But you know what?" Yasmeen shrugged her coat back on as if about to storm out. "Even if you're not a paranoid delusional and somebody out there's taking these shitheads out, so what? Who cares? Animals like these?" Jabbing at his list as she rose to her feet. "They tend to breed. And so when they go young? It's called the trickle-down effect, our gift to the future."

"Are you hearing yourself?" Billy sputtered.

"Are you hearing *your*self?"

The conversation was over.

"Fucking Billy." Yasmeen dropped back into the chair, her eyes suddenly shining like wet steel.

"What's wrong."

"Besides listening to you?"

"Besides listening to me."

A tremor set up house in the fingers of her right hand and Billy passed her the rest of his beer, which she drained like a Viking. He ordered her another.

"Yazzie, what's wrong."

"I'm sorry I'm just so tense all the time these days," swiping at her eyes with the dirty suede sleeve of her coat. "I think I'm going through menopause."

"What are you talking about, menopause, you're forty-three." Billy grateful for the change of subject.

"It could be early onset, you know? I lay in bed at night, I'm hot I'm cold I'm clammy I'm burning. I'm driving Dennis crazy."

"You always drive Dennis crazy."

"I have nightmares about my kids, all these bad things happening to them. I sit up in bed sometimes, I'm drenched, the whole bed. And my first thought is that it's blood, I'm covered in blood, but since about three months ago, I don't even get my period anymore. Don't get me wrong, I don't miss having it, but all this other shit that goes along with losing it? And I think animals can sense it. We went down to Florida right before New Year's to visit Dennis's parents? I took Dominique to feed these ducks and they went crazy, chased us, I swear to God it had to be a mile. If I had my gun we'd of had duck for dinner, the whole family. I just want it to be over."

"You should talk to somebody," he said.

"I am talking to somebody, you moron, I'm talking to you."

They sat there in silence for a long moment, ignoring the few students starting to wander in for lunch.

"I just want to stop having these dreams about my kids," she said, tagging the waiter for a third beer. "Sometimes I wish I never had kids, so many bad things can happen to them, but it never bothered me when I was in sex crimes, just now. This fucking menopause, maybe it's a good thing to have your period, a little blood loss every month, you know, like a pressure valve. How about Carmen, she's not menopausal yet, right? What is she, forty?"

"Thirty-eight."

"She's so lucky."

"Maybe it's not menopause," he said. "Maybe you're pregnant."

"Right. Do me a favor, ask your wife how long this thing lasts."

"She's a triage nurse."

"I don't know, Billy, you're all worried about Pavlicek? Maybe you should worry a little about me instead."

"You'll be all right," he said, running out of safe things to say.

MILTON RAMOS

Thirty minutes into packing up Marilys's one-and-a-half-room apartment, Milton more than got it: of course she was half a loon when it came to believing in her own bad dreams, the place was a virtual botanica, the high shelves above the two-burner stove and the cabinet beneath the bathroom sink housing a riot of spirit oils: Ogun, Pajaro Macua, 7 African Powers, Angel de Dinero, Angel de Amor, and Amarra Hombre, a.k.a. Hold Your Man, the last two also in mist form. And then there were the jars of spiritual floor wash in the back of the closet: Court Case, Steady Work, Money Shower, Chain Breaker, Do What I Say, Obey Me, Adore Me, and, once again, Hold Your Man, Milton wondering as he packed if she had been sneaking some of these concoctions into his house all along, washing the floors and walls but most important, he knew, the door frames, thresholds, and windowsills, in an effort to land him. He was fine with that, flattered in fact, but now that the potions had done their job, where the hell was she?

It was one in the afternoon on the day after she had boarded the bus to JFK and he was still waiting for her call from Guatemala City. At first he told himself, Third-world country, travel chaos, shitty to non-existent cell service, there could be a million reasons. But after a few hours of thinking about all the cash she was carrying, *third-world country* began to morph into *abduction, chaos* into *rape,* and *bad cell reception* into *murder.*

Deciding that he didn't want any of her mojo collection in his house, he unpacked what he had just packed, then went to work emptying her medicine chest, another cabinet of curiosities, including a few unmarked jars that he wouldn't open on a bet. But he found no over-the-counter items and, more jarringly, no pharmacy-filled vials, no recognizable medications — every bathroom cabinet on earth held doctor-prescribed meds — which meant she either didn't take any and was as healthy as she looked or she was too poor to take proper care of herself and was medicating on the medieval plan, the mystery of the absent meds once again hammering home to him how little, after all these years, he actually knew about her.

His cell rang, not Marilys but Peter Gonzalez, a half friend of his from the TSA.

"She wasn't on United, American, or Delta. There were four other airlines flying out of the New York area with a connecting flight to Guatemala last night and this morning, but I figured those three were both direct and had the cheapest fares so . . ."

"So . . ." Milton sat on her bed.

"Aeromexico out of JFK last night had two Irrizarys on their manifest, a Carla and a Maria — are you sure Marilys is her legal name? It could be a nickname, a childhood name, or something."

"Hang on," he said, putting the phone down and quickly rustling through her garbage until he found a rent receipt and a Con Ed bill.

"Yeah, Marilys Irrizary, keep looking." Then: "Hello? You still there?"

"You're welcome," Gonzalez said.

"Sorry. Thank you."

Going back to packing, he returned to her closet and then went through her dresser, both of which were half empty, leaving Milton struck by how few actual possessions she had. Lastly he collected her crucifixes, icons, and religious statuary: Saints Michael, George, Lucy, and Lazarus, the Infant of Atocha and Our Lady of Guadalupe, all the usual suspects. Then, after surveying the rest of the apartment one last time and not finding anything else worth taking, he began to carry her stuff down to the street, needing only four trips to complete the job, six medium-sized boxes going into the back of a rented U-Haul with a capacity for ten times that amount.

Gonzalez called back a few hours later, while Milton was in the process of unpacking those same boxes in his house.

"Spirit, Avianca, Taca, Copa, no Irrizarys on any of them."

"All right," Milton said. "Thank you."

Fighting down panic, he busied himself with unwrapping her saints until he dropped and shattered the Black Madonna and Child, at which point he lost his shit in earnest.

Whatever happened to her, it had happened here.

She had never even made it out of the city.

"We can't start looking until forty-eight hours," Turkel, the lone detective on duty in the Missing Persons Unit said. "You know the drill."

Milton had never been on the customer side of a squad room desk before, and he hated it.

"You can't jump the clock for me?" Redundantly flashing his tin.

"Last time I did someone a favor, they put me on desk duty for three months."

"What am I asking here," Milton said, thinking, You're behind a fucking desk right now.

"Look, how about you fill out the report, give it to me, if she's still missing tomorrow midnight, give me a call and I'll bump her to the top of the list."

Twenty minutes later, while still waiting for Turkel to find the right form, Milton left the office and returned to his squad in the 4-6.

"I understand where Missing Persons is coming from with the forty-eight-hours rule," Milton said, sitting between mountains of manila folders on Dennis Doyle's couch. "But I'm not talking about some teenage runaway here, and I was hoping you could reach out to somebody for me."

He knew his boss didn't like him, would have happily had him transferred out of the squad in a heartbeat if he could, but Milton couldn't think of anyone else to go to on this.

Doyle leaned back in his office chair, his head encircled by the framed portraits of his own bosses on the wall behind him.

"Who do I know there," he said, scowling into the middle distance, then picking up his phone, putting it down, picking it up again. "I got the guy. Remember that Night Watch sergeant was in here that morning I was asking you for the 494s on Cornell Harris?"

Milton slid his ass to the edge of the sofa. "Vaguely."

"Billy Graves, he spent a lot of years in the ID Squad, he's got to have a few friends in Missing Persons."

Milton got to his feet.

"Boss, you know what? Maybe I'm hitting the panic button too early on this."

"Your call." Doyle shrugged.

"I appreciate it though, thank you," he said, walking back into the squad room.

"Who is she, anyhow?" his boss called out after him.

Back in Marilys's apartment, he scoured dressers, drawers, and trash receptacles for anything that could help him find her, turning up nothing beyond those bullshit elixirs, a never-used datebook, and a set of keys that didn't fit her door. It was only after overturning half the furniture and getting down on his stomach with a Maglite to peer beneath whatever he couldn't move that he discovered the three phone numbers written in pencil on the wall above her mini-fridge.

The first was to a local deli, the second to a Chinese restaurant that delivered, but the third, with an outer-borough area code, was to an older female Hispanic with good English.

"Good afternoon, this is Detective Milton Ramos from the New York Police Department Missing Persons Unit. I'm looking for a Ms. Marilys Irrizary?"

"Not here."

"Who am I talking to?"

"Who am *I* talking to?"

Milton took a breath. "Detective Milton Ramos, NYPD, your turn."

"Anna Goury," then: "Josepha Suarez."

"Which."

"Both."

"Do you know Ms. Irrizary?"

"*Ms.?*" Sardonically dragging out the *z* sound. "Yeah, she's my sister, what's going on?"

And when Milton, overwhelmed by the

question, was unable to answer, she asked, "Are you really a cop?"

Anna Goury/Josepha Suarez lived with her husband, three kids, and what Milton thought might be a wolf in a federally funded prefab ranch house on Charlotte Street in the former anus mundi section of the Bronx, all six rooms of her home spotless to the point of parboiled. She looked a lot like Marilys, but then again all Indio women of a certain age seemed to him born of the same womb.

The three small cups of rocket-fuel Bustelo she served him at the kitchen table both helped and hindered his getting the full story out, breaking down his inbred reticence but making him stammer.

"I don't understand," she said after he finished. "Why would she be going to Guatemala?"

"Why? I told you, to bring back . . ."

"Our mother? Our mother's dead fifteen years," she said. "Besides, we're from El Salvador."

"Hold on, hang on," the sweat caught in his mustache suddenly reeking of coffee.

"Well, all I can say is," Goury/Suarez delicately rotating her demitasse cup on the

smooth tabletop, "I hope you didn't give
her any money."

CHAPTER 13

Rolling onto his own street after a four-thirty a.m. police shooting in Herald Square had extended his tour nearly until noon, Billy was so jacked from all the liquid speed he had ingested that he clipped a neighbor's garbage can and then just kept on driving, his house at the end of the curved block shimmering like a mirage. Oddly enough, the sight of Pavlicek's Lexus parked in his driveway settled him down rather than sending him over the edge, artificial adrenaline, in the end, no friend to genuine alertness.

They were having coffee in the kitchen, Carmen in her nursing whites, Pavlicek in dry-cleaned jeans and a sport jacket.

"I didn't know Carmen went to Monroe," Pavlicek said as if Billy had been sitting with them all along. "Did you know that?"

"Well, yeah, she's my wife," he said carefully, looking to her for a read on the situation.

"My parents went there in the sixties, they met in tenth-grade journalism class," looking past Billy into the living room. "How's that for staying power."

"Must have been a whole different school in those days," Billy said, still trying to catch Carmen's eye.

"No, they told me it was crap back then too."

"He was asking me if I remembered any of the teachers," Carmen said. "I told him I didn't even remember going there."

"Yeah, you never talk about it," Billy too tense to take a seat in his own kitchen. "So, John, to what do we owe the honor?"

"Hey, look at this guy," Pavlicek beaming as Declan wandered into the kitchen, then pulling the boy close. "How old are you, now?"

"Eight." Always a sucker for adult attention, Declan didn't resist, standing there between Pavlicek's legs, an expectant half-smile on his face.

Billy finally caught his wife's eye: What gives? Carmen, thrown by the query, just shrugged.

"You got a girlfriend yet?" Pavlicek asked.

"I hate girls," Declan said, stating a fact.

"Yeah? What's your favorite team?"

"The Rangers."

"Baseball Rangers or hockey Rangers."

"Hockey. I hate the baseball Rangers."

"My boy's sport was football."

"I like football. I'm on a team," Declan said, then walked out of the room.

"What a guy you have there," Pavlicek said to the space between the parents.

"Well, yours is no slouch," Carmen said.

"Yeah," Pavlicek said faintly, smiling down at his coffee.

Billy finally took a seat. "So, John, what's up?"

Pavlicek took a breath, then folded his hands on the table. "Do you remember that Memory Keepers national convention Ray Rivera was talking about that time on City Island?"

"I know that group," Carmen said. "We give them a conference room for their meetings. So sad, you know?"

"Well, I went there as a guest of the Bronx-Westchester chapter, the one that meets at St. Ann's," nodding to Carmen. "It was in a Marriott outside of St. Louis and the first night they had a ceremony in this huge banquet hall, fifty, sixty tables, maybe five hundred parents from all the local chapters coast to coast. And, once everyone got settled, they passed out these cheap see-through plastic roses attached to batteries, one to a family, then they turned out all the lights in the hall and started to project a slide show onto a movie screen up front, sort of a death carousel. Each slide was a photo of someone's murdered child, could be anywheres from an infant to a forty-year-old, with name, birth date, then the 'murdered' date, printed below. 'Murdered,' not died, not killed. They'd hold the photo for twenty seconds or so, and when you saw your son's or daughter's face up there, your grandchild's, you turned on your battery-powered rose. One by one, those roses going on in the dark, here, over there, in the corner, in the back, and all the while they're playing this sappy theme music over the sound system, Michael Bolton, Celine Dion, the Carpenters, Whitney Houston, roses clicking on for infants, gang-bangers, little girls, teenage boys, grown women, black, white, Chinese, "You Light Up My Life," murder date, rose, "Memories," murder date, rose, "Close to You," murder date, rose, "I Will Always Love You," murder date, rose, murder date, rose . . . And people for the most part were pretty composed, but every once in a while a face would come up on the screen and you'd hear somebody gasping in the dark or moaning, then race-walking out of the room. I think they had an understanding, if you're going to lose it, you need to leave, because it could create a chain reaction . . . So, the ceremony is going on and on, more and more roses lighting up this huge grief cave, and by the end of the slide show the whole room was, like, blazing with roses, I mean that fucking slide show went on for something like an hour and a half — twenty seconds a life, you do the math."

A silence came down, everyone staring at the table until Billy couldn't take it anymore.

"John, what's wrong with you."

"I lost you," Pavlicek blinking at him.

"I'm right here."

"Then be more specific."

"The hematologist."

Carmen looked from one to the other.

"I know you're seeing him."

"Me? No."

"John Pavlicek," Billy said. "I'm sorry, but I have the records."

"Junior."

"What?"

"That would be John Pavlicek Jr.," Pavlicek said. "It's called T-cell prolymphocytic leukemia, no one beats it, and it's fast. Six months at the outside."

"No!" Carmen's voice fluty with shock.

"Are you sure?"

"I come back from a two-week business trip four months ago, December sixteenth, I hear him in his bedroom, I walk in there," looking directly at Billy now. "I thought he had got stomped by a gang. Rings around his eyes, lumps and bruises all over his body, he can barely move, raise his eyes to me."

"Wait," Billy's hand out like a stop sign, "hold on, you told me . . ."

"I know what I told you," he said flatly.

Carmen started to cry, the sight of a weeping nurse bringing home the death sentence for Billy.

"So," Pavlicek sighed, "you ask around to Yasmeen, to Whelan, to Redman, do you know what happened to this animal, to that animal, do you think Pavlicek caught some kind of disease and lost his mind, do you think . . ."

"John, you have to understand . . ."

"Who the fuck cares, Billy. I mean, where's the scales, where's the justice in it?"

Billy closed his eyes, dreamed of sleep. "Are you telling me something?"

"I'm *asking* you something." Pavlicek leaned across the table and touched the back of his hand. "Because from where I'm

400

sitting? If God or whoever else could just point a finger at a kid like John Junior, then all bets are off, because no one's minding the store. So, someone like me, what you do is, you take care of all your unfinished business, you do what you have to do to balance the books, so that maybe, just maybe, when the time comes, you might manage not to jump in the grave with him."

"Sometimes with that kind of leukemia . . ." Carmen began, then faded.

"My boy will be rotting in the earth while Jeffrey Bannion is getting laid? I don't think so. While Eric Cortez is going to a Yankees game? While Sweetpea Harris is becoming a father?"

"What are you telling me," Billy repeated numbly.

"You're a detective," Pavlicek said. "You figure it out."

Billy went away again, came back. "John, I swear to God, you know how much I love you, and I'm devastated for your son, but if you killed any of those . . ."

"You'll what, you'll lock me up?" Pavlicek finished his coffee and got to his feet. "You want to hear the worst, the very worst about this fucking type of leukemia he's got?" Looking around the kitchen as if trying to decide what to smash first. "The median age at onset is sixty-five. Imagine that."

They sat in silence long after the Lexus had disappeared.

"You're not going after him, are you?" Carmen finally asked.

Billy didn't answer.

"*Are* you?"

"Can you give me a goddamn minute?"

Carmen punched him so hard his arm went dead.

"*Jesus,* Billy!" she wailed, shoving back her chair and leaving the room.

Later that day, unable to sleep, Billy returned to Columbia Presbyterian, headed over to the information desk, and asked for John Junior's room. He dreaded seeing the kid in the state his father had described, but after Pavlicek's visit he had no choice.

The clerk sent him up to the oncology ward, where a nurse — once Billy had said that he was Junior's uncle and showed her his ID — told him that Junior had been checked out a few days ago. For a fleeting moment Billy thought that meant he was on the mend.

"He's home?"

"Transferred to Valhalla."

"To *where*?" Billy thinking she had chosen

a sick way of telling him that Junior had died.

"The Westchester County Medical Center in Valhalla."

"Is that good or bad?"

"It's just closer to his family," she said breezily enough, but he'd been around nurses for the last twenty years of his life: John Junior was never going home again.

On his way back down the corridor, Billy noticed, through open suite doors, that some of the patients' rooms had second beds that sat lower to the floor and on collapsible legs for easier storage. On one, an older woman in street clothes was sleeping next to her daughter's sickbed. In another suite, a man was unpacking a suitcase as his wife watched him with near-lifeless eyes. He had slept on one of those beds himself for two nights at Lenox Hill after Carmen had given birth to Declan.

Billy returned to the nurses' station. "Family can sleep over?"

"If they want," the nurse said.

"How about the Pavlicek boy?"

"Johnnie? When we had him, his dad just about moved in. Very nice man, given the circumstances."

"Slept here every night?"

"I think that's why he moved his son. The

403

commute was too hard on him."

"Did he need to sign in?"

"Only if he was coming in after visitors' hours."

Without too much cajoling, Billy got her to find the guest log for March 17, the night of Bannion's murder. Pavlicek had signed in at nine p.m.

"Do they sign out when they leave?"

"No need."

"So if, say, a visitor wants to go home at midnight, two in the morning . . ."

"Then they go."

Which left him with nothing.

"All right, then," offering his hand.

"Tell the Pavliceks I'm still praying for them," she said, her responding grip startlingly strong.

Back home, Billy headed upstairs to take another shot at sleep, passed his father's open bedroom door, and wandered in. Billy Senior lay on his bed, fully dressed for a change but snoring, flayed sections of the *New York Times* scattered around him on the bedspread.

Taking a seat at the small desk his father had brought with him from his last home, Billy scanned the spines of the books that lined the top shelf. Beside the old man's poets were luridly written original guides to nineteenth-century New York City; a first-person account of the Civil War draft riots of 1863; a hardback reissue of *1866 Professional Criminals of America;* and three fat novels about Ireland written by Thomas Flanagan, two of which Billy had actually read and somewhat enjoyed.

"Which is catching your eye?" Billy Senior murmured from the bed.

"Dad, you know me." Billy blushed.

"The dummy act doesn't become you," Senior said. "I've been telling you that since you were a kid."

"You know me," Billy unthinkingly repeated. Then, catching himself: "Must be an echo in here."

"What's on your mind?"

"Why does something have to be on my mind for me to come visit?"

Billy Senior quietly waited him out, his eyes unwavering, reducing his son, as in the old days, to a bucket of tells.

"Dad, let me give you a hypothetical situation," he began, then faltered. "If you knew that a certain friend crossed the line . . ."

"Which line?"

"The legal line . . . And you were having a real problem looking the other way . . ."

Flat on his back, his father frowned at the

ceiling. "Is this friend on the Job?"

Billy didn't answer, which was answer enough.

"How good a friend is he?"

"Like a brother."

"Then first off, you have to ask yourself what would happen to him."

Billy felt his heart lurch, but he wasn't sure in which direction. "No matter what he did?"

"It's that bad?"

Again, Billy didn't answer.

"What are we talking about, mass murder?"

"Just some nonsense," he said, getting to his feet. "I should sleep."

"That was fast," his father said.

"No, I'm just . . ."

"Are you all right?"

"Yeah, no, I'm great." Billy patted his father's arm, turned, and was halfway out of the room when the old man began talking to him as if he were still seated.

"Back in June of sixty-four, there was a cop in Harlem, I won't say his name, he's passed anyhow, and this individual, he killed someone pretty much in front of his partner."

Billy sat back down.

"A pimp, had some Indian moniker, Cochise, Cheyenne, Geronimo, maybe. They had him in the back of the patrol car, and he starts mouthing off, just wouldn't stop. So this cop, let's call him Johnson, it was at night, he drives over to Morningside Park, drags him out, busts him up bad, and leaves him there to die, which he did."

"Because the guy was mouthing off?"

"Well, that and because there wasn't a girl in this man's stable over sixteen, because he had a habit of slashing Achilles tendons when any of them tried to run away from him, because he was so arrogant that he threatened Johnson's family. And yeah, because he wouldn't shut the hell up back there."

"What happened to him?"

"What happened to who."

"Johnson."

"Nothing."

"Walked away clean?"

His father propped himself up with a second pillow. "You have to understand, my son, the summer of sixty-four was red hot uptown, and this Cochise individual had more enemies than a Roman emperor. The squad pretty much went through the motions of looking into it for a few days, but nobody really gave a damn, and then a lieutenant from the One-nine, Tom Gilligan, shot and killed a fifteen-year-old black kid in the street, and we had almost a week of rioting on our hands, so the pimp was totally forgotten."

"Johnson's partner didn't say anything?"

"I can't say what it's like now, but back then? You looked the other way. Always."

"How about the partner, what happened to him?"

The old man was so long in answering that Billy almost repeated the question.

"Looking back after all those years?" his father finally said. "He could've been a better father to his kids, maybe, a better husband to his wife, but other than that?" Looking Billy in the eye now. "He sleeps like a rock."

Walking into Harlem Hospital at three a.m. in order to follow up on an agg assault that had come into the office an hour earlier, Billy wandered the halls until he found his point man, Emmett Butter, standing outside one of the ORs, notebook in hand, watching as a trauma team worked on his victim.

"What do you got."

"Bekim Ismaeli," Butter reading off his notes, "nineteen, stabbed twice in the chest."

"Is he likely?"

"Wobblin'."

"Where'd it happen."

"They're not sure, they said they were walking on either St. Nicholas or Amsterdam, all of a sudden five or six black guys jumped out of a car, stabbed Ismaeli, snatched his chain, then took off."

"Who's they."

"What?"

" '*They* were walking.' Who was walking."

"The other Albanians, his buddies. They brought him in."

"Can any of them ID the car?"

"I don't think so."

"Make, color, nothing?"

"Apparently not."

"Guys are walking down a street, middle of the night, five, six other guys jump out of a car, stab their friend twice, steal his chain, then jump back into the car and take off."

"Apparently."

"And these friends who brought him here, not one of them knows what street they were on, and nobody can even say what color car it was. Do I have that right?"

"Apparently," Butter looking away now.

"What does that sound like to you."

"Like they're selling a story."

"I agree. So where are these Albanian friends?"

"They left."

"They left. Did you interview any of them?"

"Just as far as I told you. Then I went to check with the doctor and when I came back out they were kind of gone."

"Kind of gone. You got their names though, right?"

"I was about to," Butter said, blushing with humiliation, then: "I'll put it all in the report."

"How about you don't."

"What?"

"Do everybody a favor and say you got here after they left."

"Yeah?" Butter looking at him now with dog's eyes.

"But we're clear about what happened in here, yes?"

"Yeah, yes."

"My people get to screw up once."

"I understand," Butter said, then again: "I understand."

"All right," Billy said, turning away, "stay with Ismaeli, see if he comes around."

"Hey, boss," Butter called out. "Thank you."

Thinking that there was a good chance the kid would screw the pooch on this, his first run, Billy had made sure to wait until something came in north of Ninety-sixth Street before sending Butter out, knowing that grievously fucking up anywhere south of that, where the press began to give a shit, would have resulted in him being transferred to Missing Persons or worse. But if Butter was ever going to be of any use to him or any other squad boss, he had to start cutting his teeth somewhere.

His wife would never admit it to him, but Billy's guess was that interns killed patients all the time, and their supervisors, with an eye for the long-term healer to come, mainly looked the other way. Well, it was the same with him. In order to get the greater job done, to mold your people as you saw fit and prepare them to effectively do the job in the years to come, you tolerated error, you turned a not-quite-blind eye to the actions of others and to your own actions. You created secrets and you kept secrets.

Out on the streets, same thing: depending on the individual and the situation, sometimes you threw the Thor hammer at a misdemeanor, other times you let an individual walk who had no right to sleep in his own bed that night. You did all these things and more because as a boss, if you weren't willing to play fast and loose when required,

411

if you weren't willing to make a discreet hash of the rule book now and then, on this job you might as well call in sick.

That's just the way it was.

Carmen called as he was walking to his car. "Hey."

"Hey," Billy bracing himself.

"Look," she said, "I don't want you to do anything or not do anything because I pressured you. You'll resent me forever."

"I appreciate that."

"That being said, you know how I feel."

"Right."

"Just come to it on your own."

MILTON RAMOS

Marilys Irrizary Ramos.

Even her pregnancy was probably bullshit.

Another family taken away from him. And for what: fifteen hundred for the bogus plane tickets, eighty-five hundred for the bogus bribe.

A lousy 10K.

Fuck her.

It was time to get back in the game.

Here's what he didn't like about giving his daughter away to Anita:

1. Her two-story clapboard was only a curb's width distant from the city-bound service road of the Staten Island Expressway, cars flying by as if the first to reach the Verrazano Bridge was entitled to free head.
2. She was a smoker.
3. She drank. As far as could tell,

nothing harder than white wine, but still . . .

And here's what he did:

1. Her husband, Raymond, was a nice enough guy who owned a gas station and made decent money.
2. She was a thirty-five-year-old teacher's aide who worked at a K-4 public school but who couldn't have children of her own, and her eyes always had that slightly tense quivery thing going on, which hopefully meant that she desperately wanted a kid before her time ran out.
3. The house was not just neat but clean, the velour couch and matching chairs in her living room sheathed in vinyl, the wall-to-wall carpet as pristine as a putting green.
4. And lastly, she was slender, at least by his standards, and the most fattening things in her refrigerator, which he opened on the pretense of getting a soda, were a still-sealed log of Cracker Barrel cheddar cheese and a small bubble pack of Genoa salami.

"What do you mean you're being targeted, what does that mean?" Anita asked him.

They were sitting at her dinette table, Sofia watching cartoons in the dustless living room, a small overstuffed suitcase at her feet.

"Some big-time banger I put away sent down orders from upstate for his crew to take me out. Gang Intel found out about it from a CI."

"But what does that mean?" Anita nervously playing with the cellophane on a new pack of Merit Lights.

"Probably nothing. I spoke to the NYPD Threat Assessment Team, they already had TARU put up surveillance cameras around the house, plus a directed patrol unit rolls by once an hour twenty-four/seven. I'm not really worried about it? But that doesn't mean nothing's going to happen."

"Milton, Jesus."

"It comes with the territory." He shrugged. "The thing is . . ." looking to Sofia, who was quietly eating mozzarella strips, eyes on the screen. "The thing is, if something does happen to me? Sofia . . ."

"Of course."

"So I was thinking . . ."

"Of course."

"Or if I'm unable to take care of her for whatever reason . . ."

"Of course of course of course."

Milton felt relieved but also freaked, his cousin going for it way too fast. "Don't you want to talk to Ray first?"

"Why. We've being trying to have a child for the last five years."

"Still . . ."

"He'd be doing handstands, trust me."

"And you like her, right?"

"Do I like Sofia?" she whispered. "The bigger question is does she like me."

Good question. Sofia hardly knew her.

"Don't be ridiculous, you're her favorite aunt."

"I'm her second cousin, if you want to get technical about it," Anita said, still whispering.

"Whatever," Milton said, "blood is blood."

"Wow," Anita said.

"It would be a simple matter of writing you into my will as Sofia's guardian."

"We have that second bedroom, I mean Ray's just using it as an office, you know?"

"Good," Milton said tightly.

"I mean what does he need it for?"

Too fast, too fast, Anita just going with the

excitement without a moment's reflection, as if Milton were offering her a puppy. And she didn't seem too worried about his own dangerous situation, horseshit story that it was.

"And I have to say, the schools around here?"

"Terrific."

"Plus I've been around kids Sofia's age five days a week for the last five years, so it's not like I don't . . ."

"There you go."

This was a life-changing commitment, how could she not hesitate?

"I mean I would really love her up, Milton, you know I would," Anita's hands trembling a little as she finally opened the pack of cigarettes. Then, catching him staring, she tossed the whole thing in the sink.

"No more of these, I can promise you that."

"Relax, I'm still alive."

But she was a good person and he had to believe that if things went south for him — *when* things went south for him — Sofia would have a soft landing here.

"Wow." Anita shivered. "This is almost enough to make me want to bump you off myself, you know?"

The impact, a heartbeat after he blindly backed out of her driveway into the expressway service road, spun his rear end a full ninety degrees so that he was suddenly facing the oncoming traffic and the smashed front grille of the Ram 1500 that had T-boned him. The driver, big enough to star in TV ads for his own ride, was out of the truck so fast that at first Milton thought he had been ejected. It was all he could do to stow his weapon under the seat before Bigfoot reached his car.

"The fuck!" the guy shouted, pounding on Milton's hood.

Like she was some goddamn rescue dog . . .

Milton got out of his car. Behind the damaged truck, the nonstop honking of the city-bound cars now trapped in the one-lane road was like the sound track for his fury.

"It was my fault," Milton said. He took out his wallet, but the guy slapped it out of his hands before he could even start to fish for his insurance card.

"I feel like stomping your ass."

"You can try," Milton said.

Like she was a puppy in a cardboard box . . .

Thrown by Milton's matter-of-fact invitation, the big man hesitated.

"I think you should try."

Anita was nuts, was a child herself. She was just jumping on this without a thought in her head.

"You're crazy."

"And you're a fucking cunt," Milton said.

Red-faced with throttled violence, the guy started to tilt forward from the hips like a dipping bird, his breath puffing Milton's hair. Praying for the punch to come, Milton stood his ground and waited for it, even though he pretty much knew he had already cut off the guy's balls and that nothing would happen. And nothing did, Ram Tough man settling for a string of low face-saving curses as he returned to his front-mangled ride and took off, leaving Milton feeling so thwarted he thought his heart would break.

Milton stood in Sofia's bedroom, surveying the scatter of dolls and books and games. She would need things, obviously, but he could only send over a little of her previous life at a time in order to allow everyone, his daughter and her new parents, to gradually become accustomed to their roles. He didn't want anyone to panic.

But what did she need right away. Clothes.

What kind of clothes. What did an eight-year-old girl wear. Even when she was a toddler he had never dressed her, barely took notice of what she had on unless it was something too tight for her frame.

Socks. They didn't take up much space, so he figured he could get away with three pairs without raising eyebrows. Underwear, T-shirts. Again, three of each, everything tossed into a large Hefty bag. Her floral corduroy jeans, into the bag. How about a dress, a skirt. No, two skirts; no, one, but where did Marilys keep them? This should be Marilys's job, Milton at first mildly annoyed about that, and then the irony kicked in, making him sit down before he fell down.

A moment later, once again galled to the edge of his teeth by the divide between the grief givers and the grief takers, the fuckers and the fucked, by the eternal inevitable of his violently miserable life, Milton walked out of the room dragging the half-full garbage bag behind him and headed for the basement.

A few minutes later he was out on the street, the bag, much heavier now, spackling the sidewalk red from his front door to the trunk of his car.

CHAPTER 14

It was turning out to be another nothing of a tour, the only job so far a four a.m. outdoor scene in the West Village, where a home owner had been shot by his lawn mower while cutting the backyard. The live .357 shell, previously asleep in the grass, had been sucked up into the rotary blades, ignited, then fired itself out the back end of the machine into his nuts.

By the time Billy and Stupak made it to the scene — shots fired was shots fired — Emergency Services was already combing the yard for any other stray ordnance and some joker had handcuffed the high-end mower to a lamppost.

"Who the fuck mows their lawn at four in the morning," the patrol sergeant said.

"Myself, I'd be kind of interested in finding out how the bullet got to be in his backyard in the first place." Billy yawned. "Any ideas?"

"We had a problem last month with some subhumanoids coming over the PATH from Jersey City, but nothing with guns."

"There's that indoor rifle club on Mac-Dougal," a uniform said. "That's only a block over."

"A, it's indoor; B, the house rifle's a .22," the patrol sergeant said.

"Just the one so far?" Billy asked one of the ESUs scouring the grass.

"Found a quarter and a roach clip," the cop said. "That's about it."

Billy sent Stupak over to Beth Israel on the off chance that the victim would be able to talk between now and eight a.m., then, after deciding not to canvass the neighbors at this hour, headed for his car with the intention of going back to the office and grabbing a nap.

But the e-mail that came in over his phone a few minutes later as he was pulling out of his space knocked any notion of sleep into the next week.

There was no message, only an attached JPEG, Billy opening it to see a flash-lit snap of Curtis Taft lying cuffed and gagged on a wooden floor, his red-dot eyes buzzing from above the fat strip of electrical tape that had been slapped across his mouth. The photo had been sent from Taft's own phone, but

Billy had to be an idiot not to guess who the shutterbug was.

After reversing back into his spot, he threw the car into park and immediately started to dial.

"What did you do."

"Come and see," Pavlicek said.

"Is he dead?"

"Come and see."

"Where are you."

"Fifteen twenty-two Vyse."

In the heart of their old precinct, in a building Pavlicek owned.

"Fuck you. Don't move."

"I wouldn't dream of it."

Thirty minutes later, flying down Vyse Avenue the wrong way, Billy sideswiped the length of Pavlicek's Lexus, continued until he was a few feet past the taillights, jumped out, and came racing back on foot.

Pavlicek was out of the car waiting for his charge, but all he did when Billy threw a sloppy haymaker was deflect the blow, then pull him into a bear hug. When it came to hand-to-hand, Billy never could fight for shit.

"What did you do," he hissed, his arms pinned to his sides, Pavlicek's bristle like sandpaper along his jaw.

423

"Calm down."

"What did you *do.*"

Pavlicek thrust him backward, Billy totter-
ing nearly the length of the SUV before
regaining his balance and charging him
again. This time Pavlicek whipped him
chest-first into the Lexus's side-view mirror, the pain like a punch.

"You want to keep going with this?"

"Are you trying to jam me up?" Billy
barked, ripping the side mirror off its mount
and throwing it at Pavlicek's head. "You
think that'll do it?"

The mirror had glanced off Pavlicek's
temple, drawing a little blood. Bracing for a
brawl, Billy set his feet, but instead of warring back, Pavlicek simply stanched the thin
flow with the heel of his hand, then looked
off down the street. At first Billy was thrown
— Pavlicek had been erratically explosive
for weeks — but now it was as if anger over
his son's impending death had somehow
gone beyond expressible fury to a higher,
finer level, making Billy's rage in comparison seem so pedestrian that it hardly mer-
ited a reaction.

Three silent but alert white men in jeans
and sweatshirts came out of 1522 into the
predawn stillness and headed toward the
Lexus, Billy recognizing one: Hal Gurwitz,

carrying a Yankees bat bag, a defrocked cop who had done some time for putting a handcuffed prisoner in the hospital with a ruptured spleen. He guessed that the other two, younger and a little more tense, might still be cops.

They eyed the long scrape on the SUV's body and then Billy's sedan, slant-parked in the wrong direction.

"Everything OK up there?" Pavlicek asked.

"Yeah," Gurwitz said, taking the question as an all-clear sign. "I believe the moving van should be coming somewheres around midmorning."

"Everything OK down here?" the youngest of the three asked, looking directly at Billy.

"Absolutely." Pavlicek pulled out a wad of cash as thick as a rolled washcloth and distributed what looked like a few hundred dollars to each of them. "I'll be in touch."

The men walked off as a group, each in turn casting an eye back toward Billy and the cars, until they all piled into a minivan in front of an elementary school at the far end of the block.

"Some of my tenants on the fifth floor were confusing their apartment with a dopeteria," Pavlicek said, stooping to pick up his side mirror, then tossing it into the backseat. "You'd think everyone around here would know the score by now."

The van slow-rolled past them on its way to wherever, the three cops inside throwing deep shade Billy's way one last time.

"Do they know?"

"Know what." Then: "What do *you* know?"

"Just . . ." Billy felt his adrenaline abandon him in a reverse rush. "Where is he."

Pavlicek took a breath, tracked the last of the moon as it slipped between two dead walk-ups at the end of the street.

"You know, when I heard Bannion bought it at the train station that night? I wept with happiness. To go to Thomas Rivera's parents and bring them news like that: Somebody sliced up your boy's murderer, he died in his own blood on a filthy subway platform . . ."

"Did you tell them you killed him?"

"I didn't kill him."

"Right, that's right, you were sleeping at the hospital that night. I saw your name on the sign-in."

Pavlicek threw Billy a look that had him taking a step back.

"I didn't kill him, and that's a fact. But justice, real justice, Billy, it's like the getting of grace. The closest thing to peace on earth."

"Where is he."

Pavlicek crossed the narrow street to 1522, then waited at the entrance until Billy understood to follow.

Cuffed hand and foot like a bagged deer, Curtis Taft lay curled on his side in the smaller bedroom of a ground-floor vacant, his eyes widening then narrowing at a rapid tic-like pace, the tape across his mouth tugging redly at the trapped curls of his beard. A second strip, half the size of the gag, was pasted across his forehead.

"Jesus!" Billy hissed, backing up until he hit a wall.

At the sound of Billy's voice, Taft's eyes slowed and then focused on a section of baseboard inches from his face.

Billy knew he should leave and call it in, but he didn't. He knew he should cut Taft loose, but he didn't do that either.

Taft twisted his head so he could look at Billy directly, the oh-shit sight of his five-year hunter making his chest begin to rise and fall — but not so intensely that anyone could describe it exactly as *heaving* — and despite everything Billy found himself nakedly wanting some kind of more — a tape-muffled plea, a widening eye, a stream of uncontrolled piss — and he found it enraging that his White wasn't giving it to him.

"Cut him loose," he said faintly.

Pavlicek dropped into a squat alongside Taft, peeled the smaller strip of tape off his forehead, and held it between his fingers.

"I heard that the only family member who showed up for Shakira Barker's arraignment last week was her grandmother," Pavlicek said, his eyes never leaving Taft's face. "The same for the funeral of the kid she killed. No one but Grandma. Thank God for the grannies, huh?"

"Get him up."

Pavlicek removed the tape from between his fingers and placed it across Taft's nostrils, Billy's already gagged White immediately beginning to writhe, his eyes bulging like eggs.

Billy finally started across the room, but Pavlicek removed the tape before he could get there.

"It's not my place," he said, extending the strip to Billy on a fingertip.

Billy returned to his spot on the wall.

"It's nothing," Pavlicek said, still offering the tape. "It's like applying a band-aid."

"Get him up, John," Billy said, looking away.

"Peace on earth," Pavlicek said, rising to his feet, crossing to Billy, and pressing the tape into his bruised chest on his way out of the room. "Nothing like it in the world."

A moment later the apartment door slammed shut, Pavlicek leaving Billy and Taft staring at each other from opposite corners of the empty room.

Helplessly trussed though he was, Taft sensed that Billy wasn't going to take the bait. His eyes began to recede back into their sockets, then droop with supreme contempt, the same contempt that had allowed him to kill those girls and then go back to bed, the same contempt he'd displayed whenever Billy's efforts to bring him to justice invariably came to nothing.

Billy plucked the strip of tape from his chest, stepped forward, and then, as Pavlicek had, hunkered down above his prisoner.

Taft began to look bored, his eyes dimming in his head. Billy affixed the tape to his nostrils. Taft's expression remained the same.

Like he had Billy's number. Had it since day one.

Billy got up and left the room to explore

the rest of the apartment, the smell of the freshly painted walls reminding him of the day he had moved into his first home with his first wife.

When he returned to the bedroom, he saw that Taft no longer looked so bored, and that a pinkish mist had begun to seep into the whites of his eyes. Billy left again, this time to splash cold water over his face in the kitchen, wiping away the excess on the sleeves of his jacket, then drying his hands on the back of his slacks.

When he settled over Taft this time, the pink of his eyes had turned poppy and completely flooded the scleras. A few seconds after that, his hog-tied body began to repeatedly jackknife, then arch in pure animal spasm.

Billy stood up and returned to his original position against the far wall. "If you even think of flagging down a patrol car," he said evenly, "or walking into a police station? Or picking up a phone and calling 911?"

The room abruptly blossomed with the stench of involuntary evacuation.

"You see how easy he found you? You see how easy that was?"

Standing next to the Lexus, they watched in silence as Curtis Taft, mustering as much dignity as possible given the circumstances, walked toward the intersection of Vyse and East 172nd Street, his stride a little off-kilter.

He was smart enough not to look back.

"I didn't really expect you to go through with it," Pavlicek said after Taft finally turned the corner. "But you got a taste of how it would feel, right?"

Billy didn't answer.

"Oh yes you did."

Billy started walking to his car.

"Looking at me like you did when I came to your house . . ." Pavlicek called out after him, sounding both imperious and resentful. "Fucking saint that you are."

Billy came back. "This shit is what heals your grief, John?"

Turning away, he noticed, for the first time, the Westchester Community College decal on Pavlicek's rear window. "This is how you honor your son?"

He had no idea how he came to be lying on his back. His jaw felt as if it was now located behind his left ear. When he managed to find his feet, he was immediately thrown belly-down onto the hood of the Lexus, his kidneys being pounded from behind. By the time he rallied enough to defend himself, twisting his hips and whip-

431

ping a high and ineffective elbow to the side of Pavlicek's head, the deep one-note whoop of a patrol car brought it all to an end.

"Go ahead, tell them what's the what," Pavlicek wheezed. "Now's your chance. Go on."

Billy, gasping himself, intercepted the young cops, both Asian, as soon as they stepped out onto the street. Holding out his gold shield, he slurred, "Family feud, it's under control."

After the uniforms reluctantly rolled off, Billy tottered back to his sedan and drove away, Pavlicek watching him go with the scowling concentration of someone trying to memorize a license plate.

Coming home directly from the Bronx, his exploded jaw pulsing like a drum, Billy saw the red carnage on his front porch and flew into the house to check on his family, racing bedroom to bedroom, the animal priority of who he loved most coming in the order of rooms entered — Carmen before his kids, his kids before his father.

All sleeping, all breathing.

Back in the kitchen, Billy chugged down a glass of tap water, then stepped outside to verify what he thought he'd seen.

The front of the house looked like a

slaughter pit, the cedar planks on the south side of the porch, the exterior wall directly behind it, and Carmen's pink-and-blue Easter banner all peppered with blossoms of gore. A split trash bag, its guts still puddled with paint, lay between the front legs of his father's rocking chair, looking, to anyone driving by, like a sleeping dog. But it was the scatter of children's clothes that froze his heart: a top, a pair of jeans, another top, another pair of pants, and a slurry of underpants and socks, all so red-drenched and twisted that he had no idea whether they were for a boy or a girl.

He went into the garage, gathered up two lawn bags, a wire-whisk brush, an aerosol bottle of Strip-All, and a joint-compound bucket filled with hot water. Checking the time — six-fifteen — he quickly set to work.

It was only later, while carefully going through the paint-stiffened clothes, looking for shop labels or laundry marks and finding nothing more than the ubiquitous Gap Kids tag, that it came to him that his family's tormentor had chosen red twice now, the porch and the children's clothes bathed in the same arterial shade as the handprint on the back of Carlos's jacket.

It made him think about the Jews in Egypt smearing their doors with lamb's blood to fend off the Angel of Death — except in this case, the message seemed to be the opposite.

After dutifully driving his kids to school — *Carmen before his kids* — Billy sat in the kitchen on a straight-backed chair watching his wife wrap her thumbs in heavy layers of gauze, which she then secured with surgical tape.

He had told her that his dislocated jaw had come from a roll-around with a five a.m. Dusthead in the course of making an arrest, but doubted that she believed him.

"Tilt your head back and open your mouth as wide as you can."

"This is going to hurt, right?"

"Like a bitch, but only for a second."

When she put her thumbs in his mouth, each one settling on a back molar, and then rose up on her toes in order to put her whole body into it, he thought he would puke.

"Billy, relax."

"I am."

"No you're not. I tell you what . . ." she said, lowering herself, then quickly rising up again and bringing her thumbs down so hard on his back teeth that he screamed.

"Fucking hurts, right?" Carmen said a

moment later as she unspooled the tooth-shredded gauze from around her thumbs. He thought he had bitten them off.

"Guy wasn't even that big," he said, the red-hot throbbing of the last few hours miraculously down to a run-of-the-mill sore-ness.

"No, huh?" Avoiding his eyes.

He didn't understand why she wasn't pressing him for the truth, which made him even more edgy than he already was.

"I must've had three inches and forty pounds on him," Billy doubling down on the story. "They should have called animal control."

"We had a guy brought in last week?" she said, staying in the game. "He was so cranked on PCP he shattered both of his femurs just by tensing his legs. We go to lift him off his gurney, he jumps up and starts running down the hall like a track star. Didn't feel a thing."

Billy bent over and started to retch.

Carmen offered him an unwashed cereal bowl from the sink.

"I'm good," he said, accepting it.

"So where are you at?" she asked.

"With what." Billy blinked, hoping to duck the subject.

Choosing to let it be, at least for now, Carmen handed him three Advils and a glass of water.

"I want you to go over to Saint Joseph's for an X-ray."

"Right now I need to sleep," he said. Then, gingerly probing his jaw: "Thank you."

While Carmen was upstairs changing into her work whites, Redman called.

"I need to come by," he said.

"What for?" As if he couldn't guess.

"I need to talk to you. I'll drive up."

"Hang on," Billy said, putting the receiver to his chest. He'd had enough of visitors, announced and unannounced, coming to sit or stand in his kitchen and dump all kinds of dark drama on his head.

"I tell you what," raising a hand to Carmen as she walked out of the house, "I need to take care of something, then I'll come down to you, how's that sound."

"All right," Redman said reluctantly. "Just, until you get here? Don't do anything."

Billy walked out the front door a few minutes later, intending to take the paint-stiffened clothes over to the Yonkers precinct that was overseeing the directed patrols. At first he was startled to see Carmen still on the porch, then not, given her missing banner.

"I saw that when I came in," he said as offhandedly as he could. "Some kids must've taken it last night."

But rather than raise hell about it, she seemed distracted, barely acknowledging that he had said anything at all. Then he saw what she was focused on: a rivulet of red paint that he'd missed earlier had settled into the seam between house and porch, looking like a boundary line on a map.

She walked to her car, unlocked the driver's door, then spoke to him without looking his way. "I don't want Millie picking up the kids from school this afternoon," she said numbly. "You do it."

The night-vision surveillance footage from the previous evening, both chalky and luminous, was eerie enough to pass for paranormal activity. Billy watched the tape three times, the mysteriously launched garbage bag sailing as clumsily as an overweight turkey through the fuzzy air before erupting on his porch and spewing out its contents.

"Those patrols are bullshit. I want a twenty-four-hour posting in front of the house," Billy said, regretting the "I want" as soon as it came out of his mouth.

"Not happening." The detective, Evan

Lefkowitz, shrugged.

"What do you mean, not happening."

"We're undermanned as it is."

Billy reached into the bag of clothes lying on an unoccupied desk, pulled out the pair of girls' corduroy pants, and held it in his fist.

"Let me tell you what that guy did. He sat on his ass until he saw your doughnut eaters roll by, knew he had a good fifty-five minutes, ate a sandwich, did the crossword, bloodied up my porch, took a piss, washed his car, and went home. I want, I need, *my family* needs, a twenty-four-hour fixed post."

"Doughnut eaters?"

Billy took a breath. "Look, I'm sorry about that, I swear to you I'm not one of those NYPD assholes who thinks every cop outside the five boroughs is some eeba-geeba related by blood to Barney Fife."

Without excusing himself, Lefkowitz stepped off to talk to another detective about a different issue, Billy taking it to mean that maybe his Mayberry riff had been a little too lovingly delivered.

"Hey, this is my town too," he said when Lefkowitz returned. "I'm living my life here, raising my kids here, paying my taxes, and all I'm asking you for is just a little bit more protection."

"Like I said, we're undermanned as it is."

"All due respect, but could I speak to your boss?"

"She'll just tell you the same."

"Nonetheless . . ."

"Fine by me," Lefkowitz said, walking away. "She'll be in next week."

As Billy came up on Brown's Family Funeral Home that night, Redman, wearing a full-body apron and latex gloves, was standing in the narrow doorway swapping cash for Chinese takeout with a delivery boy.

"You mean to tell me you're OK walking the streets like that?" Redman said without raising his eyes from the exchange.

"Like what?"

"Don't you have a mirror at home?" Redman counted out his change. "Come in here."

Once they were inside the chapel, Redman had Billy take off his shirt and lie down on a somewhat clean gurney. Then, reaching into his cluttered cosmetics cart, he found a jar of Standard Caucasian camouflage cream and went to work on the constellation of bruises that, between Pavlicek and Carmen, had erupted across Billy's face since the morning.

"You ever notice how the storefronts line

up in this neighborhood?" Redman said. "Dunkin' Donuts, Popeyes, Roy Rogers, Ashley Stewart's big women shop, then a funeral parlor, all cheek to cheek like a de-evolution cartoon."

"They have fat people in Nebraska too, last I heard," Billy said, wondering when they were going to get to Pavlicek.

"My point being," Redman stepping back to assess his work, then peeling off his gloves, "I had two bodies coming in this week, a five-hundred-pounder and a four, but when I added the weight of the casket I realized that my front steps would collapse, so I had to farm them out to Carolina Home up the block because the director over there was smart enough to put in reinforced steel."

Rafer came rolling into the room, made two quick circuits around his father, then charged at an old man sporting a Masonic fez and apron, who was lying in his casket parked by the piano.

"So." Billy sat up and reached for his shirt. "Why am I here."

Redman took a limping stroll around the chapel, straightened out a few folding chairs, then slowly came back.

"Look, I'm going to save you a lot of trouble."

"How's that," Billy said, feeling the cadaver cream starting to grip.

"It's done."

"What is."

"All what you've been looking into."

Billy was quiet, waiting for more. Then: "How am I supposed to let him get away with this."

"Who, the lone gunman?"

"What?"

"You think we all sent Pavlicek out there like that?"

"What then."

"All of us."

Billy swiped at his caked jaw with a shaking hand. "Who's all of us."

"Pavlicek didn't do anything more than his part."

" 'All of us.' Including you?"

"Why not me?"

"Look at you," Billy said cruelly.

And then he was aloft, Redman holding him two feet off the ground with those harpooner's arms, the guy wheeling so fast on his cracked hips that Billy hadn't even felt the long fingers slip under his arms.

"Why not me?" Redman holding him up in the air like a baby.

"Put me down, please?"

Redman deposited him in a folding chair,

Rafer immediately raising his arms to his father: My turn.

"You did Sweetpea," Billy said. "Bullshit. The wit said the doer had straight hair. Nothing about a fucking Afro."

Redman picked up his son, held him in one arm. "That wit was six floors up and off-his-ass high. You said so yourself."

Billy grabbed a rag and swiped at his face, but the makeup had turned to cement. "His girlfriend said she heard a white voice over the cell."

"Do I sound, do I *ever* sound like some mush-mouth street nigger to you?"

"You kind of did, right there," Billy said.

Rafer started to wail.

"What you cryin' for, man?" Redman hitch-limped over to the Samsung and found something on the Cartoon Network.

Billy went momentarily south, checking his watch — ten p.m. — wondering if this kid even had a bedtime.

"Why," he said.

"Because it felt right. It felt fair."

"Why."

"Pavlicek's boy. We all known him since he was wearing a diaper. First of the kids born to us."

"Redman . . ."

"It's not like playing God, because me

442

personally? To tell you the truth, the only time I believe in God is when something shitty happens, like Little Man here and his g-tube or John Junior catching leukemia. I'm in here sending people off three, four times a week to meet Jesus or whoever, but . . . You know what I believe in? Earth. Dirt. This right here. All the rest is a story. I guess I'm in the wrong business."

"So everybody . . ."

"Was in on it."

Billy went away again, telling himself that there had always been something off about Redman. Look how he chose to make a living, look how many wives he'd had, look how many kids . . .

"Billy, we all saved each other's lives one time or another, including me yours."

And to let the kid play around dead bodies all day . . . Redman and his wife — what was the child-rearing philosophy here?

"Billy," Redman bringing him back, "I am telling you all this because it's over." He held his long basketball hands in front of his belt, gently tamping down the air like shushing a baby. "So let it be."

Billy made it back home by midnight, but unwilling to go in and risk a conversation with Carmen tonight, he parked halfway down the street, intending to sit tight until the bedroom window went dark.

An hour into the wait, he reached for his notebook and made out the chart:

Redman — Sweetpea
Yasmeen — Cortez
Pavlicek — Bannion

Tomassi's death by bus kept Whelan's name off the chart, and Curtis Taft didn't make it either, though Pavlicek had served him up to Billy hoping he would complete the sweep. But as he continued to sit there and study the neat matchups, he began to wonder if Redman, in order to protect Pavlicek, had been selling him a story back at the chapel, thinking that if Billy bought the conspiracy angle and thought he'd have to bring down three friends instead of just one, he might lose heart and walk away.

The 24/7 directed patrol unit cruised past his car without noticing him in the driver's seat, slowed down in front of the house, but never came to a stop in order to allow the cops to get out and inspect the grounds. It was the third pass he had observed since parking here, each more lax than the one before.

As he reached for his cigarettes on the

444

dash, the pack slipped through his fingers and landed between his feet. When he bent over to retrieve them, his forehead touched the steering wheel and that was that, Billy sitting up an hour later with a pink streak above his eyes as vivid as a brand.

He checked the time: two a.m. The bedroom window was dark.

Stepping from the car, he discovered that the asphalt beneath his feet was dappled with dried paint — the leakage from the clothes bag before it had been thrown onto his porch. Whoever had done the deed last night had chosen the same observation point as he had, a spot far enough away to avoid detection but near enough to track the life of the house.

Using the Maglite he kept in his glove compartment, Billy tracked the drippings from his car toward his house until they came to a stop thirty yards out from the front porch. Here the spatter took on a roughly circular pattern, the elongated drops at the outer edges suggesting that the actor, having picked this place for a launching pad, had then gone into a hammer-throw spin to build up enough centrifugal force to hit his mark ninety feet away.

Billy sat in his father's rocker on the

porch, imagining their stalker, their Fury, whipping that goddamn bag around and around himself before letting it fly, just sat there running and rerunning the film until he found himself suddenly flooded by a powerful halo of light, the search beam of the directed patrol car coming by for its three-thirty a.m. look-see.

When Billy raised his hand, they cut the beam and slowly rolled off, but not before the driver called out, "Here, I'm full," and then tossed something onto the lawn. Once the car was out of sight, he walked through the damp grass and found a crumpled paper bag, inside of which was a half-eaten doughnut.

When he finally entered the sleeping house, the silence was so absolute that it created its own sound, a high even hiss like static from a distant source. Walking into the kitchen, Billy decided, once he opened the freezer, that he didn't need a drink tonight — well, maybe just a pull — wiping his lips afterward, then heading for the stairs.

Soft-stepping into the bedroom, he jumped when he saw Carmen in silhouette sitting on a chair beneath the window, her hands flat on her thighs.

"What are you doing?" he whispered.

"What's wrong?"
"I saw him," she said.
"Saw who?" Then: "You saw him? Where."
"In a dream."

MILTON RAMOS

The evening had started out OK enough,
Anita and Ray bringing Sofia and a little
friend to meet him at a diner in Staten
Island so that he could hand over his care
package of new clothes, DVDs, and favorite
animals. His daughter seemed excited to
see him, crawling into his lap to eat her low-
fat mock sundae, but the whole time he
feared that at the end of the meal she
wouldn't ask him to take her home, not that
he would have done it.

At first, Sofia's new friend had thrown
him. The kid, Jen or Jan, a scrawny little
thing with no more personality than a
hamster, lived two houses down the street
from Anita, and the girls, once introduced,
had apparently become instant blood sisters
and were, in fact, having a sleepover tonight.
Sofia had never had a sleepover in her life,
let alone a best friend. Their caged house in
the Bronx had never been a home to other

kids, even for a few hours after school, and this realization made him wince.

When the bill came, Ray nearly snatched it out of the waitress's hand. "No arguments," he said.

"Fine with me," Milton said.

Sofia slid off his lap and moved to the other side of the table.

"When we go home?" she said to Anita. "Can we call Marilys?" Then to her mouse of a friend: "She's my other mom."

"I *know*!" Jan or Jen said with delighted exasperation. "You tell me all the time!"

It was the third time Sofia had brought up Marilys since the waitress had taken their orders, and it would be the last.

"Listen to me," Milton said, his sleeve sliding through the dregs of his dessert as he reached across and took her wrist. "Marilys isn't your other mom. Marilys isn't anything. She doesn't love you, she doesn't even care about you, OK?"

"Hey, Milton," Ray said.

"Can you get that through your head?"

Sofia was too shocked to do anything other than stare at him in red-faced astonishment, but the other kid, after a breathless second, started to cry as if the world had come to an end.

Mortified, he got up from the table,

walked out the door, and marched into the diner's parking lot. Weaving his way through an army of parked cars to an unlit spot, he seethed in the dark for a few minutes, then pulled out his phone and called Marilys's sister.

"This is Milton Ramos, you remember me?"

She said she did, but she didn't sound too happy about it.

"I'm going to call you back in a half hour. When I do, you're going give me the names, addresses, and phone numbers of everybody in your family living in New York."

Milton stepped deeper into the shadows as Ray came out of the diner, and a moment later pulled out of the lot with a carload of mutes.

"If I call back and for any reason you don't pick up? I'm coming back to your house. Do yourself a big favor and save me the trip."

At eleven that evening he sat across the oilcloth-covered dinette table, glaring at Marilys and her so-called cousin Ottavio, a balding runt with amphibious eyes.

They were in Ottavio's one-bedroom apartment in Astoria, Milton's former fiancée and her kinsman anxiously looking everywhere but at him.

"They were going to kill him," Marilys said numbly, staring first at Milton's hands with their paint-rimmed nails the color of blood, then at the greasy bat he had placed between them on the table.

"Who's they," he said. Then: *"You,"* making Ottavio jump. "Who's they."

"Some individuals I got steered to wrong."

"They were going to kill him," Marilys repeated, forcing herself to meet his eye.

He didn't know what angered him more, the fact that she had so heartlessly ravaged his life for money and dismissed his daughter's need for her like it was nothing or the fact that, despite his desire to slaughter her, she was treating him like a total stranger.

"You're living here now?"

"Just for a little bit," her voice down to a hush.

"You really her cousin?"

"Distant," Ottavio said, unconsciously glancing toward the sole bedroom.

"I want my money back," he said.

"It's gone," Marilys said, once again staring at his bunched hands.

Milton went off into his boiling head long enough for Marilys to add, "We can start paying you back a little each week."

We.

And the thought of having to see her, or him, every week or month to maybe collect twenty dollars here, thirty dollars there, the excuses, the no-shows, the constant, snake-headed presence of them in his life . . .

"I don't want your fucking money."

He took up his bat and slowly got to his feet, Marilys raising her eyes and then asking in a breathless monotone, "What are you going to do."

Nothing. Whether it was some perverse residual feelings he still had for her or just a failure of nerve on his part, he would do nothing.

He reached for his coat.

When it became apparent that she was in no physical danger this night, she added more softly, "Milton, I made a mistake. I'm sorry." And then a PPS as he turned toward the door: "How's Sofia?"

When Victor Acosta finally left the Bryant Motor Lodge at four o'clock in the morning, there was a three-woman, two-man smackdown going on in a corner of the parking lot and Milton, who had already been waiting on him for two hours, maybe longer, understood that he had no choice right now but to remain in his car. Which, he figured, was probably just as well, since

452

he'd been hitting the thermos steady and was temporarily too drunk to not fuck this up.

While Victor was busy stowing his gear in the Range Rover, Milton, in hopes of sobering up, put all four windows down and the AC on full blast and then rolled out of the lot directly onto the southbound New England Thruway, driving from the Bronx to Queens to Brooklyn. Thirty-five minutes later, freezing but still wasted, he pulled up across the street from Victor's apartment building on Palmetto Street in Bushwick and settled in, taking one last nip of the 'Treuse to chase the chill.

He didn't have to wait long, Victor's Range Rover slow-cruising right past him while he was still feeling around the floor after dropping the thermos cap. At first, it looked almost too easy, Victor parking the Ranger one block ahead, then walking back in his direction. But when Milton stepped from the car he immediately fell back against the driver's door, weakly waved his bat at the sky, then hinged forward to puke into the roadway as Victor, wide-berthing the mess, made it to his front door unmolested and disappeared into the building.

Just as well, just as well.

When his vomiting came down to a few

ropy strands of saliva and his eyes began to lose their strained filminess, he slowly raised himself up and took a few raw breaths.

Just as well . . .

Then, unbidden: *I don't want your fucking money.*

Why did he say that to her? It was *his* fucking money. She might have scammed him out of it, but he had said *your money,* as if she had taken his sense of self along with the cash. Had date-raped his brain. And he had just walked out the door, don't mind the wet spot.

He slammed the bat into his own car door, was about to do it again, do anything to fend off his other memory of tonight — Sofia's shell-shocked silence, her stunned poke-hole of a face — when the magnified clack of a turned latch abruptly brought him back, Milton looking up to see Victor returning to the street with a small dog.

It was like he was asking for it.

Like he was insisting on it.

The dog, some kind of small pug, immediately squatted and pissed on the pavement, the streetlight too bright right there to risk anything. But when Victor turned the corner, Milton, keeping his distance and sticking tight to the shadowed building fronts, followed. They walked in a two-man

454

stagger nearly the length of the street before Victor, absorbed in his dog's doings, came to a complete stop with his back to him.

The distance between them was next to nothing, but he was still too wasted to close in fast, and the broadcasted wheeze of his lungs, the sloppy scrape of his bat against the pavement had Victor fully turned around and reaching for something on his belt before Milton could make contact.

And then came the invisible jolt to his torso, a white wallop of phosphorescent pain emanating from somewhere between his left hip and armpit that lifted him like a backhand into the side of a building. But he was too drunk and too determined to let it distract him for long, and after shutting down what needed to be shut down, Milton once again began to close in. The dazzling burn in his side made it difficult for him to really bring the bat around like he wanted, and the lead-pipe impact of the heavy-booted side kick that Victor delivered to his thigh at some point didn't help, but when he was done, Carmen's brother lay curled at his feet, blood bubbling from his nostrils each time he took a breath, an ivory shard of bone that had broken through the sleeve of his shirt winking in the moonlight.

By the time Milton managed to circle

around and slowly drive past the scene, a small crowd had already formed: dope fiends, joggers, dog walkers, and what have you, everyone on their cells, either calling out or making iPhone videos, the flashers of an approaching ambo lighting up the street like a midway. From the car, he spotted his bloodied bat lying up against the curb, but there was nothing he could do about that now.

It wasn't until an hour later, while standing outside the cage-gate of his house and woozily patting himself down for the keys, that he finally noticed the dual Taser darts still buried between his ribs, their attached wires dangling down his side like extruded nerves.

CHAPTER 15

There were six people in the visitors' waiting room outside the OR of the Maimonides Medical Center: Billy, Carmen, Bobby Cardozo, a detective from the 8-0 Squad, and three of Victor and Richard's friends — gym rats, by the look of them — everyone waiting for Victor to come out from under the knife. The damage — a shattered left humerus, a fractured right collarbone, the left lung pierced by the lowest and smallest of his three broken ribs — was gruesome, the only good news being that the actor had stayed away from his head.

"Bobby, can you get prints off the bat?" Billy asked Cardozo, whose black eyes, goatee, and kettle-drum gut made him look like a villain in a silent movie.

"We're sending it to the lab this afternoon. So, hopefully."

Richard Kubin came into the waiting room with a vending-machine coffee, his anger making him look broader and taller than Billy had ever seen him.

"Your friend . . ." Cardozo began.

"My husband."

"He carried a Taser?"

"You would too if you saw where he worked."

"I'm just asking."

"Look, we know who did this," a short, red-bearded weight lifter said.

They didn't, but Billy did, as did Carmen, who, rather than browbeating Cardozo and the entire hospital staff, was sitting silently on a tatty couch, staring at her hands.

"These little mutants from the Knickerbockers," the bearded guy said. "They sport-hunt us like we're their personal buffalo herd."

"What are you talking, gay bashers?" Cardozo reared back. "You sure? I pass your friend Mr. Acosta on the street, I'm not thinking gay."

"Meaning what," Richard snapped.

"I'm just saying," Cardozo retreated.

"Saying what."

Cardozo threw Billy a quick helpless look, then stepped away to regroup.

At first, Billy didn't understand why he was refraining from volunteering information about the stalker in order to help

458

refocus the investigation. And then he did: simply put, he felt ashamed.

As far as he knew, they had all been victimized, but somehow over the course of the last few weeks, the innocence of the people living under his roof had gradually come to feel tainted, as if they all in some way deserved what had been happening to them. It was a classic reaction, he knew, the victim falling into self-loathing and self-blame, but now that the family contagion had reached out and claimed Victor, he felt as guilty as if he had swung the bat himself. And Carmen — sitting there so uncharac-teristically withdrawn — had to be feeling something of the same.

"These kids . . ." Cardozo said, taking out his notepad.

"Kids?"

"These individuals. Any names? Street tags?"

"There's two," said another friend, wearing a Bucknell T-shirt. "I know them by sight."

"And the other one," the weight lifter said. "The moron with the hat."

"How about this," Cardozo said, stowing his pad. "Why don't you all come in, we'll set you up with some photo trays, then we can do a ride-by around the Knickerbockers, see if you can maybe make some IDs that way."

"You know what?" Bucknell said. "Forget it. We'll take care of it ourselves."

"How about you don't," Billy volunteered.

"Do you know how many assault complaints we filed with your precinct this year?" Bucknell wheeling on Billy. "Do you know how many times I've been in that building? You people just don't give a shit."

"First I'm hearing about it," Cardozo said.

"Exactly."

Billy looked to Richard, hoping that he could help cool out his friends, and saw that the anger in his eyes was beginning to give way to exhaustion and sorrow. Reaching through the scrum, Billy took his arm and steered him to a second couch, directly opposite his wife.

"He'll be all right," Billy said.

"How do you know?"

"You know how I know? I'll tell you how I know." Billy hesitated, then: "The nurses' station. If Victor was in any kind of touch-and-go situation, all those nurses over there, they'd of been throwing our crowd a lot of looks by now, trying to figure out how to handle us in case things turn out bad. And I'm just not picking up that vibe from them, so relax."

It was total bullshit, but it seemed to do the job, Richard faintly nodding, then sliding back deeper into the cushions. Nurses: Billy stole another peek at his wife, not six feet away from them but still so pulled into herself that he doubted she had heard one word of his nonsense.

"So when are the twins coming?" he asked Richard.

"What?"

"When are . . ."

"Ten days," he said, then, sitting up: "Jesus."

"I'll come over," Carmen said dully. Raising her eyes to him, she added, "Every day."

Leaving his wife and Richard behind, Billy went along with everyone else to the 8-0. Once there, unable to bear withholding information about the family nightmare any longer, he took Bobby Cardozo aside.

"I need to talk to you about something."

"About what, the gay thing?" Cardozo whispered. "I said the guy didn't look gay. What the fuck, it was a compliment."

Billy's cell rang — Carmen — Billy stepping away from Cardozo to take the call.

"Hey," her voice as flatlined as it was when he left her.

"What's going on?"

461

"He's out of surgery. It went OK."

"Good. Excellent."

"I'm sleeping here tonight," she said.

"OK."

"I need you to do me a favor. When you get home make up a bag with some clothes and my meds. You know which ones?"

"The Traz and the Cymbalta."

"The Traz and the Abilify."

"When did you go on Abilify?"

"Can you just do it for me? Give it to Millie, let her take your car, punch in the address on the GPS for her, and send her over."

"All right, I'll be home in about two hours."

"Thank you."

"Carmen, what's wrong?"

"What's wrong?"

"I mean besides. You've been in a trance for days."

The silence on the other end was so absolute that Billy thought she had hung up on him.

"Hello?"

"Just, not now, OK?" she said, then added, "I'm sorry," sounding like she meant it.

Billy found Cardozo pulling up mug shots on a desk monitor.

"This kid here?" he said, tapping a shave-

462

headed teenager with a wandering eye. "He's a stone skull-cracker. Pipes, rebar, a golf club one time. Told me that he didn't like guns because they could get you in trouble."

"Just hold off on all that for a bit," Billy said, pulling up a chair. "You need to hear this."

It took close to half an hour for him to lay it all out: the accosting of his son, the abduction of his father, the red assault on his porch, the entire systematic and now expanded tormenting of his family.

"I don't see it," Cardozo said. "With all the three-legged meat eaters we got running around this precinct? I'm shopping local."

Yasmeen rang him at home as he was sorting through Carmen's side of the medicine chest.

"You called me yesterday?" she said.

"I did?" Then, remembering the world as it was before this morning: "Yeah, I did."

"What's going on?"

"I need to talk to you."

"Again?"

"Just . . ."

"Jesus, I talk to you more than my husband. What are you trying to do, get back with me?"

"Right."

"Just say, we'll get a room."

"Cut it out."

"With how stressed I am? No shit, let's go."

"I seriously need to talk to you."

"You don't even have to kiss me."

"Where are you going to be today," Billy said. "I'll come to you."

"Redman's nuts. *I* shot Eric Cortez? Are you on drugs?"

They were sitting on a bench overlooking the playground in Riverdale where Yasmeen's younger daughter, Simone, was trying to master double Dutch with some other girls.

"You know what? I don't like to talk about people, but since he's already talking about me? I think Redman's smoking his own product."

"What product," Billy shielding his eyes from the unfamiliar midday sun.

"Embalming fluid. Dipping his cigarettes in that shit. It's like eating your brain with an ice cream scoop."

"Redman doesn't smoke."

"Then maybe you're doing dip. What the fuck, *I* shot Eric Cortez?"

Billy sat with his arms draped along the

top slat of the bench, listening to the kids behind the mesh fence shrieking as if they were about to be butchered.

"You're drinking like you want to kill yourself, Yasmeen, why is that."

"Because I already said to you I'm going through life changes and I'm depressed. I confessed to you about that. I confided in you about that. And now you're going to use it to accuse me of some bullshit like this? Who do you think you are?"

Billy slumped forward on the bench, his head in his hands. "Tell me again about your night sweats, how you wake up thinking you're all bloody, how someone's going to hurt your kids," his voice monotone with gloom.

Yasmeen sat there for a moment, her lower face flexing and bulging as if her mouth was stuffed with marbles.

"I tell you what," she said, getting to her feet, "here's what you do. You go to your good buddy in Brooklyn Narcotics and share your, your findings with him, you tell him all about me fucking up the Del Pino investigation, you tell him all about my nightmares and my drinking, you tell him how Cortez being brain-shot just about makes me wet, and then you let him come for me, how's that."

Yasmeen went to the fence, collected her protesting daughter, then walked past him on her way out of the park. "You're like some stranger to me, you know that?"

And then she was gone, Billy sitting there, thinking, So are you. Thinking, So are you all.

After a busted four-hour sleep and a tasteless dinner Billy found himself watching a football game on NFL Classics, his sons in full peewee league gear, cleats to helmets, seated on either side of him. They were all strung out, Billy over everything and the kids just because they had — no, they were — exquisite antennae when it came to in-house agitation.

The game, from 2012, was a great New York Giants come-from-behind victory, 41–34 over Tampa Bay, but when watching these old games, Billy never told his boys the final score in advance; it would be like telling a joke punch line first. Tonight, unfortunately, that meant subjecting them to three Eli Manning second-quarter interceptions with no hope in sight; by the second pick, Carlos began to cry, which got Declan, also on the verge of tears, throwing a punch and hurting his hand on his younger brother's helmet, and before Billy could intervene they were both wailing like paid mourners while blindly trading shots across the bow of his gut.

"What are you hitting him for?" he squawked at Declan. Then, turning to Carlos: "What you crying for?"

Neither kid had the words or the self-control to stop belting the other, which resulted in him pushing them off to the far sides of the couch.

"Everybody stop hitting and crying, all right? Just, please, OK?"

Pausing the game, he waited for them to subside. He knew he should turn the TV off altogether before the third interception sent them completely over the edge, but he also wanted them to hang in there, so that they could experience the thrill of the fourth-quarter comeback. So they all could.

"You guys want to keep watching or do you want to go play?"

"Watch," Declan wept.

"Watch," Carlos said, aping his brother's tragic delivery.

"You sure?"

"Yes."

"You have that new game upstairs you could play."

"Watch," Dec said in a shuddery hush.

"Watch."

"OK, watch," reaching for the remote. Then: "You know what? Let's see it tomorrow instead."

No one protested.

"Tomorrow will be better."

And it would be, Billy intending to fast-forward the DVR'ed version directly to the fourth quarter for them, all joy and no pain.

John MacCormack called an hour later as Billy was coming out of the kids' bedroom after having told them their favorite story, about the time when, as a rookie, he had chased down and subdued a riderless police horse in Times Square — leaving out, as he always did, the most heroic part of the adventure, the fact that he was off-his-ass drunk at the time, otherwise he'd have never been so idiotic as to bolt from his window seat at the bar and start running like a maniac down Broadway.

"Just thought you might want to know," MacCormack said, "Eric Cortez went out of the picture."

"What happened?"

"Pulmonary infection. The fucking guy survives being left outdoors overnight, brain-shot in January weather, then goes and gets pneumonia in a warm hospital three months later."

"So now it's a homicide?"

"So now it's a homicide," MacCormack said. "Just grabbing at straws here, you sure you don't have anything for me?"

"Wish I did," Billy said, surprised by a surge of protectiveness toward Yasmeen.

"All right then."

"Let me ask you, what day was he found?"

"Cortez? The fifth, why?"

"January fifth?"

"Yeah, why?"

"No reason," Billy said. "Thanks for the update."

As soon as he got off the phone with Mac-Cormack he began putting a call through to Yasmeen, then hung up and called her husband instead, Dennis blowing up at him halfway through "Hello."

"What the hell did you say to her today? She came home half out of her mind."

"What did she say I said?"

"She didn't, but what the fuck, Billy, she's just starting to do good again."

"It was nothing, just some bullshit I was thinking I wanted to talk to somebody about, but I shouldn't have picked her. Can you apologize for me?"

"Apologize yourself."

"No, you're right, you're right, I'll call her. Everything OK otherwise?"

469

"Same ol'," Dennis sounding calmer.

"So, the reason I called you, she said you took your family to Florida?"

"Yeah, Boynton Beach, to spend New Year's with my parents. And people say I don't know how to party, can you imagine that?"

"I hear you . . . How long were you down there?"

"From like the thirtieth to the eighth. Why?"

"I was thinking of taking the kids, they've never been."

The thirtieth to the eighth, Billy thinking, Good news for her. Thinking, Fucking Redman. And back to thinking: All Pavlicek, all the time.

He had the option of taking the night off, but he didn't want to be alone, didn't want to think about Pavlicek, Victor, the stalker, his father, or even his wife, and so, with Millie sleeping over and the slapdash 24/7 patrols at least going through the motions, he drove into the city at midnight, hoping, for a change, that the general malice out there would keep him busy until the morning.

But in the way of these things, the night, as of three in the morning, was another dud

— a home invasion on West Forty-sixth Street in which the home invader got his ass beat by the home owner, and a brawl at Complications, a pole-dance club on the West Side Highway where a few visiting Memphis Grizzlies had been throwing back Dom and stuffing hundreds, although none of them were involved in the fight.

The Wheel called as he was driving back across Twenty-third Street to the office.

"We got a stabbing homicide in the Three-five."

"Indoors or out."

"In. Fort Washington and One ninety-first."

"Fort Washington and One ninety-first?" Billy straightened up. "What address."

"I just said."

"The building number, for Christ's sake."

By the time he showed up at Esteban Appleyard's apartment, it was a party: CSU, patrol, Stupak, Butter, and Jimmy Whelan himself, his retired gold shield hanging by a bead chain over a pullover sweatshirt. Jimmy had no business being there, but Billy wasn't going to say anything, and the others bought his expired tin at first sight even though he was wearing flip-flops.

The small dining table in the living room

471

was a tabloid tableau: two abandoned hands of cards, a knocked-over bottle of Tattoo Spiced Rum, three used glasses, and an ashtray bearing the remains of five Kool filter tips and a hollowed-out cigar wrapper that still held shreds of skunk.

The body, belly-down on the carpet in a pool of not quite dried blood, was crammed into a corner of the room as if Appleyard had tried to escape his killers by crawling through the wall. There were multiple stab wounds to his back and buttocks. Rigor had locked his mouth into a savagely wide grin.

As the two CSU techs turned him over, they all saw that he was still holding his last hand, five cards clutched tight in a frozen grip beneath his chin.

"What's he got?" Billy asked.

One of the techs carefully prized the arm away from the body. "Aces and eights. Just like Wild Bill."

"Bullshit," Whelan said.

"Take a look."

Whelan stooped over the body and squinted at the hand.

"A pair of threes," he announced. "You assholes."

"Dead man's hand, baby," the tech laughed.

"Who's Wild Bill?" Stupak said.

Moments later, as the techs started to inventory the frontal devastation, a small intact balloon of intestine began to peep shyly out of a puncture wound above Appleyard's navel, then slowly began to expand, those in the know quickly covering their noses and mouths before it could burst.

Wanting to avoid the explosion of stench, Billy retreated into the bedroom, which, like the rest of the small four-room apartment, had been utterly ransacked — plants torn out of their pots, underwear, shirts, and sweaters hanging from open dresser drawers, along with VHS porn tapes and an upended shoe box that had been filled with small serrated-edged snapshots from Appleyard's childhood in Puerto Rico.

Whelan wandered in and picked up a ripped-out peace lily, the soil that was still clinging to its roots drizzling onto the unmade bed.

"How much money you think he could've hid in this pot, thirteen dollars?"

"You sure this was about the lottery?" Billy asked.

"Of course it was. Fuckin' guy. I told him a thousand times, you heard me yourself."

Whelan picked up one of the old photos fantailed around the shoe box, a black and white of the victim as a little kid standing

473

with his mother by a seawall.

"I swear, when God said he was passing out brains, Appleyard heard 'trains,' didn't want any, and hid under a table."

"Any thoughts on the actors?"

"Yeah," Whelan said, "but not here."

When they left the apartment, the hallway was filled with tenants.

"He's dead?" a neighbor asked Whelan.

"You bet."

"See, I told him," another one said.

Whelan clapped his hands once. "Everybody, just go back home."

"This *is* my home."

"Inside."

"You're not the boss of me."

"Got February's rent together yet, Alvin? How about March?"

"Jimmy, you disrespect me like that?"

"Whoever owes me two months' rent. Inside."

Out on the street, they slipped into Whelan's cigarette-smelling Elantra.

"There's these shitheads, the Alvarez brothers, in 2015 over there," pointing to another prewar across the street, also with a deep H-block entrance. "Out of the blue they've been buddying him up all this last week like a lost cousin."

"Apartment?" Billy writing.

"Fifth floor's all I know. The youngest brother, Marcus, just got back from upstate, Tomas I once caught trying to jimmy a storage lock in my building with a gravity knife."

"So prints are on file."

"You could say that."

"Anybody else?"

"Around here?" Shrugging as he reached for the door handle. "Start with them."

Stepping from the Elantra back out onto the street, Billy wandered to the rear of the car, paused to light a cigarette, then saw the bullet holes in the trunk, moonlight brightening their jagged edges, some curling in, some curling out.

"Come here," he said.

Whelan came around, regarded the constellation of punctures, then lit a cigarette himself.

"Can you pop it, please?"

"You're kidding me."

"Jimmy."

"You think there's something in there?"

Billy stared at him.

"If you want to be a prick about it, get a warrant."

"Sweetpea wasn't even yours."

"I don't know what you're talking about."

"You did it for Redman?"

475

"I don't know what you're talking about."
Then, again, before Billy could say anything
more, "I don't know what you're talking
about."

Deaf to the occasional horns and blind to
the oncoming headlights, Billy took a brief
walk down the center of Fort Washington
Avenue, his hands clasped on top of his
head.

Yasmeen was in Florida when Eric Cortez
was shot. Pavlicek was at the hospital with
his son when Bannion died all over Penn
Station. Sweetpea ended his days in the
boot of Whelan's car. He himself was at a
crime scene in Manhattan when Curtis Taft
was being hog-tied in the Bronx.

Redman had been telling the truth after
all, but only the partial truth. They were all
in on it, but no one was anywhere near the
scene when their own demons had gone out
of the picture.

They had swapped Whites.

Two hours later, as he and Stupak were
escorting Tomas and Marcus Alvarez out of
their apartment house for questioning, the
uncuffed brothers shouting in each other's
face not to say shit, Billy saw that Whelan
had made no effort to move his car from in
front of the building, their entire convoy

having to walk past it in order to get to the waiting van.

MILTON RAMOS

The call from Anita came in as he was sitting on the side of his bed, rewrapping the Ace bandage on his empurpled thigh, Victor's boot print there still so clearly defined on his flesh that he could have accurately ordered him a pair of shoes.

"Milton, your daughter left three messages on your phone. Why aren't you calling her back?"

"I've been drowning in work," he said, reaching for the Chartreuse on his night table. "Is she OK?"

"Other than you not calling her, she's fine."

Milton threw back a shot, got up, and began looking for his car keys. "Is she mad at me for last night?"

"She hasn't said anything."

Dropping to the floor, he felt around beneath the bed. "I have to apologize for my behavior. I was upset."

"It's OK. I just figured with all the terrible stress you have on you right now."

He stopped moving. "What do you mean."

"That gang contract."

"Contract . . ." Crouching there confused, then remembering his story, rising to his knees. "I have to ask you again. Sofia, do you still want her?"

"Do I want her?" Anita sounded unsure of his meaning. "Sure, she's a delight."

"Good," returning to his search.

"Just give me an idea of when you'll be taking her back."

"It's almost over," he said, spotting the car keys in one of his tossed-off shoes.

"I just don't understand why you don't call her."

He was pretty sure he could drive.

The cemetery was one of those unending necropoli that lined the ride into the city from JFK, a crowded mouthful of gray teeth, unkempt and askew. But up close, say, if you found yourself kneeling before a loved one or two or three, it wasn't that bad. And that's where he found himself, in a catcher's squat before the stones of his mother and two brothers, desperate to get his bearings.

He was no great master planner of revenge, no fiendish calculator; he was nothing more than an increasingly violent and out-of-control wreck whose hands shook all the time now from drinking, nothing more than a raging borderline wet-brain, so constantly tired these days that he could barely get in or out of bed. And assuming they had recovered his bat from the scene, it would only be a matter of days before they matched his prints.

In high school, his English teacher didn't think anyone in class could get through *Moby-Dick* without tossing the book out a window, so she had brought in a Betamax tape of the movie, drawn the blinds, and played it on a roll-down screen. Most of the students were bored stupid by the black-and-white film, but not him. He had been riveted by the metal-eyed captain, his blazing doggedness, and in the end, when he went down into the sea strapped to the beast that he had lived to kill, it had struck Milton as the perfect outcome.

And that's how it should end between him and Carmen.

Sofia was with the right people, and this patch of earth, right here among his brothers and his mother, looked so inviting. He was so tired, all the time now. He just had to move fast before he was unable to move at all.

CHAPTER 16

When Billy returned to the funeral home the next morning, Redman and his wife, Nola, were sitting on facing folding chairs across the aisle from each other in the darkened chapel, both staring at the carpet while Rafer flew around the room waving a cosmetic stippling brush in his hand.

"It's ten in the morning," Redman said. "I was expecting you at dawn."

Nola stood up and left.

Billy waited while Redman got to his feet, took the brush back from his son, then lifted him in his arms.

"If I could have, I would have, you better believe that," he finally said. "Fact of the matter is, I can carry a two-hundred-and-fifty-pound body across this room from the prep table to the casket, no problem, but if I go more than a block to buy a beer? I need a walker. End of the day? All I could do was disappear him."

"Could you put Rafer down, please?"

Redman gave him a look as if Billy were about to slap on cuffs.

"I can't talk about this with the kid in your arms," Billy said.

Bending stiffly from the waist, Redman complied, Rafer taking off for his grandfather's cubicle, where the old man was once again playing poker on his computer.

"What do you mean, disappear him," Billy said. "Disappear him how."

"He left here in a casket. Underneath someone else."

"Underneath who."

"That girl you had me bury."

"You did that to her?"

"I did it to him."

All he needed was an exhumation order, find out if Martha Timberwolf had any company beneath her stone. And when the forensics came back on Whelan's trunk, they were bound to find something.

"You knew what Whelan was up to before he did it?"

"I got up one morning, went out back for a smoke, and there's Sweetpea Harris laying in the yard. And that's all I'm saying about it."

"Did you ask him to do it?"

"I said that's all I'm saying about it."

483

"How about the others."

"Which others."

"I want to know who did who."

"Why."

"Why?"

Redman opened a box of cheap hand fans advertising the funeral parlor, then began depositing them on chair seats.

"I'm just curious," Billy said. "Did you embalm him?"

"Either that or let him stink up the joint."

"Jesus Christ, Redman, where's your heart?"

"Where's yours. You pursue this, you'll be taking people away from their kids, so where's yours," he said, walking off before Billy could walk out.

At Maimonides, Victor was asleep in his bed, Richard lying next to him, wide-eyed but withdrawn. On a sofa at the opposite end of the room, Carmen was also asleep, hands curled under her chin, her face pressed so deeply into a cushion that he had to resist moving her head back.

Billy stood against a wall, dutifully stared at the three of them until he thought he would go crazy.

Who did who . . .

Stepping out into the hallway, he called

Elvis Perez.

"Are you in?" he asked.

"For about an hour or so. What's up?"

"Do you still have the tapes from Penn Station?"

"Of course."

"I never took a look at the one under the information boards."

"That's because I told you it's a waste of time."

"I'm leaving now."

"Really, if I thought . . ."

"I'm leaving now."

"Where's Waldo, right?" Perez said, standing over Billy's shoulder as they viewed the rescued tape of the scene beneath the LIRR track information board. "See what I'm saying?"

Billy had to agree: the scrum of plastic-derby-wearing revelers was so tight under the board that when he was finally able to ID his vic, Bannion was already leaving bloody shoeprints on his way to the subway, dead man jogging.

"Where's Waldo in hell," Elvis said.

When Perez left with his partner on a witness interview run, Billy remained at his desk and reran the tape. Again, nothing, just Bannion popping out of the periphery and taking off. There were others coming and going under the board besides Bannion: staggerers, stragglers, latecomers to the party, and those who just wandered away as if having lost interest in getting home. But not one of these wanderers, all leaving the crowd at the same time or just after Bannion made his stumbling dash to nowhere, exhibited any kind of suspect body language, no one running or even walking off at anything more than a dawdling pace, no one even glancing back at the crowd they had just left.

Most of the people whose faces were turned to the camera and could be identified had already been interviewed by Midtown South, including all of Bannion's friends that night. Teams of detectives had either traveled out to Long Island or caught the potential witnesses at their workstations in Manhattan, not one of these sit-downs yielding a single helpful lead.

Billy reran the tape. Then ran it again, this time in slow motion. On his sixth viewing someone caught his eye — one of the commuters, exiting the throng a moment before, not after, Bannion, which made sense given that it must have taken the stupefied vic a moment or two before he realized what had already happened to him.

The figure, its back to the camera as it briefly lingered at the bottom of the frame before leaving the scene altogether, looked like nothing so much as a small, upright bear.

"They finally salvaged the tape," Billy said.

"What tape?" Yasmeen asked from behind her desk in the university security office.

"From Penn Station."

"I thought they had that tape."

"The other one."

"What other one."

Tired of the dance, Billy showed her the printout of the shaggy form walking away from the crime scene before anyone there knew it was a crime scene.

Yasmeen looked at it, then — unconsciously, Billy assumed — glanced at her Tibetan coat draped over an empty chair.

"It was either you or Janis Joplin coming out of that crowd."

"Do you know how many coats like this . . ."

"Don't jerk me around," he said wearily. "Not now, all right?"

She was a long time in responding.

"You have those two little boys," she finally said. "Could you imagine me ever coming up to you like this?"

"I didn't kill anybody, Yasmeen."

"The hell you didn't. And what did we do? Closed ranks and protected your ass."

"It was a justified shoot. I didn't need you to."

"Oh yes you did, cokey boy."

One of the other retired detectives working at the school came into the office and dropped a folder on her blotter, Yasmeen getting to work on it before he even left.

Billy sat there for a while studying the photographs push-pinned into her wall: campus trespassers, a trashed dorm lounge, the facades of problematic East and West Village bars.

"Yasmeen, the story's going to come out one way or another."

"Well, one good story deserves another," she said, flicking the side of her nose.

Billy got up to leave.

"You know, Dennis, he's a good guy, a good dad, I'll give him that . . ."

Billy stood there, waiting for the punch line.

"But I could've been with you all these years, you know? I could have been your wife, Dominique and Simone could have been your daughters."

"I'll give you a week to get a lawyer," he heard himself say.

"You'd do that for me?" she said sweetly, Billy almost positive she was being sarcastic.

"So you say," Carmen said, looking down at the Penn Station printouts spread out on the kitchen table before her.

"So I know," Billy looking at her. "And you know too."

Carmen shifted her gaze from the table to the window. "Do you remember when I couldn't get out of bed for close to three months? What did she do for us."

"This has nothing to do with that."

"No? What's it have to do with?"

"Do I even have to answer that?"

Resting her brow in the heel of her palm, Carmen looked as if she'd rather be any-where else than in this room with this man right now.

"Do I even have to answer that?" Billy pleaded.

"Why did you marry me," she said.

"Why did I what?"

"What did you see in me."

"I don't know. I saw you. Where are we going with this?"

Carmen swept the printouts to the floor. "Jesus, Billy," her voice clotted with tears, "sometimes people just need to be for-given."

489

More cryptic and distance-making shit from his most intimate of intimates, Billy watching her climb the stairs to the bedroom and feeling more isolated on this than ever before.

Three bodies, and so far everyone was either defying him, threatening him, or tossing off pronouncements fit for a Sphinx. Everyone acting like they had his number.

Billy called first Redman, then Whelan, got the machine for both and left the same message: one week to lawyer up. He started to dial Pavlicek's number, then hung up in mid-dial. This one had to be face-to-face.

Not really thinking about what he would see when he walked into the private suite at the Westchester Medical Center in Valhalla, Billy took one look at the patient, then turned and retreated, hoping no one inside had noticed. Out in the hallway, he caught his breath and then reentered, having no choice but to accept that the sallow-skinned, seemingly inert stick figure lying in the bed, with its distant, unresisting eyes, was, still was, John Junior, only six months ago a bear of a young man who'd often had to sidle through doorways.

Speechless, he floated across the room and stood in a corner.

"You know, I was trying to describe to Johnnie here," Pavlicek said, his eyes never leaving his son's face, "what it was like for us back in the nineties, the bust-ass blocks, the gangs, the dope lines going right past the precinct house, that whole rodeo."

He was seated on the side of the bed, one hand on the kid's thigh, the other on his forehead, as if he was afraid his son would start to levitate.

"John," Billy whispered, "I had no idea."

"I'll never forget the day I bought my first building on Faile Street, five thousand dollars, the old guy running down the street with the check in his hand, 'You'll never make a dime!' But then the fun began, remember? All those all-nighters, me, you, Whelan, Redman, Charlie Torreano, God rest his soul . . . Stripping, sanding, uncovering that beautiful wood, the moldings, the sconces, then that morning light coming in . . ."

Billy stepped to the bed and lightly touched Junior's hand, the kid turning his head in response but too deep in his medicated drift to raise his eyes.

"Billy, I swear to you, twenty-six buildings later and nothing ever felt as good to me as rehabbing that first dump on Faile. Well, what the hell, I made my dent."

491

There was no way Billy could bring up what he had come to say, not here and not now.

Pavlicek let him get halfway to the door. "Redman told me that you couldn't drop the bomb on him this morning until he put his kid down," looking at Billy for the first time since he came into the room. "So I can imagine what a bitch this must be for you right now."

"That all can wait," he said.

"For what, Junior to die? You're going to make this into a death watch before you turn me in?"

"What I meant . . ."

"I know what you meant," Pavlicek cut him off. "Just let it happen."

Billy took a seat on the edge of the narrow visitor's bed wedged under the far window, dress shirts and sweaters spilling out of a Gladstone bag on the blanket.

"John, what do I do."

He had always looked up to Pavlicek for guidance; they all did.

"It looks like you're doing it."

"How can you make me carry this?"

"In all honesty? You weren't exactly on my mind at the time," Pavlicek said. "Besides, you did it to yourself. No one told you to go fucking investigate."

492

"You shot Cortez?"

"Do you need me to say it?"

"I do."

"I shot Cortez. I screwed it up, but that there was definitely me."

"I can't sit on three bodies," Billy said. "I can't live with it."

"Then don't."

"Are you serious?"

"Tell me you're not asking for my permission."

But he was, he had been asking for permission all along from everyone: from Carmen, from his father, from Redman and Whelan and Yasmeen, and having finally received it from Pavlicek, no less, he felt the tension go out of his body like air from a slashed tire.

"After Taft in the apartment," Pavlicek said, "you said to me, 'This is how you honor your son?' "

"John, in all fairness . . ."

"You think I don't understand what I did? You think I don't know there's a price to pay? So let me pay it."

"All right," Billy said after a while. "All right."

"Let me be done with it."

"All right," Billy said yet again. Then: "I gave the others a week to lawyer up."

"A week's fine."

John Junior whispered something indecipherable to Billy's ears but not to his father's, Pavlicek slipping a straw through the spout of a water bottle, then raising his son's head just enough for him to take a few sips without drowning. Junior then said something else Billy couldn't understand but that made his father nod in agreement.

The room descended into silence, Billy watching Pavlicek alternately minister to his son and just hang at his side, the ticking of an unseen clock underscoring the stillness.

"Yasmeen's pulling the coke card," Billy finally said. "She said she'd use my history."

"She's full of shit," Pavlicek said without looking at him.

Billy got up, walked over to the bed, then bent down to kiss John Junior's forehead. "I should go."

"What the hell," Pavlicek said. "I made my dent."

MILTON RAMOS

He had always been somewhat indifferent about what he wore to work. Usually it was one of the three sport jackets he had bought from Men's Wearhouse the week he'd been promoted to detective, a white or blue dress shirt, pleated chinos or gabardines, and, always, the black Nike lace-up boots — good for running if the need arose and sober-looking enough to pass inspection. But tonight he was going for the suit, charcoal wool and last worn when he had spoken to Sofia's third-grade class on career day — what a clown show that was — a nice blue knit tie, and a pink broadcloth button-down from his one trip to Brooks Brothers. But he would no sooner swap out the Nikes for any other footwear than he would exchange his Glock for a slingshot.

Just past midnight, after finally nailing the Windsor knot he'd been striving for, he threaded his holster through his belt, slipped his flask into his ankle holster, dropped a mini-bottle of Scope into his inside jacket pocket, and left the house.

Forty-five minutes later, he walked into the Fifteenth Precinct, headed for the desk, and presented his ID to the duty sergeant.

"It's been a while," he said. "Where's the Night Watch office again?"

CHAPTER 17

Tonight's hell mouth seemed to be situated in Union Square, three runs to that area in less than five hours. The first, at one a.m., on Irving Place, involved the discovery of a middle-aged lawyer who had been found nude, bound, and asphyxiated facedown in his own bed, the word ABUSE with either an R or a D at the end — a mystery for the day tour — carved into his back with a scissor blade. The second run, coming in at three, was in response to the theft of a two-hundred-pound bluefin tuna worth seven thousand dollars from the kitchen of a sushi restaurant on Park Avenue South. And the third and hopefully last run of the night, coming in at four-thirty, was a nonfatal double knifing in the park proper, directly beneath the statue of Gandhi, the actor on that one a seventy-five-year-old panhandler, the victims two drunken tourists from Munich who thought it would be a real howl to hand the old piss-bum a pre-euro ten-mark German note instead of a few American dollars.

"You should have seen them, laughing at me like they was giving a cell phone to a monkey," Terence Burns said over a five a.m. Coke in the Sixth Squad interview room a few blocks from the scene. Bug-eyed and sporting a steel-colored goatee, he was nearly doubled over with arthritis but somehow still agile as a cat. "Like I wasn't gonna know what a motherfuckin' deutsche mark looks like. Hell, I seen plenty, I had plenty, and I spent plenty when I was over there with the Fortieth Tank back in sixty-one."

"You were there?" Billy both liking the guy and needing the distraction.

"Didn't I just say that? Had a good time too for most of it," Burns said. "The whores used to call us hamburgers, the white boys, cheeseburgers. They'd see a bunch of us coming to the club, they'd start throwing out all the shitkickers, 'No cheeseburger! Hamburger only!' "

"For real?"

"Oh I'm always for real."

"Another Coke?"

"Fanta if you got it," Burns said. "Grape or orange."

Billy went out of the room to hit the vending machine and returned with a Mountain Dew.

"So what else was going on back then?" he asked.

"What else? You don't know your history? You don't know about Checkpoint Charlie?"

"I heard of it."

"You don't know nothing about the tank standoff with the Russians? I was a machine gunner, they had me set up outside the hatch of a M-48 staring right into the cannon of a T-55 for sixteen motherfuckin' hours, couldn't have been more than seventy-five yards away. I swear, as scared as I was? If I hadn't been so drunk, we'd of had World War Three right then and there."

Returning to the park to pick up a copy of the Crime Scene Unit report, Billy noticed that the small trucks from upstate and New Jersey had begun to arrive for the Union Square Greenmarket, the vaguely hippieish farmers dragging out their folding tables and canopies in the predawn dark. He also saw one of his supplementals, Milton Ramos from Dennis Doyle's squad in the 4-6, standing on the edge of the scene watching the techs stow their gear.

Billy had been trying to keep his distance from the guy all tour; like a number of one-offs, there was something not quite right about him. He seemed to be both on edge and spacey, plus Billy was pretty sure that he'd been slipping off fairly steadily to drink. Not that Ramos would have been the first detective on Night Watch to sweeten the long hours and boredom that way; Feeley's eyes often looked like two cherries floating in buttermilk, but that was Feeley.

The CSUs, both female, were hunched over the hood of their van now, sorting through their report forms.

"So how was the great tuna robbery," Billy asked Ramos. "Anything fishy about it?"

"I think it was an inside job," Ramos said flatly.

He was short and thick but too powerfully built to be called fat, his slitted features hidden beneath thick brows and a permanently impassive expression. Billy had him pegged as a complete loner, on the job and off, the type of uncommunicative humorless near blank that made everyone in his home squad uncomfortable.

"You know," Ramos said, looking around the park, "I used to work midnights my first two years, but now? I don't know if I could handle it anymore. How does your wife put up with it?"

"She's a nurse," Billy said, "she can put up with anything short of me having a second family."

"Oh yeah? What kind of nurse?"

"ER, but over the years she's done it all."

"Done it all, seen it all . . . Easygoing?"

Billy gave him a look. "Philosophical about things," he lied.

"Philosophical." Ramos nodded, still looking away. "Shit happens."

"Something like that."

Billy saw Stupak, coming from the Irving Place homicide, enter the park and head toward the tents and tables, waiting for someone to open up.

He raised his cell to call her.

"She always want to be a nurse?" Ramos asked.

"What?"

"Your wife."

"What is this, an interview?"

"No, I'm sorry, I just . . . My wife? She passed seven years ago."

"I'm sorry to hear that," Billy said, killing the call.

"Yeah. Hit-and-run."

"I'm sorry."

"We have a daughter, she's eight," he said, then: "If the mother's dead and you say 'we,' is it 'We *have* a daughter' or 'We *had* a daughter'?"

The guy was definitely sauced, but he was talking about losing his wife.

"Grammar wasn't my strong suit," Billy said.

"You have kids?"

"Two boys."

"Two boys, double the trouble."

Billy impatiently checked the time, six-fifteen in the a.m., the crime scene techs still hunched over the hood working up their reports.

"Back when we were kids?" Ramos moved closer to him. "Me and my brother, we were the terror of the neighborhood."

"Oh yeah?" Billy tried to call Stupak again. "What neighborhood was that?"

Ramos either didn't hear him or didn't want to answer.

"What are you doing," Billy asked Stupak.

"Where are you?"

"By the Gandhi statue waiting on CSU. Bring me a coffee, cream and sugar, and a buttered roll."

"You know," Ramos plowed on, "before she died, my wife was an X-ray technician at Beth Abraham for five years, so I know a little about nurses. And, the little I know is that they're not like cops, you know what

502

I'm saying? You don't become a nurse because your mother and grandmother were nurses, so forgive me for getting personal and you can just tell me to mind my own business, but I'm curious, why do you think your wife became a nurse?"

"Now I'm supposed to say, 'Because she likes to help people'?"

"Not at all, I was just wondering if there was any one moment where she, you know, like an event or something . . ."

Billy gave him another long look.

"Like with me," Ramos said quickly, "I never thought I was going to be a cop, I was a troubled kid, a fighter. But when I was seventeen, I lost my mother and two brothers all like within a month's time, and I needed a place to hide."

"What do you mean, hide."

"Not hide, more like I needed a structure, you know, be part of something that would give me all the dos and don'ts, keep me from going over to the dark side. It took a few years, but here I am."

"Here you are," Billy said, not liking this guy at all, him and his copious tragedies.

One of the techs finally came over, peeled off a copy of the report for Billy, then headed off to the greenmarket with her partner.

"Beautiful, right?" Ramos said, as the sun began to paint the tops of the ancient office buildings at the western edge of the square.

Billy loathed sunrises; he knew them as cruel mirages, each one a false promise that a tour had come to its end when, in fact, depending on the time of year, there were anywhere from one to three hours left for that phone to ring with a fresh disaster. Sunrises, like Ramos here, made him tense.

They made him feel fucked with.

"Listen to me," Billy said abruptly. "You've had liquor on your breath all night."

Frowning, Ramos looked away.

"I'm not going to write you up, but I don't ever want to see you on my tour again. In fact, you can take off right now, I'll sign you out when I get back to the office."

At first, Ramos didn't respond, his frown deepening into a scowl, but then he began nodding his head as if having come to some kind of decision.

"I apologize," he said quietly, turning back to Billy and handing over the keys to the squad sedan, "and I appreciate the courtesy."

Ramos walked off toward the Fourteenth Street subway entrance without another word, Billy watching him all the way, wondering if he had been too hard on the guy.

Then, tired of waiting for Stupak to deliver his breakfast, he wandered over to the market himself, where he discovered that almost all the cops involved in the three wee-hour local felonies were now cruising the food stalls as intensely as if they were at a gun show.

Walking into the house with two biodegradable bags filled with agave-sweetened muffins, crullers, and doughnut holes, it seemed to Billy that the only one up and about was the six-year-old, Carlos sitting in the dining room and eating the breakfast he had made for himself: a teacup of orange juice and an unthawed Eggo.

"Where's your mother?" Billy asked, dropping the waffle into the toaster. "Is she still sleeping?"

"I don't know."

"Where's your brother?"

"At Theo's house. He slept there on a sleepover."

Through the kitchen window Billy saw his father sitting on a lawn chair beneath one of the TARU cameras in the backyard, the old guy, as usual, reading the *New York Times.*

"How's Grandpa today?"

"I don't know," Carlos said, then: "A

teacher in my school got quit."

"What do you mean, got quit?"

"He's not a teacher anymore."

"Oh yeah? What teacher."

"Mr. Lazar."

"Mr. Lazar quit? Or got fired?"

"I don't know."

"Why?" He couldn't imagine that the school would can him for being gay.

"He hurt some guy," Carlos said.

"What do you mean, hurt. Hurt what guy?" Billy trying to remember the name of Lazar's potential blackmailer.

"He got took away," Carlos said.

"Lazar?"

"Mr. Lazar."

"Who took him away?"

"The police guys at release time. I'm going to the basement. Dec said there's a mouse."

Billy went up to his bedroom, quietly crept past his wife, her flank beneath the sheets swelling and dipping like a chain of dunes, and stowed his weapon and handcuffs in the closet. Then, intending to call the Yonkers PD to find out about Lazar, he went back down to the kitchen.

A few minutes later, while he was still on hold with the Second Precinct Detective Squad, the doorbell began to chime. Assuming the callers were either evangelists or Con Ed, and worried that a second round of chimes would wake Carmen, he stepped briskly into the hallway and swung the door wide to see Milton Ramos standing on his doorstep, stone-faced and thick as a stump, his razored eyes staring past Billy and into the house as if he weren't even there.

Thinking that he was probably stuporously drunk by now and angry about having been booted from Night Watch three hours earlier, Billy was about to try to talk him down when Ramos reached behind his back — Billy vaguely thinking for some kind of letter of complaint — and came out with a Glock.

"Where is she," Ramos said.

Billy took a step outside the house, then made a big show of holding up his hands for the TARU cameras, though he had no idea whether anyone was even monitoring them.

"Where is she," Ramos repeated, muzzle-shoving Billy back inside as far as the living room while efficiently patting him down with his free hand even though they were both still in motion.

So, not stuporously drunk.

"Ramos." He couldn't remember his first name. "What are you doing?"

"Where is she."

This time Billy heard the question. "Where's who."

"Your wife."

"My wife?"

"Your wife, your wife, your wife," he said, as if fed up with a blockhead.

"Hang on, hang on, I'm the one who gave you grief."

Done with the basement, Carlos wandered into the room and without looking at either Ramos or his father, took a seat on the couch and picked up the remote.

"Hey, buddy, not now," Billy said, his voice starting to float. "Go outside."

"He stays," Ramos said, letting the kid settle in and find his show.

"Look, just say," Billy struggling not to plead, "what do you want."

"I told you already," Ramos said. Then, tilting his chin to the sound of footsteps coming from above, "She's up there? Call her down."

"She still doesn't recognize me."

Ramos was addressing Billy but his eyes were on Carmen, sitting across the room from him as stiff as a pharaoh, her own gaze fixed on the floor. "How can that be."

Carlos, absorbed in his cartoons, was sitting alongside Ramos on the couch now, the automatic hidden beneath a throw pillow between them.

"What do you need the kid for," Billy said, striving for an offhand tone. "Just let him come to me."

Ignoring Billy, Ramos leaned forward to get Carmen to look at him. She wouldn't.

"But you remember Little Man, right?" he said.

"You're Milton," Carmen whispered dully.

"Maybe I'm Edgar."

"Edgar's dead," she said in that same downcast hush.

"So you know," he said.

Billy, barely listening, finally became aware that there was a real conversation going on, neither Ramos nor his wife raising their voices.

"My whole family, in the ground, where you put them," Ramos said to her, "and all these years I never knew why."

Carlos half-stood to reach for the remote again, Ramos slowly raising a hand to grab him in case he decided to bolt, but the kid fell back into the cushions on his own.

"Milton, I'm right in front of you, I'm right here," Carmen's voice, despite the danger, still jarringly flat. "Please don't hurt my son."

"He's not going to hurt him," Billy said lightly, his heart blowing like a bellows. "He's got a daughter of his own, right?"

The sound of the back door opening had Ramos half-rising, the automatic now down at his side. But at the sight of Billy Senior standing in the doorway, ruffled sections of the weekend paper tucked under his arm, he eased himself back down, slipping the gun once again beneath the pillow.

"What are you coming so early for?" Billy Senior said, stepping into the den. "I'm on nights this week. Didn't they tell you?"

"I just came by to visit your son," Ramos said easily. "I'll be back for you later."

"Well, see you then, my friend." Billy's father gave a short wave and left the room the same way he came in.

At first Billy was baffled, but then he realized that his father had been talking to his replacement driver, and that Ramos was the one who had been torturing them for weeks.

Milton, she had called him.

There was a glass snow globe from Jiminy Peak on the windowsill, a brass candlestick on a side table, the snow globe closer but still too far away.

"Tell me why you did it," Ramos said.

Carmen tried to raise her eyes to Carlos, couldn't. "Milton, I'm scared to look at him. Please."

"Carlos, buddy, come on over to me," Billy said. "Ramos, be a good guy, just let him come."

"Tell me why you did it."

"I never meant to," she said. "You have to believe that."

"Ramos, be a good guy . . ."

"Why."

"Ramos, you do something here, how much time do you think you'll ever have to be with your daughter? She's already lost her mother, you told me yourself."

"Why."

"Because he broke my heart," Carmen said, her voice barely carrying across the room.

"He what?" Ramos cocked his head, draped an arm atop Carlos's shoulders.

"Think it through," Billy said, eyes back to roaming for weapons.

"Broke my heart."

"Broke your heart," Ramos said. "He got you pregnant?"

"No."

"But he was fucking you." More a question than a statement.

Carlos started to fidget under the weight of his arm, but Ramos was too absorbed to even notice.

"Be cool, buddy," Billy said to his son.

"He never even looked at me but once," Carmen said.

Out the window, Billy saw a fleet of patrol cars and a Yonkers ESU van rolling up to the house, their presence, prayed for earlier, now heightening his sense of danger.

"I was fifteen years old," Carmen said heavily. "They came up to me on the stoop, he had just hurt my feelings, I was mad, and I said what I said."

Astonishingly, understandably, Carlos fell asleep against Ramos's shoulder.

"You were fifteen, he had just hurt your feelings . . . And you just said what you said," Ramos recited to himself. "Hurt your *feelings*? That's it?"

"You want a better story?" Carmen softly crying now. "I don't have one."

The house phone rang; hostage negotiators for sure, Billy knew, no one making a move to answer it.

"You know something?" Ramos said to Carmen, his voice filled with wonder. "I believe you. Fifteen years old . . . I don't know what I was expecting to hear all these years."

The fax line began to ring in the den, followed by Carmen's cell phone in the hallway.

"Would it be too little for me to say that I pray for him every day of my life?" she asked listlessly.

"Yeah," Ramos getting to his feet, the Glock rising in his fist, "it would."

Before Billy could launch himself, his father reappeared in the doorway, this time with his ancient .45 double-gripped and leveled at the back of Ramos's head. When Ramos wheeled to the threat, then kept coming, Billy Senior fired, although the fucking thing might as well have had a BANG flag pop out. Billy lunged for the snow globe on the windowsill, then giant-stepped forward and cracked it against Ramos's near temple, sending him milk-eyed to the floor, the side of his face shining with viscous liquid and glitter.

For a moment, Carmen just stood there as if still lost in whatever they had been talking about; then, snapping out of it, she scooped Carlos from the couch, screamed, *"Billy, come!"* and when he wouldn't — his father was in the house too — remained in the doorway, her legs trembling like jackhammers, until he shoved her out of the house, toward the cops.

Having no idea where the Glock had gone, Billy snatched his father's .45 out of his hands, then dropped down to straddle Ramos's broad back, the sheer breadth of it stretching the tendons in his groin.

Billy Senior headed up the stairs.

"Dad!" Billy yelled, but the old man kept climbing.

With all the phones in the house continuously ringing as if to announce a royal wedding — all the phones except, strangely, Billy's own — Ramos began to come around, his eyes slowly opening and closing like something in a terrarium. Billy pressed the .45 hard into the nape of his neck, then searched him for his cuffs. Nothing.

He had to get to a phone and give Yonkers the green light to come on in before he lost control of the situation, but he couldn't risk rising up with Ramos unsecured, couldn't risk him seeing the barrel-plugged gun full-on and recognizing it for what it was, couldn't risk him finding his own live piece somewhere in the room.

"There's like a fucking army out there, OK?" Billy said, trying to keep the tremble out of his voice. "So just take it easy, OK?"

Ramos winced, then slightly, effortlessly, shifted beneath Billy's weight, Billy knowing right then that he wasn't physically strong enough to keep him down if it came to that.

"Milton, right? Milton, think of your

daughter, OK? Just think of your daughter and everything is going to be OK, OK?"

Ramos was fully alert now, but he made no further effort to move, just lay there with the side of his face half-buried in the high nap of the carpet, staring off as if thinking about something unrelated.

"Your daughter, what's her name," Billy chattered. "Tell me her name."

Clearly the calmer of the two, Ramos continued to stare off, Billy's bulk and the pressure of the muzzle no more distracting than pecking birds on the back of a rhino.

"Come on, Milton, tell me her name."

Ramos cleared his throat. "If somebody in your will is down as your kid's guardian," he said, his voice half-muffled by the pile, "and you go to jail instead of dying, do they still get the kid?"

"Yeah, sure," Billy said automatically, ducking then swiveling his head in a low search for the cast-off automatic.

"Or does jail throw the whole guardian arrangement out the window."

Billy thought he saw what might be the gun lying deep under the couch, but it could just as easily have been one of the kids' toys.

"She likes it out there with her aunt," Ramos continued. "I don't want her going to foster care."

"Sure," Billy babbled. "She stays wherever you decide."

"What do you know," Ramos said calmly, then threw Billy off his back as easily as doing a push-up.

The Glock, now pointed at Billy, had been under Ramos the whole time Billy had been riding him.

"Over there," Ramos said. "On the table."

Billy did as he was told, putting his father's gun on the low coffee table.

"The fucking thing's plugged anyhow," Ramos added.

If he knew that all along, Billy thought dreamily, *and his own live piece was right under his gut . . .*

"We can get out of this, no problem," Billy said. "Just let me pick up the phone. Or pick it up yourself."

"Turn to the wall, please?"

Billy did as he was told, so stupid with fear he felt high.

"Did you know?" Ramos asked him from behind.

"Did I know what."

"She never told you," Ramos marveled.

"Tell me what," Billy said, then: "So tell me now. I want to know."

"Never said a word . . ."

As fine cracks in the wall paint, inches

from his face, imprinted themselves on his brain, as the hell choir of endlessly ringing phones faded to a weak, sickly carousel tune in Billy's ears, Ramos took two steps back.

"You see?" his voice tearing up blackly. "All these years, and you fucking people, you just sail on, sail on."

Billy tried to shut himself down and just let it happen, but then he heard Ramos stepping back farther. Then farther. Then heard the front door swing open, the murderously pregnant silence out there rushing into the house like a tornado.

He wasn't sure what he experienced first, the staggered report of the volley or the sight of Ramos charging the ESU cops with Billy Senior's dummy gun. Either way the outcome was the same.

Either way the phones finally stopped ringing.

As the house filled with footsteps and radio squawk, Billy, intent on finding his cell phone, tuned out the calming voices, shrugged off the reaching hands that were screwing with his concentration.

"Where did it go."

"Where'd what go, Billy," someone said.

"My goddamn phone, I just had it this morning."

"It's in your front pocket," the voice said. "Why don't you come sit down."

Pulling out his cell, Billy saw that there was someone on the line.

"Who's this."

"Graves, is that you?" a familiar voice said.

"I asked who this is," Billy said, finally allowing someone to guide him to a chair.

"Evan Lefkowitz, Second Squad."

"You're calling me?"

"Actually, you called me, us, about an hour ago, then left the line open," Lefkowitz said. "We've been listening in ever since."

"Hey, while I have you?" Billy said brightly, waving off the hovering EMTs. "I was talking to my son earlier . . . What's the deal with Albert Lazar?"

A new call came in while the medics were debating whether to shoot him up with three mikes of sodium nitroprusside or let his blood pressure come down on its own.

"Hey, Billy, Bobby Cardozo from the Eighty Squad. We finally got a match on the prints from the bat."

"Good," Billy said, watching the needle go in.

"Are you sitting down? Because you're not going to believe your ears."

By the time they finally laid eyes on each

other in the trauma room of Saint Joseph's, Billy was so dizzy from the Nitropress, Carmen so bombed on Ativan, that for a while all they could do was stare.

"Who's got the kids?"

"Millie," she said, then: "Billy, I'm so sorry."

In the ensuing stoned silence, fragments of her conversation with Ramos began to revisit him.

"You knew he'd be coming for you?"

"I knew something would be coming for me," she said. "I just didn't know what."

Billy nodded, then nodded some more. "So," clearing his throat, "who's Little Man?"

It took two days of her pretty much sleeping around the clock before she was prepared to answer the question, Carmen announcing her readiness on the third afternoon by coming downstairs in a long plain white nightgown, silently drinking two cups of coffee, then inviting him back upstairs.

Once they were inside the semi-darkened bedroom, Carmen immediately slipped back under the covers. But Billy, intuiting that she might need some breathing room for whatever was to come, opted for the lone chair, lugging it across the room from its spot beneath the far window to the side of the bed.

"When I was fifteen," she began, "I would've done anything, anything to have Rudy Ramos like me, just like me. You have no idea what I thought of myself back then. My father was so rotten, such a lousy human being, and my mother was his dishrag. Then my father left her for another woman and moved to Atlanta. Which was good, I thought, because now it would get better between us, but she just, overnight, turned into this sour old widow. I would be like, 'Mommy, be happy, you're free,' but no, she just, 'Who'd want me now,' I mean, she was good-looking, thirty-seven years old, but she shut herself down, started yelling at me and Victor nonstop over nothing, anything, just never let up . . ."

Despite the marathon hours she had spent recuperating in this room, Billy thought he had never seen her look so exhausted, her eyes like swollen almonds beneath half-mast lids.

"And I knew Rudy, Little Man everybody called him, from the building and from school, not 'knew him,' he was a year ahead of me, but . . . And I didn't think about him all that much, then one day I just did

and I couldn't stop, it was like I had suffered a stroke, but I was nothing to him,
just some ghost of a girl who lived where he
lived and went to Monroe . . . He was a big
deal on the basketball team, and between
games and practices he'd hardly ever leave
school before five o'clock, and a lot of those
days I'd find things to do in the after-school
program so I could go home when he did. I
mean, I was so fucked up that I wouldn't
even walk on the same side of the street as
him, but I'd always manage to enter the
building when he did so we'd go up the
stairs at the same time, and I hated that I
lived one flight below him because if I lived
on his floor or the one higher then that
would be one more flight I'd have to be near
him, just day after day like that, agonizing
over how maybe tomorrow I should walk in
front of him instead of behind him, behind
him instead of in front of him . . . And his
bedroom was right above mine, 3F and 4F,
and I'd hear him walking around above my
head and sometimes he'd be doing himself,
and the bedsprings would creak and I'd lay
down in my own bed and . . ."

"Whoa, whoa."

"Billy, please, let me tell you."

"Carmen, I can't hear this."

"Why? You're the man I love, the father of

my children, and I'm telling you things about me that I never could before."

"OK, OK, Jesus."

"What, are you jealous? He's been dead more than twenty years."

"Don't be ridiculous," Billy scoffed, thinking, She's been cheating on me with this kid, walking around with him in her head since the day they met.

Then as quick as the feeling had come down on him it lifted, Billy recognizing that what was really getting to him was not jealousy but the realization that if he hung in for this right now, that baffling and invisible dragon he'd been protecting her from all these years might finally begin to take on form and he might not to be able to handle its appearance.

"Are you angry at me?" she said. "Do you want me to stop? I'll stop, I will, just tell me to."

"Don't be ridiculous," he repeated.

"I'm serious, Billy, I will."

"I'm serious, too," he said, then forced himself to add, "I want to hear it all."

For a long moment, she looked at him like the liar he was, then carried on.

"It took me maybe two months before I had the courage to say something to him, even just bullshit, and I decided this one day, I was going to say, 'Your sweater's so fly.' I thought about saying 'so tight,' 'so dope,' 'so gangsta,' 'ill,' 'phat,' 'snap,' 'the bomb,' '*da* bomb,' but I liked 'fly' the best, and at lunch I finally went up to him in the cafeteria, but instead of saying, 'Your sweater's so fly,' I was nervous and I said, 'My sweater's so fly,' and the kids at his table heard it and they all started laughing, and he was, he said, 'Your sweater's so fly?' but looking at them not at me, 'I'm happy for you,' still looking at them, like to get their approval, and in that moment when he looked at them instead of me, with that stupid grin on his face? I saw him for what he was, a self-centered immature boy with a little bit of a cruel streak. But I had been in love, so the realization hit me like a train . . . I don't know if I felt like I actually *hated* him? But God, did he put a hole in my chest that day."

Carlos came into the room, climbed into bed, curled into Carmen's side, and quickly fell asleep. Although his son still hadn't said a word about the other day, he'd been sleeping, since then, almost as much as his mother.

"Later, after school, I saw him go into our building and I didn't want to go inside, I didn't want to walk up the stairs with him, didn't want to be in my room and hear his creaky bed over my head, so I just sat on the stoop remembering his face when he said that, 'Your sweater's so fly?' not even giving me the consideration of eye contact. And I'm just sitting there like that, feeling more and more humiliated, more and more like an invisible nothing, and then at one point I looked up and I saw these two guys coming towards our building, and the way they were carrying themselves made me nervous. Hoodies, sunglasses on a cloudy day, hands in pockets, they looked like surveillance photos of themselves, and then they stopped a few feet away, had a conversation, then one of them came up to me, says, 'Where's Eric Franco live at, what apartment,' and I knew, everybody in the building knew, Eric Franco dealt coke, but these guys didn't look like they were there to score, they looked like trouble."

Carlos started to talk in his sleep, nonsense words addressed to his brother. Billy was deaf to it, but Carmen waited until her son was finished before going on.

"But instead of giving them his apartment, 5C . . . I don't remember *consciously* thinking about what could happen if I said 4F? But that's what came out of my mouth."

Billy stood up.

"Where are you going?"

"What? Nowhere."

"You're leaving?" Carmen saying it like, leaving her.

"No, I was just stretching," he said idiotically.

"Can you sit down?"

"I'm down," he said, "I'm right here."

He began to reach for her hand, then withdrew, sensing that whatever she needed right now, physical contact was not on the list.

"I don't know if I really heard the gunshot from the fourth floor or just imagined that I did — I don't see how I could have, it was a .22 handgun going off inside a six-story building, but all of a sudden I felt this, this gripping sensation inside my chest, and a minute or two later those two came back out of the building the same way they went in, not rushed, looking around without seeming to be. And after they walked past me they stopped and had another one of those side-mouth conversations, and I knew they were discussing what to do about me, the witness . . . I was staring at the ground, I could no more run at that moment than I could fly, I was totally theirs whatever they wanted to do with me, but when I finally managed to raise my head they were gone."

"Carm . . ."

"What happened was that they rang the bell and when Rudy opened the door they shot him through the eye and the bullet went into his brain."

"Carmen . . ."

"But I killed him. Nobody could tell me different. I knew what I knew before I knew it . . . '4F,' I said."

"Carmen, listen to me, the killers were the killers."

"Billy, don't."

"They're the ones who had the guns."

"Billy, I'm begging you . . ."

"Carmen, you were a kid, fifteen, you said so yourself."

"The cops came to our door later that day, doing a canvass of the building, nobody could figure out why this basically no trouble to anyone boy was executed. And when they came to our apartment I hid in the bathroom while they talked to my mother, and when they left I told her that I saw the killers, I talked to them, and first she turned white, then, without even giving me two minutes to pack or say goodbye to my brother, she dragged me out of the apartment and into a cab for Port Authority, and put me on a bus to live with my father in Atlanta. And when I was down there I heard that Milton and Edgar killed the guys that killed their brother, then later I heard that Edgar was killed in return, and that their mother died soon after, and now, now Milton's gone."

"He's gone? He was here to kill you."

"And now you understand why."

"Carmen, how many lives have you saved in that hospital. How many people are still walking the earth because of you."

"So, whatever the law thinks of me, and it doesn't think anything of me at all about this, I know what I did."

Billy's impulse was to once again try to defend her from herself, but he finally accepted the fact that all he'd be doing was causing her more pain.

"So," she said after a long moment, "you tell me about Pavlicek, about Yasmeen, about Jimmy Whelan, what they did and why. But I've got more souls to answer for than any of them, and I live with that every day. I see the Ramos family every day, I say I'm sorry to them so many times in my head from morning to night it's like I have a chemical disorder."

Billy finally, cautiously, lay down next to her.

"I know you want to give me absolution, Billy, but you don't have that power. I wish you did." Then: "But at least now you know."

Too early the next morning, Billy found himself sitting alone at the kitchen table, staring out the window at the askew backboard in the driveway, his coffee as cold as a pond. Immediately after unloading to him about her part in the destruction of the Ramos family, Carmen had proceeded to pass out, was still passed out, Billy checking the wall clock, fifteen hours later. He couldn't count the times he'd seen that in murderers who'd finally owned up to what they had done — straight back to the cell and their first peaceful sleep in weeks, months, years. You couldn't wake them with grenades.

His phone rang — Redman — Billy killing it directly.

The day before, Yasmeen and Whelan had tried to call him too. If he had picked up for either of them, his guess then was, the conversation would center strictly on asking how his family was doing. For them to ask where he was at in regards to turning them in, so soon after what he'd been through, would have been a grievous error in judgment on their part and they'd know that. Nonetheless, the seven-day grace period he had given them to get ahead of their situations was more than half over, but as far as he knew not one of them had even walked into a lawyer's office yet, let alone stepped into a precinct with a story to tell. His take was that they were all banking on the trauma, hoping that in the aftermath of what had happened to him and his family he would be thrown into such a state of emotional chaos that he would no longer have the time, the brain cells, or the heart to follow through on his own ultimatum.

Hearing the thump of his father's *New York Times* landing on the porch, Billy opened the door and saw a Chevy Tahoe sitting silently at the foot of his driveway, Yasmeen staring out at him through the windshield.

At least she knew enough not to come to the door.

Billy walked down the driveway, taking his coffee with him, and settled into the passenger seat without a word.

She had barely brushed her hair and was wearing nothing more than a heavy sweater thrown over pajamas, the first time he'd seen her without the Tibetan coat in months.

"Hey, I called you so many times, you didn't answer, I just had to come by."

Billy looked at his watch: five forty-five a.m.

"I know, I'm sorry, I couldn't sleep," she said. "I just want to know how everybody's holding up."

"We'll get through."

"I can't imagine, that must have been such a nightmare for you."

"I don't want to talk about it."

"No, I understand," she said quickly. "I understand. I should go home," running her palms along the top of her steering wheel but making no move to start up the car.

She had no more driven up here to ask after his family than she had come for the latest NBA scores, the musk of her anguish growing so intense that he had to crack his window.

"Sorry," she said, "I just ran out of the house."

"This picture," Billy tapping the laminated photo of her daughters that hung from the neck of her rearview mirror, "was that always there? Or did you just put it up this morning?"

"No," she said faintly, "that's just my girls, you know."

The first oriole of the season caught his eye, a dash of bright against the early spring drab.

"Just my girls," she murmured, looking off.

He removed the photo from its bead chain, flipped it into her lap. "You see them? What the hell were you thinking?"

"It was do what I did or go kill myself. Better a mother in Bedford Hills than in a grave."

"I can't hear this shit," he said, reaching for the door handle.

Yasmeen grabbed his hand. "You don't think I know what I did?" she warbled. "You think I didn't know how I'd be after that? But at least I'm alive. It was me or him."

"Which him."

"What?"

"Cortez or Bannion."

"I didn't go near Cortez," she said.

"So, clean hands on that one, right?"

Up on the porch, Milton Ramos was leaning against the front door at an impossibly low angle, his rigid body inches from the ground, Billy taking him in and then lifting his eyes to the bedroom window, to Carmen up there desperately trying to exorcize her history via hibernation.

And all he wanted to do right now was join her.

All he wanted to do right now was to be free of himself, free of all the bodies, and

531

tend to his family.

"What happened to your coat," he said his gaze still fixed on the window.

"What? I burned it."

"Just as well."

"What do you mean?" she said quietly.

"I mean, next time you buy a jacket, take a girlfriend."

"Billy, say what you mean," Yasmeen tilting toward him now, as taut as a bird.

Billy took a sip of the cold coffee, then opening his door, tossed the rest onto the driveway.

"You know," he said, "sometimes when I draw a slow night and I can duck out early, I'd be coming around that curve right about now, sliding for home."

"Billy, please . . ."

"Sitting out here like this?" he said. "It's like I'm waiting for myself to show up."

"Fucking Billy," Yasmeen blurted as she keyed the ignition. "Fucking Billy."

The unexpected blast of Mariah Carey coming through the car speakers made her scream.

Enough.

"You get a lawyer yet?" he said, turning off the radio.

"There's a guy," she said sullenly. "I'm going to see him today."

"Save your money," he said, finally stepping out of the car.

"What?"

But she knew what, Yasmeen clamping a hand across her mouth like a muzzle, the tears running over her knuckles.

"And do your crying at home."

Carmen stumbled into the kitchen an hour later, her face a blur.

"How long was I out for?"

"Long enough."

"Then why am I still so exhausted?" she said, wandering over to pour herself some coffee.

"I heard Victor's going home tomorrow," he said.

"He is."

"Does he know?"

"About Milton?"

"About you," he said.

"Me? No. I couldn't ever tell him."

"Well, maybe you can now."

"Now I need to."

"Just wait a little while until he settles in with the babies."

"Of course," she said. "Of course."

"Yasmeen drove up this morning."

"This morning?" Lowering herself into the chair next to his. "I didn't hear anything."

"She stayed in her car."

"Did you talk to her?"

"Yeah, I did."

"And?"

"And it's over," he said.

"Over. What do you mean, 'over.' " Then: "With just her or all of them?"

Billy shrugged.

They sat in silence for a while, Carmen joining him in looking out at the backyard.

"I'm glad," she finally said. "Thank you."

He wanted to say that he didn't do it for her, but who knew.

Milton Ramos reappeared, this time sitting on the living room couch, immobile yet full of murderous despair.

Well, Billy told himself, what did you expect.

And if Carmen hadn't seen him yet, she'd see him soon enough.

"I think I got up too early," he said.

"Me too," she said, reaching for, but missing, his hand. "Let's go back to bed."

The call from Stacey Taylor came a week later.

"I need to tell you something."

"What's that."

"Have breakfast with me. It's a long story."

"Give me the headline."

"Just have breakfast with me," she said. "You'll be glad you did."

"You said that the last time."

"This time I mean it."

"I have a therapy session at two."

"Physical?"

"Family."

"Where."

"West Forties."

"Then come after."

"Your whale, Curtis Taft?" she said to him over a four p.m. breakfast in another one of her tin-can diners. "He shot his girlfriend last night."

"Girlfriend or wife?" Billy asked, thinking of Patricia Taft, big and stately, pushing a stroller that day through the atrium of the hospital.

"Girlfriend."

"You have a funny definition of good news."

"She'll live," Stacey said, fondling an unopened pack of Parliaments, "but he also clipped the first EMT coming through the door, so he's most likely going away just this side of forever."

So, yeah, good news, he guessed, but it left him flat. "He got away with a triple," he said. "Skated like Brinker."

"You catch them for what you catch them for," she said. "You told me that."

"Memori Williams, Tonya Howard, Dreena Bailey," he said loudly enough to turn heads.

And Eric Cortez, Sweetpea Harris, Jeffrey Bannion, if he was taking a true tally.

The food came, two omelets that were so oily they looked shellacked.

"So, in other news," sliding her plate to the side. "I've been hearing some wild rumors."

"About . . ."

"Bad guys getting taken out by frustrated cops."

"Frustrated, huh?" Billy thinking, Maybe the center would hold for them and maybe not, but if she had really called him here hoping he would help her out, she was dreaming. He would no more talk to her about any of his friends than they would have talked about him eighteen years earlier.

Ignoring the food, he took a sip of coffee. "Where'd you hear that?"

"You know I can't say."

"Journalistic ethics?" he said with more of an edge than he'd intended.

The dig deflated her like a pin. "Yeah, well, we used to hear bullshit rumors like this all the time back at the *Post*. They rarely came to anything."

He wanted to remind her that *rarely* wasn't the same as *never,* that eighteen years ago, when she was young and mad ambitious, words like *rarely, unlikely, implausible* would never have slowed her down — but what would have been the point.

The woman sitting across from him — gray in face and grown so bony in middle age that he could count the knobs of her spine through her pullover — just didn't have the heart for the chase anymore; *rarely,* these days, justification enough for her to fold her tent and go home to her wine and her cigarettes and her death-wish drunk of a boyfriend.

"I need to tell you something," he said, before he could stop himself.

"Tell me something?" Stacey looking at him warily, not liking his suddenly breathy tone.

"It's about me and you," Billy thinking, She can get back in the game with this. Get back in the game and redeem her good name.

"Can I go outside for a smoke first?" she nearly pleaded, her eyes pierced with dread.

Her resistance to finally hearing the words that would vindicate the last two punishing decades of her life at first baffled him, then sobered him. What the hell was he thinking? The consequences for his family and for himself . . .

"Forget it, it's nothing."

He knew she wouldn't press, and she didn't, Stacey masking her relief by pretending that something out on the street had caught her eye. And Billy, playing his part, started attacking his eggs as if they were edible.

"Let me ask you something," she said after a while. "Whether you were or weren't high that day and that psycho with the pipe was still bearing down on you like that . . . Would you have done anything differently?"

"Hypothetically?" he said. "No, I don't think so." Then: "No, I wouldn't."

Stacey went back to gazing out the window, her thin features vanishing in the late afternoon sunlight that slanted through the glass.

"I mean, it's not like I never think about getting back into some kind of reporting," she said, tentatively pressing her fingertips against her throat. "But that sex advice column for men that I write? We had nine thousand hits last issue. Up from fifty-five hundred the issue before, up from three thousand the issue before that. So, I think it's safe to say that I'm onto something."

Billy nodded in gratitude.

"Can I go out and have my cigarette now?" she said.

Pavlicek tried to ring through as he was leaving the diner, the only one of them who hadn't attempted to contact him in the days after Ramos. The others had stopped calling directly after his talk with Yasmeen, Billy assuming that no one wanted to risk a conversation that, if they said the wrong thing or adopted the wrong tone, might prompt him to change his mind. Yet Pavlicek hadn't called even once, and so on the third attempted ring-through, coming forty minutes after the first, Billy yielded to his curiosity and picked up. But instead of getting Pavlicek on the other end, the voice Billy heard was Redman's.

"It's John Junior," he said. "The funeral's here on Thursday."

Unlike the Homecoming for Martha Timberwolf, Junior's service was standing room only.

At first, when he entered the already crowded chapel with his wife and kids, Billy wondered if he had it in him to let himself go, even just for this day. But when he saw Pavlicek, lumbering wild-eyed between the casket and Redman's piano like a chained bear, he couldn't help but wade through the crowd and grab him.

"It's over now, right?" Pavlicek said too brightly, his breath rank with grief. "All over but the shoutin'."

"Sure," Billy said, wishing it were so.

"Come here," Pavlicek taking Billy by the elbow and steering him to the side of the open coffin. "Look at this, can you believe this?" Touching his son's rigid left pinkie sticking out from the folded repose of his crossed hands. "He looks like some fucking fop holding a teacup, and this here," running a finger down the left side of Junior's jaw, the skin there three shades darker than on the right, "and his hair, I don't know what Redman was thinking but this kid never had a pompadour in his life."

Pavlicek's tone was crisp and snappy and jarringly unaffected by the tears that slipped down his face in sheets. "I mean, I never thought our friend was the greatest mortician on the planet, but this is ridiculous."

"Maybe he just doesn't get to work much on white people," Billy said carefully.

"And see, I put this in," pointing to his own gold shield tucked into a corner of the casket. "And this," lifting out a framed photo of the two of them taken in Amsterdam a few years earlier. "And this," a snapshot of Junior as a toddler with his mother before she tried to drown him. "I really debated putting that one in, but . . ."

The disconnect between voice and tears continued, Billy wondering how long he could keep it up.

"You ever read that?" Pavlicek asked, pointing to a paperback copy of *Steppenwolf* near Junior's feet. "Last year he told me that it changed his life, so I tried to get through it a few times to see what he saw," the tears finally beginning to climb into his throat, "but honestly? I thought it was crap. Anyways it's all over now, right? All over but the shoutin'."

"Johnny," Billy said, stepping back from Junior's body. "I'm dying for you."

Embarrassed by his choice of words, Billy began to apologize, but he needn't have bothered, given that Pavlicek had already turned away and was now engaged in giving Ray Rivera, father of the murdered Thomas, the same manic tour of the coffin and its contents as he had given Billy.

They were all there with their families, those who had families: Yasmeen, Dennis, and the girls; Redman, who had prepared the body but turned the service over to his father so

541

he could participate purely as a mourner, standing with Nola, Rafer, and two of his six or seven other sons; and Jimmy Whelan, who at least had the sense for once not to bring a date.

They all made some sort of contact with Billy, mostly sober nods, a few terse greetings, Yasmeen going so far as to hug Carmen and make a quiet fuss over the kids. But for the most part they kept their distance, which he thought was more about letting sleeping dogs lie than anything else, and he was fine with it. He preferred it.

"I believe it's time," Redman's father announced with soft authority, "for us all to be seated."

Junior apparently had been utterly indifferent to the notion of any kind of God, and so Pavlicek, no Bible beater himself, passed on having any kind of religious celebrant and instead turned the program over to his son's friends, who served up half a dozen well-spoken homages, an acoustical duet on "I'll Fly Away," and a teary solo of "Angels Among Us," sung by a young woman who had been the closest thing Junior had had to a girlfriend in the last year of his life.

When the woman returned to her seat, a retired detective from Bronx Homicide, not on the program, spontaneously got up and sang an a cappella version of Eric Clapton's "Tears in Heaven," which had half the room weeping like babies, including Carlos and Declan, hardly more than babies themselves. Billy didn't know what unnerved him more, his two sons' intuitive empathy in a room beyond their experience or the sight of Jimmy Whelan, the childless, mateless, eternally diffident ghetto harem keeper, sobbing more loudly than anyone else. As for Billy himself, the last couple of weeks had utterly tapped him out, and it would take a lot more than a sad pop tune with a painful backstory to get him weeping.

Redman Senior, seemingly singing directly to Junior's father, closed out the concert with "The Battle Is Not Yours."

And then it was his time, Pavlicek rising from the front row, giving his back to the room as he silently leaned over the coffin — Billy could hear him whispering something to his son, but too indistinctly for anyone to make out — then finally turning to the assembled, the expression on his face near homicidal.

"I don't know if anyone came here to celebrate John Junior's life, but I certainly didn't," he said, gripping the podium as if he wanted to crush it. "I am here before you, I am here among you, to rage and curse

God for the arbitrarily murdering fuck that he is, not that I'm the first parent ever to feel that way, and to grant myself at least one afternoon where suicide would be logistically difficult."

Tickled by the profanity, Carlos looked up at Billy and grinned.

"You know, you read the papers after a young man dies in this city, someone's always saying, 'He was just starting to get his life together, he was just talking about going back to school, getting his GED, getting a job, talking about being a real father to his daughter, talking about getting away from the 'hood, about enlisting, about marrying his fiancée, he was just about to do this, to do that . . .' All these 'just's, whether they were true or not, because they all died young and 'just' was all they had, tomorrow was all they had. And the same could be said for my boy. He was 'just' about to finish his schooling, he was 'just' about to find his own way in the world, 'just' about to show me the man that now, now, he'll never get to be, the man that over the years would have null-and-voided every hardship, every heartache I've ever endured in my life."

Pavlicek paused, returned to the coffin as if for a quick consultation, then turned back to the seats. "You want to hear what a great kid he was? How his heart was pure gold? How he loved life, loved people, loved a challenge, all that boilerplate et cetera, et cetera? For those of you who want to hear all that, consider it said. The fact of the matter was that he was just about to be, and now he's not."

Looking around the room Billy noted that all three of the WGs were in tears, their faces in various states of contortion. Even Redman, king of the poker face and impresario of seventy-five to a hundred memorials like this every year, was swiping at his cheeks with those mile-long fingers of his.

They had all killed or been complicit in a killing, out of passion but clear-eyed and purposefully, but they had no problem giving in to their grief when it came to one another. He had nearly lost his mind trying to bring them to justice, turning on his longtime friends in order to do what was right, what he thought was right, and as a result his own eyes on this day were as dry as sand. Still, they had all been so tight over the last two decades, had gone through so much together, and for one mad minute, Billy's anger at them for excluding him from their murderous plans trumped his outrage at what they had done. But instead of passing, the anger lingered, Billy wondering if this pop-up fury he was experiencing over having been shut out from this most desperate of compacts between friends hadn't been a part of his anger at them since the beginning.

"There's some people in this room right now," Pavlicek said, "who gave twenty years or more to the Job, myself included. We've seen it all, handled it all, and when a young person dies we've all walked up the stairs, knocked on the doors, and delivered the news, between us, to an army of parents. We've caught them on their way to the floor, carried them into the bedroom or living room, then gone into their kitchens and brought them water — over the years, an ocean of water, glass by glass by glass. And so, after all that, we think we understand what it must feel like to be one of those parents, but we don't. We can't. I still can't. But I'm getting there."

Billy reflexively looked across the room at Ray Rivera, expecting him to be nodding in agreement, but instead saw a profile carved in stone.

"But so my son . . ." Pavlicek paused, looking about himself as if he had misplaced something, then seemed to give up on finding it. "I think I just want to read this," he said, pulling an envelope out of his jacket pocket and removing a single page cut from a book. "This was handed to me today by a friend, and it's as good a farewell to him as anything else."

And then, after giving it one last silent read, Pavlicek began to recite, tone-deaf to the rhythm of the words:

> These hearts were woven of human joys
>   and cares,
> Washed marvellously with sorrow, swift to
>   mirth.
> The years had given them kindness. Dawn
>   was theirs,
> And sunset, and the colours of the earth.

It was Rupert Brooke's sonnet "The Dead" — "The Dead (IV)," actually, Billy knowing this because his father had read it to him, more than once, when he was a kid, and when Billy became older, more than once he had read it himself.

> . . . He leaves a white
> Unbroken glory, a gathered radiance,
> A width, a shining peace, under the night.

At the end of the service, Pavlicek chose to stand at the head of the open coffin to once again receive mourners, the line extending from the front of the chapel to the small windowless vestibule and out into the street.

"It's over now, right?" Pavlicek chanted to Billy. "All over but the shoutin'."

"It's over," Billy said. "Everything."

Despite his state, Pavlicek picked up on his meaning right away. "Billy. I know what I did to you. What we all did to you. And I'm sorry."

"Not for today," Billy said. "Today is today, all right?"

"We just knew if you ever . . ." Pavlicek began, then cut himself off, leaving Billy to wonder how he had intended to finish that sentence.

"Another day, OK?"

"All right," Pavlicek said. "Another day."

As Billy turned to step away, Pavlicek grabbed his wrist.

"You hear about Curtis Taft?"

"I did," Billy said.

"I don't know, maybe that day we gave him PTSD, maybe we drove him to that."

"Not today, OK?"

"I mean, I sure fuckin' hope so," Pavlicek rasped with a kind of black glee, Billy looking into his eyes and absolutely knowing that if time ever folded in on itself and Pavlicek had it to do all over again, to put another bullet into the back of Eric Cortez's skull, or to re-murder any of the other Whites by gun, blade, or with his bare hands, he'd go about it with joy.

Turning back to the mourners, Billy saw that Whelan, Redman, and Yasmeen, each standing in a different part of the room, had all been quietly observing the conversation, their expressions, before they one by one turned away from him, flat-eyed and alert, Billy thinking, And so would they all.

The car was parked four blocks uptown from the funeral home, and as they headed north on Adam Clayton Boulevard, the boys serpentined like loons before them, racing up every stoop and making a show of high-jumping over every minuscule bit of crap on the sidewalk.

"That poem he read?" Billy said to Carmen. "It's from World War One. It made me think of my dad."

"Well, it should. He gave it to me this morning to give to John."

"My father did?"

"I was right there when he gave it to me."

"I didn't even know he knew about the funeral." Then: "Why didn't he give it to me?"

"I think he knew, he knows, what's going on with you and the others, so he gave it to

549

me instead."

"And how the hell does he know that?"

"Don't ask me," Carmen said, "he's your father."

Later, as they unloaded the kids in the driveway and then entered the house, Billy remembered that he was supposed to go in tonight, his first tour back after two weeks on medical leave.

"I'm thinking about calling in sick," he said to Carmen in the kitchen. "I don't really want to go."

"I think you should," she said.

"I don't think I'm up for it."

"I think you should," she repeated on her way to the freezer for the vodka, then to the cabinet for two juice glasses.

"Yeah? How about you?" Billy watching her pour out too much, a sure sign of a non-drinker, which, under normal circumstances, she was.

"I already called the hospital, told them to put me back on the schedule starting tomorrow."

"You sure you're up for it?"

"Keep calm and carry on," she said, raising her glass.

"What?"

"I saw it on a refrigerator magnet," Car-

550

men taking a sip and making a face. "I mean Jesus, Billy, what else can we do?"

His third run that night was on Madison Avenue, a four a.m. smash-and-grab of a tiny jewelry store set inside the exterior arcade of an office building in midtown, almost all of the stock snatched out of the brick-bashed window, nothing much to see now but bare earring trees and daggers of broken glass.

At this hour, the canyoned street was a ghost town, and Billy easily spotted the late-model Nissan Pathfinder slowly approaching from three blocks south. When it finally pulled to the curb, an elderly woman sporting a high helmet of frosted tangerine hair, lipsticked and dressed in a nubby plaid skirt suit as if she had been sitting up all night waiting for the phone to ring, stepped carefully out of the passenger-side door onto Madison. The driver — her husband, Billy assumed — remained behind the wheel with the engine still running, staring straight ahead as if waiting for the light to change.

She absorbed the carnage without expression. "I been here thirty-seven years and nothing ever happened," she said quietly, a soft thread of old Europe running through her words.

When Billy was a kid all of his aunts had filigreed birdcage hair like hers, and he could never figure out how they slept.

"How's your insurance?"

The woman blushed. "It only covers jewelry that's in the safe."

"How much is in the safe?"

"I have arthritis. Every little piece, in and out, in and out, morning and night, takes me two hours, I can't do it anymore." She was wiped out.

"Is that your husband?" Billy asked.

She glanced at the old guy still behind the wheel but said nothing.

"And where was he tonight?" Theodore Moretti asked.

"Do I even have to answer a question like that?" The woman addressed Billy, more amazed than insulted.

He had no idea how Moretti had gotten back on the sign-up sheet after being black-balled just the month before, but he had. "I thought you were at the Three-two," Billy snapped.

Moretti's cell rang and he walked down the block, hissing into his shoulder.

"What happens now?" she asked, Billy picking up on that near-buried refugee inflection again, thinking, This is nothing for her.

Before he could respond, a patrol car flying the wrong way down Madison came to a rocking stop in front of the store. One of the uniforms jumped out, holding a black plastic garbage bag.

"We caught the guy running on Park," he said, gesturing to the head-down, handcuffed thief in the backseat. "I feel like goddamn Santa Claus."

The woman took the bag and peered inside at her life, then up at Billy.

"Who would do such a thing?"

"I hate to say it," Billy said, "but all of this has to be vouchered as evidence."

She looked at him blankly, Billy unable to tell whether she didn't understand him or didn't care; nonetheless, he decided, it was a reasonably happy ending.

ACKNOWLEDGMENTS

My editor, John Sterling, a highly incisive and diligent master builder — and as ruthless as ever.

To all the friends and guides who have schooled me over the last few years —
First and always, John McCormack.
Irma Rivera, Barry Warhit, Richie Roberts, Rafiyq Abdellah, John McAuliffe.
And to my street-writer heroes — Michael Daly and Mark Jacobson.

ABOUT THE AUTHOR

Harry Brandt is the pen name of acclaimed novelist Richard Price, whose eight previous novels — including *Clockers* and *Lush Life* — have won universal praise for their vividly etched portrayals of urban America. He lives in Manhattan with his wife, the novelist Lorraine Adams.

THE INGENUITY GAP

THE
INGENUITY
GAP

Thomas Homer-Dixon

Alfred A. Knopf

New York • Toronto • 2000

THIS IS A BORZOI BOOK
PUBLISHED BY ALFRED A. KNOPF
AND ALFRED A. KNOPF CANADA

www.aaknopf.com
www.randomhouse.ca

For Alfred A. Knopf (U.S.) edition
ISBN: 0-375-40186-5
Library of Congress Control Number: 00-134715

Canadian Cataloguing in Publication Data

Homer-Dixon, Thomas F.
    The ingenuity gap

ISBN 0-676-97148-2

1. Twenty-first century.   2. Social change.
3. Civilization, Modern — 1950–   .
I. Title.

CB161.H653 2000   303.49'09'05   C00-930375-8

Manufactured in the United States of America
First Edition

10 9 8 7 6 5 4 3 2

To my students
and the future they will make their own

CONTENTS

THE INGENUITY GAP

PROLOGUE

MOST OF US occasionally suspect that the world we've created is too complex and too fast-paced for us to understand, let alone control. Most of us sometimes guess that even the "experts" don't really know what's going on, and that as individuals and as a species we've unleashed forces that we cannot manage. The challenges facing our societies range from international financial crises and global climate change to pandemics of tuberculosis and AIDS; they cross the spectrum of politics, economics, technology, and ecological affairs. They converge, intertwine, and often seem to be largely beyond our ken—incomprehensible even to our leaders and specialists.

In this book I'll argue that the complexity, unpredictability, and pace of events in our world, and the severity of global environmental stress, are soaring. If our societies are to manage their affairs and improve their well-being they will need more ingenuity—that is, more ideas for solving their technical and social problems. But societies, whether rich or poor, can't always supply the ingenuity they need at the right times and places. As a result, some face an *ingenuity gap*: a shortfall between their rapidly rising need for ingenuity and their inadequate supply.

Ingenuity gaps tend to widen the already yawning gulfs of wealth and opportunity within and between our societies. Many societies, groups, and people adapt reasonably well to our swiftly changing world, but others have fallen behind and risk being overwhelmed by converging pressures. In the twenty-first century, the growing disparities between those who adapt well and those who don't will hinder our progress towards a shared sense of human community and erode our new global society's stability and prosperity. The next century is likely, for this reason, to be a time of fragmentation and turmoil, of divisions and rivalry between winners and losers, and of humanity's patent failure to manage its affairs in critical domains.

This picture does not correspond to today's received wisdom—at least, not the wisdom espoused by many members of the economic, political, and journalistic elites of Western societies. The opinion and commentary heard from these circles has lately had a distinctly triumphalist tone. A glorious future for all is predicted, thanks to the leadership of the West. The success of the United States, in particular, has revealed the path to universal well-being; all that remains is for other societies to follow its lead.

The West certainly has every reason to be proud of its successes; its capitalism, science, and liberal democracy are marvelous institutions that have made extraordinary contributions to human prosperity and freedom. And certainly Western societies, and again the United States in particular, have seen a remarkable string of economic and political achievements in recent years. But Western triumphalism is partly based on a selective reading of the evidence. Problems and issues that don't fit into this optimistic worldview tend to be downplayed or ignored. Moreover, a significant part of the West's current success is the result of a confluence of events and processes that its elites neither controlled nor really understand. Western triumphalism is dangerously self-indulgent, and even delusional; it assumes agency where there may be mainly good luck.

This book does not present a fully developed theory, because I have not tried to address all relevant issues or tie off all loose ends. Instead, I have tried to elaborate an intuition or feeling about our future. The ingenuity gap, as I call it, is a way of thinking about the very real chasm that sometimes looms between our ever more difficult problems and our lagging ability to solve them. The ingenuity gap is also a metaphor for the human predicament, a metaphor that can be explored and understood in a multitude of ways—analytically, empirically, emotionally, and spiritually. As a new millennium unfolds before us, it is my hope that this book, in a small way, will give us better tools for understanding who we are and where we are going.

Ingenuity, as I define it here, consists not only of ideas for new technologies like computers or drought-resistant crops but, more fundamentally, of ideas for better institutions and social arrangements, like efficient markets and competent governments. How much and what kinds of ingenuity a society *requires* depends on a range of factors, including the society's goals and the circumstances within which it must achieve those goals—whether it has a young population or an aging one, an abundance of natural resources or a scarcity of them, an easy climate or a punishing one, whatever the case may be. How much and what kinds of ingenuity a society *supplies* also depends on many factors, such as the nature of human inventiveness and understanding, the rewards an economy gives to the producers of useful knowledge, and the strength of political opposition to social and institutional reforms.

A good supply of the right kinds of ingenuity is essential, but it isn't, of course, enough by itself. We know that the creation of wealth, for example, depends not only on an adequate supply of useful ideas but also on the availability of other, more conventional factors of production, like capital and labor. Similarly, prosperity, stability, and justice usually depend on the resolution, or at least the containment, of major political struggles over wealth and power. Yet within our economies ingenuity often supplants labor, and growth in the stock of physical plant is usually accompanied by growth in the stock of ingenuity. And in our political systems, we need great ingenuity to set up institutions that successfully manage struggles over wealth and power. Clearly, our economic and political processes are intimately entangled with the production and use of ingenuity.

The past century's countless incremental changes in our societies around the planet, in our technologies and our interactions with our surrounding natural environments, have accumulated to create a qualitatively new world. Because these changes have accumulated slowly, it's often hard for us to recognize how profound and sweeping they've been. They include far larger and denser human populations; much higher per capita consumption of natural resources; and far better and more widely available technologies for the movement of people, materials, and especially information. In combination, these changes have sharply increased the density, intensity, and pace of our interactions with each other; they have greatly increased the burden we place on our natural environment; and they have helped shift power from national and international institutions to individuals and subgroups, such as political special interests and ethnic factions. As a result, people in all walks of life—from our political and business leaders to all of us in our day-to-day lives—must cope with much more complex, urgent, and often unpredictable circumstances. The management of our relationship with this new world requires immense and ever-increasing amounts of social and technical ingenuity. As we strive to maintain or increase our prosperity and improve the quality of our lives, we must make far more sophisticated decisions, and in less time, than ever before.

When we enhance the performance of any system, from our cars to the planet's network of financial institutions, we tend to make it more complex. Many of the natural systems critical to our well-being, like the global climate and the oceans, are extraordinarily complex to begin with. We often can't predict or manage the behavior of complex systems with much precision, because they are often very sensitive to the smallest of changes and perturbations, and their behavior can flip from one mode to another suddenly and dramatically. In general, as the human-made and natural systems we depend upon become more complex, and as our demands on them increase, the institutions and technologies we use to manage them must become more complex too, which further boosts our need for ingenuity.

The good news, though, is that the last century's stunning changes in our societies and technologies have not just increased our need for ingenuity; they have also produced a huge increase in its supply. The growth and urbanization of human populations have combined with astonishing new communication and transportation technologies to expand interactions among people and produce larger, more integrated, and more efficient markets. These changes have, in turn, vastly accelerated the generation and delivery of useful ideas.

But—and this is the critical "but"—we should not jump to the conclusion that the supply of ingenuity always increases in lockstep with our ingenuity requirement: while it's true that necessity is often the mother of invention, we can't always rely on the right kind of ingenuity appearing when and where we need it. In many cases, the complexity and speed of operation of today's vital economic, social, and ecological systems exceed the human brain's grasp. Very few of us have more than a rudimentary understanding of how these systems work. They remain fraught with countless "unknown unknowns," which makes it hard to supply the ingenuity we need to solve problems associated with these systems.

In this book, I explore a wide range of other factors that will limit our ability to supply the ingenuity required in the coming century. For example, many people believe that new communication technologies strengthen democracy and will make it easier to find solutions to our societies' collective problems, but the story is less clear than it seems. The crush of information in our everyday lives is shortening our attention span, limiting the time we have to reflect on critical matters of public policy, and making policy arguments more superficial. New communication technologies are also shifting power away from governments, which boosts the ability of subgroups and individuals to block useful institutional reform. In many poor countries, the spread of lighter and more lethal weapons has contributed to a similar shift of power away from governments towards violent insurgents and secessionists. As it becomes easier for small numbers of people to inflict massive trauma—often in the form of massacres of civilians and terrorist bombings—more poor societies are likely to become locked in downward spirals of violence that make democratic reform virtually impossible.

Modern markets and science are an important part of the story of how we supply ingenuity. Markets are critically important, because they give entrepreneurs an incentive to produce knowledge. But this incentive is often skewed or too weak—our energy prices, for instance, don't begin to reflect the potential cost of climate change to future generations—which means we often get the wrong kind of solutions to our problems. As for science, although it seems to face no theoretical limits, at least in the foreseeable future, practical constraints often slow its progress. The cost of scientific research tends to increase as it delves deeper into nature. And science's rate of advance depends on the characteristics of the natural phenomena it investigates, simply because some phenomena are intrinsically harder to understand than others, so the production of useful new knowledge in these areas can be very slow. Consequently, there is often a critical time lag between the recognition of a problem and the delivery of sufficient ingenuity, in the form of technologies, to solve that problem. Progress in the social sciences is especially slow, for reasons we don't yet fully understand; but we desperately need better social scientific knowledge to build the sophisticated institutions today's world demands.

Our species' scientific and technological prowess is nevertheless extraordinary. We create miracles from raw nature, and we have revolutionized our existence in a few lifetimes. These accomplishments are to be celebrated. Unfortunately, they have also made us overconfident of our ability to solve the problems we face. Today, a disturbingly large proportion of people in rich countries seem to believe that our ingenuity is practically boundless and that our technical experts have all the authority and knowledge they need to deftly manage our ever more complex world. These beliefs and the complacency they produce are often completely unwarranted: in fact, we often have only superficial control over the complex systems we've made and critically depend upon.

This delusion of control arises from overconfidence, but it has other sources too. We have subordinated a large portion of the planet's resources and ecology to our interests, we live increasingly in cities, and our modern economic system compresses our perceptions of time and space. These changes attenuate and distort the signals we receive from our surrounding environment. As a result, we often misunderstand the character of the problems we face; sometimes we don't see them as problems at all. In turn, we make mistakes about the kinds of ingenuity we need, mistakes that restrict and distort the amount of ingenuity we supply.

In rich countries, modern capitalism has created an astonishingly variegated mosaic of overlapping and fragmented realities. These realities have one thing in common: they're all extensions of our egos; in other words, nearly everything we do and create through capitalism is made to the measure of our human needs and aspirations. The apex of this achievement is the postmodern capitalist city. We design our cities to block out the intrusions and fluctuations of the natural world so that they will work as smoothly and efficiently and with as little discomfort to their residents as possible. We like to be comfortable, after all. But the disturbing result is that many urban residents no longer care about, understand, or recognize the importance of this natural world. Our modern cities are vital engines of ingenuity supply, producing much of what is best and most beautiful, but they also produce self-absorption, introversion, and hubris.

This tendency is exacerbated by another feature of modern capitalism: the rising economic importance of people with certain cognitive skills has combined with the greater integration of the world's economies to create a planetary "super elite." This group is increasingly homogeneous in its values and aspirations, and it controls an ever-growing fraction of the world's wealth. Most opinion leaders in rich countries are drawn from this elite, and their exposure to the difficulties confronting the majority of the world's population, which lives in poorer societies, is limited and extremely selective. So, not surprisingly, they often underestimate these societies' requirements for ingenuity, misjudge the kind of ingenuity they need, and overestimate their ability to supply it. The super elite is also a largely self-enclosed and self-referential group—making it vulnerable to internally generated intellectual fads, which it then disseminates to the rest of the world's population.

These are some of the ideas I'll discuss in this book, with each chapter focusing on one or a few of my key arguments. These pages also tell the story of a journey of discovery—a quest—that took me around the world and to the farthest reaches of our knowledge. This journey was a search for the pieces of a puzzle—pieces that when fitted together would give me a picture of how we use our practical knowledge—ingenuity in all its variety—to adapt to rapid and complex change. I hoped, too, that the completed puzzle would afford a glimpse of our prospects for survival and happiness. I bring the reader into this story in 1997, but my quest actually began long before then, and my narrative must sometimes cast back to earlier events.

Because it's a puzzle, each piece plays an important part, and I must describe them in detail. They include recent theories of turbulent systems, of Earth's ecology and atmosphere, of the evolution of the human brain, of how we produce wealth, of the factors that shape and reshape our technologies, and of the forces behind war and terrorism. I tell a story about the many forms of complexity around us and about our biological capacity to grasp, manage, and benefit from this complexity. I also tell a story about how we are altering our planet's most fundamental rhythms and processes. Six metaphors are woven through this story—metaphors of flight, faces, light, the night sky, pyramids, and water. For me, these metaphors have enormous emotional and spiritual power, and I hope they can aid us in answering one of the most basic questions humanity faces: How can we solve the problems of the future?

To give flesh to the bones of my story and support the book's arguments, I have drawn evidence and ideas from a wide array of today's research and from many of the world's great thinkers. (All these materials and people are cited in the endnotes, where I also elaborate on technical issues and discuss important questions raised by the book's main argument; readers can find further information at www.ingenuitygap.com.) In the epilogue, I offer some general suggestions about the principles that might help us reform our institutions and strengthen our global community.

The distinction at the heart of my ingenuity gap idea—between the difficulty of the problems we face (that is, our requirement for ingenuity) and our delivery of ideas in response to these problems (our supply of ingenuity)—is, I hope, a valuable tool for understanding our situation in a rapidly changing world. Although I argue that we can't always solve our problems, I cannot say enough for our astonishing adaptability and ingenuity, characteristics common to all human beings and all societies.[1] Throughout history, pessimists have far too frequently underestimated human creativity and resourcefulness. We certainly have it in our power to produce widespread prosperity and justice on this planet. But it is not at all clear that we will use this power properly. When we look back from the year 2100, I fear we will see a period when our creations—technological, social, and ecological—outstripped our understanding, and we lost control of our destiny. And we will think: if only—if only we had had the ingenuity and will to choose a different course. There is still time, I believe, to muster that ingenuity and will, but the hour is late.

PART ONE

How Are We

Changing Our

Relationship to

the World?

CAREENING INTO THE FUTURE

A T 3:16 P.M. on 19 July, 1989, the jet's tail engine blew apart. Twelve thousand meters above the U.S. Midwest, shards of the engine's fan rotor cut through the rear of the aircraft, shredding its hydraulic systems. As fluid bled from hydraulic tubing, the pilots in the front of the plane lost command of the rudder, elevators, and ailerons essential to stabilizing and guiding the craft. Immediately, the plane twisted into a downward right turn. United Airlines Flight 232 from Denver to Chicago—with 296 people aboard—was out of control.[1]

By itself, the failure of the tail engine was not catastrophic: the DC-10 had two other engines, one under each wing. But cockpit gauges showed a complete loss of hydraulic quantity and pressure. When the first officer tried to halt the right turn, the plane didn't respond. As the rightward bank became critical, the captain took over, pulling back on the control column and turning the wheel hard left—but still there was no response. In a last-ditch effort to regain command, he cut power to the left engine and boosted it to the right one. The right wing slowly came up, and the plane rolled back to a horizontal position. The right turn stopped.

Yet the situation remained critical. The plane was no longer turning, but it was still losing altitude. The captain sent crew members to look out of the windows in the passenger cabin. They saw that the inboard ailerons were slightly up, the spoilers were locked down, and the horizontal stabilizers were damaged. None of the main flight-control surfaces were moving.

And it appeared that the airframe might have suffered structural damage severe enough to cause it to break apart in flight.

Back in the cockpit, the captain and first officer worked the flight controls feverishly—they still believed they could change the plane's trajectory. But their efforts produced no obvious effect. The captain also manipulated the thrust of the two remaining engines, sometimes giving extra power to the left engine, sometimes to the right engine. This action *did* have a noticeable effect. It helped keep the plane level and countered its tendency to turn right. But changes in engine thrust gave the captain only minimal control. In fact, from the perspective of the passengers, the plane was moving in three dimensions simultaneously: it was rolling from side to side and pitching up and down, as if riding long waves across the sky.

A flight attendant opened the cockpit door to say that an off-duty United Airlines pilot, seated in first class, had offered to help. He was a "check airman" who flew with flight crews to assess their performance. The captain acknowledged that the unexpected assistance was urgently needed, because he was finding it impossible to work the flight and thrust controls simultaneously. When the airman entered the cockpit, the captain briefed him on the aircraft's critical situation in a staccato of abbreviated phrases. "Tell me what you want, and I'll help you," he replied. The captain asked him to take over the thrust controls. Grasping an engine throttle in each hand, the check airman then stood between the captain and first officer's seats, and—with his eyes fixed on the flight instruments—began to manipulate the power of the two wing engines.

About fifteen minutes had passed since the explosion. The nearest airport was at Sioux City, Iowa. But the plane had lost nearly 7,000 meters of altitude and—despite the best efforts of the check airman—was still describing a series of clockwise circles over the Iowa countryside.[2] In various parts of the United States, clusters of people had gathered around microphones and speakers to follow United 232's plight and to offer suggestions. The crew particularly wanted to hear from the United Airlines System Aircraft Maintenance (SAM) facility in San Francisco.

> Second Officer to United Airlines Chicago Dispatch: "We need any help we can get from SAM, as far as what to do with this. We don't have anything. We don't [know] what to do. We're having a hard time controlling it. We're descending. We're down to 17,000 feet. We have . . . ah, hardly any control whatsoever.

But the SAM engineers didn't have a clue how to help. They had never heard before of a simultaneous failure of all three hydraulic systems. They kept asking, in disbelief, if there really was *no* hydraulic quantity or pressure. And they asked the second officer to flip back and forth through the pages of a thick flight manual, to no avail. The crew's frustration with ground support rose.

> Captain to Second Officer: "You got hold of SAM?"
> Second Officer: "Yeah, I've talked to 'im."
> Captain: "What's he saying?"
> Second Officer: "He's not telling me anything."
> Captain: "We're not gonna make the runway, fellas, we're gonna have
>   to ditch this son of a [bitch] and hope for the best."

Almost thirty minutes into the crisis, SAM had finally assembled a team of engineers around the speaker and asked the second officer for yet another

Flight Path of United Airlines Flight 232

full report. He provided a detailed run-down of the aircraft's status. After a period of radio silence, SAM again asked, "United 232, one more time, no hydraulic quantity, is that correct?" The second officer replied in exasperation, "Affirmative! Affirmative! Affirmative!" The engineers on the ground, the crew decided, could offer no help. United 232 was on its own.

Yet, at almost exactly the same time, the check airman accomplished a miracle. He managed to bring the plane around in a single broad turn to the left, lining up the plane for the shortest runway at the Sioux City airport. This was the only left turn the plane was to make following the explosion. The captain called the head flight attendant forward and explained the procedures for an emergency landing.

> Captain: "We're going to try to put into Sioux City, Iowa. It's gonna be tough . . . gonna be rough."
> Flight Attendant: "So we're going to evacuate?"
> Captain: "Yeah. We're going to have the [landing] gear down, and if we can keep the airplane on the ground and stop standing up [i.e. stop right side up] . . . give us a second or two before you evacuate. 'Brace, brace, brace,' will be the signal . . . it'll be over the PA system: 'Brace, brace, brace'."
> Flight Attendant: "And that will be [the signal] to evacuate?"
> Captain: "No, that'll be to brace for the landing. And then if we have to evacuate, you'll get the command signal to evacuate. But I really have my doubts you'll see us standing up, honey. Good luck, sweetheart."

Thirty-five kilometers from the airport and at 1,300 meters altitude, the plane was still roughly lined up for the runway. Sioux City air traffic control suggested a slight left turn to produce a better approach and to keep the plane away from the city. "Whatever you do, keep us away from the city," the captain implored. Almost immediately afterward, as if in defiance, the plane began its tightest rightward turn, a complete 360-degree circle. The crew desperately tried to bring the nose around to face the runway again. As the aircraft rolled to a severe angle, the check airman exclaimed, "I can't handle that steep of bank . . . can't handle that steep of bank!" For five excruciatingly slow minutes, the plane turned in a circle. Working the throttles, the check airman leveled the wings once more and got the plane back to its original course.

Sioux City control: "United 232 heavy: the wind's currently three six zero at one one. Three sixty at eleven. You're cleared to land on any runway."

The runway that they were heading towards was closed and covered with equipment. Two minutes before touchdown, airport workers scrambled frantically to clear the equipment away. It was also short, at just over 2,000 meters; and, without hydraulic pressure, the plane had no brakes. But Sioux City control assured the captain that there was a wide, unobstructed field at the end. The cockpit crew struggled with the controls through the flight's last seconds.

Captain: "Left turns! Left turns! Close the throttles."
First Officer: "Close 'em off."
Captain: "Right turn. Close the throttles."
First Officer: "Pull 'em off!"
Check Airman: "Nah. I can't pull 'em off or we'll lose it. That's what's turning ya!"
Unidentified voice: "OK."
First Officer: "Left throttle ... left! Left! Left! Left! Left! Left! Left! ... Left! Left! Left!"
[Ground proximity alarm sounds]
First Officer: "We're turning! We're turning! We're turning!"[3]
Unidentified voice: "God!"
[Impact]

The plane hit the ground at the runway's leading edge, just to the left of the centerline. The right landing gear touched the ground first, then the right wing. As the plane skidded across the runway to the right it lost its right engine, chunks of its right wing, and its tail engine. It plowed across the grass, lost its left engine and tail section, and hit the pavement of another runway. The cockpit nose broke off. The remainder of the fuselage cartwheeled away and exploded in flames, coming to rest upside down in the middle of a field.

Of the 296 people on board, 111 died, including one flight attendant. The entire cockpit crew survived.

At first, United 232's experience seems to be no more than an isolated, harrowing event in the skies of the United States—a tale of heroism in the face of terror, of discipline and skill in the face of unforeseen catastrophe. It was a dramatic front-page story that had everybody talking and astonished for a day. Then it receded from public consciousness and was enveloped by the rational, bureaucratic procedures of accident investigators.

But when I read about United 232, something struck a deeper chord. The event could serve, I suspected, as a crude but vivid metaphor for the situation we are all facing, individually and collectively.

When the plane's tail engine disintegrated, the flight crew immediately faced a staggeringly complex task. Multiple, simultaneous, and interdependent emergencies converged in the cockpit. Some were recognized and understood, some were misunderstood, and some didn't even cross the crew's threshold of consciousness. As the crew members tried to make sense of their instruments and the data they received via their eyes and ears, problems cascaded into other problems with almost overwhelming speed. The crew was swept along by a tightly coupled chain of cause and effect. For forty-four harrowing minutes the captain and his officers assessed a prodigious flow of incoming information, made countless inquiries and observations, and issued dozens of commands. Even with extra help from the check pilot, it was all they could do to keep the plane aloft and roughly on course to a crash landing.

Of course, our daily lives don't have nearly the same drama or urgency. But most of us feel, at least on occasion, that we are losing control; that issues and emergencies, problems and nuisances and information—endless bits of information—are converging on us from every direction; and that our lives are becoming so insanely hectic that we seem always behind, never ahead of events. Unexpected connections among places and people, among macro and micro events, connections that we barely understand in their true dimensions, weave themselves around us. Most of us also sense that, just beyond our view, immense, uncomprehended, and unpredictable forces are operating, such as economic globalization, mass migrations, and changes in Earth's climate. Sometimes these forces are visible; more often they flit like shadows through our consciousness and then disappear again, behind the haze of our day-to-day concerns.

Yet the flight of United 232 is more than a vivid metaphor for a world of converging complexities and connections, of decision-making at high speeds in conditions of high uncertainty, and of the difficulty of managing in such circumstances. It is also a metaphor for crisis—for the sharp, unexpected, blinding events that sometimes send us reeling. Investigation after the crash revealed that the engine explosion was caused by a fatigue crack in the tail engine's stage-1 fan disk, a large doughnut of titanium alloy out of which the blades of the jet engine's fan radiate. The crack started near the center of the disk, at the site of a tiny metallurgical flaw formed when it had been cast seventeen years before. Slowly, imperceptibly, during 38,839 hours of flying time (about 7 billion revolutions of the disk), this flaw turned into a crack, and the crack grew in length.[4] At the time of the disk's last inspection, in April 1988, it was over a centimeter long and should have been noticed by United's inspectors. But it was not.[5] And 2,170 flight hours later, in a split second, the crack shot outwards to the edge of the disk, and the disk blew apart.

In our personal lives we sometimes see similarly sudden and shocking events: physical or mental disease unexpectedly affects a loved one, companies we deal with abruptly go bankrupt, and computers, televisions, and cars suddenly break down. Within the larger society, stock markets crash, revolutions break out, and floods devastate communities. The simple mental models in our heads, the models that guide our daily behavior, are built around assumptions of regularity, repetition of past patterns, and extrapolation into the future of slow, incremental change. These mental models are the autopilots of our daily lives. But no matter how much we plan, build buffering institutions and technologies, buy insurance, and develop forecasts and predictions, reality constantly surprises us. Sometimes these are happy surprises; sometimes they are not. Rarely are our reactions neutral.

United 232 also offers some reassuring lessons about our ability to react. Faced with sudden calamity, the crew members used their wits and their courage to save almost two-thirds of the lives aboard. The U.S. National Transportation Safety Board (NTSB) declared that "under the circumstances, the UAL flight crew performance was highly commendable and greatly exceeded reasonable expectations." The situation they faced was unprecedented: they hadn't trained for it; no airline crew had ever trained for it. Such a disaster was thought too unlikely or too catastrophic to justify specific training. The pilot and his officers therefore had to invent, on the spot, a method for controlling the plane. They also had to assess the plane's damage, choose a place to land, and prepare their passengers for a crash landing.

The moment the engine exploded, crew members had to meet a sharply higher requirement for *ingenuity*—that is, for practical solutions to the problem of flying the aircraft in new conditions.

The decision-making process they used to meet this ingenuity requirement has been studied in minute detail by Steven Predmore, currently a manager of human-factors analysis at Delta Airlines in Atlanta.[6] Predmore examined the transcript produced from United 232's cockpit voice recorder. He reduced the thirty-four minutes of recorded conversation to a series of "thought units"—that is, "utterances that deal with a single thought, action, or issue." He then classified these thought units by type, speaker, and target, which allowed him to analyze the crew's response to the emergency. Since thought units are almost the same as individual pieces of information, his technique created "a rough index of the rate of information transfer" among crew members.[7]

Predmore found that the number of thought units averaged about thirty per minute with peaks of fifty to sixty per minute. In other words, with every one or two ticks of a watch's second hand, a chunk of information flew across the cockpit. (For comparison, during demanding moments of routine flight, aircraft crew members rarely transmit more than fifteen thought units per minute.) The thought units came in all forms: commands by the captain; advocacy of actions by junior officers; observations about the state of the plane; requests for information concerning, for example, possible landing sites; statements of intent; and expressions of emotional support. Much of the communication was in parallel, with independent, simultaneous conversations overlapping and intersecting. The highest rate of flow during United 232's flight—almost one thought unit per second—occurred fifteen minutes after the explosion. "This represents the point," Predmore says in the doctoral dissertation he delivered at the University of Texas in 1992, "where the check airman enters the cockpit after his visual damage inspection, and he is immediately brought into the loop with regard to damage to the flight control systems, corrective action that is ongoing, decisions about where to land, and instruction on the manipulation of the throttles."[8]

For the entire duration of the crisis, the crew members were close to a human being's peak cognitive load: they were processing information, making decisions, and supplying ingenuity about as quickly as humanly possible. The load was extreme in part because the crew was enveloped by uncertainty and lacked a clear understanding of the aircraft's state: expert analysis later showed that the cockpit's flight controls were completely useless. "Both the captain and first officer were fighting the stick to maintain control," Predmore told me, when I interviewed him eight years after the crash, "but it turns out that they could have actually let go of the stick entirely. The only thing that helped was the check airman's use of differential engine thrust."[9] Given the circumstances, however, the captain and first officer were right to keep manipulating the controls. "It's easy to look back and say it was a simple problem, because there was actually very little they could do to control the aircraft," Predmore went on. "But they didn't know that there was little they could do. They had some sense that they had flight control, but they didn't know which systems were working."

Ingenuity requirements were so high that the check airman quickly became indispensable. "The demands created by the use of differential engine thrust to control the aircraft" made it almost impossible for either the captain or the first officer to attend to other tasks.[10] The addition of the check airman to the crew allowed the captain to assign priority to tasks, divide and delegate them among crew members, and monitor the crew's performance. "The captain was an amazing leader," Predmore noted. The check airman's extra help, combined with the captain's effective organizing of the resources he had, allowed the crew to act like a precisely coordinated team; they became almost a single mind, and supplied enough ingenuity to direct the plane to a crash landing.

United 232 was also blessed with a great deal of luck. The crisis occurred during daylight, in good weather, and in reasonable proximity to an airport. "Had any one of these factors been different, the outcome would have been different," Predmore concluded. "The captain said the number one factor was luck. After the accident, they reprogrammed the scenario into a flight simulator, and on thirty-five attempts, they couldn't get anywhere near the runway."[11] In fact, based on these simulator exercises, the Safety Board concluded that "landing at a predetermined point and airspeed on a runway was a highly random event. . . . [Such] a maneuver involved many unknown variables and was not trainable, and the degree of controllability during the approach and landing rendered a simulator training exercise virtually impossible."[12]

_____

Is our world becoming too complex to manage? Can all societies supply the ingenuity they need to meet the challenges they face? Sometimes it seems that we are collectively careening into the future, very much as United 232 careened to a crash landing. Must we, in response to the challenges before us, turn ourselves and our societies into analogues of the United 232 crew? Must we become tightly integrated decision-making units, hypercharged with adrenaline and fighting to stay on top of events?

My long-standing interest in how societies adapt to complex stresses dates back more than two decades. For many years this interest remained unfocused and uncrystallized in my mind; it was barely more than a background concern that created a fragile connection between disparate current events that I read about in newspapers. But a specific intellectual challenge I faced after I finished my doctorate at MIT in 1989 led me to put boundaries around my interest in social adaptation and give it more definition.

I grew up in a rural area outside Victoria, British Columbia, in the 1950s and 1960s. My father worked as a forester, and my mother was an artist and illustrator of wildlife, so as a young boy I learned to love the outdoors and take an interest in environmental issues. Both my parents were also attuned to the ebb and flow of current affairs, and we spent hours talking about what was going on in the world. It may have been watching the unfolding, televised horrors of the Vietnam War, or perhaps our family discussions of the century's history, especially of events surrounding World War II, but something instilled in me a deep curiosity about the causes of human violence. When I arrived at university, many years later, I focused my studies on a phenomenon that truly bewildered me—the nuclear arms race between the United States and the Soviet Union.

Eventually I entered the political science program at MIT, where I continued my studies of international relations and defense and arms control policy. But gradually I shifted away from these issues to return to the deeper, underlying question: What makes people fight each other? I was especially intrigued by the processes behind "group-identity" conflicts, which involve a stark distinction between "us" and "them." This category includes violence that centers on nationalist, ethnic, racial, or other ethnocentric identities. In my dissertation, I carefully analyzed and tested several of the best theories of group-identity conflict.

In my first research project after graduation, I combined my two chief interests: conflict and the environment. I decided to explore whether violence inside poor countries could be traced to critical environmental problems. Many poor countries in the developing world suffer from severe pollution, scarcity of fresh water, erosion of cropland, deforestation, and depletion of fisheries. Could this environmental stress, I asked myself, increase the risk of insurgencies, ethnic clashes, urban riots, and coups d'état? For about seven years, with the help of a wonderfully talented group of researchers and advisers from fifteen countries, I worked to answer this question, with considerable success.[13] But once I was deep into the issue, I found that environmental problems cannot, by themselves, cause violence. They must combine with other factors, usually the failure of economic institutions or government. Some societies, it turns out, adapt quite smoothly to environmental stress, while others succumb to confusion and deterioration. Why, I wondered, did some succeed and others fail?

Over time, I came to the conclusion that a central feature of societies that adapt well is their ability to produce and deliver sufficient ingenuity to meet the demands placed on them by worsening environmental problems. Basically, I proposed, societies that adapt well are those able to deliver the right kind of ingenuity, at the right time and place, to prevent environmental problems from causing severe hardship and, ultimately, violence.

Within this rudimentary theory, I defined *ingenuity* as ideas that can be applied to solve practical technical and social problems, such as the problems that arise from water pollution, cropland erosion, and the like. Ingenuity includes not only truly new ideas—often called "innovation"—but also ideas that though not fundamentally novel are nonetheless useful. Social theorists have long known that something like ingenuity is key to social well-being and economic prosperity. Experts in history, economics, organizational theory, and cognitive science recognize that an adequate flow of the right kind of ideas is vital, and that we need to understand the factors that govern this flow. For example, Paul Romer, a Stanford economist who pioneered the field of New Growth theory, argues that ideas are a factor of economic production just like labor and capital.[14] For him and like-minded economists, ideas have intrinsic productive power and are responsible for a significant part of economic growth.

Taking Paul Romer's argument as a starting point, I began to think of ingenuity as consisting of *sets of instructions* that tell us how to arrange the constituent parts of our social and physical worlds in ways that help us achieve our goals. We need copious ingenuity to address the commonplace challenges around us. Every day, for instance, an average city receives thousands of tons of food and fuel, tens of millions of liters of water, and hundreds of thousands of kilowatt hours of electricity. Huge quantities of wastes are removed, hospitals provide health services, knowledge is transmitted from adults to children in schools, police forces protect property and personal safety, and hundreds of committees and councils from the community to the city level deal with governance. The amount of ingenuity needed to run this system is, of course, not the same as the amount needed to create it, because at any one time an enormous array of routines and standard operating procedures guides people's actions.[15] But our urban system, with its countless elements, is the product of the incremental accretion of human ingenuity. It was created, over time, by millions of small ideas and a few big ones.

I soon realized that ingenuity comes in two distinct kinds: the kind used to create new technologies, like irrigation systems that conserve scarce water, or custom-engineered grains that grow in eroded soil, and the more crucial kind used to reform old institutions and social arrangements and build new ones, including efficient markets, competent and honest governments, and productive schools and universities. I called these two kinds *technical* and *social* ingenuity.

Technical ingenuity helps us solve problems in our physical world—such as requirements for shelter, food, and transportation. Social ingenuity helps us meet the challenges we face in our social world. It helps us arrange our economic, political, and social affairs and design our public and private institutions to achieve the level and kind of well-being we want. The crisis aboard United 232 nicely illustrates the difference between the two kinds of ingenuity. The captain initially used differential engine thrust to control the plane—an example of technical ingenuity, because differential thrust was a strictly technological solution to the problem. But he recognized that the load of tasks in the cockpit was simply too great for the three people there; a technological solution, by itself, was not enough. So he accepted the check airman's unexpected offer of help and created a new allocation of tasks within the cockpit—an example of social ingenuity that allowed him to devote time to integrating the crew's performance. It also helped him think farther into the future.

Social ingenuity, I came to understand, is a critical prerequisite to technical ingenuity. We need social ingenuity to design and set up well-functioning markets; and we need market incentives to produce an adequate flow of new technologies. Astute political leaders bargain, create coalitions, and use various inducements to put new institutional arrangements into place; competent bureaucrats plan and implement public policy; and people in communities, towns, and households build local institutions and change their behavior to solve the problems they face: they are all supplying social ingenuity.

I was making good progress, I thought, in understanding ingenuity's role in our ability to adapt to environmental stress. But once I had grasped the fact that ingenuity was key, a host of new questions arose. Two in particular drew my attention, and would remain with me as I explored this issue in coming years. First: Is humanity's *requirement* for ingenuity rising as its environmental problems increase, and if so, how fast and why? My research so far had strongly suggested that ingenuity requirement goes up as environmental problems worsen, because societies need more sophisticated technologies and institutions to reduce pollution and to conserve, replace, and share scarce natural resources.[16] Second, can human societies *supply* enough ingenuity at the right times and places to meet this rising requirement, and if not, why not?

Our supply of ingenuity, I soon recognized, involves both the generation of good ideas and their implementation within society. It's not enough for a scientist, community, or society simply to think up an idea to solve an environmental problem; the idea must also be put into practice— the hybrid corn must be planted, the new farming credit system must be set up and operated, the community must educate itself to change its behaviors—before the ingenuity can be said to be fully supplied. I soon discovered that many of the critical obstacles occur not when the ingenuity is generated (there is usually no shortage of good ideas) but when people try to implement new ideas. The biggest obstacle is often political competition among powerful groups, which stalls or prevents key institutional reform.

In 1995, I brought all these elements and questions together in an article I published in a leading academic journal.[17] I suggested that many of the societies around the world that are currently experiencing severe environmental problems, from China and Pakistan to Egypt and Haiti, are locked in a race between their soaring requirement for ingenuity to solve these problems and their uncertain ability to deliver it. If a society loses this race—if, in other words, it cannot supply sufficient ingenuity to meet its needs—it develops an *ingenuity gap* between requirement and supply. Societies with severe ingenuity gaps can't adapt to or mitigate environmental stress. And mass migrations, riots, insurgency, and other forms of social breakdown often result.

About this time I had a conversation with a leading trader of financial instruments in Toronto, a conversation that told me something about the factors boosting our need for ingenuity in today's world, and made me realize that I could extend my ingenuity argument beyond poor societies and their environmental problems—that indeed, our rich societies today face ingenuity gaps sometimes even more critical than those facing poor societies.

Over the previous dozen years the trader had climbed the corporate ladder, to his current pinnacle of success as head of a large bank's derivatives trading group. The location of his office, at the apex of a skyscraper, reflected his group's importance to the bank. The entire top floor of the building was packed with advanced computer workstations for the derivative, bond, and currency divisions. Floor-to-ceiling windows offered a spectacular 360-degree view across the city; massive air-conditioners worked frantically to remove the computers' heat. It was an otherworldly scene: advanced technology and ingenuity from sky to sky.

The day had gone particularly badly for the trader. Over dinner, he poured himself another glass of wine. "It only took fifteen seconds," he groaned. "For fifteen seconds my mind went blank, I just couldn't focus, and I lost it."

Five minutes before the close of a crucial trading window at noon, his mother-in-law had called for an update on her portfolio. "I like my mother-in-law, but she phones at the worst times, and she's very insistent. I was keeping my eyes on the trading screens and trying to focus on her questions at the same time. I had a perfect set-up and was ready to move. But she kept talking and talking. When I finally got her off the phone, I had only fifteen seconds to make the calculations and trades. I could have done it—I've done it so many other times—but this time I froze. It cost me a quarter of a million dollars."

Our unlucky trader had recently convinced his skeptical bosses that the bank needed a major upgrade of its analytical capability to stay one step ahead of its competitors in the cutthroat global derivatives markets. He had bought ranks of $25,000 computers and advanced software; and he had hired a clutch of Ph.D.'s in mathematics, some trained by the top institutions in the world, to generate models of trading strategies. They sat for hours in front of giant computer screens producing numerical models and three-dimensional graphic images that looked like weird topographies from another planet. The topographies, which changed their shape like plastic throughout the day, represented shifting profit opportunities on combinations of variables that gauged investment risk, such as foreign exchange rates, interest rates, and commodity values.

To me, the trader's unfortunate experience with his mother-in-law—and his highly developed work environment in general—pointed to a key factor driving up the ingenuity requirement in our world, especially in rich countries. "When I started this business," the trader said, "there was time to reflect, to think through our strategy. Now there's never enough time. Things happen so fast, and I have to hire the smartest people in the world to help make the best decisions at lightning speed." When things happen faster, in greater numbers, and with greater interactive complexity, we need more ingenuity to make the right decisions at the right time.

Only three lifetimes ago—about the year 1800—an average person met no more than a few hundred people in a lifetime. Almost everybody lived in rural areas, personal transport speed was equivalent to the speed of a horse or a sailing ship, and almost all information was communicated directly through speech. At the turn of the twenty-first century, a citizen of a technologically advanced society probably meets hundreds of thousands of people in a lifetime. Most people live in urban areas of extraordinary density by historical standards, they can reach the other side of the planet in less than a day, and they can transmit information instantly by the gigabyte. These changes have multiple effects on ingenuity requirement and supply.

On the requirement side, the advent of billions more people on the planet, each consuming more energy and materials and each with more technological power to produce, invent, communicate, travel, and destroy, has sharply increased the density, intensity, and pace of human interactions; it has helped shift power from states and governments to individuals and subgroups; and it has generated a multitude of environmental and epidemiological stresses, some of them global in scope. In response to this ever more intertwined, unpredictable, and urgent array of technical and social issues—from international financial crises and global climate change to the AIDS pandemic—we must continually make faster and more sophisticated decisions about technologies, policies, and institutional arrangements.

Many of the factors that thus raise our need for ingenuity can simultaneously boost its supply: for example, high population densities greatly increase the flow of useful ideas and thereby generate economic growth. In fact, large, crowded cities are the main engines of wealth production in most economies, because they provide dense and synergistic concentrations of capital, talent, and entrepreneurial opportunity. Increased international trade and faster personal transport speed allow the easier transfer of knowledge and ideas among societies. And many people argue that new information technologies, like the Internet, are unleashing immense creativity as untold millions interact electronically. Around the world, for instance, non-governmental organizations empowered by the Internet are actively working to reform our institutions and solve environmental, human-rights, and other problems.

But a variety of factors, including some of those mentioned above, can restrict our ability to respond with more ingenuity. As new communication technologies swamp us in information, we often devote more time to managing information and less to producing new, high-quality ideas. Subgroups empowered by the Internet and, in some societies, by increasingly lethal means of violence, can more easily block vital institutional reform. Most poor countries, especially in Africa, are desperately short of financial capital, while their human capital—their skilled technicians, educators, and civil servants—hemorrhages towards rich countries. Yet financial capital is essential to fund universities and research institutes and to grease the wheels of institutional reform; and human capital is needed for almost all social improvements. Similarly, despite humanity's progress in reducing global hunger, hundreds of millions of children in poor countries remain malnourished. Many of them suffer cognitive stunting that puts them at a permanent disadvantage in our increasingly knowledge-intensive world. And in many poor countries, creeping scarcities of natural resources, such as water, cropland, and forests, result in political turmoil and violence, which derail the economic reforms needed to deal with these very scarcities.

So an adequate supply of ingenuity at all times and places is not assured; ingenuity does not always appear in the right amounts when and where it is needed. To one degree or another, all human societies are locked in a race between a soaring requirement for ingenuity and an uncertain supply. (The illustration opposite is no more than a very simple schematic representation of the ingenuity gap idea; it raises a variety of technical issues—including the question of how we measure ingenuity—that I will address later.) Some societies are doing better in this race than others: they are preventing their ingenuity gaps from opening too wide, which means they are adapting reasonably well to rapid change, either by keeping their requirement for ingenuity from rising too fast or by raising the rate at which they supply ingenuity. Other societies—mainly those that are very poor—are losing the race decisively. As they fall far behind the leaders, the already huge differentials and contrasts among human societies grow ever wider.

While poor countries are particularly vulnerable to crippling ingenuity gaps, rich countries and global society as a whole are by no means immune. Wherever and whenever they occur, ingenuity gaps tear the fabric of our societies, making them more polarized, intolerant, and unstable.

The Ingenuity Gap

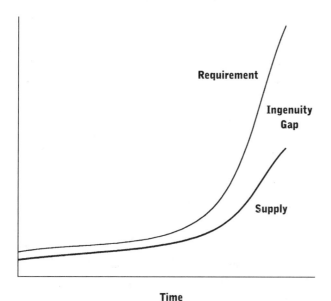

As I was exploring this idea through the mid-1990s, I realized that at its core it was not new. Writing in 1945 at the end of his long life, the novelist H. G. Wells (a man of extraordinary prescience) somberly reflected that "hard imaginative thinking has not increased so as to keep pace with the expansion and complications of human societies and organizations." This was, Wells went on, "the darkest shadow upon the hopes of mankind."[18] In the mid-1980s, the famed historian William McNeill similarly commented that "intelligence and ingenuity . . . run a race with all the nasty eventualities that interfere with human hopes and purposes; it is far from clear which is winning."[19] And in 1997, a large group of scholars brought together to identify humanity's major challenges concluded that "Today many believe it is possible to shape the future, rather than simply prepare for a future which is a linear extrapolation of the present or a product of chance or fate. [Yet the] complexity, number, and frequency of choices seem to grow beyond the ability to know and decide. Skills development in concept formulation and communications seems to be decreasing relative to the requirements of an increasingly complicated world."[20]

Although my argument's core idea wasn't new, to my knowledge no one had developed it farther, at least not in a way that gave real insights into humanity's situation. No one seemed to have clearly distinguished between, on the one hand, changes in the difficulty of the problems we face and on the other, changes in our delivery of ideas in response to these problems.[21] Perhaps, I thought, the idea hadn't been developed because it is utterly at odds with the prevailing wisdom in Western societies in the 1990s.

A statement I had recently come across seemed to epitomize this wisdom. In a book published by the Brookings Institution, a leading Washington think tank, the prominent Harvard economist Richard Cooper declared that "only two inputs are ultimately required to satisfy all man's material needs on earth: brainpower and energy." And "since energy is one resource with respect to which the earth is not a closed system, receiving from the sun vast amounts daily, both inputs will be in ample supply if society manages its affairs sensibly."[22]

I was already familiar with and respected Richard Cooper's thinking. I knew him to be an insightful commentator on international economic policy, who had been chairman of the Federal Reserve Bank of Boston in the early 1990s and Under-Secretary of State for Economic Affairs in the Carter administration. But here I found his ideas disturbing. His sweeping statement seemed simultaneously important, ill-informed, and evasive.

It was important, because it nicely summarizes the worldview widely shared by many economists and others who are resolutely optimistic about the human condition. Over the long term, everything will be fine, these optimists say, because human beings are ultimately smart enough to solve all of their societies' problems. Yet Cooper's statement also struck me as ill-informed, because it shows little grasp of certain basic physical realities, realities that can't be changed no matter how smart we are. He suggests that solar energy could give us all the power we need, but the energy density of sunlight (that is, the amount of energy per square meter received on the surface of the planet from the sun) is so low that each modern city would require an immense sprawl of solar panels to supply its needs. Even with highly efficient solar panels that convert almost all the sunlight they receive to electricity, the sprawl would be many times larger than the city itself.[23] It is true that the surface of Earth receives from the sun each day several thousand times the amount of energy consumed by human beings. But because of its distribution and relatively low intensity, this sunlight is often not a useful energy source for modern, energy-intensive cities and industries (a fact overlooked by most solar-energy enthusiasts).

Finally, I found Cooper's remark evasive because it avoids the issue of "brainpower" entirely. He leaves a host of key questions unaddressed: What is the trajectory of humanity's need for brainpower? Is this need rising, stable, or falling? Are brainpower and its products (including ingenuity) infinitely available on demand?[24] Or are there critical obstacles to the delivery of enough of the right kinds of brainpower at the right places and times? Brainpower will be in ample supply, Cooper states, "if society manages its affairs sensibly." But doesn't this phrase beg the question? The sensible management of our societies is the very task that will require immense amounts of human brainpower in the future!

Cooper's statement reveals an unalloyed faith in human ingenuity. He's not alone in this faith: he is, in fact, a good representative of a broad group of scholars, analysts, and commentators who wield great influence in Western countries, especially the United States. These *economic optimists*, as I have come to call them, see the human experience as a grand story of exuberance, energy, and expansion—the surmounting of hardship and misery. They correctly point out that, on average, humans have never been so well off, and they generally go on to argue that given enough time, we can solve all our problems—that is, supply the ingenuity we need—through a combination of free markets, science, and liberal democracy. Markets provide incentives for entrepreneurs to solve economic problems; science builds an essential foundation of knowledge about our physical and natural worlds; and democracy broadens the range of people empowered to identify and address social and technical challenges. As markets, science, and democracy spread around the world, they say, the trend towards human betterment will continue indefinitely, and why not? In these circumstances, swift technological change is normal, and all humanity will eventually be brought within its ambit.

Economic optimists usually dismiss any less upbeat assessments of humanity's prospects as little more than hand-wringing. Problems like global climate change or the social dislocations caused by markets might be serious, they concede, but they add that every generation feels it lives on the cusp of chaos. People invariably believe that change is too rapid and that the world is becoming too complex and unpredictable, but in the end they usually manage well. The past two centuries have been a period of astonishing material and social progress for much of humanity—why should the future be different from the past? As the late Julian Simon, one of the optimists' standard-bearers, wrote in 1995, "Almost every absolute change, and the absolute component of almost every economic and social change or trend, points in a positive direction, as long as we view the matter over a reasonably long period of time. That is, all aspects of material human welfare are improving in the aggregate."[25]

In light of humanity's astonishing accomplishments in its short history, such faith in human ingenuity is entirely understandable. As I thought about how societies adapt to complex stresses, the optimists' concepts and theories powerfully influenced me.[26] I took these people very seriously; there was a great deal of *prima facie* evidence they were right—evidence about the past and present states of humanity and about the successes and failures of different forms of social organization. And I wanted to believe them. The elements of their worldview came together with an appealing simplicity and seamlessness that spoke to my fundamental hopefulness, my belief that we can improve our lives if we want to. It also spoke, less admirably, to my ethnocentrism: the social arrangements it trumpets as exemplars are precisely the economic, scientific, and political institutions of the Western civilization in which I live. All the same, I eventually decided that this untempered faith in human ingenuity was often grounded in a partial and selective reality.

Economic optimists usually draw on only a limited slice of today's human experience. Theirs is the hermetic, manufactured world of urban malls, office buildings, and advanced technologies that we see all around us in rich countries. (Indeed, a disproportionate number seem to live and work in the megalopolis of the U.S. northeast, especially New York

City.) When they do travel beyond their high-technology urban cocoons, they usually visit regions or enclaves of similar techno-dynamism. Their travels, the machines they use, the television they watch, the newspapers and magazines they read, and the Web sites they visit all reflect this artificial world.

Such partial exposure to the world can lead us to quite astonishing conclusions. I have heard eminent social scientists of this persuasion say that natural resources "aren't important anymore." Resource extraction industries and resource processing, they argue, make up an ever smaller fraction of the gross domestic products (GDP) of modern industrial countries. Prices of key non-renewable resources, such as metals and petroleum, have fallen over time. And human technical ingenuity has found adequate substitutes for many resources that have become critically scarce.

These assertions are correct as far as they go, but, once again, they capture only part of the reality. They neatly glide by the fact that about half the people on the planet—some three billion, all told—rely on agriculture for their main income, and that perhaps one billion of these agriculturalists are mainly subsistence farmers, which means they survive by eating what they grow. Over 40 percent of people on the planet—about 2.4 billion—use fuelwood, charcoal, straw, or cow dung as their main source of energy; 50 to 60 percent rely on these biomass fuels for at least some of their primary energy needs. Over 1.2 billion people lack access to clean drinking water; many are forced to walk kilometers to get what water they can find. And about a billion people depend directly on fishing for a large proportion of their animal protein.

These people live mainly in Asia, Africa, and Latin America. They depend on local natural resources for their day-to-day survival, and they have little access to the vast technical ingenuity so abundant in the rich countries of North America, Europe, and East Asia. Deforestation, polluted water, depleted fisheries and eroded cropland harshly affect their lives in countless immediate and intimate ways, and natural resources will remain critically important to their well-being for decades to come. Yet many of us manage to ignore the contradiction these people present to our rosy worldview, because we rarely see them or go to the places where they live.

Enclosed within a limited and selective reality, economic optimists tend to make a number of mistakes about the nature of the problems humanity faces and our capacity to solve them—four mistakes in particular, I concluded. First, they tend to take the truly extraordinary improvements in human well-being over the past two centuries and project them linearly into the future, without much questioning or reflection. Yet if we look back over a longer period of time, human affairs have been marked by many sharp changes in economic, social, and environmental conditions, some of which severely harmed our well-being. Linear extrapolation is a dangerous game: the last two centuries' progress is not the only evidence we should use to predict our trajectory into the future. Second, they generally present only highly aggregated statistics about major trends in human well-being, usually statistics on things like life expectancy or per capita GDP averaged across whole societies or regions of the world. But when these statistics are disaggregated—that is, when the averages are broken into subsets—the story is less clear than they suggest. For example, although it is true that the number of hungry people in the world fell in the first half of the 1990s, the progress was concentrated in thirty-seven countries (including the world's largest, in terms of population, China and India); but in nearly sixty countries the number of hungry people actually increased.[27]

Third, economic optimists usually downplay events and facts that raise serious questions about their worldview. Problems like global climate change are dismissed as scientifically groundless or, at worst, minor inconveniences that can and will be surmounted by human creativity. They are the annoying side effects of the explosive improvement in human well-being. Any region (like sub-Saharan Africa) that seems to be moving in a decidedly negative direction is declared an anomaly. Africa is, well, Africa. Attention instead shifts to the bounding economies of North America, Europe, and, until late 1997, East Asia. These regions represent the future of humanity.

Fourth, economic optimists tend to regard markets, science, and democracy as panaceas. But they are not. Most of today's markets are riddled with market failures: the true costs and benefits of the goods and services traded are often not reflected in their prices, and so the ingenuity response of our economies is skewed. Moreover, although conservative commentators often assert that setting up well-functioning markets is a relatively straightforward matter of reducing government interference, modern markets are actually exceedingly complex institutions, and policymakers need enormous ingenuity to put them in place. Science faces serious practical constraints, including human cognitive limits, the varied rates of scientific progress in different domains, rising costs, and vulnerability to social turmoil. Finally, depending on a society's character (that is, on its culture, ethnic cleavages, and the like) and the specific form of its political institutions, democracy can contribute to policy gridlock and even social disintegration.

These four mistakes lead economic optimists to underestimate how much ingenuity human societies need to maintain or raise their well-being, and to overestimate the ability of societies to supply this needed ingenuity. As a result, they are often oblivious to actual and potential gaps between ingenuity requirement and supply.

———————————

Today's overwhelming volume and variety of information makes it possible—by selecting and connecting data points carefully—to paint practically any picture of the world and make it seem accurate. So the pictures we paint are often more a reflection of our deepest personal orientation, especially of our basic optimism or pessimism, than of empirical evidence.[28] All the same, amidst the welter of information that sometimes seems to point in every direction, certain facts about long-term trends around the world ultimately shift the balance of evidence, in my mind, against the economic optimists. These facts indicate that there are chronic and widening ingenuity gaps in a number of domains of human activity. Significant problems, some of them fundamentally new in their character and scope, remain unsolved or are getting worse, in part because we haven't generated and delivered enough ingenuity to address them.

For instance, although average incomes and quality of life around the world are improving, these statistics—which are, again, highly aggregated—hide extreme and growing differences in wealth. Income per person, averaged globally, currently rises by about 0.8 percent per year, but in more than one hundred countries in the last fifteen years income has actually dropped. Some 1.3 billion people—about 30 percent of the population of the developing world—remain in absolute poverty, living on less than a dollar a day.[29] And the gulf between the poorest and wealthiest people on the planet is widening very fast. In 1960, the income of the richest 20 percent of the world's population was thirty times that of the poorest 20 percent; in 1998, it was eighty-two times greater. The combined wealth of the world's richest 225 people (a total of $1 trillion) exceeds the annual income of the poorest 47 percent of the planet's population, about 2.5 billion people. Indeed, the assets of the world's three richest individuals or families—Microsoft's Bill Gates, the Walton family of Wal-Mart stores, and renowned investor Warren Buffett—are now greater than the combined GDPs of the forty-eight poorest countries.[30] Meanwhile, as the rich get richer in developed countries, average household consumption in Africa has plummeted 20 percent over the last twenty-five years. In India, an estimated 60 percent of all newborns are in such poor condition from malnutrition, low birth weight, and other causes that they would be immediately placed in intensive care were they born in California.[31] Never in human history have we seen such differentials between rich and poor. And these differentials are the main cause of huge and often disruptive migrations of people around the world in search of a better life.

Partly as a result of these wealth gaps and migrations, we're managing global medical threats badly. As health care and sanitation systems disintegrate in parts of Africa because of civil turmoil, and as they are stretched beyond their limit by megacities and government failure in South Asia and Latin America, we see sudden outbreaks of infectious disease like cholera, ebola, and the plague. Tuberculosis, the top killer among infectious diseases, has infected 1.75 billion people worldwide, nearly a third of the human population; it kills 3 million a year (a remarkable 5 percent of total deaths from all causes), and its incidence is growing fast. Although researchers in both rich and poor countries have made striking progress in campaigns to eradicate some diseases, including Guinea worm and river blindness, they are only a few steps ahead of potentially devastating strains of drug-resistant bacteria and malaria. Studies in the United States show a thousandfold jump in the resistance of pneumococci bacteria to penicillin in less than ten years. "We need novel antibacterial agents urgently," says Dr. Alexander Tomasz of Rockefeller University. "The new numbers are astonishing."[32]

Meanwhile, the international community has made scant progress developing the collective means to stop mass violence and major violations of human rights: in the Balkans, Iraq, Rwanda, Congo, Angola, Kashmir, Sri Lanka, and North Korea in recent years there have been hundreds of thousands of deaths. Nor has the international community developed the means to manage global flows of financial capital: daily trades on foreign-exchange markets have soared almost one-hundredfold, from $20 billion in the mid-1970s to about $1.5 trillion now. But fewer than 5 percent of transactions relate to materially productive economic exchange. As shown by the 1994–95 Mexican peso crisis and the 1997–98 Asian financial debacle, currency speculation—although often triggered by legitimate weaknesses in a country's economic fundamentals—can overwhelm the stabilization efforts of national central banks. The herd behavior of money traders produces extreme currency volatility, which depresses economic growth and ultimately causes severe harm to the economies affected.

Global environmental problems probably provide the clearest evidence that we are generating challenges that we can barely understand, let alone adequately address. By transporting rock and soil, logging forests, damming rivers, and releasing chemicals into air and water, we are now producing enormous changes in Earth's systems. The geographer Robert Kates and his colleagues note that "transformed, managed, and utilized ecosystems constitute about half of the ice-free earth; human-mobilized material and energy flows rival those of nature."[33]

The results are sometimes quite surprising. When scientists discovered the hole in the stratospheric ozone layer over the Antarctic in the 1980s, they were shocked: they hadn't anticipated it, and they didn't understand the chemical processes that produced it. (Several years of hard investigation were needed to produce a full explanation.) The hole's sudden appearance was a spectacular example of how complex natural systems can respond to relatively small human impacts by changing their behavior in sharp and unpredictable ways. Despite claims by some that the problem has been solved by international agreements to control the release of ozone-eating chlorofluorocarbons, the 1998 hole was the biggest on record (the 1999 hole was almost as large), and the current best estimates suggest that ozone concentrations around the planet will remain depleted for several decades.[34]

And how serious is the loss of ozone over the Antarctic and elsewhere? It's believed to raise the amount of ultraviolet (uv) radiation that penetrates the atmosphere and reaches the surface of the planet. Relative to the 1970s, increases in surface erythemal (sunburning) uv are estimated to range from 4 percent in the Northern Hemisphere mid-latitudes, in the summer and autumn months, to 130 percent in the Antarctic spring. The biological effects are still uncertain, but probably include higher rates of human skin cancer; lower productivity of phytoplankton, macroalgae, and zooplankton in oceans; and changes in the cycles of carbon in aquatic ecosystems.[35]

Some research suggests that higher exposure to ultraviolet radiation is contributing to a sharp drop in the populations of many species of amphibians, especially frogs.[36] From the rainforests of northern Queensland

and Costa Rica to forested mountains in California and Oregon, frog populations are collapsing and some species have disappeared entirely.[37] The causes probably include habitat destruction, climate change, higher exposure to ultraviolet radiation, and widespread contamination of breeding areas by agricultural and industrial chemicals, with all of these factors interacting to weaken amphibians and increase their vulnerability to infections by funguses and parasites.[38]

Numerous other forms of plant and animal species are declining because of human activities, and it is likely that in the next one hundred years at least 25 percent of the biodiversity on Earth will disappear.[39] This will rank among the half-dozen greatest extinctions in the history of life on the planet. And we are living within it. On land, about one in eight plant species is in danger of vanishing.[40] Well-known animals such as the jaguar, rhinoceros, and mountain gorilla may soon be largely eliminated from the wild. At sea, higher ocean temperatures, possibly caused by human-induced global warming, are contributing to the bleaching and death of tropical corals around the world; meanwhile, two-thirds of the world's fisheries are already exploited up to or beyond their sustainable limit, and catches are falling in many of these areas.[41]

This is a grim list of economic, social, and environmental challenges. But our societies, especially the rich ones, will generate and deliver enough ingenuity to solve many of them. As for the problems that can't be solved easily, we will often learn to live with the consequences. Usually this won't be too difficult, because human beings are very good at adjusting to new conditions. Wealthy countries will build more secure frontiers to keep out poor migrants. Strict quarantine procedures will isolate patients who don't respond to drugs. We will wear hats to protect us from the sun, modify our crops to survive in eroded soils, and grow fish in huge aquaculture ponds. Some problems, like the loss of biodiversity, won't have much immediate effect on our quality of life: we will easily and comfortably adjust to a world without jaguars, frogs, gorillas, and many of the species alive today.

To me, though, there is little cause for optimism in these remedies. Nor do I think we have to accept such a future.

By early 1997, I had decided that we might usefully think of human societies as "knowledge factories"—some more successful than others. And I thought that by looking at the ingenuity requirement-supply balance we could gain a new understanding of the problems our societies face. But as I tried to put together the pieces of this ingenuity puzzle, I foresaw a chorus of skeptics gathering round. The claim that humanity is facing serious ingenuity gaps is not proved, I heard them saying; history is a long litany of gloomy forecasts and predictions that did not come true because they underestimated humanity's creative potential. In any case, it's not lack of ingenuity that prevents us from solving our economic, social, and environmental problems, but political struggles over power and values—struggles over what we want, where we should go, and who should benefit. If we resolve these struggles, then the problems we face become largely technical, and are in most cases fairly easy to solve.

These were powerful objections. I knew that I had to tackle them, and many other tough questions, to solve the puzzle. How can we measure ingenuity, and how can we distinguish different types and qualities of ingenuity? How much ingenuity do societies actually need? What, precisely, drives this need? Who are ingenuity's main suppliers? And what are the main obstacles to its supply? With enough time, research, and thought, I felt hopeful that I could answer these questions and concerns.

A good deal of my inspiration to continue came from a poster-sized photograph hanging on my office wall—a photograph of a little girl, no more than two years old. She is sitting in a dusty street, dressed in a plaid tunic, and holding a small clay pot in her lap. In the background, just behind her, a clutch of other pots glows in the sunlight. The photo shows little else. Yet there was something about the look in the girl's eyes—at once sad, angry, and distant—that haunted me.

I had taken the photograph myself, a few years earlier in a street in Patna, the capital of the state of Bihar in India. After a long walk down a noisy, impossibly crowded, and garbage-strewn thoroughfare, I had spotted her on the other side of the road. I crossed over, knelt down beside her, and took five quick shots. The moment lasted no more than thirty seconds. Then I kept on walking.

Bihar, one of the most wretched states in India, is racked by crime, violence, and disease. Its politicians and elites are staggeringly corrupt, even by Indian standards; its pathetic infrastructure of roads, sewers, water pipelines, and electricity grids is collapsing; and its tired croplands must support some of the highest-density farming populations in the country. I went there to study the links among population growth, cropland scarcity,

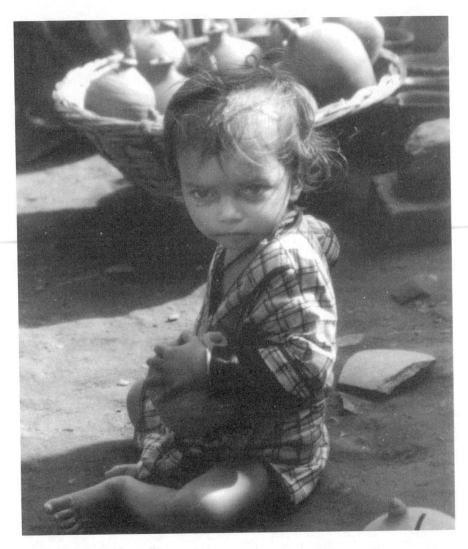

The Little Girl in Patna

and what I soon understood was the utter ineffectiveness of the state's institutions. I left with a wealth of information and ideas provided by the many extraordinary people I met; I also left with photographs of the little girl.

I enjoy taking photographs of children when I travel and have dozens of shots stacked in boxes around my office. A few of these shots, some almost twenty years old, have made it onto my walls. When I look at them, I often wonder who the children are. I wonder about their names, whether they have grown up healthy and happy, and what they are doing now. As I sat at my desk trying to make sense of my ingenuity puzzle, I asked myself these questions about the little girl in the photograph. After a while, I realized she was watching me too. She did not look happy: although she was less than two, her face already betrayed an immense weariness and distance. But I became convinced that she held some of the key pieces to my puzzle—that the story of her life would help me address the tough questions that remained and answer the skeptics.

I decided I would go back to Bihar and try to find her.

First, though, I had to visit other places. There were experts I needed to interview and things I needed to see in England, Canada, and the United States and across East Asia. Only after I had traveled to these places would it make sense to try to find the girl.

The adventure took shape. I wrote letters, lined up interviews, and laid out my itinerary. Colleagues and friends gave me helpful advice by phone, fax, and e-mail. On large sheets of butcher paper, I scribbled plans for my travel and outlines of my ingenuity argument. I tacked the sheets across the walls of my office, nearly obscuring the picture of the girl. Other sheets ended up scattered across the floor, mixed with hundreds of books, papers, and magazine articles.

Under the girl's gaze, I began trying to put my puzzle pieces together: statistics and facts about global forces, historical trends, and huge populations. But it soon dawned on me that my perspective had become so sweeping that I risked losing her: in my mind she was starting to disappear in a vast and undifferentiated crowd of billions of faces. At that moment, she became more to me than simply an arbitrary end point for my adventure. She reminded me daily that while writing my larger story about ingenuity I should remember to see individual faces in the crowd, and make my ingenuity theory meaningful at the level of real people in the real world—farmers in Kansas, bond traders in London, and little girls in Patna.

―――――――――

When United 232's right landing gear hit the runway, it smashed through the concrete and gouged a half-meter hole in the ground. The tip of the right wing broke off, spilling aviation fuel that burst into flames as the plane skidded along the ground. Three times, the plane bounced on its nose, at one point becoming completely airborne again. With each successive impact the fuselage weakened, finally breaking into five separate pieces. By the time the severed cockpit tumbled to rest, it had been compressed into a waist-high piece of scrap metal. Thirty-five minutes passed before rescuers realized that crew members were still alive inside.[42]

Pandemonium reigned inside the main section of the fuselage. Surviving passengers found themselves strapped in their seats hanging upside down. The ceiling of the cabin was now their floor. "Even in the dim light and gathering smoke, the scene was shocking," wrote one passenger later. "Some [people] were struggling to break free. Others were hanging limp and lifeless. From one dangling passenger, blood trickled to the floor. From another still body, it poured in a steady stream. And from yet another lifeless form, an arm hung by a thread while flames consumed the rest."[43]

The crash of United 232 was a terrible accident. The passengers and crew of United 232 were tremendously unlucky that the plane's fan disk disintegrated and wrecked all its hydraulic systems; experts put the odds of such a failure at a billion to one. But they were also amazingly lucky: subsequent analysis showed that nobody, let alone nearly two-thirds of the people on board, should have survived. The crash was one of those events in our world—and there are many of them—that can be interpreted either optimistically or pessimistically, depending on one's starting point.

Nonetheless, at the beginning of my adventure in early 1997, I knew that many people would find my parallel between United 232's experience and the human condition far too pessimistic. At the time, elite opinion in Western countries held that, for the most part, everything was going fabulously—democracy and capitalism were spreading, markets were booming, the Cold War was long in the past, and humanity's future seemed extraordinarily bright. The idea that we were actually spinning around in circles, barely under control, would have seemed ludicrous.

As my travels and research unfolded over the next two years, though, the United 232 metaphor started to seem less absurd. Starting with the Asian financial crisis in mid-1997, a cascade of economic and political events revealed some of the shaky assumptions underpinning elite opinion. Country after country was thrown into recession, and the spread of democracy in places like Africa suddenly seemed less than inevitable. It became clear that, at the very least, humanity's trajectory towards a bright future would not be simple and linear.

During this period, I was struck by other similarities, some of them almost uncanny, between United 232 and our broader situation. With its flight surfaces frozen, the damaged aircraft oscillated up and down through the air, much like a porpoise jumping over ocean waves—a phenomenon that aeronautical engineers call the "phugoid." As a result, the plane responded to changes in engine thrust with a delay of twenty to forty seconds, making a precise landing impossible. Similarly, policy-makers in today's world must often face excruciating delays between the time when important decisions are made and the eventual response of the slow, unwieldy political and economic systems they are trying to manipulate. Meanwhile, events within these systems race ahead. Moreover, because crew members weren't sure which actions in the cockpit improved their situation and which were useless or worse, they faced a skyrocketing cognitive load. The same appears to be true for today's policy-makers, who have available to them a wide range of policy tools, almost all of uncertain effectiveness. And finally, during United 232's last forty-four minutes, the SAM experts on the ground could not help; likewise, one of the most disturbing things about our current world is that the people we anoint as experts constantly fall short of our expectations, especially in times of crisis.

It was only towards the end of my travels that I came to see how United 232's experience also provides a host of positive lessons. Reflecting on the accident, the plane's captain identified a number of factors—including luck, good communications, advance preparation, and close cooperation among crew members, passengers, and ground staff—that allowed them to salvage relative success from what looked like inescapable disaster. His conclusions and those of others convinced me that there are many things we can do to close our ingenuity gaps.

OUR NEW WORLD

I STROLLED up a gently inclined street and emerged on a parade ground overlooking the sea. In front of me, the muscular arms of two huge points of land embraced a magnificent harbor. The view beyond the points out to the horizon was sparkling and clear. On this sunny and breezy September morning, tugs ushered small freighters past a breakwater, Navy vessels maneuvered their way out to sea, and tourists strolled across the broad, brilliant lawn in front of the Citadel.

I was in Plymouth, a relatively small city on England's southern coast that has played a disproportionately large role on the world stage; its story is, in some ways, a synoptic history of the modern Western world. From this harbor sailed armies that conquered France in the fourteenth century, and a fleet that defended England against the Spanish Armada in the sixteenth. From this harbor, too, sailed Drake, Cook, and Darwin to explore the most distant reaches of the planet. Convicts were hustled off to Australia, and half a million emigrants—including those on the *Mayflower* in 1620—streamed past the two points to populate the New World. Napoleon was held prisoner here on his way to St. Helena. English troops departed from this harbor for the Crimea and the Falklands, and Americans for the beaches of Normandy on D-Day. During World War II, Hitler repeatedly bombed the city, starting firestorms that wrecked the downtown, destroyed half the schools and churches, and killed more than a thousand people.

I sat down on a bench to admire the view. In the center of the parade ground, called the Hoe, there is a grand old lighthouse.[1] Largely untouched by the bombing and rebuilding of the city, it was originally constructed

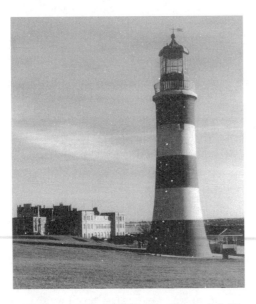

Smeaton's Tower, Plymouth, England (with the MBA building in the background)

on Eddystone Reef, a treacherous shoal about twenty kilometers into the English Channel from Plymouth. Before the mid-eighteenth century this reef had claimed the lives of hundreds of sailors and fishermen on their way to and from the harbor. Local entrepreneurs and merchants had made several attempts to build a lighthouse there, but construction technologies were primitive and the circumstances under which construction had to take place—a reef underwater at high tide, often battered by ten-meter waves—were appalling: many died in the various attempts, and the early lighthouses were destroyed time and again by storms.

Then in the 1750s John Smeaton, a leading English engineer, built a new kind of lighthouse. Large stone blocks were cut to dovetail together, which gave the whole structure much more strength. Standing almost twenty-five meters above high water, the Smeaton lighthouse had a flared base and a beautiful hyperbolic arc to its sides; its design was to become the standard for stone lighthouses around the world. This new tower was not dashed to pieces by storms, and about 120 years later, when the time came for a bigger and more powerful light, the tower's upper portion was dismantled and rebuilt on a new base in the middle of the Hoe, where tourists admire it today.[2]

Climbing the tower's narrow internal stairways, I came to an octagonal, glass-enclosed upper deck. From the ceiling hung the crude chandelier-like rack for the candles used in the original lighthouse. When Smeaton finished his gem in 1759, twenty-four tallow candles in the rack produced sixty-seven candlepower of light—a tiny, flickering beacon to sailors beating up towards the dangerous reef in a storm. Upgrades in 1810 and 1845 added oil lamps, reflectors, and lenses that increased the light flow to 3,216 candlepower. The replacement lighthouse built in 1882 at first produced 79,250 candlepower, and today the same tower generates 570,000 candlepower in two staggeringly powerful bursts of light every ten seconds. In other words, the passage of 250 years—only three and a half lifetimes—has seen a ten-thousandfold increase in the lighthouse's power.

I'm fascinated by our progress in making and using light, but I had not come to Plymouth to admire Smeaton's Tower. I was there, on the first leg of a European trip, to interview Professor Michael Whitfield, the director of the Marine Biological Association of the United Kingdom.[3] The MBA was founded in 1884 and is currently housed in a sturdy stone building on the seaward side of the Citadel. Its first president was the renowned scientist and humanist Thomas Huxley, who in his early twenties had himself gone to sea as a young assistant surgeon on the H.M.S. *Rattlesnake*. Today, the institution remains one of the leading marine research centers in England, focusing on basic marine science, including the biology of invertebrates, the locomotion and feeding of zooplankton, the communication of schooling fish, and human impacts on ocean environments.

Mike Whitfield had come to my attention through a brief article he wrote in the scientific journal *Nature*.[4] He had objected, with poetic vigor, to some remarks published in 1945 by the eminent Russian scientist Vladimir Vernadsky, who was one of the founders of modern geochemistry. Vernadsky's thinking about the complex cycles of elements and energy within Earth's biosphere was decades ahead of its time: he had warned that our impact on the planet's ecology had become so large that it was time to think seriously about human management of the natural resources and cycles of the biosphere. Our impact, in his words, raises "the problem of the reconstruction of the biosphere in the interests of freely thinking humanity."[5] Like him, many people now believe that we can manage the biosphere and should do so in our own interests. Yet in his *Nature* article, Whitfield had been scathing about such grandiose notions: "I recoil from this vision!" he declared. "We should rather understand our dependence on [Earth's] grand cycles, and learn to tread softly in their presence."

I left the Hoe and the view across Plymouth's harbor and walked to the utilitarian building that houses the MBA. A public aquarium occupied the ground floor, and demonstration tanks full of fish and sea anemones lined the upstairs corridor. I found Mike Whitfield's office, and he greeted me at the door. A genial man of fifty-seven with bushy gray hair surrounding a bald pate, he welcomed me to morning tea at a large oak table covered with journals and scientific articles.

"The first thing people must grasp," he said, after we had spent a few minutes getting acquainted with each other, "is that we must view Earth's systems as a functioning whole. We must learn what makes them tick as a whole, not merely the mechanisms of their component parts." There is a critical distinction, he asserted, between a narrow, analytical understanding of how the individual components of Earth's systems work—the understanding pursued by most contemporary science—and the more holistic perspective that he believes scientists and laypeople need to adopt. Moreover, he stressed, "complex systems exhibit emergent properties: as elements are added, complex behavior emerges. And even advanced and sophisticated models of these systems cannot capture their inherent unpredictabilities. We often know that the system will operate within a certain envelope of behavior—but not exactly where it will be within that envelope."

The key idea here, it seemed to me, was the *emergence* of new and unexpected properties as individual components are combined into increasingly complex systems. "Emergent properties" have long fascinated philosophers of science. They commonly use the wetness of water as a good example: wetness is a property of neither the hydrogen nor the oxygen that together make up water, but when these elements are combined, the resulting water has the entirely novel characteristic of wetness. (To use the common aphorism, the whole is more than the sum of its parts.) Moreover, water's wetness, some philosophers claim, cannot be predicted. We cannot anticipate that the combination of hydrogen and oxygen will be wet, even if we have complete knowledge of these elements' individual properties. Similarly, as Mike Whitfield explained to me, when the multitude of components of Earth's biosphere—the forests, soils, atmosphere, oceans, and phytoplankton—are brought together into various interlinked systems, they interact to produce complex and often unanticipated properties and behavior.[6]

"Many of these complex systems," he continued, "are governed by feedbacks, and if stressed too much they can move to radically new equilibria. The feedbacks often allow Earth's biosphere to operate as a control, as a thermostat if you like, on interactions between the atmosphere, land, and oceans."[7] In other words, they provide stabilizing mechanisms, dampening negative interactions among system components and reinforcing positive interactions. But I would be very surprised if these systems didn't have the capability to shift to entirely new equilibria if they are pushed too far.

"Take the Mediterranean, for example. A combination of factors—including reduced river runoff (especially from the Nile), salty brines coming in through the Suez, and perhaps climate change—has caused a large shift in circulation patterns. Whether this is an unusual occurrence is hard to say, and we don't know what its potential consequences might be. But some researchers think that the higher salinity of deep Mediterranean water could affect the stability of water formation as far away as Iceland. Laypeople think that the Mediterranean is isolated from outside oceans, but it's just not true: a huge amount of water pours through the Straits of Gibraltar. Great boluses or globs of this water—called *Meddies* by specialists—migrate along the continental shelf towards Iceland."

"What do you mean," I asked, remembering his comments on Vernadsky, "when you say that we should 'tread softly in the presence' of Earth's grand cycles?"

"We really don't know how many important features of Earth's grand systems work," he stressed. "For example, the MBA has begun a program to gather information on the impact of human beings on marine ecosystems along the English Channel. We're asking: What is the assimilative capacity of the coastal sea? How much rubbish can we dump? And how much fish can we take out? But this is an almost impossible task because we don't really know which species inhabit the waters of coastal Europe. We don't have a proper count of the species there; of those species we have identified, we often don't know what they do; and we therefore can't possibly know how the whole coastal ecosystem operates. We do know, from our studies of other ecosystems, that some species aren't essential to the overall functioning of the ecosystem. But others are *keystone* species, and if we remove them we will gravely damage the whole system. In the case of the English Channel, determining a particular species' role is often staggeringly difficult.

"Our ignorance is compounded by the fact that human societies and many natural systems operate on radically different time scales. It takes countless millennia for nature to build up biological capital—to build up, for instance, the capital represented by the diversity of species in the English Channel—yet we can wipe out much of that capital in an extraordinarily short time. As we exploit these systems of natural resources at a very high rate, we don't appreciate the length of time it took nature to create the resources in the first place." As he spoke, I could see the Channel behind him through the windows of his office. He paused, pensively, before going on. "It takes between one hundred and one thousand years to create one to two centimeters of topsoil, yet we can strip that soil away in a few years. It can take tens of thousands of years for rainwater to fill water-bearing aquifers in the ground, yet we often deplete these aquifers in decades. Moreover, because many of Earth's systems operate on time scales of hundreds, thousands, and millions of years, they are very slow to recover from human insults. Consequently, we don't know how we are changing the long-term relationships between ourselves and our environment."

We had talked for almost two hours, and soon I rose to leave. But before I went, Mike Whitfield wanted to emphasize a central point. "Fundamentally, humanity's approach to the ecosystems on which it depends arises out of arrogance. We have a misplaced optimism about our abilities." Global ecosystems, he noted, cannot be managed consciously, just as we can't manage our own bodies consciously. "Inside our bodies, a lot of things are ticking over without much thought, and if we had to manage consciously all these things—the beating of our heart, the flows of hormones, the cellular repair processes—we would be utterly overwhelmed. The same is true of global ecosystems. The irony of the situation is that in the end we may actually be condemned to manage these ecosystems because we have perturbed and destabilized them so much. And I am certain that we won't be any good at it."

A few minutes later, I stood on the Hoe again, looking out across Plymouth harbor. Somehow, I was sure, Whitfield's comments, the splendid yet inscrutable sea in front of me, the grand history of Plymouth and Smeaton's lighthouse were all part of one story. Yet I wasn't sure how these individual threads wove together to make that story, or even what the story said. It would be months before I knew.

Over the next days, while I talked to other experts across England—economists, demographers, and specialists on the problems of poor countries—my mind returned again and again to that moment on the Hoe. I realized I had already grasped one of the Plymouth story's threads: it had wound its way through Mike Whitfield's comments.

Humankind is entering a fundamentally new world. Many changes have opened the door to this world. Some have been sharp and conspicuous—the demise of the Soviet empire, for example, or the widespread use of the World Wide Web. Other changes, most in fact, have been small and incremental. Individually they aren't particularly novel or interesting; indeed, they are almost unnoticeable. Yet these countless small *quantitative* changes in the nature of our technologies, in the character of our societies, in the size of our population, and in our impact on the ecosystems around us add up, over time, to major *qualitative* changes in our lives, communities, and surroundings.

This new world has arrived insidiously, creeping up on us while we were distracted by day-to-day activities and passions. We gave it little thought or self-conscious reflection, because human beings adjust smoothly to incremental changes in their circumstances. We didn't really notice that things had become vastly different from the way they were. Instead, we turned around and the new world was simply here, part of our lives, a *fait accompli*.

Nonetheless, taken together, these small changes have produced spectacular results: they have dramatically raised the complexity, unpredictability, and pace of events around us. These trends, in turn, have had a huge impact on our need for ingenuity and our ability to supply it. Moreover, because this new world is, in important respects, essentially different from the one we knew in the past, the signposts we used previously to guide our behavior will not necessarily be good signposts in the future.

A particularly important quantitative change behind this qualitative change has been the growth of the human population. During the twentieth century this population nearly quadrupled, from 1.65 billion to around 6 billion people. Never before have our numbers increased so fast in absolute terms, as the eight-century span in the illustration on the following page shows. In 1900, the annual growth of our population was about 10 million people; at the beginning of the twenty-first century, it is just under 80 million (it peaked in the late 1980s at 87 million).[8] This growth has intimately influenced the lives of people and societies in every corner of the planet.

Yet beyond our vague intuition that 6 billion is a very large number, most of us can't really grasp the statistic's true meaning. Perhaps it's easier if we imagine this population evenly distributed across the planet's 60 million square kilometers of habitable land—across Earth's prairies, rangelands, farms, and urban landscapes; across its coastal plains, terraced hillsides, and temperate forests. Spread out this way, each of us would nevertheless remain within easy calling distance of our neighbors: we would be dotted across the landscape barely one hundred meters from each other.

World Population Soared in the Twentieth Century

The world has become a crowded place. But it will not become more crowded indefinitely; population growth will not last forever. In fact, as we can see in the illustration above, it's already ending. In the last two decades, as education, economic development, and modern ideas have spread and the status of women has improved in poor countries, the average number of babies born to each woman (what demographers refer to as the *fertility rate*) has fallen very fast—indeed, much faster than even the most optimistic demographers predicted. Countries like Thailand, Bangladesh, and Kenya, where women used to have an average of six or more children, have seen that number drop to three and, in some cases, even two. Meanwhile, in many rich countries, especially in Europe, fertility rates have fallen far below the 2.1 births per woman required to replace the population (in Italy, the 1995 rate was 1.17).[9]

The 1998 United Nations' "medium" projection suggests that world population will grow from the current 6 billion to 7.8 billion in 2025 and 8.9 billion in 2050. (Its "low" and "high" projections for 2050 are 7.3 and 10.7 billion respectively.[10]) But the medium projection doesn't necessarily represent the most likely outcome.[11] Given recent fertility data, and given the very real possibility of higher mortality rates in poor countries than the UN projections anticipate, my guess is that the 2050 population will be closer to the low end of the UN's range—around 8 billion—than to the high end.[12]

Yet it is wildly and irresponsibly premature and simplistic to declare—as some commentators have—that "the population explosion is over" and that we should begin worrying about a global "birth dearth" or "population implosion."[13] These commentators are referring mainly to the situation in rich countries, where today's below-replacement birth rates will lead to tomorrow's rapidly aging societies, posing major challenges for economic and social policy.[14] The global situation, however, is very different: the world's total population will not level out, at the earliest, before the third decade of the twenty-first century. It will grow by about 720 million people in each of the next two decades (2000-2010 and 2010-2020), and about 95 percent of this increase will occur in poor countries. Around 50 percent of poor countries' growth, in turn, will result from sheer *demographic momentum*: the large number of girls still to reach reproductive age—girls born during the 1980s and 1990s, when the biggest annual increments were added to the world's population—guarantees further population growth even if the best family planning technologies are widely available, which usually they are not.[15]

Many countries' underlying populations are now so large that even small annual growth rates, in percentage terms, still mean large increments in total population. For example, although India's growth rate is now under 2 percent per year and China's is under 1 percent, their respective populations still grow by 15 and 10 million people annually. We should also not forget that the drop in birth rates has not happened to the same degree in all poor countries; in some, birth rates remain very high: in 1997 thirty-three countries, including twenty-five in Africa, still had rates of six children per woman. At least seventy-four countries—including Nigeria, Syria, and Honduras—will likely double their populations in the next two or three decades.[16] Whether we like it or not, therefore, within the lives of today's children, Earth will almost certainly have a human population at least 25 percent and perhaps almost 100 percent larger than it is now.[17]

This population growth does not have to be a bad thing. As many economists rightly point out (and as I will explore more closely in the chapter "Ingenuity and Wealth"), larger populations can boost economic development by generating scarcities of goods, services, and natural resources—scarcities that, in turn, stimulate entrepreneurship and technological innovation. Larger populations also provide more labor to produce goods and services, bigger markets to buy those goods and services, and more heads to generate useful ingenuity.[18] The twentieth century's dramatic growth in human population has been accompanied by history's most astonishing growth in human prosperity, and the two things are, undoubtedly, causally linked. And the causal links probably go in both directions, since larger populations often generate more wealth and more wealth supports larger populations.

Yet population growth is not always a good thing. Whether it contributes to economic prosperity depends on its institutional context—markets, governments, and laws. In combination with inefficient, incompetent, or corrupt institutions, population growth and large populations can harm social well-being. Within the individual family, a larger number of children can mean less investment per child in nutrition, medicine, and education. It can also mean that the pool of family resources—in rural communities, for example, the family's plot of cropland—is divided into smaller and smaller parcels as it is passed to each successive generation of children. At the level of the society as a whole, high fertility rates can divert the economy's savings away from investment towards consumption.[19]

When European populations grew rapidly in the nineteenth and early twentieth centuries, many people who could not find good jobs emigrated to the Americas and to colonies in Africa and Asia. But a similar escape valve is, for the most part, no longer available to today's poor countries, and their extra population must be largely absorbed and employed at home. Many of these people are moving into cities. And combined with the natural growth of the population already living there, these cities are expanding so rapidly that water systems, roads, electrical grids, sewers, and other essential infrastructures of daily life are severely overtaxed.[20]

Data from the 1980s and 1990s suggest that population growth now markedly threatens the quality of urban life in poor countries.[21] Megacities like Karachi in Pakistan have become largely ungovernable.[22] Their potential political instability is magnified by the age structure of their populations: rapid growth has produced a "youth bulge," which means there is a disproportionately large number of young people compared to other age groups. In Africa, for example, over 40 percent of the population is under fifteen years old. Underemployed, urbanized young men are an especially volatile group that can easily be drawn into organized crime or mobilized for violent political action.

Finally, larger human populations usually place a greater burden on the natural environment that surrounds them, and local effects can have global repercussions for the planet's climate, its fisheries, and its supplies of fresh water, cropland, and forests. There are strong reasons to believe that some countries—like China, India, Pakistan, and Egypt—do not have enough high-quality environmental resources to sustain their enormous populations indefinitely. Total population size, however, is not the only thing that determines environmental burden: what the people in the population do is also important. Are they, on average, consuming a lot of natural resources, like petroleum, water, trees, and fish? And are they, on average, producing a lot of waste, such as sewage from houses, nutrients leaching from agricultural land, and heavy metals emitted from factories?

We can estimate, very roughly, the size of our impact on the environment by multiplying our population's size by its per capita level of resource consumption and waste output.[23] When we do this for the whole planet, the results are impressive. From 1900 to 1999, during a century that saw the advent of cars, air conditioners, and luxury vacations at Club Med, per capita annual resource consumption and waste output increased more than fourfold. Taking into account the concurrent fourfold growth in the world's population, the total annual human impact on the planet's environment at the end of the twentieth century was therefore nearly *sixteen* times that of 1900: the population was four times as large and each person consumed each year, on average, more than four times the natural resources and released more than four times the waste.[24]

Of course, responsibility for this outcome was highly unequal. By 1999, some people in rich countries were consuming thousands of times the 1900 average, while many in poor countries were consuming far less than that average. In countries like the United States, Germany, and the Netherlands, the production of goods and services today requires, *for each person*, over eighty metric tons of natural resources annually.[25] Much of this resource requirement is hidden from us, as consumers: for instance, producing food causes about fifteen metric tons of soil erosion for each U.S. resident each year, while building roads and other infrastructure requires moving another fourteen tons of rock and soil.[26]

If we project these figures into the future, by 2050 the world's population will probably have grown to about eight billion, a third larger than it is now. Even assuming only moderate economic growth in poor countries, we can also expect our per capita consumption of resources and our output of waste, averaged across all the people in the world, to at least double. Taking these two factors into account, by 2050 the total quantity of energy, resources, and waste moving through the world's economy each year will have nearly tripled, and Earth's environment will have to withstand nearly three times today's annual impact.[27]

But the most striking fact of all emerges when we look at the entire century and a half between 1900 and 2050. In this period, barely two life-times long, our annual impact on the planet's environment will have increased more than *forty*fold, and almost two-thirds of this increase will have occurred in the first five decades of the twenty-first century—that is, in the next fifty years.[28] This analysis tells us that we have experienced, so far, only the earliest stages, just the leading edge, of the planet's environmental crisis. Far, far greater environmental challenges are still to come.[29]

The combined activities of our enormous population are already producing breathtaking effects.

Our planet is only 12,700 kilometers in diameter—about three times the distance between New York and Los Angeles—and we can easily travel halfway around it in less than a day. We have turned much of its land surface into a patchwork of cities, industrial parks, farms, and rangeland. We have laid on this land a web of roads, canals, and pipelines. We have dug out of it hundreds of billions of tons of material, moved this material around, processed it, and dumped it. Our factory ships and trawlers crisscross the world's oceans to exploit every valuable fishery. Our planes and satellites weave themselves around its sphere.

We are moving so much rock and dirt, blocking and diverting so many rivers, converting so many forests to cropland, releasing such huge quantities of heavy metals and organic chemicals into air and water, and generating so much energy, carbon dioxide, methane, and nitrogen compounds that we are perturbing the deepest dynamics of our global ecosystems. Between one-third and one-half of the planet's land area has been fundamentally transformed by our actions: row-crop agriculture, cities, and industrial areas occupy 10 to 15 percent of Earth's land surface; 6 to 8 percent has been converted to pasture; and an area the size of France is now submerged under artificial reservoirs. We have driven to extinction a quarter of all bird species. We use more than half of all accessible fresh water. In regions of major human activity, large rivers typically carry three times as much sediment as they did in pre-human times, while small rivers carry eight times the sediment. Along the world's tropical and subtropical coastlines, our activities—especially the construction of cities, industries, and aquaculture pens—have changed or destroyed 50 percent of mangrove ecosystems, which are vital to the health of coastal fisheries. And about two-thirds of the world's marine fisheries are either overexploited, depleted, or at their limit of exploitation. The decline of global fish stocks has followed a predictable pattern: like roving predators, we have shifted from one major stock to another as each has reached its maximum productivity and then begun to decline.[30]

Regional Fish Stocks Have Declined in Succession

Fishing Area	**Year of Maximum Harvest**	**Maximum Harvest (000 metric tons)**	**Recent Harvest (000 metric tons)**
Atlantic, Northwest	1967	2,588	1,007
Antarctic	1971	189	28
Atlantic, Southeast	1972	962	312
Atlantic, Western Central	1974	181	162
Atlantic, Eastern Central	1974	481	320
Pacific, Eastern Central	1975	93	76
Atlantic, Northeast	1976	5,745	4,575
Pacific, Northwest	1987	6,940	5,661
Pacific, Northeast	1988	2,556	2,337
Atlantic, Southwest	1989	1,000	967
Pacific, Southwest	1990	498	498
Pacific, Southeast	1990	508	459
Mediterranean	1991	284	284
Indian Ocean, Western	1991	822	822
Indian Ocean, Eastern	1991	379	379
Pacific, Western Central	1991	833	833

But such a string of statistics and facts can numb the mind. By themselves they don't give us a visceral understanding of how we have transformed the planet, subordinated it to our ends, and made it tiny in the process. They don't really tell us how every corner of Earth is now our backyard.

In September 1997, the United States military gave us a sensational display of this human dominion. In a joint war game with Central Asian countries, five hundred U.S. paratroopers from the Eighty-second Air-borne Division dropped out of the sky onto the deserts of Kazakhstan, in the farthest reaches of the former Soviet Union. American transport planes delivered these troops directly from North Carolina to the other side of the planet, refueling from air tankers along the way. Once the planes had disgorged their cargo, they returned to the U.S. as they had come, completing the longest military expeditionary flight in history. After this triumph, the commanding officer, General John Sheehan, exulted, "There is no nation on the face of the Earth we cannot get to."[31]

If every corner of Earth is now our backyard, it's also now our garbage dump. We produce a truly prodigious flow of waste. The largest human-made structure on the planet is not an Egyptian pyramid or a hydroelectric dam but the Staten Island Fresh Kills landfill near New York City, which has a depth of one hundred meters and an area of nine square kilometers. Although each of us makes only a tiny quantitative contribution to the total flow of human waste, these contributions add up, once again, to produce a major qualitative difference in our world. The source of my own visceral understanding of this truth was not a gigantic garbage dump or a list of impressive facts and statistics but, ironically, a lowly plastic bottle.

The summer before my trip to Europe, a friend and I had visited a wild and isolated part of Canada's Pacific coast—the Brooks Peninsula, a rectangular extrusion of mountains, forests, and beaches that juts out into the sea from northwestern Vancouver Island in British Columbia. We arrived by herring skiff and pitched camp at the junction of a long, sandy beach and a river tumbling out of the mountains. The setting was truly grand: in front of us stretched the open Pacific; behind us rose the steep, darkly forested peaks of the peninsula and Vancouver Island.

We expected such a remote place to be relatively pristine. As a child growing up on Vancouver Island thirty years before, I had spent many hours beachcombing with my parents along stretches of coast farther south and closer to major settlements. On these occasions, we had seen few signs of humanity.

But this time things were different. My friend and I found countless pieces of junk strewn across the beach. Everything plastic available in supermarkets was there, and much, much more. Bleach bottles, toys, light bulbs, fluorescent tubes, hard hats, car tires, bicycle tires, chunks of Styrofoam, foam coffee cups, yogurt containers, rubber thongs, plastic water pipe, storage containers, oil drums, plastic milk boxes, dishsoap bottles, disposable diapers, tampon applicators, and fishing floats. Torn and tangled wads of nylon fishing net wrapped themselves around logs tossed to the back of the beach by winter storms. Higher up the shore, in the underbrush of the coastal rainforest, plastic debris littered the forest floor, also blown there by storms. And everywhere there were thousands upon thousands of clear plastic water and soft-drink bottles. Plastic bottles of engine lubricant appeared in huge numbers too, all chucked off the decks of fishing boats, trawlers, and freighters. Plastic bottles were inescapable.

Jutting out into the Pacific as it does, the Brooks Peninsula is well positioned to catch debris from the North Pacific, Alaska, and California currents that cycle past Vancouver Island. The peninsula acts a bit like a net thrust into a stream full of garbage. Sometimes interesting things arrive in the stream, such as the old glass fishing floats from Japan that West Coast beachcombers prize. But we were unlikely to find any such treasures during our visit: each spring, after the big storms have passed, private helicopters now scour even the most distant shores of British Columbia for all valuables. And in contrast to thirty years ago, we were also unlikely to be alone. Human populations are now much larger and wealthier. Brooks is a long boat ride from the nearest launch point, and float planes are banned from the area, but lots of people (including my friend and me) now have the leisure time and modern wilderness technologies to reach the area. Every day we were greeted by a new round of happy kayakers paddling up the coast.

We had a wonderful holiday. We found that we could ignore the plastic on the beach and turn our attention easily to the glorious sea and mountains. And the adventurers paddling by were without exception pleasant people who respected the outdoors and our privacy.

After a few days, the herring skiff returned. Reluctantly, we started back to the city. Our skipper, Esmo, was a taciturn old Scandinavian who had come with his family in the 1920s to the northwest coast of Vancouver Island—a place that must have seemed, in those days, like the end of the world. During our long trip down the coast he loosened up a bit. Occasionally he pointed out a feature of the land or sea and told us a story about the local natives in the early days or about his life as a fisherman. He had a delightfully wry view of the coast and the diverse peoples who had settled there. We mentioned the amount of junk on our beach, and he agreed that the problem had become much worse. A few years before, he said, a freighter bound from Asia had lost a container of shoes off its deck. When the container broke apart, shoes washed ashore up and down the coast. People from isolated hamlets and villages rushed to pick them up, and a brisk trade in individual shoes began as the scavengers tried to create matching pairs.

We laughed at that story. But the sea and shore were sending poignant messages too. On our way home, we were reminded yet again how small the planet has become and how humanity has changed it. We passed dozens of small rocks and islands just offshore. At one time, Esmo told us, they had been covered with birds—puffins, gulls, cormorants, and other species. Now the islands were completely bald, with not a bird to be seen. "Minks, rats, or less feed," he explained. Perhaps minks and rats were raiding the nests. But in the last few years Canadian and American overfishing had helped cause a collapse in fish stocks off the coast. It was hard to avoid the conclusion that the birds had gone, at least in part, because the fish had gone.[32] (In the single month of July 1918, just one of the dozens of fish traps strung along the southwest coast of Vancouver Island caught over thirty metric tons of spring salmon; eighty years later, sports fishermen in the same area were allowed to catch just one fish per day.)

Continuing southeast, we cruised by a chain of thousand-meter mountains that rose directly out of the sea and ran parallel to the coast. Soon we were opposite some of the world's most notorious logging clear-cuts. Featured in major television documentaries and multiple-page photospreads in magazines like *National Geographic*, these clear-cuts must be seen to be believed. From the shoreline up to the mountain peaks, and for kilometers of coastline, every tree had been felled or burnt. Logging roads cut across the slope in long diagonal lines, like the slashes of a giant's saber. When these side hills were originally logged, the timber company had followed standard practice and intentionally lit fires to clear away the remaining debris of stumps and broken branches. But the fires had escaped their boundaries and swept to the tops of the peaks. The resulting denuded mountainsides, easily visible from the sea, became a public relations disaster. Anti-logging crusaders sent photographs around the world, and the site became a potent symbol in a remarkably effective European campaign against British Columbia's wood products.

Esmo told us that some of the people who caused the mess were fired. The logging company began an expensive reforestation and land restoration program, planting trees, obliterating logging roads, and rebuilding creekbeds. We could see that much of this work had succeeded: in the thirteen years since the catastrophe, the lower slopes had begun to go green with new Douglas firs, some more than seven meters tall. But there was irreparable damage too. The region receives some of the highest rainfalls in the world. With the trees gone and residual logging roads forming channels for storm runoff, thousands of tons of topsoil had washed directly into the sea. On a single side hill, I counted nine major erosion slides—including one that appeared to have carved off the whole corner of a mountain. Creeks and gullies were plugged with fallen rock and logging debris. And the upper quarter of the slopes showed little evidence of forest regeneration—there was hardly any soil left there to support the planted trees.[33]

The extreme anti-logging hyperbole of many environmentalists has always struck me as a bit hypocritical. Anti-logging activists often live in wood houses, and they all use reams of paper to disseminate their publicity. To support an adequate standard of living, humankind still needs huge quantities of wood and wood products, from planking and beams and fibreboard to paper. We need trees, lots of them, and we must therefore use a good fraction of Earth's surface as cropland for tree farms. Indeed, British Columbia's terrain and temperate climate are ideal for growing softwood suitable for construction. I know that we can grow and harvest trees sensibly: during his career in B.C., my father worked as a forester and built a reputation as an innovator of logging and reforestation techniques that cause minimal damage to the land. As a child and young man, I spent many hours watching his employees use these techniques, and for two summers I worked in the B.C. forest industry myself, surveying tracts of timber for logging.

But on that sunny afternoon, the clear-cuts southeast of Brooks looked less like tree farming and more like pillage. Along with the vanished fish and birds and the endless plastic junk on the beach, they told us more clearly than any statistic that humankind has seized this tiny planet in its grip and made the whole of it its own. What we saw in that little patch of western Canada was not unusual: similar things are happening practically everywhere, from the Baltic to Siberia, the Amazon, and Indonesia.

What we saw there also reinforced something I'd seen on every continent in my travels: humanity can no longer escape from itself and its doings. There was a time when the adventurous and pioneering could go to a new land, open up a frontier, and try again. In many of these frontier lands in Canada, Australia, Latin America, Africa, and elsewhere, the population densities, including both indigenous peoples and the first waves of colonists, were extremely low. As recently as the middle of the twentieth century, the planet seemed large enough to offer room for such escape. In the last few decades, however, the global frontier has closed. There is nowhere new, untrammeled, and unexplored to go. There is nowhere that loggers, American paratroopers, or happy kayakers can't reach. We are trapped with each other in Earth's biosphere, a life-supporting layer no thicker, proportionately, than the skin of an apple. But we are still treating this world as if it were endless.

Along the coast of Vancouver Island, my friend and I saw a few of the changes human beings are producing in their physical world. The sights had a palpable emotional effect: we were thrilled by the beauty of the mountains and sea, alarmed by the now-bare rookeries, and appalled by the ugliness of the clear-cut mountains. But our Vancouver Island experience, by itself, could not give us a full appreciation of the scale, multiplicity, and gathering speed of environmental changes around the planet.

If it were possible to compare satellite photographs of Earth taken before large-scale human activity with photographs taken today, several differences would be immediately obvious. One would be the astonishing amount of light humanity emits at night—something I will explore later. Another would be the extent of deforestation. This deforestation has occurred through logging (as on Vancouver Island) and more significantly, through the conversion of forested land into cities, cropland, and pasture for cattle, sheep, and goats. Forest fires started by human beings have also taken a huge toll. The earlier photos would show woodlands and closed forests covering about six billion hectares—about 40 percent of Earth's land surface, or over six times the total area of the United States.[34] Today's photos would show that about a third of this forest cover has disappeared.[35]

This aggregate figure, however, is misleading. Up to the middle part of the twentieth century, most forest loss occurred in the temperate zones of North America and Europe, and in some parts of Asia, especially China and India. In the last several decades, replanting, natural regeneration, and more efficient use of wood have reversed this trend in North America and Europe. (Standing timber volume in the United States has actually increased 30 percent since the mid-twentieth century, thanks in large part to plantations of fast-growing trees in the southern states.[36]) But, at the same time, deforestation has skyrocketed in tropical developing countries, as rural populations in those regions exploded and worldwide demand soared for mahogany, teak, sandalwood, and other exotic woods. In the thirty years between 1960 and 1990, Asia lost nearly a third of its tropical forests, while Latin America and Africa lost almost a fifth.[37] During the single decade of the 1980s, an area of tropical forest nearly three times the size of France (more than one and a half million square kilometers) was converted to other uses.[38] Although the rate of deforestation then declined a bit, a swath of tropical forest larger than New York State (121,898 square kilometers) nevertheless disappeared each year between 1990 and 1995.[39]

Satellites take photographs from space that show the depletion of forests around the planet. On the ground, this loss of trees causes visible changes in people's surroundings and has direct effects on the quality of their lives. People who depend on trees for their well-being can see that forests are gone, that soil erosion and flash floods are worse as a result, and that fuelwood can't be found.

But humanity is producing other slow and incremental changes in Earth's natural systems that are far less visible and that have far less obvious consequences. Especially important are changes in the amount of certain trace gases in the planet's atmosphere—gases such as carbon dioxide, methane, and nitrous oxide. These gases occur naturally, but in very low concentrations of parts per million or parts per billion. Human activities, however, are sharply raising these concentrations. Carbon dioxide is released when we burn fossil fuels, cut down forests, and manufacture cement. Methane is released by rice fields, petroleum production, termites eating wood waste in recently logged regions, and a billion flatulent cattle. And nitrous oxide is released when soil bacteria consume nitrogen-based fertilizers.

These gases are important, in part, because they affect the transparency of the atmosphere to various wavelengths of light. Even in very low concentrations, each helps make the atmosphere opaque to long-wave infrared radiation, which means that heat radiated from the surface of the planet has greater difficulty escaping into space. This is the notorious *greenhouse effect*: Earth's atmosphere acts like a blanket that traps heat and warms the surface of the planet.[40] In fact, if it weren't for the naturally occurring greenhouse effect (caused largely by water vapor), the average temperature of the planet would be about 33 degrees Celsius lower than it is now, and most of the life we see around us could not survive.

The release of extra amounts of trace gases—like carbon dioxide and nitrous oxide—makes the warming stronger than it would be otherwise. Many scientists believe that this enhanced greenhouse effect will significantly change Earth's climate in coming decades and produce more frequent droughts, floods, and perhaps major storms, which could disrupt our economies and societies. But our planet's climate is an extraordinarily complicated phenomenon and our understanding of it is seriously incomplete. Scientists don't know, for instance, exactly how oceans and clouds affect the global warming process.

Over the last few years, though, a consensus has developed among the experts: assuming no major changes in the trend of human emission of greenhouse gases, we will likely see the atmosphere warm between 1 and 3.5 degrees Celsius by 2100, with a "best estimate" of a 2 degree increase.[41] This may not seem like much—after all, on an average day we hardly notice a couple of degrees difference in temperature—but even a small increase could have major consequences for the behavior of Earth's climate. For example, the difference between today's climate, which is very warm by historical standards, and the coldest period of the last ice age, around eighteen thousand years ago, is only about five degrees.

Climate modelers also predict that the warming of the next hundred years will probably happen faster than any warming of the last ten thousand years.[42] Already, the average air temperature at the planet's surface has risen between 0.3 and 0.6 degree Celsius since the late nineteenth century, and the last decade has seen a number of the hottest years on record, with 1997 and 1998 possibly the hottest of the millennium.[43] Evidence of warming comes from many quarters: in temperate zones, nights are becoming warmer relative to days and spring is arriving earlier, while in the Arctic, sea ice is rapidly thinning—by almost 40 percent over the last four decades.[44]

Most climate experts now believe that a global warming "signal" has emerged from the "noise" of natural climate variation. Although these experts still debate whether this warming is caused by human activity (it could, for instance, be caused by changes in the intensity of the sun's radiation), many have decided that, on balance, the evidence indicates we are influencing the global climate.

Data gathered near the South Pole show, in particularly dramatic fashion, how far and fast humankind has pushed up the atmosphere's levels of carbon dioxide. In the 1970s and 1980s at the Vostok station in East

Antarctica, Soviet and French scientists drilled down into one of the ice sheets that cover much of the southern continent. They extracted a two-kilometer-long cylinder or "core" of ice that represented a record of Antarctic snowfalls going back more than 160 thousand years. Recently, an international team extended the drilling to 3.6 kilometers, for a record of the last 420 thousand years. Over this immense period of time, each new snowfall compressed the previous one beneath it, and the layers upon layers of snow accumulated into the vast ice sheets we find in Antarctica today. By analyzing the ancient snowfalls in the ice cores, including the air bubbles trapped in the snow, scientists were able to determine both the atmosphere's carbon dioxide concentration and its average temperature over Antarctica at the time the snow fell.[45]

The scientists' findings were disturbing: they had unlocked from the ice evidence that humankind might be throwing the planet's climate completely out of kilter (shown in illustration on following page). During the 420 thousand years registered in the ice cores, the concentrations of carbon dioxide in the snowfalls had varied up and down, between a low of 180 and a high of 280 parts per million (ppm). Four 280 ppm peaks occurred 420, 330, 240, and 130 thousand years ago; a slightly lower fifth peak of about 275 ppm occurred in the ice at the top of the core, closest to the present. Ambient air temperature varied almost in lockstep: as the carbon dioxide concentration rose, the temperature rose; as the carbon dioxide concentration fell, the temperature fell. The scientists knew that this close correlation between carbon dioxide levels and temperature didn't necessarily mean that changes in carbon dioxide levels *caused* the changes in temperature—it was conceivable that causation worked in the reverse direction, or that both changes in carbon dioxide level and temperature were produced simultaneously by an unknown, third factor. But the cores provided impressive *prima facie* evidence of the link between carbon dioxide concentration and temperature.[46]

In some ways, however, what made these ice cores most disturbing was an item of information that they didn't contain. As it happens, it takes centuries for accumulating snow to seal off air bubbles, so the bubbles trapped at the top of the cores, and therefore closest to the present, were still about seventeen hundred years old. They didn't show carbon dioxide levels for the most recent centuries or decades. Yet in the mid-1980s, when scientists first analyzed the cores, they knew that human industrial and other activities had already pushed the atmosphere's carbon dioxide concentration to about 350 ppm—far above the range of fluctuation of the last 420 thousand

CO$_2$ Concentrations and Temperature Have Varied in Lockstep

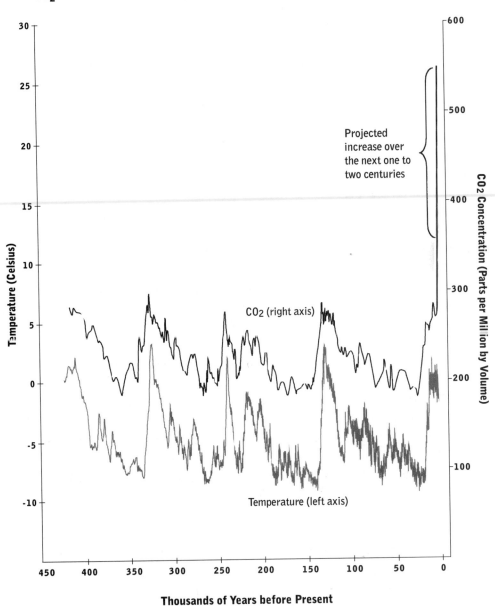

Thousands of Years before Present

Note: The zero-degree point of the temperature scale (left axis) represents the present ice-core temperature of minus 55.5 degrees Celsius.

years. Today, this concentration is about 370 ppm and is rising steadily by 1 to 2 ppm each year. Most experts believe that in the next one to two centuries we will see at least a doubling, and perhaps a quadrupling, of concentrations from preindustrial levels. Since this increase is happening in the blink of an eye—relative to the time span of 420 thousand years—the projected level of atmospheric carbon dioxide shown in the illustration opposite rises almost vertically.[47]

Experts can't say for sure what effect this increase in carbon dioxide concentration will have on the planet's average temperature. But the Vostok ice cores suggest temperature will rise, and perhaps rise fast. And one thing *is* certain: with each incremental ton of carbon we emit from our cars, power plants, and logging operations, we are producing, inexorably, an atmosphere that is significantly different from the one that influenced human civilizations in the past. In fact, in the next two hundred years we may produce an atmosphere with carbon dioxide levels that Earth hasn't seen in hundreds of millions of years.[48]

Since 1988, when a brutally hot North American summer pushed the issue into newspaper headlines and onto the agenda of the U.S. Congress, greenhouse warming has been in the news a lot. The public in rich countries has, for the most part, heard about carbon dioxide's role as a contributor to warming and about the potential consequences for the world's climate. They may have only a vague and fragmented understanding of the issue, but they have some understanding, nonetheless. Unfortunately, people are far less aware of many other changes we are producing in our global ecosystem—changes that may affect our future as much as, or even more than, greenhouse warming. One such change is the rapid accumulation of nitrogen compounds in our environment.[49]

Nitrogen is the sixth most common element in nature, the principal constituent of air, and the fourth most common element in living matter (behind oxygen, carbon, and hydrogen). It is a crucial constituent of DNA, RNA, and the proteins on which life depends. But in its most common form, two nitrogen atoms combine to form a nitrogen molecule (N_2) that is quite stable and cannot be absorbed or used by most plants and animals. Various natural processes, including lightning and the actions of bacteria in soil and on the roots of leguminous plants, break this molecule apart and incorporate the separated atoms into ammonia (a process called *nitrogen fixation*), and other bacteria convert ammonia into nitrates. Plants then extract the nitrogen from these compounds to make proteins, and the vital element is passed through the food chain to animals. Nitrogen fixation is essential to all higher life. It is key to Earth's grand cycle of nitrogen from the atmosphere, through the soil, into plants and animals, and eventually back to the atmosphere via the decomposition of these organisms and their wastes.

Although there is a lot of nitrogen around us, those natural processes fix only a limited amount. Farmers have found that insufficient nitrogen often restricts crop output, and they have developed various methods to add more to their fields. They have used human and animal waste as manure, and they have grown legumes and plowed them back into the soil. But these methods of organic recycling—employed widely by all traditional agricultures, and particularly by those in Europe and East Asia—limit the amount of plant protein that one hectare of land can produce. This limit means that a hectare can feed, for all practical purposes, a maximum of about five people.

During the nineteenth century, entrepreneurs started looking far afield for other sources of fixed nitrogen: they excavated deposits of saltpeter in Chile and guano in Peru, and they recovered ammonium sulfates from ovens used to produce metallurgical coke. But it was the work of two German scientists that finally removed the natural nitrogen constraint. In 1909, Fritz Haber, a university chemist, developed a method to synthesize ammonia (NH_3) out of nitrogen and hydrogen, and Carl Bosch, an industrial chemist, transformed the laboratory process into an industrial one. The first commercial ammonia factory began production in Oppau, Germany, in 1913.

Following World War I, and especially following World War II, the Haber-Bosch synthesis was widely adopted to produce chemically useful nitrogen, mainly for fertilizer. As the world's population soared, production of fixed nitrogen also soared, from under 5 million metric tons in the late 1940s, to 10 million tons in the 1950s, and to more than 100 million tons in the late 1990s. Growth in fertilizer output was similarly astonishing: in fact, between 1984 and 1996 alone, the world's farmers applied as much synthetic nitrogen fertilizer as they had applied in all prior years.[50] Today, the amount of nitrogen fixed by humans rivals that fixed by nature: natural processes fix between 90 and 150 million metric tons each year, while human activities fix another 130 to 150 million tons. (The remainder of the nitrogen fixed by humans, above the 95 million tons produced industrially, comes from planting legumes and recycling crop residues and manures.[51])

The Haber-Bosch process is a wonderful example of human technical ingenuity—ingenuity that has brought huge benefits to us all. Vaclav Smil, a geographer at the University of Manitoba, has calculated that about 40 percent of all protein in humanity's diet depends on synthetic nitrogen fertilizer.[52] Put another way, nearly two and a half billion people are alive today because "the proteins in their bodies are built with nitrogen that came from a factory" using the Haber-Bosch process.[53] Smil also points out that many land-scarce countries with large populations are utterly dependent on nitrogen fertilizer for their existence. "As they exhaust new areas to cultivate, and as traditional agricultural practices reach their limits, people in these countries must turn to ever greater applications of nitrogen fertilizer."[54]

But there have been costs too. We have doubled the flow of chemically reactive nitrogen in the global ecosystem, with many unanticipated effects. Nitrogen fertilizers contribute to soil acidity and loss of vital soil nutrients. Soil bacteria acting on these fertilizers release a small fraction of their nitrogen as nitrous oxide into the atmosphere, which depletes the ozone layer and enhances global warming (a molecule of nitrous oxide is about two hundred times more powerful as a contributor to global warming than a molecule of carbon dioxide). Moreover, nitrates leach out of fields into nearby bodies of water and aquifers. Groundwater contamination is now widespread in the U.S. corn belt and Western Europe.

Nitrogen compounds that leach into lakes, rivers, and the sea often cause eutrophication—an increase in the water's nutrient levels that leads to excessive plant growth. Algae blooms appear, blocking sunlight, and their decomposition sucks oxygen from the water, killing fish and other organisms. Such effects can be seen everywhere, from New York's Long Island Sound to the Baltic Sea and the Great Barrier Reef of Australia. Nutrient flows off coastal lands may also be responsible for an apparent upsurge of red tides and toxic blooms of protozoa around the world that make people sick and kill fish and marine mammals.

Each spring and summer in the Gulf of Mexico, populations of phytoplankton and zooplankton explode, and oxygen levels collapse along the Louisiana coast. In a swath of ocean that sometimes reaches a total area of

Each Spring and Summer, a "Dead Zone" Appears off Louisiana

Bottom Dissolved Oxygen (mg/L)
July 23 – 28, 1996

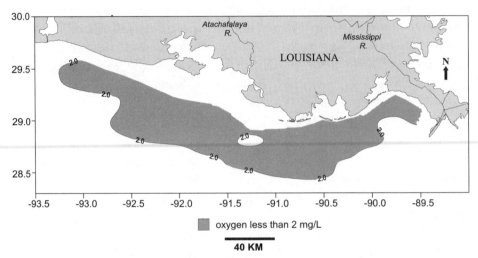

20 thousand square kilometers (about the size of the state of New Jersey), fish populations plummet and most bottom-dwelling creatures, including crustaceans and starfish, move away or die.[55] The bottom sediments turn black and are covered with mats of sulfur-oxidizing bacteria. The region becomes so devoid of fish and other large life forms that scientists and ecologists now call it "the dead zone," and fishermen worry about the threat to the Gulf's $26 billion annual catch (see illustration above). The disaster's cause is clear: the Mississippi River, which drains 40 percent of the area of the contiguous forty-eight states, pumps thousands of tons of nitrogen and phosphorus into the Gulf from upstream farms and cities. Experts estimate that nearly 60 percent of this excess nitrogen is due to fertilizer runoff, especially from the upper Midwest and the basin of the Illinois River, over one thousand kilometers away.

As we add billions more people to the world's population, and as these people—quite reasonably—strive for a higher standard of living that includes a protein-rich diet, the global output of synthetic nitrogen will far surpass today's already huge output. Bioengineering breakthroughs may be of great importance, but we cannot predict with any confidence how soon they will come and how much difference they will make. Nitrogen is essential for crops and for the growth and survival of human bodies. Although biotechnologists are working to develop grains that harbor their own nitrogen-fixing bacteria, their widespread use is probably decades in the future.[56] Meanwhile, a huge flux of human-produced reactive nitrogen is seeping into every corner of the biosphere, with consequences we only barely understand.[57] This massive release of nitrogen, the geographer Vaclav Smil notes, "amounts to an immense—and dangerous—geochemical experiment." In the span of just one lifetime, he concludes, humanity itself has developed a profound chemical dependence.[58]

––––––––––––––––

High output of reactive nitrogen. Soaring levels of carbon dioxide. Relentless tropical deforestation. Distant beaches covered with plastic bottles. These are all aspects of the new world we have created for ourselves, one step—one more baby, one new car, one additional paper factory, one extra Coke bottle—at a time. After talking to Mike Whitfield, in his office overlooking the English Channel, I had teased out for myself an important thread of his story: these small, almost imperceptible changes, when taken together, fundamentally alter key relationships in the complex ecological and physical systems surrounding us. Cumulatively, our demands on our environment have never been so great, and they are escalating fast.

But when large changes happen in increments we don't see them as readily, and so we often don't recognize their importance. In some respects, our brains adjust too easily to the incremental evolution of our surroundings.[59] And even when we are aware of such change, we usually remain deeply ignorant of its possible consequences. We have only a rudimentary understanding of how the ecological systems around us work and of how our actions affect them. In particular, we are rarely able to predict the sharp shifts in the behavior of complex systems—shifts like sudden algal blooms, forest blights, and extreme climate events—that can arise when many small pressures accumulate over time. These *threshold events*, as experts call them, are much like the explosion of United 232's fan disk. Everything seems to be fine and progressing normally until, out of the blue, a major shift in the system's behavior occurs that requires huge amounts of ingenuity in response.

We will need a far better understanding of our planet's complex systems, and much more sophisticated technologies and institutions, if we are to achieve a relationship with our surrounding natural environment that is economically and socially sustainable. Ever greater amounts of ingenuity will be required; we will have to be, in other words, increasingly smart, indefinitely into the future.

But we have not yet shown that we can supply even a small fraction of the ingenuity we need to understand and manage the forces we have unleashed across the surface of Earth. In many respects, we really don't have a clue what we're doing. The relationships in complex, evolving ecosystems—systems seriously perturbed by human activities—may be too numerous and intricate to be fathomed, much less manipulated, by the human brain.[60] Using the brain for such ends, suggests the renowned entomologist Edward O. Wilson, is a bit like trying to unscramble an egg "with a pair of spoons." He points out that it is impossible for today's scientists to reconstruct and manage even fairly limited ecosystems. "To move ahead as though scientific and entrepreneurial genius will solve each crisis that arises implies that the declining biosphere can be similarly manipulated," he writes. "But the world is too complicated to be turned into a garden. There is no biological homeostat that can be worked by humanity; to believe otherwise is to risk reducing a large part of Earth to a wasteland."[61]

THE BIG I

O N A WARM mid-September evening in 1997, not long after my trip
to Plymouth, I took a walk through the Isle of Dogs. I went there
strictly on intuition: somehow, I thought, the place might give me
insights into the forces changing our world.

Just over a decade before, this isolated tract of East London had been a
wasteland of derelict wharves, warehouses, and run-down housing tight by
the Thames. Now it was erupting with office buildings, high-tech industry, light manufacturing, and expensive new housing. It aspired to be one
of the preeminent symbols of the new England, representing the drive and
dynamism of modern capitalism, with its capacity to reclaim and reinvent
the world, to create jewels out of dross.

Lying in the heart of the old Port of London, in a part of the city now
known as Docklands, the Isle of Dogs (so called because more than six hundred years ago, Edward III made the marshland the burying place of his
greyhounds) is a large peninsula formed by the meandering Thames. In the
nineteenth and twentieth centuries, engineers cleaved the peninsula with
immense enclosed docks and quays for the loading, unloading, construction, and repair of ships. The Isle became a hub of the British Empire, and
continued to bustle with trade from around the world till the 1960s
and 1970s.[1] But its fate was sealed by intense competition from other ports
and by the advent of roll-on/roll-off container ships with drafts too deep
to make it up the Thames. One after another the docks were closed and
abandoned, the Port of London went into irreversible decline, and 150
thousand jobs vanished.

When she came to power, Margaret Thatcher could not abide the blight of the rotting, impoverished former Port: for Conservatives, it was a reminder of the lost British Imperium, of the grandeur that seemed forever gone. The London docks had been, for centuries, a place of commotion and energy, where the greatest trading ships had brought the world's commerce to the city's very door; Thatcher resolved that the Docklands would be reborn. Over the objections of local activists and the Labor Party, she created a development corporation empowered to attract business to the area by offering tax concessions and cheap land.

But despite the incentives, and the stratospheric office rents in the City only a few kilometers away, business was slow to come. The Isle of Dogs and other parts of the Docklands farther east were too distant from London's bustle. The Isle in particular had no subway or passenger train links to the rest of London, and it needed immense infrastructural investment—including completely renovated electricity, sewer, and road systems—before it could support high-density office towers. Developers also had to overcome the East End's deeply entrenched reputation as a zone of intractable unseemliness, crime, and poverty, where as recently as the nineteenth century the bodies of executed pirates and sea rovers had been left to hang in the water until "three tides" had washed over them. As a result, when an American developer proposed a sprawling complex of towers, tenants were unwilling to sign leases in advance, and the scheme didn't get off the ground.

Enter the Reichmanns, the famous Canadian family of real estate developers. In 1987, Paul and Albert Reichmann arrived in London, fresh from building the World Financial Center near Battery Park at the southern tip of Manhattan. The project had been a great success; many thought the complex comparable in importance and vision to Rockefeller Center in midtown. The Reichmanns seized upon the Docklands as a suitable stage for their next grand performance. They persuaded Thatcher and the London authorities to let them build a new financial center for London at Canary Wharf, smack in the center of the Isle of Dogs. Their plan included a cluster of office towers tall enough to stand above the rest of the zone and, for that matter, above the rest of London.

What happened next is well known. The tale of the Reichmanns and Canary Wharf is one of hubris, even megalomania, and of the spectacular collapse of the world's preeminent real estate empire—a $10-billion implosion that shattered the Reichmanns' fortune and forced their departure from the Docklands in disgrace.[2]

But ten years later, by the time of my evening stroll in September 1997, most of the complex's first stage had been completed, and Canary Wharf and the Isle of Dogs were alive with business. The Reichmanns had regained control of the development, and Paul Reichmann had justifiably been labeled "one of the most resilient and tenacious entrepreneurs of the twentieth century."[3] As I walked past the towers and looked upon the project's apparent success, I found it hard to grasp the audacity of the Reichmanns' gamble ten years before. Such monumental daring often seems sensible in retrospect, with all the dangers and risks hidden under well-crafted masonry.

I walked south from Canary Wharf: away from the glass-and-chrome foyer and transit station, through a construction site, and across a futuristic pedestrian bridge that spanned a wide stretch of water—a bridge constructed in a long horizontal spiral like a writhing snake. I arrived in a light industrial zone and then passed row upon row of new buildings. "A secure managed office environment," shouted a hoarding on a fresh low-rise office complex next to Millwall Dock. Secure from what I wondered. But as I looked around, it was clear. Hemmed in on each side by the new development was a redoubt of low-income housing, perhaps four or five streets of row houses and municipal apartment buildings, surrounded by fences and walls. On one side, the redoubt abutted the new printing plant of the *Daily Telegraph*, *Financial Times*, and *Guardian* newspapers, plants moved to the Docklands in the 1980s in an effort to break the crippling power of British printing unions. The walls between the houses and the printing plants were topped with rolls of barbed wire.

Here on the Isle of Dogs was a microcosm of the new postindustrial economy—of the two new economies, in fact. One comprised the workers in the fast-moving knowledge industries: the information and symbol analysts of the banks, investment houses, law firms, accountancies, advertising companies, and design studios that had moved into the new buildings around me. Through the windows of their offices, I could see people working, faces illuminated in the dusk by the light of their computer screens. They worked here, and for the most part lived elsewhere. The other economy comprised the laborers and low-paid service employees in the nearby houses. They lived here, and for the most part worked (if they worked) elsewhere—in stores and at lunch counters and on construction sites throughout the city, as cashiers, laborers, guards, and cleaning staff. Before Thatcher and the Reichmanns arrived, it turns out, the Isle of Dogs was not exactly a decrepit wasteland. It was a populated and vigorous community—poor, no doubt; run-down, yes; but nonetheless animated with people and families, and home to many thousands.

I walked away from the working-class redoubt, and along the edge of the many renovated waterways. A row of abandoned loading cranes had been restored and repainted as sculptures; in the gloom, they resembled enormous black praying mantises hovering over the water. I turned back to look at the buildings of Canary Wharf. Standing above everything else, bathed in floodlight against the night sky and topped with pulsing aviation lights, the central tower and surrounding buildings hardly looked real. They were too monumental, and there were simply too many floors and windows, piled one on top of the other.

Canary Wharf represents a weird combination of architectural styles that seem to have only one central theme—grandiosity. The central tower dominates everything else. Clad in stainless steel, its fifty stories are as brutal, sheer, and modernistic as any New York skyscraper, but the tower lacks the context of the rest of New York's skyline. It stands by itself: a blunt chisel pointing into space. Improbable, arrogant, almost absurd. Near its base rests a more elegant neoclassical building with rounded corners; it, too, is colossal, but next to the tower it seems small. Nonetheless it startled me: it looked as if it had been cut by a knife and pulled into two sections. The Docklands' elevated railway runs through the gap between the sections. As my eye followed this rail line into the heart of the Canary Wharf complex, the building's separated halves seemed like two sides of a great door that had been slid open, ever so slightly, to reveal a glimpse of the power inside.

The sight was impressive, and I knew I was supposed to be impressed. But it was also discomforting. The Reichmanns had laid out a detailed master plan for Canary Wharf, but the complex seemed nonetheless entirely ununified. Architectural themes and ideas are jumbled together: the modernist central tower stands against the lower neoclassical office blocks, and all Canary Wharf's buildings are laid out along a treed avenue that resembles a grand, Haussmann-like Parisian boulevard. As my eyes scanned the broader Docklands landscape, I realized that all the renovated zones of the Isle of Dogs are a similar architectural jumble. Here a futuristic printing plant, there an apartment building that looks like a ship's bow, all around glass-sheathed office blocks. The place has the appearance of a frontier land, where each architectural ego has staked a claim and raised a

Canary Wharf

meretricious monument to itself. Thatcher's development corporation imposed on developers only minimal common requirements. Before me, in consequence, was the urban design of economic deregulation: exciting and vigorous, but also raw and full of jarring contrasts and transitions.[4] It gave no comfort or sense of place.

My eyes were drawn back to the central tower, crowned with a four-sided pyramid, red beacons flashing to warn passing planes. I noticed that there were pyramid-like peaks and structures on top of other new buildings nearby. I had seen similar devices on modern buildings elsewhere too. But where? Then I realized that an almost identical pyramid caps the World Financial Center's main tower in New York.

Both buildings, I later learned, were designed by Cesar Pelli, the prize-winning Argentine-born architect who was Dean of the Yale School of Architecture from 1977 to 1984. The Reichmanns' success with the World Financial Center led them to hire Pelli's firm again for the main building at Canary Wharf. But on seeing Pelli's plan, many Londoners thought that the tower's form and dimensions were unsuited to the city. They criticized in particular its height relative to St. Paul's Cathedral four kilometers away. But Pelli remained unabashed: "The important buildings," he proclaimed, "are not in the scale of the body of man, but in the scale of his ideas. St. Paul's was like that, and, I hope in its own way, the tower will be as well."[5]

As I walked back to Canary Wharf—across the writhing bridge, through the construction site, and towards Pelli's tower—the image of pyramids remained in my mind. What were the architects trying to do here? Taken together, the architecture on the Isle of Dogs is less than the sum of its parts. It is a cacophony of competing styles and themes, each with a different historical lineage, each carrying its own world of associations and meanings, and each exhibiting no sense of responsibility to nearby style. In this cacophony, nothing prevails, and the rich histories and meanings of each style tend to cancel each other out. The viewer is left with a muddle of motifs—an anarchy of columns, angles, arches, soaring glass walls, and thrusting towers that is simultaneously stimulating and senseless.

The architecture around me seemed to exemplify postmodernism, that reaction against the eighteenth-century Enlightenment's effort to privilege human reason and to reveal the underlying mechanisms of the natural and social worlds. In his brilliant book *The Condition of Postmodernity*, the geographer David Harvey cuts to its core. Postmodernism, he notes, rejects all efforts to identify objective truths, universal and enduring patterns in nature and human history, and ideal forms of social order. Its hallmarks are "fragmentation, indeterminacy, and intense distrust of all universal or 'totalizing' discourses (to use the favored phrase)." Postmodernism extols the ephemeral, the fragmented, the discontinuous, and the chaotic: it "swims, even wallows, in the fragmentary and the chaotic currents of changes as if that is all there is." As a result, it "abandons all sense of historical continuity and memory, while simultaneously developing an incredible ability to plunder history and absorb whatever it finds there as some aspect of the present."[6]

Looking at the clutter of architecture around me on the Isle of Dogs, I felt the force of Harvey's metaphor: history had been plundered, and I was walking through a vast dumping ground of trophies seized from the past. But there was a rich irony in this chaos too. Capitalism ruled in the Isle of Dogs that evening, and the tract around me was a full-throated chorus of its energies. Yet fragmentation and disorder are not, in general, what individual capitalists want, at least not in the degree I saw on my walk. The maximization of profits generally requires considerable control, order, and predictability; chief executives want, for example, controlled (even restricted) competition, ordered markets, and predictable supplier and production costs. Successful capitalists also privilege human reason: they are calculating and rational in pursuit of material ends. They usually believe that the market is—objectively and universally—a good thing. The market's "totalizing discourse" surrounds, penetrates, and saturates capitalism; and it gives people within this economic system a set of lenses through which they can interpret and evaluate all human interactions.

How could contemporary capitalism, I wondered, with its desire for order and predictability, produce such a world of fragments? David Harvey provides a plausible answer. First, he argues, contemporary capitalism's hyperflexible methods of producing wealth have sharply compressed our conceptions of time and space: we expect things to happen faster, and we perceive our reach across geographic space as greatly extended. Second, capitalism is simultaneously caught in a recurring crisis of overaccumulation: it generates wealth so successfully that it tends to produce too much stuff for the economy's level of demand.

But, Harvey goes on, the first of these processes can help solve the problems created by the second. As time is compressed, the turnover rate of capital rises, and new tastes and consumption patterns arise and disappear more quickly, which boosts demand.[7] Similarly, as space is compressed, new markets become available, and excess capital can be spread across larger regions. Capitalism thus solves the problem of overaccumulation by creating an ever more quickly shifting kaleidoscope of wants and needs across an ever wider geographical space. But this hyperactivity produces fragments and ephemera. Time compression rams together the past, present, and future; and it chops our temporal reality into small segments, as one orchestrated consumer fad follows another in ever more rapid succession. Space compression jumbles together the world's diverse cultures; they bump against and overlap one another in bewildering confusion. Since many of these cultures can't easily coexist in the world marketplace, capitalism tends to strip away their essential characteristics, leaving only the faintest and most innocuous cultural afterimages. The result can easily be an endlessly changing postmodernist collage of production and consumption, of rootless images and motifs.

Pelli's pyramid was, for me, as I stared up at it, just such a fragmented symbol or rootless motif. Yet it also revealed something about the underlying insecurities of the system that was busily re-creating the Isle of Dogs.

Thanks to the ancient Egyptians, the pyramid is the ultimate human-made symbol of timelessness, of permanence, and of the authority that comes with durability. It is also a symbol of undemocratic power and immense wealth. Whether they were conscious of their motives or not, I felt that Pelli and the Reichmanns had seized upon this symbol, and elevated it to the pinnacle of the highest building in the land, in a vain effort to assert authority over the welter of fragments and contradictions below: not only did the pyramid celebrate capitalism's wealth, it also provided a serene image of eternity set against capitalism's corrosiveness. It was a reaction to the system's tendency to overturn, jumble, and render mundane and temporary everything it produces—an attempt to assert order and immortality in a land of fragments and ephemera. Capped by the pyramid, the whole Canary Wharf complex reflected not only its creators' arrogance but also their darkest fears. Those fears had helped make the complex's architecture grotesque; the buildings were almost fascistic in their boldness, lack of subtlety, and relentless striving.

Back in Canary Wharf's heart, I sat in a café near the base of the central tower. It was now about 8 p.m., and I watched the "knowledge workers" and "symbol analysts" leave at the end of their long day. Many were only in their twenties and thirties. It was clear that they came from every country of Europe and often from countries far beyond. I assumed that most of them spoke several languages and were worldly, interesting, and conscientious people. I wondered how many had a strong attachment to a particular land or culture. They seemed exemplary citizens of the postmodern world: so multicultural as to be almost non-cultural. In a zone of London that pell-mell development had made rootless and ahistorical, they too seemed rootless and ahistorical. Some of them, at least, belonged to an endlessly fungible international super elite of investment bankers, corporate lawyers, and equity traders whose members are equally comfortable working anywhere on the planet, as long as they have the right computers, software, and communications equipment.

They were going home, I imagined. Going home to places like Butler's Wharf, a set of renovated warehouses overlooking London's Tower Bridge. After changing out of their suits, they would fan out to the city's most expensive restaurants, to choose their dinners from menus offering uncommon and delicate combinations of flavors, textures, and colors. They would have meats, fish, fruits, and vegetables brought to their tables from around the planet; they would know and drink the very best wines; and they would discuss the day's trades and their vacations in the Seychelles and Maldives. For this super elite, the exceptional and exotic are now daily fare. For them, everything is possible; everything is available. I wondered if, away from the competitive thrill of their eighty-hour-a-week jobs, they would fall prey to ennui.

I was jolted out of this speculation: Paul Reichmann had just walked into the café. He stayed only a moment—just long enough to buy a takeout coffee—before returning to his waiting car, but I was struck by how old and stooped he seemed. Here was one of the world's great entrepreneurs, a person who had single-handedly changed the face of London by erecting a mighty pyramid-capped tower in the middle of an industrial wasteland. Yet, in the end, he appeared to be little more than an old man drained of vigor by age and financial calamity. All the pyramids he could construct seemed feeble in light of his obvious mortality.

What was I to make of all this? Was this place telling me anything relevant to my investigations?

I felt it was. In Canary Wharf and the Isle of Dogs, capitalism has created a bewildering nightmare-scape of contradictions and mixed symbols that seem designed to distract people's senses and prevent reflection—designed, in other words, to substitute adrenaline, giantism, and raw audacity for subtlety, care, and reflection. And as hyperkinetic capitalism compresses time and space and pillages history for motifs, and as it relentlessly fragments reality and makes ephemera of the fragments, it blurs the line between reality and illusion, making it ever harder to discriminate fact from fantasy. Because, while the architecture of Canary Wharf is in some ways grotesque and fascistic, it is simultaneously fantastic. The place resembles a Disney theme park. Closing my eyes I could imagine a medieval castle here, Aladdin's cave there and, just around the corner, a spaceship waiting to leave for the stars.

Inside the fantasyland, an increasingly homogenized, transnational super elite is at work, earning an ever-larger slice of the global economic product. As some of the best and brightest of their generation, these men and women must play a leading role supplying the ingenuity we need to solve our problems. Yet the world in which they work is unlikely to give them a firm grip on the reality of those problems: in countless ways, they are separated from reality, isolated in a land of human construction and human ideas, where reality and illusion are intermingled.

I got up to leave the café, thinking about the stooped old man I had just seen. He was so palpably mortal. No matter how much we try to isolate or distract ourselves from reality, it has a way of intruding into the lives of even the smartest and most powerful among us.

———————————

The train surged up from under the English Channel and sped on through the Artois countryside of northwest France. I was on my way from London to Paris to visit friends. A few minutes later, a conductor announced that we'd reached our maximum speed of three hundred kilometers per hour— we would be in the Gare du Nord in less than an hour.

The farms and towns stretched like rubber streaks as they flashed by the windows. Cars traveling in the same direction as our train on a parallel expressway seemed as if they were crawling. Occasionally I glimpsed a person in a field or a street, but only for a millisecond. They didn't even look up to see us pass.

The machine that encapsulated me, the new Chunnel train, was marvelous in every respect. The seat design, the ergonomics of the washrooms, the public address system—all bespoke thousands of hours of thought, inventiveness, and ingenuity. I wondered at it all. Then I watched the countryside.

There was haze in the air. It was everywhere outside the train. I had seen it before—most of us see it, most of the time, but we don't notice it anymore, if we ever did.

It's the haze of industry, of modern life. It rises from our power plants, factories, cars, and sometimes from our burning forests and fields. As I flashed by in the train, it sat between me and the ever-so-brief reality of the French countryside. It bled the life out of the landscape. Greens and blues and reds were a deadened and dull brown, as if they'd been mushed together on a painter's palette. Edges were indistinct. The scene before me was not only temporary in the extreme—each image of the countryside passed in front of my retinas barely long enough to register in my brain— it was also flat, insipid, and weary.

In the last days of the summer of 1997, haze was a problem in that part of Europe; a combination of weather conditions had locked pollution close to the ground across much of France, the Low Countries, and Germany. But the problem wasn't peculiar to that time or place. A large fraction of the world's population now finds it difficult to escape such haze. It's distinct from the localized air pollution, or smog, that we're familiar with in cities. Haze covers whole continents, stretching from urban and industrialized areas out across the countryside, and often deep into what we normally regard as wilderness regions, like the northern Canadian tundra and Arctic.

Global haze has become something of an obsession of mine. I first noticed it on a flight from Europe to Boston in the summer of 1986. Sitting by the plane's window as we approached North America, I admired the forested ruggedness of the Labrador coastline and the crystal blue sky above. We flew across northern Quebec and turned southwest to follow the Saint Lawrence River. A few minutes later we were directly over Quebec City. For a moment, instead of looking down at the old walled city that I love, I looked horizontally out of the plane. There, in front of me, pointing lazily northwards at ten thousand meters, was a brown tongue of airborne sludge, the leading edge of the cloud of North American haze that sits over much of the continent. As we penetrated farther into the heavily populated regions of the northeast, the cloud stretched out to the horizon in all directions and the crystal blue sky disappeared entirely. It became a sickly brown.

At the time I forgot about the matter. But a few weeks later, on the Fourth of July weekend, I happened to be sailing with some friends off Shelter Island, between the eastern jaws of Long Island. It was a sunny day, and there were dozens of boats on the water, making a cheerful scene of colorful sails and happy families enjoying the holiday. But the water was brown from an ongoing red tide in Long Island Sound, and the sky, I noticed, was tinged with brown too. It wasn't the vivid blue sky that should accompany a sunny day; it was half blue—a pallid, feeble approximation of a blue sky. We were, I realized, sandwiched between brown and brown: an ocean made brown by nitrogen overloading from coastal runoff (or so I assumed), and a sky made brown by the industrial emissions of North America's population, blown by prevailing winds across the continent and over our heads.

Could anybody on the water with me that day remember what a really blue sky was like? I stretched my mind and tried to recall the clear skies of my childhood on Vancouver Island, skies swept clean by fresh winds arriving from the endless Pacific Ocean. Most of us on the boats had lost touch with such memories, if we had ever had them. The natural world was now always behind a veil, always less vivid and vital than it could be.

Since that time, I have become acutely aware of haze. Traveling across the broad plain of northern China, I have found it so thick that I could barely distinguish the gushing smokestacks of factories and power plants only a kilometer away. Along the heavily populated and industrialized flatland around the River Ganges in northern India, rice fields, villages, cities, and sky all blended into each other with a seamless grayness. And in my favorite wilderness parks in eastern Canada and the United States, once splendid landscapes often appeared washed out and dull.[8]

Our industrial activities spew a host of substances into the atmosphere, including sulfur dioxide, nitric oxide, nitrogen dioxide, volatile organic compounds, and soot. Some of these substances, such as soot, scatter or absorb light directly. Others, most importantly gaseous sulfur dioxide and nitrogen compounds, are transformed by complex chemical processes into tiny particles and droplets (commonly called *aerosols*) that remain suspended in the air for days and that are almost the ideal size to scatter and weaken the sky's light.[9] When they scatter light, these aerosols tend to make the sky appear white when viewed horizontally from the ground; when they absorb light, they give the sky the brownish hue that is especially common in cities. There is a certain irony in the fact that sulfate aerosols, because they reflect some sunlight back into space, actually help counteract the effects of global warming in heavily industrialized regions.[10]

Most of us in rich countries don't have the faintest idea how widespread human-generated haze has become or how much it affects visibility. Yet it is now omnipresent in most of the industrialized world. "Much of the time," says Glen Cass, an air-pollution specialist at the California Institute of Technology, "a widespread mass of haze-producing airborne particles sits over the entire eastern United States."[11] The U.S. National Research Council reports that "the average visual range in most of the western United States, including national parks and wilderness areas, is 100 to 150 kilometers, or about one-half to two-thirds of the natural visual range that would exist in the absence of air pollution. In most of the East, including parklands, the average visual range is less than thirty kilometers, or about one-fifth the natural visual range."[12] Since 1988, pollution control efforts in the U.S. have cut sulfur dioxide emissions by 12 percent and have greatly reduced smog in many urban areas, such as the Los Angeles basin. But, in general, the rural haze in the United States, especially in the east, has either stayed the same or diminished only slightly.[13]

The problem is not limited to the United States and Europe, although elsewhere its causes may be different. In poor tropical countries, widespread burning of forests and rangeland creates smoke clouds that sometimes blanket whole sections of the planet; fires in Indonesia in 1997 and 1998 burned some 4 million hectares of timber and generated a pall of smoke that stretched across Southeast Asia.[14] Even in remote parts of the globe, human-made aerosols—including smoke, soot, and sulfate and nitrate particles—at concentrations of only a few micrograms per cubic meter "can shorten visual range by tens of kilometers."[15]

Why am I so concerned about haze? To me, it signifies something more general than just pollution or atmospheric processes. As haze cuts us off from vivid skies and landscapes, it attenuates our ties to the wider, external reality in which we are embedded. It is just one of the many ways we are constructing—inside that wider reality—an artificial and self-referential world.

Increasingly, only the collective human ego—what I call "the Big I"—bounds and defines this constructed world. We subordinate, alter, and reinvent almost everything around us according to our own interests, from the mountains of Vancouver Island to the Isle of Dogs and the very sky overhead. Seduced by our extraordinary technological prowess, many of us come to believe that external reality—the reality outside our constructed world—is unimportant and needs little attention because, if we ever have to, we can manage any problem that might arise there. And, in any case, as the pace of our lives accelerates, we have less time to reflect on these broader circumstances. All these trends can push us into narcissism, as they weaken our sense of awe at the universe beyond our human ego; and what is perhaps more important, they also weaken our receptivity to critical signals from the external reality that might awaken us to our deep ignorance of the potential consequences of our actions, and warn us against hubris. Without this awareness we have a less accurate understanding of how much and what types of ingenuity we will need to meet the future's challenges.

The incremental changes we have produced in our natural environment— from the depletion of our forests, to soaring levels of carbon dioxide and reactive nitrogen, to creeping haze in our atmosphere—are paralleled by, and often partly caused by, incremental changes in our technology.

We forget how different today's technological world is from that of the past. Just as we easily adjust to the hazy skies above us, we easily adjust to—and soon take for granted—the stupendous array of manufacturing, transportation, medical, office, communication, and household technologies around us. Many of these technologies could not even have been imagined by previous generations. At the turn of the twentieth century, barely one and a half lifetimes ago, the horse and buggy was still standard transportation, household food was cooled with blocks of ice, a severe septic wound in an arm or a leg often meant amputation, and transoceanic communication was by telegraph. Today, only a hundred years later, our daily life includes cars, jets, refrigerators, antibiotics, and multimedia presentations carried by fiber-optic cables. None of these technologies seems particularly unusual or worthy of note; after an initial sense of surprise and sometimes delight when they were first introduced, we adopted them smoothly into our lives without further remark. The miraculous quickly becomes commonplace; the extraordinary is normalized.

The sweep of technological change, however, is the most tangible evidence of the fabulous power of human ingenuity. And I have always thought that a particularly good example of technological change is humankind's progress in making light, which was why I found Smeaton's Lighthouse in Plymouth fascinating.

Over thousands of years, humans and their ancestors have produced countless small improvements—and some big ones—in light-making technology. Around half a million years ago, the hominid Peking man (*Homo erectus*) generated light with open fires. During the Paleolithic period, about 40 thousand years ago, fat-burning stone lamps appeared; then, around 2000 B.C., Babylonians used sesame oil lamps; and in the Middle Ages in Europe tallow candles became widespread. After the late eighteenth century, the means for making light developed rapidly: first with coal-gas lamps in homes and streets, later with incandescent bulbs, and by the 1930s, with fluorescent tubes and sodium vapor lamps. The 1980s and 1990s, in turn, brought compact fluorescent bulbs and halogen lamps.

As we moved from open fires to tallow candles and then to compact fluorescent bulbs, the efficiency of light-making rose steadily. William Nordhaus, an economist at Yale, has studied this trend.[16] The model of an enterprising academic, he couldn't find published information on the light

Milestones in the History of Lighting

1,420,000 B.C.	Fire used by Australopithecus
500,000 B.C.	Fire used in caves by Peking man
38,000–9000 B.C.	Stone fat-burning lamps with wicks used in southern Europe
3000 B.C.	Candlesticks recovered from Egypt and Crete
2000 B.C.	Babylonian market for lighting fuel (sesame oil)
1292	Paris tax rolls list 72 chandlers (candle makers)
Middle Ages	Tallow candles in wide use in western Europe
1784	Discovery of Argand oil lamp
1792	William Murdock uses coal-gas illumination in his Cornwall home
1798	William Murdock uses coal-gas illumination in Birmingham offices
1800	Candle technology improved by the use of stearic acid, spermaceti, and paraffin wax
1820	Gas street lighting installed in Pall Mall, London
1855	Benjamin Silliman, Jr., experiments with rock "oil"
1860	Demonstration of electric-discharge lamp by the Royal Society of London
1876	William Wallace's 500-candlepower arc lights, displayed at the Centennial Exposition in Philadelphia
1879	Swan and Edison invent carbon-filament incandescent lamp
1880s	Welsbach gas mantle
1882	Pearl Street station (New York) opens with first electrical service
1920s	High-pressure mercury-vapor-discharge and sodium-discharge lamps
1930s	Development of mercury-vapor-filled fluorescent tube
1931	Development of sodium-vapor lamp
1980s	Marketing of compact fluorescent bulb

produced by open fires and sesame oil lamps, so he built his own fire, obtained his own Roman lamp (similar to a Babylonian lamp), and made his own light measurements with a Minolta illuminance meter. He concluded that the efficiency of light production—measured in terms of light output per unit of energy input—has improved by a factor of thirty thousand from the cave-dwellers' open fire to today's compact fluorescent light bulb. Since the time of the Babylonian sesame-oil lamp, efficiency has improved twelve-hundredfold. And the rate of improvement appears to have accelerated. "The overall improvements in lighting efficiency are nothing short of phenomenal," he writes.[17]

He also gauged changes in light's cost, measured in terms of the number of hours of work required to produce or buy a given amount of light. His own experiments with fires and lamps "provide evidence that an hour's work today will buy about 350 thousand times as much illumination as could be bought in early Babylonia."[18] He continues: "One modern one-hundred-watt incandescent bulb burning for three hours each night would produce 1.5 million lumen-hours of light per year. At the beginning of the [nineteenth] century, obtaining this amount of light would have required burning seventeen thousand candles, and the average worker would have had to toil almost one thousand hours to earn the dollars to buy the candles."[19]

These technological changes have brought huge improvements to our lives. Not so long ago, our existence was strictly governed by the cycles of day and night. Candles and oil for lamps, if available at all, were expensive and carefully rationed. They could perhaps extend the day by an hour or two after sunset, but then economic prudence demanded that the flame be extinguished and everyone go to sleep. Technologies for making cheap and abundant light have therefore been one of history's great liberators. They have opened up vast numbers of hours for work, family, and leisure activities; for invention and idleness; and for developing one's full potential as a human being. Indeed, since Roman times, light (*lux*) has been closely associated with luxury (*luxe*).[20]

But there have also been costs, many of them unanticipated. As light became easier to produce and far cheaper, we flooded our world with it. Not only are our houses ablaze—so are our streets, parking lots, playing fields, highways, office buildings, factories, shopping malls, racetracks, and construction sites. We now produce so much light that a photograph of the night-side of Earth from space shows the outlines of the continental U.S., Europe, Japan, and China clearly delineated by the light of coastal cities.

Nighttime Lights of the USA (top) and Europe (bottom)

The megalopolis of New York City forms a huge white blob on the photograph, as do London, Paris, the Rhine Valley, the California coast from Los Angeles to San Diego, and the eastern coast of Japan.

So much light now pours from our bulbs, lamps, and headlights that our urban night skies are no longer black but a dingy gray or orange. Most stars have become invisible. The growing slice of the human population that lives in the world's cities thus has little or no exposure to the glory of a cloudless night sky with its sweep of stars. Ironically, the light that we use to see our world blinds us to the universe.

More prosaically, our use of modern technologies for producing light conflicts with our fundamental biological nature. Human bodies and brains evolved over millennia, probably in Africa, in a natural-light regime of days and nights of roughly the same length. The lives of our distant hominid ancestors moved according to the cycle of sunrise and sunset, and over untold generations the human species genetically adapted to this light environment. Compared with the speed of genetic evolution, artificial light has arrived in the blink of an eye, disrupting, in the process, those ancient and biologically rooted circadian rhythms and sleep patterns. In combination with technologies like television and the Internet, the result is now chronic sleep deprivation and sub-optimal cognitive performance for a large proportion of the population of industrialized countries.[21] (An average American accumulates a five-hundred-hour sleep deficit each year. A third of U.S. adults say that lack of sleep interferes with daily activities, and nearly a quarter admit to falling asleep while driving at least once in the previous year.[22])

This qualitative change in our world—the fact that it is now flooded with light—has multiple effects on ingenuity supply. Since our societies can now work, and think, twenty-four hours a day, we can supply vastly more ingenuity to deal with the challenges around us.[23] Those lighted office buildings, construction sites, and factories are full of people— knowledge workers—producing, implementing, and delivering practical ideas. The lighted streets, highways, and airports allow the exchange of ingenuity, and of the products of ingenuity, around the clock.

One has to wonder, however, about the quality of some of this ingenuity. Our sleep-deprived and cognitively addled brains may simply be generating and delivering ever larger quantities of stale, mediocre ideas. And the creeping, insidious occultation of the stars is but one more contributor, like the dulling of the sky by atmospheric haze, to that broader and more fundamental qualitative shift in the character of our lives: the loss of reference points beyond the human-created world.

———————

The technology of making light was not on my mind as the train pulled into Paris's Gare du Nord in the early evening. Rather, I was thinking about all the places I treasure in Paris. I hadn't been back in many years. During my early twenties, I rented a tiny room in the Neuvième Arrondissement, only a few hundred meters from the Opéra and not much more than a kilometer from the Louvre. It was one of the best times of my life—a chance to make friends from all over Europe, to wander late into the night through the Latin Quarter and, only incidentally, to work on my French. As an unsophisticated Anglo-Canadian, I have always envied Parisian passions for food, love, art, and politics. There is a depth of history and culture in Paris, and an aesthetic sensibility, far greater than one easily finds in North America.

A friend met me on the platform, and we caught a cab to a hotel. Dusk came, and bulbs and lamps across the city were turned on; viewed from space Paris emerged as one of Europe's big blobs of light. Our taxi wound through the heavy evening traffic towards the Place de la République. I was thrilled to be there, but I have always found cities a bit claustrophobic. When I was young, my parents and I entertained ourselves mostly out-doors—fishing, hunting, camping, and playing in western Canada's magnificent rural areas. I have spent most of my adult life, though, in large cities in North America, Europe, and Asia, and my attitude towards them has always been ambivalent. They energize part of me, but they suffocate another part.

Cities are the source of countless good things in our lives. They are where we generate most of our creativity and wealth; they are the location of most of our greatest art and architecture; and they are full of diversity, adrenaline, and excitement. They are embodiments of our social nature and monuments to our ingenuity.[24] We go to cities to meet people, make money, and gain knowledge; cities are where we have things manufactured and sell our products, and where we go to be inspired and entertained. For these and many more reasons, most of us now prefer to live in cities. In rich societies, 80 to 90 percent of the population lives in urban areas, and in poor countries the urbanized percentage is quickly rising to the same level, with hundreds of millions of people moving from the countryside.

Today's cities also represent, in many ways, the apex of human ego-centrism, the most elaborate and potent expression of the Big I. Our cities are made to human scale—even the huge skyscrapers of Canary Wharf or La Défense in the outskirts of Paris are examples of monumentalism on a purely human scale—and everything is designed for or shaped to our interests. Things that get in the way of our interests, like bad weather, are resolutely shut out of our lives. As a result, as urban dwellers we inhabit an entirely *meso-scale* world, a world constructed entirely in the middle range of nature's space and time scales. Because this middle range best suits the physical needs of human beings, the upper and lower ranges—the micro and macro ends of the space and time scales—are lopped off. We no longer experience them. For all intents and purposes, micro and macro phenomena no longer exist, and the meso scale becomes the only real world. This leaves us with an astoundingly impoverished awareness of the small and large systems that intimately affect our lives.

Take, for instance, soil. Few urbanites can appreciate this complex, fragile ecological system, but it is crucial to our well-being. Soil's realities are micro-phenomena, and to the urban consciousness they are, quite simply, nonexistent. We see little soil in cities like Paris, London, New York, or Toronto. Asphalt, concrete, and cobblestones cover the ground and surround our trees right up to their trunks; flowerbeds are usually small and their soil obscured; even in North America's suburbs, soil is resolutely buried beneath turf. When we pass fields of grains and vegetables on our visits to rural areas, the soil in the distance is, to us, little more than the stuff that plants must stick their roots into to hold themselves upright. We have a vague notion that anything else soil provides is no longer particularly essential, because farmers can easily use fertilizer to substitute for its nitrogen, potassium, and other nutrients. Soil is dirt. It's the brown stuff that has to be washed out of our children's clothes. It's not particularly interesting. More often than not, it's a nuisance.

But if we could break out of our urban cocoons, we would learn that healthy soil is more than dirt and that it provides plants with much more than a place to put their roots. As the Dutch professor of soil biology Lijbert Brussaard and his colleagues write, "soil provides the physical substratum for virtually all human activities, [for example] agriculture, buildings, transport; it provides resources for industrial use and waste management; and it is central in elemental cycles, without which agriculture would not be possible."[25]

The creation of soil begins with the inorganic grindings of rock generated over millions of years of weathering and chemical action by the elements. Time and life contribute organic, rotted debris from plants. But in addition—and this is often the most surprising fact to the average urbanite who regards soil as inert and lifeless—a cubic meter of good soil is also a vibrant, living ensemble of billions of interdependent organisms linked together by unbelievably complex flows of energy, water, carbon, sulphur, oxygen, and nitrogen.[26]

Bacteria that live in the film of water around soil particles are at work decomposing plant litter and promoting vital chemical processes. Other bacteria form nodules on the roots of legumes and fix the atmosphere's nitrogen so that it can be used by plants. Fungi produce webs of filaments that enhance soil structure. Protozoa feed on bacteria and fungi; and nematodes—tiny unsegmented worms—in turn eat bacteria, protozoa, and plant debris. The busy routines of mites, millipedes, centipedes, and termites help mix and aerate the soil. Earthworms chew through tons of organic matter a year, leaving in their wake casts that improve soil tilth. Slugs, snails, beetles, insect larvae, and moles consume these smaller creatures, thereby producing nutrient-rich wastes.

Healthy soil teems with these animals: a single gram of soil may contain between a million and a billion bacteria; a square meter of grassland soil can harbor two hundred thousand arthropods (a category that includes mites, millipedes, and termites) and close to a thousand earthworms.[27] Together they help ensure that plants have the things they need to grow— that air penetrates deeply, that water doesn't drain away or evaporate too quickly, and that an adequate range of nutrients clings to the immense surface area provided by the soil's countless particles.

Scientists know a great deal about the chemical and physical properties of various soils, but they know much less about the types and functions of soil organisms. As Lijbert Brussaard says: "The number of existing species is vastly higher than the number described."[28] We do know that many human agricultural practices, especially the heavy use of pesticides, herbicides, and artificial fertilizers, harm this vital riot of life. We also know that most of these agricultural chemicals give us, at best, only rudimentary substitutes for the essential services that soil creatures provide.

In cities, we don't see or think about soil, how it works, how our actions affect it, or how little we understand it. Nor, usually, do we think about anything else in the external world that is really small or really large. This is one reason that people like the kayakers my friend and I met at the Brooks Peninsula head for the outdoors. For these adventurers, modern technologies and wealth haven't reinforced the self-referential, human-constructed world, but have instead allowed them to move beyond it.

When outdoors, they escape a bit from the Big I. They will not find true wilderness, because human activities have fundamentally altered, either directly or indirectly, all regions of the planet. There is no true wilderness, in the sense of pristine nature, left.[29] But outdoor adventurers do become more aware of their micro and macro surroundings, as space and time scales are briefly restored to their full dimensions.[30]

In the city, for instance, we aren't confronted by the micro-reality that frog populations are declining across much of the world. This reality becomes clearer only if we regularly observe life outdoors—we are then more likely to encounter the tangible reality that there are fewer frogs around. Similarly, in the city most people don't notice the macro-reality of weather very much, except when a severe heat wave or storm arrives. As urbanites, we spend almost all our time indoors. We encounter the elements for only brief intervals between car and office or between buildings. But in the rural outdoors, sky and clouds take on new meaning. We become acutely aware of how they unfold during the day: Is that smoldering line of thunderheads moving our way? Do those threads of high cirrus clouds herald a storm? Will that patch of clear sky grow to give us sun?

When I'm outdoors and a long way from the city, I often sit in one place for an hour or more, consciously focusing on small and large things around me, such as a hawk circling for its prey or water lapping along the shore of a lake. After the sun sets in the evening, I sometimes use a star chart to find the constellations and the solar system's visible planets—Jupiter, Venus, Mars, Saturn, and occasionally Mercury. I hope, above all, to find the planets, because I can use them to shift my mind to a less anthropocentric view of Earth's position in the universe.[31]

I start by building a three-dimensional image in my mind. Earth and the planets orbit the sun along roughly the same plane, which slices through Earth roughly at the equator. I face south (the direction of the equator from Canada) and imagine that I can see this plane, stretching from the point in the east where the sun rises to the point in the west where it sets, and sweeping across the southern sky. It intersects the dome of the night sky along a line astronomers call the *ecliptic*. Since the visible planets all lie on this same plane, by linking them together across the night sky I can identify the line of the ecliptic, and along that line I imagine Earth's orbital plane vanishing to infinity. Once I have found the planets and the ecliptic, I bring the sun into this three-dimensional mental image: it's somewhere below the western horizon to my right, a position usually indicated by the residual glow of the sunset in that direction. Since the sun is the pivot around which everything in the solar system rotates, it's on the same plane as Earth and the rest of the planets.

With all these elements firmly in mind, I take a mental leap. Instead of taking Earth as a stable reference point for observing everything else, as we all usually do, I mentally place the sun in a fixed position below the horizon, and then envision Earth and the planets above me turning counterclockwise around it, as though they and I were embedded in a giant disc that cuts the heavens in two and revolves around the sun at its center.[32] It usually takes a while to build this image correctly. But once all the elements fall into place, I am rewarded with a surge of vertigo, because the new image dramatically overrules my everyday "folk" intuition about the world. I become abruptly aware that I am not firmly planted on stationary ground but am actually flying through space on my small vehicle, the Earth, at thirty kilometers a second, in a huge arc around the sun.[33]

Our everyday intuition about the relationship of Earth to the planets and to the rest of the universe is pre-Copernican: we know rationally that Earth orbits the sun, but to our senses and our intuition, the ground beneath our feet is stationary.[34] It's jarring to be reminded that Earth is actually in motion. Not only does my mind-game induce vertigo, it extends my spatial dimension outwards from the narrow human-made world. Suddenly, the stars and planets are no longer simply points of light on the two-dimensional surface of the night sky; they become, instead, our neighbors in three-dimensional space.

This neighborhood is unimaginably vast, and within it Earth is absurdly minuscule. Beyond the planets, and within the volume of space visible to astronomers, are, at latest estimate, 125 billion galaxies, each containing perhaps 50 billion stars.[35] (Such stupendous numbers are almost impossible to grasp, but a person counting the stars in the currently visible universe would need about five thousand times the estimated age of the universe to enumerate them all.[36]) If we could shoot into space and watch our planet as it recedes from us, we would find that Earth and the solar system inhabit the outer edge of a spiral galaxy, the Milky Way. We would see that this galaxy is a member of a gravitationally bound group of twenty-six galaxies, known as the Local Group, that sits on the periphery of a far larger cloud of galaxies. This cloud itself lies near the edge of the Local Supercluster, a macro-structure in space encompassing some ten thousand galaxies. Light, the fastest thing in the known universe, takes hundreds of millions of years—literally millions of human lifetimes—to cross this supercluster.[37]

There is weirdness and wonder at both ends of nature's spatial spectrum, from the sky overhead to the soil below our feet. But in our modern cities we obscure the sky behind haze and light, and we pave over the soil. A wall of technology and its products now cuts us off from much of the universe around us. At the same time that we are altering our natural world one increment at a time, we are separating ourselves from this world. As a result, it seems less and less real, and we are less able to pick up the signals from our environment that could warn us of trouble; oblivious, we become yet more arrogant and sure of our powers. Arrogance distorts our ability to see which challenges around us really need our attention; and that, in turn, distorts the amount and kinds of ingenuity we supply.

Some skeptics might respond that it is simply not true that our ties to external reality are increasingly attenuated. Modern science and technology provide us with innumerable devices that allow us to probe and understand that external reality as never before and to communicate the results to specialists and the public. The Hubble space telescope extends our vision far into the universe, and electron microscopes allow us to investigate the biochemistry of soils. The Internet permits faster and more intensive dialogue among scientists about emerging ecological problems—like the disappearance of frogs. And the World Wide Web makes all this information far more accessible to the interested layperson. In fact, these skeptics might conclude, humankind is more connected with non-human reality than ever before.

In many respects, these arguments are correct. But, while our knowledge about the external world is undeniably greater and more widely available than ever before, it is still not reaching very many of us. Most of it is known only to particular interest groups and communities of specialists. And when it dribbles out of these communities, it usually goes no farther than the intellectual elites of the wealthiest countries in the world, or is lost in the torrent of factoids distributed by popular media (something I explore in the chapter "Vegas"). The everyday experience of a person living in industrialized countries or, more generally, in the planet's mega-cities, barely touches on the natural world. On a day-to-day basis, most of us in rich countries are increasingly sealed within the hermetic and sometimes illusory world of the human-made, the human-scaled, and the human-imagined.

We are losing a sense of our place in the scheme of things; a sense of how strange the world is, and of the limits, ultimately, of our knowledge and control. We are losing the awe, the respect, and the recognition of mystery that remind us to be prudent.

On a few occasions in my life I've had such a feeling, and I realized I was deeply fortunate, as we all do at such moments. Sometimes it has been evoked by nature's straightforward grandeur—by an enormous waterfall in a jungle or by a range of mountains at dawn. Other times, outright intimidation has done the job. A friend and I were once trapped all night in the middle of a herd of wild African elephants. As we sat in the dark in a two-person tent, a bull elephant ripped branches out of a tree a few meters away. Without weapons, adequate shelter, or any way to escape, we felt puny. In an age when humans seek to subordinate every intrusive aspect of nature, the tables were briefly turned and raw nature was, once again, clearly the master. (The tables were soon turned back: most of the elephants around us that night were eventually slaughtered by gangs of poachers using military rifles and submachine guns.)

But sometimes something more subtle—an encounter with something small, easily missed or ignored—can trigger the feeling. I remember one occasion particularly well. It was a brilliant fall day, and I was hiking along an uninhabited part of the north shore of Lake Ontario. The afternoon was warm, so I stopped and stretched out on a large rock to enjoy the sun. As I watched the sky and clouds, a butterfly flittered across my field of vision. A few minutes later, another zigzagged by. Then another and another. Curious, I sat up and looked around. The milkweed on the shore of the lake behind me was alive with monarchs, their distinctive orange-and-black-veined wings gently fanning the afternoon breeze. They were gorging themselves. Then, one by one, they ascended hundreds of meters into the sky to begin their long and perilous trek across the lake.

Quite by accident, I was in the middle of one of nature's most extraordinary spectacles—the migration of monarch butterflies. It's not noisy, grand, or intimidating. Actually, it's very easy to miss: at any given place along the migration route, it occurs for only a few days. But each year, from August to October, millions of these butterflies begin their journey to southern wintering grounds. West of the Rockies they move to sites along the Pacific coast from Monterey to Los Angeles. From eastern North

America, they converge on a few clumps of fir trees in the highlands of central Mexico. In the process, some of these half-gram animals travel up to four thousand kilometers—roughly equivalent, in human terms, to walking one and a half times around the planet.[38]

But the distance they cover is not their most astounding accomplishment: even more remarkable is the fact that the monarchs arriving back in the north the following spring are not those that went south the previous fall. In fact, more than once during their return trip in the spring, the migrants will reproduce, the old ones die, and the newborns continue the journey northwards—as if each butterfly's life is just one segment of an endless relay race. A full migratory cycle involves from three to five generations. Somehow, each generation knows where it is in the cycle, whether or not to migrate, and if it must migrate, in which direction it should go. And somehow those that migrate are able to navigate across lakes, bogs, forests, fields, freeways, suburban tracts, and cities to get to their destination.

Recent research shows that, on sunny days, monarchs choose their direction by combining signals from an internal clock that measures the time of day with visual cues regarding the sun's changing azimuth—its changing position along the horizon.[39] Combining these two measurements into a workable indicator of orientation is not a trivial task, especially since the sun's position in the sky, at any given time in the day, changes as the seasons progress. Moreover, on cloudy days monarchs can still navigate effectively, which suggests their sun compass is supplemented by something else, perhaps a sensor that detects changes in their orientation to Earth's magnetic field.

For a moment, as I watched those tiny, fragile creatures begin their journey across Lake Ontario, I felt I was in the presence of something infinitely larger and more impressive than all human accomplishment and all the postmodern pyramids and dazzling light technologies we can muster. Those insects were following a pattern of behavior that was visibly linked to hundreds of millions of years of evolution. A window into those past eons opened in front of me. There, in their barely potent but ardent flitterings over the lake, I could see real power and timelessness, unlike anything humanity could ever hope to match.

But who sees the monarch migration anymore?

My European travels had nearly ended. After Paris, I returned to London for a conference of specialists on population growth. Over dinner at a posh hotel, I had a fascinating, wide-ranging conversation about humankind's future with John Bongaarts, vice president of policy research at the Population Council in New York.

John Bongaarts is one of the world's leading demographers. Currently, he is noted for research in which he differentiates the fraction of future human population growth that could be prevented by wide distribution of contraceptives from the fraction that is more or less "locked in" because of the large number of girls still to reach their reproductive years (the problem of "demographic momentum" that I mentioned in the last chapter and that will account for about 50 percent of population growth in poor countries over the next two decades). He is an attractive fifty-five-year-old Dutchman, with well-groomed white hair and, despite his three decades in the United States, a slight Dutch accent.

"The next twenty-five years will be very difficult," he stressed. "We'll see continued rapid population growth, about seven hundred million people per decade for the next two decades. We're also going to see many simultaneous changes in the global ecosystem—things like deforestation, soil erosion, dying coral reefs, climate change, and pollution of coastal zones with nitrogen. What's worse, most of these changes occur slowly and so won't be noticed: we're gradually drifting into a world where we've lost many valuable things. On the global scale, we can expect big differences between winners and losers—a patchiness, I would say, of the global landscape—and perhaps some big local catastrophes, like droughts, famines, and genocides."

"I agree," I replied, "but there's also the likelihood of sudden changes in the economic, political, and ecological systems that we live within. After long periods of slow change, those systems can flip to radically different states or equilibria if pushed far enough. And we're now so interlinked on the planet that a shock or flip in a key system in one part of the planet can propagate to every other part in the blink of an eye."

Bongaarts wasn't convinced. "Well, we saw an interesting example only a few years ago," I suggested. "The 1994 Zapatista rebellion in Chiapas, Mexico, helped trigger a collapse of the Mexican peso. It's true the peso was very vulnerable because of the country's huge current-account deficit. But the rebellion reminded the world that Mexico wasn't the next economic tiger, and the peso collapse ricocheted around the world, forcing currencies down from Canada to Southeast Asia."

"But the density of connections in these systems—their very complexity—produces resilience," he argued. "In a highly complex, networked system like the world financial system, chunks can be damaged, removed, and even destroyed, yet the rest of the system can often step in to contain and repair that damage. Even if, God forbid, New York City were destroyed or simply disappeared, the loss would certainly have a staggering effect on the world, especially its financial management, but human civilization wouldn't collapse. The rest of the human system would move in to repair the damage and replace the loss."[40]

He paused and thought for a moment. "Nonetheless, we aren't currently seeing sharp, dramatically visible changes in our systems, and their seeming stability is probably lulling us into complacency. These systems aren't giving us clear negative signals. So people aren't being given the information and incentives to reflect properly on the challenges we'll face in the future. And we can be certain of one thing: the golden future proposed by certain economists and techno-optimists will not come to pass. The ecological stress we're putting on the planet and the trend towards widening gaps between rich and poor ensure we'll see a future altogether more mixed and ambiguous."

Back in my hotel room, I decided Bongaarts was probably right, at least in part: we weren't getting strong enough signals from the complex systems we depend upon. But as it turned out, we didn't have long to wait. It was only September 1997; the Asian financial crisis had just begun. Within a year, the signals, at least those from the international economic system, would be dramatic enough for everyone to see.

PART TWO

Do We Need

More Ingenuity

to Solve the

Problems of

the Future?

COMPLEXITIES

WHEN I RETURNED to North America, Mike Whitfield's world of zooplankton, emergent properties, keystone species, and the ecology of the English Channel seemed far away. But I knew that many of his points were relevant to our daily lives. They were also important pieces of the ingenuity puzzle, although I wasn't yet sure how to put them together.

Mike Whitfield had spoken of the intrinsic complexity of the ecosystems we depend upon and of characteristics common to complex systems in general. In our daily lives, we often shut ourselves off from the natural world (as I suggested in the last chapter), but most of us are at least intuitively aware that we are surrounded by a multitude of other complex systems—economic, technological, and social—created by human beings. Most of us also have the impression that these human-made systems are becoming immensely *more* complex over time. Yet it's hard to put our finger on exactly how or why.

One factor that increases complexity in our lives is the relentless march of technology.[1] The ferocious competition of modern capitalism—its inexorable "creative destruction," as the economist Joseph Schumpeter once labeled it—propels technology's development and generates the wealth that allows new technology to be used by more and more people. When taken individually, the new devices that surround us seem reasonable and helpful: microwave ovens, voice-mail systems, and jet planes help us get more done, save time, communicate with friends and colleagues more easily, and get where we want to go faster. But when taken together, and when used not just by ourselves but also by everybody else in our society, these devices sometimes make our lives more complex and, surprisingly, more difficult. In Whitfield's terms, increased complexity is an emergent property that arises when discrete elements—in this case, individual new technologies—combine and produce unanticipated effects.

These effects are insidious, creeping in from the edges of our reality in ways we don't immediately notice. For example, new communication technologies steadily widen the circle of people each of us can contact: today we can reach out to a far larger number of people than we could even twenty years ago, and a far larger number of people can easily reach us. As a result, we find ourselves more rushed and facing an expanding range of obligations and responsibilities, because it is easier for other people to make demands on our time. Voice-mail messages, e-mail letters, and faxes pile up. Meetings proliferate. Scheduling calendars and Palm Pilots are crammed with appointments and conference calls. And when these new communication technologies are combined with new technologies of travel and production, everybody moves more, makes more things, and communicates more in interaction with more people. Since we can all do more, we feel we *must* do more, because if we don't we will be left behind by our colleagues, neighbors, and competitors. Thus the technologies that save us time and labor individually—that empower each of us—bind us collectively into a frenetic, mad race in which we often feel more caged by obligations and demands than before. The tools of our liberation often seem to imprison us. Harvard economist Juliet Schor, author of *The Overworked American*, makes a similar point. "Technology," she says, "reduces the amount of time it takes to do any one task, but it also leads to the expansion of tasks that people are *expected* to do. This is what happened to American housewives over the twentieth century as they got new appliances. They didn't actually do less work—they did more things. It's what happens to people when they get computers and faxes and cellular telephones and all of the new technologies that are coming out today."[2]

The people who succeed in this new, technologically hypercharged environment make up a narrow elite that thrives on constant stimulus. They tend to be young, urban, aggressive, and highly competent, like the people I saw at Canary Wharf. But, like most of us, they usually don't think a lot about who they are, about what their ultimate aims are, or about the broader consequences of what they are doing. Instead, they thrive on the competition and change of the moment, on the mad race that is the essence of today's world. Even if they want to ponder bigger issues, the compressed and complex conditions of our modern lives don't give them much room to do so.

But one fact is clear: as our lives and our world become faster-paced and more complex, our need for ingenuity rises. Both as individuals and as societies, we must deal with more issues simultaneously and make decisions faster. We must deliver an ever greater range of problem-solving ideas at an ever higher rate, and to accomplish this task we must rely on increasingly sophisticated time- and decision-management tools.

The march of technology is the most obvious, immediate cause of the greater complexity of our lives. But the ultimate answer to the question, What produces increasing complexity? is both deeper and more general. We can't answer this question, though, without taking a short detour into the rapidly developing field of *complexity theory*. Much of the pioneering work in this new field is taking place at the Santa Fe Institute in Santa Fe, New Mexico, an organization that has developed a worldwide reputation for bringing together top thinkers from diverse disciplines to study how complex systems, from economies to ecosystems, work.

The institute has a number of resident thinkers, and one of them, the economist W. Brian Arthur, has studied the sources of complexity with great subtlety. In a path-breaking article, he identifies three critical processes that make systems more complex.[3]

We can think of a system as a group of things or "entities," as Arthur calls them, interacting with each other over time.[4] These entities might be, for example, individual species in an ecological system like Whitfield's English Channel, or specific communication technologies in an information system such as the Internet, or corporations in an economic system. Arthur argues, first, that such systems become more complex through a process he calls *growth in coevolutionary diversity*. In a "coevolutionary" system, the entities that make up the system—organisms, corporations, or whatever—compete fiercely. Those entities that don't do well in this competition don't survive. At the same time, though, competition isn't simply a "war of all against all." Over time, the system's entities can also develop webs of interdependence: corporations learn to work together and use each other's products, for example, and some species of fish in the English Channel will have symbiotic (or mutually beneficial) rather than predator-prey relationships. As these interactions proliferate—whether they are competitive, cooperative, or symbiotic—new opportunities or niches emerge among the existing entities. (The image that comes to my mind is of a row of children's building blocks on a table, each block spaced slightly apart from its neighbors; every time a new block is added to the row, a new space is created too, and this space is analogous to a new niche in the system.) As new niches emerge, new entities evolve to exploit them. "By this means," Brian Arthur writes, "complexity, in the form of greater diversity and a more intricate web of interactions, tends to bootstrap itself upward over time. . . . With entities providing niches and niches making possible new entities, it may feed upon itself; so that diversity itself provides the fuel for further diversity."[5]

He uses the apt example of the modern computer industry. Here, the entities in the coevolving system are discrete computer technologies. The arrival of microprocessors—that is, computer chips—produced niches "for devices such as memory systems, screen monitors, and bus interfaces that could be connected with [microprocessors] to form useful hardware—computing devices." Computers in turn created needs for operating systems, programming languages, and software. The interaction of hardware and software then permitted the development of technologies from desktop publishing to computer-aided design. And all these developments fed back to stimulate improvements in microprocessor technology.

Brian Arthur stresses that the potential for new entities to develop is often a function, not so much of the number of other entities in the system, as of the possibilities for interaction among them. For instance, only the conjunction of lasers, xerography, and computers made possible the invention of laser printer technology. He also argues that some types of coevolutionary system can generate an explosion of niches; in other words, the number of possible interactions and, consequently, the number of niches can multiply stunningly fast. This increase, in turn, boosts the diversity of entities within the system and the complexity of the system as a whole. In short, diversity begets diversity, and complexity begets complexity.[6]

What does all this mean for the ingenuity gap? This first process described by Arthur tells us that virtuous circles may take hold in some societies, in which these societies experience an explosion of creativity, ingenuity, complexity, and diversity. At the same time, those societies that never reach a critical rate of development of new entities—whether they be technologies, corporations, or forms of social organization—and that therefore do not develop new niches rapidly either, will remain quiescent indefinitely. Arthur's first mechanism implies that we will see a widening gap between highly adaptive societies able to generate immense amounts of ingenuity and those that remain poor backwaters.[7]

Although coevolving systems tend to become more diverse and complex as time passes, Brian Arthur also notes that there are fluctuations around the upward trend. On occasion, a new entity replaces another more basic or fundamental one within a system, and this change eliminates the niches linked to that more basic entity. A century and a half ago, for instance, the bureaucracies of corporations and governments were sustained by elaborate systems of copiers and scribes. They wrote and rewrote important documents, such as contracts and correspondence, by hand. But the development of typewriters and carbon paper eliminated this entire interdependent edifice of institutions, technology, and personnel—a change that produced, in turn, a sharp but temporary drop in the system's complexity.

Arthur's second process that increases complexity, which he calls *structural deepening*, occurs not within whole systems but within single entities. An entity like an organism, technology, or corporation becomes steadily more sophisticated in order to improve its performance; this trend is driven by fierce competition with other entities in the ecological, economic, or social system. "The steady pressure of competition," he argues, "causes complexity to increase as functions and modifications are added to a system to break through limitations, to handle exceptional circumstances, or to adapt to an environment itself more complex."[8]

The introduction of radically new, simple systems can sometimes sweep away complex earlier systems that have become encrusted with additions and complications. By the 1930s, for example, the piston engine in airplanes had become hugely complicated: engineers were trying to make these engines operate effectively at high speed in the thin air of high altitudes. The revolutionary Whittle jet engine, in contrast, had one moving part. So, eventually, as the performance advantages of jet engines became obvious, they supplanted piston engines in planes. But the desire to make jet engines perform even better inevitably led to the addition of further subsystems and sub-subsystems, including cooling devices, airflow control, extra compressors, and afterburners. Today's advanced jet engines have over twenty thousand parts. Brian Arthur sums up: "In evolving systems, bursts of simplicity often cut through growing complexity and establish a new basis upon which complication can again grow. In this back-and-forth dance between complexity and simplicity, complication usually gains a net edge over time."⁹

Arthur's third process—*capturing software*—is completely different from the previous two. Sometimes, he contends, systems take over or "task" simpler systems, exploiting the entities that make up these systems and also the set of rules or "grammar" that governs interaction among the entities.[10] This process is less obscure than it sounds. Arthur uses the example of human societies and electricity: we have learned to task electrons by understanding the physical rules (or grammar) that govern electricity. Humans exploit electrons and their grammar of electromagnetism as "programmable software" for an ever-broadening array of technologies.

He extends this idea to the immensely complex social systems we have constructed around us. National and international securities markets, for instance, have invented a grammar of options, indexes, and futures that can be applied to different objects of underlying value (often called "underlyings"). At first, these underlyings might be straightforward things like pork bellies, U.S. dollars, or shares of IBM. But when securities markets apply their grammar of options, indexes, and futures to them, new objects of value, often called "derivatives," are created. The markets can then again apply the same grammar to these derivatives to create further objects of value in a progressively thickening hierarchy of complexity. In other words, markets recursively apply the same set of rules, over and over again, to the very things that they have produced through those rules. Some derivatives become so remote from their original underlyings that only the most analytically astute financial managers have any grasp of what they are or mean.

So three processes produce greater complexity in our world: competition and interdependence among entities creates niches that new entities can fill; this competitive environment also encourages individual entities to breach performance limits by adding new subsystems; and large systems of entities can capture or task simpler systems, adapting and building on the grammar of these simpler systems to boost performance.

These processes are constantly at work in the technological, political, and economic systems around us. We see them operating simultaneously in local communities, the domestic market, and the international system of states. The results are often new and performance-enhanced technologies and institutions. When taken individually, these technologies and institutions can be very useful. But when taken together, the combined effect is a faster-paced, more densely linked, increasingly interactive, and often overwhelmingly complex world. Produced by our ingenuity, it is a world that often demands from us ever greater amounts of ingenuity. It is also a world where, increasingly, most of us have handed over control to specialists who are able to supply this ingenuity.

Evidence is nearby—in fact, it's under the hood of our cars.

———————————

When I was a teenager in the early seventies, I had a boy's fascination with cars. I lived in a rural area on Vancouver Island, where friends and parties were widely dispersed. Social life and the pursuit of girls demanded a good set of wheels. On turning sixteen, I got my driver's license and inherited my parents' 1952 Oldsmobile—a car with a powerful (for the early fifties) V-8 engine and a four-barrel carburetor. The engine, or "mill," as we called it, was hardly compact: it weighed perhaps 150 kilograms and stood almost a meter high from oil pan to air filter.

As a budding mechanic, I cut my teeth on that car. Over a period of months, I busied myself grinding its valves, reboring its cylinders, rebuilding its carburetor, and fitting new rings on its pistons. I rebuilt the suspension system, sandblasted and bolted on new fenders, and rechromed the ornaments. That was happiness!

As part of this project, I found a derelict '52 Oldsmobile and ripped it to pieces for parts. Eventually the derelict's engine found a home in the middle of my father's carport, wrapped in a chain and rigged to a block and tackle connected to a beam. As I unbolted the machine heads and broke the engine into pieces, oil and sludge pooled on the plywood underneath and seeped across the floor. My father was hardly pleased with the hideous mess, but I was determined to understand this greasy chunk of hardware. I can remember my epiphany when I realized, in a flash, how all the pieces functioned together: the pistons, the crankshaft, the timing chain and gear, the camshaft, hydraulic lifters, and valves. I stared at the engine sitting in its brown pool of muck. I was astonished by its ingenuity, by the extraordinarily clever way the pieces were integrated into a whole to convert chemical energy into mechanical energy.

From that moment on, the mechanistic metaphor of how things work in the universe—a metaphor of deterministic cause and effect, of the functionality of the individual parts making up the whole—was firmly rooted in my mind. To be sure, it was only one metaphor among many at my disposal, one whose usefulness varied according to the task at hand, but I am still impressed by its intuitive power.

I later learned that this metaphor had its origins in our great intellectual transition from medievalism to modernity. This transition began with Copernicus in the sixteenth century, gathered momentum through Galileo, Descartes, and Spinoza, and culminated in Newton's grand synthesis in the late seventeenth century. The new view emphasized the simplicity of nature, the interpretation and representation of natural phenomena by mathematical law, and, most fundamentally, the machinelike character of the natural world.[11] (In those days, the paradigmatic machine was the clock and not, of course, the internal combustion engine!) Although this revolution reached its apogee with Newton, René Descartes was its earliest clear exponent. "Give me extension and motion, and I will construct the universe," he proclaimed. As John Herman Randall Jr., one of the preeminent intellectual historians of the middle twentieth century, writes, "To Descartes thenceforth space or extension became the fundamental reality in the world, motion the source of all change, and mathematics the only relation between its parts. . . . He had made of nature a machine and nothing but a machine; purposes and spiritual significance had alike been banished."[12]

But dismantling that Oldsmobile engine was more, for me, than a greasy introduction to the Cartesian revolution. It also taught me that it was possible to analyze machines and the other things in our world; to break them apart, piece by piece, and grasp their inner workings; and to reduce complexity to simpler building blocks.

Today, however, such an enterprise wouldn't be so easy, or so satisfying, at least when it comes to cars. Look under the hood of any modern car, and you'll see why: Brian Arthur's structural deepening is at work. In order to breach performance limits, the complexity of the modern automobile engine has soared. Automotive engineers have generated a never-ending accretion of additional features, ranging from pollution-control devices to computer-controlled fuel-injection systems. As a result, today's cars are far quieter, safer, more comfortable, and more efficient than those of the early fifties. But there have been costs too. As a teenager I could easily identify and reach the main engine, steering, and brake components under the hood of my Oldsmobile. Today, the engine compartment is a sinister tangle of hoses, wires, and tubing, a proliferation of electronic devices and computers, all incomprehensible to the amateur.

In fact, even most professional mechanics are little more than diagnosticians now. The modern car is trundled into the shop and hooked to computerized diagnostic systems, and faulty engine modules are replaced in their entirety. If the faulty modules are repaired at all—rather than simply junked—they are rarely fixed in the shop but instead shipped to specialized facilities with the specific expertise needed. As the complexity and sophistication of our cars have increased, we can no longer repair them in our backyards or in our garage grease pits. Instead, we increasingly rely on distant expertise and knowledge. In short, the rising complexity of our machines has reduced our independence and self-sufficiency. It's ironic that as technology does its job better and empowers us in various ways, it leaves us with less control, power, and freedom in other ways.[13]

Sometimes structural deepening can lead to truly perverse and counterproductive results. Several years ago, I came across a pithy example. I often travel from Canada to the United States to speak at conferences and workshops, and occasionally I am reimbursed for my time. More often than not, though, my hosts and I end up entangled in cumbersome Internal Revenue Service rules covering fees to foreigners. After one excursion, my hosts asked me to fill out IRS Form 1001, which was titled "Ownership, Exemption, or Reduced Rate Certificate." I had never seen this form before (although I gathered that it was widely used), and I really didn't know what to do with it, especially since none of the boxes I was supposed to fill in had any relevance to my situation. I was asked to indicate, for instance, whether my income came from rent or royalties on natural resources and patents; I was asked for detailed information on bonds that might pay me interest; and finally I was asked to sign as the "beneficial owner, fiduciary, trustee, or agent." The form's reverse side was densely packed with incomprehensible instructions.

As I looked over this curious document, I was particularly struck by a band of text across the bottom. It bore the title "Paperwork Reduction Act Notice" and read:

> The time needed to complete and file this form will vary depending on individual circumstances. The estimated average time is:
>
> | | |
> |---|---|
> | Recordkeeping: | 4 hr., 32 min. |
> | Learning about the law or the form: | 1 hr. |
> | Preparing and sending the form: | 1 hr., 7 min. |

The text then cheerfully concluded with a note that if I had comments "concerning the accuracy of these time estimates or suggestions for making this form simpler" the IRS would be happy to hear from me. It provided an address in Washington, D.C., where I could send my comments.

The Paperwork Reduction Act, passed in 1980 in the waning days of the Carter administration and amended in 1995, is a classic example of structural deepening gone awry. The law was supposed to improve the efficiency of the U.S. federal government and lighten the burden of paperwork on citizens. In Brian Arthur's terms, the additional complexity introduced by the law was supposed to improve government performance. But it has not worked. Although the U.S. Office of Management and Budget hired a special staff to review and approve every form and information request of every agency of the federal government, the estimated total time that the U.S. public invested each year fulfilling federal paperwork requirements rose from 4.7 billion hours in 1980 to 6.7 billion hours in 1996.[14]

More perversely, Form 1001 showed how the law makes government *more* inefficient and confusing to the average person. My first reaction to the notice at the bottom was to add up the time allotments. Was I really supposed to spend over six and a half hours on this form? The suggested times seemed so precise, and the total amount so daunting, that Form 1001 practically leapt at me with self-importance. And what records, exactly, was I supposed to spend four hours and thirty-two minutes keeping? I hadn't a clue. In its entirety, Form 1001 resembled the jumble of hoses and wiring under the hood of a modern car, and the "Paperwork Reduction Act Notice" at the bottom was a particularly forbidding clump of complexity.

I imagined that most law-abiding U.S. citizens confronted with Form 1001 would simply hand it over to a tax expert. In other words, they would deal with the matter just as they would deal with the complexity of their modern cars: they would have it fixed by someone with specialized knowledge.

Instead, I just ignored it. There were advantages, I decided, to being Canadian.

But even if we can identify the processes that make the world more complex over time, we still don't have a good grasp of what complexity is. How do we know complexity when we see it? What are its key features? Again, the field of complexity theory can help: thinkers there have identified a number of important features shared by complex systems. Some are already familiar to us from Mike Whitfield's remarks in Plymouth and Brian Arthur's analysis above. But we need a better grasp of these key features—six of them, in all—if we want to understand how complexity drives up our need for ingenuity or, indeed, if we want to understand many of the confusing events in our new world.

An obvious feature of complex systems is that they are composed of a *multiplicity* of things; they are made up of a large number of entities, components, or parts. And systems with more components are generally more complex than those with fewer. A square kilometer of an Amazonian jungle has vastly more species, and is therefore a far more complex ecosystem, than an equivalent patch of Sahara desert. A 1999 Oldsmobile engine, with its computerized control and advanced fuel, cooling, and pollution abatement systems, has far more parts, and is therefore far more complex, than my 1952 Rocket 88. Over time, as Brian Arthur shows, a coevolutionary dynamic within a system can boost the number of components and, in turn, the system's complexity. So the great range of coevolving species in the Amazonian jungle creates niches and opportunities for the evolution of yet more species; and the accretion of subsystems to the Oldsmobile engine generates needs for further subsystems to optimize performance.

The second feature common to complex systems is the dense web of *causal connections* among their components; in other words, their components have so many links to each other that they affect each other in many ways. The more causal connections, in general, the greater the system's complexity. As Mike Whitfield indicated, a particularly important result of all this dense connectivity is causal *feedback*, in which a change in one component affects others in a way that eventually loops back to affect the original component.

Feedback can be positive or negative. By "positive" feedback, complexity theorists don't mean that the feedback is always a "good" thing. Instead, they mean that the feedback reinforces or amplifies the initial change, and in the process it creates a virtuous or vicious circle. Stock markets, for example, are often driven by positive feedbacks: in a bull market, rising stock prices reinforce the confidence of investors, which causes them to buy more stocks, which further boosts prices; more begets more. This interaction is a virtuous circle, since most people become wealthier. In a bear market, falling prices undermine investors' confidence, which causes them to sell stocks and further drives down prices; less begets less—a vicious circle, since most people become poorer. Because the crowd psychology that governs short-term stock prices can sometimes get out of control, the institutions that oversee many stock markets have introduced mechanisms that interrupt the positive feedback in a bear market (including "circuit breakers," which halt trading when prices drop too far too fast). The important thing about positive feedbacks is that they are inherently unstable: they create self-reinforcing spirals of behavior, and can cause systems to become overextended or unbalanced.

Negative feedbacks, on the other hand, help maintain the stability or equilibrium of a system by counteracting the initial change: more is balanced by less, or vice versa. When stock prices fall, investors often seize the opportunity to buy newly cheaper stocks, which can counteract the drop in prices. Conversely, when stock prices rise, investors often sell to take their profits, which can slow the increase in prices.

Sometimes components in a highly connected system are *tightly coupled*. This means that a change in one component has rapid, multiple effects on other components of the system. The change branches out through the web of components, producing distant and often unexpected results.[15] There is little natural buffering capacity in the system to prevent the original change from affecting other components. A great example is available in our everyday urban lives: when drivers tailgate at high speed on a freeway, they create a tightly coupled system. A mistake by one driver, or a sudden shock coming from outside the system, such as a deer running across the road, can cause a multi-car accident. None of the drivers in the system has enough space in front of his or her car to avoid rear-ending the preceding car should it stop suddenly. But if all the drivers open up more space in front of their cars, the entire system's buffering capacity increases as it becomes more loosely coupled.

A third key feature of complex systems is the *interdependence* of their components. A good way of measuring interdependence is to divide a system into pieces and then see how the change affects the properties and behavior of the pieces. The human body is an excellent example of a highly interdependent complex system. Cutting it into pieces—severing its limbs from the torso, for instance—dramatically changes the behavior of the resulting pieces and their ability to function. It changes their very nature. Speaking generally, the larger the part that can be removed from a complex system without affecting the overall system's behavior, the more resilient the system.[16] During our dinner in London, John Bongaarts argued that the world's complex social and financial systems are relatively resilient, because large pieces can be removed or destroyed without causing entire systems to collapse.

The fourth feature of complex systems is their *openness* to their outside environments: they are not self-contained, but are affected, sometimes profoundly, by outside events. As a result, it's often hard to locate a complex system's boundary—that is, the point where the system ends and the outside world starts.[17] Where, for instance, do we draw the line between a human society and its encompassing, vitally important ecosystem of other living things, like the soils in which it grows its food and the forests that help recycle water through its environment? When we study or work with complex systems, the boundaries we draw around them are often arbitrary, so we tend to neglect important factors that affect the way they function.

Complex systems normally show a high degree of *synergy* among their components—a fifth common feature. Synergy means, in everyday language, that the whole is more than the sum of its parts.[18] Likewise, when we talk about complex systems, synergy means that the combined effect of changes in two or more of a system's components differs from the sum of their individual effects. We find many good examples in ecological systems.[19] Severe erosion of cropland caused by the action of wind or water, as is happening in many parts of Africa and Asia, reduces the depth of soil available for the roots of plants (what experts usually call "rooting depth"). This change can lower the yields of wheat, corn, and other grains. Inadequate rainfall can also lower yields. But because the loss of rooting depth makes crops particularly vulnerable to reduced rainfall, the combined or "synergistic" effect of these changes, if they occur at the same time, is much larger than the sum of their independent effects. Put another way, loss of rooting depth multiplies the effect of drought on crop output, and drought multiplies the effect of loss of rooting depth. Similarly, the rising prevalence of deformed and missing legs in some frog populations around the world has almost certainly been caused by a synergistic combination of factors. Biologists have proposed, for instance, that higher levels of ultraviolet radiation, due to ozone depletion, can make some otherwise innocuous chemical pollutants in the environment extremely toxic to frogs.[20]

Sixth and finally, complex systems exhibit *nonlinear* behavior—we can't count on things developing in tidy, straight lines. Nonlinearity is a notoriously difficult concept that even complexity specialists have difficulty explaining, but in the simplest terms it means that a change in a system can produce an effect that is not proportional to its size: small changes can produce large effects, and large changes can produce small effects.[21] Nonlinearity is important and has practical consequences, because experts in many fields commonly base their predictions of future developments on the linear projection of past developments. For instance, the economic optimists we encountered in the first chapter assume that the steady improvements in human well-being seen in the past two centuries will continue indefinitely into the future. But complex systems, like our national and international economies, are nonlinear, which means they can alter their behavior quite unpredictably. They might evolve slowly over time, with no more than incremental changes in their key components and variables, and then suddenly exhibit a sharp shift in behavior as they cross a critical threshold. In lay terms, we might say that the last incremental change was "the straw that broke the camel's back." Since many complex systems exhibit such threshold effects, it's risky to use straight-line extrapolations to predict their future behavior. (As a physicist friend of mine said, when he was explaining nonlinearity to me, "the world looks flat till you step off the edge.")

During our conversation in Plymouth, Mike Whitfield referred to threshold effects in nonlinear systems when he talked about Earth's grand ecosystems flipping from one equilibrium to another. In the 1970s, we got a dramatic demonstration of such behavior when the Peruvian anchovy fishery—one of the world's richest—abruptly collapsed because of the combined effect of many factors, including overfishing and changes in Pacific currents due to El Niño.[22] A similar flip happened in the late 1980s and early 1990s when the cod stocks off the northeast coast of North America were suddenly and massively depleted.

But perhaps the most striking evidence of how we can push the natural environment across a critical threshold was the hole in the stratospheric ozone layer that appeared over the Antarctic in the mid-1970s.[23] At that time, scientific models of ozone depletion, for the most part, assumed a roughly linear relationship between chlorofluorocarbon (CFC) emissions and stratospheric ozone depletion. In other words, atmospheric scientists assumed that an increase in CFC emissions would produce a roughly proportional decrease in ozone concentrations. They simply did not anticipate that ozone destruction could occur on the surface of ice crystals in the stratosphere when certain temperature and light conditions combined with particular concentrations of water, nitrogen compounds, and CFCs.

As a result, scientists did not identify Antarctica's sudden and severe weakening of its ozone layer until the mid-1980s—nearly ten years *after* the hole first opened up. Despite having abundant data on ozone concentrations from satellites orbiting over the South Pole, scientists had programmed the computers that analyzed these data to assume the linearity of ozone depletion—that is, that the ozone layer would only be depleted in proportion to the amount of CFCs we had pumped into our environment. The computers therefore automatically discarded all anomalous results, including measurements indicating a dramatic fall in ozone concentrations.[24] But, as it turned out, if conditions are right, ozone destruction occurs at lightning speed, stripping the gas from thick layers of the Antarctic's high atmosphere in a matter of weeks.[25]

What does it mean to say that a given ecological, social, or technological system is more complex than another? We understand some of the key features of complex systems and some of the forces that seem to be making our world more complex, but we still need a good measuring stick for complexity. Then we'll be better able to gauge how much more complex our world is becoming and how much more ingenuity we'll need to meet this new world's challenges.

We might be able to use information theory to develop a measuring stick. This theory has been around for over fifty years, but it has received lots of attention lately because of the explosion of new communications technologies. Information, in the context of this theory, has a very specific definition, so the amount of information communicated by a message or an event can be precisely measured. Roughly speaking, the information content of an event varies inversely with the probability of that event occurring; in other words, the more unexpected the event, the greater its information content.[26] The "message from the Sahara" is a well-known example: a message telling us that there have been heavy rains in the Sahara desert communicates much more information than one telling us that there have been no rains, because the probability of rain in the Sahara is very low.[27]

Using this theory, we can estimate a system's complexity by looking at the minimum amount of information needed (or the minimum length of the statement needed) to fully describe the system.[28] The more information or the longer the statement, the greater the system's complexity. But it's hard to turn this appealing idea into a practical measuring stick.[29] So researchers have proposed various alternative approaches: some estimate the length of the underlying set of rules or "grammar" that would describe a complex system's behavior, and others focus on how the features of complex systems vary when observed at different distances or scales. Each of these approaches, though, has weaknesses.[30]

Another way to estimate a system's complexity is to measure the difficulty of creating a mathematical model of it. Such a model is, in part, a set of equations that describes all the system's main components and the causal links among them. Some systems are extremely difficult to model because they have so many components; to use the specialists' awkward phrase, they are "mathematically intractable." As the number of components, variables, or "dimensions" in the equations goes up, the length of time it takes to work out, or solve, the equations rises even faster. This is vividly known as the "curse of dimension," and the curse resonates wickedly through many areas of scientific research crucial to our well-being, from climate modeling to medicine.[31] Although modern supercomputers can help solve this problem, even the fastest computers are often quickly overwhelmed. As two top experts, Joseph Traub and Henryk Wozniakowski, say, "the curse of dimension can elevate tasks to a level of difficulty at which they become intractable. . . . Even though scientists have computers at their disposal, problems can have so many variables that no future computer speed will make it possible to solve them in a reasonable amount of time."[32]

But the "curse of dimension," besides providing us with a rough indication of degrees of complexity, also tells us something about how much ingenuity we must have to manage the complex systems around us. These systems have so many components and so many different potential behaviors that we often require huge amounts of ingenuity to understand how they work and to predict what they will do in the future.

Modern biology gives us a good illustration. To cure and manage human disease, we frequently need very accurate knowledge of how our bodies produce key molecules, such as proteins; we also need to know how these molecules behave and function. We might assume that all this information about proteins is contained in our DNA—since DNA provides the basic template from which proteins are made—and that as molecular biologists better understand human DNA, we will develop a complete blueprint

The Folded Hemoglobin Molecule is Extraordinarily Complex

of the way our proteins are made and the way they work, biologically and chemically. Unfortunately, knowledge of our DNA is only a first small step in such understanding.

When a protein molecule such as hemoglobin is manufactured in a cell, it only briefly remains a long, linear chain of atoms. Quickly, it folds itself into a characteristic shape or bundle (shown in the illustration above), and it is this shape that determines the protein's biochemical function—in the case of hemoglobin, the ability to carry oxygen in our blood and release it to cells throughout the body. The folding process is not well understood.[33] But we do know that as the number of amino acids in the protein increases, the complexity of the folding skyrockets. Even today's fastest computers are not remotely up to the task of figuring out which, of all the different folding possibilities, is the right one for the molecule to function properly. Relatively simple proteins can fold in many places along the chain of atoms, and each fold can occur in many different directions. An average protein of about one hundred amino acids presents an unimaginable number of folding possibilities, and a supercomputer would need a billion billion billion years to test every one.[34] Nonetheless, nature *does* successfully fold these proteins into useful shapes, often in only a few seconds. While the mathematical problem of modeling protein folding is intractable, clearly the physical problem in the real world is not. We just don't know how nature solves the physical problem.

Can we use any of these rudimentary measures of complexity—a system's information content, the length of its underlying grammar, or its mathematical intractability—to tell us whether our world is really becoming more complex? Some experts believe we can.

We should keep in mind, though, that human beings have always been surrounded by great complexity: the planet's weather and climate systems and the natural ecologies around us, for instance, are intrinsically complex. And anthropologists have learned that our social interactions, even among our hunter-gatherer ancestors, have also always been complex. Some experts have even proposed that the human brain grew rapidly over the last two million years precisely because we needed to understand and manage the social complexities of our communities (success at social intrigue, it turns out, takes a lot of brainpower).

But our common feeling today that things are becoming far more complex, and our common preoccupation with complexity in general, are new phenomena. Langdon Winner, a wonderfully insightful theorist of politics and technology, argues that the world *has* changed in some fundamental ways to provoke these concerns. "If there is a unique quality to the modern era," Winner writes, "it is that the conditions of existence have changed to such a degree that something explicitly recognized as 'complexity' now continually forces itself into our awareness."[35]

Most of the changes Winner refers to have occurred incrementally (as I argued in the "New World" chapter); sometimes, as a result, they have gone almost unnoticed. One change is simply the steady growth of the human population: as our numbers and population densities have risen, our interactions have become more numerous and more complicated. In addition, as I suggested at the beginning of this chapter, new technologies have also boosted the complexity of our lives. Brian Arthur's processes of coevolution and structural deepening have created an ever-widening array of lighter, cheaper, easier-to-use, and more powerful technologies. These new technologies extend our power and options as individuals, communities, and societies. They allow us to live longer and healthier lives; travel farther and faster; control the world around us more completely; and send more information to more people, faster, over greater distances. In other words, they extend our *agency horizon*, as I call it, which is our reach in both time and space.[36]

In combination, these changes have sharply raised the density, intensity, and pace of our interactions with each other and with our environment. The *density* of interactions has increased, because our systems now have many more entities—including people, groups, organizations, and technologies—and these entities have more links to each other. The *intensity* and *pace* of interactions have also increased, because these entities are more powerful, and because they pass materials, energy, and information among themselves in greater quantities and more quickly.[37]

Nearly every statistic that gauges the degree of connectivity among human beings or the movement of information, people, and things shows exponential growth. When I first used e-mail at MIT in the mid-1980s, the whole world contained only a few thousand host computers for the Internet; by 1999, the number had soared to nearly 50 million.[38] In 1977, about $18 billion worth of foreign exchange was traded every day in the world's financial markets; today the figure is $1.5 trillion—a nearly hundredfold increase in less that twenty-five years.[39] Between 1960 and 2000, a period during which the planet's population doubled, worldwide traffic volume—that is, the total number of kilometers traveled by people in cars, buses, trains, and planes—increased more than five times; and between 1950 and 1988, worldwide volume of air transport alone increased almost one hundred times.[40]

These trends have in turn boosted the complexity of our social and economic systems. Greater complexity isn't necessarily a bad thing, though. In many cases, as Brian Arthur shows, we deliberately make our systems more complex in order to make them perform better. And higher connectivity among a system's components, as John Bongaarts suggests, can make it more shock-resistant. But the steep and seemingly endless rise in the connectivity and in the level of kinetic activity in our world generally makes the social and economic systems we depend on more tightly coupled, synergistic, and likely to exhibit abrupt and unexpected nonlinearities.[41]

This rising complexity may already be having a profound effect on the way we organize ourselves. The American theorist Yaneer Bar-Yam, one of the most thoughtful people working on these issues, argues that higher complexity is making many of our social and economic hierarchies unworkable. As a result, it is catalyzing a worldwide shift towards cooperative networks and weblike arrangements. He estimates that the complexity of large, modern societies now exceeds that of any one individual (as measured by the information content of a person's DNA and brain), making it impossible for a single person or small group of people to control these societies effectively. Instead, we see hierarchies collapse; he points to the examples of the Soviet Union and of large, private corporations in the West that decide to downsize. Often, networks of cooperating units take their place. This "complexity transition," he asserts, "implies that various collectives of human beings are now behaving in a manner that is more complex than an individual. This statement could not be made tens or hundreds of years ago."[42]

So there's a lot of evidence that our world is becoming enormously more complex, and fast. This change is fundamentally shifting the way we organize ourselves, the way we solve problems, and the way we perceive ourselves and the world around us. Whether, on balance, it's a problem or a good thing remains to be seen. But, at the very least, we can say that humanity must now make more and better decisions faster than ever before. The rising complexity and pace of our world demands more ingenuity from us of all kinds.

AN ANGRY BEAST

THE ULTIMATE CONSEQUENCES of complexity are hard to fathom, and sometimes more than a bit disturbing. For this reason, most of us remain avid captives of the Cartesian model of the world as a relatively simple, mathematically tractable, and predictable machine. As I stood over the rusty old V-8 in my father's carport, I found this model—this theory of reality—vivid and sweet. It stayed with me for many years. In fact, it grew stronger as time passed.

In the mid-1970s, I worked intermittently in resource industries in Western Canada, as a compassman on a crew of forest surveyors, and as a roughneck on oil and gas drilling rigs in northern British Columbia and Alberta. By the summer of 1978, I had found my way to the little town of Swan Hills, two hundred kilometers northwest of Edmonton. During the day I was part of a team of men stringing kilometers of natural gas pipeline across the swamps and scrub of the Canadian wilderness.

During the evenings I stretched out on the bed in a tiny, grubby room in a trailer. There was nothing to do in town except drink oneself silly in beer parlors, so my main entertainment was a never-ending stack of novels and popular science books.

As we cut a path through the bush and forest, dropping tons of tubular steel into the earth, our work was forceful, managed, and directed; it was clearly grounded in the common-sense notion that observable causes produce, deterministically, observable and predictable effects. And it was satisfyingly in keeping with the mechanistic model of how the world works that had dominated my mind for years.

One evening I had an insight. Perhaps it arose from the brute prowess of our pipeline work. As I lay on my narrow bed, it occurred to me that if at one precise moment in time—say, midnight of January 1, 1979—humankind were to have complete knowledge of the position, direction, and velocity of all the objects in the universe and all the fluxes of energy, and if we also had highly accurate theories about how these objects and fluxes were interacting at that instant and could interact, and what the results of these interactions would be, we would be able to predict all events in the universe, both forwards and backwards, from that one specific moment. Of course I knew that we would never have such finely detailed knowledge, but I was still struck by the theoretical possibility that if we did, we could produce a complete map of the entire history and future of the universe.

It was only many years later that I learned that I had stumbled upon an idea, first proposed by the eighteenth-century French mathematician Pierre-Simon de Laplace, of a fully deterministic world. The son of a peasant farmer in Normandy, Laplace left behind his humble origins and rose to be one of the great mathematicians of his time. Often called the Newton of France, Laplace pioneered probability theory and used Newton's theory of gravitation to account for the planets' deviations from their predicted orbits. In 1773, he wrote, "The present state of the system of nature is evidently a consequence of what it was in the preceding moment, and if we conceive of an intelligence which at a given instant comprehends all the relations of the entities of this universe, it could state the respective position, motions, and general affects of all these entities at any time in the past or future."[1]

Laplace's vision was entirely at one with René Descartes's mechanistic worldview. But within decades the fabric of this worldview began to fray. As scientists searched for patterns and laws governing the workings of the natural world, they learned to rely less on rigid, logical deduction from mathematical axiom and more on careful experimentation and gathering of real-world data. Also, Charles Darwin's theory of evolution suggested that things in the natural world could adapt and change their essential character over time—something that simple, clocklike machines, with their endlessly repeated cycles, cannot do. And the new physics of the early twentieth century brought with it the theories of relativity and quantum indeterminism, which radically undermined earlier ideas of time, space, and causation.

In the late nineteenth and early twentieth centuries, a key contributor to these intellectual shifts was another Frenchman, Henri Poincaré. A man of truly prodigious intellect who was widely thought to be the greatest living mathematician of his day, Poincaré not only made major contributions to celestial mechanics, topology, and number theory, he also produced many of the basic results of the special theory of relativity quite independently of Einstein. Moreover, he was a fine writer and was keen to communicate the value and methods of mathematics and science to popular audiences.

In 1903, Poincaré proposed a critical revision to Laplace's deterministic view of nature:

> A very small cause which escapes our notice determines a considerable effect that we cannot fail to see, and then we say that the effect is due to chance. If we knew exactly the laws of nature and the situation of the universe at the initial moment, we could predict exactly the situation of that same universe at a succeeding moment. But even if it were the case that the natural laws had no longer any secret for us, we could still only know the initial situation *approximately*. If that enabled us to predict the succeeding situation with *the same approximation*, that is all we require, and we should say that the phenomenon had been predicted, that it is governed by laws. But it is not always so; it may happen that small differences in the initial conditions produce very great ones in the final phenomena. A small error in the former will produce an enormous error in the latter. Prediction becomes impossible, and we have the fortuitous phenomenon.[2]

Poincaré's suggestion in this passage is of monumental importance: some natural systems, he points out, magnify small changes in starting conditions, which makes it very difficult to predict accurately how they will behave over time. As a graduate student at MIT in the mid-1980s, I was fascinated when I came across Poincaré's argument in a tight twelve-page article titled "Chaos" in the magazine *Scientific American*.[3] Written by the leading theorists James Crutchfield, J. Doyne Farmer, and Norman Packard, it was among the first in a wave of articles and books that popularized the technical concept of chaos, and it is still among the finest summaries of this idea.[4] Although the concept has been widely taken up by today's media, it is often misunderstood and misused. But for scientists, engineers, and theorists, chaos has a very precise meaning and refers to specific behavior in the natural and social worlds. It is also a concept vital to our purposes in this book: I argue here that we generally need more sophisticated technologies and institutions—that is, more ingenuity—if the economic, social, technological, and ecological systems we critically depend upon sometimes behave chaotically.

Chaotic systems are not always complex (in fact, chaos can be observed in some very simple systems), and complex systems are not always chaotic. Nonetheless, the phenomenon is common in complex systems. Chaotic behavior arises from a conjunction of some of the key characteristics of complex systems I identified in the previous chapter: multiple components, dense causal connections among these components, feedback loops, synergy, and nonlinear dynamics.

A chaotic system magnifies the effect of small perturbations: as a result, the way the system develops over time is highly sensitive to minute differences in initial conditions, just as Poincaré proposed at the turn of the last century. The further one tries to project the system's behavior into the future, the harder accurate prediction becomes. But chaos should not be confused with randomness—that is, with events and behavior that have no specific cause. In chaotic systems, the basic processes of cause and effect still operate among the system's components. But how the interactions of these components unfold over time and what kinds of large-scale behavior these interactions produce are nevertheless, in important respects, unpredictable.[5]

Crutchfield and his colleagues gave a vivid example of how a system can magnify tiny perturbations. Suppose, they suggest, we play a game of billiards on a standard table with standard balls. But this game has an unusual feature: the interaction of the balls with one another and with the table is frictionless. Once set in motion, the balls continue their merry paths around the table, bouncing off each other and off the sides of the table indefinitely. If we follow the impacts and trajectories of the balls after the initial break of the rack, the authors ask, "For how long could a player with perfect control over his or her stroke predict the cue ball's trajectory?" Not very long, it turns out: "If the player ignored an effect even as minuscule as the gravitational attraction of an electron at the edge of the galaxy, the prediction would become wrong after one minute!"[6]

In the daily world around us, chaos is most noticeable in the vagaries and unpredictabilities of the weather. In a famous paper in 1963, the meteorologist Edward Lorenz showed that an astonishingly simple mathematical model of Earth's atmosphere—a model consisting of only three calculus equations—produces chaotic behavior.[7] After studying the implications of such models, Lorenz introduced his now famous "butterfly metaphor": the global atmosphere is so sensitive to small perturbations, he suggested, that the flap of the wings of a butterfly in Brazil might cause a chain of events eventually culminating in a tornado in Texas.

Meteorologists now recognize that chaos in the atmosphere severely limits their ability to predict the weather (although it may not impose such severe limits on prediction of the more general phenomenon of climate[8]). Despite the advent of extremely powerful, high-speed computers for modeling changes in the atmosphere, meteorologists remain conservative in their estimates of how many days into the future they can forecast the weather. Even under the best circumstances, the theoretical limit of detailed weather forecasts is about eighteen days.[9] Forecasts of average weather conditions might be extended to thirty days. Beyond that limit, useful weather prediction is, and will probably remain, impossible.

As the wave of books and articles about chaos and complexity has moved through popular consciousness in the last decade, many commentators—and even some scholars—have jumped to the conclusion that chaotic processes operate in human society too. Markets, crowds, popular protests, and the international system have all been declared to exhibit chaotic behavior. But we should be cautious about applying chaos theory to human society. Unlike natural systems, humans can learn, so they can change their behavior to avoid chaos. Although it is true that many social systems are extraordinarily complex and nonlinear, they are not wholly disorganized systems; rather, they exhibit at least partial self-organization. As we will see later in the chapter "White-Hot Landscapes," human social systems *do* learn and, as a result, are often able to keep themselves at the fecund boundary between chaos and order.[10]

Some systems flip back and forth between chaos and order. And a system's shift between these modes can be a good example of a nonlinear or threshold response to small outside perturbations.

The phenomenon is visible in your kitchen. Remove the screen from the nozzle of your kitchen tap and turn on the water to low volume. The water will drop into the sink in a smooth stream that flares near the tap and tapers as it falls away. This is called "laminar" flow, since the currents of water inside the stream are all aligned in roughly the same direction. Slowly increase the volume of water coming out of the tap, and the stream will suddenly twist into a sinuous, ropelike form as the flow becomes turbulent. Whereas the behavior of laminar flow is largely predictable, that of turbulent flow often is not.

Turbulence—the apparently random eddying and twisting of the flow—is now regarded as a special case of chaotic behavior. Laminar flow occurs when a fluid's viscous forces dampen its chaotic behavior. But as the speed of flow passes a key threshold, these forces are no longer strong enough, and turbulence appears.[11] This is not necessarily a bad thing; in the cylinders of a gasoline-powered car, turbulence helps gasoline vapor mix with air (both of which are, technically, fluids). And the dimples on a flying golf ball produce turbulence around its skin, which shrinks the volume of low-pressure air behind the ball. A dimpled ball travels more than twice as far as a smooth sphere of the same size and weight.

Nevertheless, engineers often want to reduce, eliminate, or at least better understand turbulence. Around the hull of a boat or over the surface of an airplane, it produces drag that raises fuel consumption. Turbulence must also be managed to improve the combustion efficiency of our automobile, train, jet, and rocket engines. As engineers Parviz Moin and John Kim write: "Many of the environmental or energy-related issues we face today cannot possibly be confronted without detailed knowledge of the mechanics of fluids."[12] As we will see, our ability to understand and control turbulence becomes more important as humanity's environmental situation becomes more complicated.

The first step in controlling turbulence is to predict where it will appear and how it will behave. This is not an easy task; in fact, it has long been regarded as one of the most difficult problems in classical physics. Experts in fluid dynamics start with a set of equations discovered independently in the nineteenth century by a French engineer, Claude Navier, and an Irish mathematician, George Stokes. Based on Newton's laws of motion, the Navier-Stokes equations should (at least in theory) allow engineers to calculate the velocity and pressure of a moving fluid, such as the air passing over an aircraft's wing.

To do this, engineers represent the space through which the fluid is moving, in this case the space over the wing, using a three-dimensional grid of points. The Navier-Stokes equations generate data on the air's velocity and pressure for each point during a sequence of moments in time.[13] In this way, engineers create a picture of the flow of air across the wing as a step-by-step stream of data for each point, then use this information to calculate the lift and drag forces affecting the plane.

Modern supercomputers greatly aid in the calculation of these forces for complex surfaces, like those of a plane. The size of eddies in turbulent flow can vary by a factor of a thousand, and aerodynamic engineers need a grid of high enough resolution to capture both the smallest and largest eddies in the boundary layer between the plane's skin and the air rushing over its surface. The higher the density of grid points—that is, the closer they are to each other—and the shorter the simulated period of time between each moment in the sequence, the more accurate the data provided by the calculations. But as the total number of points goes up and the length of the time interval goes down, the computational burden rises very fast (much as we saw with the protein-folding problem in the last chapter).[14]

The total number of grid points depends on a number of factors, including the density and viscosity of the air moving over the plane and the size of the plane itself. When all these factors are taken into account for a modern aircraft, the results can be astonishing. For example, a standard transport plane with a fifty-meter fuselage cruising at 250 meters per second at ten thousand meters altitude would require a grid of about ten quadrillion points (that is, ten million billion points). Even the most advanced supercomputers available today—computers capable of trillions of calculations a second—would have to work for thousands of years to simulate the air's flow for only one second of flight.[15]

This is clearly an impossible task. It will probably remain impossible for many years, if not decades. So engineers, being eminently pragmatic, take various shortcuts: for example, they focus on only a portion of the aircraft, and they use experimental data and *ad hoc* models to estimate the effects of small eddies. These techniques have allowed major advances in the precision and speed of aircraft design, permitting much less trial-and-error and expensive wind-tunnel testing.

All the same, there is a salutary lesson here. Scientists and engineers have major difficulty dealing with the fluid turbulence in our daily lives—the turbulence around our planes, in our car engines, and even in our blood vessels. In their designs for new technology, they need extraordinary ingenuity to predict and manage the behavior of these relatively small-scale phenomena; and even with extraordinary ingenuity, they often don't do it well. Yet some technological optimists, dating back to the Russian geochemist Vladimir Vernadsky, whose "vision" Mike Whitfield scorned when I met him in Plymouth, argue that we can manage the vastly larger, infinitely more complex, and often highly turbulent cycles of energy, materials, and life surrounding us on Earth. Commenting on our capacity to manipulate Earth's climate, the American physicist and well-known science-fiction writer Gregory Benford says that "now is precisely the time to take seriously the concept of *geoengineering*, of consciously altering atmospheric chemistry and conditions, of mitigating the effects of greenhouse gases rather than simply calling for their reduction or outright prohibition."[16] Such plans are, surprisingly, already afoot: some private firms have announced their intention to fertilize large areas of ocean to create phytoplankton blooms that absorb atmospheric carbon dioxide and boost fish production.[17]

We should hope that the optimists are right—that we can, if we want, geoengineer the planet. As Whitfield told me, we may discover that we've perturbed and destabilized Earth's systems so much that we have no choice but to take on the task of managing them. And, adds Benford, "as we begin correcting for our inadvertent insults to Mother Earth, we should realize that it's *forever*. . . . Once we become caretakers, we cannot stop."[18]

But in light of what we now know about complexity, chaos, and turbulence, grand plans for geoengineering would seem audacious at best and folly at worst. The requirement for technical and social ingenuity would be enormous, and perhaps far beyond anything humankind can hope to supply.

Once we begin to look at the world around us using our new understanding of chaos and nonlinearity, we find many examples of systems whose behavior we cannot accurately predict or manage.[19] For instance, until the mid-1980s seismologists were reasonably confident that earthquake prediction was possible. They believed that if we invested in good science and adequate time for research, experts would eventually be able to warn of major earthquakes, giving public officials the chance to evacuate regions at risk and launch emergency plans.[20]

At the time, a dominant explanation of earthquakes—an explanation still popularly accepted today—was the "seismic gap" hypothesis. According to this idea, geological stresses accumulate along fault lines between two giant tectonic plates moving in different directions. When the pressure between the plates reaches a critical level, it is released in an earthquake; the plates slip into a new position, and the pressure between them temporarily eases. In the 1970s and early 1980s, some seismologists used this idea to suggest that major earthquakes would occur along certain sections of the San Andreas Fault, which runs through heavily populated areas of California (slippage along this fault caused the disastrous 1906 San Francisco earthquake).

But major California quakes have not occurred as expected; and careful measurements using instruments buried deep in California faults show that stresses prior to earthquakes are actually quite weak. Although the seismic gap hypothesis did take account of the fundamentally nonlinear character of earthquakes (earthquakes are, in many ways, the paradigmatic nonlinear event, because they involve a sharp and sudden change in a system's behavior), it did not allow for the underlying chaos of the process. Each year, tens of thousands of tiny earthquakes do affect a heavily faulted region such as California. Sometimes, it appears, a cascade of events can turn one of these tiny quakes into a major one. As Thomas Heaton of the U.S. Geological Survey says, "A big earthquake is simply a small one that ran away."[21] Whether or not such a cascade of events occurs depends on local geological conditions: the type and porosity of the rock, the density and orientation of cracks, the prevalence of water in the rock, and the types of substances dissolved in the water.[22] Ever so slight, unknowable variations in these initial conditions can make the difference, according to this new way of thinking, between an unnoticeable tremor and a building-shattering catastrophe.[23]

If this new hypothesis about earthquakes is right, it raises insurmountable problems for earthquake prediction. We may be able to generate rough probability estimates of when and where major quakes will occur, but we probably won't ever be able to judge which of the countless small quakes in a region will cascade into a large one.[24] Yet there's still a widespread public belief, often promoted by uninformed non-scientists, that precise prediction is possible. One of the strongest critics of this misplaced faith is Robert Geller, an American professor of earth and planetary physics at the University of Tokyo. "The public, media, and government authorities must be clearly informed," Geller insists, "that earthquake prediction in its popularly understood sense is impossible at present, that all attempts to predict earthquakes to date have been failures, and that there are no reasonable prospects for prediction in the near future."[25]

Chaos and nonlinearities also make prediction exceedingly hard in the field of ecology, which deals with relations between the world's diverse organisms and their natural environments. Studies of wild grass on the prairies, and mathematical analyses of Dungeness crab populations, show unexpected booms and crashes in population.[26] In recent years, scientists have found similar behavior in a wide range of natural systems: coral reefs in the Caribbean, fisheries along the East coast of North America, and predator-prey populations in Africa all exhibit highly synergistic, nonlinear, and often chaotic behavior.

When they analyze the dynamics of complex ecosystems, most ecologists now reject traditional ideas of balance and stability—like the idea that, over time, populations of predator and prey in an ecosystem (for example, the numbers of caribou and wolves in the Alaskan wilderness) will achieve a rough balance with each other.[27] They have developed a new understanding of ecological complexity that recognizes that such systems are in constant flux and have many possible stable states—in other words, that these systems have, as ecologists say, *multiple equilibria*. We often can't predict the direction and character of such systems' behavior, which makes efficient management of them exceptionally difficult. This new understanding—if it accurately reflects the underlying ecological reality—has staggering implications for our ability to govern our relationship with our natural environment.[28]

Over several decades, one of the trailblazers of this new ecological thinking has been the Canadian ecologist C. S. "Buzz" Holling, currently at the University of Florida. Holling makes a key distinction between our approach to understanding how complex natural systems work—our *epistemology* as philosophers of science would call it—and our simple mental models of the systems themselves. Our epistemology is distinct from, but nonetheless often subtly related to, our simple mental models of nature.

Echoing Mike Whitfield's remarks in Plymouth, Buzz Holling contrasts two dominant epistemologies, or "streams of science." These streams are most obvious and distinct in biology. The first, exemplified by molecular biology, is a "science of parts." It stresses careful analysis and data collection and the precise statement and rigorous testing of theories; it is, as Holling says, "essentially experimental, reductionist, and narrowly disciplined in character." The second, exemplified by evolutionary biology and ecology, is a science of the integration of these parts. It builds on the products of the first kind of science, but it is less interested in the properties of the individual parts than in what happens—what emergent properties can be identified—when these parts are combined into a whole system. This second stream of science is more pluralistic, more comfortable with and interested in gaps in knowledge, and more accepting of uncertainty and surprise. It is fundamentally interdisciplinary, in that it draws on many fields and many approaches—historical, comparative, and experimental—to understanding the natural world. The premise of this second stream, Holling stresses, "is that knowledge of the system we deal with is always incomplete. Surprise is inevitable."[29]

When scientists are dealing with complex natural systems, they need to have a high comfort level with surprise and uncertainty. They need to be comfortable using a variety of theories and research methods, and they need to accept—and maybe even delight in—the possibility that they will never fully answer some of their deepest scientific questions. Holling believes that this attitude is possible only for scientists who have in their minds a certain model of nature and of the relationship between nature and humankind.

According to Holling, four models of nature roughly mark the chronological stages of ecologists' advancing understanding. The model he calls Nature Balanced prevailed early in the twentieth century. It assumed a tendency on the part of natural systems to evolve towards a stable equilibrium: "It was an image of self-regulated populations in 'balance' with themselves and their environment, an image whose simplicity and ordering power provided the directions for a flood of research in field and laboratory."[30] This mechanistic, Cartesian-like model was widely embraced by governments and corporations. It provided the intellectual backbone for widespread policies in Western countries to extract "maximum sustainable yields" from fisheries, forests, and other renewable resources.

Inevitably, the intellectual dominance of Nature Balanced, combined with its failure to accurately predict many phenomena in the real world, provoked a backlash among experts. An alternative view emerged, which Holling calls Nature Anarchic. This view holds that organisms within ecosystems are highly diverse and don't maintain a self-regulating balance among themselves; instead, pressures coming from outside the ecosystem, for instance changes in climate or intrusions of foreign plants and animals, can produce wide fluctuations in the relationships among its organisms.[31]

But this theoretical framework too was eventually found wanting: the concept of anarchy implies disorder, but nature exhibits many kinds of order, and variations in populations and ecosystems clearly arise from internal as well as external forces.

Nature Resilient was the next mental model—one that, Holling argues, dominates ecology today and represents a major step forward. An ecosystem is resilient, in this view, if the relationships among its organisms persist even in the face of sharp shocks from outside.[32] It hasn't been easy, though, for ecologists to adopt this new view: they have had to shift to the second epistemology mentioned above—that is, to an approach that allows for uncertainty and emphasizes the integration of a system's parts. In Nature Resilient, complex ecosystems are understood to consist of many intimately interlinked and "nested" subsystems. In other words, a large ecosystem, such as a region of Amazonian rainforest, has embedded within it smaller systems, such as the cycles of energy and life operating on a specific hillside or along a specific portion of riverbank. In turn, these subsystems incorporate ever smaller sub-subsystems, all the way down to soil bacteria. Nested systems thus contain everything from sweeping macrosystems to the minutest microsystems, and they are structured and controlled by a range of factors, including "keystone" species (that is, species that are crucial to the whole system's operation), periodic outbreaks of insects and wildfires, and the underlying decade- and century-long geophysical cycles of elements like carbon, nitrogen, and sulfur.

With Nature Resilient, the essential characteristics of complex natural systems—uncertainty, surprise, and constant change—emerge front and center once again. Holling writes, "Any of the realistic representations of the key processes [governing biological populations and systems] show the existence of thresholds, limits, and other nonlinearities. . . . Once the models incorporate three or more population variables or species, together with realistic representations of the key processes, a very wide range of complex population behaviors is produced. Even in the simplest models, multiple stable states are the rule, not the exception, and behavior can range from extinctions, to stable limit cycles, to boom-and-bust flips between stability regions, even to chaotic behavior. . . ."[33]

Although complex ecosystems can have multiple stable states or equilibria, these equilibria are often surprisingly robust. The very complexity of ecosystems often makes it harder for them to flip from one equilibrium to another.[34] So, if a forest ecosystem has lots of redundancy in keystone species—such as birds that prey on harmful insects—it will be much less likely to collapse if some of these species are lost through logging. Similarly, if the organisms making up a prairie ecosystem vary substantially from one part of the landscape to another, then a blight or pest that harms certain organisms won't spread as quickly or as far.

Unfortunately, the very resilience of nature may be a trap for us. It may lull us into believing that our natural environment is infinitely robust and endlessly abundant and that we don't need to limit our plunder of forests, fields, rivers, and fisheries. "Therein lies the irony of ecological resilience," Holling asserts. "On the one hand, it provides the buffer for incomplete knowledge, therefore allowing experiment and recovery; but on the other, it also exacts few penalties fast enough on the greedy or stupid."[35]

It's also important to realize that the resilience of natural systems is not unlimited. We have ordered our landscape and simplified the ecosystems around us since time immemorial, but today our huge populations and extraordinary rates of resource consumption are reducing ecosystem redundancy and diversity as never before. We are, in fact, homogenizing ecosystems on a planetary scale, turning forests and prairies into monocrops of trees and grain, paving across wetlands for subdivisions and malls, and replacing our depleted fisheries with aquaculture pens. "For the first time," Holling writes, "humanity and nature are transforming each other on the whole planet, are beginning a co-evolutionary experiment on a planetary scale."[36]

So Buzz Holling gives a fourth and final model: Nature Evolving. This model doesn't deny the idea of ecosystem resilience, but it suggests that we have entered a new era—an era marked by the mutual, almost dialectical evolution of nature and humanity. Although our impacts on Earth's ecosystems have increased incrementally over a long period of time, these impacts are now so large that they are changing, and often compromising, our ecosystems' underlying functions and processes. In turn, these altered ecosystem processes—such as collapsed fisheries and a warmer climate—force us to change our behavior. We cannot say how this dance between nature and humanity will evolve, or where it will take us, because we don't have a good enough grasp of the natural systems in which we are embedded. As Holling concludes, "not only is the science incomplete, the system itself is a moving target."[37]

Biosphere 2 Taught Us a Lesson about Managing Complex Ecosystems

In the early 1990s, humanity learned a lesson—a practical and profoundly revealing lesson—in the difficulty of constructing and managing complex ecosystems. It unfolded at Biosphere 2, an ensemble of buildings resembling a huge, futuristic greenhouse in the Sonora Desert of Arizona (shown in the illustration above). Built with $200 million from the Texas billionaire Edward Bass, the structure covered 1.3 hectares and enclosed a volume of more than 200,000 cubic meters. Biosphere 2's designers wanted to create within this space an artificial and materially closed ecosystem—a miniature version of the material and life cycles of Earth (which they labeled Biosphere 1).

A team of ecologists and engineers collaborated with experts from the Smithsonian Institution, the New York Botanical Garden, and the University of Arizona to predict the synergies among the enclosure's 3,800 species of plants and animals and its air, water, and soils. Thirty thousand tons of dirt were moved in from a nearby pond; workers created a little rainforest, marshland, desert, ocean, and farm; and on September 26, 1991, with great fanfare, four men and four women, who called themselves "Biospherians," were sealed inside for a two-year period.

Things did not go well. Temperatures in the upper reaches of the eight-story structure were much higher than planned, while light levels throughout were much lower. For reasons no one could figure out, oxygen concentrations plummeted; by January 1993, they had dropped from a normal level of 21 percent of the atmosphere to a potentially debilitating 14 percent, a concentration normally found at an altitude of 5,300 meters, or nearly nine-tenths the height of Mount McKinley, the tallest peak in North America. To avoid a medical emergency, Biosphere 2's external managers pumped into the building a total of twenty-three tons of pure oxygen in January, August, and September 1993. Carbon dioxide levels oscillated wildly from day to day and season to season. Nitrous oxide in the atmosphere soared to concentrations that could reduce the Biospherians' synthesis of vitamin B_{12} and damage their brains.[38]

Excessive artificial rain turned the desert into grassland; aquatic habitats were polluted with nutrients that caused algal blooms; and soils became infested with pathogenic nematodes that destroyed the roots of crops, causing Arizona authorities to place Biosphere 2 under quarantine.[39] Morning glory vines, with their lovely, startlingly blue flowers, originally introduced to absorb carbon dioxide, ran amok in the carbon-rich environment; the Biospherians had to weed constantly to maintain space for their food plants. Trunks and limbs of trees became brittle and apt to break suddenly. Nineteen of twenty-five vertebrate species went extinct, as did all pollinators, which meant that most of the complex's plant species could not reproduce. Almost all species of insects, including crickets and grasshoppers, disappeared. Cockroaches filled the void, along with teeming numbers of crazy ants (*Paratrechina longicornus*), which swarmed over Biosphere 2's vegetation.

Some of these failures were later attributed to the zealotry of project planners. Researchers at the University of Arizona had used powerful computers to mathematically model the interactions among the installation's organisms and materials, but they had assumed in their calculations that Biosphere 2's soil would contain no more than 4 to 5 percent organic matter—about the standard level of enrichment in the external world. As it turned out, though, Biosphere 2's leaders fervently believed in principles of organic farming and therefore promoted the ecological value of soils rich in compost; the dirt they had extracted from the local pond and brought into the Biosphere contained 30 percent organic matter—between five and ten times the normal level.[40]

The results were horrendous. Bacteria and microbes flourished in the highly fertile soil. As these bugs broke down the soil's carbon compounds, they sucked up oxygen from the surrounding atmosphere and released large amounts of carbon dioxide. This process explained the plummeting oxygen levels, but it left project managers with a puzzle: concentrations of carbon dioxide in Biosphere 2's atmosphere should have been much higher than those actually measured. Only after much debate and contention did researchers realize that the extra carbon dioxide was reacting with calcium in the building's ten thousand square meters of exposed concrete to form calcium carbonate. As two expert, external evaluators later reported, "The original atmospheric oxygen, in effect, became locked up in the walls of the structure."[41] To cap it all, this reaction raised the concrete's acidity, which threatened to corrode internal reinforcing bars and eventually weaken the entire building.

The original eight Biospherians, hardy, healthy, but considerably thinner, emerged from Biosphere 2 in September 1993. They were greeted by recriminations among project staff, officials, and outside experts. Eventually, New York's Columbia University took over the complex and implemented a series of more cautious and controlled ecological experiments. But despite the spectacular failure of the original plan, most knowledgeable commentators were charitable. They recognized that the Biospherians had tried heroically to keep their world liveable. They also noted that mistakes were inevitable. As a leading geochemist said, "Anybody else would have made equally bad blunders, but different ones."[42]

Nevertheless, Biosphere 2 had revealed some sobering truths about the limits of our understanding of complex ecosystems. "Despite the enormous resources invested in the original design and construction . . . and despite a multimillion-dollar operating budget," the two outside evaluators finally wrote, "it proved impossible to create a materially closed system that could support eight human beings with adequate food, water and air for two years. The management of Biosphere 2 encountered numerous unexpected problems and surprises, even though almost unlimited energy and technology were available to support Biosphere 2 from outside." They concluded: "At present there is no demonstrated alternative to maintaining the viability of Earth. No one yet knows how to engineer systems that provide humans with the life-supporting services that natural ecosystems produce for free."[43]

Our inability to accurately predict and manage the behavior of complex natural systems has immense consequences for our well-being. These consequences are potentially most ominous in the case of Earth's grand ecological, biophysical, and geochemical systems.[44] As I learned during my travels in Europe, just as we are recognizing our interdependence with these systems and our deep ignorance of how they work, we are altering their basic dynamics in ways that could, in time, seriously hurt us.

Take, for example, ocean currents. Most people don't realize how their lives are intimately affected by the ocean currents and their accompanying atmospheric systems. They may have a vague awareness—based on press reports—that El Niño events in the South Pacific cause havoc around the world, but awareness ends there. Nor do most people realize just how little we actually know about these systems. Yet a quick review of a few issues of leading scientific journals such as *Nature* and *Science* shows that the debate about currents is vigorous and that the stakes are enormous.

For nearly twenty years, a key figure in this debate has been the eminent geochemist Wally Broecker, currently the Newberry Professor of Geology at Columbia University in New York. He pioneered the study of nonlinear behavior in ocean currents and is now one of the world's leading specialists on the subject.[45] In 1984, while listening to a lecture by a German scientist, he had an important insight. The lecturer was discussing ice cores extracted from deep in Greenland's ice sheet—cores similar to those extracted by the Soviet scientists at the Vostok base in Antarctica. He explained how close analysis of the ancient and stratified ice in these cores showed that Earth's historical climate had often jumped or "flipped" from one relatively stable state to another. These jumps were sometimes remarkably fast and dramatic: for example, at the end of what is called the Younger Dryas cold event, which occurred around 11,500 years ago, the average temperature of the region stretching from North America across the North Atlantic to central Europe warmed by seven degrees Celsius in just thirty years (shown in the illustration on the following page).[46] Broecker was intrigued. He asked himself what might cause these abrupt changes. After reflecting on the question for a while, he realized that they could be related to abrupt changes in another of Earth's major systems—the mighty cycle of water in the Atlantic Ocean that operates *between* the surface and deep sea. Eventually, he and another scientist, Arnold Gordon, dubbed this cycle the "conveyor belt."

The Atmosphere's Temperature Rose Abruptly at the End of the Younger Dryas Cold Event

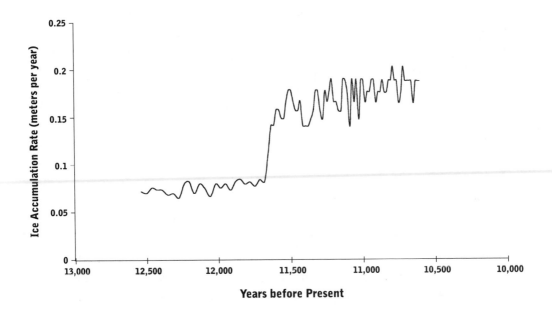

Note: Ice accumulation rates correlate with ambient atmospheric temperature. Because warmer air holds more water vapor, the warmer the atmosphere's temperature over Greenland, the greater the precipitation in the form of snow, and the faster the rate of ice accumulation.

The conveyor belt works in the following way. Water warmed in the equatorial region of the Atlantic Ocean flows northward in the upper part of the ocean towards Iceland and Greenland. There, it is cooled by winter air from Canada and Greenland. As the water's temperature drops from about 12 degrees Celsius to between 2 and 4 degrees, it becomes increasingly dense and sinks in vertical plumes to the bottom of the ocean thousands of meters below. It then flows southward again, in a slow but prodigious stream, all the way to the Southern Atlantic, where it joins the current that flows west to east around the Antarctic continent. Pushed around the Cape of Good Hope, across the southern Indian Ocean and around southern Australia, the water eventually moves north into the Pacific basin and returns to the surface in a massive upwelling. Now on the surface of the Pacific Ocean, the same water follows a return trip north of

Australia, around Southern Africa, and back into the Atlantic to begin the cycle once more.

The sheer size of this grand, continuous movement of water is hard to grasp. The deep flow from North to South Atlantic consists of 20 million cubic meters of water per second, which is roughly the same as the planet's total rainfall at any given moment or, using a different measuring stick, to one hundred Amazon Rivers. The flow of water is also slow, often taking many decades to move from one part of the Atlantic basin to another. In fact, the conveyor needs 180 years to replace the Atlantic basin's water completely.

From the point of view of our well-being, the most important fact about this flow is its effect on climate. As the conveyor's warm southern water drops into the depths of the North Atlantic, it releases a huge amount of heat into the atmosphere—an amount roughly equal to 25 percent of the solar energy that falls on the North Atlantic. This heat raises average annual temperatures in Europe by five to ten degrees Celsius. In other words, if the North Atlantic conveyor were to stop operation, Europe would be thrown into a climate crisis: a city like Dublin would experience the temperatures of the desolate islands of Spitsbergen, far north of the Arctic Circle, and agricultural production would plummet across Europe.

Other than the North Atlantic, there are only a few places on the planet where deep ocean water is created (another is the sea around the perimeter of the Antarctic continent). Since these regions are critical to the operation of the conveyor belt girdling Earth, they are also critical to the global movement of heat energy, especially from the tropics to the poles. Moreover, since the descending water is rich in carbon dioxide absorbed from the air, these vertical flows powerfully influence the amount of carbon in the Earth's atmosphere; they act like huge pumps sucking carbon out of the air and delivering it to the deep sea.

Experts such as Wally Broecker call the movement of water between the upper and deep ocean the *thermohaline circulation*. It depends, as I mentioned above, on the heating and cooling of the ocean's waters, because changes in water temperature change its density, and because relatively dense water sinks, while less dense water rises. It also depends on salinity, because as water's salinity increases its density increases.

The interaction of water temperature and salinity can be complicated. In the North Atlantic, for example, rain falling in Siberia and the Canadian Arctic drains down innumerable rivers and streams into the Arctic Ocean.

It then combines with rain that falls directly on the Arctic Ocean itself to make the water in the polar basin relatively low in concentrations of salt. This low-salinity water, in turn, gushes through the basin's constricted outlets to southern oceans—the Bering Strait between Alaska and Eastern Siberia, and the gaps between Canada, Greenland, and Scandinavia. As it floods into the North Atlantic, it mixes with water arriving from the Atlantic's equatorial region and lowers the overall density of water in the North Atlantic. This tends to counteract the effect produced by the cooling of the southern water, which is to raise the water's density. Luckily for the climate in Europe, the cooling effect prevails, and the combined waters from the Arctic and the south become sufficiently dense to sink to the bottom of the ocean. The conveyor belt continues to function.

But whether it will continue to function as the Earth's climate warms is another question. Global warming, among its many effects, increases the vigor of hydrological cycles, which are the movements of water between soil, vegetation, bodies of water, and the atmosphere. More vigorous cycles in the Northern Hemisphere mean more precipitation over Siberia, the Canadian Arctic, and the Arctic Ocean. And more precipitation in these areas means, in turn, even less saline water in the Arctic basin. (Indeed, in recent decades fresh water flows into the Arctic basin have increased substantially.) Eventually, the water pouring out of the Arctic basin might become so fresh that it overwhelms the cooling effect in the North Atlantic, causing the conveyor belt to slow or stop.

Wally Broecker and other scientists have used large, computerized *general circulation models* to gauge the effects of this greater volume of low-salinity water on the currents and climate of the North Atlantic. These models, which incorporate causal links between the movements of the atmosphere and ocean, are not unlike the three-dimensional grids used to study turbulence over the wings of an airplane. The scientists have found, to their great concern, that relatively small changes in salinity can radically change the behavior of the North Atlantic thermohaline circulation.[47] Some models show the circulation shutting down entirely. Without doubt it has more than one stable configuration or equilibrium (it may, for instance, break up into smaller currents or eddies in the North Atlantic), and sudden shifts among these equilibria have probably produced the climate flips discernible in the Greenland ice cores.[48]

So this recent climate research points to a paradox: global warming could plunge Europe into a deep freeze. The story isn't limited to the

North Atlantic, however. Because the region's thermohaline circulation is crucial to the operation of the conveyor belt of water that snakes around the planet, its reorganization could precipitate a chain of nonlinear climate events all over the world. Evidence of simultaneous shifts in climate is visible in ancient coral growth in the Northwest Atlantic, in deep sediments off the coast of Santa Barbara, and in the detritus left by glaciers in New Zealand.[49] Since Wally Broecker's remarkable insight in 1984, researchers have begun to see more and more connections among such events.

Wally Broecker spends most of his time at the Lamont-Doherty Earth Observatory. Located in Palisades, New York, Lamont-Doherty is a division of Columbia University dedicated to improving our understanding of the biological, geophysical, and chemical processes affecting our planet. I visited him on a grim, drizzly morning in early November that was made tolerable by the glorious fall colors shining through the rain along the Interstate Parkway out of New York City.

My shuttle bus from Columbia University stopped in front of a cluster of low buildings in a parklike setting, and the graduate students and researchers aboard dispersed in every direction to find their offices, research benches, and computers. I located Wally Broecker in the geochemistry building—a weary, one-story rectangular structure dating from the 1950s. Dressed in blue jeans and a cotton vest, the sixty-six-year-old Broecker came out of his office to greet me. I was struck immediately by his crusty self-confidence; he looked and acted like a man who would be happier on the deck of an ocean-going research vessel than in a landlocked scientific center.

We chatted a bit and I explained my research interests. Then I came directly to the point: "I hope you can help me address several questions that have been on my mind for some time. What, in your opinion, is the state of our understanding of ocean-atmospheric systems and how fast is this understanding progressing? Do you think we're going to be able to predict changes in these systems? And finally, to what extent are we going to be able to manage these systems?"

He replied without a moment's hesitation. "Although our knowledge is advancing, the target is retreating faster than we're advancing. It's baloney to suppose that we will understand ocean-atmospheric systems by, say, the year 2010. We're learning all the time that we have to understand new things—things that we didn't realize were important before. We were naive to think that this was a solvable problem.

"As for prediction," he continued, "I don't think we can predict even the smooth, incremental part of the global warming, which is what everybody talks about. There will be a warming; I can't see any way out of it. But its magnitude is open to a lot of questions. And abrupt, nonlinear changes are totally unpredictable because we understand so little about them—except we know that they happen, because we see them in the ice-core records."

Then Broecker turned to my question about our capacity to manage these changes. Most economists, he argued, are wrong to believe that straightforward market mechanisms and technological fixes will allow humanity to meet the challenge of global warming. Nevertheless, it is essential to find alternative sources of energy that produce much less carbon dioxide than fossil fuels do. Another possibility is to strip the carbon dioxide from these fuels, liquefy it, and pump it into the deep sea or into wells and caverns on land, where it can be held indefinitely.[50] "We have to start a very aggressive program to find substitute sources of energy. Such a program would be a politically neutral step, it would not cost all that much money, and it could start immediately. It would symbolize that there is a real problem, and it could be advantageous to industry, because there would eventually be big money in these new technologies."

Then he came to an idea, outlined in his 1985 book, *How to Build a Habitable Planet*, that had always struck me as bizarre.[51] "We can counterbalance global warming by purposely putting sulfur dioxide into the stratosphere. To me, that's the only viable solution. If you don't like the sulfur dioxide, don't worry, it eventually goes away, because rain washes it out of the atmosphere. The main thing that we have to determine is whether it would affect the ozone layer."

Sulfur dioxide reacts in the atmosphere to form sulfuric acid, which condenses into small droplets that stay suspended in the air as an aerosol (a process I discussed in the "Big I" chapter). The droplets tend to reflect sunlight back into space, but they are relatively transparent to infrared radiation emitted from the surface of the planet. In other words, droplets of sulfuric acid in Earth's atmosphere act like a one-way mirror to counteract global warming. Wally Broecker had estimated that an annual injection of 35 million tons of sulfur dioxide into the stratosphere would offset the warming effect of a doubling of atmospheric carbon dioxide. Surprisingly, a fleet of 747s, working more or less nonstop, could do the job for a total cost of about $30 billion a year (in 1985 dollars), a figure that incorporates the cost of both producing and transporting the sulfur dioxide gas. At the time, he concluded this was not an insurmountable sum for a $20 trillion world economy.

"But when you think of global solutions such as this," I asked, a bit incredulously, "are you serious about them, or are you suggesting them, in part, just to be provocative—to get a reaction? Are you saying, in essence, 'Watch out, people—if we go down this road, and produce substantial global warming, we will have to look seriously at options like intentionally injecting huge quantities of sulfur dioxide into the atmosphere?'"

"Yes, that's the point." he replied. "If we had to, we could implement the sulfur dioxide response in a year. If we want less radical solutions, we will need major scientific research and major international agreements. Getting these things under way will take a long, long time, and we are not moving the process along fast enough."

"Wouldn't the sulfur dioxide cause serious acid rain problems?"

"No. The amount you need is comparable to the amount already injected into the troposphere [the atmosphere near Earth's surface] by natural processes, and the acid rain would be spread out—roughly two-thirds of it would fall over the ocean, assuming you did both hemispheres."

"But what would it do to the color of the sky?" I persisted.

"It would bleach the sky. That would be a real psychological disadvantage, no doubt." He went on with a wry chuckle, "We would get beautiful sunsets, but sunsets only last an hour a day. In a world that is overly warm, it's a price that will have to be paid till carbon dioxide levels come back down or we think of some other mitigation strategy."

I imagined the haze I detest covering the entire planet, turning blue skies milky white everywhere. It was an appalling prospect. And Wally Broecker's apparent optimism about our ability to manage Earth's complex systems also disturbed me. "If we respond by putting large amounts of sulfur dioxide into the atmosphere, or by undertaking other large-scale interventions, we would still," I suggested, "face the possibility of unanticipated, nonlinear changes resulting from our own interventions."

"Yes, that's true, although I don't think there will be more than one of these abrupt changes, whether we intervene or not. But the most alarming thing about such changes is that, when they happened before, the ocean-atmospheric system flickered or chattered during the transition. And the flickerings lasted for a few decades—the transition was thirty to forty years long—and during that time the system was not gradually going from mode A to mode B; instead, it was jumping back and forth. If such flickering happens in the next century, when we have eight billion or more people on the planet, and when we need to produce two to three times more food for each unit of cropland, we will be in a really tough situation. The chances of major social conflict will soar."

I tried to pin him down on the likelihood of nonlinear changes. "In your career, have you become more concerned about abrupt changes or less?"

"Oh, much more concerned."

"Does that mean that you think there is a higher probability of an abrupt change occurring, or that you've increased your estimate of the costs to us of such a change?"

"Well, it means several things. We only realized in 1985 that abrupt changes could occur. The first article I wrote about them appeared in *American History* magazine and dealt with the cause of the Younger Dryas [the cold spell that occurred 11,500 years ago, at the end of which the temperatures from North America to Central Europe increased by seven degrees Celsius]. I was furious when the article came out, because the editor had put the question 'Will It Happen Again?' across the front cover. I was angry because I had not mentioned the future in the article at all! I thought that the editor was too lazy to read the article, or didn't care, and I thought it was terrible journalism. But now, here I am saying the same thing."

"So, over the last couple of decades, your estimate of the probability of an abrupt change occurring has increased?"

"No, I haven't concluded that these things are more probable or predictable. I have become more concerned about them because the general circulation models linked to ocean-atmosphere models show a serious sag in thermohaline circulation. Maybe it is simply the fact that I understand the phenomenon better than I did before—occasionally things take a long time to settle in your mind."

He paused, then continued. "I had to get one question, in particular, clear in my mind: What fraction of the future warming is going to come smoothly and what fraction abruptly? We are beginning to realize now that a major fraction of past changes in climate was abrupt. The graphs of these temperature changes tend to have a rectangular shape, with a sharp vertical movement as the temperature suddenly rises or falls, and then a leveling off (shown in the illustration on page 138).

"In one of our linked ocean-atmospheric models, if you induce a mode flip in the ocean, then climate change occurs mainly over the North Atlantic basin. We thought the change was restricted to that region, but when we looked at sediments in cores and other evidence from diverse regions around the world we realized—lo and behold—that the effects appeared all over the planet. The past changes in the climate were triggered from below, I think, by changes in ocean circulation, but none of our models can accurately reproduce these past worlds. We can't get glacial ice to Cincinnati, we can't get dust levels in the atmosphere to be twenty times higher, and we can't get the tropics to be three and half degrees colder—we can't get any of this climate behavior in our models unless we actually write it, directly, into the models.

"So, over the years I have been asking myself: What is it about the world that allows it to change simultaneously in so many places? I have a feeling that the water vapor content of the atmosphere was much lower during these past changes, and that there were much higher levels of dust. [Water vapor helps trap heat within the atmosphere, whereas dust often reflects the sun's heat back into space.] For some reason the residence time of water molecules in the atmosphere dropped. Even if evaporation stayed about the same, water's residence time was less, so the standing crop of water vapor in the air was smaller.

"This was not a chicken-and-egg situation: those parts of the system that could reorganize, reorganized all at once. One year the system was operating one way, and the next year it was operating another. Until we can understand how the system can do that, we have no way of even studying these things. A better understanding will not be a panacea, but it will be step one.

"That's how bad it is," Broecker concluded. "We're fooling with a system we don't understand. If humanity commissioned an environmental-impact assessment on the effects of high levels of carbon dioxide emissions into the atmosphere, the assessment would have to reject the emissions, because we couldn't rule out extremely harsh consequences."

As I left his office, Wally Broecker handed me one of his most recent articles. Back on the bus to New York City, I pulled it out of my bag, flipping through the pages while the bus passed the spectacular fall foliage along the Hudson River, crossed over the Washington Bridge, and re-entered the bedlam of Manhattan. Just before the final stop at Columbia University, I reached the concluding paragraph. Broecker wrote:

> My lifetime of study of Earth's climate has humbled me. I'm convinced that we have greatly underestimated the complexity of this system. The importance of obscure phenomena, ranging from those that control the size of raindrops to those that control the amount of water pouring into the deep sea from the shelves of the Antarctic continent, makes reliable modeling very difficult, if not impossible. If we're going to predict the future, we have to achieve a much greater understanding of these small-scale processes that together generate large-scale effects.[52]

Given Plymouth's latitude, its climate is remarkably warm. The Devon and Cornwall counties that make up the long peninsula jutting out from southwest England greatly benefit from the North Atlantic conveyor belt's magnanimous contribution of heat to the atmosphere. Many people regard the region as the prettiest part of England: the land is lush and productive (with palm trees growing in Cornwall), the people are charitable, and the sea still offers a rich harvest of fish.

In the heart of Manhattan, I understood the story Plymouth had tried to tell me months before. The fishermen dashed against Eddystone Reef, the heroic masons who built Smeaton's lighthouse, and the sailors, emigrants, and explorers who sailed from Plymouth's splendid harbor were all struggling against the most ferocious forces of nature. They were trying, each in their minuscule way, to improve their lot in the face of astonishing odds. The benignly sparkling ocean I saw that September morning hosted nature at its most primal; and over the centuries the men, women, and children of Plymouth had come to know primal nature well.

Although a marvel, Smeaton's lighthouse was only a tiny, defensive riposte to nature's ferocity. But today, collectively, our ripostes are aggressive and no longer tiny. We have multiplied the cleverness and ingenuity of Smeaton's lighthouse a trillionfold, and with this ingenuity we are rampaging across the surface of the planet and altering the basic character of our physical world. We have been so dazzled—blinded even—by the light of our endless technologies that we often blithely disregard our staggering ignorance of how our natural world works. We will not be able to disregard it for long. Nature won't let us. And, if the North Atlantic thermohaline circulation collapses, places like Plymouth will see the signs of nature's wrath first. "Climate is an angry beast," Wally Broecker has said, "and we are poking it with sticks."[53]

GLIMPSING THE ABYSS

O N THE MORNING of Monday, October 19, 1987, I woke in a hotel room in La Jolla, having just finished a week of doctoral research at the San Diego campus of the University of California. The work had gone well. I was looking forward to returning to MIT to write up the results.

At around 7:45 a.m. I turned on the television. To my surprise, I found Dan Rather hosting a special news report from the East Coast. He looked astonished. The New York stock market had been open for just over an hour, he reported, and the Dow Jones Industrial Average had already fallen nearly 10 percent. Astonished myself, I watched the television as I packed. In a restaurant over breakfast I found another television to follow the market's oscillations. During the next hour a rally began, and by 8:45 Pacific Time the Dow had recovered about half the morning's losses. But the rally had no momentum, and at 9:00 the slide resumed. In three successive, accelerating waves, the market collapsed through the remainder of the trading day. In the final fifteen minutes alone, in one mad frenzy of selling, the Dow lost 5 percent of its value.

At 1:00 p.m. I arrived at the airport. In a bar along the main concourse, a group of people several deep pressed against the counter to watch a television hanging from the back wall. Dan Rather was still on the air: the market had just closed, and he was wrapping up the day's events. The Dow had finished down 508 points—a 22.6 percent nosedive, bigger than any since World War I and far larger than the 12.8 percent drop on the worst day of the 1929 crash. In a single day, the equity value of America's stock portfolios had plunged $500 billion.

But these statistics were not the thing that really disturbed me: it was the look in Dan Rather's eyes as he signed off. There was more than astonishment there now; it seemed to me there were also bewilderment and fear.

On the flight back across the country, I couldn't concentrate on my work. Instead I wrote a letter to a close friend, scribbling down my immediate thoughts about the day's main event. Even if the market recovered fully the next day, the crisis seemed to reveal a larger truth—it had been apparent in Rather's eyes. This heralded successor to Walter Cronkite was a tacit symbol of the predictability, stability, and basic reasonableness of American institutions and society. His bewilderment, even if only momentary, revealed something awful, something that none of us readily admits and that most of us work hard to deny or avoid.

No matter how much we believe in our institutions and in the regularized procedures of our societies, no matter how just, rational, and durable we think them, they are at best only loosely grounded on some form of bedrock reality or immutable truths that endure beyond human beings. To a considerable degree, they are sustained by collective belief and consensus, by tacit, unquestioned, and often grossly simplistic assumptions about how the world works, and often by mutual and willful self-delusion. Our societies cohere and function in no small part because most of us want them to cohere and function, and because the alternatives are, for most of us, literally unthinkable.

We all eagerly assume there exist people, somewhere, who unlike ourselves *do* have a grip on the bedrock reality that underlies our societies, who understand how things work and will take care of us if severe problems arise. We also deeply fear the possibility that it isn't true, and there are no such people; this was what I thought I'd seen in Rather's eyes. I scribbled to my friend, "The facade cracked for a moment. The illusion of regularity, sameness, and security cracked for a moment. I could just glimpse beyond the illusion, in Rather's dumbfounded face, the realization that nobody really is in control, nobody really understands the horrendous complexity of this world we have created. Where are the experts? Where are the leaders? Surely they're going to make things right again!"

It turns out that the experts and leaders really had lost control that October day. Trading computers were overloaded, phone systems were clogged, sell orders remained unfulfilled because there were no buyers. Buzz Geduld, a partner in Herzog, Heine, Geduld, Inc., recalled "a continuous onslaught of sell order after sell order after sell order. . . . [All] we knew was, we were seeing a big panic, and we were just hopeful and praying that somewhere this was going to stop."[1] The experts who were expected to step in with reassuring pronouncements were either unavailable or unwilling to comment; Alan Greenspan, the newly appointed Chairman of the Federal Reserve Board, was on his way to make a speech in Dallas. Other top policy-makers in Washington made no public statements.

By late Monday afternoon, the specialist firms on the New York Exchange's trading floor responsible for maintaining an orderly market in specific stocks were facing an unprecedented liquidity squeeze. Having bought tens of millions of shares that they couldn't sell, shares that had depreciated in value throughout the day, some firms couldn't meet the Exchange's minimum capital requirements. Michael Rosen, a teacher of business management, later wrote, "Many specialist firms surviving Monday ended the day with stock inventories several multiples higher than their average holdings, all of which had to be paid for within five business days. Prestigious firms turned to their normal lenders, similarly prestigious New York banks, only to find that the banks were not interested in lending."[2] And James Maguire, the chairman of a large specialist firm handling about seventy stocks, said, "From 2 p.m. on, there was total despair. The entire investment community fled the market. We were left alone on the field."[3] During that single day, the market had erased two-thirds of specialists' total buying power of $3 billion.

To make matters worse, the nation's payment system—the network of banks and clearing houses that actually transfers funds following market trades—was in danger of buckling. Mismatches in payment schedules among the stock, futures, and options markets exacerbated this strain: stock purchases in New York had to be settled financially five days after the trade, but margins on futures and options purchases in Chicago had to be posted before the start of the next trading day. As a result, many traders arbitraging stock and futures indexes between the two cities didn't have the funds available from their stock sales in New York in time to meet margin requirements on their purchases of index futures in Chicago.[4]

One of the key people out of town on this critical day was Jerry Corrigan, the forty-six-year-old president of the Federal Reserve Bank of New York, the most important of the twelve U.S. Federal Reserve Banks. Corrigan had been in Venezuela for several days to discuss the Latin American debt crisis, and he arrived back in New York on Monday only after the markets closed in chaos. After conferring with Greenspan in Texas, he agreed to work with Fed officials in Washington to draft a statement reassuring the markets. In order to achieve maximum impact, the statement was issued in Greenspan's name shortly before the New York Exchange opened on Tuesday morning. It said, "The Federal Reserve, consistent with its responsibilities as the nation's central bank, affirmed today its readiness to serve as a source of liquidity to support the economic and financial system."

Following standard practice, the Federal Reserve then bought government securities from banks, which increased these banks' reserves for lending. This action drove down short-term interest rates and effectively injected money into the banking system. If the banks could be kept liquid, Jerry Corrigan and his colleagues hoped, the banks would ensure that specialists, arbitragers, brokerage houses, and everyone else in the system stayed liquid too.[5] Between October 20 and November 2, in "open-market operations" under Corrigan's direction in New York, the Federal Reserve therefore created $12 billion in new reserves, permitting up to $100 billion in new lending by banks.[6] The intervention was designed to be as dramatic as possible: on the morning of Tuesday, October 20, there was to be no doubt of the Fed's commitment to maintaining liquidity in the financial system. Corrigan and his aides personally phoned big New York banks and leaned on them to lend liberally. Ever so slowly, the message began to take hold, and during the remainder of the week, the ten largest New York banks almost doubled their loans to securities firms, from $6.5 to $12 billion.[7]

Alan Greenspan's one-sentence statement, however, had been an explicit acknowledgment of the enormity of the crisis: the run on the markets had placed the American economy at grave risk. And by 12:30 p.m. on Tuesday, it had looked like another rout was under way in New York. *The Wall Street Journal* reported that "specialists didn't have any buy orders, and many simply stopped making markets. Many believed that their capital . . . was gone or nearly gone."[8] A ferocious wave of selling coupled with a lack of buyers forced trading to halt on more than 160 stocks, including blue-chip firms like IBM, Merck, Sears, Eastman Kodak, USX, and Philip Morris.[9] According to the *Journal*, printouts of New York trading on Tuesday morning painted "a harrowing picture of a market in disarray."[10]

Under immense pressure from securities firms and specialists who lacked the capital to keep the market operating, John Phelan, the chairman of the New York Stock Exchange, held a meeting of top officials in his office to consider closing the entire Exchange. He placed a round of phone calls to key people—including Jerry Corrigan and Howard Baker, the White House chief of staff—warning them that the stock market might have to be shut down. The Chicago Mercantile Exchange heard this news and feared such an action would trigger a tidal wave of futures selling; it therefore halted trading of Standard & Poor's 500 futures contracts. In Washington, Howard Baker ordered White House lawyers to draft the legal document the president needed to declare the Exchange closed.[11] But he also asked John Phelan to do everything he could to avoid this outcome: closing the Exchange would be an admission of defeat, it would exacerbate the panic, and it would deal a severe blow to confidence in the entire U.S. economy.

Then, miraculously, the market began to turn. There was a sudden spurt of purchases of a thinly traded stock-index future at the Chicago Board of Trade. "In the space of about five or six minutes, the Major Market Index futures contract, the only viable surrogate for the Dow Jones Industrial Average and the only major index still trading, staged the most powerful rally in its history."[12] There was also a flurry of small but well-timed purchases of blue-chip stocks in New York. These events were so opportune that they led some analysts later to suspect a coordinated manipulation of the market.[13] But whatever the cause, within an hour large institutional buyers had returned to snap up bargains and short sellers had begun covering their positions. By the end of trading on Wednesday, the Dow had recovered over half of Monday's loss.

The worst of the crisis had passed. Yet most people at the center of events during those two days were horrified by how close they had come to disaster. Felix Rohatyn, the famed partner in the investment banking firm Lazard Freres & Company, told *The Wall Street Journal* that the stock market had been "within an hour" of disintegration. "Tuesday was the most dangerous day we had in fifty years."[14]

Despite a subsequent torrent of reports and analyses, the exact causes of the crash remain obscure. Was it an example of crowd psychology gone wild in an age of instant communication and computer-driven arbitrage? Or did it reflect a sudden but entirely rational change in people's interpretations of the market's underlying fundamentals?[15] The best explanation, it seems, takes into account the complexities and nonlinearities of modern market behavior. Over the previous months, a host of small worries— about the American budget deficit and trade balance, about prospects for inflation and interest rates, and about the long, unbroken rise in stock prices—had accumulated in investors' minds. In this environment of pent-up concerns, a few relatively minor events, such as the release of alarming trade-deficit figures or the rumors of an impending U.S.-Iran war, easily triggered a disproportionate avalanche of selling.

But several other factors combined to make the subsequent panic far worse than it might have been. More powerful computer and communication technologies, coupled with trading strategies like portfolio insurance, had sharply boosted the complexity, volume, and speed of market transactions. The market's infrastructure, including such things as the nation's system for settling payments, just didn't have the capacity or flexibility to respond adequately to these new pressures, especially under the unprecedented peak loads of October 19. The crash was caused, at least in part, by an ingenuity gap: the market had become too complex, nonlinear, big, and fast for the financial institutions guiding it at that moment. Put differently, the need for ingenuity to keep these markets stable had risen faster than the amount of ingenuity the financial and regulatory institutions could supply.

The crash was stunning, but calamity was averted. Acting as lender of last resort, the Federal Reserve undoubtedly saved the day, and within two years the stock market had largely recovered. But the story of the crash carries some enduring lessons.

First, it reminds us that individual events and decisions—often small and sometimes accidental—can have a major effect on the development of large social phenomena. The unfolding of these phenomena is often not determined by some kind of inexorable inner logic, but is highly contingent on the character of specific, sometimes chance events. Such sensitivity to individual events is, of course, especially common in chaotic social systems, like stock markets in the midst of mass panic. If Greenspan, Corrigan, and their colleagues had delayed a day before acting, if key banks had been slightly more resistant to regulators' entreaties to increase lending to specialists, or if Phelan had closed the Exchange prematurely, the crash's outcome could have been far more dire. It could have sent the American economy into a tailspin, taking the world economy along with it.

In the terminology of social scientists, the evolution of social systems is often *path dependent*: a decision, delay, or mistake at a critical moment can direct the system down a path that diverges widely from the one it otherwise would have followed. And once the system is well down this path, jumping to an alternative path, to a path not taken, is almost impossible.[16] To put it another way, where the system *is* at any given time depends crucially on where it *was*—that is, on the accumulated events and decisions, small and large, accidental and deliberate, that have made up the system's history to that point. And looking back on that history, we have a natural tendency to see an underlying logic operating—even though there may have been none present. The events of history often look inevitable in retrospect, but in general they aren't.

So the first lesson of the crash was that many of history's big events are highly contingent. For a few hours, the stock market and American economy were on a knife-edge. But the crash held another lesson too: in the minds of the people directly involved, and in the minds of many others—like Dan Rather, the travelers pressed against the bar in the San Diego airport, and me as I watched Rather's face—some of life's guiding regularities were briefly rocked to their foundations. We glimpsed a void. Few things are scarier than the sudden recognition that the social world around us is not really founded on anything solid or tangible but is largely constructed in our minds, out of shared beliefs and, frequently, delusions. In his assessment of Black Monday, Michael Rosen writes:

> That which appears objective—the naturalness of organizations, the structuring of hierarchies, the immutability of economic laws, the stability of order—is illusory, where fronts are maintained through the management of common backstages of meaning. Nevertheless, at times disorder raises its head, the mask of everydayness fades, we peer over the edge into the abyss of uncharted terror.[17]

Luckily, we were all quickly able to banish terror from our minds. Thanks to the fortuitous intervention of Greenspan and others, the crash of '87 was safely pushed into the past and out of sight; and, surprisingly soon, the event seemed only a momentary correction in the steady upward surge of American and world markets over the next decade.

By 1997, Alan Greenspan was widely hailed as the hero of '87 and the individual most responsible for the subsequent equity boom. He had become the financial system's omniscient and omnipotent guardian against terror, its bulwark against the abyss. Yet at the very time of this idolatry, interesting things were happening on the other side of the planet that raised serious questions about the actual ability of experts like Greenspan to manage this system.

During the 1980s and the first two-thirds of the 1990s, the economies of East and Southeast Asia boomed. They were models of a new form of capitalism, many commentators claimed—a form characterized by high savings rates, openness to foreign investment and ideas, commitment to developing their human capital through family planning and education programs, and tight, collaborative relations among state economic managers and business elites. From Jakarta and Bangkok to Seoul and Shanghai, Asia was on the move. Cities sprouted forests of construction cranes. Urban planners unfurled grand designs for new airports, high-tech economic zones, and the world's tallest buildings. Modern expressways carved through the countryside's grain fields and rice paddies. And rural people—most born into subsistence poverty—flooded into the towns and cities. The region's economic growth was amazing: never in history had so many people seen their living standards rise so fast.[18]

Foreign banks poured hundreds of billions of dollars into these economies. Lending grew by 20 percent or more a year. "There was a huge euphoria about Asia and Southeast Asia," *The New York Times* reported Dennis Phillips of the German Commerzbank saying, "it was the place to be." And Klaus Friedrich of Dresdner Bank agreed: "All the banks would be standing in line—J. P. Morgan, Deutsche Bank, Dresdner. We were all standing in line trying to help these countries borrow money. We would see each other at the same places. We all knew each other."[19]

During this period, I spent a lot of time in the region. On one trip in the summer of 1995, I traveled for several weeks by train across the Chinese countryside. Like so many other visitors, I was intoxicated by the energy and excitement of the Asian boom. It was almost impossible not to succumb. I remember strolling along Shanghai's waterfront late on a misty June evening. The newly rebuilt promenade—the Bund—on the bank of the Huangpu River was crowded with well-dressed young Chinese out for a walk. Facing the river was a crescent of financial buildings and hotels constructed by Europeans in the early part of the century, each splendidly flooded with golden light. And rising out of the Pudong Special Economic Zone across the river was the Oriental Pearl TV Tower, the symbol of the new Shanghai. Looking like something conjured up by the fevered imagination of a science-fiction writer, the tower thrust hundreds of meters into the sky, its three huge spheres sparkling with colored lights.

Shanghai's Oriental Pearl TV Tower in 1995

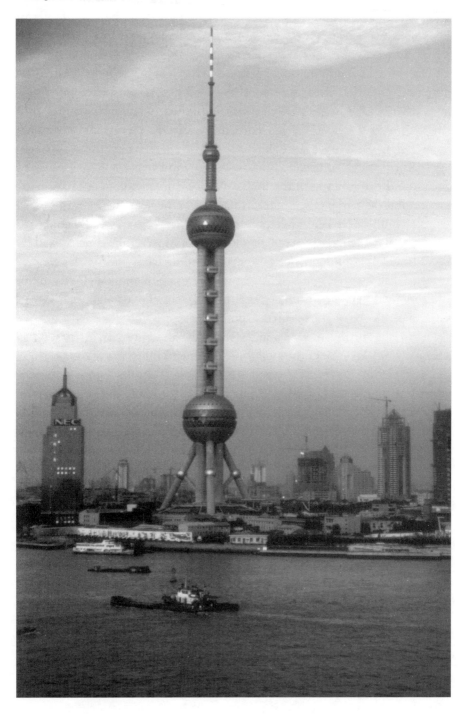

The ancient, cultured city of Shanghai was exploding with energy. It vibrated, gleamed, and seethed with entrepreneurial exuberance. It was an end-to-end construction zone, a nonstop medley of cranes, jackhammers, and bulldozers creating skyscrapers, elevated expressways, subway tunnels, and luxury apartment buildings. It boasted some of the most impressive architecture in Asia, with massive glass-faced hotels and office buildings, swathed in scaffolding, shooting skyward. Billboards and banners plastered the shopping districts, blaring advertisements for everything from blue jeans and diapers to hot-water heaters and American whiskey.

In 1995, much of urban China, especially in the coastal zones, looked the same. From the top of the fourteenth-century city gate in the provincial capital of Nanjing, I counted thirty-three heavy construction cranes within a radius of five kilometers. Looking down from the wall, I could see roads being widened, trees felled, and sewer and water pipelines installed. The streets of Nanjing, Zhengzhou, and Beijing were lined with new private stalls and stores, and brightly lit shopping malls and arcades were full of every imaginable consumer good. Roads were choked with Audis, Jeep Cherokees, Volkswagens, Volvos, and Mercedes.

My visits during this period to other urban centers in Asia, such as Hong Kong, Jakarta, and Bangalore, produced the same feelings. I was dazzled by these societies' transformation and raw exuberance. Yet in 1997, only two years later, everything turned abruptly upside down. In the summer and fall of that year a currency crisis began in Thailand and ricocheted across the region. International investors and speculators laid siege to one currency after another—the Thai baht, the Hong Kong dollar, the South Korean won, the Malaysian ringgit, the Indonesian rupiah, the Filipino peso. The region's stock markets crashed. Suddenly the experts knew—it seems they had known all along—that Asia had been ripe for a downturn. Banking systems, they concurred, were unstable, corrupt, and overwhelmed with bad debt, much of it short-term; currencies were artificially inflated; investment patterns were dictated by cronyism and connections, not economic rationality.

As a result, the region was awash in underused office buildings, factories, and infrastructure. Fully 40 percent of Shanghai's office space was vacant—space in the very buildings I had seen shooting skyward only two years earlier. And in Kuala Lumpur, just as Malaysia's economy imploded, the world's tallest office buildings had opened for tenants. The Petronas Twin Towers, designed by our redoubtable architect Cesar Pelli, added nearly fifty football fields of office space to an already glutted market.[20] The Asian miracle and that special version of Asian capitalism, so widely hailed only a short while before, suddenly appeared tawdry and tattered.

(The construction of tall buildings seems to be a leading indicator of economic downturns. The Chrysler Building and the Empire State Building soared into New York's skies in the 1930s just as the U.S. economy sank into depression. Similarly, the construction of the World Trade Center and Chicago's Sears Tower in the 1970s preceded a severe slump, as did construction of Canary Wharf in the late 1980s. This correlation isn't surprising: at the height of an economic boom, showiness and extravagance tend to trump substance and economic fundamentals.[21])

Like the 1987 crash, the Asian economic crisis contained several disturbing lessons. For one thing, it showed that the world's top financial and economic experts were just as susceptible as the rest of us to fad and the whims of crowd psychology.[22] Although many experts said later—with much self-assurance and impressive jargon—that the Asian crisis had been inevitable and clearly foreseeable, few had taken such positions beforehand. Even the world's top credit rating agencies had given little hint of a problem: in the year and a half leading up to the crisis, Moody's and Standard & Poor's hadn't downgraded the long-term debt ratings of Indonesia, Malaysia, or Thailand. (But they did downgrade these countries' debts after the crisis broke, which made the ensuing panic worse.) In the patronizing language of its annual report, issued in September 1997, the International Monetary Fund had declared that the Fund's directors "welcomed Korea's continued impressive macroeconomic performance [and] praised the authorities for the enviable fiscal record." The IMF had been equally effusive about Thailand: "Directors strongly praised Thailand's remarkable economic performance and the authorities' consistent record of sound macroeconomic policies."[23]

But only three months later, with the Thai baht and the Korean won being hammered through the floor, the economist Robert Johnson could write in *The New York Times*: "Today, where once everyone saw efficiency and vitality, now the image is one of widespread corruption and waste. How could anything so good turn so bad so quickly? If Asia's vibrant economies can collapse, what other assumptions about economic conditions anywhere can we count on?"[24] The world, he recognized, had changed in the blink of an eye, and the world's experts were riding on the same Zeitgeist bandwagon as everybody else.

If economic experts are susceptible to fads like the rest of us, it's partly because economic theories, data, and institutions are often weak. That's the second lesson of the 1997 Asian crisis. Current economic theories do not give us an accurate understanding of the nonlinear and hypercomplex behavior of the international economic system; key data on the economic performance of countries and their banking and private sectors are often poor or nonexistent; and critical institutions of global economic management are frequently overwhelmed by the demands they face. In the absence of strong theories, data, and institutions, facile economic nostrums and fads become received wisdom. Confronted with rapid and confusing changes, experts and policy-makers cling to this wisdom. Hardly surprisingly, it usually supports the short-term interests of powerful economic elites.

Although the kind of currency run that occurred in Asia appeared to arrive out of the blue, there was actually a rudimentary plan in place to prevent just such an event. In a world of tightly integrated financial markets, "hot" capital can flow like quicksilver in and out of economies. The computer-driven speculations of currency traders and capital managers often wildly exaggerate the market's response to underlying weaknesses of economies, which makes rational economic planning and reform impossible. In late 1994 and early 1995, the world was given a nasty preview of this new reality of financial globalization, when a run on the Mexican peso caused a hemorrhage of capital out of the country and shook currencies around the world. Shortly afterwards the IMF took a number of steps to discourage currency volatility. It instituted an "early warning system" to give international banks, corporations, and currency traders advance information about countries with potential problems. This early warning system had several components: the IMF encouraged countries to provide more information about their economic fundamentals, some of which was posted on the World Wide Web; it increased its surveillance of emerging economies; and it started publishing some of its background studies of these economies.

Unfortunately, the system didn't work when it was really needed. As speculative pressures mounted against the Thai baht in early 1997, spurred by a severe current account deficit and an overhang of short-term foreign debt, Thai economic managers refused to heed IMF warnings. There seemed little need: after all, foreign banks were still pouring money into the country. More deceitfully, in mid-1997 Thailand blocked the release of a scathing IMF report on its economic policies. But within weeks, waves of speculation had nevertheless forced the Thai government to devalue the baht. By the end of July, the Thais had to turn, humiliated, to the IMF for help to stabilize their currency. But it was too late: the quicksilver of hot capital was gushing out of Asia. "Frankly, the early warning system failed," concluded C. Fred Bergsten, the head of the Institute for International Economics in Washington. "The Thais did not listen to the Fund and the markets were very slow to send Bangkok warning signals, even though they knew there was trouble coming."[25]

By early December 1997, the IMF, the United States, and Western governments had fallen back to Korea. They were desperately trying to save that country, and perhaps the world, from an economic debacle. The panic must go no further, they realized; it had to stop at Korea. Yet the eleventh-largest economy was on the ropes: in the week after the IMF announced the largest stabilization package in history, the Korean won dropped 30 percent against the U.S. dollar. The shortcomings of the IMF and the entire edifice of world financial management were now all too visible, and a raging debate among economists, bankers, and government officials filled the world's newspapers, magazines, and airwaves. Two questions dominated the debate: What should the IMF and other relevant agencies be doing? And did these agencies have the management capacity to do anything effective at all?

Positions on the first question were all over the map. In each of the affected Asian countries, the IMF had sought to reestablish confidence in the country's economy by imposing a standard package: fiscal austerity, high interest rates, managed failure of weak banks and corporations, privatization, and reform of banking systems.[26] Critics like Harvard's Jeffrey Sachs and the World Bank's Joseph Stiglitz argued that, in some respects, these prescriptions were precisely the opposite of what was needed. The IMF policies were fundamentally deflationary: high interest rates and restrictions on credit were sure to depress economic activity, yet these economies needed increased economic production, exports, and confidence to pull out of their tailspin. Other critics argued that the market "correction" should be allowed to take its course, producing widespread bankruptcies if necessary: those who had been profligate or corrupt should reap what they had sown. If the IMF's interventions covered the losses of crony capitalists within Asia and of foreign banks outside the region, they would just encourage more irresponsibility in the future.

But the second, and more interesting, question lurked under the surface. Did the crisis represent a fundamental failure of management capacity at both the national and international levels? Many believed so. "National supervision of complex global firms and global markets is inadequate to meet the requirements of the times," said John Heimann, chairman for global financial institutions at Merrill Lynch, who was leading a team of experts to study this risk.[27] The team concluded: "Given the speed with which market participants can react to events anywhere in the world, reaction times in the event of a shock are virtually instantaneous. Managers and regulators have very little time to analyze the problem and formulate and implement a response. The sheer velocity with which international transactions take place may increase the risk of misjudgment."[28]

So what should be done? John Heimann and his colleagues proposed an answer: major commercial and investment banks should undertake more self-regulation and self-supervision, and regulators in national governments should collaborate more with these institutions; in other words, government regulators should delegate some of the task of managing the international economy to the very same large commercial and investment banks that helped cause the Mexican and Asian crises in the first place. "The speed and complexity of innovation in the markets," Heimann's team concluded, "the [government] supervisors' inevitable position 'behind the curve,' and their real handicaps in competing for talented staffers all argue for private institutions to take on greater responsibility."[29]

But what about international financial agencies like the IMF? Couldn't they pick up the pieces if regulation and supervision by national governments failed? The Asian crisis suggested not. Even the IMF's first deputy managing director, Stanley Fischer, conceded that "the amount of detailed knowledge it takes to understand a system is beyond the capacity of a single multinational organization [such as the IMF] to deal with."[30] Others were harsher. In a series of caustic attacks in *The Financial Times* and elsewhere, Harvard's Jeffrey Sachs railed against the secrecy and lack of accountability of the IMF's decision-making process. "The world accepts as normal the idea that crucial details of IMF programs should remain confidential, even though these 'details' affect the well-being of millions." But beyond this secrecy, he pointed to a more distressing problem: the IMF and other keystone agencies of the international financial system didn't have the human capital to properly discharge their responsibilities.

The situation is out of hand. However useful the IMF may be to the world community, it defies logic to believe that the small group of one thousand economists on 19th Street in Washington should dictate the economic conditions of life to seventy-five developing countries with around 1.4 billion people.

These people constitute 57 percent of the developing world outside China and India (which are not under IMF programs). Since perhaps half of the IMF's professional time is devoted to these countries—with the rest tied up in surveillance of advanced countries, management, research, and other tasks—about five hundred staff cover the seventy-five countries. That is an average of about seven economists per country.

One might suspect that seven staffers would not be enough to get a very sophisticated view of what is happening. That suspicion would be right. The IMF threw together a draconian program for Korea in just a few days, without deep knowledge of the country's financial system and without any subtlety as to how to approach the problems.[31]

But Jeffrey Sachs's concerns were not widely heeded. In the early months of 1998, as the Korean rescue package seemed to take hold and Asian economies stabilized, doubts were quickly buried. Experts confidently trumpeted that the region would boom again, and perhaps soon. We were assured that the economic fundamentals of the region's countries were very strong and that the financial crunch would weed out weak corporations and banks, while cheap currencies would spur an export surge. Indeed, the experts said, the Asian panic was a normal corrective to the excesses of the 1980s and 1990s. Currency traders and speculators had done everyone a service by bringing the world's attention to the lack of adequate national oversight of Asia's banking systems. Markets and freewheeling international capitalism had worked well.[32]

This self-congratulation, however, revealed the third lesson of the crisis. The experts and elites at the apex of modern capitalism have a practically boundless capacity for after-the-fact rationalization. As soon as evidence allows, they paper over any cracks that have developed in their worldview. They rush to backfill the voids of doubt. Anomalous data that deserve close attention are quickly explained away or forgotten in the stampede back to exuberant money-making. An abrupt, nonlinear shock like the 1997 Asian financial crisis is absorbed into a modestly adjusted worldview with only a moment's pause. One day Asia is golden. The next it is a pariah. But there's no need to worry, say the experts and elites as they reassure themselves and others, because Asia's problems are unique, isolated, and easily fixed.

There's no doubt that most of us in rich countries are deeply indebted to markets and capitalism. They are the wellspring of much of the modern world's opportunity, health, and wealth. And markets and capitalism are essential to successful economic development in the world's poorest regions. Yet the economic ideology of modern capitalism is, as philosophers of science would say, almost "non-falsifiable." It is a worldview that is virtually impossible to refute or challenge, because it is infinitely adaptive and malleable. Almost every event or possibility can be subsumed within its relentless energy and optimism. It's also largely ahistorical: the crash of '87, the later financial calamities in Mexico and Asia, and other annoying surprises are quickly relegated to the past, and the past is of little consequence. The only things that matter are the present and future; and the present and future (as Canary Wharf revealed) can be constantly reinvented.

Eventually, reality does correct such self-indulgence. But this reality hits home hardest not at the top of the capitalist heap, but at the bottom. The emergency stabilization package urgently negotiated among the United States, commercial banks, the IMF, and Mexico in 1995 shoved a floor under the value of the peso, allowed the country to deal with its current account deficit, and laid the foundation for renewed economic growth. Commentators outside Mexico turned to other issues. The crisis had passed; the system had worked; most important, foreigners' loans were covered. But the stabilization package achieved its results at a huge cost—a cost borne, for the most part, not by Mexico's corrupt elites or foreign lenders, but by the country's middle class and poor. As the country tipped into an appalling recession, the average wage dropped by almost 15 percent, and already-high levels of criminality, violence, and militarization skyrocketed. Afraid that they would be robbed if they stopped at red lights, drivers in Mexico City began speeding straight through downtown intersections. Assassinations and kidnappings for ransom soared. The military became increasingly involved in policing civil society, with much of the country's south taking on the appearance of an armed camp.

In the wake of the IMF's ministrations in late 1997 and early 1998, a similar story unfolded in Southeast Asia. Depression gripped Thailand and doubled its unemployment rate. Economic activity slowed to a crawl, construction in cities like Bangkok stopped almost completely, and a million migrant villagers returned to their rural homes, only to find no jobs there either. The country ejected three hundred thousand illegal workers, mostly back to Myanmar. Malaysia also sent back to Indonesia boatloads of construction laborers who had been providing raw labor for the country's building boom.[33]

Indonesia was hit especially hard, as the country suddenly faced multiple, converging crises. When the rupiah plummeted in value, the government reluctantly moved to close a number of insolvent banks, triggering a run on other banks. Credit evaporated from the economy. By mid-January, 260 of the 282 corporations listed on the Jakarta stock exchange were technically bankrupt. Millions lost their jobs, and at the same time basic dietary staples shot up in price. In only two months, the price of rice and cooking oil increased between 30 and 100 percent, and the price of chicken, the principal meat, rose 50 to 100 percent. The falling rupiah also forced up the cost of imported insecticides and seeds. The higher cost of these agricultural inputs, combined with the impact of a severe drought and forest fires that were blanketing much of Southeast Asia in haze, drove down rural food output. Nonetheless, the central government wanted to move people out of cities like Jakarta to reduce the risk of urban violence. It cut the price of tickets on trains leaving the cities, so many of the newly unemployed flooded back to the already overcrowded farms and terraced hills of rural Indonesia.

Not surprisingly, in February 1998 food riots and ethnic clashes erupted across the country. Analysts started to talk about the possibility of widespread starvation in a society that only shortly before had boasted of its self-sufficiency. The riots climaxed in May with an orgy of looting and attacks on ethnic Chinese that resulted in the deaths of five hundred people in Jakarta, and damaged or destroyed nearly five thousand buildings. The violence had the perverse effect of creating more upheaval in the country's food distribution system, because it had been largely controlled by the Chinese minority.

The violence also revealed something more general—and more disturbing—about the social strains in our modern world: the rioters attacked mainly symbols of affluence. They were principally young men who had come from the countryside looking for jobs and had suddenly found themselves on the street. "As they sit idly on benches above open sewers that run through the slums," wrote a journalist in *The New York Times*, "the young men complain not so much about President Suharto as about their frustration that they are being laid off just as prices are going up." The rubble of the recent violence surrounded the slums, and many of the rioters, the journalist continued, "seemed to derive satisfaction from the idea that the air-conditioned department stores, monuments to the wealthy, have gone up in flames. Some of the idle young men sound less interested in political warfare than in class warfare."[34]

In mid-1997 and early 1998, world financial markets exhibited many of the characteristics and behaviors that I described in the chapter "Complexities."[35] It was as if someone had opened the tap slightly, and the fluids coursing through the international financial system had flipped from laminar to turbulent flow. The system's innumerable components—including the banks, the trading houses, corporations, and governments—interacted intensely to produce vicious circles and sharp nonlinearities. The couplings among these interdependent components had been tightened by lightning-fast computer and communication technologies and round-the-clock, round the-world trading, which meant that the financial system as a whole had little slack to absorb errors or sudden shocks. The system amplified small perturbations far beyond expectations, and it often behaved in totally unexpected ways, as damage to one system component spread rapidly to others. A relatively small event—the devaluation of a minor currency or a corporate bankruptcy in Hong Kong—produced a cascade of repercussions around the world. Rapid-fire surprises blindsided financial managers and policy-makers. Rumors, misinterpretations, errors, and lies tore across the planet, causing wild market swings before they were corrected. Alan Greenspan seemed well aware of these dangers and was worried by them. Computer-driven global markets, he noted, have "the capability of transmitting mistakes at a far faster pace throughout the financial system in ways that were unknown a generation ago."[36]

Volatility, surprises, and cascading repercussions are not always bad. A certain amount of chaos in global markets and most other social systems is inevitable (and as I discovered later in my investigations, even desirable). But system fluctuations sometimes exceed acceptable bounds, causing real suffering to real people in real communities around the world. Some of the managers of our corporations and of our national and international financial institutions are charged with keeping such things from happening. Yet these people are facing truly enormous and constantly growing management demands. As markets, financial systems, and corporations become faster and more sophisticated, managers need faster and more sophisticated management tools, including better data-gathering and interpretation technologies, so they know what's going on in the systems they are trying to manage. Better decision-making procedures are also essential, so they can quickly focus the best expertise on their problems and ensure all stakeholders are heard. Finally, they need better implementation tools, so they can give practical effect to their carefully crafted solutions.[37] In other words, as market and social systems get more complex, the requirement for management ingenuity rises concomitantly.

Can managers and management systems meet this rising need for ingenuity? The Asian financial crisis revealed that the answer is sometimes no, and the result can be a serious ingenuity gap that leads to terrible suffering, conflict, and insurrection. By 1997, at both the national and international levels, technology-driven changes in the speed and complexity of financial transactions had surged ahead of the relatively slow pace of improvement in the capacity of governmental and intergovernmental institutions to manage these transactions. As Allen Sinai, the top global economist at Primark Decision Systems, an investment advisory group, said, "What makes this problem so distinct is that it is . . . laced with every type of financial crisis and instability that has ever shown up in the real world or any textbook. And while there are some brilliant minds working on it, no one can deal with it."[38]

Perhaps the clearest evidence of soaring management demands in modern globalized markets is corporations' mounting reliance on high-powered consulting firms, like McKinsey & Co., the Boston Consulting Group, and Anderson Consulting. When faced with a complex new problem beyond the ken of their own full-time managers, firms are increasingly seeking outside help. A team of consultants, each of whom makes more than $100,000 a year, sweeps in. They bring with them the diverse expertise the firm needs but doesn't have itself—expertise on everything from just-in-time inventory management to foreign banking regulations, from advanced information technologies to health-care insurance schemes. The use of such services is rising fast: from 1990 to 1997, the revenues of the consulting industry as a whole grew 10 percent or more a year, with some of the top firms seeing growth of 20 to 30 percent annually. These firms now gobble up many of the best-and-brightest graduates from business schools, and, lately, from medical schools, technical schools such as MIT and Caltech, and humanities Ph.D. programs at first-tier universities as well. Recruits receive, in effect, a gilt-edged entrance ticket to the new global super elite. As *The Economist* notes, "McKinsey's five thousand alumni form a quasi-Masonic network at the top of businesses and governments alike: former McKinsey men run organizations as disparate as IBM, American Express, and the investment arm of SBC Warburg."[39]

Why is the consulting industry prospering? "The answer," *The Economist* continues, "can be summed up in two words: complexity and uncertainty. Complexity creates confusion; uncertainty creates fear; and both create a booming demand for outside advice." Lowell Bryan, a senior partner at McKinsey, says, "Other people's problems are our opportunities, and there's a bull market in problems at the moment."[40]

———————

If people thought they had seen the end of the Asian financial crisis by the spring of 1998, they were sorely mistaken. Downward pressure on East Asian currencies and stock markets returned during that summer, leading a senior official of the World Bank to declare that the region could slide into an economic depression. An American bailout of the Russian economy went awry, and then in August Russia defaulted on some of its foreign debts. The Russian default, in turn, pushed a major American investment fund, Long-Term Capital Management, to the edge of bankruptcy. With the Western financial system teetering on the brink, the Federal Reserve Bank of New York scrambled to organize a $3.6 billion private bailout of the fund. Meanwhile, North American and European stock markets plunged. As September gave way to October—a month that has historically witnessed more than its share of stock market crises—many commentators and policy-makers, including President Clinton, openly acknowledged that the world faced the worst economic crisis since the Great Depression. Only three interest rate cuts by Alan Greenspan in quick succession reassured investors that markets would remain liquid and that stability would prevail.

In Asia, a critical bulwark against a deepening of the crisis had been the nonconvertibility of the Chinese currency, the yuan. If currency traders had been able to trigger a run on the yuan, it would likely have caused a further, truly catastrophic decline in currency values across the region. Ironically, China's policy of insulating its economy from global capitalist pressures helped protect the capitalist system from itself. But staggering damage had already been done, and, once again, Indonesia was the worst affected: by the end of 1998 the country's GDP (in U.S. dollars) had shrunk to less than half that of 1997, twenty million people had been thrown into poverty, and hysterical groups of vigilantes were sweeping through remote towns and villages seizing, torturing, and executing anyone they suspected of "sorcery."[41]

In Western financial centers, the crisis, as it waned, left experts breathless and bewildered. Alan Greenspan admitted, "I have learned more about how this new international financial system works in the last twelve months than in the previous twenty years."[42] Yet, as before, people quickly suppressed their doubts about the ability of financial elites to manage this system; when economic calm returned in 1999, people forgot how grim the situation had appeared only a few months previously. Some analysts did argue that it was just a matter of time before another crisis hit, and that an overhaul of international financial institutions was urgently needed, but nevertheless the momentum for truly substantial reform quickly dissipated. The World Bank, the IMF, and the American administration instead turned to blaming each other for making the crisis more severe than it might have been.

It was Kofi Annan, the United Nations Secretary General, who seemed to best capture the broader implications of what had happened. At a glittering meeting of the world's business leaders in early 1999, he issued a somber warning—a warning that, interestingly, pointed to an ingenuity gap between the demands placed on societies by global economic change and the capacity of societies to respond effectively to these demands. "The spread of markets far outpaces the ability of societies and their political systems to adjust to them, let alone guide the course they take," he cautioned. "History teaches us that such an imbalance between the economic, social, and political realms can never be sustained for very long."[43]

UNKNOWN UNKNOWNS

MY FIRST INTUITION that there could be something disturbing about the unfathomable complexity of our modern, human-made world came on a backpacking trip through Europe in 1977. I had stopped in Strasbourg, France, for several weeks, where I earned myself a small wage making kitchen cabinets and cooking meals for a local family. The father was a physicist. He worked at a nearby research laboratory that included a particle accelerator designed to pry open the deepest secrets of the atom. One sunny afternoon in August he took me on a tour of the facilities.

Although tiny by comparison with accelerators elsewhere in the world, the Strasbourg machine seemed mammoth to me, stretching through room upon room filled with computers, wiring, tubing, and heavy magnets. I asked my physicist guide about one queer-looking component after another, and he tried to explain the machine's operation in simple terms. After an hour or so, however, a larger puzzle came to my mind.

"Is there anybody," I asked, "who understands this thing in its entirety?" My distinguished guide clearly had expertise about some of the accelerator's components, but only a general grasp of the whole thing. "Is there anyone who has expertise about all the components and who can put those individual bits of knowledge together into a truly complete understanding of the entire machine?"

"No," the physicist answered, with a look that showed he thought the question a bit peculiar. "No, no one understands this machine completely." I felt some discomfort about his answer at the time, but I didn't know exactly why.

More than twenty years later, as I gathered pieces of my ingenuity puzzle in North America, the reasons for my discomfort became clearer when a pair of articles in the journal *Foreign Affairs* in the summer of 1997 brought the issue into sharp focus. The Berkeley political scientist Steven Weber and the MIT economist Paul Krugman were discussing whether modern postindustrial economies had eliminated the business cycle—that long, repeating wave of economic boom and recession, and sometimes depression, that began in the early nineteenth century when paper credit became widely used in the newly industrialized economies.[1]

Steven Weber argued that several developments in today's economies dampen the boom-bust swings of the business cycle. Our workforce is more flexible and less vulnerable to recession, he claimed. As well, new information technologies allow companies to better control their inventories, while the globalization of finances, production, and economic demand makes the world economy less sensitive to economic conditions in any one country.[2]

At the time the U.S. was in the midst of its longest peacetime economic expansion, so Weber's optimism seemed justified. Paul Krugman pointed out, however, that the business cycle had been declared dead before. In the late sixties, as America pumped up its economy with Vietnam War dollars, and shortly before the first major oil shock kicked off a decade of stagflation, a number of experts made claims similar to Weber's. "Why does the business cycle persist?" Krugman asked. "Because, as the bumper stickers don't quite say, stuff happens: the world refuses to stay put, and policy is always playing catch-up. To look at the causes of booms and slumps since the business cycle was last declared dead is to be awed by the sheer variety of curve balls history throws at us." He went on, "Who in 1969 imagined that a recession could be triggered by a war in the Middle East—let alone a fundamentalist revolution in Iran? Who would have thought that the ever-so-controlled Japanese economy could be whipsawed by a financial bubble that drove land and stock prices to ridiculous levels, then burst? Who could have predicted that two well-meaning projects—the political unification of Germany and the monetary unification of Europe—would interact to produce a disastrous slump?"

Paul Krugman's insightful comments, it seemed to me then, led to a more general conclusion. When things are going well, as they were for most people in the United States for most of the 1990s, it's easy to forget that we live in a world of *unknown unknowns*. Not only are we often ignorant of critical components, processes, and possibilities in the complex systems surrounding us, we're also often ignorant of our ignorance. Wally Broecker, when I spoke to him in his lab outside of New York, made this point about the North Atlantic's conveyor belt; and the point is equally true of the Strasbourg particle accelerator, Biosphere 2, and the global economy. We often don't know what we don't know.

Crudely speaking, three kinds of system—natural, social, and technological—make up our world. Prior to our arrival on Earth, most natural systems already existed in some form, including the planet's grand geophysical and geochemical systems, like the climate and the ozone layer; and its biological and ecological systems, like forests, fisheries, and soils. In contrast, our social systems are entirely the products of our actions. Our national and international markets, our governments, and our court and judicial institutions cannot exist independently of us; we have constructed them within, and they remain largely internal to, our societies. Technological systems usually inhabit the boundary between these natural and social worlds; as physical entities (for example, my car) they exist independently of us, but they have meaning and utility only for us.

Over time, as I argued in the "New World" chapter, we have produced incremental, quantitative changes in all three types of system. By themselves, the changes have usually been tiny in degree or amount, but together they have produced shifts in the quality of these systems' basic character and behavior. For instance, as we've evolved from the agricultural to the industrial and then postindustrial stages of development, we've made our social and technological systems so much more complex and fast-paced that they are qualitatively different from previous ones. And as our impacts on Earth's natural systems have become immense, we've sharply increased the chance of severe nonlinearities in the behavior of these systems—such as sudden changes in the world's ocean currents. Together, greater complexity and pace and a higher chance of nonlinearities tend to boost the number of unknown unknowns in the natural, social, and technological systems around us. These systems have more components and processes that we don't even know exist, and these components interact more frequently in surprising and ill-understood ways.

Generally speaking, we're not eager to admit how little we understand the systems we construct, live within, and depend upon. When it comes to unknown unknowns, we are masters of avoidance and denial. We easily convince ourselves that we know enough to manage the systems around us effectively, or, at least, that there are experts who do. We also easily accept a consensus regarding the basic constituents of our natural, social, and technological systems and the basic principles by which we can manage and master these systems. (The creation of this consensus is made easier by, and is itself part of, our increasing separation from natural systems.) We are truly terrified, as we were on Black Monday, when this consensus and, in turn, our constructed reality are seriously threatened. And we seize upon any opportunity, as we did after the 1997–98 Asian financial crisis, to rationalize away critical anomalies and convince ourselves that, after all, we really are in control.

Because we tend to delude ourselves that we understand the complex systems around us better than we actually do, we are often less prudent than we should be when we deal with them. "The system works," we say to each other after a crisis, in relief and self-congratulation, and continue doing things as we always have. We introduce changes not to reform but only to refine our institutions, practices, and technologies, to increase their performance and efficiency; and these refinements (like the ever greater speed of international currency transactions) often make the systems affecting us even more replete with unknown unknowns. And our sense that we are working to improve things leads to a complacent belief that our management of our affairs is excellent—thoroughly sound and scientific.

Take, for instance, how we handle natural resources important to us, like our fisheries and forests. The people we charge with managing these resources—such as government fisheries officers or logging company foresters—have usually learned, as part of their technical training, that it's possible to have precise and detailed knowledge of how these resource systems work. They have been taught, basically, that these systems have few if any unknown unknowns. So when they get into the field, they tend to treat fisheries and forests as if they were relatively simple machines, and they try to operate these machines to maximize the steady output of tons of fish or cubic meters of wood. As well, for efficiency's sake they usually make the government agencies and industries that regulate and extract the resource increasingly complex (much the way we make our car engines more complex to improve their performance). But this whole approach has many bad results. Among other things, it makes our societies increasingly dependent on constant and predictable flows of food and fiber from these resources, and it makes the government agencies and industries less flexible in the face of rapid change. Most important, though, as managers try to turn our fisheries and forests into simple machines, they make these systems more homogeneous and less resilient to shock: fisheries become more likely to collapse, and forests become more susceptible to insect blights and wildfires that cover vast areas.[3]

The science writer and historian Edward Tenner has a label for such behavior: he calls it the "pathology of intensity," which is "the single-minded overextension of a good thing," in this case the single-minded effort to achieve the highest stable output from a resource.[4] Time and time again we find that such monomania produces results we don't expect and ultimately don't like.

A classic example is our use of antibiotics. When these drugs were first developed in the middle decades of the twentieth century, people thought they were miraculous. It was widely believed, by professionals and laypeople alike, that we would soon be able to vanquish all bacterial disease. So, once again, in a single-minded overextension of a good thing, antibiotics became widely used not just to cure illness but also to prevent illness in both human beings and livestock. (In 1997, treatment of livestock with antibiotics for purposes of nutrition, therapy, and prophylaxis accounted for half of the world's antibiotic consumption.[5]) In the process, most of us forgot that humanity and its diseases together make up a coevolving system—a system that is actually one part of Buzz Holling's larger coevolving system of humanity and nature (which I described in the "Angry Beast" chapter).[6] Inevitably, as we have introduced powerful antibiotics into our arsenal—a total of more than one hundred drugs at the moment—bacteria have evolved ways of defending themselves. Today, as a result, we're facing a crisis of antibiotic resistance in bacterial species ranging from common strains of salmonella to the often lethal *Staphylococcus aureus* and *Mycobacterium tuberculosis*.[7]

Because coevolving systems constantly change, often in their most basic characteristics, they usually present particularly severe problems of unknown unknowns. And when it comes to diseases, as we have become more urbanized and as we have started traveling farther and faster using new transport technologies, we have greatly accelerated both the rate at which diseases can spread through our populations and the rate at which they can evolve into drug-resistant forms. Prior to the wide use of airplanes, people who contracted infectious diseases during overseas travel would normally show symptoms before arriving home. Transit times by sea were generally longer than disease incubation periods, and travelers who showed symptoms on arrival could be isolated in quarantine stations. But now an infected traveler can spread a disease through large communities before anyone even knows he or she has it. So we not only need more biomedical ingenuity to deliver new antibiotics at a faster pace than ever before, we also need more social ingenuity to develop new institutions, often international in reach, for disease detection and tracking.

Edward Tenner's pathology of intensity often multiplies unknown unknowns. It also often produces another condition that is particularly pernicious: narrowing of expertise. Our never-ending quest for efficiency, speed, and productivity causes overspecialization and fragmentation of knowledge, and it reduces the availability of general expertise, and thus ingenuity supply within our management elites.

We find some of the best illustrations in modern financial markets. New computer and communication technologies have increased the speed of financial transactions; they have also made possible new financial instruments, from innovative kinds of options and futures to mortgage bonds and interest-rate swaps. There's no doubt that these things bring many benefits: they allow the world's money managers to boost flows of capital for investment, give corporations trading overseas a wide range of hedges against currency fluctuations, and reduce market inefficiencies, like arbitrary differences in the exchange values of, say, U.S. dollars trading in London and Tokyo.

But these technologies and instruments promote people with narrow technical and analytical skills, and at the same time displace people with the experiential knowledge—some might call it wisdom—needed to produce market order, stability, and the steady creation of wealth. On October 19 and 20, 1987, as the Dow crashed through the floor and federal regulators fought for control, experienced traders intervened at key points to calm the market. Today, there are far fewer people around with the necessary experience. The men (and they are mostly men) who dominate global financial systems are increasingly computer jockeys. They are unquestionably brilliant in their narrow domains, but they have had virtually no exposure to the world beyond their keyboards and monitors. Says Gene Rochlin, a professor of energy and resources at the University of California, Berkeley: "As skill with the computer and its models becomes more important than accumulated experience, power and influence are shifting to a generation of younger traders more familiar with electronics than trends, less concerned with preserving long-term market stability than with developing and mastering better, quicker models with which to outmaneuver the competition.... [Experienced] traders with a vested interest in making and stabilizing markets are increasingly being displaced by a new breed of 'paper entrepreneurs,' computer wizards who depend on their computers rather than experience, seeking to make short-term profits by anticipating small market movements rather than long-term ones by creating a pattern of stable investments, driving the market in response to trading programs with little or no concern for the underlying economic activity."[8]

We're now all acutely aware how (in many fields) more experienced managers are actually intimidated by a younger generation steeped in the arcana of computers and their magical, number-crunching software.[9] As early as 1992, Alan Greenspan warned of the risks. Reflecting on a recent European currency crisis, he urged regulators to "guard against a situation in which the designers of financial strategies lack the experience to evaluate the attendant risks, and the experienced senior managers are too embarrassed to admit they do not understand the new strategies."[10] The irony, of course, is that the experienced managers are deferring to people who are, in reality, extraordinarily ignorant of the real workings of the global financial system. This new breed of speculators and traders, Gene Rochlin writes, "transfer funds, securities, bonds, or derivative instruments over the face of the globe, along electronic networks whose details and structure they do not understand, between computers and computerized databases they do not fathom and cannot program or query without professional help."[11]

Experiential knowledge consists of intuitions, subtle understandings, and finely honed reflexes gained through years of intimate interaction with a given natural, social, or technological system. A manager may not have to draw on the full depth and richness of this knowledge to meet the system's everyday demands when it's functioning at equilibrium and behaving predictably. Experiential knowledge may therefore seem redundant and unnecessary, especially to engineers hoping to improve efficiency. They may eliminate the people who possess it from the system by automating managers' tasks. But when the system is confronted with a crisis—a sudden and dangerous nonlinearity—experiential knowledge can make the difference between successful resolution of the crisis and catastrophe. The flight of United 232 is a good example. The aircraft's situation was unprecedented, but the captain drew on intuition gained from countless flying-hours to use differential engine thrust to stabilize the plane. And his intimate knowledge of interpersonal dynamics in the cockpit allowed him to allocate tasks effectively to deal with the emergency. Without such wisdom to draw on, the crew would have failed to save anyone at all.

When we fragment management expertise into subspecialties and squeeze out broad experiential knowledge, we become more vulnerable to unknown unknowns. This is the story of the modern automobile engine, which can no longer be repaired by the lay mechanic but only by specialists who are expert in the engine's subcomponents; it is the story of the modern airline cockpit, where the tasks of crew members are increasingly automated; and it is the story of today's financial markets.

———————————

In addition to analyzing the pathology of intensity, Edward Tenner catalogs what he calls "revenge effects." These are "the ironic, unintended consequences of mechanical, chemical, biological, and medical ingenuity." The technological world we have created around us has a tendency, he argues, "to get even, to twist our cleverness against us."[12] Over the years, I've gathered my own favorite examples of revenge effects. The catalytic converters on modern automobiles have done much to reduce urban smog in rich countries; but they turn out to be a major source of nitrous oxide, a powerful greenhouse gas.[13] Efforts in the U.S. to eradicate the ferocious fire ant using an arsenal of pesticides wiped out its parasites and competing species of ant; there followed an explosion of the fire ant population across hundreds of millions of hectares of the U.S. South and Southwest.[14] And in only a few decades, our use of space has cluttered low-Earth orbits with more than one hundred thousand bits of debris, ranging from fragments of derelict rocket bodies to centimeter-sized spheres of frozen coolant that have leaked from the nuclear reactors of defunct Soviet satellites. Traveling at tens of kilometers per second, these objects can be lethal to our spacecraft, forcing designers to start shrouding them in shielding.[15]

I would argue that revenge effects often arise when we add components and functions to our technologies to improve their performance, which can make them behave in unexpectedly perverse ways. Modern computer software offers some dramatic examples.

On June 4, 1996, the European Space Agency launched the massive Ariane 5 rocket into space on its maiden voyage from the agency's center in French Guiana.[16] Thirty-seven seconds later, the rocket's two inertial guidance systems delivered diagnostic error messages to the on-board computer responsible for controlling the steering. The computer mistakenly interpreted the messages as flight data and concluded that the rocket had taken a sharp turn. It tried to correct course by ordering the rocket's boosters and main engine to swivel their exhaust nozzles to an extreme angle to redirect their thrust. But the unneeded correction produced violent aerodynamic pressures that began to rip the rocket apart, triggering its automatic self-destruct mechanism. Developed over ten years at a cost of $7 billion, the *Ariane 5* blew up thirty-nine seconds into its flight, destroying the four uninsured satellites aboard.

How could such an extraordinarily sophisticated technological system—a system produced by literally tens of millions of hours of human labor and ingenuity—fail so spectacularly? Investigators found that the guidance system's computers had malfunctioned when they tried to convert data on the rocket's horizontal velocity from 64- to 16-bit format. Normally, built-in error correction software handles conversion problems swiftly. But in this case, software engineers had decided such protection wasn't needed because the velocity figure would never be large enough. They hadn't reckoned on *Ariane 5* being a more powerful and faster rocket than *Ariane 4*. Ironically, the calculation that caused the two guidance systems to crash was only needed to align them prior to launch. But when programmers developed software for an early version of the rocket, they decided to leave the calculation running for the first forty seconds of flight to allow for a quick restart of the countdown in the event of a launch hold.

In their postmortem analysis, the Europeans acknowledged the difficulties presented by software complexity. Jacques Durand, head of the *Ariane 5* project, admitted that "very tiny details can have terrible consequences. That's not surprising, especially in a complex software system such as this."[17] The investigative board chose not to blame any particular contractor, and it explicitly recognized the danger of unknown unknowns: "A decision was taken. It was not analyzed or fully understood." And "the possible implications of allowing [the calculation] to continue to function during flight were not realized."

At the time, the conversion error that caused *Ariane 5* to self-destruct was probably one of the most expensive software bugs in history. But it paled beside the notorious Y2K problem, which, according to most estimates, cost corporations and governments around the world $250 billion. Although, contrary to what many Cassandras had predicted, no widespread disasters occurred on January 1, 2000, few experts doubt that there would have been severe problems if repairs hadn't been made in advance.

The Y2K problem originated in a seemingly innocuous decision in the early years of the computer revolution to conserve computer memory by representing years with two digits instead of four. Programmers had no idea that this decision would haunt the world decades later. As one technology consultant, Peter de Jager, commented: "Many of us truly believed (incorrectly so) that the software we were writing would long be retired before the new millennium."[18] In too many cases, however, it's the programmers who retire first, not their programs. As experience and wisdom about older software slowly fades, as source code and documentation are lost, and as compiler programs change, the ability to revise older software degrades. Yet the *Ariane* experience shows that the software *itself* can be surprisingly durable, and it's hard to predict which parts will endure and how those parts will be employed in the future. Bits and pieces are used and reused—if they did the job well before, we reason, let them do the job again. Thus software tends to accrete over time, almost like alluvial soils deposited in layers; and often the inner workings of older software are not completely understood by programmers using it later.

Also, the machines running older software often remain in use. The problem is particularly acute with "embedded systems," the computer chips built into our industrial machinery, alarms systems, medical testing equipment, stoplights, and navigation beacons, and into consumer products ranging from watches and VCRs to cars and microwave ovens. The Y2K problem highlighted how these chips have infiltrated every aspect of our lives in ways few people recognized. Unfortunately, companies that make these embedded systems sometimes go out of business, and the expertise on these systems can disappear with them. This can make it extraordinarily hard to figure out, after the fact, how embedded systems might fail. Such unknown unknowns made the Y2K bug much harder to manage.

Writing and repairing software generally takes far more time and is far more expensive than initially anticipated. "Every feature that is added and every bug that is fixed," Edward Tenner points out, "adds the possibility of some new and unexpected interaction between parts of the program."[19] De Jager concurs: "If people have learned anything about large software projects, it is that many of them miss their deadlines, and those that are on time seldom work perfectly. . . . Indeed, on-time error-free installations of complex computer systems are rare."[20] Even small changes to code can require wholesale retesting of entire software systems. While at MIT in the 1980s, I helped develop some moderately complex software. I learned then that the biggest problems arise from bugs that creep into programs during early stages of design. They become deeply embedded in the software's interdependent network of logic, and if left unfixed can have cascading repercussions throughout the software. But fixing them often requires tracing out consequences that have metastasized in every direction from the original error.

As the amount of computer code in our world soars (doubling every two years in consumer products alone), we need practical ways to minimize the number of bugs. But software development is still at a preindustrial stage—it remains more craft than engineering. Programmers resemble artisans: they handcraft computer code out of basic programming languages using logic, intuition, and pattern-recognition skills honed over years of experience. Their techniques are neither measurable nor consistently repeatable.[21] So programmers' productivity has improved only slowly in recent decades, and the quality of code varies greatly from one programmer to another. The software industry realizes it must do better and is introducing a range of techniques to improve performance. It's adopting common standards to evaluate programming teams and measure software complexity, and some software developers now use mathematics, especially set theory and predicate calculus, to test their early programs.[22] This approach helped produce the computer code directing the high-speed rail system I traveled on in France. Other software developers are trying to make interchangeable, reusable software parts. Like Eli Whitney's invention of interchangeable parts for muskets in the early nineteenth century—a key step in the industrial revolution, because it allowed people to specialize in producing specific parts rather than whole machines—this development could be immensely important.

The difficulties presented by unknown unknowns in software are often compounded in networks (or what specialists call "distributed systems") made up of many computers. Networks can consist of huge numbers of interconnected parts, each a potential point of failure, and with many not known to the system's managers.[23] Stories of troubles with such systems are legion. In January 1990, software bugs in the AT&T telephone network produced a U.S.-wide shutdown that lasted nine hours and blocked 70 million calls.[24] And in July 1997, a database failure at a Virginia company responsible for maintaining the central directory of Internet addresses caused bad address information to propagate around the world, blocking access to Web sites and making countless e-mail messages undeliverable.[25]

Problems in computer networks arise not just from the failure of individual parts or components—such as individual computers—but also from failure of links among them. The loss of one link means that the information it's carrying must be offloaded to other links. If some of these other links are already operating near peak capacity, the additional load can cause them to fail too, which displaces their information to yet other links. This can cause a rapid cascade of failing links. And it's a problem not limited to computer networks: other kinds of networks, like electricity grids, are also vulnerable. In August 1996, the loss of the Big Eddy transmission line in northern Oregon caused overloading on a string of transmission lines down the west coast of the U.S., triggering blackouts affecting four million people in nine states.[26]

Vicious circles (the positive feedbacks we encountered in the "Complexities" chapter) often exacerbate such cascading failures. On Black Monday, some links within the U.S. financial system became overloaded with information. They slowed to a crawl and occasionally failed entirely. These failures generated more panic in the market, prompting more sell orders, and ultimately causing an even greater load of information to pour into the financial system.

Engineers can improve the reliability of networks by building into them extra hardware, software, and data, thus making them less vulnerable to the failure of single components.[27] They can also program the network's nodes and connections to respond to various types of crisis by selectively shutting down or isolating parts of the system and conserving core functions (a response similar, in some respects, to the way the human body reacts to shock). Ideally, systems with such features would behave as John Bongaarts suggested over our dinner in London: individual components could be damaged or even destroyed, yet the rest of the system would contain and repair the damage. But the experts who build reliable networks concede that it's impossible to anticipate and make plans for all possible failures.

The U.S. air-traffic control system illustrates most, perhaps even all, of these problems—and potential dangers. This network of personnel, radars, beacons, computers, and communications equipment guides airplanes along invisible highways in the sky crisscrossing North America and beyond. Over the decades, the system has maintained an extraordinary safety record, each year directing hundreds of billions of passenger miles of accident-free traffic. But by the late 1990s, its controllers and technicians were overworked and much of its hardware was creaky. In some cases, machines at critical nodes were decades old; they failed regularly, and the expertise needed to repair them had largely disappeared. As one commentator wrote in *Scientific American*, "Maintenance is becoming a black art. Parts are scarce. Old equipment has to be cannibalized. Many of the technicians and support staff who were schooled in the subtleties of 1960s vintage computers are retiring and have not been replaced."[28]

Air-traffic control failures are bad enough in themselves, but they can generate other failures that cascade through the system. During the morning of December 18, 1997, a technician's error interrupted power to radar displays in Kansas City's high-altitude control center. Radio links to pilots and dedicated phone lines to other centers also went dead. For four minutes, controllers could not see, hear, or speak to the planes in their charge. When electricity suddenly flashed on again, the power surge damaged several radar screens and a circuit board in an IBM mainframe, a machine no longer manufactured. For the next two hours, technicians scrambled to cannibalize the board from a backup computer. By that time, however, flights had been disrupted across the continent. People were still experiencing delays late that evening.[29]

At the time of this incident, the U.S. Federal Aviation Administration (FAA), the government agency responsible for the air-traffic control system, had long known that the entire system needed an overhaul. When President Ronald Reagan sacked 11,500 striking controllers in 1981, the FAA faced a chronic shortage of controllers and decided to substitute technology for personnel. It proposed an extraordinarily ambitious project to overhaul the system's computer and communication technologies. The specifications for the project, called the Advanced Automation System (AAS), required it to run 99.99999 percent of the time; in other words it couldn't be out of operation for more than eighty seconds in twenty years. The new system also had to support "continuous operation"—that is, it had to keep running if a workstation or mainframe crashed, and it had to permit software updates even while the software was in use.

After seven torturous years of technical argument and litigation, IBM was finally hired as prime AAS contractor. But almost immediately things went awry. The company allowed its scores of programmers to work largely independently of one another, without adequate coordination. Technical problems, meanwhile, overwhelmed the FAA. It deluged IBM with changes in specifications as it laid plans for the perfect system and then abandoned these plans when they proved too ambitious.[30] As one engineer later said: "I think we were asking IBM to do things in the AAS system that actually violated the laws of physics." The contract with IBM eventually needed 290 changes, and the FAA's pile of documents listing system requirements was six meters high. To make matters worse, during this entire process the people who would be using the new equipment were not adequately consulted. "Mesmerized by the flood of detail," one observer wrote, "both contractor and customer failed to pay attention to how a more automated system would change the way an individual controller performs."[31] By the early 1990s, the project's anticipated cost had doubled to $7.6 billion (cost was rising as fast as expenditure), and the completion date was slipping three and a half weeks for every month of work. Finally, in 1994, the FAA administrator acknowledged that the project had become a monumental debacle and shut it down—wasting more than ten years of effort and $2 billion spent on software and equipment design.

But the problems didn't end there. In the place of the defunct project, the FAA introduced a scaled-down plan to replace screens and workstations in terminal air-traffic control stations across the country. By 1998, reports began to appear of design and software flaws in this project too, and in January 1999, only two months before the new equipment was to be deployed, the FAA announced an indefinite delay to boost the software's speed.

Meanwhile, the agency faced headaches on other fronts. It had to postpone its plan to use satellite signals to guide airplanes, in the face of widespread concern about such a system's resilience and vulnerability to sabotage. Writing the software, an administrator admitted, was "a much greater challenge than originally anticipated."[32] And, as January 1, 2000, approached, the FAA conceded that many of its aging mainframes might not be free of the Y2K bug. The manufacturer of the mainframes, IBM, announced that they should all be retired before the millennium. "IBM remains convinced," the company announced, "that the appropriate skills and tools do not exist to conduct a complete Year 2000 assessment."[33] Many date functions were buried deep in the computers' micro-code, some of which had been written in the early 1970s. Only two programmers familiar with the code were still around, and both were retired. Concerned that it couldn't replace the machines on time, the FAA hired one of the retired programmers to help find the Y2K bugs and rewrite the code.

Taken together, the FAA's difficulties are a sobering example of an ingenuity gap. Several factors had converged to raise the air-traffic system's ingenuity requirement, including the shortage of controllers, deregulation (which sharply boosted air traffic), and rapid changes in the computer and communication technologies used by airlines. The FAA was ill-equipped to supply this ingenuity: it was saddled with poor and inconstant leadership, reward systems that didn't encourage employees to be frank about problems with the AAS and its successor systems, and personnel procedures that made it difficult to hire the experts it needed. From the early 1980s, it lagged far behind events. "The agency has been outpaced by users of the system," noted one commentator. Its difficulties "raise the question of whether decade-long planning cycles, ideal for building roads and bridges, can accommodate the rapid changes in computer and communications systems that are the foundations of air-traffic control."[34]

Yet, amazingly, the air-traffic control system has so far remained exceedingly safe. It is an exemplar of what experts call a *high-reliability organization*. These are organizations that can carry out extraordinarily complex tasks quickly with few errors and almost no catastrophic failures.[35] In theory, such organizations shouldn't be possible. Yet high-reliability organizations maintain failure-free performance by investing a large slice of their resources in preventative planning and careful analysis of their mistakes (non-catastrophic though they may be). They also display certain common behaviors in their day-to-day operations. For example, during periods when the pace and complexity of decision-making are high, as in a control tower during heavy traffic hours, the norms of hierarchy are pushed aside. Authority shifts to front-line equipment operators, because superiors recognize they don't know enough about rapidly changing events to intervene effectively.[36]

During these periods, operators perform extraordinary feats of cognition. They construct and maintain in their minds a complex map of the events they are managing. This map, according to Gene Rochlin of Berkeley, "is not easily describable, even by controllers." A novice arriving in an air-traffic control room is overwhelmed by diverse information and cannot possibly make sense of what is happening. "The novice is totally incapable of forming any visual map of the reality that is represented. That is a very special and highly developed skill possessed only by trained operators. To them, the real airspace is being managed through mental images that reconstruct the three-dimensional sector airspace and all of its aircraft. The consoles are there to update and feed information to the operator, to keep the mental image fresh and accurate; they neither create nor directly represent it."[37]

In the combat-operations centers aboard ships of the U.S. Navy, operators say they "have the bubble" when they have successfully created a mental map of the flight paths, aerial tactics, and weapons use of the carrier-based fighters they are managing. The term likely derives from earlier days of fighting ships when weapons were aimed using an air bubble trapped in a tube of fluid, much like the tube in a standard carpenter's level. Now it indicates that operators have been able to accomplish the amazing feat of constructing and maintaining "the cognitive map that allows them to integrate such diverse inputs as combat status, information flows from sensors and remote observation, and the real-time status and performance of the various weapons and systems into a single picture of the ship's overall situation and operational status."[38] Operators face a constant risk of "losing the bubble," of having the comprehensible and predictable suddenly become opaque and bewildering. We've all had similar experiences at one time or other. We have found ourselves in a complex situation where we have suddenly "lost it"; one moment the scene makes sense, but the next it is totally unfamiliar.

Operators invest great cognitive effort to construct and maintain their complex mental maps, and they often rely on years of accumulated experiential knowledge. Unfortunately, efficiency-driven efforts to automate high-reliability systems, like the Federal Aviation Administration's AAS Program, tend to reduce the amount of experiential knowledge available. Again, in day-to-day operations, this may not matter much. But what if something unexpected happens? "For the operator in an emergency," Gene Rochlin contends, "deprived of experience, unsure of context, and pressed into action only when something has already gone wrong, with an overabundance of information and no mechanism for interpreting it, avoiding a mistake may be as much a matter of good luck as good training."[39] This problem is compounded if, as is common, automation is seen as a way of increasing the system's throughput, which in air-traffic operations means increasing traffic loads and density.

As our world becomes increasingly complex and fast-paced, we will need more high-reliability organizations to manage not only our air-traffic control systems, but also our communication and energy grids, our national and international financial systems, our military and security organizations, and our stressed ecological relations with nature. Yet as we try to improve the efficiency and performance of these systems, we tend to erode the very characteristics that make them highly reliable. And as these systems become more automated and complex and contain more unknown unknowns, we frequently don't understand them well enough to maintain their reliability.

In the end, we may come to rely more and more on luck to avoid serious failures of the complex systems that we have created and depend upon. This may not be as dangerous as it sounds. "The puzzling thing about accidents and especially large catastrophes is that they are so few," writes Charles Perrow, a Yale sociologist famed for his thinking about accidents in human-made systems. "It is hard to have just the right combination of system failures and environmental conditions to kill a lot of people in one blow. For this reason, countless risky systems successfully skirt disaster, skimping on safety and putting other interests first, while regulators fuss."[40] But in the final analysis Perrow's argument doesn't seem very reassuring: while luck may have often been our friend in the past, in a world of proliferating unknown unknowns, we would be grossly imprudent to assume it will always be there when we need it in the future.

PART THREE

Can We Supply

the Ingenuity

We Need?

BRAINS AND INGENUITY

T HE OFFICE where I write is well equipped. It's a large room, on the top story of a house, and has built-in file desks and cabinets, exten-sive bookshelves, a window, and a sealed skylight. It also has a fine, marble-trimmed fireplace and a number of pictures on the walls, including the one of the little girl from Bihar. It's a comfortable place—which is a good thing, because while writing this book I spend much of my life there.

My office is also a useful stage for a mildly amusing thought experi-ment about ingenuity (during those not infrequent moments when I'd rather be outside doing something else). I imagine that a nasty person has locked me inside the office and cut the phone line. I can't leave through the door, and the only window opens ten meters up in a sheer wall at the back of the house and faces directly onto the blank façade of another building, so I can't escape that way either. I could stand at the window and shout for help, but chances are no one would hear me. Somehow I have to signal my presence in the office to people on the street in front, so they can enter the house, open the door, and rescue me.

Inside my office I have certain raw materials or "resources." These include a large number of books, journals, and newspaper clippings; a thick pad of large sheets of white butcher paper on which I write chapter outlines; an assortment of pens, markers, paper clips, and sticky tape; my notebook computer; a cordless telephone; a desk lamp; a small compact disc player; various bits of electrical cord; a small table; and a long alu-minum pole with a special connection on the end that allows me to close the blind on the skylight. This is all I have at hand to signal the world outside. How can I save myself?

I see that the metal pole unscrews into several sections. I realize that I can unscrew it and reassemble the sections inside the fireplace and up the chimney. Then I could tape a sheet of butcher paper on one end of the pole with a large message on it saying that I'm trapped, push it up the chimney, and wave it vigorously enough that someone outside will notice. I gauge the length of the pole and then look up the chimney (trying to avoid getting a faceful of soot) to see if the pole is long enough. It looks like it is. I'm in luck!

There's a simple problem here in terms of ingenuity requirement and supply. I have a practical problem (I'm trapped in my office) from which arises a practical goal (to make contact with the outside world, alerting someone to my predicament). In the limited world of my office, I have certain physical things to work with—such as butcher paper, tape, and a pole—and I can apply my own labor to these things. I also have another, truly spectacular asset: a human brain. Like every other human being, I am equipped with the most sophisticated problem-solving device in the known universe. Once I set my brain to work on the task, it will produce a stream of immaterial ideas that can be thought of as discrete sets of instructions, almost like recipes, that tell me how I can combine and use the material things around me to achieve my goal. These ideas are just as important to the solution of my problem as the butcher paper, the pole, and my labor.

Now, assume that I'm able to draw up a list of all possible solutions to the problem I face. Each solution can be represented, again, by a discrete set of instructions—that is, a sequence of commands of the form "First, do X, then do Y, and finally, do Z." In turn, these various sets of instructions can be ranked according to their length: some solutions require that I carry out a fairly limited sequence of actions to combine and use the things in my office, and the corresponding set of instructions is therefore fairly short; others involve a much more elaborate sequence of actions, implying a much longer set of instructions.

Such sets of instructions are what I mean by "ingenuity." More elaborate solutions require longer and more complex sets of instructions. In turn, longer sets of instructions generally (but not always) represent more ingenuity. Simpler solutions require shorter sets of instructions that generally represent less ingenuity. I can therefore define the minimum *ingenuity requirement* to solve my problem as the amount of ingenuity represented by the shortest set of instructions on my list, which is the problem's simplest solution.

Let's say that putting a paper flag on the pole and waving it out of the chimney is the simplest solution to my problem. To escape my office, I must *supply* at least that much ingenuity, which means I must generate *and* implement the set of instructions for that particular solution. If I can't or don't, I experience an *ingenuity gap* between requirement and supply, and I stay in my office forever. But notice that supplying sufficient ingenuity is not just a matter of generating and implementing a set of instructions of a certain length. The set must also include the right instructions in the right order. It's not going to help, for instance, if I tape the butcher paper to the bottom end of the pole after I have put the pole up the chimney. Although the length of a solution's set of instructions is a crude but useful measure of the relative *quantity* of ingenuity required by the solution, it is not a good measure of the *quality* of that ingenuity. To measure quality, we must use other criteria.[1]

What happens if the problem I am facing becomes more difficult to solve? Maybe my nasty jailer starts adding layers of bricks to the top of the chimney to make it taller. Soon the chimney's length exceeds that of my aluminum pole. All is not lost, though, because the small table in my office has detachable legs that I can join to the bottom of the pole to make it longer. A tricky task: I need to figure out some splint-like arrangement— perhaps using stiff book covers, tape, and pen bodies—to join the segments together. As the chimney becomes taller, so the length of my set of instructions must increase, which means my ingenuity requirement rises. Eventually, the chimney becomes so tall that, no matter how ingenious I am, I cannot achieve my goal. No set of instructions, no matter how long or elaborate, can tell me how to combine the things in my office to signal my presence to the outside world. Essentially, my requirement for ingenuity has become infinite, while my supply, even though I've expanded it to the utmost of my ability, has reached its limit.

The amount of ingenuity we require to achieve a given goal depends critically on two things: first, the intrinsic difficulty of achieving the goal and, second, the kinds and amounts of resources that we have available and that we can manipulate to achieve the goal. As the goal becomes harder to achieve and resources more scarce and inappropriate, our requirement for ingenuity rises.[2]

We can see how our world is, in many ways, becoming more complex, fast-paced, and unpredictable. As a result, the problems we face are getting more complicated as well, and (as in my thought experiment), we need longer and more elaborate sets of instructions for technologies and institutions that can effectively solve them. Or, to put it in terms of complexity theory: the greater complexity of our world requires greater complexity in our technologies and institutions. As the American complexity theorist Yaneer Bar-Yam writes, "We must understand that . . . human systems exist within an environment that places demands upon them. If the complexity of these demands exceeds the complexity of a system, the system will fail. Thus, those systems that survive must have a complexity sufficiently large to respond to the complexity of environmental demands."[3]

The human brain is the ultimate source of the ideas, ingenuity, and sets of instructions we need to cope with this greater complexity. And it is, itself, a vastly complex system. Through a sophisticated set of senses, the brain receives a flood of information about the body's internal state and its external environment. It interprets this information and commands appropriate responses. Although we think of the brain primarily in terms of its role in conscious thought and decision, it also handles a wide array of routine and unconscious tasks, from guiding motor activity to regulating visceral, endocrine, and somatic functions.[4]

This amazing information-processing machine consists of a dense and intricate network of tens of billions of discrete nerve cells or "neurons."[5] Each neuron has a cell body that receives signals from other neurons through an array of slender filaments called dendrites; it can send its own signal down a long, thin projection, called an axon, that connects with the dendrites or cell bodies of other neurons. Although most neurons' cell bodies are tiny, averaging between 0.01 and 0.05 millimeters in diameter (it would take between forty and two hundred of them in a row to add up to the diameter of an unsharpened pencil lead) their axons range from a few thousandths of a millimeter up to a meter in length.[6] The most impressive fact about the brain is not, however, the number of neurons we have packed into our skulls, or the size of these neurons, but the number of connections or "synapses" among them, currently thought to be close to 100 trillion. A single neuron can, in fact, have tens of thousands of synaptic connections to other cells. These synapses are key to the brain's computational and information-processing power—they help the brain store the knowledge, make the decisions, and generate the ingenuity that helps us survive and prosper.

Despite its complexity and astonishing capabilities, the brain is a small organ relative to the human body: it weighs only about 1.4 kilograms, or about 2 percent of a person's total mass. All the same, the human brain is about six times larger than we would expect for mammals of our size, which ranks us at the top of the list of vertebrates, along with the dolphins, in terms of relative brain size.[7] And this nervous system is resource-hungry, consuming about 20 percent of the body's oxygen and energy.

From the point of view of generating ingenuity, it appears that the *cerebral cortex* is the brain's most important region. This outermost layer of the brain's wrinkled surface seems to be where our capacity for creativity, novel associations, and improvised solutions resides. At first glance, though, the cerebral cortex doesn't seem to deserve such plaudits: it is just two millimeters thick and, flattened out, would cover just four sheets of standard typing paper. But under each square millimeter of this sheet's surface are an astounding 148,000 neurons—totaling some 14 billion neurons in all—connected in perplexing ways to each other and to distant regions of the brain. Neuroscientists are just beginning to understand how these cells work together. But they do know that the size and complexity of the cerebral cortex is a distinguishing characteristic of human beings. The flattened cerebral cortex of a chimpanzee (our closest living relative among the primates) would cover only a single sheet of typing paper, and a rat's would barely cover a stamp.[8]

The human brain is the product of millions of years of evolution that took place in ecological circumstances different from those around us today. Experts differ sharply over what imprint these circumstances left behind. But there are compelling reasons to believe that the deep past endowed the brain with characteristics that powerfully shape our ability to respond to modern challenges.

Perhaps the most salient of these characteristics is the brain's sheer versatility. William Calvin, an American theoretical neurobiologist whose interests branch into evolution, the origins of language, and climate change, has identified a cluster of defining features of human intelligence. These include imagination, the use of symbols and language, the capacity to engage in multistage planning, and a broad base of knowledge from which to draw solutions. At the top of Calvin's list, though, is our extraordinary ability to improvise in novel situations, to "guess well" when confronted by unexpected circumstances. "The best indicators of intelligence," Calvin writes, "may be found in . . . those rare or novel situations for which evolution has not provided a standard response, so that the animal has to improvise, using its intellectual wherewithal." Intelligence, he goes on, "implies flexibility and creativity—in the words of the ethologists James and Carol Gould, an 'ability to slip the bonds of instinct and generate novel solutions to problems.'"[9]

Where does the human brain's versatility come from? It's actually quite unusual in nature. When faced with the brutal pressures of evolutionary competition, most species survive not by generalizing—that is, by doing many things well—but by specializing. They exploit, ever more efficiently, a relatively narrow ecological niche. Specialization gives the species a competitive advantage in that niche, but also makes it less versatile and flexible and thus more vulnerable to changes in its environment. Human evolution evidently did not follow this standard route. We are exemplars of generalists: we can eat a wide variety of foods; we can thrive in a wide range of climates; and we have an astonishing ability to produce the things we need to survive from materials at hand.

The evolution of this generalist took place over a period of 6 million years, beginning with an animal roughly like today's chimpanzee and ending with the arrival of *Homo sapiens sapiens*, somewhere around 100,000 years ago. The last 4 million years have seen between eight and thirteen distinct species of bipedal hominids, of which maybe four were part of the direct line of descent leading to modern humans.[10] In other words, the long and twisting evolutionary route that produced us included a lot of dead ends. In the last 2 million years of this period, the adult hominid brain more than tripled in volume, from about 400 to 1,400 cubic centimeters (cc). This growth occurred in two bursts: the first, from 400 to about 900 cc, took place between 2.0 and 1.5 million years ago; and the second, from 900 to 1,400 cc, happened between 700,000 and 100,000 years ago (shown in the illustration opposite). Some of this growth was associated with an increase in the overall body size of evolving hominids (larger animals tend to have larger brains). But the second spurt—a surge of around 50 percent in brain volume—was unrelated to changes in body size and was therefore largely dedicated to increased cognitive function.

Something happened during the last two million years—a period that encompasses what experts call the Pleistocene epoch from 1.8 million to

Hominid Brain Volume Has Expanded in Two Bursts

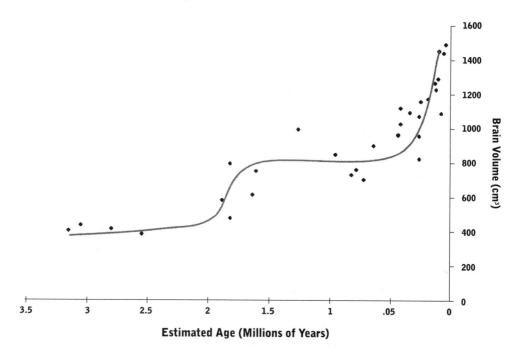

Note: Each data point on this graph represents a specific skull from which brain volume has been estimated. The line drawn through the points illustrates only one possible interpretation of the path of hominid brain growth.

10,000 years ago—to drive the growth of the hominid brain. Some powerful evolutionary pressure selected for the ferocious intellectual powers that modern humans deploy. The orthodox explanation, first proposed by Charles Darwin and named the *savanna hypothesis*, focuses on the shrinking of the forests in Africa caused by the climate's cooling and drying around the beginning of the Pleistocene. As vast tracts of savanna opened up, early hominids were forced to descend from the trees and survive on the plains. Eventually they evolved to walk on two feet, eat meat, use language, and make tools and weapons to feed and defend themselves. Brain expansion accompanied the evolution of this tightly integrated set of characteristics common to modern human beings.

The transition from life in trees to life on the savanna required us to stand on two feet, possibly to reduce the thermal stress produced by long periods in the sun.[11] Bipedalism, in turn, set in motion a cascade of consequences that aided and encouraged brain growth. For example, it allowed hominids to carry tools over long distances and to scavenge carcasses of game during hot periods of the day when carnivores sought shade. Because meat has a higher density of nutrition and energy than vegetable matter and is more easily digested (which is why some plant-eaters, like cows, have multiple stomachs), hominids were able to evolve a smaller gut and reduce the energy they needed for digestion. This metabolic energy was then available to support an enlarged and energy-hungry brain.[12]

The savanna hypothesis might explain the first spurt of brain growth, but can it explain the second, which was unrelated to changes in body size or stance? Paleoanthropologists have generally assumed that, following the hominids' shift from forest trees to the savanna plains, the natural environment—the climate, vegetation, and the like—stayed relatively stable in its overall characteristics, maintaining a relatively constant evolutionary pressure on hominids. Indeed, most hypotheses regarding brain growth are underwritten by this key, but often tacit, assumption of environmental stability. It raises a problem, however: a stable environment cannot be used to explain one of the most distinctive features of the advanced hominids that evolved in the last million years—that they are large-brained generalists. Such an environment tends to produce specialists, because in a stable environment species have time to exploit and occupy available ecological niches. Over time, these specialists prosper, and generalists are disadvantaged.

Experts have proposed several ways that large-brained generalists could evolve despite a relatively stable savanna environment. Perhaps savanna life produced an "evolutionary arms race" between hominids and competing species that encouraged brain growth.[13] Maybe selection pressure arose from the complex interpersonal challenges of hominid social life—such as negotiating divisions of resources, creating alliances, and manipulating potential enemies.[14] Or possibly hominids needed larger brains to calculate and sequence the ballistic hand movements needed to throw rocks at prey.[15]

More recently, however, some scientists, in particular the paleoanthropologist Rick Potts, Director of Human Origins at the National Museum of Natural History in Washington, D.C., have suggested that the environment in which hominids evolved was *not* stable. Careful study of sedimentary clays, fossilized pollens, and other evidence indicates that the mid- to late-Pleistocene—from about 700,000 years ago till the appearance, some

600,000 years later, of *Homo sapiens sapiens*—was also a period of extreme climate variability. It was a time of ice ages, of alternating warm and cold intervals when immense ice sheets repeatedly invaded the middle latitudes of North America and Eurasia. Earth's crust was depressed under the burden of ice; sea level fluctuated wildly as glaciers and ice caps sucked water from the oceans; and huge lakes formed and then vanished in normally dry areas. This variability, which may have been triggered by the kind of non-linear shift in Atlantic currents described by Wally Broecker, affected the climate around the planet, including the tropics. Distant reaches of Africa saw sharp changes in average temperature, the availability of water, and in the dominant species of plants and animals. In fact, the environmental fluctuations during this period were some of the most rapid and severe since the time of the dinosaurs, 64 million years before.[16]

Organisms—human and otherwise—can respond in two general ways to such sharp fluctuations: they can migrate to places offering more familiar and favorable environments, or they can stay in the same place and evolve generalist strategies for survival, strategies that allow them to thrive in a wider range of conditions. They might, for instance, evolve physical attributes that permit them to eat a broader diet or survive in extreme temperatures; they might adopt behaviors that promote greater sharing of resources among community members; or they might develop the cognitive ability to invent tools that buffer them against the vagaries of their surrounding environment.

Rick Potts argues that the rapid growth of the human brain aided such generalist responses to severe environmental turbulence. "Each major shift in global climate created unfamiliar rearrangements of water, food, and other resources," he notes. Hominids with larger brains that could remember and interpret huge amounts of environmental data were better equipped to respond to environmental change. Eventually, our direct ancestors came to rely on more than just large memories: they also evolved the mental and social means to generate novel responses to their surroundings and to crises—a real advantage in an unstable environment. "The shifting, unforeshadowed settings of the Pleistocene favored faculties sensitive to environmental change and capable of stabilizing human needs," Potts writes. "During hominid evolution, the mental, social, and ecological paradigms of our early ancestors were altered in ways that heightened the flexibility of response, the reading of environmental nuance, and the heterogeneity of behavior."[17] As Yaneer Bar-Yam suggests, the human system (in this case, the hominid brain) developed a level of complexity commensurate with the complexity of the environmental demands placed upon it.[18]

But the environment was not always fluctuating and harsh during the mid- to late-Pleistocene. There were long periods when it was relatively benign. At these times, hominid populations expanded, and their genetic diversity increased. Hominids with new combinations of genes—combinations that produced novel physical characteristics and behaviors—were more likely to survive to reproductive age. Then, often with little warning, the environment would turn unforgiving again. Evolution's grim process of selection would start afresh, and those genetic strains that were least fit in the new environment would die off. But because the selection process was operating on a more diverse gene pool, there was a higher likelihood that some of the new substrains would be better adapted to the changed environment. So these boom-and-bust cycles permitted rapid evolution of hominid genomes.[19]

"In the surviving species," Rick Potts concludes, greater cognitive capability and behavioral versatility "ultimately blossomed into symbolic coding, complex institutions, cultural diversity, technological innovation, human occupation of Earth's diverse biomes, an ability to recover from disturbance and grow by colonization, a greater awareness of self and of external factors, and the tendency to buffer environmental disruption by altering immediate surroundings."[20]

The evidence pieced together by Rick Potts suggests that a highly variable natural environment encouraged the second burst of hominid brain growth. By 100,000 years ago, Earth was home to several species of hominid, including archaic *Homo sapiens*, the Neanderthals, and *Homo sapiens sapiens* (often called, by experts, "anatomically modern humans"). Archaic *Homo sapiens* disappeared shortly thereafter, while Neanderthals survived for another 70,000 years. These various species probably encountered each other, and they may have even produced hybrids, but the archaeological record does not yet give a clear picture of the nature of their relationship.[21]

Both Neanderthals and *Homo sapiens sapiens* had very large brains; in fact, with a volume between 1,200 and 1,750 cc the average Neanderthal brain may have been slightly larger than the modern human's. Neanderthals were stout and very strong, with bodies adapted to the harsh climates of ice-age Europe and the Near East. Survival depended on a sophisticated ability to live in relatively large and complex social groups; to map their geographic domains in their minds; to identify the locations of resources, animals, and cave shelters; and to read the signs of nature around them.

There seems little doubt that Neanderthals used some form of spoken language.[22] They were also adept tool-makers, being apparently the first hominids to haft a sharpened stone onto a wooden shaft to make a thrusting spear. And they developed a method of fashioning stone points, called the Levallois technique, that demanded great cognitive skill. The maker of a Levallois point had to be able to visualize the intersection of multiple planes within a suitable piece of rock, plan a complex sequence of blows to produce the right fractures, and adjust the plan as the sequence unfolded and revealed new information about the nature of the rock. "Even today," says archaeologist Brian Hayden, "there are few students of lithic technology that ever achieve a Neanderthal's level of expertise in producing good Levallois cores or flakes, while the number of contemporary flint knappers that have successfully mastered the technique for producing good Levallois points probably number less than a score."[23]

Nevertheless, the archaeological record indicates that the Neanderthal mind was very different from that of modern humans. Despite their evident skill in making and using stone points, their tools remained very simple, rarely combining more than one or two components, varying little in form, and never incorporating bone, antler, or ivory. Moreover, Neanderthals apparently had little art or religion; and they seemed not to decorate their bodies or engage in ritualized burial.[24] In many respects, despite their brain size, Neanderthals seem strangely rigid and uncreative.

In his brilliant book *The Prehistory of the Mind*, the British archaeologist Steven Mithen explores the differences between the Neanderthal and the modern human mind. Drawing on the new fields of evolutionary psychology and what he calls *cognitive archaeology*, he develops a compelling theory of how the hominid mind evolved, from the early australopithecines of Africa to today's *Homo sapiens sapiens*.[25] He begins with a central thesis of evolutionary psychologists: in response to its natural and social environment, the hominid mind developed specialized cognitive capabilities to deal with certain common problems. These specialized capabilities— often called *modules, cognitive domains*, or *intelligences* by experts—allowed hominids to interpret their surroundings quickly and with a minimum of error. They were not necessarily located in any specific region of the brain, but were rather emergent properties of the joint operation of many regions. They were also rich in content; that is, they contained a lot of innate or hard-wired knowledge about the Pleistocene world, knowledge that enabled young hominids to learn the essential features of their environment very fast.[26]

In line with the current thinking of leading evolutionary psychologists, Steven Mithen suggests that hominids evolved four specialized capabilities in particular: a *technical intelligence* that incorporated a basic understanding of principles governing their physical reality—like solidity, gravity, and inertia—and helped hominids make tools and predict events in their physical world; a *natural history intelligence* that helped them identify and categorize plants and animals; a *social intelligence* that helped them interpret social arrangements in their complex communities; and a *linguistic intelligence* that allowed them to use symbols referring to the external natural and social worlds. These intelligences can still be identified within the modern human mind, although some are little more than vestigial remnants.[27] They are most easily seen in the learning behavior of young children. Mithen notes that "there is a mass of ever-accumulating data from developmental psychology that children are indeed born with a great deal of information about the world hard-wired into their minds."[28]

But the evolutionary psychologists' model cannot be a complete account of the human mind, Mithen continues, because our knowledge and thought are not as severely compartmentalized as the model implies. In fact, he points out, one of the most striking things about our minds is our capacity for analogy and metaphor—two cognitive tools among the most powerful in our mental armory. The abilities to see similarities among diverse things and combine ideas from different domains are essential elements of human creativity. Knowledge flows back and forth abundantly between our vestigial intelligences: if we want, we can think of animals as people, of people as physical things, and of physical things as living beings. Mithen labels this remarkable ability *cognitive fluidity*. "When thoughts originating in different domains can engage together," he writes, "the result is an almost limitless capacity for imagination."[29]

The modern human mind's obvious flexibility has led some experts to reject the evolutionary psychologists' argument that it is powerfully shaped by its evolutionary heritage. The mind is not made up of a cluster of genetically programmed specialized intelligences, they say. Rather, it is a single, extraordinarily flexible, general-purpose problem solver—much like an extremely powerful computer—whose behavior is almost entirely determined by inputs from its environment.

The debate between these two camps has at times been bitter.[30] But Steven Mithen's theory of hominid evolution suggests how they might be brought together. Building on archaeological evidence of hominid tool-making, hunting, and habitation, he argues that the early hominid, australopithecines, who lived between 4 and 2 million years ago, had a brain that consisted of a general-purpose problem solver and a social intelligence module, both relatively sophisticated. With *Homo erectus* (from 1.8 million to 300,000 years ago) and especially with the Neanderthals (from about 200,000 to 30,000 years ago), evolution added natural history, technical, and linguistic intelligences to this core. The linguistic and social intelligences worked together—indeed, language may have evolved to communicate social knowledge—but the other dedicated intelligences operated largely in isolation from each other. There were, in a sense, cognitive walls between them, and these walls probably explain the odd rigidity of the Neanderthal mind.

Little changed when *Homo sapiens sapiens* first arrived, about 100,000 years ago. The new hominids made some bone tools and engaged in slightly more ritualized burial, but otherwise they behaved similarly to their predecessors and to their contemporaries, the Neanderthals. But around 60,000 years ago something startling happened: the archaeological record shows an explosion of art, ritual, and complex tool-making. This, Steven Mithen contends, is the first evidence of full communication among the various intelligences within the hominid mind. The vehicle for that mind, the hominid brain, hadn't become any bigger—its last burst of growth had concluded tens of thousands of years before. But suddenly we see the lineaments of modern human thought—its creativity, its flexibility, and its extraordinary ingenuity. "A cognitive fluidity arose within the mind," he argues, "reflecting new connections rather than new processing power. And consequently this mental transformation occurred with no increase in brain size."[31]

How did this extraordinary thing happen? Drawing on the work of the cognitive scientist Dan Sperber, Mithen speculates that some hominids began to use their language to talk about things beyond the social world— "nonsocial" things like animal behavior and the technical problems of tool-making. These "talkative individuals" gained an evolutionary advantage because they could use language to learn about, communicate, and put to use the non-social knowledge of other individuals, rather than simply rely-ing on observations of their behavior.[32] In the process, they imported, bit by bit, snippets of nonsocial knowledge into their social-intelligence mod-ule. Gradually this module became a clearing house for ideas from other modules and for new ideas and knowledge that couldn't easily fit anywhere else.[33] It became a place where creative combinations could arise.

The change in the social-intelligence module's role was propelled by the development of consciousness—an awareness of self in time and place that probably arose fairly late in hominid evolution. Some experts believe that consciousness originally evolved to help hominids predict the behavior of other members of their community. Later, Mithen argues, consciousness was adapted to manage "a mental database of information relating to all domains of behavior."[34] The joint operation of language and consciousness in the central clearinghouse of the social-intelligence mod-ule allowed the hominid mind to produce recursive, or self-referential, "metarepresentations" of the world—that is, concepts of concepts and symbols representing symbols—causing an explosion of conceptual nov-elty and creative power. Language was extended to many domains of human intelligence and experience, it became a medium for metaphor and analogy, and it enabled early humans to refer to things beyond their immediate senses, allowing their imaginations to transcend space and time.

According to this theory, then, and in some contrast to Rick Potts's argument above, the most striking features of the modern human mind—its versatility, capacity to improvise, and generalized ability—developed circuitously. The brain's evolution followed an oscillating path, from a largely generalized intelligence 4 million years ago, to the specialized intelligences of archaic *Homo sapiens* prior to 100,000 years ago, and finally back again to the far more powerful generalized intelligence of today's modern humans.[35] This path was marked by several nonlinearities, includ-ing two surges in brain volume and, around 60,000 years ago, a sharp change in the interrelationships of the mind's parts. At that time, the mind jumped from being a cluster of specialized intelligences, which were largely compartmentalized and separated from each other, to a highly flex-ible and powerful generalized problem solver, within which the specialized intelligences still operated as subcomponents.

Steven Mithen writes that our cognitive fluidity—which is exemplified by our capacity for analogy and metaphor—is "the defining property of the modern mind."[36] Its arrival opened up enormous possibilities for human development. But perhaps most important, it permitted a type of rapid, nonbiological evolution—*cultural evolution*—that further helped hominid societies adapt to diverse and changing circumstances.

Culture is an amorphous concept at best, but the scholars Robert Boyd and Peter Richerson provide the definition I've found most succinct and useful: according to them, culture is "information—skills, attitudes, beliefs, values—capable of affecting individuals' behavior, which they acquire from others by teaching, imitation, and other forms of social learning."[37] By this definition, the sets of instructions that I call "ingenuity" are often key components of a society's culture. And the transmission of these sets of instructions from one generation to the next, as well as their slow evolution over time, is an important part of my story about ingenuity supply. A society's ability to solve its everyday problems critically depends upon the amount and quality of knowledge it has received from previous generations; the society then adjusts, fine-tunes, and passes this accumulated knowledge to posterity. So culture is a bit like a pipeline carrying knowledge from the past into the future.

But how, actually, is culture transmitted, and how does it evolve over time? Robert Boyd and Peter Richerson give us a powerful theory.[38] They argue, very much in the manner of Rick Potts and Steven Mithen, that the social and physical environment in which hominids evolved was highly complex. Individual hominids, despite their large brains, could not adequately sort and assess the bewildering amount of information they received. And, since a decision based on a mistaken interpretation of the environment could be fatal, they had little room to learn by trial and error. They were better off imitating the behavior of other, usually older members of their group, because these members had more experience and had already shown that they could survive. The result was an evolutionary pressure that favored hominids endowed with the cognitive capacity to communicate information from one generation to the next. Individuals who could learn this way disproportionately survived to reproduction age and were able to pass to their offspring the genes for this capacity.

In modern human societies cultural communication from one generation to the next occurs not only from parents to children but also from other adults to children. And parents and other adults, taken together, usually embody a fairly wide range of different cultural "models" (or sets of interrelated skills, attitudes, beliefs, and values).[39] If children simply imitate their parents, the process of cultural selection is "unbiased," and the range of cultural models in the society will tend to remain the same. If, on the other hand, children adopt cultural models other than those of their parents, the process of cultural selection is "biased." In this case, the range of society's cultural models, and as a result the character of the society's overall culture, will gradually change—in fact, it will often converge to a smaller number of favored cultural models. So, for example, if significant numbers of young people adopt the cultural model of their society's high-status members (a model that incorporates, say, certain styles of fashion and attitudes towards work and leisure), then the society's overall culture will slowly shift in the direction of that high-status model. After extensive research, however, Boyd and Richerson conclude that cultural transmission in our societies is only weakly biased: in other words, most people get most of their cultural information directly from their parents. Still, they point out, even weakly biased cultural transmission can produce big changes in culture, given enough time.

There's another interesting way to think about cultural change. The evolutionary theorist Richard Dawkins draws a close analogy between biological and cultural evolution. He proposes that chunks of information—from tunes and catchphrases to ideas for making things, growing food, and curing illness—are themselves self-replicating entities, just like genes. These chunks of information, or *memes* as Dawkins calls them, inhabit our brains; and they use our brains as vehicles, he argues, to spread from one brain to another, very much the way viruses propagate by exploiting the genetic machinery of their host cells. As memes are thereby communicated, copied, and combined, they mutate. On top of this, memes must compete with each other for brain resources, because our brains have limited memory and processing power. In this competition, those memes with features that favor survival and propagation tend to become widespread in the general population of brains. For example, Dawkins, who is intensely anti-religious, argues that the meme of faith, an idea central to most religions, tends to be self-perpetuating because it unconsciously discourages the rational inquiry that could lead people to reject that very meme.[40]

Dawkins' theory of memes is intriguing, and it's controversial. It downplays the role of human creativity, because it emphasizes the roles of random mutation and impersonal selection processes in the evolution of ideas.

In other words, memes, rather than our creative brains, become the agents of change. "A complex meme does not arise from the retention of copying errors," argues one critic, the cognitive psychologist Steven Pinker. "It arises because some person knuckles down, racks his brain, musters his ingenuity, and composes or writes or paints or invents something."[41] I believe there's real merit to this criticism. All the same, the meme theory shows us how some ideas, including perhaps important bits of ingenuity, can develop and persist in our societies without much conscious creativity and direction by human beings.

One way or another, all these theories—by Potts, Mithen, Boyd, Richerson, and Dawkins—give us fascinating glimpses of the evolution of the modern human brain, and they say much about the brain's ability to supply the ingenuity we need to adapt to complex and rapidly changing conditions. Its multiple intelligences, its cognitive fluidity, and its capacity for cultural evolution are remarkable endowments left us by our Pleistocene forebears.

We evolved in a period of environmental turbulence, when little was certain or stable. Each of us has, inside each of the countless cells in our bodies, genes from those unknown hominids who scavenged across the fluctuating African savanna and eventually migrated around the planet. These genes guide the growth and development of each of our brains, and our brains give us our unparalleled power to loosen our ties to specific environments and habitats and strike out for new territory.

For Rick Potts, the message from the Pleistocene is a message of optimism—one that rings out like a clarion call: "The strange buoyancy of the hominids is in us, a hopeful heritage of response to novel environmental dilemmas," he declares. "Our genetic blueprint enables our brains and societies to live creatively in an uncertain world."[42]

Flash forward hundreds of thousands of years from the Pleistocene savanna to early December 1993.

I'm in a grubby office building in the southern outskirts of New Delhi, waiting to see the Indian minister of state for the environment. After an hour's delay, an aide hustles me into his office. The room is huge but shabby—like the building—with an overlay of opulence that befits the minister's status. The walls are panelled with hardwood veneer, the dirt-brown wall-to-wall carpet is rippled and worn, and the only decorations are faded poster-size photographs of India's endangered flora and fauna. The minister, fiftyish with bushy dark hair, stands up behind his desk and thrusts his hand out to greet me. He radiates energy.

It has taken three months to schedule this half-hour meeting, so I'm well prepared. We sit down and I quickly explain that I'm in India to study whether scarcities of water and cropland lead to violence, and I ask for his support and advice. An assistant creeps shyly from a side room, placing a document in front of him to sign. With this duty dispatched the phone rings, and the minister is lost in an animated conversation in Hindi. A few minutes later, the phone rings again. Then another assistant appears, wanting information.

During these interruptions my eyes wander the office. The desk in front of me is a good three meters long, and at one end, taking up a third of its surface, are tall stacks of file folders, each as thick as my hand. There are more than one hundred folders in all, perhaps half a cubic meter of paper, I calculate.

My half hour is soon up, yielding only a dozen minutes of useful conversation. As I rise to leave, I glance at the file folders. "You have quite a bit of work there," I remark.

"Yes," he answers, exasperated, "that's today's work."

The minister's brain, with its array of cognitive tools adapted for hominid life in the late Pleistocene, was clearly not up to the task confronting him that day on his desk. Even allowing for the inefficiencies and clutter of the Indian bureaucracy—a bureaucracy that generates more than its share of useless paperwork—the issues and problems were piling up faster than he or his staff could solve them. They faced an ingenuity gap.

Most of us are familiar with this situation. Working in modern business, academic, or government offices, we are perpetually swamped under a tidal wave of incoming information. In the last twenty-five years, word processing technologies have probably doubled the average writer's output of memos, reports, articles, and books. Not only can people generate more information faster, they can now deliver this information through many more conduits. Twenty-five years ago most offices received information in only three ways: by speech, mail, and phone (with messages often taken by a secretary). Today, offices get information through at least three more conduits: fax, voice mail (which has largely replaced secretaries), and the Internet (including e-mail and the Web). And in their short lifetimes, the delivery capacities of these new technologies have leapt upwards. An average voice mailbox can now receive and hold dozens of long messages; e-mail accounts often stack up hundreds of letters a day; and lobbyists, corporations, and nongovernmental organizations regularly blast-fax thousands of people at a time.

More information plus more conduits plus greater capacity per conduit equals inundation—which is how most of us feel much of the time: inundated, drowning in information. Decisions have to be made faster, because transmission times have been reduced. The result is that we flit from task to task like the Indian minister of the environment, desperately trying to sort and answer incoming messages and scrambling to deal with the issues they raise. On one hand, the requirement for ingenuity steadily climbs: we need a higher quantity and rate of delivery of good problem-solving ideas. On the other hand, our capacity to generate and deliver ingenuity drops. An average person in our modern information economy spends ever more time on basic tasks of managing information, and ever less time producing creative ideas and truly useful knowledge.

This *info-glut*, as many experts now label it, is not just a problem in our daily lives; it has implications for our well-being generally. Most of the critical challenges humanity faces can be addressed only by combining knowledge from many disciplines. Yet information management problems are particularly acute in highly interdisciplinary fields.

I experienced these problems myself in the mid-1990s, when I hired a team of researchers to investigate the links between environmental stress and political instability. As our work moved forward over the months, we found ourselves sitting at the convergence point of multiple streams of books, academic papers, statistical data, and computer documents produced by at least a dozen disciplines, from economics and demography to soil science and forest ecology. As this material filled our computers, piled up on our desks, and overflowed from boxes and filing cabinets crammed into our offices, a stark truth presented itself to my mind: the problem in our information economy is no longer information delivery—we've solved that problem with multiple information conduits and extraordinarily high capacity per conduit. The problem is the interface between the material in our computers and desks and our cerebral cortexes. The critical bottleneck is cognitive; we simply can't shove information into our brains fast enough and cognitively process it fast enough to keep up with the speed of delivery.

Technological optimists and other fans of the communications revolution would probably upbraid me for a lack of faith. For them, the greatly increased flow of information is an unalloyed boon: as the world is linked together by satellite telephones, fax machines, and the Internet, our individual brains are connected into one vast network. Through this network, we can borrow from an enormous global store of ideas generated by other people's brains, and we can create synergistic combinations of what were previously discrete ideas; through this network, too, we can generate and distribute many more of the sets of instructions, or ingenuity, that we need to solve our problems.

But our day-to-day personal experience, whether in government bureaus in India or in corporate offices in the West, is something we ignore at our peril. It suggests that the present story is more complicated than optimists claim: that for every contribution to the supply of ingenuity we gain from a new link between people or between ideas, we may lose ingenuity because of the complexity, pressure, and pace of our information-glutted world. In the end, we may be inexorably exchanging the peace and quiet needed to generate high-quality ingenuity for the adrenaline-charged hyperactivity produced by waves of low-quality data.

Thirty years ago, Alvin Toffler tackled the problems of information glut and cognitive overload in his famous book *Future Shock*, and in the late 1990s, David Shenk extended the argument in *Data Smog*.[43] But underlying these discussions is the infrequently acknowledged, more encompassing worry that human beings have created circumstances—from the info-glut in our offices to financial crises that flash around the world in the blink of an eye—whose complexity, unpredictability, and pace exceed the cognitive abilities of the human brain. That extraordinary endowment of mental creativity and fluidity given us by our Pleistocene ancestors may be no match for the challenges of the world we have created for ourselves.[44]

Some interesting evidence in the field of paleoanthropology supports the claim that our brains are not equal to modern demands. The anthropologist Robin Dunbar tested the hypothesis that brain growth was stimulated by the demands of social interactions within groups. Working with living primates, he found a statistical relationship between the average size of the neocortex of a primate species and the average size of that species' social group (defined as the set of other members of the species that an individual knows socially and is able to monitor successfully).[45] Extrapolating backwards, he and his colleague Leslie Aiello then predicted the average size of hominid social groups from the size of their brains. By their estimates, the australopithecines who roamed Africa three million years ago had, on average, the capacity for social knowledge of 67 other members of their species. Over time, the size of the social group increased: *Homo habilis*, about a million years later, had a brain large enough to permit social knowledge of 82 others; *Homo erectus* of 111; Neanderthals of 144; and modern humans of 150.[46]

A capacity to monitor 150 other people was probably quite satisfactory for most human beings until the twentieth century. But today's information technologies have extended our reach to a far vaster community—indeed, the community is, for all intents and purposes, infinitely large. And there's an implicit expectation that we should be able to smoothly manage our complex interactions with all the members of this community. Given our evolutionary heritage, it's not surprising that most of us fail to live up to this challenge. It's not surprising, either, to hear that the rising incidence of depression and other anxiety-related mental illnesses in our societies may be partly caused by this failure.[47]

Yaneer Bar-Yam, the American complexity theorist, uses very different evidence to reach much the same conclusion. He argues that the level of complexity of modern human society has recently overtaken the complexity of any one person belonging to it (see the chapter "Complexities"). But our individual complexity, as we've seen above, serves an important function: it helps us adapt to changes in our circumstances, because it gives us a wider repertoire of responses to those changes. "The degree of complexity of the individual," Bar-Yam asserts, "reflects the extent to which independent responses can be made to distinct conditions." So as modern human society becomes more complex than we are individually, it begins to exceed our adaptive ability. In effect, we have too short a repertoire of responses to adjust effectively to our changing circumstances. As a result, we try to simplify our social environment by limiting our exposure to it in various ways. In our everyday lives, for example, we retreat into tightly bounded subcommunities, and in our work we specialize in narrow subprofessions. But another result is an increased sense of insecurity. For many, Yaneer Bar-Yam concludes, the inability "to develop an effective set of responses to the environment will lead to frustration. Indeed, such frustration has become widespread."[48]

It's likely that you've often heard people draw an analogy between the human brain and modern computers. Both are information-processing machines, they say; the only real difference is the materials they are made of. But the truth is that metals, plastics, and silicon enable computers to process information far faster and with far more raw power than the biological materials of the human brain. The nerves of our body carry information along their axons in the form of electrical impulses, and transmission between nerves occurs through the diffusion of chemicals across their synapses. Depending on the type of nerve fiber, transmission speeds range from 0.5 to 160 meters per second, compared to hundreds of *millions* of meters per second through human-made electrical circuits.[49] And, although huge amounts of information can pass into the brain through its sensory pathways—vision, hearing, touch, and the like—very little of it can be processed at any one time. The optic nerve has a potential transmission capacity of 400 million bits of information a second, which is about the amount of information in fifty copies of this book; but peak processing rates within the brain (measured in tasks like piano-playing or reading random words) average around twenty to twenty-five bits per second, which is little more than the information contained in the last three letters of this word.[50]

The brain is also surprisingly limited in its ability to discriminate between stimuli within one category of stimulus: when people listen to a sequence of different pitches of musical tones, for instance, most can accurately distinguish only five or six. Results are—remarkably—similar for loudness of sound, brightness of light, hue of color, taste, touch, and the length, direction, and curvature of lines. This led the psychologist George Miller to argue, in a famous 1956 article, that the human brain has an identifiable *channel capacity* or "upper limit." In general, he showed, people can distinguish a maximum of about seven alternatives within a given category of stimulus.[51]

These are pretty severe information-processing constraints. One might reasonably wonder how we could even read a sentence at reasonable speed, let alone survive in an information-inundated world. To cope, the brain has evolved a range of rough-and-ready techniques for speeding information processing and decision-making.[52] Basically, it searches out and identifies patterns in its environment and stores records of these patterns; this way, it can respond more quickly when it perceives the patterns again. It combines information into chunks, and then combines these chunks into further chunks. Language itself is a good example of this "chunking" process:

phonemes are combined into letters, letters into words, and words into phrases that can be handled as whole units. The brain also adopts various rules of thumb, or heuristics, for reaching decisions. For example, when confronted with a complex problem, it usually accepts the first satisfactory solution that it finds, rather than searching for the best of all solutions (a heuristic called "satisficing"). And to overcome the limits of its channel capacity, the brain uses multiple dimensions of comparison to distinguish among stimuli, rather than just one. That means it distinguishes among sounds, for instance, not only by their pitch but also by their loudness, duration, and location in space. Given what we know about the Pleistocene environment, this approach makes sense. As George Miller writes, "In order to survive in a constantly fluctuating world, it was better to have a little information about a lot of things than to have a lot of information about a small segment of the environment."[53]

These strategies help turn the relatively slow biological material of our brain into an extraordinary cognitive machine. As a result, despite the raw processing power and speed of modern computers, the brain still produces far superior performance on many tasks—especially those involving pattern recognition, inference, strategic planning, and creativity.

One part of our brain is particularly important to humankind's intellectual and creative abilities. Residing under the skull forward of the temples, the *frontal lobes*, as specialists call them, are the brain's most recently evolved region. They are far larger in humans than in any of our closest primate relatives—making up about 30 percent of the cortex's total surface area and possessing a multitude of complex and reciprocal connections with other parts of the brain.[54]

Although the frontal lobes are uniquely large in humans, scientists have only recently begun to understand their functions. As the frontal lobotomies performed so commonly in the fifties, sixties, and seventies showed, they can often be damaged or partly removed without producing debilitating changes in cognitive ability or behavior. But decades of careful observation of brain-damaged patients and experimentation with animals have led researchers to conclude that the frontal lobes fulfill an executive or supervisory function. They allow us to undertake complex behaviors that require integrating multiple and simultaneous streams of incoming information. They prevent distraction by extraneous events and thereby help us maintain attention on the task at hand, yet they also manage our smooth shifts to new tasks and concepts as necessary.[55] Perhaps most important, the frontal lobes seem to be the place where we consciously initiate thought and action in response to novel or nonroutine challenges—where, in other words, we respond to the question "Gee, what should I do now?" The frontal lobes do this partly by creating a concept of the self as something that has continuity through time. They also integrate cognition and emotion, which gives visceral relevance to events affecting the self. The brain can then recall specific episodes involving the self in the past—along with the feelings these events evoked at the time—and can imagine alternative episodes in both the past and future. The frontal lobes allow us to travel in time mentally and manipulate the world in imagination: two abilities that are key to planning and creative action in a complex world.

The Left Cerebral Hemisphere

People with frontal-lobe lesions are often confused by simultaneous streams of information. They act on information fragments rather than on an integrated understanding of their situation. They also tend to be impulsive—trying to solve problems without reflection or planning—and apathetic about themselves, the past, and the future. They seem not to have a clear sense of who they are or of their continuity over time.[56] As one researcher writes: "When the frontal lobes are damaged, only the perpetual present remains."[57]

The frontal lobes appear to be a key source of humankind's remarkable cognitive versatility and fluidity. They are, perhaps, the place where Steven Mithen's multiple intelligences talk to each other—the ultimate wellspring of the ingenuity we need to cope in our new world. So, in the next step of my quest to put together the pieces of the ingenuity puzzle, I decided to learn more about them.

It turns out that one of the world's experts on the frontal lobes is in Toronto. Dr. Donald Stuss is the vice president of research at the Rotman Research Institute, a center located in a geriatric hospital in the north of the city. I visited him one morning in early spring, just as the leaves were appearing on the trees and shrubs around the building. But his office was hard to find; I was soon lost in a confusing warren of corridors and stairways. I wondered, in passing, whether his office had been hidden as a fiendish test of his visitors' frontal-lobe ability. When I eventually discovered his suite, I was quite late for our meeting. But Dr. Stuss, a cheerful fifty-seven-year-old, quickly put me at ease with coffee and banter as he sat at a paper-strewn desk and talked about his work.

"It's hard to pin down exactly what the frontal lobes do," I began, "but how would you describe their functions?"

"I've been studying them for about thirty years, and the answer still isn't entirely clear to me," he replied. "But we've learned that they integrate information from diverse parts of the brain. And, most important, that they combine cognition with emotion, or what psychologists refer to as *affect*. We know, too, that as a task becomes more complex, more areas of the frontal lobes are recruited to work on it. We often refer to the region as serving an executive function, but we've eliminated, I think, the idea that there is an engineer sitting there."

"The frontal lobes are not a homunculus, then? There's no little guy, sitting in the front of our brains, bringing everything together and making choices?"

"That's correct, there's no homunculus. It's a nice metaphor, and one that we sometimes use for lay audiences. But we can explain frontal-lobe function strictly in terms of integrative processes." Taking out a sheet of paper, he quickly sketched a diagram of the brain, circling three areas. "Several areas of the brain are considered to be high-level association cortices—the parietal, temporal, and frontal. The frontal lobes have a higher integrative role than the others." He drew lines between the three circled areas. "Even though there's cross-talk between the parietal and temporal lobes, there's greater convergence of information in the frontal lobes, and certain processes take place only there. The frontal lobes, in particular, have the major access to affect, whereas these other two regions have less access. And it's the integration of cognition with affect that appears to be key to self-awareness."[58]

"You seem to be suggesting," I said, "that affect, or emotion, is very important for the brain's high-level integrative and executive functions. Yet conventionally people think of emotion as a primitive aspect of human psychology. They believe the highest level of human intellectual function is rationality—cold, detached, and instrumental. And this conventional perspective suggests that, ideally, we should strip emotion out of our decision-making and cast it aside."

"Exactly. I've spent decades studying the role of frontal lobes in logical cognition, but I'm now bringing in affect. We've shown that the polar region of the right frontal lobe—a region long regarded as useless—is a place important for humor and intentionality. The frontal lobes are also the source of our 'gut feeling,' which is something largely dissociable from knowledge and logic. The essence of human life is the integration of these things."

"And how does psychological stress affect the frontal lobes, for example the stress produced by our inundation with information and the increasing pace of our lives?" I'd read that chronic stress—especially stress arising from feeling that critical events in one's environment are both unpredictable and uncontrollable—hampers the function of the hippocampus, which is the part of the brain critical to spatial learning and declarative memory (roughly, memory of explicit facts).[59] Stress also appears to contribute to neuron death in this vital brain region.[60] But I knew little about stress's effects on the frontal lobes.

"Well, stress affects sleep and the arousal system, and the arousal system involves the frontal lobes. Sleep deprivation reduces metabolic uptake in the frontal lobes, throwing off one's ability, not to do common tasks, but to do frontal-lobe-type tasks that involve sequencing and shifting among problems. Amy Arnsten at Yale and other researchers have also found that stress significantly impairs working memory, which is a critical function of the frontal lobes. Working memory is often called 'scratch-pad' memory—it's a bit like the RAM in our personal computers—and it helps us govern our behavior."[61]

I saw an opportunity to bring together some pieces of the ingenuity puzzle. "I am particularly interested in situations that involve multiple streams of incoming information, where decisions have to be made very fast, as for example in air-traffic control or even in the management of major financial crises. These tasks recruit the frontal lobes, as I understand it. You seem to be suggesting that sleeplessness and stress . . ."

An aide entered with a sheaf of scholarly articles and draft papers. Stuss reviewed the material with me for a couple of minutes; then we returned to the conversation—but I struggled to find the thread. "Where was I going with this question? . . . I can't remember what I was going to ask."

"Aging!" Stuss declared, and we both laughed—a bit nervously on my part, since I'd recently turned forty-three. "Aging and frontal lobes," Stuss continued. "Yes, I said to myself, I shouldn't interrupt him, he's going to lose it!"

"Aging produces results similar to frontal lobe lesions?" I asked, scrambling for a new line of inquiry.

"In some regards. Our humor research is important here: the elderly have the same type of cognitive deficits as patients with damage in the right frontal lobe, but their emotional responsiveness is normal. When they get a joke, they laugh, but they do have difficulty getting it sometimes. The individual differences in aging are enormous, however. It's not like a specific, focused lesion."[62]

"The one thing that does happen," he went on, "is that processing slows down, probably because of the deterioration of the white matter—the insulation around the neurons in the brain. When things come at older people too fast, they can't process them.[63] In fact, you can make a young person look like he has frontal lobe damage by just cranking up the speed and difficulty a little bit."

"I would term that kind of thing cognitive overload," I said. "Is that an appropriate term?"

"Yes."

"Speaking very generally," I continued, "it seems that there is more information in the world, that information is flowing faster, and that any one individual is facing a larger number of tasks on a daily basis. There are some individuals in our society who must handle truly prodigious cognitive loads—for instance in the investment and financial industries. Many of the people in these industries are young. My guess is that they have to be young to handle complex derivative models, have six screens in front of them at the same time, and yet stay more or less on top of things."

"You've got it."

"Gene Rochlin, a professor at Berkeley, argues that computer and communication technologies are squeezing out experiential knowledge in favor of sheer, raw cognitive ability. But it's experiential knowledge that in many cases provides real adaptability to novel challenges: the recognition that I've seen this pattern before, that it's not good, and that we must stay away from it."

"I agree," Stuss responded. "With regards to aging, we've got things reversed. As you move up the ladder in most organizations, you get more and more stressed and more and more to do, whereas it should be *exactly* the opposite way around! As you move up, you should be starting to do larger conceptual, pattern recognition tasks that involve less stress and less cognitive input but that draw on your rich history of emotional experiences."

"Our studies with the elderly show that the one thing you get with age is wisdom. You've got this affective responsiveness, this emotional experience. Somebody once asked me whether there was any benefit to aging, because there seems to be little that's positive about the body's physical deterioration. I answered by saying that there is something positive, but it's more spiritual than physical. If your physical stuff gets peeled away, what do you have left? You have your self, your memories, and your history; and those are your spiritual parts. What is a midlife crisis—it's preparation for aging. Some people say it's an assessment of 'What have I done?' I would say it's an assessment of 'Who am I?' You are forced, if you can meet the challenge of aging, to develop truly as a human being."

———————

As I left the office and wound my way back through the warren, I reflected on something I had read in Donald Stuss's articles. He had once been asked to evaluate the cognitive abilities of a postal clerk who had suffered a serious frontal-lobe injury. Oddly, the brain damage hadn't affected the clerk's performance on IQ tests at all; in fact, he remained a member of Mensa, the high-IQ society. But he could no longer sort mail. Although he had passed every government exam, he could not do a job that demanded planning, organization, and the integration of complex information to perform sequential tasks.

What did this incident say, I wondered, about our meritocratic testing procedures? Tests like the Scholastic Assessment Test and the Graduate Record Exam—indeed, the whole panoply of standardized tests we use in rich societies to sort and assign people to categories—are very similar to IQ tests. They are also institutionalized gatekeepers, providing "objective" criteria that allow our societies to parcel out opportunities for upward mobility. Yet the work of Stuss and his colleagues suggests that these tests can't measure key frontal-lobe abilities—abilities that we generally regard as essential to human intelligence and that make us truly flexible, adaptable, and surviving beings in a complex world.[64] In fact, although IQ scores correlate reasonably well with school grades, they correlate only weakly with measures of creativity, and they generally account for only about 10 percent of variation in individuals' later success in life.[65]

The more I thought about this problem, however, the more I saw two distinct and somewhat contradictory processes operating in our rich societies. On one hand, the people who succeed at our meritocratic tests are empowered in our social hierarchies, despite the fact that these tests don't properly measure some key frontal-lobe abilities. Over time these people, through their decisions and actions, tend to reproduce the institutions and procedures, including the testing procedures, that empowered them, thus putting more of exactly the same kind of people into positions of influence.

On the other hand, the direction of change in our world appears to demand ever greater frontal-lobe abilities from all of us. These abilities are not distributed evenly within our societies: the subtle interaction of nature and nurture during the development of each person's brain leaves some people better endowed than others. Consequently, as the complexity and pace of our world increase, the fraction of our population truly capable of meeting our world's challenges decreases. The people who best meet these challenges tend to rise to the top of our corporate and administrative hierarchies. They also tend to thrive in hypercomplex, time-compressed circumstances. In fact, Brian Arthur's theory (reviewed in the chapter "Complexities") suggests that these people tend to make their circumstances even more complex and compressed as they improve their strategies and technologies in competition with each other.

If I'm right about these two processes, then two distinct types of people, with quite specific cognitive abilities, climb the ladders of our social hierarchies. Our meritocratic testing procedures may not be aligned with the mental demands of our modern world, but our societies are nevertheless developing, inexorably, an ever more rarefied and selective cognitive elite, some of whose members I saw leaving the towers that September evening at Canary Wharf. The rest of us, those of us who don't excel at IQ-like tests or thrive in hypercomplex environments, are left behind. And some of the people left behind probably have mental abilities critical to our survival. They might have, for instance, the ability to integrate their factual grasp of the startling events in our new world with a powerful emotional appreciation—an appreciation grounded in wonder, awe, hope, and perhaps even fear—of what these events could mean for our future. This emotional appreciation could help us make better choices about which path, of the countless paths before us, we should follow into that future.

INGENUITY

AND WEALTH

I T WAS A GLORIOUS, SUNNY DAY in mid-August as we unloaded our gear from the float plane. At the water's edge, a friend and I heaped our tent, packs, fishing rods, and all the other paraphernalia of modern camping. We'd flown to an isolated lake a few kilometers inland from one of the most rugged parts of Canada's Pacific coast, and we planned to hike to the coast and camp for several days by the sea.

The unloading finished, we said goodbye to the pilot. He started the engine and revved it to a howl, turning the plane away from the shore to make a run down the lake's full length. We watched the plane lift off the water at the far end, shrink to a dot, and vanish behind the mountains rimming the lake. Then there was complete silence.

We were thrilled to be starting our holiday, but our plans quickly unraveled. The trail that was supposed to take us to the coast was nowhere to be found. The creek out of the lake was impassable, choked with fallen trees and debris. And the shoreline where we had heaped our gear was surrounded on all sides by a band of virgin West Coast rainforest—a profuse and chaotic tangle of fir, cedar, hemlock, rotting windfalls, and exuberant underbrush. Beyond this forest was a wide expanse of land logged twenty years before that had naturally regrown with alder and dense brush. It formed an impenetrable wall of vegetation six meters high.

I've had a lot of experience hacking my way through the temperate rainforests of the northwest coast of North America, but on this occasion—expecting to find a trail—I was foolishly unprepared. We'd brought no axe, compass, or flagging tape. We had no radio to signal distress. All we had was a cheap machete. And after I had flailed at the brush for ten hours, cutting a path no more than a hundred meters long, the machete was so dull that it bounced off the stems uselessly.

Trapped on the lake's shoreline, we had no choice but to wait several days for the plane to come back and collect us. The glories around us soon lost any charm or romantic appeal. The mountains became brooding and sinister; the wind in the trees sounded ancient and icy cold; and the pleasant riot of vegetation in the forest turned into a vicious struggle for light and space among trees, ferns, and fungi. Raw nature showed us its brutal face; it was inscrutable and infinitely more powerful than the two of us in our soft bodies. Time was on nature's side; it had endured forever, and it could wait forever. But we could not.

We had ample food and a good tent. But I found myself thinking for hours about our impotence, acutely aware how thin was the line between survival and death. The nights were cold and wet. Without our tent and sleeping bags, we would probably have died of hypothermia before the plane returned. These, and our pots, matches, and camping knives, suddenly became precious, miraculous instruments—nothing like them could be found nearby and we were utterly dependent on them.

As I considered our fragile defenses against death, it dawned on me that all of them—tent, pots, matches, and knives—were themselves made out of raw nature. All the material artifacts we take for granted in the modern world, from the cars in our driveways and the furniture we sit on to the food in our refrigerators, are produced or extracted from five material constituents of our natural world: rock, soil, wood, water, and air. Human beings have used ingenuity, energy (mainly in the form of hydrocarbon fuels), and the genetic information in the life around us to manipulate and reconfigure these five constituents into the infinite array of things that serve our needs.

My friend and I were duly rescued by the float plane and safely returned, chastened and chagrined, to civilization. Several years later, back in that marvelous womb of artifacts called Toronto, I stumbled upon a book titled *Stuff: The Materials the World Is Made Of* by the science journalist Ivan Amato. It captured the same idea that had come to me on the lakeshore. Amato notes that humans extract about fifteen billion tons of raw material from the planet each year, and from that material "they make every kind of stuff that you can find in every kind of thing":

Mined ore becomes metal becomes wire becomes part of a motor becomes a cooling fan in a computer. Harvested wood becomes lumber becomes a home. Drilled petroleum becomes chemical feedstock becomes synthetic rubber becomes automobile tires. Natural gas becomes polyethylene becomes milk jugs and oversize, multicolored yard toys. Mined silica sand becomes silicon crystal becomes the base of microelectronic chips. Each kind of stuff is a link to enormous industrial trains whose workers process the world's raw materials into usable forms that constitute the items of our constructed landscape.[1]

We take the raw materials around us and mix them with ingenuity to create the miraculous things that serve our needs. They can be physical things, like the knives and stoves we use to survive outdoors and the cars and buildings we use in our cities. They can also be social things, in which case the raw materials are people, and we use our ingenuity to motivate, coordinate, and combine the actions of these people in the various institutions—from markets to parliamentary democracies—that help us define and achieve our goals.

––––––––––––

Having an abundance of physical things that serve our needs is an important part of what most of us mean by "wealth." Wealth is something we generally like and want, but few of us have a clear idea where it comes from. Indeed, for over two and a half centuries, economists have found it surprisingly hard to answer the question "What are the sources of wealth?" For economists the increased production of wealth is the same thing as economic growth, and they generally group their theories about the sources of wealth into a broad category called theories of "long-run economic growth" (where the "long run" is a period of decades). Recently, some economists have focused on how ideas, specifically, contribute to economic growth. So if we want to understand the relationship between ideas (or ingenuity) and the production of the physical things that serve our needs—from camp stoves to cars—we need to take a quick look at how economists have thought about economic growth in the past and how they think about it today.

Theories of long-run growth have an illustrious pedigree.[2] Some of the most important early ideas were developed in England in the eighteenth and early nineteenth centuries. In 1776, Adam Smith attributed the "multi-plication of the productions of all the different arts" to the increasing division of labor into specialties, to technological change, and to the accumulation of capital (for him, capital consisted of savings used to secure future benefits).[3] He believed that these factors could produce "universal opulence" for all groups and classes, as long as government ensured the administration of justice, refrained from restricting commerce, and provided basic infrastructure and public education. But a few decades later, his compatriots David Ricardo and Thomas Malthus sounded a more pessimistic note. Ricardo argued that *diminishing returns* to factors of production—such as land, labor, and capital—would constrain prosperity. A farmer could try to increase his farm's food output by hiring more laborers, but beyond a certain point the additional food produced by one more laborer (what economists call the *marginal product of labor*) would start to decline; eventually, hiring extra labor wouldn't boost the farm's output at all. Building on this idea of diminishing returns, Malthus claimed that population growth would inevitably outstrip the productive capacity of the economy's limited natural resources, in particular that of agricultural land, and in the end would cause widespread misery and death.

Ricardo and Malthus didn't foresee that capital accumulation (especially in the form of productive machinery) and technological change would help England's farmers escape diminishing returns and dramatically raise their food output, in spite of the country's small, restricted area of agricultural land. Compared to their eighteenth-century counterparts, farmers in today's advanced nations use far more machinery of vastly greater power; they plant faster-growing, more disease-resistant seeds that yield much more grain per hectare; and they apply powerful fertilizers, pesticides, and chemical weed-killers. In other sectors of advanced economies, people have similarly learned to use more capital and better technology to surmount the physical limits of resources other than agricultural land—of coal, oil, and minerals, for instance. As Harvard economist Mike Scherer writes, our capital investments and inventiveness have repeatedly "bailed humanity out of seemingly impending crises from diminishing returns," allowing economic growth to surge ahead.[4]

But it would be a while before economists had a good understanding of this whole process. For almost a century following the pioneering contributions of Adam Smith, Ricardo, and Malthus, mainstream economists paid little attention to the factors that determine and sustain long-run economic growth. Then, in the mid-1950s, Robert Solow raised the issue's profile with two crucial articles that became a foundation for modern neo-classical theories of growth, and eventually brought him a Nobel prize.[5] Until these articles appeared, most economists had assumed that increases in the output of an economy's workers, and the higher standard of living that these increases produce, were due to workers' greater use of capital (mainly, again, industrial machinery) in their production activities.[6] In one of his articles, Solow examined this proposition. With elegant mathematics, he measured how much workers' greater use of capital had actually raised their hourly output between 1909 and 1949. To the surprise of most of his colleagues, he discovered that capital explained only 12.5 percent (later revised to about 20 percent) of improvements in labor output. The remainder, which came to be called the *Solow residual*, he put down to technological change, that is, not more machines, but better methods involving better machines.[7]

Economists now generally agree that new technologies boost labor productivity and, in doing so, boost long-run growth.[8] All the same, they still dispute whether the innovative ideas embodied in new technologies play an independent role in raising productivity. Some skeptics try to eliminate the Solow residual by simply tinkering with conventional growth theory: they change the theory to allow for qualitative—not just quantitative—improvements in capital (that is, better, not just more, industrial machinery), and they broaden capital's definition to include human capital, which consists of skills acquired by the labor force through training and education. In the 1980s and early 1990s, however, an alternative view emerged, generally called New Growth or Endogenous Growth theory. The economists who pioneered this new view argue that technological ideas should be treated as an independent factor of production. Ideas, in and of themselves, they say, have the power to produce economic growth.

One of the leaders of the New Growth school is Paul Romer, a brilliant and charismatic Stanford economist who has thought more incisively about the role of ideas in economic growth than perhaps any other person alive. Early on, he threw down the gauntlet before the conventional growth theorists:

> Our knowledge of economic history, of what production looked like one hundred years ago, and of current events convinces us beyond any doubt that discovery, invention, and innovation are of overwhelming

importance in economic growth and that the economic goods that come from these activities [i.e., ideas] are different in a fundamental way from ordinary objects. We could produce statistical evidence suggesting that all growth came from capital accumulation, with no room for anything called technological change. But we would not believe it.[9]

For a decade now, conventional growth and New Growth theorists have been locked in a sometimes heated debate. But Paul Romer has made several telling points that I believe shift the balance in favor of the new perspective. He begins by arguing, much as I did in the previous chapter, that ideas are instructions that "let us combine limited physical resources in arrangements that are ever more valuable."[10] He is a master of colorful examples to support his arguments. "We once used iron oxide (ordinary rust) as a pigment in cave paintings," he writes. "An elaborate set of ideas now lets us use it to store magnetic signals on audio cassettes, video cassettes, and computer disk drives."[11] Sometimes astonishingly productive ideas are sitting right under our noses, he points out, drawing an analogy between improvement in competitive sports and economic growth. Until around 1900, for instance, people in the Western world thought that the breast stroke was the most efficient way to swim. Yet the simple technical innovation of the crawl, in which the swimmer brings his or her arms forward out of the water, dramatically increases swimming efficiency and speed. In sports, better technique (the analogue of useful ideas in an economy) often generates far greater returns than sheer physical conditioning (the analogue of capital accumulation).[12]

As a factor of production, ideas often supplant labor by raising labor's productivity; for instance, a manufacturer might rearrange a production process to make workers more efficient, allowing employment of fewer workers. On the other hand, ideas usually accompany physical and human capital: a manufacturer's investment in machinery and trained workers generally boosts the local stock of ideas and instructions.

Paul Romer goes on to show that economically useful ideas cannot be reduced to human capital, because they are *non-rival*, whereas human capital is *rival*. Something is rival if its use by one person reduces the amount available for use by another person. Most economic goods are rival—if I fully use a patch of farmland to grow corn, for example, someone else can't use that patch, at the same time, to grow wheat. (Rivalry is distinct from *excludability*: a good is excludable if access to it can be prevented, through physical means like fences and barriers or through legal means like property rights. Romer notes that ideas may be partially excludable, using such devices as intellectual property rights or temporary monopolistic control of ideas through market power. A pure *public good*—such as national defense—is both non-rival and non-excludable.[13])

Ideas are non-rival because they are immaterial, which means that any particular idea can be used by an infinite number of people at the same time. As Thomas Jefferson famously wrote: "He who receives an idea from me, receives instructions himself without lessening mine; as he who lights his taper at mine receives light without darkening mine."[14] Human capital, on the other hand, is rival, because skills are inseparable from the material things—the brains—in which they reside. For example, if one company fully employs a particular pool of human capital—say, the skills of a group of highly trained engineers—then that human capital is not available to other companies.[15] Ideas are also more durable than human capital. When a person dies, his or her skills are lost, "but any non-rival good that this person produces—a scientific law; a principle of mechanical, electrical, or chemical engineering; a mathematical result; software; a patent; a mechanical drawing; or a blueprint—lives on after the person is gone."[16]

Romer concedes that it is tempting to combine ideas and human capital, because they are "so closely related as inputs and outputs," but argues that they should be treated separately. "Ideas," he goes on, "are the critical input in the production of more valuable human and nonhuman capital. But human capital is also the most important input in the production of new ideas." While physical capital—for example, computers, telephones and laboratory equipment—often helps human capital, "a trained person is still the key input in the process of trial and error, experimentation, guessing, hypothesis formation, and articulation that ultimately generates a valuable new idea that could be communicated to others and used by them."[17]

If one accepts Romer's argument that ideas are non-rival and have independent productive power, it both solves and creates problems for conventional growth theory. It solves problems by explaining how advanced economies have avoided a slackening of long-run growth due to diminishing returns to capital investment. Conventional theory suggests that if labor and technology remain constant, any additional investment in productive machinery and factories will eventually bring declining benefits, because an economy will become saturated with these capital goods. But economic data show no tendency over the long term for the returns on capital investment or the growth rates in advanced economies to decline; in fact, the evidence seems to indicate that growth rates have increased. In these economies, Paul Romer contends, technological ideas generated by skilled people (human capital) in private firms tend to spill out of these firms to enlarge the general stock of public knowledge. This growing, non-rival stock can then be used over and over again by skilled people in other firms to raise the productivity of their machines and manufacturing processes (their physical capital). Thus, if an economy is well endowed with human capital, it can exploit the non-rival character of technological ideas to counteract the natural tendency of capital investment to produce diminishing returns. In essence, Romer argues, ideas are a factor of production unlike labor or capital, because they actually exhibit *increasing* returns; in other words, the economic benefits derived from investment in the production of useful ideas do not decline over time.[18]

Romer's argument solves another problem for conventional growth theory: he makes technological change *endogenous* to the economy—in other words, he places this change inside his theory and explains it as an integral part of economic growth. He explicitly shows that in a given economy the flow of ideas leading to useful technologies is a direct result of investment in human capital (in education and research and development, for example).[19] In contrast, although Robert Solow's Nobel–prize winning theory acknowledges the importance of technology to productivity and growth, it doesn't actually explain how or why technological change happens; instead it treats this change as a purely *exogenous* process. Technological ideas are assumed to originate outside the economy, a kind of natural resource freely available to all firms and societies, much like manna from heaven or fruit growing wild and easily plucked from the tree.[20]

But if it solves some problems for economists, Romer's theory creates others. In particular, once economists bring into their standard mathematical models a non-rival factor of production that exhibits increasing returns—like ideas—they have great trouble explaining why technological innovation occurs at all. If firms can simply replicate ideas from a public stock when they need them, and if any ideas they produce quickly become part of that public stock, then they have no incentive to generate new ideas. So if Romer is right, a purely competitive marketplace will not produce rewards large enough to sustain private technological entrepreneurship.[21] And there *is* lots of evidence that he's right: for instance, interchangeable and reusable software parts (discussed in the chapter "Unknown Unknowns") have been slow to appear on the market: precisely because the parts can be easily copied, software entrepreneurs can't capture adequate returns on investment.[22]

Romer addresses this problem by breaking with the economists' sacrosanct assumption of pure competition. Building on the thinking of the radical mid-twentieth-century economist Joseph Schumpeter, he argues that technological innovation takes place mainly within firms that are able to reap gains from the temporary monopoly of their ideas.[23] This monopoly can arise from a firm's ownership of intellectual property rights (like patents), or because the firm is able to gain an advantage in the marketplace in various ways. It may have, for example, brand-name recognition, an established network of distributors, or, most simply, a head start as the creator of a new technological idea. The "creative destruction" (as Schumpeter called it) of capitalism sustains this monopolistic competition: because technological innovations are continually being overthrown and replaced, each turnover of technology creates an interval during which the innovator can exploit its temporary dominance of the marketplace.[24] In other words, it is a race in which there can be no ultimate winner—but significant rewards go to whoever is in the lead.

Faced with this challenge to their thinking, conventional growth theorists have not deserted the battlefield: they have mounted several attacks on Romer's arguments and those of other New Growth theorists.[25] In turn, these theorists have recently replied with more elaborate and rigorous models.[26] The debate is far from settled, but the propositions that ideas are key to economic growth, and that they have a fundamentally different character from other factors of production, are now well established among economists.

––––––––––

In the early to mid-1990s, when I first started thinking about the capacity of human societies to adapt to complex stress, especially environmental stress, I was powerfully influenced by the arguments of New Growth theorists. Much of what they said made sense. But the term "ingenuity," I decided, served my purposes better than "ideas." On one hand, it was narrower: I wasn't interested in all ideas—after all, they can range from Stephen King plotlines to chemical formulae for anti-cancer drugs—but only in the subset of practical ideas that we apply to our practical problems.

On the other hand, ingenuity was broader than "innovation," another favorite concept of economists. Innovation implies that the ideas in question are new. Although my notion of ingenuity certainly doesn't exclude new ideas, it assumes that ideas don't have to be new to be useful.

I also realized that what counts as a practical problem that needs to be solved—and therefore what counts as ingenuity—can vary from society to society. It's partly determined by a society's values, which are influenced by its culture. An idea for eradicating a blight that affects grapevines will legitimately be considered ingenuity in a society that values fine wines, but not in a society of teetotalers. Nevertheless, there are limits to this cultural plasticity, because all humans share certain requirements for ingenuity— we all, for instance, have basic needs for food, water, and shelter.

I knew too that ingenuity would be difficult to measure precisely. We might measure it, I speculated, by gauging the length of the sets of instructions we use to solve our problems (as I realized when I was planning my escape from my office). Or we might measure the information content of ideas more directly. I was particularly struck by one of Paul Romer's metaphors, in which he described how a chemistry set could represent the range of raw materials available to us in nature. In this metaphor, each chemical is assigned a position in a string of bits of information. When the substance is included in a given mixture of chemicals, the position shows 1; when it is absent, 0. The sequence of 1s and 0s is the formula for the mixture—Romer's analogue of an economically useful "idea."[27] Could ingenuity be measured by these approaches? They seemed promising, but I knew that both were essentially measures of ingenuity *quantity*—that is, of raw numbers of instructions or amounts of information. Neither approach told me how to measure ingenuity's productivity or intrinsic *quality*. Ideas are more than raw information: when someone offers us advice about solving a practical problem we quite sensibly distinguish between "good" and "bad" ideas. I knew that we had to be able to measure quality—to distinguish the good ideas from the not so good—if we wanted to develop powerful models of ingenuity requirement and supply.

We could measure an idea's quality, I thought, by assessing how well it works in practice: better ideas solve problems better. But this measure doesn't work so well, it turns out. For one thing, it means that the concept of ingenuity requirement becomes conflated with the concept of ingenuity supply: it suggests that as a society's problems become harder to solve (and its ingenuity requirement rises), successful solutions are harder to generate—that is, ideas that work become scarcer, which would *seem* to mean that the supply of ingenuity falls. But clearly, that isn't true; ingenuity requirement can rise without causing supply to fall. It's just that the ingenuity supplied doesn't solve the problem. To avoid this and other difficulties, I decided that ingenuity consists of ideas *applied* to solve society's practical problems; whether these schemes succeed is another matter. So, an idea's success or lack thereof is not a measure of its ingenuity content. Some solutions are extremely ingenious, and yet may fail where a simpler, cruder idea turns out to be effective.

In my early, rudimentary theory, an increase in ingenuity supply simply meant an increase in quantity—crudely speaking, in the number and length of the sets of instructions a society applies to its practical problems—not an increase in quality. I reasoned that an adequate quantity of ingenuity was a necessary but not a sufficient condition for adaptation to our world's complex stresses. But given that it's common for people to talk about ideas in terms of their quality, I knew that this restricted concept of ingenuity was missing an element of the word's conventional meaning.[28]

It may seem a simple thing, but it isn't always helpful to "think big": focusing on the total quantity of ingenuity that a society supplies shouldn't lead us to underrate the value of "small" ideas. When we think about the effect of technological change on growth, we tend to imagine that big ideas—like the steam engine, the telephone, or the Internet—are "better" ideas, because they create vast new industries and precipitate major economic revolutions. In modern economies, big ideas for technologies like the transistor and genetic cloning usually emerge from big industrial or government research enterprises. Such ideas and the "general-purpose technologies" they produce are immensely important, but most of our innovation and ingenuity actually comes in the form of countless small ideas—like the square-bottom paper bag, invented in 1870, that revolutionized U.S. retail sales.[29]

What's more, many of these small ideas take the form of *tacit knowledge*. This is uncodified knowledge that people often don't recognize they possess.[30] It's embodied in things like people's habits, organizational cultures, and companies' standardized procedures for solving problems. Tacit knowledge isn't written down. It may actually be impossible to reduce such knowledge to sets of instructions—just as it's very hard to write down instructions for tying one's shoelaces. Sometimes tacit knowledge can't even be communicated verbally, so transmitting it from one person or organization to another can be very difficult.[31] Sometimes it can be learned only by a kind of apprenticeship: living in and working with the knowledgeable group, firm, or society over an extended period, which allows the knowledge to be slowly absorbed through imitation.[32]

Eventually I decided—and this is a key departure from the concepts underlying New Growth theory—that the practical ideas used to create, reform, and maintain institutions and social arrangements were just as important as technological ideas—or perhaps, even more important. To capture the difference between these two types of practical idea, I distinguished between *technical* and *social* ingenuity. A society facing food shortfalls because of cropland and water scarcity could, for instance, respond with technological solutions, like better grains and deeper wells, or with institutional and policy solutions, like special banks to give farmers emergency credit, or short-term arrangements to transfer food from productive to food-scarce regions.[33]

Social ingenuity is supplied by people at all levels of society, from international and national political leaders to government bureaucrats and corporate managers or people running community organizations. Much of it consists of ideas for solving various kinds of *collective action problems*. These problems commonly arise when groups of people or societies try to provide public goods for their members, things in whose benefits everybody shares, like national defense and fire and police services. Societies find it notoriously hard to supply public goods, because people tend to "free ride" on the contributions of others: even though each person knows he or she will benefit if a particular public good is available, each nevertheless has an incentive to let others do the work or pay the cost of providing it. So social ingenuity is needed to create the right balance of carrots and sticks, of rewards and punishments, to keep free riding to a minimum.

The two kinds of ingenuity, social and technical, are intimately interconnected. In fact, I came to understand that social ingenuity is a key prerequisite to technical ingenuity. We need social ingenuity to set up and maintain public and semi-public goods such as markets, funding agencies, educational and research organizations, and effective government. If this system of institutions operates well, it provides psychological and financial incentives to technological entrepreneurs and innovators; it aids regular contact and communication among experts; and it channels money to those technological projects with the greatest prospect of success.[34] Society therefore needs ingenuity to get ingenuity, which means it is both an input to and output of the economic system. (Surprisingly, this claim often perplexes people. But a moment's reflection shows that many economic factors are both input and output—for example, physical and human capital. An economy needs factories to produce the components for further factories, and it needs engineers to train engineers.)

My use of ingenuity to cover ideas applied to both social and technical problems is a significant modification of New Growth theory. Paul Romer and other theorists in this school are mainly interested in technical ideas, such as manufacturing techniques, industrial designs, and chemical formulas, especially those developed and applied within companies. But even Romer acknowledges that ideas about social arrangements—social ingenuity, essentially—are immensely important to economic growth. "The word technology invokes images of manufacturing, but most economic activity takes place outside of factories," he writes. "Ideas include the innumerable insights about packaging, marketing, distribution, inventory control, payments systems, information systems, transactions processing, quality control, and worker motivation that are all used in the creation of economic value in a modern economy."[35]

New Growth theory helped give me a better understanding of how ingenuity improves our well-being, but a key question remained largely unanswered in my mind: What factors determine ingenuity's supply? Many optimists, including many economists, seem to implicitly believe that "necessity is the mother of invention"—that a society's need or demand for ingenuity largely determines its supply and that an increase in this need or demand will produce, almost automatically, an equal increase in supply. But I felt that the story was more complicated than that. My work in poor countries showed that societies don't always supply adequate ingenuity in response to severe environmental problems, like critical scarcities of fresh water and good cropland. Factors other than need clearly determine supply.

To understand these factors better, I turned to the long debate over the capacity of human societies to adapt to scarcities of natural resources—a debate that goes back to Confucius and Plato, but which took its modern form with the writings of Thomas Malthus and David Ricardo in the late eighteenth and early nineteenth centuries. Two positions dominate today's version of this debate.

On one side are neo-Malthusians—often biologists or ecologists—who claim that finite natural resources place a strict ceiling, or upper limit, on the growth of our population and consumption. If this limit is exceeded, poverty and social breakdown result. But evidence from recent history seems to have refuted the neo-Malthusian view: during the last two centuries, humankind has repeatedly smashed through resource barriers that appeared unbreachable. Time and again, societies have surmounted scarcity crises predicted by Malthusian Cassandras, including the feared timber shortage in America in the late nineteenth century and the "energy crisis" of the 1970s and 1980s.[36] Many energy-cost predictions made in the 1970s are now, in fact, truly embarrassing. The Cornell ecologist David Pimentel and his colleagues asserted in 1973 that "if current use patterns continue, fuel costs are expected to double or triple in a decade and to increase nearly fivefold by the turn of the century." But by 1999, real petroleum costs were little higher than in 1973.[37]

On the other side of the debate we have a diverse group of economic optimists consisting mainly of neoclassical economists, economic historians, and agricultural economists. (At some point during the last two centuries, economics transformed itself from the "dismal science" of Malthus and Ricardo to a doctrine of hope and optimism for humanity.) Loosely extrapolating from the historical record, this group argues that there are few, if any, strict limits to population and prosperity. As the late Julian Simon, the standard-bearer of the economic optimists, once put it: "There is no physical or economic reason why human resourcefulness and enterprise cannot forever continue to respond to impending shortages and existing problems with new expedients that, after an adjustment period, leave us better off than before the problem arose."[38]

According to these theorists, if markets are working well, as a resource like cropland becomes more scarce—perhaps because soil erosion has reduced its supply or a growing population has pushed up cropland demand—its price will rise. The higher price will encourage people to tap new sources of the resource, for instance by opening up new lands for agriculture; it will promote resource substitution, like the use of fertilizer to compensate for nutrient-depleted soil; and it will stimulate conservation, for example by encouraging people to use contour plowing to reduce soil erosion. The higher price will also give people an incentive to substitute labor and physical capital for the scarce resource: cropland shortages often stimulate farmers to work harder, and farmers can raise the output of their limited amount of land by using more capital, such as farm machinery.[39] Finally, the higher price can lead people to invent new technologies, like better tractors and hybrid grains that grow in poor soil, to effectively stretch the resource's availability.[40]

In its popular form, the debate between neo-Malthusians and economic optimists has become sterile. But it isn't frivolous, because the paradigms underpinning the two positions have tremendous influence in the world. The neo-Malthusian view prevails in the mass media and in the Green movement. Economic optimism, on the other hand, guides the World Bank and other development agencies in their responses to problems involving natural resources in poor countries; and it also informs the commentary we get in influential business-oriented books, newspapers, and magazines.[41]

After looking carefully at the arguments in this debate, I became convinced that the economic optimists provide a powerful theory of innovation and, essentially, of the supply of ingenuity, and that they seem better able to explain human societies' remarkable ability to adapt to resource scarcity. But their view has three important implications, each of which is both disturbing and questionable.

First, their view implies that there are few intrinsic differences among natural resources—at least from the point of view of economic utility—because we live in an "age of substitutability," in which our technological creativity permits virtually unlimited substitution of one resource for another.[42] Whether we are talking about forests, fish, iron ore, or petroleum, we can treat natural resources as largely identical; in fact, we can think of them, together, as one huge, homogeneous resource pool. We can substitute silicon for copper in our telecommunication wiring; and we can use hydrocarbons to produce polymers that replace wood in construction. Some economic optimists even argue that all resource scarcities will eventually be reduced to energy scarcities, because with enough energy we can extract all basic elements from common rock and transmute one element into another. And human ingenuity will eventually find a boundless source of energy. (We have seen ideas like this before in this book—in the comments by Richard Cooper that I reviewed in the chapter "Careening into the Future.") As the economists Harold Barnett and Chandler Morse say in their classic treatment of this subject: "advances in fundamental science have made it possible to take advantage of the uniformity of energy/matter—a uniformity that makes it feasible, without preassignable limit, to escape the quantitative constraints imposed by the character of

Earth's crust."[43] So we shouldn't worry too much about resource availability for our children. "The reservation of particular resources for later use," Barnett and Morse contend, "may contribute little to the welfare of future generations." Much more valuable to posterity will be a heritage of capital, knowledge, and institutions.[44]

Second, the economic optimists' view implies that the human species is biologically exceptional and that our modern economies are historically exceptional. Economic optimists rightly celebrate the creativity and adaptability that I discussed in the last chapter and that they believe make us different from other forms of life. (Neo-Malthusians, on the other hand, emphasize the biological and physical characteristics that we share with other organisms.) And, although these optimists can accept that severe scarcity crippled some preindustrial societies, they argue that the limiting factors in these cases were actually inadequate knowledge and institutions, not a lack of resources.[45] Today, our economic and scientific institutions are well designed to deliver the ingenuity we need to adapt.[46]

This second implication leads directly to a third: that severe resource scarcity is not a problem of excessive growth of either population or consumption in a world of fixed resources, as neo-Malthusians claim, but of the failure of economic institutions and policies.[47] In particular, severe scarcity occurs when governments have not set up market mechanisms that ensure that resource prices reflect *all* the costs of resource use. Economists use the term *negative externalities* to refer to costs not included in the resource's price because they are borne by people not directly involved in buying, selling, or using the resource. For example, if a farmer's poor tilling practices cause his land to erode, he'll bear costs himself, in the form of lower crop yields and land values; but if the soil washing off the farmer's land fills local waterways and irrigation systems with silt, making them unusable, people other than the farmer will also bear costs. In general, economists say, when people like the farmer do not pay the full costs of their use of natural resources, they have an incentive to overexploit these resources and a disincentive to apply their ingenuity to conserve them. So, the economists conclude, you don't need to point to population growth, excessive resource consumption, or the limited availability of resources in the natural world to explain scarcity, only to inadequate economic institutions—in this case badly functioning markets.

There are valuable insights at the core of each of these implications of the economic optimists' view: we have developed a phenomenal ability to substitute among resources; there is no doubt that the world's rich societies, energized by science and technology, are historically exceptional; and many resource scarcities are a result, in part, of bad economic institutions and policies. Unfortunately, though, people often accept these implications, and the economic optimists' whole perspective, without nuance or qualification. In truth, the world is considerably more complicated than the economic optimists maintain.

By emphasizing possibilities for substitution, economic optimists minimize the intrinsic differences among resources. So they don't pay enough attention to the simple, crucial distinction between *nonrenewable* and *renewable* resources. Nonrenewables like minerals, metals, and petroleum consist of static and finite "stocks" in Earth's crust. In contrast, renewable resources like cropland, fresh water, forests, and fisheries consist not only of existing stocks (the area of cropland, or the volume of water or timber, for instance) but also of "flows" that replenish these stocks over time and that can provide, if used carefully, an essentially limitless stream of goods and services to human societies. Renewables are dynamic and complex natural systems, and they are often ecological systems. As the ecologist Buzz Holling has emphasized (in the chapter "An Angry Beast"), such systems are invariably intimately linked to, and nested within, interdependent webs of other natural systems.

In the case of nonrenewable resources, the economic optimists seem to be right, at least going by the evidence of the last one or two centuries. Modern economies appear to adjust easily to scarcities of these resources. We've all been aware how the prices of metals, minerals, and hydrocarbons have declined sharply in recent years as new reserves have been located, extraction and refining technologies have improved, demand has dropped because of conservation and production efficiencies, and new technologies have helped us substitute one resource for another.[48]

But for renewable resources the story is much less clear. As we've seen in previous chapters, nearly a fifth of the world's population has to deal with acute shortages or pollution of local fresh water supplies; the planet's wild fisheries are under severe strain and many have actually collapsed; and tropical forests are disappearing at an alarming rate. Cropland and water are renewable resources that are particularly important for food production, so agriculture is a good test of the economic optimists' view on renewables. On this front, considerable evidence weighs in their favor: greater investment in agriculture and the use of new agricultural technologies, like green-revolution methods, have kept the *total* food output of the world's croplands abreast of world population, holding down food prices in global markets. But a closer look at *local and regional* situations shows that cropland and water scarcities are unquestionably limiting food output in many parts of Asia, Africa, and Latin America. Poor subsistence farmers—especially those eking a living from arid savanna, steep hillsides, and other ecologically fragile areas—usually suffer the harshest effects. And while some analysts have argued that cropland scarcity caused by population growth in poor countries can encourage farmers to raise crop yields, careful studies show the association is weak.[49] In the 1980s, population growth outpaced food output in two-thirds of developing countries and in more than 80 percent of African countries.[50]

Economic optimists have a quick reply to such evidence: they say that in places where societies don't adapt smoothly to scarcities of renewable resources—and where these scarcities, as a result, cause terrible hardship—the problem isn't really one of resource limits but, once again, of poor economic institutions and policies. Most of the world's water scarcities would disappear if government subsidies and interference didn't skew water markets and make water too cheap; wild fisheries wouldn't be depleted if international agreements established clear property rights over these resources, giving specific groups and countries incentives to conserve them; and food shortfalls wouldn't occur if governments allowed farmers to receive full market prices for their products and provided adequate infrastructure for efficient grain markets.

But such responses are only partly right. Economic institutions and policies are certainly important, but that doesn't mean that resources are unimportant. Obviously we must take both into account. My thought experiment in the previous chapter told me I needed at least two things: resources (in the form of the odd collection of materials in my office with me) and enough ingenuity to put those resources together in a way that allowed me to escape. In the same way, our prosperity is a function, in part, of both the natural resources available to us and the ingenuity we apply to those resources, some of which comes in the form of institutions and policies for resource management.[51] The billions of people in poor countries who are suffering the effects of severe scarcities of renewable resources like water, cropland, and fuelwood, are essentially caught in a vise between critical failures on both these fronts. On one side, they face worsening scarcities of the resources they need to survive; on the other, they face failing markets and governments that offer them no assistance in conserving these resources or otherwise extricating themselves from their difficulties.

My thought experiment also told me that the types of resources I had in my office helped determine the amount of ingenuity I needed to escape: the less abundant and appropriate the things in my office, the more ingenuity I needed. Similarly, in the real world, the quantities and characteristics of the natural resources available to us help determine how much and what types of social ingenuity, in the form of institutions and policies, we need to be prosperous. Unfortunately, since economic optimists—while they emphasize institutions and policies—tend to deemphasize resources, they usually overlook this link between resources and our need for ingenuity.

But the link is clear when we try to manage renewable resources. Because renewables are not static stocks but dynamic systems—subsuming countless physical and biological processes—they often cannot be physically controlled or divided into saleable units. So it's often extremely hard to set up clear and enforceable property rights for them. They remain, as experts say, "open-access" resources, and vulnerable to overexploitation.[52] Fish, for instance, move around. In oceans, they cross boundaries between national and international jurisdictions, and because no one owns fish on the high seas, anyone can harvest them without restraint. This is the main reason for the catastrophic decline in many of the world's fisheries. Because fish are a dynamic resource, national and international policymakers need to be very clever to design elaborate fisheries institutions and make them work.

There's another twist: because renewable resources are complex systems, they often exhibit interactive effects, chaotic and nonlinear behavior, and unknown unknowns. The bizarre experiences of the Biospherians, sealed inside their artificial ecosystem for two years (described in the chapter "An Angry Beast"), showed that these characteristics make renewables, and the ecosystems they are part of, very difficult to manage. Our resource-management institutions and policies must be highly sophisticated, which in turn boosts our need for both technical and social ingenuity.

Resources have unique characteristics, and this affects our need for ingenuity when we try to substitute one resource for another. Renewable resources, especially, aren't easy to replicate; it can be hard or even impossible to find good substitutes for them.[53] For instance, as we saw in the chapter "The Big I," pesticides, herbicides, and artificial fertilizers are at best only rudimentary substitutes for the services provided by the myriad creatures that inhabit healthy soil. (Urbanites' limited exposure to soil probably explains why most of them assume that these chemicals *are* adequate substitutes.) Fresh water, like soil, is essential to our survival: we need it for our health and hygiene, and to grow our crops. But no substitute has water's exact range of biological and ecological properties. If water is scarce, our options for dealing with the scarcity are restricted; we can't drink anything else or grow our plants with anything else. This simply means we need more ingenuity to manage water scarcity than we would if substitutes were readily available.

We also have to remember that renewable resources have an astonishing variety of links to other renewables in the complex webs of Earth's natural systems, which means that depletion of one renewable resource can affect goods and services provided by other resources. For example, natural forests and their associated groundcover of bushes and low vegetation stabilize the underlying soil, slow the runoff of rainwater, and recycle some of this water into the atmosphere through transpiration. These patterns are disturbed by logging, especially by the construction of roads and drainage systems and by the use of fire to clear logging slash. So when a range of coastal mountains in a poor country like the Philippines is stripped bare, local people face not only a shortage of wood for fuel and construction, but also eroded soil, changes in local climate that restrict rainfall, flash floods that destroy downstream bridges and irrigation systems, and flows of silt that block river transport and suffocate coastal fisheries.[54] A full substitute for that forest must replace not just its wood but also all the other services the forest provides.

In sum, adjusting to scarcities of renewable resources like fish, water, and forests generally requires greater social and technical ingenuity than adjusting to scarcities of nonrenewables. Evidence from around the world, especially from poor countries, indicates that we often have trouble supplying the required ingenuity. So in the case of renewables, economic optimism may be seriously misguided.

The economic optimists' creed is a tightly integrated package of beliefs about the relationship between humanity and its natural world. At its heart are two assumptions: first, that little is beyond our capacity to do or figure out if we have the right incentives, and, second, that we can use markets to create the right incentives. The first assumption is essentially a claim that there are few, if any, insurmountable problems. If we really want to, for instance, we can create virtually everything we need out of the common rock around us. We have the capacity to supply more than enough ingenuity to solve any problem we face. The second assumption is essentially a claim that we have devised the institutional means—free markets—to unleash this ingenuity.

Is the first assumption reasonable? I would say not: the difficulty of the problems we face is partly determined by the intrinsic difficulty of the problems themselves (something I will look at the more carefully in the next chapter), and partly by the materials we have at hand to work with to solve these problems. And if the materials at hand are limited or inappropriate, some problems can be, for all practical purposes, impossible to solve. No matter how cleverly we structure our institutions, and no matter how powerful the resulting market incentives, we aren't going to supply, anytime soon, enough ingenuity to produce everything we need out of common rock.

The beliefs in the unlimited substitutability of resources, in the primacy of economic institutions and policies, and in the exceptionalism of human beings and their modern markets often combine to produce what I can only call unbridled hubris. In 1974, Robert Solow, the Nobel economist, famously declared that "If it is very easy to substitute other factors for natural resources, then there is in principle 'no problem.' The world can, in effect, get along without natural resources."[55] The idea that we can get along without natural resources is now widespread in rich countries. Within the next one hundred years, I believe, it will come to be seen as one of the greatest fallacies of our time.

What about the second of the economic optimists' assumptions—that markets can be relied on to unleash vast quantities of ingenuity? There is a great deal of evidence to support this idea. Economists have shown, through detailed research, that profit opportunities created by market demand are the usual motive for technological innovation.[56] (But they are not the only motive: social idealism, the quest for power, and the desire to achieve intellectual and aesthetic satisfaction also drive technological innovation.[57]) Profit opportunities appear to be greatest in imperfectly competitive markets, where people and corporations can reap large rewards from their temporary monopoly of new technologies.[58] And entrepreneurs are essential to this process: they exploit economic imbalances or opportunities in the economy—"disequilibriums" caused by rapid techno-logical, demographic, or social change or by natural resource scarcities—to create new ideas that promote growth.[59]

So an economic institution, the market, is often at the core of the ingenuity-supply process. Yet since the fall of Soviet-style communism—a system whose blatant inadequacies were a useful counterpoint to capitalist successes—we have come to think of markets as rather unremarkable social arrangements whose workings are obvious and not terribly impressive. In reality, though, a well-functioning market is a truly extraordinary institu-tion, which can help us overcome two key (and widely overlooked) difficul-ties facing any large group of economically interdependent people. First, such people usually find it hard to coordinate their economic activities, be-cause they face high uncertainty about each other's behavior; and, second, they usually find it hard to make economic decisions as consumers and pro-ducers, because the knowledge they need to guide these decisions is widely distributed among other people and firms in the economy.[60] Markets help solve these difficulties by providing rules, norms, and conventions (from property rights to contract laws) around which people can coordinate their expectations and their economic behavior, and by providing a system for setting the prices of goods and services—what economists usually call the "price mechanism"—that gathers together and communicates information about the circumstances and preferences of other people and firms.

Well-functioning markets deserve our respect; we should hold them in awe. Indeed, the relentless optimism shared by most economists in recent decades stems largely from a deep appreciation of how markets help soci-eties generate wealth and adapt to complex changes. Commenting on the price mechanism, the renowned conservative economist Friedrich von Hayek wrote in the 1940s: "I am convinced that if it were the result of deliberate human design . . . this mechanism would have been acclaimed as one of the greatest triumphs of the human mind."[61]

But markets aren't panaceas either. Sometimes they don't provide accurate price signals (a problem economists call *market failure*), either because property rights are inadequate or unenforced, or because market prices don't reflect all the social costs and benefits of people's activities. Market failures are often especially acute when we are dealing with com-plex ecological systems. As noted, these systems are often highly dynamic: fish in the oceans, water in rivers, and rain clouds in the atmosphere tend to move around a lot, which makes it hard to set up clear property rights for the things these systems give us (fish, water, rain, etc.). Also, because ecological systems have intricate webs of causal relations among their components, damage to one component can cause damage to many other components—deforestation of coastal hillsides produces silt that ruins coastal fisheries, for instance. And, finally, because ecological systems are fraught with unknown unknowns, we often don't have enough knowledge to accurately estimate the future costs and benefits of our use of them today. For all these reasons, the market prices of the goods and services that ecological systems supply us with are invariably too low. This means that entrepreneurs don't have strong enough incentives to develop ways to protect these systems, so they tend to supply the wrong amounts and types of ingenuity in response to ecological damage.

Even if market prices are accurate, entrepreneurs still often undersupply ingenuity, because it has some characteristics of a public good. If new ideas move rapidly into the public domain where anyone can use them without cost, entrepreneurs will have little incentive to produce ingenuity, because they won't be adequately paid for their creativity. In general, ingenuity will be undersupplied if the people who generate and deliver it do not receive returns equal to the benefits their ingenuity produces for society.

These challenges aren't insurmountable. We can design ways of making sure that market prices reflect social costs and benefits; we can remove structural impediments, such as subsidies, to efficient markets; we can work to increase our knowledge of the functions and behavior of complex systems; we can set up universities and research centers to boost the flow of innovation; and we can try to provide secure, enforced, and transferable property rights for both resources and ingenuity (which means it is important to improve systems of intellectual property rights, like patents).

But "getting the prices right"—as economists say—demands copious social ingenuity. Modern markets are a complicated and often fragile web of social arrangements. An astonishing range of institutions, laws, regulations, and rights are required to make up this web, including laws governing contracts, price-rigging, credit, and the excessive concentration of capital; limits on corporate liability; regulatory regimes for stock and bond markets; stable banking systems; predictable and restrained fiscal policies; strong and uncorrupt judicial systems to enforce contracts; and agreements among levels of government permitting the movement of labor and capital. Taken together, these arrangements generally increase the potential gains and decrease the potential losses of investment and entrepreneurship.

Such arrangements don't materialize on their own. They are put in place by governments, which are the essential suppliers of the social ingenuity—in the form of good economic institutions and policies—that undergirds markets. Governments also provide other key supports to markets, including skilled civil services; public education; well-regulated transportation, communication, and energy infrastructures; and relatively balanced distributions of wealth.[62] But governments must be strong and competent to successfully provide all these institutions, policies, and other market supports. As the political scientist Peter Evans says, setting up a vigorous market "demands accurate intelligence, inventiveness, active agency and sophisticated responsiveness to a changing economic reality."[63]

While economic optimists are happy to accept that certain institutions and policies are vital to well-functioning markets, they are less keen to acknowledge the central role of government in setting up and running the needed institutions, and devising and implementing the needed policies. Instead, they often imply that the relationship between government and the market is essentially antagonistic or mutually exclusive: more intervention by government means a less efficient market and, as a result, less wealth; less intervention by government means a better-functioning market and more wealth. For example, in their widely heralded book, *The Commanding Heights*, the economic analysts Daniel Yergin and Joseph Stanislaw write of the "global battle" at the "frontier" between the state and the market: "This frontier is not neat and well-defined. It is constantly shifting and often ambiguous. Yet through most of the century, the state has been ascendant, extending its domain further and further into what had been the territory of the market. . . . [By] the 1990s, it was government that was retreating. Communism had not only failed, it had all but disappeared in what had been the Soviet Union and, at least as an economic system, had been put aside in China. In the West, governments were shedding control and responsibilities."[64]

Yergin and Stanislaw do acknowledge that government must act as a "referee" among the market's competing forces, but their treatment of this vital role is grudging and limited. Their book, like books and articles published by many other economic commentators in the late 1990s, seems to be guided by the overriding conviction that the production of wealth in a modern economy is largely a matter of getting government out of the way. But the reality is not so simple. The relationship between government and the market is decidedly symbiotic: government creates the intricate conditions for thriving markets, while markets create the wealth that (when taxed) strengthens government. Today's most sophisticated and vigorous markets don't operate in zones that government has completely evacuated, or where its intervention is minimal. Even in the most laissez-faire capitalist economies, markets float on a sea of complex institutions, regulations, and government interventions.

Government is important. Differences in governments' competence and capability—and, consequently, in the kinds of institutions and policies that prevail in an economy—help explain why some societies are rich and others poor.[65] Yet economic theories have generally not identified government as an important determinant of growth. For example, standard neoclassical theories of the kind proposed by the Nobel–prize winner Robert Solow focus mainly on a country's endowments of labor and capital. As a result, these theories generally predict that poor countries will grow faster than rich ones; there should be, in other words, *convergence* between poor and rich countries.[66] Unfortunately, evidence does not support this prediction.[67] Recently, analysts have explained this awkward fact by showing that poor countries *can* and indeed do grow faster than rich ones, but only if conditions are right: a number of factors have to be favorable, including rates of population growth, stocks of human capital, and government economic policies. Experts now say, therefore, that countries exhibit "conditional convergence." We might question the value of this finding—conditional-convergence theories simply leave to one side some of the most intriguing possible explanations of economic growth. In particular, government is acknowledged to be important, but its role is left largely unexplored.[68]

Ideological commitments seem to keep many economists from going beyond this point. Their distaste for government, based on a deeply held assumption that it is the antithesis of the market, leaves them unwilling to analyze thoroughly its often constructive role. Yet in the mid-1990s, the American economist Mancur Olson boldly argued that this role deserves much more attention. National boundaries, he wrote, "mark the borders of public policies and institutions that are not only different, but in some cases better and in other cases worse. Those countries with the best policies and institutions achieve most of their potential, while other countries achieve only a tiny fraction of their potential income." Poor countries, he continued, have economic institutions and policies that provide the wrong structure of incentives. "The structure of incentives depends not only on what economic policies are chosen in each period, but also on the long run or institutional arrangements: on the legal systems that enforce contracts and protect property rights and on political structures, constitutional provisions, and the extent of special-interest lobbies and cartels."[69]

If economic institutions and policies are key, then so is government; and if government is key, then so are the political and social forces that shape how government works. The evolution of economic institutions and policies is affected by factors far outside the conventional domain of economists, such as the balance of social power among ethnic groups, the level of government and business corruption, or the extent of xenophobia about foreign investment. Such factors fundamentally determine whether a society can realize the full economic potential inherent in the capital, labor, natural resources, and the economically useful ideas—ingenuity—available to it. If a society is riven by internal ethnic conflicts, debilitated by corruption, or paranoid about foreign investment, it will be far poorer than it could be.

So, in our search for the sources of wealth, we have been dragged inexorably away from neat, clean, and quantifiable analyses of the roles of capital and labor in economic growth. We have had to consider, in addition, the profound effects of economic institutions and policies, and we have found ourselves, in the end, in the murky and analytically intractable world of government and politics. What early economists quite reasonably thought could be reduced to numbers, mechanism, and Cartesian equilibrium turns out to be vague, path-dependent, nonlinear, and phenomenally complex.

It was this train of thought that led me to my final adjustment to the premises underlying New Growth theory: the flow of economically useful ideas in our societies—those very ideas that tell us how to reconfigure the rock, soil, wood, water, and air around us into the miraculous things that serve our needs—is a consequence not just of economic but also of social factors, like the political struggles that shape market institutions and policies. Modern markets are, without doubt, an important part of the solution to the ingenuity supply problems faced by both rich and poor societies, but they are not simple beasts: they are intricate, fine-tuned, and vulnerable to the vagaries of politics, social conditions, and struggles for power. Our governments must be competent, strong, and ingenious if we are to set them up and get them working right.

TECHNO-HUBRIS

E CONOMIC OPTIMISTS not only place great faith in markets; they also place great faith in that ingenuity-producing powerhouse, modern science. They argue that our scientific practices and institutions—especially when directed and energized by free markets—are largely responsible for our societies' extraordinary flexibility in the face of resource scarcities and other technical challenges.

Science is certainly a key part of the story of humanity's adaptation and prosperity, but economic optimists rarely acknowledge that science faces certain fundamental constraints. Recently, I was prompted to think about these constraints when my family discovered the memoirs of my great-great-grandfather, Thomas Dixon.

A prominent English merchant in the Dutch coastal town of Flushing during the Napoleonic Wars, Thomas Dixon saw the town shift repeatedly between British and French rule as the two powers fought over the Low Countries. During periods under French occupation, he regularly smuggled captured English officers back across the Channel. At one point, he saved a portion of the British fleet blockading the Dutch coastline by rowing out at night to warn of the imminent launch of French fireships.

In May of 1810, Napoleon and his entourage arrived in Flushing with great fanfare. The keys to the town were freshly plated with silver and presented to His Majesty on a platter. As a leading figure in the community, Dixon escorted him on a tour of the town's newly reconstructed ramparts. But the emperor suspected something was amiss with the English businessman, and had him arrested at bayonet-point, taken to Paris, and imprisoned. He escaped execution by the merest fluke.

Thomas Dixon

Dixon was a gifted writer, and he makes the extraordinary events of his time sound as if they took place yesterday, not almost two centuries ago. But two centuries isn't really very long, after all—it's easily within the span of three lifetimes. And during those three lifetimes, technological change has rocketed ahead. We can get a rough impression of this change by comparing its rate across four domains of technology: military explosives, long-distance communication, personal transport, and agriculture.

In 1809, a British fleet of sixty frigates, ships of the line, and mortar vessels bombarded Flushing from offshore, leveling a good portion of the town. A near-miss buried Dixon's father up to his waist in debris. Later, a mortar shell lobbed by the British landed in a small boat in the canal outside Dixon's house.

> I had two vessels laying before my door in one of which a bombshell fell and lodged in the Cabin, when one of our servants—a bold scotch girl who from curiosity had been watching the balls as they were flying through the streets—immediately ran on board with a pail of water, snatched out the match which was still burning, poured the water on the shell, and brought it as a trophy into the house.

The standard 8-inch mortars of the time had a maximum range of about 1,600 meters; they were horribly inaccurate, and the timing of the explosion (that is, whether it was an airburst or groundburst) was determined by the length of the fuse. Their 20-kilogram shells consisted of cast iron balls filled with somewhat less than one kilogram of black powder (made up of potassium nitrate, charcoal, and sulfur) into which the British gunnery specialists offshore inserted a fuse. These were principally antipersonnel weapons, killing people with flying iron fragments. Each shell released available energy roughly equivalent to half a kilogram of TNT.[1]

Today, the conventional 16-inch guns of the decommissioned battleship *New Jersey* throw shells that pack 900 kilograms of TNT equivalent; a

Tomahawk cruise missile can deliver about 500 kilograms with ten-meter accuracy over a distance of 1,850 kilometers. Nuclear cannon developed in the 1950s (and taken out of service a couple of decades later) could throw shells tens of kilometers with yields in the range of 500,000 to one million kilograms of TNT. And the average nuclear warhead in the U.S. strategic arsenal has a yield of 200 million kilograms. Although warheads with yields of well over 50 *billion* kilograms of TNT have been produced, the trend towards ever greater explosive power has plateaued. Indeed, as delivery systems such as missiles have become more accurate in recent decades, weapons designers have generally used smaller yields. Nonetheless, it is safe to say that in three lifetimes we have seen roughly a billionfold increase in useable military explosive power.

At the same time that Thomas Dixon was showing Napoleon around the Flushing ramparts, the French had the most extensive long-distance communication system in the world—a network of semaphore towers stretching from Lille to Milan and from Brest to Metz.[2] Placed at intervals of about 15 kilometers, the towers in this "optical telegraph" had three-meter arms that could be moved to different positions. Operators used a standard codebook to set the arm positions, and they passed messages visually from one tower to the next down the line.

The semaphore network was remarkably effective. But its communications rate, in modern terminology, was only 0.5 bits of information per second. Today, common "ethernet" connections among computers have rates of 10 to 100 million bits per second. Specialized linkages—fiber-optic networks or high-speed ATM networks—now exceed tens of billions of bits per second. And computer scientists recently transmitted an astonishing one trillion bits in a single second, which is roughly the amount of information contained in three hundred years of a daily newspaper.[3] So compared to the French semaphore system used three lifetimes ago, this latest technology represents about a trillionfold improvement in performance.

After his arrest on Napoleon's orders, Thomas Dixon was at first ordered to Paris on foot. The trip took six days.

> The Gendarmes told us their instructions did not say how we were to be conveyed to Paris, and they presumed therefore the intention was to have us conducted "a petite journee"—that is, on foot—five leagues [twenty-four kilometers] per day. As they could not spare a large guard, we should each of us be tied to the tail of a horse . . . and thus conveyed

from prison to prison. After considerable conversation on this subject, I found that the promise of *Louis d'or* softened their hearts so that they consented to leave their horses behind and let us hire a carriage.

Eleven years before, when Napoleon, his fleet defeated in the Battle of the Nile, decided to return to France to overthrow the Directory, it took him fifty-four days by ship and horseback. Today the trip from Antwerp (near Flushing) to Paris by train (with the portion from Brussels to Paris by high-speed train) takes three hours, and the flight from Cairo to Paris by jet four and a half hours. This represents a fifty- to three-hundredfold improvement in transport speed.

In the early nineteenth century, Dutch farmers had some of the most productive farmland in Europe (they still do). When they were able to avoid Napoleonic depredations, their average yield of grain per hectare was around 1,600 kilograms. Today, Dutch farmers regularly achieve 6,700-kilogram yields—a fourfold increase in three lifetimes.[4]

What do these comparisons tell us? Most obviously, they remind us of the astonishing changes technology has brought about in humanity's recent history. Because we adjust to change almost as quickly as it occurs, we often lose perspective on how different our current world is from that of generations not far in the past. Just as we sometimes need a jarring experience, such as being trapped on a wilderness lake, to remind us that we live in a world of human-created miracles, we sometimes need to compare past and present technologies for meeting our most familiar human needs (food, transportation and the like) to remind us how quickly we have created those miracles.

Still, such comparisons give us only the roughest impression of the speed of technological change. Brian Arthur, the economist and pioneer of complexity theory whom we met in the chapter "Complexities," has estimated this speed by drawing an illustrative parallel between the pace of biological evolution and the pace of improvement in calculating machinery.[5] The beginning of life on Earth about 3.6 billion years ago corresponds, Arthur suggests, to the invention of addition and multiplication machines by Pascal and Leibniz in the seventeenth century. Multicellular organisms appeared about 1.9 billion years ago, a development roughly analogous to Joseph-Marie Jacquard's introduction of a punchcard-controlled loom in 1805. The Cambrian explosion of 600 million years ago—an event that saw the appearance of early forms of many of today's animals and plants—

matches the 1930s introduction of electrical calculating machines, government statistical records, and mechanized accounting. The age of the dinosaurs is likened to the age of mainframe computers beginning in the 1960s. And the advanced birds and mammals of the last 100 million years correspond to the personal computers of the 1980s and 1990s. Comparing these two time scales, Arthur estimates that technology evolves at roughly "10 million times the speed of natural evolution."

Brian Arthur's exercise is wonderfully intriguing. But, given the uncertainties involved, he admits his estimate is "more whimsy than science." The more minute comparison of Thomas Dixon's world with our own tells us something that I'd wager is ultimately more significant: though the improvement was dramatic *within* each of the four domains—that is, within explosive, communication, transport, and agricultural technologies—it varied sharply *across* these domains. Advances in transport speed and food production were impressive in themselves, but slight compared to advances in explosives and communications. Arthur's use of the technology of calculating machines as his standard of comparison means that he probably significantly overestimates the speed of technological change. Calculating machines are a species of information technology, and, as the comparison with Thomas Dixon's world makes clear, information technologies have seen some of the most startling advances in capability. Arthur is, therefore, basing his estimate on an anomalously fast-developing technology.[6]

Differences in the rate of change across technological domains do not, in general, reflect unequal investments of human brainpower in solving the problems of these domains. Rather, they reflect, in part, basic physical characteristics of the world, such as the explosive energy locked in the chemicals we create, the electromagnetic properties of elements like copper and silicon, and the biological complexity of plants and soil. Given these physical characteristics, it turns out, the concerted application of human ingenuity over three lifetimes has produced a trillionfold improvement in information transfer capability but only a fourfold increase in agricultural yields.

———————————

Economic optimists are not keen to acknowledge that technology solves some problems faster than others. But the world around us provides abundant evidence to support this observation. Once again, the objects in my office help tell the story.

On one wall of my office, near the photograph of the little girl in Patna, hangs a dramatic abstract painting of a cat—a meter-high black-and-white cat against a bright orange background. He sits upright with his front feet apart, ears curled upwards almost like horns, and tail roguishly askew behind his back. With his bright yellow eyes and impertinent stance, he looks just a bit diabolical.

The cat was painted by my mother in 1966. Like most mothers, she was a remarkable woman. She combined in one person the talents of artist, writer, and amateur scientist. But in 1970, at the age of forty, she died of multiple sclerosis. The illness hit hard and fast, robbing her first of the things essential to her artistic career—her sight, the steadiness and coordination of her hands, and her balance. It took less than a year for her body and mind to disintegrate; before our eyes, she aged thirty years.

As I sit in my office, I look across the clutter of devices on my desk in front of the diabolical cat. Amidst a jumble of cords and scraps of paper are a cordless telephone, a small compact disc player, a halogen lamp, and a notebook computer. My mother, who was fascinated by technology, never saw any such devices; some of them she couldn't even have imagined. I often reflect on the contrast between my mother's world—which existed less than half a lifetime ago—and the technologies I take for granted around me.

In the mid-1960s, my mother composed a series of short stories on a new Remington manual typewriter. I remember being impressed, as a pre-teen, by its sleek design and keys with odd symbols like @ and #. In the year before her death, she said I could have the Remington if I learned to type. At the time, it seemed a daunting hurdle. But in my teenage years I found an old typing self-instruction book, and when I arrived at university in the mid-1970s I was able to touch-type all my essays on the very same Remington.

Now, as I sit at my desk, I am using a notebook computer. It is only three years old and already ancient. By the standards of the day, it has a primitive screen, too limited a memory, and a lumbering processing chip. Yet it still represents a remarkable convergence of technological accomplishments going back beyond the invention of the transistor at Bell Labs in late 1947. In one compact package, I have advanced screen, battery, memory, processor, and high-impact plastic technologies. By itself, a relatively unheralded subcomponent—the hard drive—brings together multiple developments in recording heads, magnetic media, servo mechanics, and signal processing.[7] And each of these technologies is continuing its rapid and relentless improvement in efficiency, power, lightness, and durability. The amount of information stored on a square centimeter of disk drive increased almost five-thousandfold from 1980 to 1998. Overnight, it seems, nickel-cadmium batteries changed to nickel–metal hydride batteries, which became lithium-ion cells with their own microcontrollers; the next stage, I gather, will be cells made largely of plastic.[8] Passive-matrix liquid crystal displays have given way to active-matrix displays, with field emission displays and electroluminescent panels on the horizon. The speed of the main processing chip vaults upward by a hundred megahertz every few months.

Nothing better exemplifies this progress than the history of the lowly transistor, a tiny electronic device that amplifies, controls, and generates electric signals. When John Bardeen, Walter Brattain, and William Shockley attached two strips of gold foil to a sliver of germanium and discovered they could boost an electric signal nearly one-hundredfold, they unleashed a mighty avalanche of technological change. The first commercial transistor was about a centimeter in size; by the late 1950s it was only millimeters long; and eventually, with the aid of integrated circuit technology, it shrank to less than one-thousandth of a millimeter. As physicist Michael Riordan notes: "Today the transistor is little more than an abstract physical principle imprinted innumerable times on narrow slivers of silicon." Costs of production are almost infinitesimally small—less, Riordan claims, than the cost of printing a single character in a newspaper. He goes on: "More than any other factor, the fantastic shrinkage of the transistor in both size and cost is what has allowed the average person to own and operate a computer that is far more powerful than anything the armed services or major corporations could afford a few decades ago. If we had instead to rely on vacuum tubes, for example, the computing power of a Pentium chip would require a machine as big as the Pentagon."[9]

My ancient three-year-old notebook computer—open before me on my desk—is a truly remarkable embodiment of human ingenuity, and together with my phone and CD player, it vastly broadens my agency horizon—my reach in time and space. As I tap away on my keyboard, I can pull material together from the dozens of papers and articles I have written over the years. By logging on to the Internet, I can exchange messages with colleagues from China to Norway and find information (via the World Wide Web) on virtually every subject known to humankind. With my portable phone I can reach any of more than a billion other phones on the planet, almost instantaneously. And with my compact disc player I can listen to concerts and performances by the greatest orchestras, bands, and singers in the world. All this is at my fingertips. I don't even have to move across the room.

With so much capacity and power within our individual reach, we could be forgiven for thinking that anything is within our grasp. We could reasonably suppose that we are clever enough to do anything we want and overcome any challenge we face.

Then I look up again at the cat. Despite decades of intensive medical research, I know that multiple sclerosis is still with us, and that sufferers have seen only modest improvements in treatment. Although newspapers occasionally write of major breakthroughs, the disease still cripples millions of young adults around the world. Multiple sclerosis is entangled with some of the toughest and most complex of biomedical problems—problems that remain unsolved.

It is an "autoimmune" disease—a category that includes rheumatoid arthritis and lupus. In these diseases the body's immune system, which normally aims its arsenal of responses at pathogens invading from outside, instead turns on the body itself. Autoimmune diseases are characterized by circulation in the blood of antibodies targeted against the body's own tissues. In the case of multiple sclerosis, one target is the sheath of fat and protein, called myelin, that surrounds nerve fibers in the body and brain like the insulation around electrical cords. Damage to this sheath degrades the signals carried by the nerve's fibers, especially in those pathways involving vision, sensation, and control of limbs. Recently, researchers have found that the disease also directly severs nerve cells in the brain.[10]

But perhaps the most horrible thing about the disease, especially its severer forms, is its roller-coaster development. Sufferers experience remissions and relapses in repeated succession. Hope is followed by despair and then by hope again. Yet the trend is often downwards towards permanent paralysis.

Since the 1960s, researchers have discovered that multiple sclerosis arises from a complex set of synergistic genetic and environmental factors. The action of several genes, on separate human chromosomes, plays a role, but researchers have not yet determined the specific locations of these genes on the chromosomes. Nor have they learned how they combine with each other and with a person's physical and psychological environment to cause the disease. The available treatments, based on this rudimentary information, are not very effective, reducing relapse rates by, at best, only about 30 percent.

Despite this mixed record, I am sure that medical researchers will someday humble multiple sclerosis, as they will humble all those terrible diseases—from cancer to Alzheimer's—that take away our loved ones. Scientists' recent, spectacular progress in understanding diseases of the immune system such as AIDS tells me that the long-awaited breakthrough might not be far away. But the cat reminds me of my mother, and the contrast between my mother's world and the world of technology on my desk reminds me that human knowledge and ingenuity progress at different rates in different domains.

This is not simply a reflection of differences in humanity's need for progress in various technological domains; in fact, there may be only the roughest relationship between the degree of need and the rate of technological progress. Necessity, it seems, is not the only—perhaps not even the most important—mother of invention.

The economic historian Nathan Rosenberg emphasizes this point. "Many important categories of human wants," he writes, "have long gone either unsatisfied or very badly catered for in spite of well-established demand." Comparing progress in navigation and medical technologies from the sixteenth to the nineteenth century, he acknowledges that navigation advanced in part because of the pressing demand for new techniques. "But it is also true that a great potential demand existed in the same period for improvements in the healing arts generally, but that no such improvements were forthcoming." The difference, he argues, is that the foundation of scientific understanding at the time underpinned fast progress in the development of navigation technology, but not in medicine. "The essential explanation is that the state of mathematics and astronomy afforded a useful and reliable knowledge base for navigational improvements, whereas medicine at that time had no such base. Progress in medicine had to await the development of the science of bacteriology in the second half of the nineteenth century. Although the field of medicine was one which attracted great interest, considerable sums of money, and large numbers of scientifically trained people, medical progress was very small until the great breakthroughs of Pasteur and Lister."[11]

The products of science and technology—the treatments for antibiotic-resistant disease, the advanced computer models of Earth's changing climate, the bioengineered grains that can grow in a water-scarce world—will not always be there, in the right forms, when and where we want them. History shows that just because we want a problem solved doesn't mean the problem will be solved.

_____

Basic science—that is, the research that gives us a deeper and more fine-grained knowledge of the natural world around us—must be the foundation of any new practical technology. And we are adding to our stock of scientific knowledge at a rate of 4 to 8 percent a year, as measured by publications in scientific journals—a doubling time of ten to fifteen years.[12] But the connections between this continuing effort and the useful technology it produces are often indirect and long delayed. Decades may pass before an obscure bit of number theory in mathematics or an odd finding in particle physics makes its way into a new process for compressing data or making computer chips. Sometimes cross-fertilization is key: the findings of basic science in an apparently unrelated area can turn out to be crucial for a new technology. So it's often not clear in advance what line of research will produce the biggest payoffs in practical technologies. Are we more likely to generate useful cancer treatments by investing in cellular biology or by mapping the human genome? Can we best increase the yields of our corn crops by focusing on the molecular biology of nitrogen fixation, or by searching for new genetic strains of corn in the wild?

As well, the knowledge generated by such basic science is cumulative: each new discovery builds on a host of earlier ones. Under normal conditions, scientists generate knowledge much as a bricklayer builds a wall, one brick at a time. Each brick—each new piece of well-tested knowledge—sits atop a sturdy foundation of other bricks and becomes part, in turn, of an ever growing foundation for other bricks.

The rate at which the wall grows—that is, the pace of cumulative scientific discovery—is marked by jumps and lags as scientists make breakthroughs or lose time pursuing fruitless leads. Roughly speaking, four factors affect this pace and, in turn, our supply of technical ingenuity.

The first factor consists of human cognitive limits, some of which I discussed in the chapter "Brains and Ingenuity." These limits hamper our ability to understand our world's natural phenomena, and they are especially telling when we try to unravel the workings of fundamentally complex systems like the planet's ecology and climate. We cannot fully grasp the emergent properties and behavior of these systems if we only study their component parts in isolation from each other; sometimes we must study the systems as integrated wholes.[13] But an integrated approach means that we must think simultaneously about many components and the causal links between these components; in other words, we have to be able to hold and manipulate in our minds multiple ideas at the same time, which is very hard for our brains to do. We can compensate by developing large mathematical or computer models of these complex systems, like the general circulation models that climate scientists use. Yet such models confront us with an inescapable trade-off: the more accurately they represent the reality of the complex systems we are studying, and the more accurately they track the behavior of these systems, the more complex they become, and (given our inherent cognitive constraints) the less we understand what's going on inside them.[14]

The second factor affecting science's rate of progress is the intrinsic complexity or difficulty of the research field's subject matter. Put simply, the central scientific puzzles in a particular field may be extraordinarily hard to solve, as we saw in the case of multiple sclerosis. Similarly, as Wally Broecker suggested in the chapter "An Angry Beast," our poor understanding of ocean-atmospheric systems is a result, in part, of their enormous complexity.

There are countless other examples. One of my favorites is the history of our efforts to develop power from nuclear fusion. The source of energy in the sun, stars, and thermonuclear weapons, fusion has long been the holy grail of energy researchers. In the 1950s, during the early exhilarating years of research, many experts believed controlled fusion technology could give us a cheap, clean, and virtually infinite supply of energy. Whereas conventional nuclear power produces energy by fission, splitting apart the heavy nuclei in atoms of elements like uranium and plutonium, fusion produces energy by forcing together, or fusing, the nuclei of the lightest element, hydrogen. But these hydrogen nuclei are positively charged, so to get them to fuse they must be slammed together with enough force to overcome their natural tendency to repel each other. The solution is to heat the hydrogen gas (experimenters usually use a mixture of two rare types, deuterium and tritium) to tens of millions of degrees Celsius. The heat strips the hydrogen atoms of their electrons, and the gas becomes a *plasma* of disassociated hydrogen nuclei and electrons. If the plasma is confined at a high enough temperature and pressure for long enough, fusing nuclei will generate more energy than was required to heat the plasma in the first place. This is called the *break-even* point—and if fusion technology is ever to be a practical source of energy, it must far surpass the break-even point, because only then will it generate more power than it consumes.

While the theory of nuclear fusion is well developed, the goal of making fusion technology a practical source of energy has receded into the future as fast as work has progressed. It has always seemed twenty, thirty, or forty years distant; and with each decade success seems to get no closer. In 1987, the U.S. Office of Technology Assessment concluded that after $20 billion invested in research, it would take at least another $20 billion and twenty years just to reach a stage where evaluation of the technology's economic feasibility could start.[15] By 1998, with funding cutbacks in the major countries leading the research, most experts predicted that the first commercial fusion reactor would not appear before 2050.

What went wrong? Fundamentally, the problem was that the science was unexpectedly difficult. It turns out to be very hard to confine a hot enough plasma for long enough; as soon as nuclei within the superheated and highly turbulent gas come in contact with the walls of a reactor vessel they lose heat and the fusion reaction fails. So researchers have tried several confinement methods to keep the plasma away from any material surface. The most widely used is magnetic confinement, in which the plasma is bottled within intersecting magnetic fields, often produced by a huge doughnut-shaped device called a "tokamak." But the magnetic fields are extremely difficult to control—as "wriggly as a fabric made of interwoven eels" according to one commentator—and the plasma tends to squeeze through holes and instabilities at the outer edges of the bottle.[16] As a result, to date no experimental reactor has come close to the break-even point. "After billions of dollars of international investment in tokamaks," one commentator writes, "the best machines that have been built produce, at most, one-third of the energy that they consume."[17]

We often have trouble predicting how quickly a given technology will develop, because we don't know beforehand whether key breakthroughs in basic science will come easily or with difficulty. The progress of fusion power may critically hinge, for instance, on progress in our understanding of turbulence or of advanced magnets, but the pace of this basic science can't be forced, even if the need is clear. It's true that pouring money into research sometimes helps: the last fifteen years' remarkable advances in AIDS treatment were produced, in large part, by an enormous financial investment in research. But money alone doesn't guarantee prompt results in desired directions: despite an investment of over $30 billion since President Nixon's 1971 call for a national crusade against cancer, progress in treatment has been excruciatingly slow.[18] (In any case, basic science generally becomes more costly as it delves deeper into nature; it requires more expensive scientific instruments and equipment, and it demands more specialized scientific expertise, because as our knowledge base grows, it's harder for one person to master anything more than a narrow subfield.[19])

The third general factor affecting science's rate of progress is the nature of its scientific institutions—from its laboratories to its procedures for funding research and for peer review of scientific papers. How well do these institutions function, and what incentives do they give scientists to do good work? Progress may be slow if laboratories don't exist or are badly equipped, scientists and technicians with the right expertise are in short supply, adequate research funding isn't available, or the best scholarly journals aren't accessible. Deeply embedded boundaries between disciplines can hinder creative cross-disciplinary cooperation, and such boundaries are reinforced by a host of institutions and practices, from the traditional division of universities into departments to research funding agencies and scholarly journals that look skeptically on interdisciplinary work. Even within a given discipline or field of study, researchers may be so divided into competing camps, promoting alternative scientific theories, that envy and antagonism get in the way of creativity and cumulation.

Shortages of funding and human capital affect science in poor countries especially harshly. Many of the environmental problems, diseases, and other challenges confronting these countries demand advanced science that they can't afford, which causes them to rely heavily on technologies from rich countries that are often unsuited to their needs.[20] They have little money for research laboratories and equipment: even in large and relatively prosperous countries such as Brazil and China, the simplest tools—like clean pipettes and petri dishes—are often scarce. The far more expensive devices, like centrifuges and gene-sequencing machines, that are basic equipment for a modern molecular biological laboratory can cost hundreds of thousands of dollars; they are usually available only in the country's elite institutions. As well, researchers often can't get hold of key scholarly journals and so rely on charitable handouts from colleagues in rich countries. And they find it difficult to get published in these journals, which are almost all produced in rich countries, because of a pervasive editorial bias against science from the developing world.[21]

Scarcities of human capital—highly trained researchers and skilled administrators—can also cripple science in poor countries. Sub-Saharan Africa has fewer than fifty scientists and engineers in research and development for every million people, while the figure in rich countries is around three thousand. The continent as a whole lost sixty thousand middle and high-level managers between 1985 and 1990. India, too, faces this problem: between 1970 and the early 1990s, 30 percent of graduates of the Indian Institute of Technology in Bombay emigrated, as did 45 percent of graduates of the All-India Institute of Medical Sciences.[22]

Science's social context—the economic and political institutions, values, and culture within which it operates—is the fourth factor that can affect its rate of progress. In the last chapter, "Ingenuity and Wealth," I noted that opportunities for economic profit clearly motivate much technological progress. But this profit motive won't be strong if intellectual property rights are vague, weak, or unenforced. Property rights can be tricky, though: if ownership of intellectual property is hampered by excessive regulation, technological innovators won't be able to reap the rewards of their efforts; but if innovators are allowed complete control, useful ideas may be prevented from spilling into the broader pool of public knowledge, where they can be drawn on by others. And there are strong arguments, in any case, that the private marketplace won't adequately fund the most basic kinds of science—the fundamental research that is often highly abstract and seemingly distant from the day-to-day concerns of the real world, and on which much practical technological progress ultimately depends. This basic science needs government support.[23]

Political stability is essential too, because science is a fragile activity that is extremely vulnerable to social turmoil. The recent experience in Russia provides an object lesson: the country's decade-long slide into penury and disorder has crippled its once world-class research establishment and caused a general drop in respect for analytical thought and a sharp rise in occult and anti-science movements.[24]

Finally, the broader context of social values and culture powerfully affects science. This influence is often a good thing: social values and culture can instill respect and enthusiasm for science, and they can help guide scientific activity when it raises legitimate ethical or environmental concerns. Sometimes, though, their influence is more pernicious: in the West, for instance, we have seen a groundswell of distrust, misunderstanding, and even fear of science. These feelings have many sources—some understandable and reasonable, some less so.[25] They often distort our research priorities and discourage the best and brightest from becoming scientists. And in a world increasingly dominated by technology, widespread distrust and misunderstanding of science creates serious problems for how we govern ourselves in our democracies.[26]

The above four factors affect the pace of discovery in basic science. But even when key breakthroughs have been made, many years can pass before the new knowledge is translated into practical technology that is widely used—that is, technical ingenuity.[27] Often this delay occurs, once again, because the right market incentives don't exist. Laws and regulations may have to be adapted, industrial standards established, and other, complementary technologies developed and diffused before entrepreneurs can reap adequate profits from disseminating their new technology throughout society.

A classic example is facsimile technology.[28] Most people are surprised to learn that the original idea for a facsimile machine was patented over a century and a half ago, in 1843. Alexander Bain, a Scottish clockmaker, proposed a primitive device in which a sending machine passed a stylus over a raised image on a metal block. As the stylus rose and fell, it caused an electric current in a circuit to be alternately broken and completed. The change in current, in turn, made a stylus on a receiving machine move up and down, thus reproducing the image. Over time various inventors, including Thomas Edison, improved Bain's original idea, and the development of the photoelectric cell in the late nineteenth century eventually allowed newspapers to transmit photographs over long distances.

But widespread use of fax technology had to wait for other economic, social, and technological developments. In the 1930s, the American Telephone and Telegraph Company (AT&T) decided not to develop facsimile services for its Bell system lines. Only with deregulation of the U.S. telephone network in the late 1960s could companies attach non-Bell technologies to these lines. This change, and similar deregulation in Japan, gave fax technology a natural communication infrastructure, and a multitude of companies and inventors suddenly had an incentive to perfect the technology. Fax machines didn't burst into our everyday lives, however, until several further things happened: in the 1960s and 1970s, a United Nations committee established technical standards that allowed machines made by different manufacturers to communicate with each other; in the 1980s, digital technology and other improvements boosted transmission speed and image quality, and allowed the use of plain paper; meanwhile, rising dissatisfaction with regular postal systems encouraged people to find new ways of sending information. As a result, between 1985 and 1991, U.S. sales of fax machines grew twelvefold, to six million, and by the early 1990s U.S. consumers could choose from over 600 different machines.

Fax technology is a marvelous invention, but the idea languished for many long years before it became a practical reality. The story of this technology, like that of nuclear fusion, tells us something about the limits of our ability to supply the technical ingenuity we need. I don't agree with commentators who have recently claimed that "the end of science" is near; the current pace of overall scientific discovery and the range of issues still to be explored suggest we are a long way from that point.[29] But we must nevertheless recognize that many factors constrain the progress of science and technology. And this means that, at the very least, there's a time lag, often decades long, between our identification of a problem and our delivery of a technical solution to it.

––––––––––

It can be both amusing and disconcerting to review past predictions of technological change to see where they were right and wrong. Often, it seems, the success rate of predictions, even when they are made by experts, is little better than what we'd expect from random guesses. Most predictions rely heavily on the assumption that existing technologies will improve incrementally over time. This approach makes sense for short-range projections, but over the long term it invariably misses the rare major breakthroughs, like genetic engineering and microprocessor technology, that have truly revolutionary consequences. And occasional attempts to anticipate such breakthroughs, like past claims that fusion power would produce endless energy, usually look silly with the passage of time.

An entertaining source of popular predictions about the future of science and technology is science fiction. It's often a truly jarring experience to review episodes of American TV shows, such as *Star Trek* or *Lost in Space* from the 1960s, and to recall that the future they represented didn't seem at all implausible then—in many ways, it was actually quite like the everyday world at the time. The science writer James Gleick notes that the shows were replete with gadgets and devices that were common in the 1960s but have since been eliminated from our lives, like cameras with flashbulbs, computers with reel-to-reel tape memories, and telephones with rotary dials.[30] But these shows also portrayed technologies that aren't even close to being realized today, such as warp-speed travel through space, teleporters, and robots that can engage in everyday conversation.

In Stanley Kubrick's wonderful 1968 movie *2001: A Space Odyssey*, based on Arthur C. Clarke's novel, the renegade computer HAL became operational on January 12, 1997. The passing of this actual date in 1997 was an occasion for earnest reflection by science commentators on the technological future depicted in the movie.[31] I can remember, as a twelve-year-old, being completely convinced that such a future was plausible. And this conviction wasn't just the delusion of a science-addicted boy. The year after *2001* was released, Americans landed on the moon. By 1972, only three years later, a total of twenty-four humans had already made it into space beyond low-Earth orbit (that is, beyond about 1,000 kilometers above the surface of Earth). We were on the move: a permanent colony on the moon could not be far away, and the kind of regular, commercialized travel between Earth and the moon portrayed in the movie was, almost everybody was sure, soon to come. Undoubtedly it would come by that distant year 2001!

Yet by 2000, more than thirty years later, the number of humans who have made it beyond low-Earth orbit still stands at twenty-four, and it's unlikely to rise in the foreseeable future.[32]

HAL was the unquestioned villain of *2001*. Again, the computer's abilities seemed entirely plausible at the time. In fact we didn't give the most basic of those abilities—the ability to converse in natural language—much thought at all. In 1968, it was taken for granted that computers would soon be able to talk. To the extent that we doubted HAL's plausibility, we focused on its scheming, malicious behavior, and asked if a human-created machine could develop such independence of will and become so wicked. But in 2000 we have yet to build a computer with the ability to talk. The science commentator Paul Wallich writes: "So many aspects of everyday life as depicted in *2001* have receded over the technological horizon that it should come as no surprise that even the most basic of HAL's abilities—carrying out simple conversation—is beyond modern computers. They cannot reliably convert sounds to an internal representation of meaning; they cannot even generate naturally inflected speech. Machines still lack the enormous, implicit base of knowledge about the world and the intuitive understandings of emotion or belief most people take for granted."[33]

Of course, science fiction *is* fiction—the wild imaginings of novelists and script writers with little grounding in science (although that cannot be said of Arthur C. Clarke). Some people would dismiss it out of hand as a source of credible predictions of the future. But in fact, even the best-informed prognosticators fare little better than science fiction writers. Two decades ago, notes John Rennie, the editor of *Scientific American*, most specialists believed that building a self-contained artificial heart was an achievable goal—"not a simple chore, of course, but a straightforward one." But building a heart "compatible with the delicate tissues and subtle chemistry of the body has proved elusive." Even the most expert forecasters, Rennie argues, are "sometimes much too optimistic about the short-run prospect" for technological success. More fundamentally, most technology predictions are "simplistic and, hence, unrealistic." He goes on to assert that "A good technology must by definition be useful. It must be able to survive fierce buffeting by market forces, economic and social conditions, governmental policies, quirky timing, whims of fashion and all the vagaries of human nature and custom."[34]

In 1967, two of the world's most competent futurists, Herman Kahn and Anthony Wiener of the Hudson Institute, released a set of predictions of year-2000 technologies.[35] They listed one hundred technological innovations that would "almost certainly occur." Some they got right: they foresaw video players, automated banking systems, and the use of high-altitude cameras for mapping and land-use investigations. But many of their projections were wrong, sometimes woefully wrong: they anticipated the widespread use of nuclear explosives for excavation and mining, of robots "slaved" to humans, of large-scale desalinization, and, most remarkably, of "inexpensive and reasonably effective" systems for defending against ballistic missile attack. They also missed some of today's key technologies entirely, including personal computers and video games.[36] Overall, despite their self-assurance and sense of certainty, their success rate was considerably less than 50 percent.

Given this history, can we make *any* useful predictions about the likely evolution of technology in coming decades? I believe we can, and I'm willing to go out on a limb and do so myself. I know that in ten or twenty years' time, my forecasts are highly likely to seem quaint and misguided, yet I think it's important to try to anticipate where technology will leap next: if we focus only on the constraints technology faces, we'll be ill prepared to anticipate how new technologies will close or widen future ingenuity gaps. So in the next pages I'll quickly consider four key technological domains: genetics and medicine, information processing and computation, materials engineering, and machine miniaturization.

Let's begin with genetics and medicine. The mysteries of DNA were initially unlocked in the 1950s. Over the following thirty years, scientists developed a set of powerful methods for manipulating genetic material—methods that allowed researchers to rapidly push forward their understanding of the genetic information contained in all life. As new findings tumbled out of researchers' laboratories, commentators predicted that genetic technologies would soon produce a wave of benefits—and ethical dilemmas. But in fact, surprisingly little has changed in our daily lives. Some new drugs and crops have appeared on the market, and some clever technical accomplishments, including the cloning of mammals (beginning with Dolly, the famous sheep) have prompted wide public debate. But as of 2000, the wave of benefits and dilemmas has not yet broken over us.

It soon will. Genetic knowledge and technologies have matured, and have crossed a critical threshold. Molecular biologists can now manipulate DNA with far greater precision and speed than were possible even a decade ago. We can now delete or "knock out," with relative ease, specific chunks of genetic code in an embryonic plant or animal; scientists can then study what happens as the organism develops into an adult without the deleted code, a procedure that helps determine what functions, if any, the genetic material serves. Conversely, researchers can insert new or different code into an organism's genes; in fact, they can actually move genetic code from one species to another (producing "transgenic" organisms). As a result, scientists can genetically program animals like pigs to produce human hormones, proteins, and other substances that are extracted and used as supplements.[37]

Molecular biologists have also mapped and read the entire genetic sequence of several simple organisms, including yeast, some species of bacteria, and the fruit fly, an insect that has been of interest to biologists. And by the time this book appears the Human Genome Project should have sequenced all three billion base pairs in human DNA.

These techniques and knowledge will deeply influence medicine. Victor McKusick, one of the pioneers of modern medical genetics, identifies three beneficial trends in particular. First, he says, genetic researchers are turning their attention from the specific genes that cause disease to the causal mechanism or "pathway" by which a malfunctioning gene, in interaction with other factors, produces disease. "Now that we increasingly know the why—which genes cause certain diseases—we must find out the how—how the genetic defects lead to particular problems." Second, McKusick sees more vigorous research on complex diseases, like multiple sclerosis, that involve more than one gene. To date, most research has focused on single-gene disorders, which are fairly rare. However, "disorders such as hypertension, cancer, asthma, and major mental illnesses involve a combination of genes, and that's what researchers are starting to try to understand." Third, McKusick notes that the rapid accumulation of genetic data for multiple species allows scientists to identify, far more quickly than before, what a newly discovered piece of genetic code does. "Because computer databases now contain genome information of various species, including the functions of various genes, scientists can compare a particular human DNA sequence with similar sequences of other creatures."[38]

The first quarter of the twenty-first century will almost certainly produce a self-reinforcing cascade of practical genetic technologies in medicine. Unless blocked by law, genetic screening of fetuses, for example, will become common; and we will likely see the beginning of therapies that involve altering or inserting genes in children and adults. Genetically altered animals will grow replacement organs, called "xenotransplants," that human immune systems won't reject. (Some prominent scientists are worried that xenotransplantation may allow lethal viruses to jump from their animal hosts, particularly pigs, to humans; but the demand for transplant organs is rising so fast that the technology will almost certainly be developed, albeit under scrutiny.[39]) Perhaps most significantly, we may also see germline engineering, which is the deliberate manipulation of the genetic material in human eggs and sperm to enhance or alter traits in the resulting person, traits such as disease resistance, life span, or intelligence. Since these traits could then be transmitted through the person's children to future generations, germline engineering would give humanity the astonishing ability to direct its own evolution.[40]

Such advances will not be limited to medicine, but will also revolutionize agriculture, animal husbandry, fisheries, forestry, and practically every other human activity that exploits living things. Already, for instance, fisheries researchers have injected coho embryos with sockeye genes that pump out extra growth hormone; the resulting transgenic coho mature three times as fast and weigh on average eleven times as much as their non-treated cousins.[41] (One experimental fish grew to thirty-seven times the average weight.) In the future, scientists will also undoubtedly develop food grains—such as corn, wheat, and rice—that fix their own nitrogen. Unfortunately, though, the wide use of such crops is probably two decades in the future; they will not arrive in time to prevent the massive and damaging increase in nitrogen compounds in the Earth's environment discussed in the chapter "Our New World."

Now let's play the prediction game for information processing and computation technologies. We'll see further astounding progress in this already frenetic arena, especially in the integrated circuits that lie at the heart of modern computers. For over thirty years, one rule of thumb has held true, more or less, for memory chips and microprocessors (the latter being the chips that actually do calculations and manipulate information in computers). Called Moore's law after Gordon Moore, one of the founders of the Intel Corporation, this rule says that the amount of information compressed on a given area of chip doubles every eighteen months.[42] But today, electrical components on chips are so tightly packed that this rate of improvement may not be sustainable through further miniaturization alone. One problem is that the waves of ultraviolet light used to transfer circuits to a chip—in a process called "photolithography"—are too wide to make chip features much smaller than the current one seven-thousandth of a millimeter.[43] But by using X-ray light (which has even smaller waves than ultraviolet light) engineers may be able to cut feature size further, to perhaps less than one ten-thousandth of a millimeter, or about a thousand times smaller than the diameter of a human hair. At that size—a size that chip manufacturers will probably reach around 2010—more fundamental physical limits start to kick in: because key chip components will be separated by only a few atoms, the electrical insulation among components will start to break down.[44] Nonetheless, for the foreseeable future it seems likely that we can sustain the momentum of chip improvement. Intel has recently announced, for instance, the release of "multilevel cell flash memory" that allows two bits of information to be stored where only a single bit could be stored before.[45]

The first microprocessor, the Intel 4004, was introduced in 1971 and contained 2,300 transistors; by the mid-1990s Intel's Pentium II microprocessor had 7.5 million transistors. During that period, the performance of micro-processors improved 25,000-fold. Indeed, the rate of improvement increased from 35 percent a year in the mid-1980s to about 55 percent a year (or an astonishing 4 percent a month) by the mid-1990s. In the last few years, performance improvements have come not just from packing ever more transistors onto a chip, but also from cleverly sequencing or "pipe-lining" information within the chip and from locating memory "caches" right on the microprocessor itself. The next step may be to construct single chips with multiple processors that can carry out tasks in parallel. Eventually, microprocessor and memory chips may be combined to reduce wiring and thereby the time for information transmission.

Writing in 1995, David Paterson, a professor of computer science at the University of California, Berkeley, suggested that the combined improvements discussed above could produce gains in microprocessor performance, in the twenty-five years between 1995 to 2020, as large as those in the *fifty* years prior to 1995 (that is, since the dawn of the computer age). "This estimate means that one desktop computer in 2020 will be as powerful as all the computers in Silicon Valley today. . . . The implications of such a breath-taking advance are limited only by our imaginations."[46]

But improvements in chip technology are only one part of the continuing, even accelerating, information revolution. We will soon see major leaps in computer software, artificial intelligence, and the movement of information. For example, as processors become cheaper and smaller, they'll be embedded in everything around us, from pieces of paper and light switches to our clothing; and as wireless communication improves, we'll increasingly find ourselves surrounded by a distributed network of countless small processors sharing information and making decisions among themselves—about the temperature of our office buildings, the best routes we should take home from work, and the foods we should put in our shopping carts.

In software, computer scientists are now experimenting with a technique—called "genetic programming"—in which computer programs essentially design themselves. Inside a computer the scientists create a Darwinian environment where individual computer programs compete with others to solve a problem of interest. Through a process akin to natural selection, those programs that do well are allowed to reproduce and swap computer code with other successful programs; those that don't are eliminated from the population. The best programs that emerge, after many iterations of selection and reproduction, can be completely opaque to an outside expert, containing hundreds of inscrutable expressions in computer code. But they can also work very well—in fact, even in these early days of research, some work better than expert-designed programs. Researchers are now starting to link genetic programming with specialized computer circuit boards (called "field-programmable gate arrays") that can change their own wiring designs when directed to do so.[47] The simultaneous and interdependent evolution of software and hardware could completely overturn our conception of computers and could produce startling progress on a whole range of mathematical and technical problems.[48]

One of these problems is artificial intelligence. The field of artificial intelligence (or AI, as insiders call it) seeks to develop computer systems that can mimic human cognitive abilities, like the ability to order a meal at a restaurant, to make one's way down a crowded street, or to read and understand a newspaper. As a graduate student in political science at MIT in the 1980s, I wanted to explore the inner workings of people's understanding of political events, and I thought AI could help. The core task was to get computers to understand "natural" language—that is, the language that you and I use on a day-to-day basis. In other words, the task was to make the key linguistic abilities of Arthur Clarke's HAL a reality. In the early to mid-1980s, the field was abuzz with ideas about how to reach this goal. But as I noted about HAL, grasping the meaning of even simple statements in natural language—say, a newspaper story about Al Gore's presidential election campaign in 2000—is a far more complex process than most experts initially imagined. We bring an immense store of beliefs, assumptions, and commonsense knowledge about the world to any statement we hear or read, and we are also influenced by many other factors, including the context of that statement and the speaker's or writer's intentions. In the 1980s, the task of representing and managing this background knowledge effectively within a computer was insurmountable, and computers running even the best natural language programs often produced gibberish in response to even the simplest questions.

Today AI is in the doldrums, but here is my prediction: AI will be back in the news repeatedly over the next decades, and it will change our lives. Douglas Lenat, leader of a large AI effort called the CYC Project (as in en-*cyc*-lopedia), believes a turnaround may be near. "Now that the world has all but given up on the AI dream," he writes, "artificial intelligence stands on the brink of success."[49] Lenat's team is developing effective ways to represent background knowledge in huge, carefully partitioned databases. These databases allow computers to correctly answer complex questions about texts, even when the answers demand long strings of inference. Much work remains to be done, but I share Lenat's optimism: coupled with advanced voice recognition software (perhaps designed by genetic programming), natural language processing will allow us to perform everyday tasks by simply talking to the machines around us, to our cars, houses, and computers. We will be able to send intelligent software "agents" into computerized libraries and the World Wide Web to gather, interpret, and deliver to us information on specific issues. Eventually, we may even be able to embed small devices in our ears (much like hearing aids) that will translate into our native tongue speech in foreign languages (*Star Trek*'s universal translator, or almost). HAL is not, I believe, just a figment of our science-fiction-dazzled imaginations. He may be a late arrival at the party, but he is on his way.

———————

Taken together, these impending advances in computer hardware and software guarantee that within a relatively short time we will be able to process, store, and interpret quantities of information that are truly staggering, even by today's astonishing standards. We will also be able to send more of it, faster, to more places than we can currently dream of.

Inside all modern computation and telecommunication devices—from microprocessors to satellites—are radically new materials that conduct electricity and emit light (the carriers of information) in precise amounts and frequencies. The key materials in semiconductors, lasers, and optical cables are now custom designed, sometimes almost atom by atom, to perform the specific tasks required by electrical engineers. For example, the process of "molecular beam epitaxy," invented in the early 1970s and used to create semiconductor material, has become so precise that a square centimeter of semiconductor crystal containing over a quadrillion atoms might have just three atoms out of place. Physics, chemistry, and modern computers have converged to give scientists the capacity to build materials with specific properties, on demand. As Ivan Amato, the author of *Stuff*, says: "The materials research community has reached a new plateau of unprecedented power in its ability to understand, control, and manipulate the material world." Do you need, he asks, "a lightweight alloy that remains strong at the searing temperatures of a scramjet operating at many times the speed of sound and able to withstand the frictional offensives of atmospheric molecules scouring the material like supersonic sandblasting? Do you need a polymeric material compatible with brain tissue that in the presence of specified levels of a specific neurotransmitter will release pharmaceutical agents previously loaded into the polymer? How about concrete ten or twenty times stronger than any available now? Call in your local materials engineer."[50]

Chemists can now design and build molecules with the exact shapes needed to serve specific functions in biological systems. Notes Peter Atkins of Lincoln College: "They can build molecules that can replicate themselves, or act as fingers, tongs, or pencil cases, or as minute containers for reactions."[51] Chemists have also discovered how to create metallocene catalysts that give them great control over the growth of the long, chainlike molecules—called polymers—that make up plastics. The resulting materials are exceptionally strong, durable, and transparent, and can be used in everything from motors to medical equipment needing repeated high-temperature sterilization.[52] The ability to build things atom by atom may also eventually allow engineers to create key electronic components, like transistors, out of only a few molecules; this new field of "molecular electronics" therefore suggests how we might continue miniaturizing our computers far beyond the physical limits inherent in today's silicon chip technology.

Much of all this extraordinary technical progress and promise, whether in the fields of biology, information, or materials, comes from advances in manipulating tiny things—DNA molecules, atoms in semiconductors, and long-chain polymers. Similarly, in the domain of machine technology, we will soon see a flood of minuscule devices that can do everything from control turbulence around a plane's wing to stabilize buildings during earthquakes. These devices, known as microelectromechanical systems or MEMS, combine microprocessor and microsensor technologies with tiny motors, called microactuators. They can be manufactured by the millions using photolithographic processes very similar to those used for computer chips.[53] Depending on their design and programming, MEMS might respond to changes in their local environment by (for example) sending a tiny electrical signal, shutting a minute valve, or moving a tiny flap or arm. Taken individually, each response is almost unnoticeable; but when the responses of many MEMS are coordinated, the results can be astonishing.[54]

For instance, it may soon be possible to stretch a skin of MEMS across the surface of a plane's wing, each device two-tenths of a millimeter in diameter, and each programmed to detect changes in air pressure, direction, and velocity preceding a turbulent eddy. On receiving the right combination of these signals, the MEMS in a particular region of the wing would raise tiny flaps—no more than a tenth of a millimeter long—to cancel out the emerging eddy's effects. Such an aircraft skin would, engineers believe, dramatically reduce the energy-sapping turbulence within the millimeter-thick layer of air surrounding a plane's wing. Skins of MEMS might, in fact, entirely replace the flight surfaces, including the rudder and ailerons, that are currently the source of much aerodynamic drag. The exterior of such a plane would have few, if any, large moveable surfaces; its flight would be controlled entirely by its skin.[55]

MEMS are already finding their way into the devices around us, from smoke detectors to medical instruments. In the future, they will have a practically infinite array of uses, turning everyday inanimate objects into "smart" machines. They will likely be used to lower turbulence and increase fluid flow in pipes and to automatically administer drugs within people's bodies. Embedded in skyscrapers' structural components, they will allow buildings to bend slightly in response to earthquakes, absorbing and dissipating earthquake shocks. MEMS will also have myriad uses in war—for example, as low-cost detectors of chemical or biological attack; as miniature gyroscopes in cheap, high-precision munitions; or as "surveillance dust" that is distributed across a battlefield and detects even the slightest enemy movement.[56]

The four domains of science and technology that I've pinpointed here—genetics and medicine, information processing and computers, materials engineering, and machine miniaturization—will each cause spectacular changes in our lives. But these are only *four* domains, and within each I've focused only on developments that seem very likely. Extending our survey to include more speculative technologies would greatly lengthen our list. During our lives we may well see, for example, computers that use the quantum fluctuations of subatomic particles to carry out their logical operations (such computers will be unimaginably faster than any yet produced and may well push back the intractability constraints discussed in the chapter "Complexities"), commercial aircraft that fly at hypersonic speeds, magnetic-levitation trains, cars powered by fuel cells, and at last, artificial organs such as hearts.

Science and technology, together, give us astonishing and relentlessly growing power. And, as I have argued earlier in this book, this power can be immensely seductive. As we reshape our world, from the atoms in silicon semiconductors to the dams along the world's great rivers, as we make miracles out of the raw nature around us, and as our technologies sweep us into the future, we may become convinced of our own invincibility and infallibility, and dream that our possibilities are truly boundless. If technological progress becomes our *raison d'être* and miraculous machines our gods, we may begin to think that we, as the creators of these machines, are gods ourselves.

———————

Almost a century ago, Henry Adams—historian, novelist, and scion of a patrician Boston family—wrote an especially eloquent comment on these attitudes, a comment that remains as pertinent today as it was then. At the Exposition Universelle in Paris in 1900 (the largest exposition in Europe to that point), Adams was seduced in the hall of electric dynamos. In a famous passage of his autobiography, written in the third person, he wrote:

> [To] Adams the dynamo became a symbol of infinity. As he grew accustomed to the great gallery of machines, he began to feel the forty-foot dynamos as a moral force, much as the early Christians felt about the Cross. The planet itself seemed less impressive, in its old-fashioned, deliberate, annual or daily revolution, than this huge wheel, revolving within arm's length at some vertiginous speed, and barely murmuring—scarcely humming an audible warning to stand a hair's breadth further for respect of power—while it would not wake the baby lying close against its frame. Before the end, one began to pray to it; inherited instinct taught the natural expression of man before silent and infinite force.[57]

Adams discerned that technology worship and self-worship can quickly become hubris. We lose our grip on reality, on what we really can and cannot do, on what we really can and cannot know. The dynamo becomes more impressive than the planet, or even nature itself. God is lost, forces and imponderables beyond us are unseen or misinterpreted, and we become the measure and the masters of all things.

Examples of such scientific and technological hubris can be found deeply embedded in our culture and guiding institutions. They take the form of subliminal assumptions about our capacities—assumptions that subtly affect our thought, symbols, discourse, and behavior. A curious case in point is the official seal of an institution Adams knew well: Harvard University.

In 1870, Adams was appointed professor of medieval history at Harvard; seven years later, he resigned to write history. During these last decades of the nineteenth century, America was beginning to flex industrial muscles swelled by the power of new technology. After the catastrophe of the Civil War, a sense of optimism and possibility began to rouse the country. In 1869, the first railroad link from the Mississippi Valley to the Pacific was completed at Promontory Point, Utah. A depression in the mid-1870s slowed further construction, but within ten years, three more railroads reached out to the West Coast, and a network of lines boosted economic development in the South. Between 1879 and 1899, the total value of all goods manufactured in the United States more than doubled, and steel production grew eightfold. By 1900 the country was producing more iron and steel than England and more than a fourth of the world's pig iron. Mineral and timber exploitation in the West, a fast-growing population, a steady flow of capital from Europe, and a host of new industrial technologies combined to create a potent economic alchemy. Indeed, this period between 1860 and the end of the century saw one of history's great surges of invention, much of it American: new technologies included the telephone, typewriter, electric light bulb, cash register, train air brake, refrigerator car, and gasoline internal-combustion engine.[58]

Right in the middle of this period, in 1885, Harvard changed its official seal. This may seem an odd event to note, but it was a change not unrelated, I believe, to the changing temper of the times.

The history of Harvard's seal had been long and tangled.[59] Shortly after the college was founded in 1636, its overseers adopted a seal showing three open books (originally perhaps supposed to be Bibles) placed in a triangle—two above and one in the middle below—with the motto "Veritas" (Latin for "truth") spelled across them. The top two books were face up; but the one at the triangle's bottom was face down. In these early years, religious education was a central part of Harvard's curriculum, and the "Veritas" referred to on the seal was almost certainly divine, not scientific, truth. Similarly, the bottom book was placed face down in recognition, probably, that some knowledge was available only to God. As the official historian for Harvard's Tercentenary, Samuel Morison, writes, "Harvard students were reminded in their college laws, and by their preceptors, that the object of their literary and scientific studies was the greater knowledge of God; and that the acquisition of knowledge for its own sake, without 'laying *Christ* in the bottome, as the only foundation,' was futile and sinful."[60]

It appears, however, that the Veritas motto didn't make this point clearly enough, and the original seal and its motto were buried in the college archives sometime in the mid-1600s and for almost two hundred years the college's motto was much more explicitly religious—first "In Christi Gloriam" ("To the Glory of Christ") and then, after 1693, "Christo et Ecclesiæ" ("For Christ and the Church"). Curiously, during these two centuries the third book was face up.

In the mid-1830s, Harvard's then-president, Josiah Quincy, came upon the original seal's design in the college archives. Excited by his discovery, he persuaded the corporation to change the seal back to its original form, with "Veritas" as the motto and the third book once again face down. But only a few years later, Harvard appointed a new president. Edward Everett harbored a keen dislike of his predecessor's accomplishments, and in a powerful fit of pique he demanded that the corporation restore the "Christo et Ecclesiæ" seal. In his words, he was proud to have removed "this fantastical and anti-Christian Veritas seal . . . to the forgotten corner of the records where it had slept undisturbed for two hundred years."[61]

There matters stood till 1878. In that year, Oliver Wendell Holmes, dean of Harvard Medical School, poet, humorist, and father of the famous Supreme Court justice, wrote two sonnets that crystallized the long-running tension in the institution between the two views of its purpose, and, ultimately, between two views of the possibility of knowledge. In the first, titled "'Christo et Ecclesiæ,' 1700" Holmes poked heartily at the elitist and obscurantist tendencies in the Church-dominated Harvard of the early years (tendencies that he clearly believed persisted in his day):

TO GOD'S ANOINTED AND HIS CHOSEN FLOCK:
So ran the phrase the black-robed conclave chose
To guard the sacred cloisters that arose
Like David's altar on Moriah's rock.

Against these lines, Holmes juxtaposed "1643 'Veritas' 1878":

TRUTH: So the frontlet's older legend ran,
On the brief record's opening page displayed;
Not yet those clear-eyed scholars were afraid
Lest the fair fruit that wrought the woe of man
By far Euphrates—where our sire began
His search for truth, and, seeking, was betrayed—
Might work new treason in their forest shade,
Doubling the curse that brought life's shortened span.
Nurse of the future, daughter of the past,
That stern phylactery best becomes thee now:
Lift to the morning star thy marble brow!
Cast thy brave truth on every warring last!
Stretch thy white hand to that forbidden bough,
And let thine earliest symbol be thy last![62]

Holmes's sonnets created a sensation. Older and ecclesiastical alumni thought the first insulting; but many others were delighted by his challenge to the old guard. In his explanation of the verse, Holmes declared:

> The Harvard College of today wants no narrower, no more exclusive motto than Truth,—truth, which embraces all that is highest and purest in the precepts of all teachers, human or divine; all that is best in the creeds of all churches, whatever their name; but allows no lines of circumvallation to be drawn round its sacred citadel under the alleged authority of any record or of any organization.[63]

Confusion followed in the years following Holmes's salvo, and during this period the college used various combinations of the previous seals. Visitors to Harvard Yard can see one version—with the third book face down and "Veritas" written across the books—on the side of Daniel French's famous statue of John Harvard, which was presented to the college in 1884. A year after this statue appeared, the corporation finally made up its mind and adopted a hybrid design by William Sumner Appleton. As in the original, the Veritas motto was superimposed on three open books, but all were face up, and all were placed on a shield encircled by "Christo et Ecclesiæ."

It is easy to understand Holmes's 1878 challenge to Harvard: religious dogma and free intellectual inquiry don't mix. But there can be little doubt that Harvard's decision, in the end, to adopt Truth as its principal motto and to turn the third book face up also reflected the surging optimism of the time. Although Holmes cast the issue as a contest between obscurantism and the free pursuit of knowledge, Harvard's action was more than just an announcement in favor of intellectual liberty. In America, the late nineteenth century was a period of stunning advances in human knowledge and enterprise. In that spirit, the university was boldly proclaiming to the world that human beings could come to know all—that they could aspire to turn over the last book and uncover the final and absolute truth of things.

In 1935, the president and fellows of Harvard voted to create a formal distinction between the university seal and the university arms. The seal, which could be used only for official business, was to follow Appleton's design. The arms were to be the same but without the surrounding Latin inscription; they could be used for "decorative purposes having association, whether official or unofficial, with Harvard University." And in both, the three books were to remain face up. The arms have since become Harvard's logo—a commercialized symbol distributed on pamphlets, sweatshirts, baseball caps, and coffee mugs around the world. Today one of the world's preeminent institutions of higher learning (with eight Nobel prize-winners currently on faculty), a keystone institution of knowledge and authority in a superpower that affects the lives of nearly every person on the planet, has as its guiding symbol a bald assertion of human immodesty.

And yet, despite our extraordinary technological and scientific prowess, it's not at all clear that we really know what we are doing in this new world we've created for ourselves. We're amazingly ingenious, but we may not be ingenious enough to manage our world and prosper within it. We charge forward, packed cheek by jowl on a tiny planet, billions of us, consuming, striving, creating, and jostling each other. We crisscross the sphere in our planes, cars, and ships, subordinating all its places and resources to our needs. We act as if the future is clear, and clearly ours. But the future is murky at best, and it's not yet ours to claim. The greatest triumphs and tragedies of our story are undoubtedly yet to come.

WHITE-HOT LANDSCAPES

I T WAS LATE AFTERNOON, and the sun outside the plane's window hung above the horizon. The captain announced that we were beginning our descent towards Washington, D.C. Slowly we dropped out of the blue sky into the shroud of brown haze over the city.

I was on the next leg of my quest to understand the ingenuity puzzle. My destination: the annual meeting of the American Political Science Association (APSA), the world's largest professional gathering of political scientists.

I had visited Washington many times over the previous ten years—my research team and I had often been asked to present our findings on the links between environmental stress and conflict to bureaucrats and policy-makers in the city. We would meet with middle- and senior-level officials of the State Department, the Department of Defense, the National Security Council, and the CIA, among other agencies, and on a couple of occasions I briefed the vice president.

As I got to know Washington, I started to have misgivings about the place. The city is a study in contrasts. Enclaves of extraordinary prosperity, power, and ritziness press hard against some of the most blighted black neighborhoods in the country. The calm of the central mall—with its lovely ponds, fruit trees, and monuments—seems a world away from nearby streets that at that time were terrorized by some of the nation's highest murder rates. Together with its adjoining metropolitan zones in Virginia and Maryland, Washington embraces probably the largest concentration of public-policy talent in the world—it's chock-full of "big brains," so to speak. Yet in the mid-1990s the city's management, under the leadership of Marion Barry, had become a nationwide symbol of official incompetence, corruption, and outright venality. We could see these contrasts as our taxis bounced along the potholed roads from one meeting to another: the islands of impressive buildings in Washington's core, with their façades bespeaking authority and assurance, were divided from each other by deteriorating streets whose repair had been short-changed for years.

These contrasts of power, wealth, and race are obvious even to a casual observer; they are an inescapable part of the city scene. The more I learned about Washington and its people, however, the more acutely I felt the force of another, more subliminal contrast that seemed to reflect an aspect of the city's deeper character. One glimpses it only fleetingly, at those rare moments when one can separate oneself from the buzz, hustle, and excitement that seem to make nearly everyone in the city a little more impressed with themselves. Then, one can see how Washington, more than any other city in the Western world, reveals the contrast between humanity's astonishing ingenuity, on the one hand, and on the other its limited grasp of the events surrounding it. Washington is a center of immense power and authority—from the Federal Reserve and the FBI to the Pentagon—yet this power seems inconsequential beside the brooding, barely recognized forces underneath the surface of our planet's economy, ecology, and society.

In some ways, I thought, when I first arrived in the city, America is a time capsule of the Enlightenment. Its original political institutions and culture were deeply influenced by thinkers like Locke and Montesquieu and by the Enlightenment's eighteenth-century emphasis on the role of reason in human affairs. While Europe moved on to the romanticism and nationalisms of the nineteenth century and the appalling totalitarianisms and barbarity of the twentieth, America remained committed to its optimistic, rational, can-do civic religion. It remained a society guided by a core belief that individuals and communities, through their intelligence and exertion, can master their circumstances and improve their lot; a society of pragmatists, of builders, engineers, and entrepreneurs who went from one technocratic triumph to another—from the Panama Canal, to the Manhattan Project and the stunning achievements of the Apollo Program. As the capital and power center of this society, Washington seemed to distill America's optimistic creed. And with the collapse of the Soviet

Union in the early 1990s, the country stood astride the world. It was thrilling—almost addicting—to be there at the center of it all.

But time capsules are anachronisms. As my visits to Washington continued over the years, a suspicion entered my mind and slowly gained ground. Most of the men and women I dealt with were tremendously bright and dedicated. Indeed, they were the very "experts" who we gladly assume are smoothly manipulating the levers of the social machines that govern our lives. Nonetheless, I was increasingly struck by how little they really grasped of what was happening in the world around them. I didn't feel smug about this observation: I certainly didn't feel that I had any better grasp of the world's events. But corralled as we were, each within our limited domain, with our narrow authority, it seemed that none of us had anything but the barest understanding of key events and processes. The rules of thumb and intellectual tools we applied to the problems of our modern world seemed feeble in comparison with these problems' complexity, opaqueness, and in social-science terminology, path dependency.

More often than not, the Washington experts and officials I encountered resembled the SAM engineers who tried to advise United 232's crew as their plane pirouetted across the Iowa sky: they were highly trained, well-meaning, but largely out of their depth. Yet these experts and officials were at the pinnacle of authority in the country that dominates Earth economically, militarily, scientifically, and culturally. In light of the ferocious changes sweeping the planet, the chasm between their understanding and the complexity of the problems they faced was creepy. If one couldn't find people here who had a good idea of what was going on, where on Earth could one find them? The question persisted, uncomfortably, in my mind. It became one of the things that galvanized my thinking about the ingenuity gap.

———————————

I had decided to attend the American Political Science Association annual meeting to explore one aspect of the ingenuity question in greater depth: What knowledge can the social sciences offer to help policy-makers do their job? Can they—especially economics and political science—help us design better institutions for this dauntingly complex new world? At the APSA meeting, I knew I would have the chance to observe state-of-the-art political science.

After checking into the hotel I didn't go to the conference immediately, however. Instead I hailed a cab and crossed town to see one of my favorite monuments in the city, the Jefferson Memorial. It was a warm evening, but only a few people were scattered around the Memorial grounds. A young couple sat on the steps beside the Tidal Basin, while a father and his two children admired Rudolph Evans's heroic bronze statue of Thomas Jefferson inside the colonnaded dome.

I wasn't sure why I had come. Perhaps it was because I always find the place peaceful and inspiring. The inscriptions on its interior walls, drawn from Jefferson's writings, seem to highlight essential features of America's self-perception. One in particular strikes me as a fierce, almost authoritarian, commitment to liberty. Chiseled into the Memorial's stone in grand letters, it completely encircles the room just below the dome. In an 1800 letter to Dr. Benjamin Rush, a member of the Continental Congress and signer of the Declaration of Independence, Jefferson famously declared: "I have sworn upon the altar of God eternal hostility against every form of tyranny over the mind of man." On this visit to the Memorial, however, another inscription caught my attention. Adapted from an 1816 letter to Samuel Kercheval and carved into the southeast wall, it reads:

> I am not an advocate for frequent changes in laws and constitutions. But laws and institutions must go hand in hand with the progress of the human mind. As that becomes more developed, more enlightened, as new discoveries are made, new truths discovered and manners and opinions change, with the change of circumstances, institutions must advance also to keep pace with the times.[1]

Jefferson had understood that institutions must change with changing circumstances. Today, his statement seems more pertinent than ever.

But what, exactly did he mean? What are "institutions"? Experts have suggested dozens of definitions, but I have always found the one offered by Douglass North, a Nobel prize–winning economic historian, most useful. Institutions, he says, are "the rules of the game in a society or, more formally, the humanly devised constraints that shape human interaction." Countless problems arise in our everyday dealings with others, and we also have endless trouble living in societies and coordinating our actions to produce public goods that benefit everybody. Institutions, consisting of sets of instructions on how we should behave towards each other, help in a number of ways. They specify the range of socially permissible, required, or recommended actions in a given situation; they also make widely available key information about what other people are doing in our social setting. Institutions are socially agreed-on approaches that make it easier for us to decide what course of action we should follow. They help us arrive efficiently at agreements among ourselves, and they encourage and coordinate our collective action to produce benefits for our whole group.[2]

To put it in contemporary terms, Jefferson, two-hundred-odd years ago, recognized that the complexity of our institutions must rise with the complexity of the human interactions they are intended to manage and the tasks they are supposed to perform. This holds true whether we are designing institutions to deal with the chronic problems in the U.S. health-care industry, the instabilities in the international financial system, or the large-scale changes we are producing in Earth's environment.

The national parks of the United States and Canada provide, I think, one of the best practical illustrations of this. Almost all the national parks have seen huge increases in numbers of visitors in recent decades; they have also faced steadily growing pressure from an ever widening range of users—groups that are very vocal and often extraordinarily antipathetic to each other—from backpackers to automobile campers to off-road vehicle enthusiasts.[3] Park managers have had the unenviable task of reconciling these competing interests. Over time, as a result, the rules and regulations (that is, the institutions) governing park use have had to become more and more complex.

I'm most familiar with the situation in Algonquin Park in Ontario, two hundred kilometers northeast of Toronto. Established in 1893 and extending across nearly eight thousand square kilometers between the Ottawa River and Lake Huron, the park is widely regarded as one of the finest wilderness canoe areas in the world. Its network of hundreds of lakes and rivers, big and small, is linked together by thousands of kilometers of portage routes. The going isn't easy: trails and portage routes are rough, campsites rudimentary, and help usually a long way away. But visitors can spend weeks exploring the interior without ever retracing the same path, and they are almost always rewarded with sightings of moose, bear, and other wildlife. Algonquin Park is one of the places I go to see the stars and planets at night. My friends and I trace their patterns in the sky, often serenaded by the distant howls of timber wolves.

But many different groups have interests in this swath of land. Canoeists have to contend with motorboat operators, day campers with wilderness hikers, duck hunters with birdwatchers, and fishermen with white-water rafters. Because the park's timber is valuable in a region where logging is a mainstay industry, logging companies are allowed to harvest trees within its boundaries, despite the fact that native groups lay claim to much of the territory. Aerial photographs show that many of the areas between the lakes have been clear-cut, with Potemkin borders of trees left standing along lakeshores and portage routes.

As pressures on the park have mounted, all users have had to abide by more precise and complicated regulations. Each year, the authorities publish a large map that divides the park into regions geared to the needs of different groups and that specifies the rules they must follow. In the last decade, this map has become an increasingly incomprehensible montage of areas and subareas designated for specific uses and governed by ever more detailed rules of conduct. Whereas canoeists used to be able to sign in at one of the park's many gates and then disappear into the interior, charting a course and changing direction as whim, weather, and provisions allowed, now they must designate in advance precisely what route they will follow, what campsites they will visit, and what day they will leave.

Park managers enter all this information into computers to monitor and control the flow of people through the area. These managers have, essentially, structurally deepened their management system (to use Brian Arthur's term from the chapter "Complexities") so that more people can benefit in more ways from the increasingly efficient exploitation of the park's resources. Once again, though, the result is a tightly coupled system that restricts users' freedom and is vulnerable to failures. A couple of days of high winds can prevent canoeists from moving to their next campsite; and when they don't vacate the area for the next arriving group they can produce a cascade of disruption all the way back to the park's boundaries.

The challenges facing the people who design and implement the rules of the game—that is, the institutions—in this remote part of Ontario may seem far removed from our daily lives, but in many ways Algonquin Park is the world in miniature. Whether they are managing national parks or the international financial system, our community, national, and global leaders are under enormous pressure to create institutions that will satisfy a rapidly growing number of competing interests and at the same time address a fast-widening array of interconnected problems. Poor countries are often particularly ill-equipped to respond to these challenges. Their governments are often weak, their judicial systems corrupt, their civil servants poorly trained, and their universities and research institutes politicized. So they have less capacity to generate the ingenuity they need to meet the demands of our modern world. And poor countries, because they start from a lower level, generally need more social ingenuity than rich countries to effect reforms.

Most of all, we need new international institutions. The ones we have were often created decades ago, for an entirely different world. In the aftermath of events like the 1997–98 Asian financial crisis, many experts began to admit that humanity urgently needs better management of its international affairs; they also began to acknowledge that there is a yawning gulf between what is needed and the actual performance of the institutions that exist now.[4] Yet in the absence of legitimate and effective government at the international level, reforming the world's economic, security, environmental, and health institutions and designing new ones is astonishingly hard.[5] Leslie Gelb, the president of the Council on Foreign Relations in New York, describes the situation starkly: "[World leaders today] are playing on a chessboard where international and domestic transactions form a seamless web, where the number of public and private players are barely countable let alone controllable, where the rules are yet to be defined, where the true nature of threats remains shrouded by their very multiplicity and complexity, and where it is hard to judge what constitutes winning and losing."[6]

All these difficulties, and more, confront our efforts to create institutions to solve global environmental problems, from species extinction to climate change.[7] If these institutions are to work well, their complexity must reflect the astounding complexity of Earth's biophysical systems.[8] And, in general, the scale of such bodies needs to match the scale of the systems they regulate: local, community institutions are better at managing small-scale ecological systems, such as particular streams or coastal fisheries, while planetary institutions should be used to address global problems, such as climate change. But because the planet's biophysical systems, from soils to climate, are linked together in webs of interdependence, the diverse institutions we design to regulate these systems must also be intricately linked so they can pass information among themselves and cooperate to achieve their goals.[9]

This is just the beginning of the difficulties facing those who are charged with creating such institutions, though. The planet's biophysical systems also operate over a huge range of time scales. The behavior of some of these systems, like the growth of forests, unfolds very slowly; that of others, like weather, can change by the minute, often in sharply nonlinear ways. As Michael Whitfield argued in Plymouth, these time scales— whether immensely long or tiny—often don't match the intermediate time scales within which people and their institutions exist. (One result is that we frequently find ourselves investing huge quantities of capital, manpower, and ingenuity trying to speed up some natural systems and slow others down; for instance, we fertilize forests so we can harvest them sooner, and we refrigerate our foods to slow the natural processes of decay.)

Additionally, when managers intervene in complex biophysical systems to change their behavior, they must often contend with delays, sometimes of uncertain duration, before the systems respond. These delays, or time lags, also plague social systems. They are analogous to the lag in United 232's response to changes in engine thrust, a lag that made precise landing of the plane almost impossible. In the social world, one of the most familiar examples is the delay between a shift in a central bank's short-term interest rate and the economy's later change in output. In the natural world, whether we're dealing with the fluctuating productivity of wild fisheries or the recovery of Earth's ozone layer, time lags are omnipresent. We need institutions that are stable and farsighted enough to cope with these lags, yet simultaneously flexible enough to deal with rapid and abrupt change.

The climate change treaty currently under discussion is called the Kyoto Protocol, because the initial agreement for emission reductions emerged from a conference in Kyoto, Japan, in late 1997. For rich countries, the protocol established a set of interim targets for future carbon emissions tied to each country's 1990 level of emissions. Since then, a vast assortment of people from governments, international organizations, corporations, NGOs, and various lobby and pressure groups has been engaged in almost nonstop consultations and negotiations on how to strengthen the protocol, make its provisions work, and bring poor countries into the agreement. The international institutions that eventually come out of this process, assuming that it's successful, will probably be the most complex in human history. For one thing, it's phenomenally hard to assign responsibility for emissions of greenhouse gases like carbon dioxide, methane, and nitrous oxide, because they are produced by countless different industrial and consumer practices. Every human being contributes to the global warming problem in some way or other, whether he or she is a rural peasant burning straw for heating and cooking in China's interior, a suburbanite driving a sports utility vehicle on the streets of Boston, or a farmer cultivating rice (and so producing methane) in Indonesia. Any set of institutions charged with controlling global warming will have the staggeringly difficult task of setting up and implementing procedures for monitoring who is emitting what, when, and where.

As well, some of the greenhouse gases in the atmosphere—an amount perhaps equivalent to about half of all human emissions—is absorbed naturally by the environment. Billions of tons of carbon dioxide, for example, are annually sucked up by the world's forests and oceans; much of the constituent carbon is then locked into tree trunks and the shells of marine organisms, where it no longer contributes to global warming. But it's not at all clear how to assign the value of these absorption processes—or "sinks" as experts call them—across countries. There is also the fact that the different greenhouse gases stay in the atmosphere for different lengths of time, sometimes for up to a century, which suggests that today's industrial countries should be held at least partly responsible for emissions they produced during their industrialization process many years ago. Yet can we really imagine any of today's rich countries accepting such responsibility?

All in all, these various complications tend to drive a wedge between the world's rich and poor societies. Negotiations are made even trickier by the scientific uncertainty about the global warming; by the fact that the costs of cutting emissions have to be paid in the present, while the rewards will come in the distant future, which naturally conflicts with most corporations' and politicians' preference for assured short-term gain; and by the need to include essentially *all* countries in climate negotiations (generally, negotiations are more likely to succeed when they involve a relatively small number of parties).[10] Any final agreement would have to satisfy not only the technical requirements for emission reduction established by scientists, but also the political demands of the countless interest groups in each country—from oil companies and fertilizer manufacturers to labor unions in automotive industries—affected by the agreement.[11] Lastly, translating intention into action will not be straightforward: a country might sign a climate agreement and then not act on its commitments. Our international and national leaders will need extraordinary political will and ingenuity to produce compliance with any agreement that demands significant changes in our lifestyles or economies.[12] One wonders who amongst them today has that will and ingenuity!

The Kyoto Protocol and its later amendments incorporate a proposal for setting up an international market for trading emission rights. Under this arrangement, a producer of greenhouse gases, say a U.S. coal-fired electricity plant that is about to overshoot its established target or ceiling, might find it cheaper to comply with its emission target by paying for reductions in a Chinese power plant's emissions than by cutting its own. In poor countries, industries that use energy wastefully could invest in relatively cheap efficiency improvements and then sell their resulting emission credits on the international market for profit. In theory, many economists argue, such a market-based approach is the most efficient and ultimately the cheapest way (in terms of overall costs to humanity) to reduce greenhouse gas emissions. And it allows the world community to set an overall target for global greenhouse gas emissions, while letting individual corporations and governments figure out amongst themselves how they are going to meet that target.

Many people, quite understandably, find the idea of creating a market for the right to pollute a bit bizarre, if not downright offensive; some see a deep contradiction between the underlying ethic of environmentalism—an ethic, supposedly, of harmony, cooperation, and peace—and the lusty, avaricious profit motive that drives markets. I'm less bothered by this contradiction: markets are, as we've seen before, powerful instruments that can be harnessed for many ends. But even the idea's advocates realize that the problems are legion. Rights to emit greenhouse gases will probably be derived from national emission targets codified in the final climate agreement. For example, each country will probably be allowed to emit a specified amount of carbon dioxide over a specified period of time. Yet given the complexities of the issue, it's difficult to see how rich and poor countries will ever agree on national targets.[13] Even if they do, the global market in emission rights will demand very careful management, because, among other things, the prices emission rights sell for in the international marketplace will not accurately reflect the dramatically different trade-offs that rich and poor countries must make to buy such rights (a dollar's worth of emission rights has much more value in a poor country than a rich one, because people in the poor country must give up much more elsewhere in their lives to buy it).[14] This and related difficulties will force the world's governments to add an elaborate layer of financial and environmental institutions to the existing international system.[15]

Again we can see parallels between Algonquin Park and the planet as a whole. In Algonquin Park, as the tide of visitors swells and users' demands soar, officials create ever more elaborate guidelines to squeeze the maximum possible benefit from the park's limited territory. Similarly, as the size of the human economy increases relative to the planet's resource base and biosphere (in this case, as our emissions of greenhouse gases rise relative to the biosphere's capacity to absorb them), we must create ever more elaborate institutions and social arrangements to sustain our standard of living, to use resources efficiently, and to manage our relations with the planet's complex biophysical systems.[16] And of course, we'll need ever larger amounts of ingenuity to design and construct these institutions.[17]

There is, however, one crucial difference between the two situations. Whereas officials in Algonquin Park have good information on all aspects of the land under their authority—on the diversity of animal and plant species and whether they are abundant or threatened, on the condition of the park's forests and the flows of water through its rivers and lakes, and on how all these elements combine to create the park's intricate ecology—the people we charge with managing global ecological affairs are operating largely in the dark.

When I interviewed Wally Broecker at the Lamont-Doherty Earth Observatory in New York, he gave me some appreciation of our ignorance of the basic dynamics of ocean currents and their effects on the atmosphere. We might be excused our ignorance in this case, because ocean-atmosphere systems are, after all, almost inconceivably complex. Less easy to excuse is our astounding lack of knowledge of much more visible features of our planet's natural resources and ecology—features that have a direct impact on our well-being. For instance, we know surprisingly little about the state of the planet's soils. While we have good information for some areas, like the Great Plains of the United States, soil data are sketchy for vast tracts of Africa, Asia, and Latin America, where billions of people depend directly on agriculture for survival. So we can't accurately judge how badly we've degraded these soils through overuse and poor husbandry, though we do have patchy evidence that the damage is severe and getting worse in many places.[18] Similarly, despite extensive satellite photography, our estimates of the rate and extent of tropical deforestation are rudimentary. We know even less about the natural ecology and species diversity inside these forests, where biologists presume most animal and plant species live. As a result, credible figures on the number of Earth's species range from 5 to 30 million.[19]

And when it comes to broader questions—questions of how all these components of the planet's ecology fit together; how they interact to produce Earth's grand cycles of energy, carbon, oxygen, nitrogen, and sulfur; and how we're perturbing these components and cycles—we find a deep and pervasive lack of knowledge, with unknown unknowns everywhere. Our ignorance, for all practical purposes, knows no bounds.

Buzz Holling practically despairs on this score. "Because we are only now beginning to understand the changing reality," he writes, "there is consequently no limit to the ability of good scientists to invent compelling lines of causal explanation that inexorably support their particular beliefs. How can even the best-intentioned politician possibly be expected to deal with that? How can even the most reflective of the public?"[20]

I had sat for half an hour on a stone bench under the Jefferson Memorial's dome, scribbling down the inscriptions on the walls. It was time to go back to my hotel. But before I left, inspired as I was by Jefferson's words, I flipped over my sheet of paper and quickly wrote out some reflections on the challenges facing us when we try to set up new institutions for our new world.

Whether we're trying to manage the global environment, national computer networks, or international financial markets—all complex systems—there are, first, challenges arising from the pace of change in these systems. The faster the pace, the more likely serious gaps will appear between the systems' behavior and our lagging management capabilities. Second, there are the challenges arising from our ignorance of how the complex systems around us work. When we know we are ignorant about an aspect of a system, like the global climate, that we need to manage, we can set up our institutions to get the knowledge we need. If we have questions about how much carbon the oceans are absorbing, for instance, then we can fund research institutes to answer those questions. But when we can only guess at the extent of our ignorance, realizing that we are almost certain to be confronted with unknown unknowns, it makes sense to build buffering capacity into our institutions: that is, to give them the slack and resources they need to respond to surprises. So, our global climate-change institutions should be designed *now* to deal with the possibility of abrupt shifts in the behavior of Earth's climate, like those that Wally Broecker argues lie in wait for us.

And third, once we have come up with a good design for an institution, we still face the often huge challenge of overcoming political opposition to it, or (to put it differently) devising the political bargain among different interest groups that will actually allow the institution to be created.

I folded the piece of paper and put it in my pocket, knowing that these are stiff challenges indeed. We need immense amounts of ingenuity to surmount them. The social sciences should be an important source of this ingenuity; they should be important tools in the toolkit we use to devise institutional solutions to our problems. Economics and political science, especially, should be able to help us create solutions. But my experience as a card-carrying social scientist told me that both of these disciplines are blunt and broken tools at best.

The Annual Meeting of the American Political Science Association was under way in one of Washington's largest hotels. There were enough of us to inundate the place. For several days, panel discussions and workshops covering every imaginable topic in the discipline's lexicon ran nonstop in dozens of the hotel's small meeting rooms, racked, one after the other, along each side of the building's infinite corridors. As I walked through the corridors, moving from one small room to another myself, I peeked into these little caverns. Most were windowless and lit by fluorescent lights. In each, ranks of chrome and vinyl chairs faced a line of tables covered with white tablecloths. Panelists and paper-presenters sat behind these tables. If they were lucky, and the topics they were addressing were hot, the chairs in front of them would be filled with earnest colleagues. More often than not, though, the audience would consist of the dozen or so true aficionados of the subject at hand.

At regular intervals, the hum emanating from these small rooms was interrupted by plenary sessions. Held in huge ballrooms with ten-meter ceilings and movable walls, the plenaries featured the discipline's luminaries expounding on topics of interest to a large number of the meeting's participants. Sometimes klieg lights, television cameras, and a clutch of microphones at the speaker's podium would make the event seem particularly exciting and important.

The conference extended vertically as well as horizontally. In the basement, a cavernous hall was filled with publishers' book displays and long rows of tables bearing stacks of xeroxed conference papers. The conference moved upwards through level after level of meeting rooms, past lobbies, bars, and restaurants alive with the roar and bustle of full-throated networking in action, and up into the hotel's many floors of bedrooms and suites. It was a three-dimensional labyrinth—a beehive almost—of air-conditioned and artificially lit passages and chambers, all completely isolated from the world. I marveled at how we could all find our way around this labyrinth and was reminded of the time I had tried to locate Donald Stuss in his Toronto office; once again, I needed a complex cognitive map to get myself from one place to another. And, just like actual bees, the inhabitants of this hive resembled each other: we were mostly white middle-class men wearing a standard uniform of khaki cotton pants, blue blazer, and red tie (with not too much pattern). There is a bland sameness to this species of professional political scientist.

Underneath this sameness, though, and underneath the meeting's busy hum, if one listened carefully and knew how to interpret the participants' signs and symbols, were sharp quarrels and angry words. Political science is a discipline divided on itself. Factions and camps contest the most basic matters of argument, evidence, and method. Some believe that the discipline is a legitimate "science," and that with careful and skilled research it can produce lawlike generalizations about human political behavior not so very different from the laws of physics and chemistry. Others respond vehemently that this is nonsense, that the stuff of politics is, in its deepest essence, unlike the atoms and molecules of the physical world. The job of political science, say these critics (who are often postmodernists), is to help us break out of rigid, mechanistic, and unified understandings of political life. Generalizations, if any are possible, apply only to subsets of human societies and over limited periods of time.

We battle not only over the scientific status of the discipline but also over the nature of the political world's fundamental building blocks, like power, the state, and nationalism. We even disagree about the most appropriate metaphors or "models" of human beings. Some of us, for instance, see human beings as little more than independent calculating machines who constantly assess the costs and benefits of different courses of action and then rationally choose the course that maximizes individual profit; others see them as rule-followers who generate public goods, solve collective action problems, and manage complexity by building institutions; and yet others see human beings as storytellers and story readers who create themselves and the world around them using the meaningful categories of their languages.

Most political scientists, however, would ruefully agree that the discipline has produced very little truly useful knowledge. Despite hundreds of thousands of person-years of research and thought, our understanding of the nuts and bolts of politics—of the factors that make democracies successful; of the pressures that shape national and international institutions; and of the causes of wars, revolutions, and genocides—has progressed excruciatingly slowly. In contrast to the natural sciences of physics, chemistry, and biology, where the wall of knowledge is built brick by brick, political science, like its social-science cousins anthropology and sociology, isn't very cumulative. We are far less likely to build on the findings of our peers; instead, we leap on our horses and ride off in all directions, eventually staking out isolated and often antagonistic conceptual territories.

The result is a dangerous lag between the natural sciences and the social sciences. The natural sciences and the technologies they spawn carry us into the future at bewildering speed, in the process remolding our understanding of ourselves and revolutionizing our relationships with each other and the natural world. The social sciences plod along behind, unable to generate fast enough the knowledge we need to build new institutions for our new world. The renowned management expert Peter Drucker sums up the problem this way: "Effective government has never been needed more than in this highly competitive and fast-changing world of ours, in which the dangers created by the pollution of the physical environment are matched only by the dangers of worldwide armaments pollution. And we do not have even the beginnings of the political theory or the political institutions needed for effective government in the knowledge-based society of organizations."[21] One of the best recent examples of a lag between technological change and institutional capability is the U.S. federal and state government antitrust suit against the Microsoft Corporation. The original consent decree signed by Microsoft and the U.S. Justice Department in 1994 was intended to maintain competition in the market for PC operating systems. But by the time the decree was negotiated and signed, it was too late: Microsoft's Windows operating system had already monopolized the market, running on about 95 percent of new PCs. Robert Hall, a Stanford economist and adviser to the Justice Department says that "to really have fostered and protected competition in the operating system market, it should have been signed in 1985 instead of 1994."[22]

The people who work in political science are, for the most part, well-intentioned and smart. Most have chosen their careers out of a genuine concern for the state of the world and a desire to make it better; and most are very bright, because even modest success in social science demands considerable breadth of knowledge and nuance of thought. Yet they have largely failed to produce any really valuable knowledge. Given the importance of the subjects they study and the resources they have invested in research, this is a truly stinging indictment.

How could this have happened? The question raises some of the most intractable and opaque problems in modern philosophy. Some explanations focus on the sheer complexity of social phenomena, on the difficulty of carrying out controlled experiments, or on the relative immaturity of most social sciences compared to major branches of natural science.[23] Other explanations note how the social sciences are inevitably entangled in matters of morality as well as fact, or how they often blur the distinction between the observer and the observed, a distinction critical to the objectivity of natural science. Certainly all these factors help to make research difficult, but none seems a decisive explanation, in itself, of the difference in success of the social and the natural sciences.[24]

Some people argue that economics is an exception to this general story. Economics, they say, provides a much more analytically precise and tightly integrated body of theory—a theory that is explicitly linked to a small set of generally accepted assumptions about human beings' motivations and decision-making procedures, and that has been rigorously tested against quantified empirical evidence. Among all the social sciences, economics alone, these boosters contend, has a defensible claim to true scientific status.

Economics certainly deserves to be regarded as the queen of the social sciences; unlike the others, it has unquestionably produced useful knowledge on a wide range of issues that affect our daily lives. Yet we should be suspicious of its bold claims to scientific status. Modern neoclassical economic theory is firmly grounded in the kind of mechanistic worldview (described in "Complexities") that sees the economy as a machine, and to explain the operation of this machine it imports many of the concepts of nineteenth-century classical physics. So it stresses the natural tendency of the economy to find a stable equilibrium and the possibility of isolating the effect of changes in different economic factors (like changes in interest rates) on economic performance.[25] As well, to achieve its simplicity and elegance, the theory focuses on the behavior of independent individuals operating in a market—individuals who are atomized, rational, similar in preferences, and stripped of any social attributes. But this makes the theory largely asocial and ahistorical: there's generally no place in it for large-scale historical, cultural, and political forces that sometimes have a huge impact on our economies—forces like the emancipation of women, rising environmental consciousness, or democratization in poor countries. Because it's insensitive to broad social forces, modern economic theory is also surprisingly insensitive to its own tight relationship with capitalism. Nevertheless, it's clearly a product of capitalism—a specific, historically rooted economic system—and it only makes sense in the context of capitalism.[26]

Some of these factors help explain economists' notorious difficulty predicting the future course of our economies. A mechanistic metaphor won't work well in a turbulent world, where countless factors interact synergistically and economic systems sometimes behave in sharp, nonlinear ways. Nor will it work well in a path-dependent world, where positive feedbacks can amplify small differences in initial conditions to create very large differences in an economic system's eventual path of development. In the same way, an economic theory that disregards the human elements (society, culture, history) won't accurately predict the behavior of systems in which these things are powerful forces. And sure enough, a review of long-range economic predictions over the last two decades shows a record of dismal failure: in 1979, forecasters widely thought that prices of commodities, especially oil, would continue rising, that the stock market was a poor investment, and that the American economy would remain beset by stagflation; in 1989, most forecasters were still leery of the stock market and almost all believed that Japan would continue to surge ahead of the United States in competitiveness and economic dynamism.[27] Ten years later, at the turn of the century, these predictions looked downright silly.

To be fair, economists are not oblivious to these problems. The shortcomings of modern economic theory have been acknowledged by no less than the world's most powerful economist, Alan Greenspan. In a speech at Stanford University in September 1997, for instance, he delivered some markedly pointed comments on the limits of economists' understanding. He reviewed the ebb and flow of monetary theory over the previous decades, before an audience that included the grand old man of monetarism, Milton Friedman. At one time, he pointed out, the Federal Reserve had fairly clear rules to guide its interest-rate policy. These rules were derived from empirical research that showed a clear and durable causal link between the economy's money supply and its inflation rate. But with the rapid technological and social change of the 1980s and 1990s, this link shattered. Financial deregulation and the quick evolution of financial instruments generally increased the speed and volatility of money's circulation in the economy. Now the members of the Fed's Open Market Committee, who together set the short-term interest rate, have to operate much more by intuition and instinct, carefully weighing, in addition to money-supply indicators, a wide range of other measures, information, and sources of data. "As the historical relationship between measured money supply and spending deteriorated," Greenspan acknowledged, "policy-making, seeing no alternative, turned more eclectic and discretionary."[28]

Greenspan's remarks on this and other occasions have been disconcerting. He is at the very pinnacle of economic policy-making, and if he doesn't know how the economic system actually functions, who does? Reading his remarks, one gets the sense that the elite policy-makers at the Federal Reserve are standing on constantly shifting ground, and are repeatedly forced to react to situations "in which incoming data have not readily conformed to historical experience."[29] And because they are often unsure which indicators are most important and deserve most attention, they are in a situation a bit like the one that confronted the pilots of United 232: they are pushed harder—their cognitive load is greatly increased—because they must pay attention to a much wider range of factors than they would if they had a better understanding of the economic system.

In my experience, economists usually don't admit that they can learn much from political scientists. But the APSA meeting did suggest some ways both disciplines might move forward. During an evening plenary, the president of APSA for the year, Elinor Ostrom, presented a paper that tried to reconcile the first two "models" (in social science terminology) of human beings mentioned above—the rational-choice model of people as calculating machines (widely accepted by economists) and the rule-follower model of people as institution builders.[30]

Elinor Ostrom is a political scientist of amazing breadth and subtlety, and her paper synthesized research findings across dozens of subfields in political science, economics, evolutionary psychology, and beyond. She began by arguing that the rational-choice model that has dominated political science in recent years fails to explain key kinds of social behavior, the most important being collective action in the face of strong incentives to free ride (discussed in the chapter "Ingenuity and Wealth").[31] How is it that people regularly create and maintain vital public goods, from effective government to health and education infrastructures, when it seems to make sense—from the point of view of the rational, self-interested individual—to let others pay the price and do the work? "If political scientists do not have an accurately grounded theory of collective action," she declared pointedly, "we are hand-waving at our central questions. I am afraid that we do a lot of hand-waving." The costs of this failure are potentially very high: "As global relationships become even more intricately intertwined and complex . . . our survival becomes even more dependent on empirically grounded scientific understanding."[32]

So she proposed an alternative, "second-generation" model of human rationality. At its core she put our human ability to learn norms and rules of social interaction and to communicate this knowledge, through culture, to subsequent generations. "Norms," she explained, are evaluations, either positive or negative, that someone attaches to a particular type of action, like our norm that lying is usually inappropriate behavior. "Reciprocity" is the key norm for solving collective action problems, because it helps build trust within social groups; if someone does something nice to you, the reciprocity norm enjoins you to do something nice back. Depending on the social context and certain other factors, which she specified quite precisely, groups can develop virtuous circles of trust and reciprocity that increase the likelihood of rational and effective collective action.

Listening to Elinor Ostrom's presentation, I found her model helped me fit together many of the pieces of the ingenuity puzzle I had gathered in my study of brain evolution and human psychology. It built on the idea that ancient hominids evolved a specialized social intelligence that is exquisitely adapted to interpreting and managing complex social relations. It incorporated advanced theories of cultural evolution. And perhaps most important, it offered the possibility of moving political science beyond the crude, stripped-down conception of human rationality—cold, instrumental, and detached—that has dominated the discipline for years. There was room in her approach for integrating emotion and reason to give us an infinitely richer understanding of human intelligence and decision-making.

But then my mind cast back to another day in Washington, D.C., several years before, and the memory left me less sanguine. I had flown in from western Canada on two days' notice, joining two colleagues (one from Hawaii, the other from California) to brief Vice President Al Gore on China's environmental crisis. It was midsummer, and the city's air was hot and heavy. The meeting was supposed to begin at 7:30 in the morning in the vice president's office in the Old Executive Office Building, a huge, almost cavernous room, with ornate windows and high, gilded ceilings. But Gore was late. The Rwanda crisis was now several months old, and that morning his wife Tipper had left to visit the vast camps of Hutu refugees that had sprung up in eastern Zaire. Gore had seen her off at the airport, and I remember that when he arrived for our briefing his shirt was glued to his body with perspiration.

My two colleagues and I sat together on one side of a long table across from the vice president and his aides, while other senior officials from the administration gathered at the rest of the chairs around the table. There were about thirty people in the room, all told. For an hour we reviewed the state of the Chinese environment—a grim story of water shortages, appalling air pollution, and widespread damage to cropland—and the implications of this mounting environmental stress for China's economic development and political stability. The vice president asked several perceptive questions, made some comments, and then opened the meeting to discussion. It went on much longer than anyone had expected; the last participants left around 10 a.m.

As we broke up, Gore came over to me. The carnage in Rwanda was on everyone's mind, and it was becoming clear that the timid and legalistic American position in the Security Council in the early days of the genocide had been one of the things that allowed the massacres to spiral out of control. Gore said he had asked the director of the CIA to conduct a large research project on the sources of major episodes of civil violence, including ethnic clashes, revolutions, and genocides. He wanted the project to gather historical data going back several decades to find any factors that were consistently correlated with such violence; environmental factors were to be especially closely examined. He hoped the project would come up with a statistical tool—maybe country-by-country estimates of the probability of violence or a world map highlighting high-risk countries—that could provide policy-makers with one to two years' warning of major violence, and perhaps allow them to prevent it. Gore asked me to bring my knowledge of environmental issues to the team. The project seemed profoundly worthwhile, so I agreed.

A few months later, I was contacted by the CIA, and I joined a small group of experts to think through the project's initial design and structure. We were christened the State Failure Task Force; the name reflected an assumption that the kind of violence we were examining was a consequence, in part, of weak, fragmented, or predatory states. The group included several of the world's leading authorities on civil violence as well as top specialists on data sources and statistical methodology. It was clear that we had substantial resources at our disposal: we could scour the world for the best data, and we could use the most advanced statistical techniques to identify correlations in those data. It was a golden opportunity—the kind of thing most academics dream of—a chance to work with the best people in the field and the best information available, on an issue of tremendous importance for humanity.

Because of unexpected developments in other research projects I was running at the time, I had to leave the task force early in its work. But I was kept informed of its progress and given a chance to make comments on its final report, which was issued in November 1995.

The results were sadly meager. In the end, the findings of the State Failure Task Force said more about the limits of contemporary social science, especially political science, than about the reasons states fail. After many months of intense work, during which the task force assembled more than two million pieces of data and examined six hundred potential explanatory variables, the report concluded that three variables, in combination, provided the best prediction of major civil violence: a country's degree of openness to international trade, its level of infant mortality, and its level of democracy. High infant mortality and low foreign trade were together associated with state failure in democracies, while low foreign trade by itself was associated with state failure in autocracies.[33] This might have been an interesting result, except that the mathematical model the team developed to predict state failure, a model that incorporated these three variables, generated a distressing number of false alarms. "Assuming the historical rates of three [state] failures per year," the task force's final report admitted, "the model most likely will correctly identify two and miss one. Of the 161 countries in the analysis, the model will correctly identify about one hundred as stable and would, on average, generate roughly fifty false alarms."[34] In other words, each year, for every two countries that the model correctly predicted would experience major civil violence, it would incorrectly predict major violence in fifty countries. In a later stage of the project, the team reduced the false-alarm rate somewhat for sub-Saharan Africa, but the overall results weren't greatly different.[35]

Also, the task force's findings were hardly new. The three variables that were isolated are well known to specialists in the causes of civil violence.

Even at the project's first meeting, I remarked to one of my colleagues that infant mortality would be one of the first variables we should test, and he agreed. Although people differ a great deal in their values across cultures, everyone everywhere is concerned about their children, and when children are sick and dying, people are always deeply upset. Infant mortality is therefore a reasonable surrogate measure of the level of grievance and frustration in a society, which is, in turn, a key precursor to civil violence.

The lessons of the task force seemed to lie elsewhere: in the research challenges posed by inadequate data, by the use of the past as a guide to the future, and by the complexity of our social behavior.

Al Gore had been right to ask us to include environmental indicators in our study. Social science rarely considers the impacts of nature on society, although these impacts are often dramatic.[36] Unfortunately, the task force's entire effort was handicapped by a paucity of good environmental data, especially on fresh water availability, loss of forests, and damage to cropland. As a result, despite the vice president's interest in the matter, environmental factors were deemphasized in the project's final analysis.

The project was also handicapped by the underlying assumption—inescapable, given its methodology—that the past is a good guide to the future. One of the most frustrating things for researchers in the social sciences, as Alan Greenspan's remarks suggest, is the tendency for apparently strong associations between factors—like the association between money supply and the inflation rate—to weaken and vanish over time. If the economic, social, and ecological characteristics of our world are changing fast, which certainly seems to be true today, then the sources of future violence could be very different from those of the past, and a close examination of countries that have experienced violence in the past may not be of any help to us in predicting where violence will erupt in coming years. My own research indicates, for instance, that environmental factors will be much more common and powerful causes of civil violence in the future than in the past.[37]

Most important, the task force failed, despite the extraordinary skills and resources at its command, to develop a theoretical or statistical approach that could cope with the complexity of human conflict. Civil violence is always the result of many interacting factors: friction between strong ethnic identities, widespread anger produced by falling standards of living, and the easy availability of weapons are often mentioned; but it's very hard to determine what contribution any one factor makes by itself, and few if any of these factors will be present in *all* incidents of civil violence. Given all this, researchers should perhaps investigate what effect different combinations or *sets* of factors have on the level of violence (say, strong ethnic identities combined with falling living standards, or falling living standards combined with the easy availability of weapons). But because of lack of time and political considerations, the task force couldn't fully pursue this approach.[38]

As Elinor Ostrom wrapped up her impressive presentation, I felt an odd mix of enthusiasm and discouragement: she had given us a host of exciting questions and a set of powerful hypotheses to explore in our research. But that day the road ahead seemed depressingly long, and the distance we had covered so far seemed almost minuscule.

———————————

Maybe I was being too quickly discouraged. There was actually evidence all around me—in Washington itself—suggesting that our societies can often adapt well to changing circumstances, and can maintain their peace and prosperity, even if we haven't got a detailed understanding of how our societies work. Maybe advanced social-scientific knowledge isn't so critical to our future after all.

In the early and mid-1990s, things looked pretty grim in the city. Public services were crumbling, crime was rife in poor districts, and the D.C. government was nearly bankrupt. The end of the Cold War had sent an electric shock through the region's economy, as defense and aerospace industries, research labs, think tanks, and foreign policy and defense bureaucracies downsized. But half a dozen years later, the city government and services had been turned around and the regional economy rejuvenated. Disillusionment with the government's disarray and a slow change in the city's demography provided a political base for a new, reformist mayor.[39] Meanwhile, in the penumbra of suburbs and towns around Washington, high-tech industries proliferated, many of them attracted to the region because of the new concentration of underemployed but highly skilled scientists and engineers. Today, with nine thousand technology companies, including MCI and America Online, employing 470,000 people (over a hundred thousand more than the federal government), some commentators suggest that the region rivals Silicon Valley as a center of high-technology dynamism.[40]

How did all this come about? Remarkably, the changes just seemed to happen. Certainly, government intervention had an influence. At the height of the city's financial crisis in 1995, Congress created a financial control board that stripped the then mayor, Marion Barry, of virtually all his powers and reestablished order in the city's finances. But many of the positive changes in the city and region occurred without a central plan and without an elaborate institutional structure based on sophisticated social-science knowledge. Instead, people initiated changes spontaneously. Companies, communities, and organizations found constructive ways to make their lives better. Their responses to the challenges they faced were diverse, decentralized, and often local.

Yet such an uncoordinated approach is rarely the first thing we advocate when we face a large, tangled social or technological problem with no obvious solution, like a regional economic downturn or violent conflict in a distant land. Instead, we usually call upon government to set up institutions or programs, like Washington's 1995 financial control board, that can take command of the problem, apply expertise to it, and solve it. We tend to accept that centralized institutions can use their power to simplify complex problems and can hire the finest minds and best technologies to analyze and tame them—technologies like advanced statistical or computer models that will find optimal solutions.[41] But institutional power doesn't always produce simplification; large, centralized organizations tend to be bureaucratic, cumbersome, and inefficient. And computer models are only as good as the knowledge that goes into them, so they miss unknown unknowns.

Another way of dealing with a tangled problem is simply to do nothing, or at least nothing large, centralized, and carefully planned. Complex systems of people and groups linked together in networks—like the network of markets, people, and corporations in the Washington region—can often adapt well to a quickly changing environment. Just let these systems operate, the argument goes, and they will deal with their problems themselves. Management often isn't necessary. In fact, in many cases it just gets in the way.

This idea is appealing, because it endorses a laissez-faire approach. We need not trouble ourselves with trying to figure out the intricacies of the problem at hand, building big institutions, or developing sophisticated and comprehensive theories and policies. Instead, after putting in place a few prerequisites (like the laws undergirding markets) that allow people and groups to help themselves, we can simply stand aside.

There are actually several different ideas that can be used to justify doing nothing or doing little. The first is that complex systems—such as societies, ecologies, and large organizations and markets—have redundancy in their key components. Just as a tropical forest may have several species of bird that help keep the populations of certain noxious insects under control, a complex market may have several corporations that provide certain critical goods and services. This redundancy helps make these systems resilient to shocks and breakdowns, as John Bongaarts suggested to me over dinner in London. And this resilience, according to the theory, means that they don't need careful tending. But just because an organization, market, or society is internally complex enough to avoid catastrophic breakdowns doesn't mean it will be able to adjust smoothly to all its new challenges. It may just limp along, resilient enough to hold itself together but unable to adapt or deal with difficult problems.

Another justification for doing little is the "incrementalist" theory of decision-making. Originally used to describe problem-solving in bureaucracies and large organizations, this theory can also be applied to whole societies. It says that decision-makers in large organizations should generally "muddle through." Because they have limited information and cognitive resources to apply to any given problem, they should make lots of small, incremental decisions, each building on what has gone before and drawing on their own and their organization's practical knowledge. If they do this, then more often than not the solutions they adopt will be quite good. So it doesn't make sense—and it's often not possible in any case—to solve problems through a comprehensive and rational evaluation of all options or by developing grand, overarching schemes.[42]

But there are powerful reasons why the muddling-through approach will not always work for problems in today's world. Incrementalism assumes that our circumstances are reasonably stable and change is slow. Because the past isn't that different from the present, decision-makers can draw on what they have learned from the past—their practical knowledge, habits, and standard operating procedures, for instance—to guide their decisions in the present. But today our circumstances are sometimes marked by sharp upheavals and swift obsolescence of technologies and past knowledge.[43] Also, today people often don't have the luxury of making small, provisional decisions and then waiting to gauge the results: as we have seen, for instance, in the Asian financial crisis, micro-events and decisions can have macro-consequences, and by the time a decision-maker realizes that the consequences of a small decision aren't good, it may be too late to change the course of events.[44]

A third argument for doing little or nothing draws a parallel between complex systems and biological organisms: according to this view, we don't have to invest a lot of energy or thought in managing the complex systems around us, whether we're talking about the global climate or the international financial system, because these systems, like organisms, have built-in ways of regulating themselves that keep them stable and ordered (mammals, for example, keep their body temperature constant).[45] An old and rich sociological literature applies this idea to societies; and one of its most recent incarnations is the Gaia hypothesis, which proposes that the life in Earth's biosphere regulates the planet's environment to keep it habitable.[46] But such arguments aren't very satisfying in the end, because they don't do a good job of explaining how, why, and when a complex system develops the ability to regulate itself.

But the fourth idea in the cluster does address this issue, and for this reason it's by far the most interesting. It is actually a broad and rapidly developing set of theories about *self-organizing* and *complex-adaptive* systems.[47] These theories start with one of the deepest questions facing science today: How does a disordered universe of inanimate matter and energy spontaneously generate highly complex, ordered, and adaptive entities—from cells, organisms, and ecosystems to cities, societies, and world-spanning technological systems?

The evolutionary theory of Darwin and later thinkers gives us only a partial answer—partial because, though it highlights natural selection and adaptation in the biological world of living entities, it doesn't really help us understand the emergence of self-organization from inanimate matter.[48] Evolutionary theory also has trouble explaining the dramatic variation in the rate of evolution over time and the degree to which natural selection favors adaptive traits.

At the core of the new theories is the concept of the *fitness landscape*.[49] The landscape has hills and valleys. These features can be relatively smooth undulations, like a British pastoral scene, or they can be rugged and sharp, marked by canyons, precipices, and high peaks, like the Himalayas. The landscape represents, metaphorically, the range of possible relationships between a species, organism, society or other complex-adaptive system and its environment. Each high point represents a high point of fitness—a point where the system is relatively well adapted to its environment—and as the system evolves or changes its form over time, it moves across its fitness landscape and up the landscape's slopes to points of higher fitness.

This metaphor nicely captures the idea that complex-adaptive systems can usually improve their fitness in a number of ways: their fitness landscapes will usually have many peaks, each representing different potential adaptations to the environment at hand. The metaphor also illustrates how it's possible to become trapped in a less-than-optimal relationship with the environment. A species or society might migrate up a slope to reach a fitness peak, but that peak might be much lower than other peaks on the landscape, which can be reached only by crossing deep valleys of low fitness. Finally, the metaphor allows us to visualize the contrast between benign and harsh environments. An environment that imposes tight and complex constraints is best represented by a rugged fitness landscape (again, like the Himalayas), with lots of dangerous cliffs and deep gorges that can lead to extinction.

Although a species, society, or other complex-adaptive system can sometimes become trapped on less-than-optimal fitness peaks, many have developed means to move from one fitness peak to another across broad territories of low fitness. Any convincing theory of evolution and adaptation must explain how this happens. In one of their most profound insights, theorists working on this problem have proposed that the systems best able to move from one fitness peak to another are those whose internal structures are neither too orderly nor too chaotic. Systems whose internal structures are highly ordered will tend to be static; once they have migrated upwards to a local fitness peak, they will tend to stay there. On the other hand, chaotic systems will roam across the countryside randomly, quite possibly to their death. The most adaptive systems tend to maintain themselves on the cusp between order and chaos; they are random and adventurous enough to strike out in new directions looking for a better life, but they are also conservative and orderly enough to take advantage of improvements once they find them.

Highly adaptive systems also tend to break themselves into parts to explore their local fitness landscape. A species, for instance, might break into several subspecies, each of which explores the landscape in a different direction. Adaptive systems are generally not hierarchical and controlled by central commands; instead, they are decentralized, with their many parts linked together in networks and operating in parallel to solve the problems of survival.[50] When one part finds a higher fitness peak, it can communicate that information to other parts in the network. So a successful subspecies can crossbreed with other subspecies and pull the whole species towards the new fitness peak.[51] As the ruggedness of the fitness landscape increases—that is, as the environment becomes harsher—adaptive systems need to break themselves into more and smaller parts to best explore the landscape.

This theory gives us tremendously rich insights into how our communities and societies adapt to rapid and complex change. They help us understand what happened in the Washington region in the last half-dozen years: the region's diverse communities, corporations, and clusters of skilled people made up a fragmented network, and they quickly explored their fitness landscape. Once one or two parts of this network identified high-technology opportunities, many other parts followed behind to this new, higher fitness peak. The process was certainly not orderly or command-centered, but neither was it entirely chaotic. Rapid adaptation occurred precisely because these networked communities and groups were poised on the cusp between order and chaos.

The theory also helps us understand the extraordinary success of Western societies in recent history. They are undoubtedly among the most highly adaptive societies that humanity has ever created. During the twentieth century alone, they experienced two world wars, a deep economic depression, massive immigration, and a hugely expensive, decades-long political competition and arms race with an implacable enemy (the Soviet Union). Yet they emerged at the end of the century not just intact, but wealthier and more powerful than ever. Western societies have an enormous and unprecedented capacity to generate ingenuity in response to their problems.

The secret to their success has been a self-reinforcing combination of institutions and culture that has maintained Western societies on the fecund boundary between order and chaos. Western economic institutions hinge on markets, which are decentralized networks that give corporations and people the information and things they need to work on their problems in parallel. Western culture and political institutions also encourage the development of a vigorous civil society—a dense web of nonstate associations, including religious groups, unions, community-service organizations, sports clubs, and the like. These groups' activities help build the trust and norms of reciprocity that Elinor Ostrom argued are key to solving collective action problems, and that other scholars say are vital to sustained economic growth.[52] The diversity and independence of firms in the marketplace and of groups in civil society let Western societies explore their fitness landscapes rapidly and continuously.

Western economic and political institutions are founded on a shared culture, and the core of this culture is the conviction that the social and technological change produced by constant competition and disorder is inevitable and generally good.[53] For individuals, living on this cusp of chaos may produce feelings of anomie and disorientation; but for the collectivity, the West has learned, it is the best place to be in a fast-changing world, because it's where societies will produce the most and best ingenuity.

According to this theory, then, some parts of humanity may be entering an age of explosive creativity, as national hierarchies around the planet collapse into Internet-linked networks of disaggregated economic and social units. These haphazard social arrangements make possible a supercharged process of decentralized innovation, where individuals and groups work in parallel, scattered across vast networks, to solve common problems and produce public goods. Perhaps the best current example of this phenomenon is the collaborative development of the Linux operating system for computers, an example of what specialists call the "open-source revolution" in software development.[54] Expressing some of the excitement of this new age, the economist and complexity theorist Brian Arthur writes: "[The] Web provides access to the stored memories, the stored experiences of others. And that's what is also particular to humans: our ability not just to think and experience but to store our thoughts and experiences and share them with others as needed, in an interactive culture. What gives us power as humans is not our minds but the ability to share our minds, the ability to compute in parallel. And it's this sharing—this parallelism—that gives the Web its power."[55]

So it's possible to build a powerful argument, backed by fascinating theoretical work, that sometimes a do-nothing or do-little approach is best when we face complex problems. But before we get carried away by our excitement over these new theories and over the possibilities offered by our newly Webbed world, a few caveats are in order. A decentralized, network-based approach won't work for all problems; instead, the various types of solutions have to be matched to different types of problems. Sometimes a centralized, hierarchical, command-driven approach is essential, even if only as a catalyst or complement to a network-based approach. It's doubtful, for example, that Washington, D.C., could have reversed its financial crisis without the intervention of Congress. And it's inconceivable that we will resolve the problem of global climate change without powerful international institutions that, at the very least, provide the legal and financial framework for a market-based emissions trading scheme.

A centralized, command-driven approach is also often needed when our societies are trapped on less-than-optimal fitness peaks. Sometimes the institutional structure of a society or its culture of fundamental beliefs—such as its religion or its political and economic ideology—constrain the society so that it can't properly explore its fitness landscape.[56] Moving away from the current peak would involve raising fundamental questions about the society's internal distribution of power and wealth, or about its ultimate values.[57] It's possible that our Western societies are constrained in this way right now: despite the triumphs of our capitalism, democracy, and science at the moment, our system may not be sustainable over the long run, either ecologically (because its high-consumption lifestyle puts immense stress on Earth's environment) or politically (because it widens income and wealth gaps between rich and poor). Yet Western societies' economic and intellectual elites have adopted a remarkably uniform consensus on core social values and on what institutions best serve those values. This consensus silently closes off opportunities for fundamental dissent, elevates questionable assumptions to the level of absolute fact, and limits space for debate—in other words, it keeps us from fully exploring our fitness landscape.

If Western capitalism and democracy confront a life-or-death crisis in the future, we will probably need the help of centralized and command-driven intervention to move us in new directions. When capitalism faced its most profound challenge of the past century, the Great Depression of the 1930s, it couldn't fix itself. Instead, state intervention—in the form of Roosevelt's New Deal—was essential.

There's another, more powerful reason why decentralized, network-based solutions might not always work: our present fitness landscape is not stable. Indeed, it may be becoming increasingly rugged. As groups, societies, and technologies evolve within our planetary network, and as the planet's biosphere and climate evolve with us, the landscape to which we must adapt is changing stunningly fast. New mountains, ridges, and cliffs push upwards, while old ones shrink and disappear. Fitness peaks, perhaps even those very peaks that we inhabit, abruptly dissolve into broad valleys of low fitness; suddenly we aren't adapted to our surrounding environment anymore. The topography of our fitness landscape resembles a sheet of metal—white-hot from fires underneath—that is twisting, bulging, and buckling from heat.

White-hot landscapes. The image was on my mind as I packed my bags to return to Toronto. I thought about the evidence gathered by Rick Potts and other paleoanthropologists (in the chapter "Brains and Ingenuity") suggesting that the human brain is extraordinarily well designed to cope with rapid changes in its fitness landscape, because it evolved at a time of wide environmental and climate fluctuation. But perhaps we're now changing our fitness landscape too fast for even our own brain's astounding adaptability.

If so, we're in trouble: regardless of whether we adopt centralized or decentralized problem-solving strategies, we won't be able to scramble across our seething fitness landscape fast enough to find and settle new peaks before they subside out of sight. Our future, in this case, will not be marked by an endless sequence of relatively smooth and increasingly refined adaptations to our world; it will instead be an endless series of gambles, approximations, and random guesses, many of which won't work, and some of which will lead to disasters like the horrible violence that Al Gore hoped we could predict. This tendency to flirt with catastrophe, the historian William McNeill says, seems to be intrinsic to our destiny: "Both intelligence and catastrophe appear to move in a world of unlimited permutation and combination, provoking an open-ended sequence of challenge and response. Human history thus becomes an extraordinary, dynamic equilibrium in which triumph and disaster recur perpetually on an ever-increasing scale as our skills and knowledge grow."[58]

PART FOUR

What Does the

Ingenuity Gap

Mean for

Our Future?

VEGAS

T HE SOUND was overwhelming. Bass notes pulsed from speakers suspended overhead. They drove the air towards me in sharp waves that pummeled my chest and almost made me gasp for air. I could barely breathe anyway: people were packed so tightly in the hall I was reminded of claustrophobic markets in Bombay and Shanghai.

I had pushed my way into the Microsoft exhibit at the Comdex convention in Las Vegas, Nevada. With an attendance of over two hundred thousand people, Comdex is one of the world's biggest computer, communication, and software trade shows, and Las Vegas is one of the few cities that can handle the meeting. But even with its vast number of hotel rooms, the city bulges at the seams: room rates soar, and every decent restaurant is booked solid every night. Vegas fills with jabbering techies, software nerds, and slick hucksters for the new information utopia.

The convention itself is housed in several huge buildings, each almost as big as an airplane hangar. It's a carnival inside, with a torrent of humanity flowing along the endless avenues among the corporate booths. I passed one gaudy display after another, surrounded everywhere by dazzling light and color, huge three-dimensional billboards and mock-ups of corporate logos rising like columns on each side, lit by strobes and floods. The biggest companies have the biggest displays, some several stories high, complete with stage shows, glamorous salesgirls eager to show off their companies' wares, endless banks of computer terminals and video screens, and nonstop lectures touting the benefits of the products sold inside. The spaces between these islands of corporate power are crammed with the booths of far smaller technology and software developers—energetic entrepreneurs trying to fill market niches, many having sent most of their staff members to the show. Men are more numerous than women at the convention, and almost all men over thirty-five are obese. The computer-driven lifestyle, it seems, is sedentary and stressful, and the people attending this high-technology cornucopia have little time or inclination to eat properly.

Comdex and Las Vegas make a fitting combination. Together, they mingle computers, gambling, and the fantasies of a postadolescent playland. High-tech exhibits spill into hotel foyers only a few meters from clattering slot machines and blackjack tables surrounded by nervous casino patrons. A bit farther along, the labyrinthine hotel passages open into a vast gambling hall designed to resemble the bridge of a *Star Trek* spaceship. The different worlds of computers, gambling, and fantasy fit together surprisingly seamlessly, as if they reflect each other's essences in some kind of triangular relationship. Gambling is, after all, about living a fantasy of sudden riches; computers allow us to create virtual worlds that erase the line between reality and fantasy; and the jackpots of the information revolution have produced the new billionaires of the 1980s and 1990s. These billionaires, Bill Gates in particular, are a palpable presence at the convention, appearing fleetingly to give a speech here or a press conference there. They are the mega capitalists of our new knowledge society, and most Comdex attendees secretly fantasize about joining their select company. The whole event is suffused with millennial boosterism and a flawless optimism about the future and the capacity of information technology to create a new world beyond us.

I had come to Las Vegas on the penultimate leg of my travels. I now had at hand most of the pieces of my ingenuity puzzle. I had learned much about the nature of ingenuity and about the forces driving up our requirement for ingenuity—the greater complexity, unpredictability, and pace of our world, and our rising demands on the human-made and natural systems around us. I had also learned something about the factors that might restrict our supply of ingenuity—in particular, about the limitations of our brains, markets, and scientific institutions. But Las Vegas and Comdex, I sensed, would help me fit these pieces together into the larger picture that I sought, and they'd also help me fill a couple of major gaps that remained. I especially wanted to know more about how the Internet and other new information technologies might affect ingenuity supply, given the importance of these technologies in the creation and dissemination of ideas—the very stuff of ingenuity.

I'd decided to stay at the Stratosphere Hotel, a tower resembling the Seattle Space Needle, which vertically punctuates the seedy north end of the Las Vegas Strip. The hotel sports a high-altitude viewing deck and revolving restaurant, all capped by a roller coaster that twists around the structure's uppermost spire. When I planned the trip, I couldn't resist booking into a hotel with a roller coaster on its roof; there was something suitably bizarre about the idea, and although I hadn't visited Las Vegas before, I expected the city to be profoundly bizarre.

Eating a late dinner in the restaurant, a friend and I looked out across a sprawling city of one million people, with lights and streets radiating in all directions away from us towards distant mountains. We seemed to be at the center of a galaxy of stars; Las Vegas and its surrounding communities together make up one of the fastest-growing metropolitan areas in the United States. The roller coaster rumbled periodically overhead, and every hour or so the Strip cycled into view, with the city's famous hotels—Circus-Circus, the Stardust, Treasure Island, the Mirage, Caesar's Palace, Bellagio, the Excalibur, and New York–New York—stretching like a string of gaudy costume jewels into the desert.

The last jewel in the string, some six kilometers away, was the Luxor Hotel—a mammoth glass-and-concrete representation of an Egyptian pyramid. Thirty-six stories high and measuring two hundred meters on each side, the hotel boasts the world's largest atrium, capable of enclosing nine Boeing 747s. But it wasn't the size of this edifice that we noticed most from our distant perch (although big, the Luxor Hotel is actually only two-thirds the volume of the great pyramid of Cheops outside Cairo). Rather, it was the mighty column of light that blasted vertically from the pyramid's peak into the night sky. In a chamber at the building's apex, thirty huge Xenon lights, consuming more than 200,000 watts of electricity, produce a beam visible by jets cruising four hundred kilometers away. This beam is nearly a hundred times more powerful than that produced by Smeaton's lighthouse in Plymouth; but shooting into space, the Luxor light isn't intended to warn anybody or illuminate anything. Its point is purely aesthetic (although it seems odd to apply that word to anything in Las Vegas). In fact, the light's appeal lies partly in its apparent pointlessness: it is, at first glance, nothing more than a crude statement of exuberance, extravagance, and power.

The Luxor Hotel, I decided, brings together pyramids, artificial light, and the night sky—three metaphors that had wound themselves like contrapuntal themes through my investigations. In my mind, our ability

The Luxor Hotel, Las Vegas

to produce, ever more cheaply, copious quantities of light had come to represent our astonishing technological prowess; the night sky, similarly, stood for the mysteries that this prowess can obscure and for the sense of awe about our natural world that our technologies often extinguish; and pyramids represented our need to convince ourselves that we retain authority over an increasingly chaotic, complex, and bewildering world. When we build pyramids—whether in Canary Wharf, Battery Park, or Las Vegas—we seem to be exclaiming that we are more than uncomprehending ephemera. We are here to stay; we know what's going on; we are champions of this universe. But the futility of this bravado seems particularly clear and poignant in Las Vegas, a city with only the most tenuous grip on history and reality. As the Harvard English professor and drama critic Robert Brustein writes, "This Nevada City, artificially created out of the desert and therefore lacking an identity of its own, is trying to resignify itself by cloning more confident places."[1]

Yet Las Vegas is undeniably fun, entirely because it is ostentatious, tacky, and over the top. There's something irrepressible about the place.

Escape and denial are often good for the soul, and we need a certain amount of bizarreness in our lives. Las Vegas is appealingly hedonistic. But as we looked across the cityscape from high atop the Stratosphere Hotel, I wondered whether Las Vegas is more than just a place for adults to escape into fantasyland. Does late-twentieth-century Las Vegas actually give us a glimpse of the future of urbanized humanity?

The next day, wandering along Comdex's endless avenues, I pondered an irony: the tens of thousands of people around me were devotees of the latest newfangled information technology, but they still felt a need to meet each other in person to conduct their business. Even today's most advanced communications media are severely restricted in the amount of information they can convey. In contrast, when we talk to someone directly in front of us, we not only receive information by hearing what the person says, but also by seeing fine details of her facial expressions and body language, including how she positions her body in relation to ours. And our noses and brains have a remarkably acute ability to discriminate among people's scents, although little of this olfactory information registers in our conscious minds. It's going to be a long time before such vital, subliminal signals can be communicated over long distances, and in the meantime person-to-person meetings remain essential.

A further irony came to mind: Comdex was spawned by the communication revolution, but communication seemed oddly impoverished at this gargantuan meeting. The event was too pressured and cacophonous to produce really useful networking and communication among its participants; instead it was mainly an occasion to boost brand recognition, announce new products, and hand out brochures. In fact, my friend, a well-known expert in Web languages, made one of his most interesting contacts not at the meeting itself but in the departure lounge of the airport as we were preparing to leave the city. The departure lounge offered a few minutes of respite from Comdex's sensory overload (although a clutch of Las Vegas's ubiquitous slot machines still clattered in the background). It was a window of opportunity for a thoughtful conversation, whereas the convention's halls and hotels offered only fleeting moments to exchange business cards.

It made me think of a comment by David Shenk, the author of *Data Smog*. "The blank spaces and silent moments in life," he writes, "are fast disappearing."[2] Comdex is not only a bazaar of modern communication technologies, it is also a microcosm of some of the profound changes these technologies have wrought in our social relationships. The crushing amount of information delivered to us, and the ease and breakneck pace of this information's delivery, force us to devote less and less time to individual interactions in our social environment. Our interpersonal relationships become truncated, abbreviated, and fragmented. Leisurely, handwritten letters have all but disappeared. Our e-mail messages are stripped of nuance and texture and reduced to Morse-like staccatos of data; we drop punctuation, capitalization, and proper spelling, and we adopt an impoverished symbolism of emoticons.[3] We snatch bits of conversation with colleagues and friends on our cell phones as we dash between meetings. We become ruder. It's now possible for people from every corner of the planet to contact us, so we simply stop responding to their messages. In fact, we delete swaths of these messages from our e-mail and voice-mail inboxes without even pausing to read or listen to them.

These general trends have been recognized for some time. In a famous 1970 study of the pressures of urbanization, for example, the renowned social psychologist Stanley Milgram observed that city life is "a continuous set of encounters with overload, and of resultant adaptations."[4] People adapt by allocating less time to each input, disregarding low-priority inputs, shifting the burden of social transactions to other parties, and blocking reception of information through strategies like delisting their telephone numbers and using unfriendly facial expressions. In general, as people become overloaded with inputs from their environment, their receptivity and benevolence towards strangers declines.

Even if the general trends are not really new, the degree of fragmentation and abbreviation of today's social relations is certainly new. While the connections among us are more numerous than ever before, the meaningfulness of these connections is decreasing.[5] The cost to our societies may be much greater than simply a rise in ambient rudeness. Dense and meaningful social connections are the stuff of what social scientists have come to call *social capital*; they are the sinews around which we develop those norms of trust and reciprocity that Elinor Ostrom highlighted during her Washington presentation (in the last chapter, "White-Hot Landscapes"), and such norms greatly enhance our ability to reform and build new economic and political institutions—that is, to supply the abundant social ingenuity we need.[6] When these connections become depleted and impoverished, the ability of our societies to adapt to rapid and complex change is undermined.

These somewhat disconnected thoughts ambled through my mind as I ambled around Comdex, reinforcing similar conclusions I had reached earlier in my investigations—conclusions that seemed particularly potent that day: the very technologies of communication, travel, and production that empower us as individuals can, paradoxically, reduce our control of events surrounding us, especially when everybody uses these technologies and, consequently, everybody's life is busier and more pressured. These technologies are examples of our extraordinary ability to supply ingenuity, but they also drive up our need for ingenuity. I had also realized, after studying what we know about the human brain's characteristics and evolution, that the sheer quantity of information we must now manage often exceeds our cognitive capacity. As a result, the hyper-abundance of information in today's world—seen as a boon by many—often steals from us the quiet moments we need for contemplation. It may actually reduce our ability to create new and useful ideas.

The late 1990s saw a wave of commentary on the consequences for our personal and family lives, and for our economies, of the greater load, pace, and complexity of tasks that we must manage on a daily basis.[7] New communications technologies were only one cause of these changes (other factors were shifts in the organization of work and the rising importance of ideas in our economies). But all told, the end result was far more stress in our lives.

We experience psychological stress when we face high cognitive or emotional demands that we feel are both unpredictable and uncontrollable. The stress is worse if we can't release the frustration that results from these high demands, and if we don't have adequate social support in the form of family and friends.[8] A famous study of bureaucrats in the British civil service found that mortality rates were strongly correlated with status in the civil-service hierarchy. Surprisingly, the higher the person's position in that hierarchy, the lower his or her risk of dying prematurely.[9] After accounting for various risk factors, the researchers attributed this result to the higher levels of control and predictability that senior managers had in their work lives. Lower-level employees felt they had less control and, therefore, experienced far more stress and stress-related illness.[10]

Many of us feel that new information technologies have in some ways increased the unpredictability of, and decreased our control over, our daily lives. If so, then perhaps these technologies are becoming a major contributor to stress. Among other things, as we saw in "Brains and Ingenuity," there may be a mismatch between the optimal size of our social groups—a size some anthropologists suggest is around 150 persons, given our cognitive capacity—and the essentially infinite social groups that the Internet and other communication technologies make available to us. As our electronic groups expand beyond that threshold of 150, the meaningfulness of our relationships degrades, our ability to adequately monitor and predict the behavior of group members declines, and stress inexorably increases.

In my investigations into the human brain, I also learned that stress contributes over time to neuronal death in the hippocampus, a brain region important to learning and memory. And even mild to moderate uncontrollable stress causes the body to release certain hormones—especially norepinephrine and dopamine—that impede the working-memory functions of the brain's frontal lobes. People with working-memory deficits are disorganized and impulsive and exhibit difficulty sustaining their attention.[11]

Disorganized. Impulsive. Exhibiting difficulty sustaining attention. Sounds a lot like an average person's reaction to today's info-glut. A wild speculation came to my mind—occasioned, maybe, by the pounding excesses of Comdex all around me: if it's true that these communication technologies create much more stress in our lives, and if stress degrades our cognitive functions, then the communications revolution may, in a final irony, be sowing the seeds of its own demise. This revolution may be creating a psychological environment that hinders our ability to focus our minds and organize our ideas; in the process, it may actually lower the output of the technical ingenuity that the revolution needs to sustain itself.

I didn't need to speculate, though, about the sometimes pernicious effects of new communication technologies on public-policy debates and governance in Western societies. In the same way that info-glut affects our interpersonal relations, it also fragments and abbreviates the deliberative processes in our democracies. So much information and so many ideas are competing for the limited space in our brains that the day's perplexing public-policy issues and controversies must be condensed to single-sentence declarations and aphorisms. In this competitive cognitive environment, ideas must be crude and unreflective to win. Slogans and dogma dominate. At the very moment that the challenges facing our societies and world are soaring in complexity, info-glut drives us to simplify and sensationalize them and to dichotomize multifaceted policy problems into raging two-sided debates.

We've all heard about the shrinking soundbite on American television: from 1965 to 1995, the average news soundbite imploded from forty-two to eight seconds.[12] But we have heard less about the compression of data and debate in print media. People simply don't have the time to read articles of even modest length now. In the last two decades, articles in news magazines like *Time* have been progressively reduced in length, and more and more space has been dedicated to punchy one- or two-column-inch chunks of news. In 1979, the average length of a *Time* cover story was nearly 4,500 words; today it's about 2,800 words—a drop of nearly 40 percent. In the same period, the length of an average op-ed article in *The New York Times* fell over 20 percent, from 730 words to 575 words. Even the highbrow journal *Scientific American* has cut its standard articles by well over 40 percent, from a 1979 average of about 5,700 to about 3,200 words today.[13]

In his illuminating book, *Governing with the News*, Timothy Cook, a political scientist at Williams College, argues that the goals of American journalists fundamentally diverge from those of the country's politicians. Whereas journalists want their stories to have concreteness, plot line, color, real people, terseness, and above all "an endless series of conflicts and momentary resolutions," politicians want to preserve nuance and room to maneuver and compromise. Info-glut exacerbates this divergence. It forces journalists to pare their stories to the bone and to put a premium on snappiness and entertainment value rather than news content. Politicians who talk about "a complex problem or, even worse, a series of problems, [run into] trouble with journalists who are looking for something easily described, and preferably an easy division between protagonists and antagonists." Furthermore, if they want to survive, politicians must supply the kind of material journalists demand: "speakers concerned about getting into the news have to craft their communications so as to be littered with soundbites."[14] Newt Gingrich, the former Speaker of the U.S. House of Representatives, once vividly expressed his exasperation with these demands. "Part of the reason I use strong language is because you-all will pick it up," Gingrich declared. "You convince your colleagues to cover me being calm, and I'll be calm. You guys want to cover nine seconds, I'll give you nine seconds, because that is the competitive requirement. . . . I've simply tried to learn my half of your business."[15]

The breathless infotainment style of the media in modern democracies is understandable in a journalistic world operating at breakneck speed and plagued by info-glut, but it is completely inappropriate in an increasingly complex world that demands increasingly sophisticated policy-making. "The digital age does not respect contemplation," writes James Naughton, a former White House correspondent for *The New York Times*. "The deliberative news process is being sucked into a constant swirl of charge and countercharge followed by rebuttal and re-rebuttal succeeded by spin and counterspin leading to new charges and countercharges."[16] Yet at the same time, the very media that revel in hype of this kind are becoming more important as conduits for communication among the various branches of U.S. government.[17] Individuals in Congress and the executive branch often make calculated use of the media, both exploiting them and borrowing their tactics. The timing and wording of announcements are designed to further an agenda and maneuver policy proposals around political obstacles.

The challenges we face—within our respective societies and collectively as a species—are tangled, dynamic, and barely understood. Our responses to them require careful deliberation. When we reduce these challenges to angry dichotomies, and when we reduce the quality of information available to us about these challenges, we limit our ability to supply the social and technical ingenuity we need.

—————————

Technologies are generally becoming more powerful, efficient, and portable, as well as faster, easier to use, and cheaper. These trends, in turn, broaden our reach in both time and space—in other words, they extend our agency horizon, as I call it.

Whether we think this is a good thing or not depends in large part on our judgments about human nature and about how the progress of technology affects that nature. In Western society since the Enlightenment, optimists have argued that advances in science and technology not only allow us to better manipulate the physical world, they also liberate us from superstition and irrationality.[18] In the process, we gain the ability to control or at least mitigate our base desires and impulses, an achievement that—ideally—could open a door to utopia.

It's a theme that in one form or another has repeatedly surfaced in America's optimistic culture. Thomas Jefferson wrote that "the general spread of the light of science [has] laid open to every view the palpable truth that the mass of mankind has not been born with saddles on their backs, nor a favored few, booted and spurred, ready to ride them legitimately by the grace of God."[19] The theme has been especially powerful since America's triumph in World War II and the advent of the communications revolution. At the end of the war, the electrical engineer Vannevar Bush—then the director of the U.S.'s Office of Scientific Research and Development—proposed new technologies for storing and accessing the skyrocketing quantity of knowledge available to humankind. "Presumably man's spirit should be elevated," Bush concluded, "if he can better review his shady past and analyze more completely and objectively his present problems."[20] And in the late 1990s, Nicholas Negroponte, the director of MIT's famed Media Laboratory, argued that new communication technologies could fundamentally alter deeply rooted attitudes. He aimed to "bring the digital world to kids seven to twelve years old in the hundred poorest nations in the world," in part by positioning a communications satellite over Africa to provide free Internet access to the continent's schoolchildren. "Ten to twenty years from now," he declared forcefully, "kids won't care much about countries."[21]

I'd say that is moot. But there's another school of thought that thinks that technology can't and won't change us, but can still lead us to a better world because after all, these people say, our nature is fundamentally benign. The economist Brian Arthur writes: "[We] use all the complicated, sleek, metallic, interwired, souped-up gizmos at our disposal for simple, primate social purposes. We use jet planes to come home to our loved ones at Thanksgiving. We use the Net to hang out with others in chat rooms and to exchange e-mail. We use quadraphonic-sound movies to tell ourselves stories in the dark about other people's lives. We use high-tech sports cars to preen, and attract mates. For all its glitz and swagger, technology, and the whole interactive revved-up economy that goes with it, is merely an outer-casing for our inner selves. And these inner selves, these primate souls of ours with their ancient social ways, change slowly. Or not at all."[22]

Arthur is probably right that our primate souls change only slowly, if at all; new technologies don't reform us, they just extend the reach of our underlying nature. But his portrayal of this creative, social, and generous nature seems a bit too rosy. We use jet planes not only to visit our loved ones but also to bomb and strafe. Quadraphonic movies are great propaganda tools for inciting hatred of others. And the Internet and other new technologies can be used as much for destructive mischief as for innocent chat or essential communication.

At Comdex, I found myself especially intrigued by the relationship between the technologies around me and how we govern ourselves. Many people argue that modern communication technologies will open up a new era of grassroots democracy. Personal computers, the Internet, fax machines, and cell phones aid local activities that create and strengthen community institutions. They help build social capital in the form of networks of trust and reciprocity, and this social capital makes governments more humane and responsive. The effects are thought to be particularly pronounced in developing countries. The New York–based group Human Rights Watch has declared that "the Internet has the potential to be a tremendous force for development—by providing quick and inexpensive information, by encouraging discussion rather than violence, and by empowering citizens."[23] In my terms, these technologies boost the flow of social ingenuity by making it easier for people to reform and create the institutions—from effective municipal councils to fair national election procedures—that they need to have happy and prosperous lives.

The wide use of new communication technologies in poor countries has certainly helped ignite an explosion of activity by nongovernmental organizations (NGOS). In countries like the Philippines, India, and Brazil, a visitor can't help but be astonished by the vigor and accomplishments of the countless NGOS working for environmental protection, human rights, and economic development. The rapid drop in fertility rates in many poor countries is attributable in no small measure to the work of Internet-empowered family planning and women's NGOS. Often these groups are linked together into powerful transnational networks that focus attention and resources from around the world on local issues, like preventing malaria or drilling wells, and that forge links between activists in rich and poor countries. Often, too, these networks are ideally suited to address rapidly unfolding problems that cross national boundaries, like pollution and refugee crises.[24]

It's important to recognize that today's advances in information technology are part of a larger process—a technology-driven shift of power from the state to individuals and subgroups. As our agency horizon widens, as our reach grows, and as the technologies we use become more powerful, easier to use, and cheaper, we become individually more powerful relative to large, cumbersome, hierarchical institutions that are weighed down by bureaucracies and rigid standard operating procedures.

Some new information technologies unquestionably strengthen the state: security cameras scan public thoroughfares, squad cars are linked directly to databases on criminals, and law-enforcement agencies can search effectively through huge numbers of fingerprint and DNA records.[25] Ultimately, though, the balance appears to tilt in the other direction—towards a weakening, not a strengthening of the state. The evidence is clearest in countries that have tried to restrict the intrusions of the Internet, like Saudi Arabia, Iran, and China. Managing their citizens' access to information, these societies have found, is exceedingly difficult. "In country after country," Dale Eickelman, a Dartmouth anthropologist, says, "government officials, traditional religious scholars and officially sanctioned preachers are finding it very hard to monopolize the tools of literate culture. The days have gone when governments and religious authorities can control what their people know and what they think."[26]

Many people, especially in Western cultures that promote individualism and personal liberty, believe this shift is indisputably a good thing—to them, anything that weakens the state relative to the individual is a positive development. People who adopt this perspective tend to downplay, even to distrust, the state's role in providing public goods—including well-functioning markets, courts, and health and educational systems—that are critical to our well-being. Their implicit assumption seems to be that individual human nature is fundamentally benign, and that human beings, even with astonishing technological power at their disposal, will behave constructively if left to their own devices.

But human nature and behavior can be malicious as well as benign. And so our assessment of the consequences of a technology-driven shift of power to individuals has to be much more complex. Whether the shift is a good thing depends (to put it crudely) on whether the people empowered by it are good guys or bad guys, and on whether the state that is weakened is beneficent or predatory. When bad guys are empowered and good states weakened, the delivery of social ingenuity—in the form of good institutions—can grind to a halt.

Even in the best of circumstances, reforming institutions, or creating new ones, is hard. Niccolò Machiavelli wrote in *The Prince* in 1513 that "there is nothing more difficult to execute, nor more dubious of success, nor more dangerous to administer than to introduce a new system of things: for he who introduces it has all those who profit from the old system as his enemies, and he has only lukewarm allies in all those who might profit from the new system."[27] The task of reform is made even harder in our time by the rising power of subgroups and vested interests that don't have the broader interests of society at heart.[28] We need sophisticated institutions more than ever, to deal with our increasingly complex and fast-changing world, but concerted and truly visionary institutional reform has become exceedingly difficult to achieve. Gridlocks surround proposed U.S. legislation on many urgent issues, including health care, campaign finance, and global warming. It's now too easy for narrow coalitions and interest groups to block change that isn't in their interest.

This is the dark side of the communications revolution: using the Internet, e-mail, talk radio, and computerized address lists of carefully targeted sympathizers, lobby groups mobilize millions of people to hobble creative legislation. Congressional offices are inundated with messages poured out by automatically programmed e-mail and fax computers. As Michael Wines writes in *The New York Times*: "Modern Washington is wired for quadraphonic sound and wide-screen video, lashed by fax, computer, 800 number, overnight poll, FedEx, grassroots mail, air shuttle and CNN to every citizen in every village on the continent and Hawaii, too. Its every twitch is blared to the world, thanks to C-Span, open-meetings laws, financial-disclosure reports and campaign spending rules, and its every misstep is logged in a database for the use of some future office-seeker."[29]

New communication technologies are particularly potent when coupled with new techniques—including scientific polling, direct marketing, and image management—for mobilizing and manipulating public opinion to support specific causes.[30] Extolling the virtues of these techniques, one Washington lobbyist exclaims: "Imagine what it would be like if you were in Congress and you got a thousand phone calls a week and letters and e-mails and faxes. Not from people all over the country, but from your constituents, people whose names you recognize, the people who were at the polls with you, who live down the street."[31] Buffeted by these pressures, politicians and policy-makers become tightly bound to the unreflective whims of constituents mobilized by special interests. Governance is gradually reduced to plebiscites. We lose the engaged deliberation among citizens essential to effective democracy. Decisions on highly technical matters of public policy are instead made by leaders glued to polling results. And given the nature of polling procedures, the poll respondents—the people our leaders now listen to—don't have a chance to discuss the issues they are being asked about, to learn about their nuances and connections to other things that matter, or to move beyond the ordinal ranking of prepared answers offered by the pollster.

The power of obstructionist subgroups and special interests is further accentuated by today's frenetic pace of social change. In democratic societies, consensus on behalf of a particular policy must usually be built slowly across interest groups, among legislators, and within the public. But as the pace of change increases, the time available for consensus-building falls, and it's easier for nimble small groups to derail agreement.

All this not only hinders our supply of social ingenuity, it also increases our ingenuity requirement: legislation, for instance, has to be more complex in an effort to strike a balance among all these competing and ever more powerful groups.[32] Michael Wines notes that lawmakers must "insert and rewrite clauses to satisfy hundreds of interests that never wrote Capitol Hill or the White House twenty years ago, and probably did not even exist." The rising complexity of legislation is reflected in the increasing length of key laws: the original Clean Air Act of 1963, for example, was ten pages long; amendments to the Act filled thirty-eight pages in 1970, 117 pages in 1977, and 313 pages in 1990.

This is a nasty mix: info-glut abbreviates our attention span and encourages people to fragment, oversimplify, and sensationalize information about policy issues; technologically empowered special interests bog down the policy process; and polls reduce governance to plebiscites. The result is a vicious circle. People dislike politics and politicians, because politics seems so corrupted by special interests, because politicians seem so craven, and because both seem too often unable to address society's deep-seated and chronic problems. People withdraw their moral support from government (as evidenced by falling turnouts at elections), and so government in turn becomes more the pawn of powerful narrow interests. Perhaps most disturbingly, high-caliber citizens refuse to enter politics because they have no desire to be considered, and treated like, scum. We are left with leaders who pander and prevaricate—brilliant soundbite demagogues with little vision and even less spine.

The ultimate consequence of this combination of factors is a reduction in the flow of social ingenuity—a breakdown of vital social processes of reform and flexibility in the face of rapid change. Governments are less able to address effectively the difficult political, economic, and technical problems they face. For the time being, the foreign policy commentator Jessica Tuchman Mathews notes, the shift of power away from states to subgroups "is likely to weaken rather than bolster the world's capacity to solve its problems."[33]

We might not have much respect for them, but we should have some sympathy for the leaders of the new world we've created. We demand that they solve, or at least manage, a multitude of interconnected problems that can develop into crises without warning; we require them to guide us through an increasingly turbulent reality that is, in key respects, literally incomprehensible to the human mind; we buffet them on every side with bolder and more powerful special interests that challenge every innovative policy idea; we submerge them in information, much of it unhelpful and distracting; and we force them to make decisions in ever shorter time frames and to act at an ever faster pace. Moreover, we expect them to do their job, in the face of all these pressures, with tools provided by political institutions that were designed to meet the challenges of the eighteenth and nineteenth centuries.

It is not uncommon, these days, to hear people asking, Where are the great leaders? We look back with nostalgia on Roosevelt, Churchill, Truman, Adenauer, de Gaulle, and Kennedy. For all their failures, these men somehow clearly defined for us the problems we faced and the paths we had to follow. We often remark that no current leader even comes close to those earlier men in stature and competence.

And yet—although it's probably true that fewer high-caliber citizens are entering politics now—the decline in the quality of leadership is, in some respects, illusory. In hindsight, our leaders at mid-century seem superior to the Clintons, Blairs, Schröders, and Chiracs who lead us today, because the world fifty years ago was profoundly different from the world today. Then, the great challenges *could be* clearly defined, and our best responses *could be* clearly articulated, within ideologies that were well rooted in our cultures. Now, the challenges before us seem fuzzy and impossibly entangled with long-term, deep, and barely understood social, economic, and ecological processes. Effective responses cannot be simple and ideologically satisfying; they must instead be as complex as the problems they address, malleable in the face of rapid change, and ambiguous enough to permit multiple interpretations by the constituencies they are supposed to satisfy. No wonder our leaders seem inadequate. Ronald Heifetz, a psychiatrist who lectures on leadership issues at Harvard University, writes: "Today we face a crisis in leadership in many areas of public and private life. Yet we misconceive the nature of these leadership crises. We attribute our problems too readily to our politicians and executives, as if they were the cause of them. We frequently use them as scapegoats. . . . Yet our current crises may have more to do with the scale, interdependence, and perceived uncontrollability of modern economic and political life. The paucity of leadership may perpetuate our quandaries, but seldom is it the basis for them."[34]

Our leaders are human beings, after all. They're equipped with the very same mental apparatus that the rest of us have. This apparatus, this extraordinary brain, has at its command the specialized intelligences and the versatility that allowed hominids to survive vagaries of climate and environment countless generations ago. But our brains—in particular, our leaders' brains—are ill-equipped for the circumstances we face now. Our capacity for easy adaptation to incremental change keeps us from seeing how qualitatively new and possibly dangerous the world we have created really is.[35] The human brain's hard-wired cognitive heuristics and shortcuts—essential tools for dealing with large amounts of information—are woefully inappropriate when we're enmeshed in nonlinear, tightly coupled systems in which small things and small events can matter a lot. Its tendency, under stress, to simplify and dichotomize issues is unsuited to snarled problems that demand subtlety and nuance of thought. And its relentlessly optimistic temperament (what the anthropologist Lionel Tiger has called our "biology of hope") shortens our time horizons and instills in us a potentially fatal imprudence.[36]

As our world becomes more and more complex, and as the political and cognitive tools that our leaders bring to this world become, relatively, less and less adequate, our leaders hunker down. They eschew boldness, because anyone who makes bold decisions will be thrown out of power. They tend to become tinkerers and managers—and not particularly good managers, at that, because the systems they seek to manage are full of nonlinearities and unknown unknowns. In sum, they become less able to make their critical contribution to the supply of the social and technical ingenuity that our societies need.

Perhaps the main job of leaders, however, is not to supply ingenuity but to help our societies resolve their deep conflicts over values, wealth, and power. In fact, some skeptics might argue that there is no shortage of ingenuity—we have more than enough, the real problem is our inability to resolve key political struggles over what we want, where we should go, and who should benefit. If we could settle those questions, the rest would be relatively straightforward and technical.

But this argument overlooks the subtle relationship between politics and ingenuity. True, political struggles must be resolved, or at least mitigated, if a society is to achieve social justice and progress. But great ingenuity is usually needed to design, implement, and operate the political institutions—voting systems, parliaments, judicial arrangements, and the like—that enable societies to deal with their political struggles. Moreover, when these political institutions fail, the resulting conflict among social groups diverts the attention and absorbs the energy of leaders, bureaucrats, and decision-makers of all kinds, and the day-to-day management that is vital to the smooth running of society is then neglected.

If political processes are intimately entangled with the production and use of ingenuity, values clearly are, too. Moral, economic, and other values affect our choice of lifestyles, technologies, and social arrangements. Some of these things need much more ingenuity to produce and sustain than others, so our values powerfully influence how much ingenuity we need. For example, if we value things like sports utility vehicles and big houses that consume lots of natural resources, then we need more ingenuity to extract and process those resources than we would if we valued a less materially-focused lifestyle. Social values also affect the supply of ingenuity by influencing the behavior of social groups. Some values—such as those that stress trust, reciprocity, and commitment to the commonweal—promote cooperative behavior among groups that aids the smooth flow of ingenuity in response to shared problems. Other values—especially those that stress self-interest or the superiority of particular ethnic, religious, or economic groups—encourage divisive and narrow-minded behavior. If powerful groups in a society hold such selfish values, they will obstruct policies and reforms that they see as damaging to their interests.[37]

Many of today's leaders seem helpless in the face of debilitating struggles among diverse social groups, and unwilling to act against powerful special interests. From the perspective of outside observers, this seems to be nothing more complicated than a lack of political will. "If only those politicians had more guts!" we often exclaim. If only our leaders had the will, there would be a way: ingenuity would flow unimpeded, institutions could be reformed, debilitating political struggles managed, and most if not all of our problems overcome.

This explanation sounds good, but it means little. Almost any failure of social policy anywhere—in my terms, almost any gap between the need for and the supply of social ingenuity—can be attributed in a general way to lack of political will. Such explanations are specious: they obscure the complexity of the real world and amount to little more than finger-pointing. They blame all our troubles on an amorphous, undifferentiated group of leaders who could fix things if they weren't so venal or cowardly, and they conveniently let the rest of us off the hook. "Lack of political will" becomes the pat formula for everything that's wrong in the world.

Our leaders' apparent failure, though, has less to do with gross character flaws and more to do with the ever greater empowerment of social groups and the generally rising complexity of our world. What we complacently identify as a lack of political will is often, in reality, a lack of *social* will: we are all part of the problem, and our societies as a whole, not just our leaders, are ineffective in providing solutions to the challenges we face.

———————

Hundreds of meters below the roller coaster that twists itself around the uppermost spire of Vegas's Stratosphere Hotel, incorporated into the foundations of the structure, is an elaborate shopping mall for the hotel's guests. One afternoon, my friend and I took a well-earned break from Comdex and diverted ourselves by wandering through the mall's shops and food courts. Pretty soon, we stumbled on a large video-game parlor.

The parlor had the usual assortment of racing, martial arts, and shoot-'em-up games. It also had a flight simulator and a wide range of conventional pinball machines. But the game you couldn't miss—it confronted you the moment you walked through the entrance—brought the dead to life.

A player with an imitation assault rifle faced a huge screen showing a background of graveyards and tombs. From this background emerged a steady stream of ghoulish zombies carrying various lethal instruments—hatchets, long knives, and the like. The player had to stop the monsters or be killed. As the zombies moved relentlessly forward, the player fired a stream of bullets from the rifle, carving off hunks of rotten flesh and splattering gore across the scenery. If the player didn't hit home with a sufficient number of slugs, a zombie would get close enough to take a swing with its weapon. Then a wide slash—gushing blood—appeared across the screen, as if the player had just been carved across the face.

I was mesmerized by this game, and so were the children playing it, who seemed to be having the time of their lives. Such games *must* desensitize children to violence, I thought. (Our visit to Las Vegas took place before the string of mass murders by schoolkids in the U.S., murders that culminated in the Columbine High School massacre, provoking much public discussion of the links between video games and childhood violence.) I had recently read the extraordinary book *On Killing*, in which Lieutenant Colonel Dave Grossman shows that most people have deep, innate inhibitions against killing fellow human beings. These inhibitions are so strong that soldiers in combat will often do just about anything to avoid shooting directly at the enemy. Militaries around the world have, however, found that certain techniques of conditioning can substantially overcome soldiers' inhibitions; these techniques parallel those used in violent video games. "Video games can . . . be superb at teaching violence," Grossman writes, "violence packaged in the same format that has more than quadrupled the firing rate of modern soldiers." Particularly harmful are the games in which "you actually hold a weapon in your hand and fire it at human-shaped targets on the screen."[38]

For impressionable youngsters, video games are now so good that they blur the line between reality and illusion. As my friend and I left the hotel's mall and walked out into the afternoon glare of the desert sun, I remembered my evening stroll many months before in the Isle of Dogs. Las Vegas, even more than Canary Wharf, is the ultimate postmodern urban unreality. In the gambling halls and twenty-four-hour restaurants, where hardly a clock can be seen, or under the famous roof at Caesar's Palace that changes from day to night every twenty minutes, it's easy to lose track of time completely, or even whether it's day or night. The Strip boasts one artificial reality after another: a volcano belching lava outside the Mirage Hotel every half hour, a pirate battle engulfing the Treasure Island Hotel every two hours, and a single hotel representing the whole New York skyline.

And Las Vegas and Comdex do complement each other. New communication and information technologies subtly shift their users' understanding of space, time, and personal and community identity. They tend to make postmodernist ideas more attractive, especially the idea that the world consists of multiple, overlapping, fragmented realities, all constructed by the human mind and all essentially ephemeral.[39] So they subtly undermine the conventional assumption—an assumption rooted in the rationality of the Enlightenment and central to modern scientific thought—that we are embedded in an objective, physical reality governed by principles that operate independently of the human mind.

The Internet, for example, separates our civic lives and our work from our physical location as never before: people can establish communities and work together without being together in the same place at the same time.[40] Communication technologies that can carry more information faster than ever before also encourage us to focus on things that happen in the present—in the immediate, palpable *now*—rather than those that happen in the past and future.[41] The Internet and the Web allow us to detach our personal identities from our real physical and psychological characteristics: in the multiple worlds of cyberspace, such as chat rooms and non-stop interactive games, people can adopt an endless number of discrete and disembodied personae. And from the Net-surfer's point of view, the Web consists of countless fragmented and coexisting realities. Its hyperlinks allow the surfer to move from one virtual world to another with the tap of a finger on a computer mouse. Identity is severed from geography: a surfer can find things and people on the Web without having a clue where they actually are in physical space.

Because each surfer has a different Web experience, the Internet's fragmentation tends to supplant the shared public experience that is a key foundation of a society-wide sense of community. As Steve Lohr of *The New York Times* so happily puts it, the Internet gives us seemingly "infinite depths of narrowness."[42]

This shift towards postmodernist attitudes will continue. Two-way video communication will combine with the ability to display several windows simultaneously on one computer screen to allow people to be "present" in many places at once. Technologies just over the horizon will extend and modify the powers of our eyes, ears, and other senses; and our nervous systems will be ever more tightly integrated into the information and communication networks that run the world (as suggested in the chapter "Techno-Hubris"). The boundary between the interior and exterior of our bodies will become less significant. "Inhabitation," says the architect and media philosopher William Mitchell, "will take on a new meaning—one that has less to do with parking your bones in architecturally defined space and more with connecting your nervous system to nearby electronic organs. Your room and your home will become part of you, and you will become part of them." And as our ability to create sensory realities indistinguishable from the physical world improves, the physical attributes of the buildings and places around us will become less important. We will combine and recombine the fungible components of our physical environment to suit our momentary needs. Mitchell writes: "The constituent elements of hitherto tightly packaged architectural and urban compositions can begin to float free from one another, and they can potentially relocate and recombine according to new logics. . . . Rooms and buildings will henceforth be seen as sites where bits meet the body—where digital information is translated into individual, auditory, tactile, or otherwise perceptible form, and, conversely, where bodily actions are sensed and converted into digital information." The task of twenty-first-century designers and planners will be, therefore, to build the *bitsphere*—a "worldwide, electronically mediated environment in which networks are everywhere, and most of the artifacts that function within it (at every scale, from nano to global) have intelligence and telecommunications capabilities. It will overlay and eventually succeed the agricultural and industrial landscapes that humankind has inhabited for so long."[43]

As we left the Stratosphere Hotel and walked down the Strip, the sharp transitions from one hotel spectacle to the next were like clicks of a mouse button on the Web. We were physically hyperlinking, in a sense, from one virtual reality to another: first we were in Italy, the next moment in King Arthur's castle, and the next in ancient Egypt. Yet after a while all these virtual realities seemed the same. All the hotels were immense, fantastic, and distinct on the outside; but on the inside they all had the same endless banks of slot machines and fields of gambling tables, the same overflowing buffets of dreary food, and the same hollow hucksterism. Perhaps this is true, too, of the virtual realities of the new information age—showy façades and lots of hype wrapped around the same ideas over and over again.

I was struck more, though, by the transience of it all. Today's capitalism and information technologies have combined to create an Age of Ephemera. Our buildings are ephemeral: even Las Vegas's Luxor Hotel, that symbol of authority and durability in a time of impermanence, will last perhaps fifty years—less than a hundredth the lifespan of the pyramids at Giza—before it is gobbled up by the city's incessant regeneration of its fragmented fantasy. And the copious information that defines and shapes today's realities is also ephemeral. Our unprecedented capacity to store information belies its modern fragility.[44] First, the material in which the information is stored deteriorates over time. Whereas acid-free paper can last five hundred years, the life span of archival-quality microfilm is about two hundred years, high-quality CD-ROMs no more than fifty years, and the best VHS tapes about ten years. Already, magnetic tapes recorded in the sixties and seventies are degenerating, and serious holes are starting to appear in our records of the past.[45] Second, as one generation of storage technology succeeds another in ever quicker succession—as, for example, we switch from magnetic tapes to floppy disks to recordable CDs to store our computer data—the information stored with the old technology must be converted into a form compatible with the new technology. Inevitably, much information is not converted and is therefore lost when the old machines are no longer available to read it. This *data migration* problem, as experts call it, generally doesn't arise with information printed on paper, because we can read or interpret this information without the aid of sophisticated technology. Books printed five hundred years ago are still quite satisfactory stores of information.[46]

My friend and I eventually reached the Luxor Hotel at the far end of the Strip. It was now dark, and the hotel's great light seemed to burn a hole in the night sky above us. We were tired to the bone, having investigated every hotel foyer, casino, and tourist site along the way, so we grabbed dinner at the hotel's basement buffet and hailed a cab to return to the Stratosphere.

The drive along the Strip was like hitting the "back" button on a Web browser, as if we were retracing our steps through the physical hyperlinks of our walk. Perhaps, I thought, postmodernism is the right perspective in this frenetic age of fragments and ephemera. After all, we are increasingly deracinated, cut off from our past and unreflective about our future. Only *now* seems real now. Then I remembered something I had read in the research papers given me by Donald Stuss, the specialist on the brain's frontal lobes I interviewed in Toronto. Patients with damage to these lobes, he found, have great trouble seeing themselves as entities that continue through time. They lose "temporal integration, defined as the awareness of a stable self from the past, through the present, and into the future." "When the frontal lobes are damaged," Stuss concludes, "only the perpetual present remains."[47]

Are modern hypermedia and hypercapitalism nullifying one of our greatest cognitive advantages—our ability to imagine ourselves through time? Are they, to put it bluntly, lobotomizing us? After the sensory barrage of Comdex and the Strip, the parallel between postmodernism and the psychological state of Stuss's patients seemed far-fetched but impossible to ignore.

At the beginning of a new millennium, America is infused with optimism. Abroad, the country's economic and military superiority is unchallenged, while at home its expanding economy rides a never-ending bull market. After the dark years of Vietnam, Watergate, and stagflation, America's elites believe, almost universally, that their country has discovered the key to sustained increases in prosperity and social well-being—a synergistic combination of furiously competitive capitalism, aggressive scientific and technological innovation, and liberal democracy. These elites hardly ever doubt that the rest of the world should follow the American path and that, if it does, the future will be golden. In the concluding words of his book *Growth Triumphant*, Richard Easterlin, an economics professor at the University of Southern California, captures this spirit: "The future . . . is one of never-ending economic growth, a world in which ever-growing abundance is matched by ever-rising aspirations, a world in which cultural differences are leveled in the constant race to achieve the good life of material plenty. It is a world founded on belief in science and the power of rational inquiry and in the ultimate capacity of humanity to shape its own destiny."[48]

I call these people economic optimists, because they generally contend the greater good will be served if economic motives and institutions predominate over political and other social forces. They also fancy themselves hard-nosed realists about human beings and society. Nevertheless, when they assert that we can construct and reshape the realities we live within by letting markets unleash our will and creativity, they sound remarkably like postmodernists rebelling against the idea that we are embedded in an objective physical reality. Given sufficient effort and inspiration, the economic optimists suggest, nothing is impossible, especially in market-driven cyberspace. In the new economy built on information, symbols, and knowledge, intangibles trump tangibles. Now we can release ourselves from age-old physical and social limitations. Natural resources don't matter anymore; our prosperity and happiness need no longer be constrained by such pedestrian matters. Nor are they necessarily conditioned by our atavistic instincts and impulses, as Nicholas Negroponte implies when he proposes to eliminate African nationalisms with a single satellite and the Internet. Abundance will diffuse to all of humankind, and all groups and individuals will be able to fulfill their unique aspirations in harmony with each other.[49]

These are fantasies, and dangerous fantasies at that. They are far more dangerous than run-of-the-mill postmodernist pipe dreams, because they have the ear of the powerful. They validate the short-term, self-serving interests of the economic and political elites of Western societies—elites that *want* to believe that the forces making them stupendously prosperous and powerful will eventually benefit all humanity.

But reality intrudes; it insists on shoving its impertinent face into the midst of these pretty pictures. Widespread poverty stubbornly persists. The international economic system flips unpredictably between stable and turbulent phases. The gaps between the wealthiest and poorest groups in our societies widen further, and fast. Our natural environment spits out annoying nonlinearities like collapsing fisheries, species extinction, and ozone holes. And no matter how much we wish it to be true, a few tons of communications hardware orbiting over Africa isn't enough to sweep aside the continent's nationalisms and ethnic identities.

Paradoxically, the new communication technologies promoted at Comdex—the kinds of technologies that are dear to the hearts of economic optimists, and that encourage the intermingling of illusion and reality—themselves create hard social and economic facts, hard realities, that contradict the economic optimists' fantasies. They do this by boosting the importance of knowledge, ideas, and information in our economies and by making it easier for buyers and sellers to find each other, agree on prices, and conclude their transactions (which makes markets larger and more efficient). Although these are good developments for the participants, they do tend to widen the gulf between the richest and poorest people in our societies by helping to create a "winner take all" knowledge economy.

In the chapter "Ingenuity and Wealth," I outlined New Growth theory, which argues that ideas are a factor of production like labor and capital. Unlike these conventional factors, though, ideas are non-rival—an idea can be used simultaneously by any or all of the people who have access to it. New communication technologies have made the distribution of ideas cheaper and easier, in turn making it easier for modern economies to capitalize on ideas' non-rival character. The initial cost of generating a useful new idea—say, a formula for a new drug or a procedure for improving inventory control in large factories—is often very high; but, thanks to technologies like the Internet, the Web, and CD-ROMs, the cost of reproducing and disseminating the idea, so that it is available for others to buy and use, is now extraordinarily low. As a result, the ideas of the very best idea-generators (whether individuals, groups, or corporations) can be brought to a much larger market than before, and these people can therefore reap much greater economic rewards. In large, highly competitive, highly efficient markets, the difference between the rewards received by the best and by the second-best idea-generators can be immense.

The academic world offers some good examples of this phenomenon: a "star" system has developed in many elite universities, whereby a few scholars and researchers are paid astronomically high salaries compared to their colleagues.[50] The same trend is visible across most industries and occupations in modern economies. As the economist Robert Frank writes: "Developments in communications, manufacturing technology, and transportation costs . . . have enabled the most talented performers to serve ever broader markets, which has increased the value of their services." These changes "have sharply increased the value of the top performers relative to their lesser ranked rivals."[51]

New communication and information technologies help widen wealth differentials in another way too—by boosting the "cognitive complexity" of the average job. Because employees now use computers a lot, they generally have to be more analytically and numerically competent; because they're dealing with increasing quantities of information flowing at increasing speed, they need to be better at using language and manipulating abstract categories; and because their radius of communication is constantly expanding, they generally interact with more people in their jobs, so their social skills have to be better developed. Moreover, studies show that the share of employment in jobs of high cognitive complexity has risen, while that in jobs of low complexity has dropped. In offices, for example, word-processing technology has reduced the need for secretaries at the same time that the faster pace of work has boosted the need for administrative assistants; in factories, robots have replaced assembly-line workers while simultaneously creating jobs for engineers and skilled technicians who design and maintain robotic systems. Investigating this issue, researchers in Canada sorted all occupations in the country into five categories, according to their level of complexity. They found that between 1971 and 1991 the share of employment in jobs in the highest category of cognitive complexity rose from 23.5 to 26.8 percent of the workforce, while those in occupations in the lowest category fell from 19.8 to 15.3 percent.[52]

Rising cognitive complexity means a rising requirement for frontal-lobe abilities. Unfortunately, as we saw in the chapter "Brains and Ingenuity," these abilities aren't distributed equally across our population. As a result, when the complexity of the average job rises, those who are less adept at handling complex tasks lose out, and they are pushed to compete for the declining fraction of low-complexity jobs in the economy. Those who are very good at managing complexity, in contrast, are in high demand. These processes help hold down wages in the menial and service sectors of the economy and boost the incomes of our societies' cognitive elites. In other words, they reinforce the stark divisions of wealth that I saw in my short walk through the Isle of Dogs.

Such divisions are a reality of modern life that no amount of postmodernist fantasy-building can obscure. In recent decades, they have deepened fastest in the United States. Experts point to a range of contributing factors: weaker trade unions, stronger shareholders, globalization (which increases the competitive pressure from cheap foreign labor), a rising number of single-parent households, the influx of lower-paid women into the workforce, and, not least, the multiple effects of new technologies, some of which I've just identified.[53] The combined impact of these factors has been dramatic. From 1969 to 1997 in the U.S., the median earnings of young white men with only a high-school education dropped 29 percent in real terms, and the fraction of this group falling below the poverty line nearly quadrupled, from 6.5 to 23.6 percent.[54] Earnings of people with more advanced educations fell too, but later in the period and not nearly as much, while those of managers significantly increased. Even more striking is how the economic growth of the 1980s and 1990s benefited the richest segments of the U.S. population. While the bottom three-fifths of American households have seen their inflation-adjusted incomes stay virtually flat for almost three decades, the income of the top fifth has risen over 50 percent, and that of the top twentieth has almost doubled (shown in the illustration opposite). The U.S. economy's strong growth in the late 1990s boosted earnings of the poorer segments of American society, but without altering the long-term trend.

Although the division is most pronounced in America, it is visible around the globe. "Almost everywhere we look," writes the MIT professor of management Lester Thurow, "we see rising economic inequalities among countries, among firms, among individuals. Returns to capital are up; returns to labor are down. Returns to skills are up; returns to unskilled labor are down." Governments acknowledge that they are largely impotent in the face of these changes, while their self-satisfied elites assert that the extraordinary economic upheavals affecting so many people are simply normal economic adjustments in a rapidly evolving world. The best that anyone can suggest, it seems, is that people must continually improve their education and skills to remain marketable in a fluid economy that needs increasingly sophisticated workers. "For individuals here are three words of advice: skills, skills, skills," says Thurow. "The economic prospects of those without skills are bleak. What we now see—falling real wages for those without skills—is going to continue. In education the needs of the bottom two-thirds of the labor force are particularly acute. In an age when brawn earns little and brains much, this part of the labor force simply has to be much better educated."[55]

But there is a problem with this prescription. Given the distribution of natural aptitudes and abilities in our societies, not everyone can be educated or trained to be an information worker or knowledge producer. A knowledge-based economy privileges certain abilities over others, and only a relatively thin stratum of the society has those abilities in abundance. We

U.S. Income Disparity Has Increased in the Last Forty Years

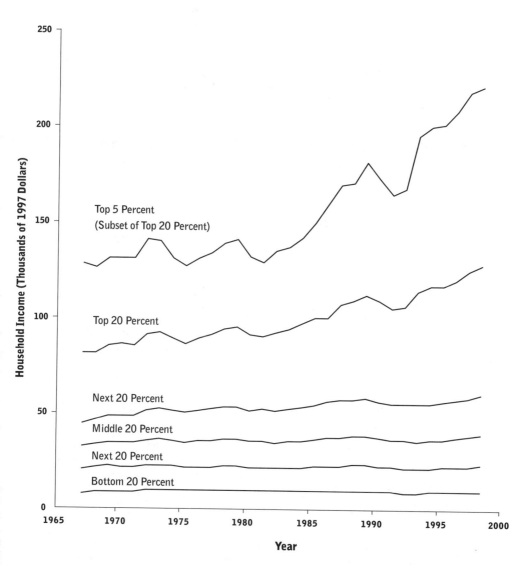

can't all be computer programmers or financial analysts or robotic-systems designers. Some people are going to be left behind, and societies with rapidly widening inequalities can't be politically stable for long.[56]

In the tourist zones of Las Vegas, reality's intrusions are kept to a minimum. Outside these zones, though, the facts of desert existence are inescapable—the glaring sun, gritty vacant lots with blowing tumbleweeds, the heat, and the dryness. From the air, as one flies into the city, it's the desert that prevails. The surrounding mountains and plains are barren and dusty brown, and they seem to stretch endlessly in every direction. Las Vegas, in contrast, is puny. Even the gargantuan hotels of the Strip, the Luxor included, form only a tiny cluster of buildings that thrusts into the desert along one street.

Las Vegas is a fragile bubble of illusion suspended in the middle of an extraordinarily harsh physical environment. The bubble survives because it is surrounded by a thick protective layer of ingenuity. Before I left the city, I decided to investigate how the city provides itself with the one thing it needs, more than anything else, to extract from its physical environment—water. In that desert, I figured, it must take some doing.

Early one morning, I drove away from the city's core to the headquarters of the Southern Nevada Water Authority, the agency responsible for supplying water to Las Vegas and several other nearby communities. A large wooden derrick of the kind once used to drill for water stood outside the Authority's buildings, at the corner of a busy intersection. After I had parked the car and signed in, an employee led me into the Authority's newly constructed rear buildings, past walls lined with charts, maps, and diagrams showing data on the status of the region's reservoirs and aquifers. Soon, I found myself in the office of Kay Brothers, the director of the resources department, which oversees long-range water planning.

Kay Brothers, a woman in her mid-forties with steel-gray hair, was cool and technical. In the course of an hour's interview, she outlined the city's complex arrangements for sharing the Colorado River, Las Vegas's main source of water, and a river whose original route passed only forty kilometers from the city center. The Colorado's waters are divided among seven states—starting with Wyoming at the headwaters and ending with Arizona and California in the south—according to allocations laid out in a 1922 agreement.[57] Today, only a small fraction of the original volume crosses the U.S. border into Mexico. The struggles over this water have been long and bitter; Nevada has never had more than a bit part in the drama. The southern Californian cities of Los Angeles and San Diego have been the big actors, regularly consuming much more than their allocation and threatening Arizona, in particular, with shortages.

The southwestern United States is an arid region with a skyrocketing urban population. It has little surface water other than the Colorado River. Moreover, the Colorado is not, by world standards, a big river, and its flow varies wildly from year to year. Already it is dammed, diverted, and managed along almost its entire length. Ensuring an adequate supply of water for decades into the future—as Brothers and her counterparts in the other six states are required to do—is a daunting assignment.

Yet she was entirely optimistic that the job could be done. She handed me reports showing water demand and supply projections for her region as far into the future as 2050. A combination of aggressive conservation efforts (a display on water-saving toilets decorated her building's foyer) and wastewater recycling were already restraining demand. And both Nevada and Arizona were working to ensure an adequate supply by banking surplus water in years of abundance. Both states, in fact, were pumping water back into previously depleted aquifers—water that could be drawn out in lean years to come. She also pointed out that much of Las Vegas's apparent extravagance with water was an illusion: the spectacular fountains, lakes, and waterfalls at the city's hotels used recycled water, often of poor quality, drawn from surface aquifers. The really big water demand, she said, came from watering of residential lawns and landscapes. For this reason, the Authority had launched an educational campaign to convince homeowners to adopt drought-resistant plants and desert landscaping. The price of water was also an important catalyst for conservation: she acknowledged that the price had gone up and would continue to go up.

Most important, Kay Brothers argued that a profound change had recently occurred in the relationships among the many stakeholders with interests in the Colorado's hydrological basin, stakeholders ranging from cities and states needing water to hydropower authorities concerned about maintaining electricity output, from tourist and river-rafting companies dependent on the river's regulated flow to environmentalists interested in protecting the area's biodiversity. In earlier years, relations among these groups had often been marked by acrimony and distrust; but today, she claimed, groups were much more willing to cooperate to solve the tough problems of managing the river's resources. Although many more groups were at the bargaining table than before, which in some ways raised the complexity of negotiation, gridlock had not resulted. Instead, cooperative solutions were easier to find, precisely because nearly all the stakeholders were represented. "You have a face and personality that you're dealing with now," she concluded. "It's still a slow, slow process, but I think it's starting to work. The stakeholders are now obtaining a respect for each other's concerns. Ten years ago that was never the case. It makes for some frustration, but overall it actually makes for a better understanding of the issues and better consideration of them." This assertion intrigued me: in this case, it seemed, the proliferation of highly empowered subgroups had not impeded the supply of ingenuity, as often happens in Washington and other capitals, but had instead improved it.

I left the meeting impressed. Even accounting for the boosterism that one expects of someone in her position, Kay Brothers had convinced me that the officials and engineers managing Las Vegas's delicate water resources were delivering enough technical and social ingenuity to keep the water flowing. And there was real reason for optimism beyond Las Vegas too: in the 1980s and 1990s, after many decades of soaring water consumption, the United States reduced both its total and its per capita water use. In fact, between 1980 and 1995, per capita use fell 20 percent, thanks in large part to much improved water-use efficiency in industry, irrigation, and thermoelectric power plants.[58]

But I wasn't convinced that the same would soon be true everywhere in the world. Each year, humanity withdraws a huge quantity of freshwater—about 4,000 cubic kilometers—from the planet's rivers, lakes, and aquifers annually. This is roughly equivalent to the amount of water that would pour over forty waterfalls the size of Niagara Falls in a year. We then return about half of this total to the original rivers and lakes, usually in a polluted condition. Because of population growth and higher personal consumption of water (for everything from showers to irrigated fruits and vegetables), our global consumption is still doubling about every seventy years. There is, nonetheless, enough water on the planet, if distributed evenly and used efficiently, to satisfy any foreseeable world population.

But this water is not distributed evenly, and it is certainly not used efficiently. Many regions, including large parts of Northern Africa, the Middle East, the Ganges basin in India, and northwestern China are already consuming essentially all their locally generated river runoff. In some of these regions the results are astonishing: the flow of water at the mouth of the Nile River dropped 80 percent in the five years from 1992 to 1997 because of Egypt's booming population and consumption; and the great Yellow River in China—once called China's scourge because of its torrential floods—is now dry at its mouth for up to five months every year because of upstream withdrawals.[59] Shortages of water can have a major effect on human health: almost one-fifth of the planet's population does not have enough clean water for basic needs, and every year a quarter of a billion cases of waterborne disease cause around 10 million deaths, mostly among children.[60]

Leading water experts believe that one thousand cubic meters of water per year per person is a useful benchmark of water scarcity. When a country falls below this threshold, its economic development is at risk. Although there are a few countries, such as Israel, that prosper with much less water, we can safely say that as average water availability drops below this level in a poor country, a substantial fraction of its population will face critical shortages of water. In practical terms this means that rural women will have to walk many kilometers from their villages for the day's water, slum dwellers will have to gather for hours around stand pipes for the few minutes when they run, and irrigated crops will die when wells go dry. Looking at the table below, we see that a number of countries already fall below this threshold and that by 2025 many more will do so, including large countries like South Africa, Kenya, and Iran.

Water Availability in 1995 and 2025

Country	Per Capita Water Availability 1995 (m³/person/year)	Projected Per Capita Water Availability 2025 (m³/person/year)
Africa		
Algeria	527	313
Burundi	594	292
Comoros	1,667	760
Egypt	936	607
Ethiopia	1,950	807
Kenya	1,112	602
Libya	111	47
Malawi	1,933	917
Morocco	1,131	751
Rwanda	1,215	485
Somalia	1,422	570
South Africa	1,206	698
Tunisia	434	288

The Americas		
Canada	98,667	79,731
United States	9,277	7,453
Barbados	192	169
Haiti	1,544	879
Asia/Middle East		
Bahrain	162	104
Cyprus	1,208	947
Iran	1,719	916
Israel	389	270
Jordan	318	144
Kuwait	95	55
Oman	874	295
Qatar	91	64
Saudi Arabia	249	107
Singapore	180	142
Yemen	346	131

The table lists selected countries where population growth will drive annual per capita water availability to 1,000 cubic meters or less per person by 2025. Figures for the United States and Canada are provided for comparison.

Driving back to the Stratosphere Hotel, I recalled my travels in China in 1995. In Beijing, I had visited the office of the vice president of a major hydrological research institute, and he had pulled out a table-sized plastic map of China that showed in raised relief the topography of mountain ranges, plateaus, and river basins. Running his fingers across the map's rough surface, he described the inescapable hydrological crisis facing his country.

"There are seven major river systems in China," he told me, "the Yangtze, Yellow, Heilongjiang, Pearl, Liaohe, Haihe, and Huaihe." Rainfall is plentiful in the south, he continued, "but it diminishes rapidly as one moves north and into the interior. Regions south of the Yangtze get one hundred centimeters per year or more; but south of the Yellow, the amount is seventy-five centimeters; and in the Beijing area it is sixty centimeters. Sometimes Beijing gets one-third of its rain in one day, and our reservoir system is completely unable to store this water when it arrives so suddenly."

The aquifers under Beijing supply 50 percent of the city's water. Originally at a depth of five to ten meters, the water table is now at fifty meters and is falling by a meter a year. As this water is extracted, the ground itself sinks throughout the region. Much groundwater is polluted by surface wastes that infiltrate downward, which causes disease and chemical poisoning in some of the region's population.

The Chinese central government has responded by announcing plans to build a giant canal to move 15 billion tons of water annually from a tributary of the Yangtze River in the south to Beijing and northern provinces, a distance of almost 1,500 kilometers. This canal will be one of the great engineering feats of human history, cutting across hundreds of geological formations, streams, and rivers; the current plan is to construct an eight-kilometer siphon to suck the water under and past the Yellow River.

But the project is enormously contentious within China. "All of the provinces along the route of the diversion scheme are upset about it," the water official said, adding that the canal and associated reservoirs would displace more than four hundred thousand people. "There is currently no agreement among the provinces on management of the canal, and management is important and difficult because canal breaks could be very dangerous to communities along the route. Already one-seventh of the project's budget is dedicated to solving environmental and social problems."

Water shortages in much of northern and western China restrict economic growth. The industrial city of Taiyan, the capital of the central province of Shanxi, is a microcosm of these problems. Situated in a valley surrounded by mountains that are rich in coal, the city is an important and rapidly growing producer of steel and chemicals. Long ago, the city's demand for water for its industries, homes, and agriculture outstripped the supply of the local Fen River, requiring ever higher extractions of groundwater from wells. As in Beijing, the water table is dropping rapidly. A large spring in the valley that has always been used for irrigation, at a site marked by one of China's best-known Buddhist temples, has almost gone dry. To make matters worse, the city and its industries produce hundreds of thousands of tons of heavily polluted wastewater each day, much of which is dumped into the Fen untreated or only minimally treated.

Because agricultural land is so scarce in the region, as throughout China, Taiyan cannot afford to stop irrigating the rice, wheat, and vegetable fields in the valley. But Fen River water is increasingly laden with dangerous chemicals and salts, most seriously cancer-causing benzene.

When I talked to local water managers, they acknowledged that the use of Fen water was slowly ruining the valley's soil, poisoning its crops, and lowering agricultural yields. The only solution was to dilute the river water with groundwater, but this resource was already overexploited. The managers had to make a dreadful trade-off: they could further damage the valley's soils and food production, or they could cut water supplies to the city's industries and homes.

Senior officials in Taiyan readily admitted the severity of their water problems. "Summer water shortages are extremely serious," said one administrator, a water engineer. "Some industries must be closed to maintain residential supply." But the potential solutions—more conservation and recycling, or pumping water 150 kilometers from the already depleted Yellow River—demanded new technologies and large amounts of capital. "We need funds and expertise from foreign countries," the engineer implored. "Otherwise, water scarcity will severely limit our economic development."

Water scarcity is only one thread in a snarled tangle of resource problems in China, from widespread deforestation to exhausted coastal fisheries and critical energy bottlenecks. And every year the country still adds over 10 million people to its population. Yet China has made extraordinary progress in liberalizing its economy, raising living standards, and feeding its people. Whether it can continue this trajectory in the face of its rising requirements for water, food, and energy depends on whether it can continue to muster the institutional reform and technologies it needs. In cities like Beijing and Taiyan, the race between ingenuity requirement and ingenuity supply is very real indeed.

———————————

Among the most spectacular sites on the Colorado River, and among the most astonishing human constructions in the world, is the Hoover Dam. On the afternoon of my visit to Kay Brothers, my friend and I decided to see the dam and its reservoir, Lake Mead, since both are an easy drive from Las Vegas.

We left the city on Interstate 93. The malls and industrial zones on each side of the highway gradually faded to suburbs, and the suburbs to a rocky and rugged desert relieved only by scattered shrubs and patches of desiccated grass. As we rose into the mountains, ravines and gullies gouged by flash floods cut across the landscape. The colors were stunning, as if a tapestry of rich browns, oranges, and ochers had been laid over the slopes.

Before reaching the dam, we stopped—once to explore an unused gravel road that twisted off into the desert, and then again to speak to the lead engineer of Las Vegas's main water treatment facility, on the shores of Lake Mead. He was open and helpful, eager to discuss his team's accomplishments in the face of the region's stunning population growth. Outside the facility, sections of a mighty water pipeline, waiting to be welded together and buried, were scattered along a newly cleared right-of-way that disappeared over the hills in the direction of Las Vegas. These were the hard-edged, practical realities of an immense city's survival in a desert.

We drove on, eventually descending around a hairpin turn carved into the ruddy walls of Black Canyon. We parked the car, and continued on foot. Farther down, the road crossed the top of the Hoover Dam and rose up again on the far side of the canyon, continuing on into Arizona.

The dam was everything it was claimed to be, and more—one of those sights, like the Taj Mahal in India or Victoria Falls in Africa, that no amount of text and no number of photographs can capture. It struck me as an expression of sheer technical exuberance, an almost religious monument to American technical capacity that was built in just over four years at the height of the Great Depression. Nestled at one end were a tasteful monument and plaque, like a roadside shrine, dedicated to the ninety-odd people who were killed during the project's construction. And despite the fact that a continuous stream of cars and trucks rolled across the top of the dam, people walking along its parapet spoke in hushed voices, as if they had just entered a grand cathedral.

Hoover Dam was built to contain the downstream ravages of the Colorado's floods and to generate power for the region's economic growth. Prior to its construction, the lack of reliable supplies of electricity and water had hobbled development in the U.S. Southwest, and the region had stagnated as an economic colony of the East. Not only did Hoover alleviate these practical constraints, it fundamentally changed the way Westerners thought about themselves and their region's prospects. "In one stroke," writes Joseph Stevens in his marvelous history of the dam, "it freed Southern California from its economic fetters and made possible virtually unlimited growth."[61]

Over 200 meters high and nearly 400 meters across at its crest, Hoover Dam contains around 3.5 million cubic meters of concrete, the largest volume ever poured in one place. Its volume, in fact, is greater than that of the pyramid of Cheops in Egypt, and like the pyramid, as one commentator remarks, it "seems to be regarded as a monument to the ingenuity of man, with intrinsic value greater than its mere functional design and construction."[62]

Nothing of its size had been attempted before, and its construction was an odyssey of technical challenges met and overcome, and of the generation and delivery of a continuous stream of ingenuity. Early on, for example, engineers realized that the heat generated by the setting of such a massive quantity of concrete could fracture the structure; so, as the concrete was being poured, workers installed a honeycomb of cooling pipes that carried refrigerated water and bled off the heat. Stevens notes that another key to success was mobility, the capacity to transport "materials and equipment to the right place at the right time so that laborers could perform their jobs smoothly and simultaneously like the moving parts of a well-oiled machine." But in the narrow dam site "such rapid, precise movement of thousands of men, tons of supplies, and mountains of concrete seemed almost impossible." Engineers solved the problem by hanging a web of cableways and buckets over the canyon that allowed materials to be continuously delivered to the workers below. An operator could "pick up anything—a truck, a bucket of concrete, a crew of carpenters, a single wrench—and lower it in a matter of seconds to any point within the mile-long construction zone." The system worked brilliantly: "there was something mesmerizing about the graceful, breathtakingly precise flight of the big buckets. Even to construction men accustomed to mechanical wonders, the site was riveting."[63]

My friend and I walked across the top of the dam to the Arizona side and gaped at the spillway tunnel, twenty meters in diameter, that disappeared into the depths of the canyon wall. In 1983, this tunnel and the opposite one on the Nevada side allowed a torrent of water from a sudden flood to bypass the dam, thus protecting it from possible breach. There was something mysteriously beautiful about the tunnel, as if it were the passage to another, unseen world. In fact, the whole dam was beautiful; it had a remarkable symmetry and aesthetic power that left me spellbound.

Back at the center of the parapet, I held on to a railing and leaned out as far as I could over the dam's face. Its vertical lines seemed to disappear to a vanishing point at the dam's base, far, far below. It gave me an exhilarating rush of vertigo. "In the shadow of Hoover Dam," Stevens writes at the end of his book, "one feels that the future is limitless, that no obstacle is insurmountable, that we have in our grasp the power to achieve anything if we can but summon the will."[64]

Yet I recalled something that had disturbed me during my interview with Kay Brothers. I asked her whether the officials and engineers in the Southern Nevada Water Authority had considered the implications of climate change for the region's water supply. She told me that they had not yet given the issue much thought.[65] I found this admission a bit surprising, because I knew that climate models suggest the region will see significantly lower rainfall and higher temperatures. As one group of experts concluded, only a few months after my conversation with Brothers, "the bottom line for the region is the expectation of serious long-term drought conditions."[66]

I pulled myself back from the precipice. My friend and I didn't speak as we went back to the car; there seemed too much to think about. Soon we were winding our way out of the canyon, and as we emerged on its lip we discovered the sun setting over the desert. The harsh mountains, valleys, and canyons around us—made vivid by golden light and stark shadows—brought to mind the idea of a fitness landscape, that imaginary topography (described in the last chapter) of mountains, cliffs, and gorges representing the struggle of complex-adaptive systems to survive.

An astounding quantity of ingenuity produced the Hoover Dam. And today people like Kay Brothers and her colleagues are delivering a continuous supply of further ingenuity to buffer the booming populations of the Southwest from the brutal physical reality surrounding them. All this ingenuity, though, assumes that environmental conditions will vary more or less as they have in the historical record. Floods won't be much bigger than the worst seen in the past, and droughts won't be much longer. This ingenuity has allowed Southwestern society to adapt itself exquisitely to a known fitness landscape. But humanity has started to deform its fitness landscapes in unprecedented and unforeseeable ways. As my friend and I drove into the lights of Vegas, I wasn't at all sure that the ingenuity I had seen that day—the pipelines, treatment plants, wells, conservation plans, even the Hoover Dam itself—would be adequate for the landscapes of the future.

PATNA

D. G. KULATUNGA was a lucky man. The senior security officer of the Central Bank of Sri Lanka was standing by the bank's front doors at 10:50 a.m. on January 31, 1996. He watched without alarm as a three-wheel motorized rickshaw and a large truck approached along the busy Colombo street that passes directly in front of the bank.

Suddenly, two men jumped out of the rickshaw and unleashed a hail of automatic gunfire at Mr. Kulatunga's guards. One of the attackers launched a rocket-propelled grenade at the bank's metal gates. The security officers returned fire, but two had already been killed. The truck then rammed the gates, trying to force its way through steel-reinforced concrete barriers that blocked the bank's entrance. It backed up and rammed the gates again but couldn't reach the building's front doors.

A moment later, as the two attackers sped away in their rickshaw, the truck erupted in a fireball. A four-hundred-kilogram bomb buried under sacks of rice in its back exploded, incinerating the truck and its driver.

The bank's two bottom floors collapsed. Mr. Kulatunga was hammered to the ground and knocked unconscious in a shower of debris. He awoke a short while later to find himself uninjured. But many others were not so fortunate. The Central Bank had erupted into flames, and the windows and façades of all the surrounding buildings had been shattered. Eighty-six people had been killed, and over thirteen hundred injured, many by splinters of flying glass. The heart of Colombo's financial district had been destroyed.[1]

It's a long way from Las Vegas to Colombo. But eight months after my visit to the desert city in Nevada, I found myself high in an office tower overlooking a hubbub of construction cranes and workers rebuilding the Central Bank. It was June 1998, almost two and a half years after the bombing. Looking out of the office's floor-to-ceiling windows, I could see the haze and cumulus clouds gathering over the ocean beyond Colombo's port. The monsoon rains that afternoon were going to be heavy.

I was on my way to find the little girl in Patna, whose photograph had inspired me in my quest to solve the ingenuity puzzle. It was a quixotic, even bizarre thing to be doing, I knew—to travel to the other side of the planet to find a single, unidentified child. I had no idea whether I'd succeed, or even whether it would be meaningful if I did. And in those moments when I was completely frank with myself, I admitted that I really had no idea *why* I wanted to find her. I was simply drawn to something about her face and her angry, enigmatic expression. People's faces, I was slowly realizing, are critical connection points among us in our increasingly fluid, atomized, and dehumanized world. Faces—as we look for them, come to know them, and remember them—can help us translate crowds into community, and selfishness and egocentrism into empathy and generosity.

I had decided not to go to India directly, though. Instead, I stopped briefly in Colombo to pursue further the answer to a key question: What happens to the supply of social ingenuity when dangerous subgroups gain power relative to the state? The attack on the Central Bank had been the work of the Liberation Tigers of Tamil Eelam—the LTTE or Tigers for short. One of the world's most aggressive and sophisticated secessionist movements, the LTTE aims to carve a Tamil homeland out of the north and east of the island of Sri Lanka, and it has been waging a brutal war towards this end for over fifteen years. The group was, I suspected, representative of a new kind of high-tech armed violence that is beginning to afflict many poor countries and that may already be spilling over into rich countries too.

An old friend of mine had arranged for me to interview Mr. Amarananda Jayawardena, the governor of the Central Bank of Sri Lanka. His office was modern, large, and spare, with an arc of huge windows behind his desk, a couple of chairs and a table for visitors, and a model of the new bank building against one wall. When we arrived, the governor, a short man of about sixty with a round face and a precise but gentle manner, welcomed us and showed us to the chairs. He said he'd been up since 5 a.m. dealing with the latest reverberations of the Asian currency crisis. After we were comfortable, he gave us his account of the bombing and its impact on the Sri Lankan economy.

He had been in his office at the back of the building when the bomb exploded. He wasn't hurt, so he spent the next several hours helping to remove the dead and wounded from the front and lower floors of the building. Clearly, the event had shaken him deeply, yet he remained optimistic about the future, and he drew from the attack some interesting lessons. All over the world, he pointed out, central banks were taking precautions against terrorist attack—not just against bombs, but also against attacks by computer hackers. Government officials and bankers had come to recognize that terrorists were keen to strike against symbols of economic authority.

I was reminded of the recent spate of bombings of financial centers, with targets including the City of London in 1992 and 1993, the Bombay stock exchange and the New York World Trade Center in 1993, as well as Sri Lanka's Central Bank in 1996. Canary Wharf had also been attacked in 1996; the IRA detonated a bomb in a parking lot near the writhing bridge I crossed on my evening walk through the Isle of Dogs. Such attacks are not, I knew, an entirely new phenomenon. In September 1920, a huge bomb ripped through Wall Street, killing forty people and injuring some three hundred others. Although at the time the attack was widely attributed to "Reds," the case was never officially solved.[2]

If the LTTE had hoped to wreck Sri Lanka's economy, however, they must have been sorely disappointed. The day after the bombing, the governor contacted the heads of the country's commercial banks and asked them to take over all international financial transactions normally handled by the Central Bank, especially foreign exchange transactions and payments on Sri Lanka's foreign debt. He also temporarily suspended treasury bill auctions. The biggest problem he faced, it turned out, was replacing records of old banking transactions. The records could be read only by obsolete technology that was no longer available in the country, so the governor had a machine flown especially from Singapore for the purpose. In general, though, the disruptions were surprisingly minor. The Colombo stock exchange registered barely a tremor, and as the commercial banks stepped in to help, the country's financial network showed exactly the kind of resilience that John Bongaarts had talked about during our dinner in London.

But the governor nevertheless cautioned against complacency. He emphasized the importance of redundancy in key components of the financial and communication systems, and he said that there had to be good integration between the financial system's internal security organizations and those of the police, army, and government bureaucracy. "A terrorist only has to be successful once," he summed up, "but we have to be alert all the time."

This was not the first time I'd visited Sri Lanka. In early 1983, I traveled with a friend and my father all over the country. It was an island paradise for tourists then, and we delighted in the country's beautiful beaches and splendid hospitality. We didn't have the faintest inkling that our paradise was about to erupt in violence, but only a few months after we left, right-wing elements of Sri Lanka's Sinhalese majority launched widespread, orchestrated attacks against the Tamil minority. It was one of the most horrific stages in the progressive dismantling of Sri Lanka's democratic institutions and rule of law.3 Over the next decade, the country spiraled downwards into an increasingly vicious civil war that involved countless massacres of innocent civilians, the almost complete destruction of the northern city of Jaffna, the arrival and defeat at the hands of the LTTE of a large Indian expeditionary force, and the assassination of many senior government officials, including the country's president. The war has left over sixty thousand people dead, displaced a million, and cost the economy annually more than a fifth of its GDP.4

When I arrived in Colombo fifteen years after my first visit, the city looked starkly different. It was an armed camp. Military checkpoints and machine-gun emplacements dotted the main roads into town. Soldiers peeked out from behind piles of sandbags, rifles at the ready, while others in camouflage flagged down rickshaws and vans to check for bombs. Armored vehicles guarded strategic intersections, and tight clusters of soldiers marched through downtown streets. Many of the city's major buildings—its military headquarters, police stations, five-star hotels, and president's mansion—were secured behind heavy four-meter-high steel barricades and rows of sand-filled oil drums that forced oncoming vehicles to weave back and forth. Watchtowers surveyed the roads in and out of the central business district, and almost all the windows of the Bank of Ceylon building—one of the skyscrapers dominating the business district—were still boarded up in the aftermath of a second LTTE bombing in 1997.

Clearly, the LTTE has grievously wounded Sri Lankan society. It has become a truly ferocious opponent of the Sinhalese-dominated status quo. Although the Tamil community has some legitimate grievances, nothing can justify, to my mind, the LTTE's horrific brutality and fanaticism. And the organization seems to be a particularly dramatic example of how new technologies can sharply boost the power of destructive subgroups relative to the state.

The LTTE uses the Internet and the Web to support a worldwide, state-of-the-art propaganda campaign and to organize the extraction of tens of millions of dollars of funding from the Tamil diaspora (one of its main sources of funds is the Tamil community in Toronto). And, technologically, the LTTE has stayed one step ahead of the Sri Lankan military. Rohan Gunaratna, an expert on the organization's tactics, notes that it was the first to use rocket-propelled grenade launchers and night vision glasses, and it pioneered the battlefield use of off-the-shelf civilian technologies—for example, in learning how to accurately target projectiles with global positioning satellite signals. The organization's leaders also use satellite telephones to link up with their combatants in the field, with their overseas cadres, and with a fleet of deep-sea freighters that maintain a flow of explosives, arms, and ammunition. The plastic explosives that destroyed the Central Bank had been purchased in 1994 from a chemical plant in the Ukraine—using funds from the Canadian Tamil community—and transported to Sri Lanka aboard an LTTE-owned and operated ship.[5]

Employing a network of front and cover organizations around the world that are coordinated out of an International Secretariat in London, the LTTE scours the world's arms bazaars for assault rifles, grenade launchers, antitank weapons, and Russian shoulder-launched surface-to-air missiles (which have been used to destroy both civilian and military aircraft in Sri Lanka). The operation has an increasingly transnational character that the Sri Lankan government is ill-equipped to counter. "How does a domestic government," Gunaratna asks, "stop an insurgent group from transferring funds from a bank in Singapore to Dresden to buy explosives or from Westpack in Australia to a Swiss account to pay for an arms consignment? Modern insurgent groups are beginning to operate like multinational firms or like intelligence agencies with a global reach."[6]

In my interviews with a wide range of intellectuals and opinion-makers in Colombo, both Sinhalese and Tamil, I found deep despair about the prospects for ending the war. While a few people I interviewed glimpsed the possibility of a peace breakthrough or believed that the increasingly obvious stalemate on the battlefield would finally prompt serious negotiations, few expressed any optimism about the country's future. Instead, they described how this seemingly endless war had profoundly polarized and embittered Sri Lankan society, severely reduced opportunities for democratic dialogue, and brought the process of real institutional and political reform—that is, the process of supplying social ingenuity—to a halt. Many despaired in particular because of what they saw as the sheer fanaticism of the LTTE—a fanaticism symbolized by the group's reliance on child soldiers and suicide bombers. As one former military officer asked me in wonder: "What is it that will lead a fifteen- or sixteen-year-old to strap high explosives around his or her waist and detonate them?"

The more people I spoke to, and the more I learned about the LTTE, the more concerned I became that this organization was a portent of things to come. Violent insurgencies and terrorist groups are becoming more high-tech, transnational, and powerful relative to the states they oppose. Gunaratna writes, "Easy acquisition of weapons with greater firepower, sophistication, and target accuracy, coupled with fanaticism of insurgents fueled by the resurgence of ethnic and religious passions can create havoc."[7] Moreover, "these transnational networks are increasingly gathering momentum and generating their own dynamic. By themselves, government bureaucracies, unlike transnational terrorist networks, are not administratively or operationally flexible [enough] to engage [these] new threats."[8]

So what, some in the rich countries of the Western world might respond: Sri Lanka is on the opposite side of the planet, and events there—or in other poor and distant countries—have little relevance to our daily lives. Unfortunately, though, cases like Sri Lanka's are not few and isolated: around the world we see a proliferation of subnational violence debilitating poor countries. Cheaper, more portable, and more lethal weapons and explosives, combined with better communication technologies and more easily available information on where to find and how to use weapons, widen the agency horizon—that is, the radius of potential destruction in time and space—of violent subgroups. Put crudely, individuals or small groups can kill more people faster, at greater range, and with greater coordination than ever before.[9] Michael Klare of Hampshire College, one of the world's authorities on the traffic in light weapons, writes: "Equipped with AK-47s alone, a small band of teen-aged combatants can enter a village and kill or wound hundreds of people in a matter of minutes."[10] In a long list of countries—including Somalia, Sudan, Algeria, Senegal, Nigeria, Congo, Rwanda, Burundi, Angola, Sierra Leone, Liberia, Russia, Bosnia, Georgia, Tajikistan, Yemen, Afghanistan, Pakistan, Philippines, Haiti, and Colombia—these technologies have increased the ability of ethnic groups, political factions, gangs, bandits, and clans to organize themselves and inflict heavy damage on each other and the state. All these societies exhibit a lethal combination of weak government, deep social cleavages, and economic hardship. All of them are also awash in small arms, from rocket-propelled grenade launchers, machine guns, and light mortars to land mines and, especially, cheap assault rifles such as the famed AK-47.

During the Cold War, hundreds of millions of these light weapons were manufactured and stockpiled by the East and West blocs. Since then, gunrunners and criminal syndicates have moved huge quantities of these weapons, along with untold numbers of cheap copies, into conflict zones in the developing world. Previously minor and manageable conflicts have, as a result, become savage, as if acid had been poured into open wounds. The result is a vicious circle: weak and illegitimate governments in these poor countries stimulate conflict, attracting an influx of light arms; the light arms then make the conflicts more extensive, bitter, and protracted, which weakens the central governments even more. As Michael Klare notes: "When societies are deeply divided along ethnic, religious, or sectarian lines and the existing government is unwilling or unable to protect minorities and maintain domestic order, the introduction and use of even small quantities of small arms and light weapons can have profoundly destabilizing effects."[11] In such situations, creating the public goods that are key to prosperity and social well-being—such as efficient markets, effective police and judicial systems, and responsive financial agencies—is next to impossible. It is too easy for ruthless opponents of positive reform to smash any progress to smithereens.

Rich countries don't benefit if significant chunks of the world become more violent and decrepit. Zones of anarchy are not only dead weights on the world's economy, they can also become sites of major humanitarian crises that demand external intervention (as in Somalia, Rwanda, and the Balkans), generators of waves of outward migration, and havens for transnational terrorist and criminal networks that target rich countries. Afghanistan, the North West Frontier Province of Pakistan, and perhaps Sudan have, for example, been staging grounds for attacks against American targets by groups financed by the exiled Saudi multimillionaire Osama bin Laden.

The rising power of individuals and subgroups to communicate, coordinate their actions, and wreak havoc means that rich countries will see more homegrown terrorism too. The Internet makes it easier and cheaper for hate groups and anti-government militias in rich countries to organize, plan seditious activities, and trade information on everything from recruiting tactics to weapons. Practically anything an extremist wants to know about kidnaping, making bombs, and assassination is now available online.[12] Often the materials needed for large-scale violence are readily at hand, as were the fertilizer and diesel fuel used in the Oklahoma City bombing. But the Internet disseminates an additional essential ingredient: the sets of instructions—the technical ingenuity—needed to put these materials together in new, destructive combinations. (One of my favorite, somewhat facetious, examples of how the right set of instructions can convert everyday materials into potentially destructive devices is the "potato cannon." With a barrel and combustion chamber fashioned from common plastic pipe, and with propane as an explosive propellant, a well-made cannon can hurl a homely spud hundreds of meters. A quick search of the Web reveals dozens of sites giving instructions on how to make this device.)

The Internet also provides access to lots of potential extremist friends. "With the phenomenal growth of the Internet," says Don Black, a white supremacist who operates the Stormfront computer bulletin board out of West Palm Beach, Florida, "tens of millions of people have access to our message if they wish. The access is anonymous, and there is unlimited ability to communicate with others of a like mind."[13] Surprisingly, even during the strong economic growth of the late 1990s, hate sites on the Web proliferated and began aiming their recruiting messages less at their traditional audiences of urban skinheads and rural, blue-collar men and more at college-bound, middle-class youth.[14] The Internet, it seems, has not only increased the scope for grassroots democracy, but also the scope for grassroots illiberalism.

These concerns are hardly new: popular media have seen ongoing commentary about the harmful effects of the Internet and the World Wide Web. Columnists and opinion leaders fret about the emergence of a netherworld of computer communication among kooks and subversives. Yet much of this concern has remained unfocused and imprecise, allowing more optimistic commentators to largely dismiss the Internet's dangers.

Not long ago, though, at the Annual Meeting of the World Economic Forum in Davos, Switzerland, I learned the dangers are real. This meeting is an extravaganza of high-powered hobnobbing, an occasion for businessmen and political leaders to discuss emerging global trends that might affect corporations and entrepreneurs. I had been invited to talk about environmental problems in poor countries. Arriving at my hotel room overlooking Davos's gorgeous alpine valley, I found on the desk a special issue of *Time* magazine that dealt with the implications of the computer revolution for global society and business. In an article titled "Dreams and Nightmares of the Digital Age," the science-fiction novelist Neal Stephenson described several possible collective futures—some bright, some dark—given today's rapidly evolving information technologies. Many popular fears about the Internet are overblown, he wrote, such as the fear that terrorists can easily find information about weapons of mass destruction on the World Wide Web. His own recent efforts "to find a nerve-gas recipe on the Internet were fruitless," because, he said, of the poor quality of much of the Web's information.[15]

He can't be right, I thought: I was sure the Web contained abundant information on chemical and biological weapons; Stephenson simply hadn't pursued the issue vigorously enough. Later in the day, I decided to check. I visited the Forum's conference center and located a bank of advanced computers hooked to the Internet. In less than two hours of browsing, I had found detailed information on anthrax toxin and mustard gas. I had also found a Cal Poly on-line seminar for an advanced course in chemical warfare, which included an outline of the steps needed to make botulinum toxin in large quantities.

Yet perhaps Stephenson is right, and popular fears are overblown. The incidence of major terrorist attacks has generally declined in the last decade (although, until 1999, the total number of deaths each year had increased).[16] And making and using chemical and biological weapons is much more difficult than commentaries in the media or even enthusiastic Web sites suggest.[17] For five years, Japan's Aum Shinrikyo cult worked to develop germ weapons without success, eventually turning to sarin nerve gas for its 1995 attack in the Tokyo subway system. Even then, the gas produced only twelve deaths, not the tens of thousands the cult wanted.[18]

Nevertheless, policy-makers in the United States and other Western countries now widely recognize that the risk of attack with nonconventional weapons—such as nerve gases and biological agents—is rising.[19] As each year passes, the knowledge, skills, and sophisticated laboratory equipment needed to succeed become more widespread. Richard Falkenrath, Robert Newman, and Bradley Thayer, three American experts, argue that the ability of groups and organizations other than states "to master the challenges associated with NBC [nuclear-biological-chemical] attack is rising in all modern societies. This gradual increase in potential NBC capabilities is in part a byproduct of economic, educational, and technological progress. Furthermore, in most modern societies, particularly those that have entered the information age, the ability of the state to monitor and counter illegal or threatening activities is being outpaced by the increasing efficiency, complexity, technological sophistication, and geographic span of the activities, legal or illegal, of non-state actors."[20]

Specialists also see unsettling evidence that a new kind of terrorist has emerged. Before the mid-1990s, most terrorist groups pursued clear political goals and were sponsored, even if only indirectly, by existing states. Now free-floating, independently funded terrorist networks are appearing, networks that express only vague political goals—often little more than a deep hatred of current institutions and authorities. For these groups, violence and destruction are not means to change the world but ends in themselves. They tend to have "amorphous religious and millenarian aims," says Bruce Hoffman, an American authority on the new terrorism, and they represent "vehemently anti-government forms of populism, reflecting far-fetched conspiracy notions."[21] "New terrorism," concurs *The Economist*, "is often just a cacophonous cry of protest against the West in general, and American government in particular—fueled by impotent rage over the Great Satan's cultural and geopolitical supremacy. Its perpetrators may be religious fanatics, or simply diehard opponents of the federal government, who might come from inside, as well as outside, American territory. They see no reason to show restraint; they are simply intent on inflicting the maximum amount of pain on the enemy."[22] Such groups are magnets for fanatical and violent individuals who have been alienated by our societies' rapid social and economic changes.

"In short," write Falkenrath, Newman, and Thayer, "the nature of terrorism is changing in a way that suggests there will be an expanding range of groups that are both capable of using weapons of mass destruction and interested in inflicting human casualties at levels well beyond the terrorist norms of the previous decades."[23] To make matters worse, these two trends are unfolding at the very time that the world's social, technological, and economic systems are evolving from hierarchies to networks and are becoming, in the process, broader in scope, faster-paced, and often more nonlinear and tightly coupled. In these interconnected networks, damage to a single node—that is, to a critical connection point in the system—can produce unexpected results. Sometimes the damage remains isolated, and the network exhibits great resilience, as was the case with the Sri Lankan financial system after the Central Bank bombing; other times the damage sparks cascading failures, as we have sometimes seen in the U.S. electrical, telephone, and air-traffic systems.

Much depends upon the system's level of redundancy—in other words, on the degree to which the damaged node's functions can be offloaded to undamaged nodes. As terrorists come to recognize the importance of redundancy, they will be better able to disable complex systems. The theorist of politics and technology Langdon Winner suggests that a first rule of modern terrorism might be "Find the critical but nonredundant parts of the system and sabotage . . . them according to your purposes." He concludes that "the science of complexity awaits a Machiavelli or Clausewitz to make the full range of possibilities clear."[24]

The rising complexity and interdependence of our world's systems, if exploited effectively, thus magnify even further the disruptive power of malign individuals and subgroups. Computer viruses are probably the best everyday evidence of this magnification effect: a single nerdy kid hacking away at his computer in the basement of a college dorm can create a virus or worm that produces chaos in interlinked communications and data systems far and wide. But there's much more to worry about than just the proliferation of computer viruses. A special investigative commission set up by President Clinton in 1997 reported that "growing complexity and interdependence, especially in the energy and communications infrastructures, create an increased possibility that a rather minor and routine disturbance can cascade into a regional outage. . . . We are convinced that our vulnerabilities are increasing steadily, that the means to exploit those weaknesses are readily available and that the costs [to an attacker of launching an attack] continue to drop."[25] The Internet, for instance, has a host of vulnerabilities; perhaps the most significant is the system of computers—called "routers" and "root servers"—that directs traffic around the Net. Routers depend on each other's accuracy as they pass packets of information along, and a software error in one router, or its malicious reprogramming by a hacker, can propagate multiple errors throughout the Net.[26]

Rising complexity also magnifies the ability of individuals and subgroups to extract illicit gains from the systems around us. National and international regulators, for example, can't possibly anticipate all the weaknesses and loopholes that criminals might exploit in the world's rapidly evolving financial systems—systems now rife with unknown unknowns. Gene Rochlin, the professor of energy and resources at UC

Berkeley, suggests that the character of today's international financial markets made it possible for Nicholas Leeson, the rogue Singapore trader for Barings Bank, to rack up $1 billion in debts, drive his firm into bankruptcy, and rattle investors around the world. "He could not have run up such huge losses," Rochlin argues, "without the access and range given him by the new [trading] techniques, or even attempted do so before the creation of global markets in futures and derivative financial instruments." As for the future, Rochlin goes on, "it is difficult at this point even to imagine what some of the possible modes of fraud and abuse might be. What we can learn from the history of human affairs in general, and markets in particular, is that this is one of those areas where human creativity exerts itself to the utmost."[27]

As I wrapped up my visit to Sri Lanka, I decided that these varied issues all revolved around a central principle: everything pointed to the rising power of malign individuals and groups, and the increasing vulnerability of the institutions that supply the public goods—the social ingenuity—that we need to be prosperous and happy.

This uncomfortable conclusion was reinforced by something that occurred during my last few hours in Colombo. The day's monsoon rains had receded into a muggy dusk, and my friend took me to a small reception and dinner put on for a tight-knit group of Sri Lanka's Anglo-educated elite. Several decades before, they had all attended one of the country's premier private schools. Today, they were all near or past retirement age, but they still represented a cross-section of Sri Lanka's top government, military, educational, and religious institutions.

As the evening wound down, I was approached by a portly gentleman with a somber expression on his face. We had spoken earlier, and I had explained the reasons for my visit to Sri Lanka. For his part, he had told me about his experiences negotiating with the leadership of the LTTE on behalf of the Sri Lankan government. Now he drew me to one side. "The head of the Indian nuclear weapons program is a Tamil," he began, alluding to the fact that the Indians had exploded a series of nuclear devices only a few weeks before, shocking the world. "I am almost certain," he went on, "that this Indian scientist has already been contacted by the LTTE." He leaned closer. "How much would it cost them to buy a nuclear weapon?"

I was shocked by the question—not so much by the idea that Sri Lankan and Indian Tamils might cooperate in such a way, but by the suggestion that the LTTE might have an interest in nuclear bombs. "What would the LTTE gain if they reduced Colombo to rubble?" I responded. "They need someone to negotiate with!"

"They would only do it out of desperation. It might be a final act of terror if the LTTE were on the ropes and saw no other options. But remember, this outfit raises upwards of $30 million a year from its diaspora. They have the cash if there are willing sellers."

Later in the evening, on the long drive to Colombo's international airport, past the checkpoints and the machine-gun emplacements, I reluctantly admitted to myself that the idea wasn't so far-fetched after all. Weapons of mass destruction are getting easier to make or buy. It's only a matter of time before terrorists or fanatical insurgencies like the LTTE start using them.

———————

Heat. Everywhere there was heat. It surrounded and penetrated me. It defined the world around me. Sweat gushed out of my body, running in rivulets down my chest and the small of my back, gluing my shirt to my skin. Everything was tangibly hot: tables, chairs, and pens were weirdly warm to the touch, because everything outside my body was hotter than my body. The water in my bottle felt like soup on my tongue. Any movement of the air—a draft, a slight breeze—was a relief; while any movement of my body or mind was an effort. Physical action, thought, even consciousness itself seemed to take place in slow motion, weighed down and dulled by the relentless, inescapable heat.

I had finally arrived in Patna. Unfortunately, it was early June, and my visit had coincided with one of the worst heat waves in India's history. Every day, the temperature soared above 45 degrees Celsius, sometimes hitting 50 degrees, while hundreds of people across the country died of heat stroke, dehydration, and heart failure. (Persistent temperatures in that range are extremely rare in populated areas of the West: a few weeks later, authorities in Dallas, Texas, declared a state of emergency after ten days of temperatures reaching only 38 degrees Celsius.[28]) In the northwestern state of Rajasthan, fights broke out over water from standpipes. Rumors of impending natural calamities, devastating fires, and World War III swept through Lucknow, the capital of India's most populous state, Uttar Pradesh.[29] In Delhi, the temperature climbed to a fifty-four-year high just as the city was afflicted with rotating water and power outages.

Residents' tempers flared, from the suburban tracts of apartment buildings that baked in the sun without water pumps or air-conditioning, to the slums and squatter settlements along the Yamuna river that stewed in their own fetid wastes. In a grand gesture, Delhi's water officials promised that no one would have to pay their water bills if they received less than thirty hours of water supply a month.

The wealthy avoided going outside, staying near their air conditioners and fans, often powered by private generators. The poor lay on the sides of the streets in any scrap of shade they could find cast by a tree or building. Many didn't have shoes to protect their feet from the blistering pavement, yet the asphalt was melting in the sun and the straight, painted lines of crosswalks and lanes were turning wavy. Through the hot middle hours of the day, these people barely moved; they slept, meditated, and waited vacantly for relief—for the evening and especially for the monsoon.

Amidst this natural trauma, amidst the power failures and water shortages, the country's political elites were preoccupied with other matters. India and Pakistan had just tested nuclear bombs, and the pages of India's leading newspapers were filled with threats, charges, and jingoistic analysis. The situation was bizarre; the country's political life and its leaders' decisions seemed utterly detached from the reality of people's lives. India could make atomic bombs, but it couldn't provide its citizens, even those in its capital city, with adequate water or electricity. One commentator exclaimed in *The Times of India*: "Already, New Delhi spends twice as much on the military as it does on health, education, and social welfare. The bomb will mean more suffering for our poor."[30]

By the time I had checked into my hotel, it was already late afternoon. To reacquaint myself with Patna, I decided to walk to the railway station, several kilometers away. But the excursion was more of an ordeal than I expected: I had visited India many times before and had traveled all over the country, but this time I found Patna's combination of heat, filth, noise, and infrastructure failure overpowering.

My hotel had intermittent air-conditioning, so walking out the front door was like being enveloped in a suffocating, muggy blanket. As usual in India, the street outside was filled with every imaginable conveyance: rickshaws, bicycles, scooters, bullock carts, cars, buses, and trucks. All the motorized traffic belched clouds of black, oily exhaust. It was a remorseless cacophony of horns, bells, radios, wailing loudspeakers, barking engines, and grinding gears.

I picked my way across a roundabout of streaming traffic and turned down the major road towards the station. Most of the city's streets have no sidewalks, just dirt margins packed with tiny, decrepit stalls selling fruits, vegetables, and dry goods. In some spots the stalls gave way to open spaces where whole families lived—mothers, fathers, children, and withered grandparents—their entire worldly possessions of a few pots and bits of clothing compressed onto a couple of square meters of dirt. Drainage was nonexistent; the few ditches and gutters along the road were inky black with human and animal excrement, garbage, and road debris. Most of the road's manhole covers had disappeared, and the openings had become waste pits. I walked past abandoned excavation sites and remnants of the city's old canals, all filled with putrid water. Along their edges scampered scrawny, shoeless kids, clothed in rags and covered in dust and sores. They crawled in and out of never-emptied dumpsters scattered along the road, some flipped on their sides and spilling their rotting contents. Families of pigs rooted through these heaps of refuse, men urinated on buildings and walls along the road, and emaciated wild dogs crisscrossed through the chaos.

I stopped for a moment on a corner and watched a mother, sitting in the dust barely a meter away from roaring vehicles, pick lice out of her daughter's matted hair. A man, dressed in the remnants of a burlap sack and so thin that I could see bones pushing through his skin, shuffled past her in disintegrating plastic thongs. Behind the mother, lining the street in both directions, were hundreds of bicycle rickshaws, battered but decked out in bright colors and chrome, their drivers sprawled listlessly on the rickshaw seats. Other drivers squatted on their haunches in small clusters, gossiping. Even the young ones seemed thin and tired. They regarded me passively—it was the first time in India that I hadn't been badgered by rickshaw drivers. Normally they would have hailed me or clustered around me, pulling me in different directions to get my business. Now, it was simply too hot to bother.

A gust of hot wind threw dust into the air and into my eyes. Street dwellers covered their heads and faces with filthy shawls to protect themselves from the grit. When the wind died down, the smell of rotting garbage and baked urine returned, strong and penetrating. I looked up and away from the street, which till then had attracted all my attention, to study the nearby buildings. Without exception they were dilapidated and grimy, many only half constructed, with forests of reinforcement bars poking out of their walls and roofs. Many façades were missing, including some of buildings five or more stories high, as if their front walls had simply collapsed. Virtually none of the buildings had been maintained or newly painted. Signs and billboards were broken, covered with muck, and often illegible. The parking lots of important businesses, like banks and the state-owned Indian Airlines, were strewn with rocks and rubble. Many of these businesses had large, decrepit generators operating outside their front doors, like beasts from the nether-world, gushing smoke as their muffler-less reports boomed down the street.

I wandered into the Indian Airlines office. It was gloomy and bleak, with a scattering of battered desks and plastic chairs. A few ticket clerks plunked away on ancient computers. The front door didn't shut properly, so the generator's fumes blew into the room, and I had to shout over its noise to make myself heard. A wave of bitterness about India swept over me—it was a feeling I had experienced many times before, but Patna, at this particular moment, seemed to distill its essence. From the point of view of a rich, pampered Westerner, the people of Patna seemed to have capitulated to ugliness, wretchedness, and inhumanity towards each other. They didn't do even the small things, like fix that front door, that would significantly improve their lives. The place was a technological, social, and *moral* calamity. It was a disgrace.

If Las Vegas is one vision of the future of urbanized humanity, I felt, Patna is another. Both are extreme and disturbing visions, but both highlight distinct and very real aspects of humanity's potential. Las Vegas is a vision of the future as a hedonistic, postmodernist fantasy sustained by the heroic application of ingenuity—a lobotomized world of distraction and diversion. Patna, on the other hand, is a vision of despair, cruelty, and vulnerability, where even rudimentary solutions to the technological and social challenges of everyday life are not provided. It is a place of the most grotesque differences in wealth between the rich and the poor where, paradoxically, even the richest aren't able to enjoy things that members of the middle class in Western societies take for granted. True, they can hire lots of servants, because labor is cheap. But they can't drink the water running from their taps, if their taps run at all. They can't rely on a steady supply of electricity. They can't escape the dust, filth, and pollution that constantly infiltrate their houses, making everything dirty and sometimes making them sick. And they live with a constant, subliminal sense of insecurity, because they are surrounded on all sides by the dispossessed.

Most important, whereas in Vegas natural and social realities are usually kept at bay, in Patna they penetrate into the deepest recesses of people's lives. Even for the richest residents, the heat, bad water, disgusting air, noise, and appalling disparities of the place cannot be avoided. And for the poorest, these things intimately define their lives and who they are.

Yet I couldn't say that there wasn't ingenuity in this place. Despite the dilapidation and squalor, there was ingenuity all around me—in people's everyday, creative adaptation to their horrific circumstances and in their everyday strategies for survival. The people on that street were doing the best they could, given the terribly limited materials and opportunities available to them. But they were supplying, at most, only fragmented ingenuity to solve their diverse, local, and immediate problems of existence on the fringe of the road. There wasn't much evidence that ingenuity was being adequately supplied to meet Patna's larger, collective needs, like effective government, well-functioning markets, high-quality public education, and good roads, sewers, and water pipelines. For whatever reason, these people had to go without these vital public goods, and so were left with no choice but to invent their own local strategies for survival.

In my luggage, I had three small copies of the little girl's photograph. The morning after I arrived in Patna, I began my search for her. I knew that I needed help. I remembered roughly where I had taken the original shot, but I couldn't simply go there myself and wave the photo around. At a minimum, I needed someone who spoke English and Bihari. I also needed the help of someone intimately familiar with the complex social customs of Indian society. Otherwise I could easily offend the girl's family and her community.

I started making inquiries to find the help I needed. But locating the girl wasn't the only thing I hoped to do in Patna: I also planned to conclude my research on the links between population growth, land scarcity, and institutional failure.

Bihar is a particularly interesting case for this research. Situated several hundred kilometers northwest of Calcutta, the state has a roughly rectangular shape that is longer north to south than east to west. Its northernmost edge abuts Nepal, while farther south the state straddles the Ganges. The Ganges is, in fact, Bihar's main geographic feature, creating a broad, fertile plain and cleaving the northern third of the state from its southern two-thirds. Patna, the capital, is situated on the river's southern shore, and the plain of the Ganges continues southward until the land rises up into the mountainous Ranchi Plateau.

With around 100 million people crammed into an area about the size of Washington State in the U.S., Bihar is the second-most-populous state in India. Eighty-seven percent of these people live in rural areas, and most farm the fertile plains north and south of the Ganges. Population densities on this agricultural land have long been among the highest in India. Because there is no new agricultural land available in the state, and Bihar's population has tripled in recent decades, population density on the existing cropland has soared. With each successive generation, growing families and communities have divided and redivided their landholdings into smaller and smaller parcels. Now the fields of Bihar's Gangetic plains resemble a patchwork quilt of tiny plots of cropland, many far too small to support a family.

This land has long been a divisive economic and political issue in Bihar. At the time of India's independence in 1947, the state's future looked exceptionally bright. It had abundant resources—rich agricultural land along the Ganges and valuable mineral deposits in the southern mountains—and it also had one of the new country's most competent civil administrations. Unfortunately, though, Bihar's society remained essentially feudal in structure: its principal economic and social relationships ran vertically between the rich and the poor. Most of Bihar's land was owned or controlled by powerful landowning castes, and groups with little or no land were almost entirely dependent on these landowners for their livelihood.

The state's political leaders realized that agriculture was key to Bihar's post-independence economic growth. To boost agriculture, and shatter the society's feudal structure, they had to break up the large landholdings and distribute them among the landless or almost landless poor. But a series of reforms in the 1940s, 1950s, and 1960s largely failed, because they were circumvented or subverted by powerful castes. Although the reforms did reduce the landholdings of the uppermost castes, the main beneficiaries were not the poorest people but rather members of middle castes, who became Bihar's new landed elite. Today, Bihar still has one of the most skewed land distributions in India. Around half of the state's cropland is locked up in about a million medium-size and large farms ("large" in Bihar terms meaning over two hectares in size), while the remaining land is divided into twelve million small farms. Over nine million of these small farms are classified as "marginal," which means they are tiny—under one hectare in size.[31]

Bihar's population exploded from the 1950s onwards, and the ranks of these marginal farmers swelled. Many were forced to abandon farming entirely when their plots became too tiny to feed their families. They then joined the state's ballooning population of landless agricultural laborers. The supply of this labor always exceeded demand. Even though farm productivity generally increased as cultivators introduced green-revolution technologies, wages for landless laborers stayed abysmally low. As the years passed, conflicts became increasingly severe between marginal farmers and landless laborers on one side, and middle- and upper-caste farmers, who still had relatively abundant land, on the other.

Beginning in the early 1970s, these conflicts turned truly vicious. Bands of Maoist insurgents called "Naxalites" gave voice to rural, lower-caste resentment by launching regular, brutal attacks against members of the landowning castes. In response, landowners organized private armies to protect themselves and to wreak vengeance on landless and marginalized communities. This cycle of attack, revenge, and counterattack has continued, with only occasional breaks, up to the present day. Residents of some of Bihar's districts west and south of Patna have now witnessed several decades of horrific violence. Whole villages have been razed; groups of women have been gang-raped; and dozens of people at a time have been shot, burnt alive, or had their throats cut.[32]

The cycle of violence has polarized Bihar's society and eviscerated its institutions. Government officials, judges, and especially the police—instead of recognizing and trying to defuse the legitimate anger of the landless and nearly landless—have usually sided with the powerful castes. Bihar's government and state institutions have, over time, become little more than extensions of the interests of landowners, the wealthy, and the politically powerful. These groups generally have no concern for the broader well-being of Bihar's society, and their utterly rapacious behavior has progressively weakened the state's institutions, from its court system and universities to its financial and agricultural bureaucracies. The practical results are visible everywhere: mafia-style gangs or "contractors" now control much of Bihar's economy and countryside; bribery and corruption are rampant; and con artists loot the state treasury. Once again, there's lots of ingenuity around, but it's ingenuity in the service of plunder for the benefit of narrow castes and cliques. So roads fall apart, irrigation and flood-control systems decay and are not repaired (because repair funds disappear through fraud), hospitals lack even the most basic supplies, and the electricity system operates at 15 percent of its capacity.[33]

While many other regions of India, especially its southern states, experienced a surge of economic growth in the 1990s, Bihar fell further and further behind. Growth was flat, more than half of the state's population remained illiterate, and malnutrition stunted the development of almost two-thirds of the state's children aged four or younger. The sociologist Bindeshwar Pathak, a native of Bihar, writes: "The state which once upon a time had the reputation of being the best administered state of the country is now synonymous with all that is worst in the country. . . . The laws seem to have been manipulated in such a way as to make them stand on their heads. The state is now a land of private armies armed to the teeth, always on the prowl looking out for the next target. The epicenter of senseless atrocities, Bihar has also turned out to be the breeding ground of killers in the red garb of revolutionaries. Fear and hatred stalk the countryside."[34]

After a few days in Patna, I visited one of the areas worst affected by this violence, the district of Bhojpur, to the west of the city along the Ganges.[35] I hired a car (no mean feat, because most drivers didn't want to leave Patna during the heat wave) and had myself driven into the countryside. Westerners traveling in poor countries tend not to leave cities, because rural travel can be uncomfortable, even dangerous, while cities usually have some semblance of Western amenities. Yet in most Asian and African countries the bulk of the population still lives in rural areas—in India, the figure is around 70 percent, or about 700 million people—so if you don't visit the countryside, you're going to miss much of what is happening in those countries.

The road out of Patna, supposedly a major east–west artery, was in hideous condition, a narrow, battered strip of tarmac, steaming in the day's rising heat and jammed with transport trucks, buses, cars, and motor rickshaws all blaring their horns. Jeeps carrying twenty or more people, some sitting on top, others hanging off their sides and back, weaved down the road, heeling over at sickening angles. Not far outside the city, the pavement narrowed to a single lane to cross a bridge over an abandoned canal, causing a kilometer-long backup of traffic on each side. Our car stalled at the entrance to the bridge, a victim of the heat. But quick action by the driver got us going again, and soon we were deep in rural Bihar.

It was the dry season, so the fields were parched and lifeless. An endless tapestry of rice paddies, their low dikes ready to trap water when the monsoons arrived, extended to the southern horizon, punctuated by clumps of palm trees. Once in a while we passed clusters of houses made of pressed mud brick and thatch, with a cow or bullock tethered outside and a hand-drawn well in the background. We crossed the river Son, a tributary of the Ganges, on a long two-lane bridge built by the British during the colonial period; the decking was almost completely worn away, so we slowed to a crawl. Eventually, after turning off the main road and following a dirt track that wound across the fields, we reached a small village.

The driver left to find himself a drink, while I wandered around the village. It consisted of no more than a few huts and stalls. There was no electricity and virtually no mechanized vehicles, such as cars or tractors. Farming here was still powered by human and animal muscles. I spied two men in the gloom of a small shed, operating, by hand, the bellows of an iron forge. The fire, contained in a pit in the shed's floor, cast an orange glow on their faces, which were streaming with sweat.

How difficult it is to make sense of the forces behind the violence in this land! As is so often the case in the social sciences, the closer I got to the problem, the more tangled its causes seemed. Some of the experts I had interviewed in Patna emphasized the role of caste, others official corruption, and still others population growth and land scarcity. Clearly, all of these factors played a role, but the trick is to figure out how they actually interact within the complex system of rural Bihar's economy, politics, and ecology.

Amidst this complexity, though, I felt that one fact was indisputable. The people around me in that village still intimately depended on their natural environment for their well-being, especially on renewable resources of fresh water and fertile soil. For these villagers, and for most people in Bihar, a long drought, the salinization of their cropland from over-irrigation, or the fragmentation of their farms by population pressure could mean destitution, even starvation. As I looked across the parched fields, it seemed to me that those of us in rich countries too easily forget that these are basic facts of life for half the people on the planet.

Nevertheless, despite the fact that scarcities of land and water were already causing terrible hardship for many people across the state, I didn't think Bihar represented a Malthusian catastrophe in the making; Bihar's soaring population hadn't collided with absolute and inescapable limits to growth. During the previous years, as I put together the pieces of the ingenuity puzzle, I had come to the conclusion that few if any societies are in danger of soon colliding with such limits to growth. Indeed, the entire neo-Malthusian rhetoric of absolute resource limits or, to use the popular phrase, of ecological "carrying capacity," has come to strike me as deeply misleading, because it implies impending, unbreachable constraints on human development. Human history is a triumphant record of people smashing through such constraints.

I had learned that the limits to growth a society faces are a product of both its physical context—that is, its context of natural resources and environment—and the ingenuity it brings to bear on that context. As populations and consumption rates rise, and as some resources become scarcer, societies can maintain or raise their standard of living by supplying more ingenuity. Scientists and engineers can respond by increasing the pace at which they deliver resource-conserving technologies. Politicians, bureaucrats, corporate managers, and community leaders can be cleverer "social engineers" by adjusting existing institutions, and by designing, building, and operating new ones that allow technical ingenuity to flourish and promote social adaptation to scarcity.

To an important degree, in other words, ingenuity can substitute for natural resources. This doesn't mean, of course, that there are no limits to growth at all, and that human populations and their appetites can expand forever. Even if our societies could supply infinite amounts of ingenuity, biological and physical laws (like the laws of thermodynamics) would eventually constrain human population size and resource consumption, at least on the surface of Earth.[36] But these theoretical limits are a long way off. In the meantime, the constraints we face are more practical: they are the result, in large part, of our limited ability to supply ingenuity. And because the amount of ingenuity we supply depends on many social and economic factors and can vary widely from society to society, we cannot determine a society's limits to growth solely by examining its physical context, as neo-Malthusians try to do. Rather than speaking of limits, it is more accurate to say that some societies are locked into a race between a rising requirement for ingenuity and their capacity to supply it.

Poor countries are more likely to fall behind in this race, because an adequate supply of ingenuity depends on having adequate financial and human capital. Laboratories need money and skilled personnel to generate technologies that can alleviate scarcity's harsh effects; entrepreneurs need credit to diffuse these technologies through the broader economy; and political leaders need financial capital to buy off special interest groups that obstruct technological and institutional reform. Poor countries usually don't have the money to pursue advanced scientific research and so must rely on technologies developed by rich countries, which are often inappropriate for their customs and economies. In addition, capital shortages frequently result in decrepit transportation, communication, and education infrastructure, which makes it hard for governments, NGOs, and corporations to put in place new resource-saving technologies, policies, and institutions.

If a society develops a serious ingenuity gap—that is, if it loses the race between requirement and supply—prosperity falls in the regions already affected by scarcity, and people usually migrate out of those regions in large numbers. Social dissatisfaction rises, especially among marginal groups in ecologically fragile rural areas and urban squatter settlements. These changes undermine the government's legitimacy and raise the likelihood of widespread and chronic civil violence. Violence further erodes the society's capacity to supply ingenuity, especially by causing human and financial capital to flee. Such societies risk entering a downward and self-reinforcing spiral of crisis and decay.

This, I reflected as I wandered around the village, was precisely what had occurred in Bihar. The state's problems had not arisen from a Malthusian crisis of population growth slamming into unbreachable resource limits, but rather from its inability to deliver an adequate supply of technologies and institutional reforms. Bihar needed efficient irrigation methods, effective agricultural extension services, and alternative jobs for people thrown off the land, but nobody had figured out how to supply them. These technologies and institutions would have loosened the grip of cropland and water scarcities on people like the villagers around me that day. They would, in effect, have loosened the coupling between those villagers and their natural environment. But in the absence of this ingenuity, the villagers' environmental constraints were as real, intractable, and intrusive as the day's insufferable heat.

Yet if the neo-Malthusians are wrong, I decided, so are the economic optimists who believe that natural resources aren't important anymore. "Few components of the Earth's crust, including farm land, are so specific as to defy economic replacement," wrote Harold Barnett and Chandler

Morse in their classic early-1960s study of the economics of natural resources.[37] The idea that we can always find adequate substitutes for any specific resource (an idea I looked at in the chapter "Ingenuity and Wealth") is now widely shared by economists in rich countries, but it struck me as meaningless, even ludicrous, in the context of the village. Even if it were technically possible, which I doubted, to find a fully satisfactory substitute for the biochemically complex soils of the Ganges plain around me, Bihar could not possibly come up with the huge investments of capital and labor that would be required, let alone the technical and social ingenuity that would support such a project—especially in the present circumstances. Bihar would remain an agricultural economy for generations to come, and during that time its soils, for all intents and purposes, would be irreplaceable.

Resources remain important because they are the raw materials that societies must work with to produce their well-being. The amount of ingenuity we must supply to achieve this depends on the properties and quantities of natural resources available to us, as I found when I wanted to escape from my office. This is clearest in poor countries where people's dependence on their natural environment is direct and obvious, but it's also true in rich countries. With their immense wealth and staggering capacity to produce ingenuity, especially technical ingenuity, rich countries have been able to resolve or manage many of their immediate resource and environmental problems. They have figured out how to substitute relatively abundant materials for scarce ones, they now produce far more food than they consume, they have made major headway cleaning up local air pollution (although they have had less success with regional haze), and they are beginning to use water more efficiently. But just when rich countries seem to have learned how to manage their natural environments, and to have forever loosened their coupling to specific physical resources, a whole new class of problems connected to Earth's natural environment has appeared, problems from climate change to major alterations of biogeochemical cycles (like the nitrogen cycle) that are generally global in scope and characterized by complexity, unknown unknowns, and non-linearities. A stable and benign climate and a normally functioning nitrogen cycle are resources important to the well-being of rich countries as much as cropland is to poor countries.

My driver came back with his drink. We got into the stifling car and bounced our way back down the dirt track towards Patna. As we passed the fields near the village, I thought about another reason why resources remain important in places like Bihar. In many poor countries around the world, scarcities of cropland, water, and forest resources don't engender waves of ingenuity, as many economists predict they should; instead, they actually reduce the supply of ingenuity, because they lead to conflicts among groups that hinder technical and institutional adaptation to scarcity. This outcome is much more likely, it seems, when societies suffer from rising scarcities *and* highly unequal distributions of wealth and power. In these cases, inequality erodes the social capital around which cooperative solutions to scarcities can be built.

Once again, Bihar gives us a stark example. The state has some of the highest population densities on agricultural land in India. Standard economic theory suggests that this land scarcity should stimulate very intensive use of all the state's cropland. Farmers should use extra labor (and machinery, if they can afford it) to eke out the maximum possible yields from their land; they should also plant multiple crops each year, as the seasons allow. Yet something curious has happened in Bihar: fallow rates are among the highest in the country. Instead of boosting the intensity of their use of their agricultural land, farmers are often leaving their land fallow! Why is this happening in a place so short of land?

During my research in the state, I thought I had found the reason: many upper-caste landowners have abandoned their land. Fearing assassination by Naxalites—or being "shortened by six inches," which means having their throats cut—they have fled to the cities, leaving private armies to keep their idle land free of squatters. At the same time, these landowners, embittered by the conflict, thirsting for revenge, and desperately seeking to maintain their privileges, have used their power over the state's institutions to resolutely block any serious proposals for land reform.

When economists analyze an economic crisis like Bihar's, they usually point to weaknesses in economic institutions, such as markets and property rights, as the fundamental causes. But I felt that the hardships of the villagers I had seen were not, first and foremost, a product of such factors. Instead, their hardships were primarily derived from inequalities of wealth and power among Bihar's castes and from the corrosive effect of these inequalities, when combined with severe resource scarcities, on the state's political institutions. And it was the debilitation of the state's political institutions that, in the end, prevented constructive reform of its economic institutions and policies.

Economic institutions and policies are ultimately subordinate to politics. And in Bihar, as in much of the developing world, politics is powerfully influenced by scarcities of natural resources.

———————————

Every morning in Patna when I woke up, I turned on the hotel television to watch the Asian version of the BBC *World News*. Even in this poorest part of India I could connect to global society, at least when the power was functioning. Over those few days a certain small item brought up the rear of each newscast: a report on the advance of a major storm that was building in the Arabian Sea off the coast of the far western Indian state of Gujarat. It had the makings of a cyclone, and each day, it grew bigger as it moved gradually nearer to the Indian coast. But no one in India seemed to be paying much attention. The country's debates and discussions focused on other issues, especially on India's fevered relationship with Pakistan.

After breakfast, my routine was simple. I spent some time making phone calls to find an interpreter and guide to help me locate the little girl. Then, around midmorning, I hailed a bicycle rickshaw to take me across the city to the A.N. Sinha Institute, a center for the study of social issues with one of the country's best libraries on Bihar's politics, economics, and land conflicts. I spent a large part of each day gathering materials there for my research.

Like so much else in the state, the institute had been allowed to decline into woeful disrepair. It was housed in a long four-story brick building on a small, treed estate on the bank of the Ganges. It could have been a beautiful setting, but the grounds weren't well tended, and the outside of the building looked weary. Inside, not only the building but the people it housed seemed weary too, shuffling from room to room, worn out by the heat. Gloomy offices and seminar rooms lined long, unlighted hallways. Everything was dilapidated—furniture, desks, and blackboards were all tattered. According to a friend of mine in the city, the state government had packed the institute with "scholars" of dubious merit, most never around, but all receiving fat salaries. The director himself, a rotund balding fellow in his forties, was apparently a friend of the state's chief minister (the equivalent of a premier or governor), whom the institute had recently awarded an honorary degree. The director's office was the only reasonably comfortable room I saw in the building, with an impressive desk, a couple of couches, and a perpetual coterie of acolytes sipping tea. On the desk sat a dysfunctional fax machine that beeped occasionally but didn't produce any faxes; it seemed more an icon of the director's power than anything else.

But the director was helpful, giving me the run of the institute and making sure that the members of the library staff were accommodating. The library itself was a surreal place, a long room with ranks of shelves for books and journals down one side, and slit windows at each end. Tables and chairs were laid out beside the shelves, and overhead hung two rows of ancient ceiling fans, interspersed with scattered fluorescent tubes, some working, some not. The electrical system appeared decades old, which didn't matter very much at the moment, since the power was out much of the day. The curtains on the windows at each end were brown with dust and rotting off their rods. From a side office, I could hear the languid tapping of a manual typewriter. A half-dozen supervisors and users populated the room, a couple listlessly reading newspapers, while the others slept with their heads on their desks. The library was a long, dark, tomblike facility, the sun beating down on it from the outside, baking its human contents in the still heat.

For hours, I would sit at one of the tables, two large water bottles in front of me, poring over detailed analyses of the state's political economy and incidents of Naxalite violence. I sat under one of the ceiling fans. When the power was on, it twirled slowly, producing a cone of moving air that made the room tolerable. When the power failed, as it did ten to twenty times a day, the air in the library was almost indescribably stifling.

In a land riven by conflict, the library's collection of materials was extraordinarily valuable. It contained historical records and careful analysis that could be the foundation for practical solutions of the state's crisis. I was deeply impressed by the quality of much of the research and scholarship I read there: it was painstakingly thorough and cautious, thoughtful yet passionate. Many of these scholars were natives of Bihar, and they were clearly anguished by what had happened to their homeland. Sadly, though, the institute's library was not a good repository for their work. The only record system for its materials was an old-style card catalog. Many of the books were piled in heaps around the room; no one seemed interested in returning them to the shelves. The books themselves were obviously deteriorating in the heat and humidity; spines were broken, and many pages were brown and crumbling. Most disturbingly, after a few days one of the librarians admitted to me that, owing to funding cutbacks, the library hadn't ordered a single new journal in five years. (The A.N. Sinha

Institute, I learned, was not the only center of scholarship in Bihar crippled by funding cutbacks: Patna University, the state's premier institution of higher learning, hadn't produced a university handbook with basic information about its courses since 1966, and now it couldn't even afford to purchase watermarked paper for awards certificates for its top students.[38]) Here again, it seemed, was another small example of the vicious cycles that plague many poor countries: Bihar's political turmoil and economic crisis was crippling a facility that could be vital to generating the ingenuity needed to resolve that very same crisis.

On one of my last afternoons at the library, when my water had almost run out, I packed up my books and notepaper and decided to head back to my hotel. The heat was particularly bad that day. There seemed to be more than the usual number of funeral processions in the streets, with bodies wrapped in colorful shawls on stretchers, carried on young men's shoulders and followed by lines of mourners. A wave of gastroenteritis from foul water, failed pumps, and spoiled food was sweeping through the city. In many of the state's urban and semiurban areas, 90 percent of water taps had gone dry.[39] Youth activists were burning effigies outside the Bihar State Electricity Board, calling for people to suspend payment of their electricity bills until the power outages stopped.

As usual, I walked out of the institute's front gate and over to a nearby group of bicycle rickshaws, in the shade of a clump of trees. None of the drivers showed any interest in me. I wasn't prepared, though, to trek the several kilometers to my hotel in the late-afternoon sun with little water, so using sign language I asked several drivers if they would take me. Eventually one agreed. He was a rake-thin fellow who seemed to be about fifty years old, but was probably only forty or so. He couldn't have weighed more than forty-five kilograms. He had graying hair, one front tooth, and a leathery, dark face with deep, reddened eyes. He wore a ragged singlet over his torso and a gray rag wrapped around his head to keep off the sun. He had battered thongs on his feet.

I got up on the rickshaw's raised and padded back seat, while the driver mounted the bicycle seat at the front and put all his weight on the machine's left pedal. Slowly, painfully slowly, we began to move.

Most Westerners who travel in India find rickshaws discomforting. Although I have used them a lot over the years, in part because I sometimes feel safer to have company in strange parts of Indian cities, I have always found the experience morally jarring. Westerners tend to be big and heavy compared to Indians, and rickshaw drivers often have to use almost all their strength to move their machines with one of us on board. It seems reprehensible to sit in relative comfort on the back of a rickshaw while a nearly destitute person pedals one around for a few rupees. On the other hand, those rupees are vitally important for the driver, and it seems just as reprehensible to walk to spare oneself guilt.

We left the vicinity of the Institute and wound our way slowly through Patna's back streets. The route to the hotel traced its way up a gentle incline through a shopping district, across several major roads, and past a park, a squatters' settlement, and a wealthier residential area. My driver worked the pedals rhythmically, rocking all his weight back and forth from one pedal to the other. He hunched over the handlebars. Big patches of sweat spread across his singlet. I noticed that he seemed to be working far harder than any of the other drivers I had used, perhaps because he was smaller or perhaps because he was older. As one kilometer rolled into another, I became convinced that he was at his limit of exertion.

Finally, across from the park, he stopped for a rest. I had a bit of water left in my bottle, so I unscrewed the top and offered it to him. It seemed an ordinary, natural thing to do, yet he was obviously surprised. After a moment's hesitation, he accepted the bottle and raised it to his lips. But just as the water crept to the bottle's mouth, a chorus of catcalls arose from the other side of the street, as a group of fellow rickshaw drivers harassed him for accepting my offer. Without drinking, he lowered the bottle and gave it back to me. Clearly, he was desperately thirsty, and I can't describe the disappointment on his face.

We continued in silence along the last kilometers to the hotel. When we arrived, I pulled out my wallet and put the rupees for the fare on the back seat; as usual, I had doubled the standard fare. But he didn't take the money. Instead, he started waving his arms, speaking in Bihari, and gesturing in a way I couldn't understand. Then it dawned on me that he wanted the water bottle. I fetched it out of my bag, unscrewed the top, and gave it to him again. This time, although he was uncomfortable touching his lips to its mouth, he drank the full amount. After handing the bottle back, somewhat sheepishly, he took his money. We smiled at each other, and he left.

Talking to a friend from Patna the next day about this incident, I learned that I had transgressed a yawning social and cultural gulf. To my driver, I was upper-caste, and members of upper castes usually regard members of the lowest castes as spiritually and physically impure. This is especially the upper-caste attitude towards people on the lowest rung of the ladder, the untouchables, and my driver was probably untouchable. He was literally too filthy to touch. He didn't want to put his lips to the mouth of my bottle, because that action might have deeply offended me. He also probably didn't know whether I'd want the bottle back after he had handled it. In his social milieu, my simple offer of a drink was fraught with difficulty.

But in that moment after he had had his drink, in the baking sun, the noise, and the dirt outside my hotel, we established a fleeting bond. When we smiled at each other, we were both nothing more and nothing less than human beings, with the same basic physiological needs. We couldn't speak to each other, our worlds couldn't have been more different, yet in this most fundamental respect we were the same: we would both die that day without water. Nature, brutal physical reality, had penetrated into our lives and made us equal—at least in that one respect, so essential to our existence—in a land with some of the most ghastly inequalities on the planet.

The next morning the satellite photographs broadcast on the BBC *News* showed a mammoth cyclone in the Arabian Sea heading north towards India. But still nobody seemed to be concerned; there was no talk of warning the communities along the heavily populated Gujarat coastline. The day's papers did, though, include some interesting commentary by meteorologists on the link between global warming and the current heat wave. As temperature records fell and as hundreds more people died each day, a consensus seemed to be emerging among the country's climate experts that India could expect more of the same in the future.[40]

This was my day to search for the little girl. With the help of a local family-planning NGO, I had finally located an interpreter and guide. We decided to look for the girl early in the morning, before the heat became extreme. The NGO provided a car, and after we got into the back seat I showed the driver one of my photographs. Just by looking at the clay pots in the photo's background, he thought he knew where to go.

As we drove across town, my guide and I talked a bit about the role of children in India's development. Children are the raw material from which poor countries fashion their human capital—that is, their skilled workforce—and human capital is an essential input to ingenuity supply. Some experts have suggested that a rapidly growing population is a good thing precisely because it means more heads to generate and deliver ingenuity.[41] But this argument assumes that growth of a society's population automatically translates into growth in its stock of human capital. Research shows that this outcome is not inevitable. At the household level, large families must often direct their resources to short-term consumption and away from long-term investments in their children's education. And at the societal level, as I had seen in Bihar, rapid population growth can contribute to environmental degradation and social instability, changes that undermine economic growth and, in turn, weaken the educational institutions that create human capital.[42]

While the effects of population size and growth on economic development are ambiguous, the effects of improvements in a population's *quality*—especially in its health, skills, and education—are not. During the nineteenth and twentieth centuries, gains in health and life expectancy were major sources of economic growth in today's rich countries. The Nobel prize–winning economist Robert Fogel has found that better nutrition and higher caloric intake boosted the fraction of the population able to work, made it possible for people in the labor force to work harder, and made the body's conversion of food energy into work more efficient (by reducing the incidence of infectious disease and diarrhea, for example). He estimates that these changes alone accounted for about 50 percent of British economic growth between 1790 and 1980.[43] And, although Fogel doesn't stress the point, longer, healthier lives clearly allowed people to devote more years to education and to the thinking and research needed to generate useful knowledge.

In the global economy of the twenty-first century, as knowledge becomes more important as a factor of production, the quality of a country's population will become an even more decisive determinant of its prosperity. The international relations theorist Richard Rosecrance argues that the global economy will increasingly differentiate itself into "head" countries specializing in generating knowledge and "body" countries specializing in manufacturing things on the basis of that knowledge.[44] Even in "body" countries, though, the workforce will have to be healthy, highly skilled, and connected to the world's knowledge networks.[45]

Looking around me at the citizens of Patna, I wasn't optimistic about their prospects in this new world. Well over half of Bihar's population, I knew, couldn't even meet India's abysmally low standard of literacy. The Internet was available to only the tiniest fraction of people in the state;

institutions of higher learning were in ruins; and almost all young people with skills and aspirations were leaving for other parts of India. Yes, some of those other parts were participating in the world's knowledge revolution, such as the high-tech triangle of the southern cities of Bangalore, Hyderabad, and Madras (recently renamed Chennai). In those cities, young computer programmers and India's new elite of information entrepreneurs crowd into swank bars and brand-name clothing stores and live in modern apartment complexes featuring health clubs and swimming pools. But these islands of economic bustle have produced little improvement in the surrounding ocean of Indian poverty, in large part because of weak state and national governments that don't collect adequate taxes on the new wealth.[46]

From the beginning of my adventure to solve the ingenuity puzzle several years before, I had had the intuition that finding the little girl in Patna would help me put in place the puzzle's final pieces. One piece that had already helped me make sense of the larger puzzle was a better understanding of the characteristics, versatility, and limitations of the human brain. So an issue that seemed particularly pertinent to me that day, as we wound our way through Patna's crowded streets to find a specific child, was the cognitive development of India's children. Would they be ready, intellectually, for the next century's knowledge-intensive, hyperdynamic, and high-pressured global economy? Would they be sufficiently adept to participate in that economy, to sell their products, services, and skills for an adequate return? These questions applied not just to India, but to developing countries in general. It's true that, on average, children in these regions are better off than ever before. But in much of Asia, Africa, and Latin America, a wide range of stresses, from violent conflict to poor nutrition, take a heavy toll during childhood mental development. Given the skyrocketing cognitive demands of the global economy, these may turn out to be dire handicaps indeed.

The human brain's extraordinary versatility is enhanced by its long juvenile period. At birth, our brain's size is similar to a newborn chimpanzee's, about 350 cubic centimeters (cc). But, while the chimp's brain stops growing at 450 cc, the human baby's keeps growing at the same rate as a fetus's, tripling in size by age four.[47] Even after this growth stops, the brain's information-processing ability continues improving for many years, as external stimuli cause the brain to prune away neurons and rewire neural connections, a process often called "cognitive sculpting." (In fact, the brain's neurons can rewire themselves throughout a human being's life; moreover, recent research shows that, contrary to long-held opinion, certain brain regions grow new neurons well into adulthood.[48]) This *neuronal plasticity* "is responsible for our mental flexibility," writes the paleoanthropologist Rick Potts. "Human beings are born into a world full of options and risks. It is the brain's lengthy out-of-womb maturation that underwrites our vast abilities to pick up data about the world."[49]

The long maturation brings risks, however, since the brain is extremely sensitive to external conditions during this period.[50] Circumstances of severe stress or traumatic violence, as experienced by tens of millions of children in the developing world's war zones, often cause long-term psychopathologies, including chronic depression, irritability, and a predisposition to violent behavior.[51] These mental disabilities are linked to changes in brain chemistry and neural connections.[52] Richard Hellie, an historian at the University of Chicago who has studied the effect of chronic violence on the development of the early Russian society, tells us that "excess exposure to traumatic violence will alter the developing central nervous system, probably by changing receptor sensitivity, similar to that seen in cocaine sensitization. This predisposes the victim to be a more impulsive, reactive, and violent individual."[53]

Of more general importance in poor countries, though, is childhood undernutrition. Because of poor diets, 40 percent of children under five in developing countries are stunted, which means they have low heights for their age; in many regions, including Bihar, the figure exceeds 60 percent. Biomedical and psychological researchers have found that, in addition to limiting height, undernutrition impairs the development of basic cognitive abilities, including locomotor and shape recognition skills.[54] It acts not only by causing direct damage to the brain (damage that is sometimes reversible if nutrition improves) but also by making children sick, lethargic, and withdrawn, which keeps them from energetically exploring their surroundings.[55] Dietary shortages of vitamins and micronutrients, often resulting from cultivation of nutrient-depleted soils, can also have a major effect on brain development. Of special concern is iodine deficiency, estimated by the World Health Organization in the mid-1990s to affect 1.6 billion people (500 million in China alone), or over a quarter of the world's population. When severe, iodine deficiency produces goiter and cretinism, and when less severe it causes persistent mental and physical fatigue and varying degrees of cognitive impairment.[56]

The child's maturing brain can additionally be harmed by a range of environmental contaminants, including pesticides and heavy metals.[57] Exposure to lead and cadmium is associated with delinquent behavior, learning disorders, and decreases in measured intelligence, including downward shifts in children's IQ scores of 4 to 5 percent.[58] The problem of lead exposure is particularly serious in countries like India that still use the metal in motor fuels and that suffer from appalling urban air pollution. A large fraction of children in cities in the developing world, it is safe to say, suffer from chronic, low-level lead poisoning that retards their mental development.[59]

We were now rumbling down the dusty Patna road, parallel to the Ganges, where I had first photographed the little girl. Thinking about the needs of the children I could see all along the road's shoulders, I started to get angry. I remembered Nicholas Negroponte's assertion that a satellite providing Internet access stationed over Africa would immediately revolutionize the continent's economic and political prospects. Only people totally entranced by the technological cornucopia of rich countries, I thought, and largely unfamiliar with what is happening in much of Africa, or in much of the developing world for that matter, could say such a thing. Outside the fantasy worlds of these technological and economic optimists, children in poor countries need peaceful societies, good diets, clean air and water, and adequate shoes before they need, or can even use, Internet access. The basics of life are the prerequisites to development. Until they are available, in Bihar and across wide swaths of the developing world, the human capital needed to create, absorb, and use new knowledge will not be even remotely adequate to meet the cognitively demanding challenges of the twenty-first century.

The driver stopped the car at the spot he thought corresponded to the scene in the photo's background. From my memory of the day when I had taken the shot, I sensed he was right, so we stepped out of the car into the hubbub of the street. It was still early morning, but everywhere there was action. A stream of scooters, auto rickshaws, carts, cows, buses, and trucks jostled past us. The wide dirt margins extending out from the road's crumbling pavement were alive with business and family life. An old barber, deftly wielding a straight razor, was shaving a younger man sitting on a stool, the implements of his trade and pan of water on a wobbly table beside him. A teenager was busily pumping up the front tire of his bicycle rickshaw. Along one side of the street were clusters of small stalls and huts, divided by narrow alleyways descending to the Ganges. Along the other side rose rickety two- and three-story buildings, of brick and whitewashed concrete, their tile roofs sloping down towards the street. Balconies hung from their upper floors, many decorated along their fronts with grates carved from brick. At street level, a series of rough-hewn wooden doors were open to reveal little shops selling clay pots, ceramic wares, and other dry goods. Overhead a tangle of electrical wires was strung from one ramshackle light standard to another.

Immediately we were surrounded by a group of inquisitive children and teenagers. The girls were dressed in colorful blouses, skirts, and saris; the boys in shorts and white singlets or grubby polyester dress shirts; most of the children were shoeless. They all jabbered simultaneously at my interpreter. She showed them the photograph, which was passed quickly from hand to hand. "He's going to use her in the cinema," declared one teenage boy. Another announced that he knew the girl in the picture and started to run down the street, beckoning us to follow. Soon we arrived in front of one of the rough doors that opened into a small house. The building's broken concrete steps bridged a gutter full of rancid water. On each side of the walkway to the steps was an array of earthen water jugs, resembling large gourds with narrow, sculpted necks.

I knew this was the place.

A moment later a mother appeared at the door, with a child in her arms. It was the girl; I would have recognized her anywhere. She was now about four years old, with closely shaved hair, brown shorts, a mauve short-sleeved shirt, and thongs. Around her ankles were silver bracelets.

The mother was bewildered and more than a little embarrassed. We explained that I'd come to give her copies of the photograph that I had taken two and a half years before.[60] Remarkably, she remembered me taking the shot, and she seemed pleased to receive the copies, interpreting the gesture as a sign of friendship and generosity. Soon the father arrived, as did the other two older daughters, along with a growing crowd of people, curious and amused, and all expressing opinions. This was clearly the event of the day.

The little girl's name was Komal Kumari. I gathered from my interpreter that Komal meant "delicate" in the local language. After talking to the parents for a few minutes, we learned that both the mother's and father's family lines came from Patna. The father worked in a small electronics shop fixing light appliances, like radios and irons. The mother sold the water jugs on display in front of their house, jugs made from clay dug out of the bank of the Ganges, across the street. In the summer when demand was high, each four-liter jug went for twenty to twenty-five rupees (about seventy-five cents). Such jugs were the standard water container for poor and middle-class households in the city.

My interpreter later estimated that the family's total monthly income was probably 1,200 to 1,500 rupees a month, or about thirty to forty dollars, which put them in the city's lower middle class. Given the state of Bihar's economy, it was unlikely that their standard of living had improved much in the last ten years. Their house was probably home to several families, each living in a single room. They likely shared a water tap and perhaps a bathroom in the back of the house, but all the household effluent drained into the gutter out front. They also likely owned a television, which, my interpreter suggested, most families valued above proper drains and clean water. "There's a lot of peer pressure to have a TV," she told me. The family's daily diet would consist of rice, lentils, flatbread, and vegetables; they would not be able to afford eggs, milk, or meat, except as a rare treat.

As I took some more photographs of Komal Kumari's family and the street where they lived, her mother told us that both older daughters were going to a government school, with the eldest, Rajani, in the equivalent of grade four. My interpreter guessed that she would probably continue in school for another five years or so, being fully literate at the end of the process. "It's a good thing that they're living beside the street," my interpreter remarked as an aside, "because the mother can have income at the same time that she manages her house."

The advantages weren't immediately apparent to me. By this point, the crowd had swelled to twenty or thirty people, and with the roaring and honking traffic right beside us, it was almost impossible to carry on a conversation. We decided to cross the street and walk down to the Ganges. Much of the crowd, especially the children, followed, and soon we were looking out across the river. It was blessedly quiet. A few people were bathing along the shore, while two young men were busy making the water jugs we had seen in front of Komal's house. Rows and rows of them lined the river's upper bank. Nearby was a small temple housing a beautiful red, green, and gold statue of the monkey god Hanuman, with remnants of flowers and other offerings strewn around its feet.

I had come all this way in my travels and my learning and exploration. Now was the moment of truth: what did it all mean? Looking out across

Komal Kumari (on the right) with her sisters

the Ganges, with a group of Indian children around me, their eyes scanning me in curiosity and silence, I understood that contradictions were at the heart of the story. These contradictions played themselves out on many levels and in many ways. Some were intriguing, and some were productive. Others were frightening. But whatever way these contradictions played out, they rendered the past, present, and future fundamentally ambiguous. I realized that there was no single right or correct interpretation of the world around us, no one answer to my quest, and no single, definitive arrangement of the pieces of the ingenuity puzzle.

Our world is a highly complex system, and complexity itself is full of contradictions. Complex systems are intricate tangles of shifting and often opposing—contradicting—forces that unfold in unpredictable and frequently totally surprising ways. The behavior of complex systems often confounds, or contradicts, our expectations. The human brain, an instrument that gives us unparalleled versatility to adapt to our complex world, is the evolutionary product of the constant shocks and volatility of an ancient African ecology, volatility that threatened, or contradicted, our prospects for survival. Similarly, the oppositions, or contradictions, in the world around us today evoke the ingenuity that we need to improve our lives—oppositions between what we have and what we want, between what we fear and what we love, and between what we regard as cruel and what we think is just.

Chatting with the children pressing up against me, I pondered the contradictions they and Komal Kumari represented. Although the standard of living of Komal's family might not have improved much in the last ten years, there was no doubt that she was much luckier to be alive today than a hundred or even fifty years ago. Only a few short decades ago, a female baby in India could expect to live to her early forties; today, Komal Kumari would probably see her mid-sixties. She was reasonably healthy, she had access to an adequate if not varied diet, and she had the prospect of obtaining a basic education. (In these respects, she was actually better off than many other children in Bihar.)

Yet as I thought about her, and about the children I'd seen in Bhojpur, I couldn't help juxtaposing their realities with the starkly different, contradictory, realities of people's daily lives in Canary Wharf, Washington, Toronto, and Las Vegas. Here on the banks of the Ganges, nature was an ever-present and intrusive force; there, it was hidden and marginalized. Here, medieval technologies, like the iron forge and hand bellows, were still in wide use; there, lightning-fast technological change was a fact of everyday life. Here, at least with respect to the Internet and modern communication technologies, a "zone of silence" prevailed; there, computers and the Internet were compressing time and space and creating vast new wealth by helping people exploit the increasing returns to investment in knowledge and ideas.[61] It might be true that the lives of Komal Kumari and most other children in Bihar were, on average, slowly improving. But, at the very same moment, children in rich countries were shooting into the future at blinding speed, and Komal Kumari was being left in the dust.

Neoclassical economists suggest that standards of living of poor and rich societies should converge over time. Yet one sees little evidence of convergence in Patna. Komal Kumari is simultaneously next door in space, but infinitely far away in terms of what she can expect from her life. How, in a converging world, could we be so close yet such strangers? For me, this was the most profound, and disturbing, contradiction of all.

Just when communication technologies and jet travel are binding our planet together ever more tightly, history's biggest differences in wealth, opportunity, and human experience are emerging. Two hundred years ago, in my great-great-grandfather Thomas Dixon's time, over 90 percent of the people on the planet lived in farming communities, and most everywhere you went the cadence of people's lives was fundamentally similar. But today, on the same tiny planet, we have subsistence farmers in Bihar next to the virtual realities of webware designers at Comdex; we have the high-tech hyperactivity of investment bankers in Canary Wharf next to the struggle for survival of rural mothers in Africa who must walk kilometers for their daily water; and we have the gated elite communities of Orange County, California, next to the bombed-out rubble of Jaffna.

Yes, thanks to economic globalization and the homogenizing effects of modern communications and travel, the planet's richest two billion people are converging in wealth and culture. But if we expand our view to encompass all humanity, all six billion of us, we see rapidly widening gulfs between the planet's richest and poorest groups and between individuals and societies that thrive in the face of our world's dramatic new challenges and those that fail and succumb. We also see that despite the miracles of modern communications, our national and global societies are, in many respects, fragmenting into a montage of discrete realities. In more ways than technological and economic optimists dare to admit, the differences among us have never been so great.

I put my camera back in its case and zipped the flap shut. It was a standard 35mm model—a single, compact package of technology worth three years' income for Komal Kumari's family. Such large disparities of wealth and opportunity do not presage a peaceful future. In times of economic and social crisis, they are likely to inspire fear and envy, ethnocentrism and ill will. As in Indonesia in early 1998, the relatively advantaged and successful will want to protect what they have, while the relatively disadvantaged, like the young men in Jakarta's slums, will want to take, or at least destroy, what they don't have. Thanks to the spread of TV, today's disadvantaged know better than ever before what they are missing. And thanks to the spread of cheap, portable, and powerful technologies of violence, they also have a greater capacity than ever before to harm the targets of their anger.

The next day, the cyclone plowed into the Gujarat coastline. Sucking energy from the hot Arabian Sea, the storm's winds and waves ripped through India's busiest port, Kandla, turning its cargo jetties, cranes, and railway sidings into twisted heaps of scrap metal. Thousands of unregistered migrants who worked in the port and surrounding salt flats and who lived in rough huts along the coast were swept out to sea. In the aftermath, a howl of protest at the lack of warning or preparation arose across the country. "The hunt for scapegoats," one journalist wrote in *The Financial Times*, "is already on." But the tragedy pointed to "a deeper malaise in Indian society: a failure of governance and of business ethics, a basic disregard for the lives of the poor. And that is likely to remain long after the port begins functioning again."[62]

EPILOGUE

A WEEK AFTER I had found Komal Kumari, my late-night flight to Europe climbed away from New Delhi and turned northwest across the Punjab. I was going home. Before long the captain told us we were flying above the Khyber Pass and would soon be over Kabul, the capital of Afghanistan. I got up from my seat, stretched my legs, and squinted into the inky darkness through the window in the cabin door.

Down below and a world away was a territory that my grandfather—Thomas Dixon's grandson—had come to know in the waning years of the nineteenth century. As a private in the Fifth Dragoon Guards of the Imperial Army's Tirah Expeditionary Force, he had served with Winston Churchill along the chaotic fringe of the British Empire between the Northwest Frontier Province and Afghanistan, fighting the Afghani Pathan on foot and horseback with carbines. That was one hundred years ago. Afghanistan at the time was ruled by Abdur Rahman Khan, the "Iron Amir," who assumed control in 1880 and began the arduous process of unifying and modernizing his country. Struggling to remain independent of British influence, he created a standing army and put down the fratricidal violence among his country's chieftains.

Now I was flying 11,000 meters overhead, surrounded by the genius of modern human engineering. The 747's six million finely crafted and fitted parts were humming in concert to carry me home.[1] But the Afghanistan we were soaring over was not the country the Iron Amir had sought to create. It was instead a country ravaged by two decades of almost continuous warfare and brutal hardship—first by Soviet invasion, then by vicious rivalries among ethnic groups armed to the teeth with leftover weaponry, and today by the medievalism of the country's Taliban government. War has ruined half the buildings in Kabul, much of the city has no municipal electricity, and only a third of its inhabitants have running water. Seventy percent of the working-age population is jobless, while one in every four children dies before the age of five.

But the desperate remnants of Afghan society were, quite understandably, the farthest thing from the minds of my fellow travelers inside the jet at that moment. Wealthy Indians and Westerners, they were on their way to make business deals, see their families, or explore tourist destinations on the other side of the world. Kabul, as far as they were concerned, could have been on the moon. But the city was actually only eleven kilometers away—straight down. Like my grandfather's world in time, it was proximate to us in space: and eleven kilometers, or a hundred years, is really not so far away. As I peered out the plane's window—seeing nothing, but trying to imagine the land and people below—I was reminded how easily we live with these contrasting realities, even acknowledge them, without *truly* juxtaposing or seeing them.

The vicissitudes of the ancient environment in Africa helped endow us with extraordinarily versatile brains. To use the paleoanthropologist Rick Potts's delightful phrase, our brains are "mirrors of nature's quicksilver." Today, they not only allow us to create miraculous machines like the 747 out of the rough materials of our natural world, but their versatility and flexibility allow us to survive, even thrive, in an astounding range of circumstances, from Baffin Island in the Arctic to the windswept deserts of the Australian interior. And they have given us an almost infinite capacity for optimism and hope, even when our circumstances are utterly miserable—as they are for families living on Patna's streets in 50 degrees of heat.

These are wonderful attributes, but they have a negative side too. We adapt so easily to changes in our world that we often forget where we've come from, and we neglect to ask where we're going. Perhaps more important, we lose sight of the sharp edges and contrasts around us. We adjust to things like the upsurge of homelessness in the streets of North American cities: once it was appalling, now we don't even see it; we walk around people sleeping on subway grates, and we ignore tin cups in outstretched hands. In the same way, we've come to accept the perpetual butchery in parts of Africa as simply a fixture of the geopolitical landscape. And we acknowledge, then forget about, the grotesque differences in wealth on this planet. The wretchedness of Kabul may be eleven kilometers away, but we can be completely blind to it. After a while, it isn't jarring anymore, and our outrage fades away.

Our brains give us other abilities, though, that can help us compensate for this tendency to adjust and forget. One is our capacity for metaphor—to see patterns and similarities among vastly different things and to allow ideas to flow across the porous boundaries of the specialized intelligences in our minds. Metaphors open windows to new ways of seeing ourselves and our situation; without them I could not have put together the pieces of the ingenuity puzzle that lie all around us. In Las Vegas, artificial light, the night sky, and pyramids became for me metaphors for our technological prowess, for the mystery of the natural world and the awe it should inspire, and for our attempts to retain authority in an increasingly chaotic world. In Las Vegas, and especially in Patna after sharing a drink with my rickshaw driver, I came to see water as not only something urgently real and essential to our lives, but also as a metaphor for our intimate dependence on the natural world and for our common needs that cut across all boundaries of class, caste, religion, and ethnicity.

And then there was Komal Kumari's face. I recalled it as she'd stood in the doorway of her parents' house just a week before. It no longer looked weary or distant as in the photograph on my office wall. She looked shy, a bit bewildered, and happy because of all the attention she was suddenly getting. While this time Komal Kumari's face seemed animated by emotions that were entirely different from those that my camera's eye had caught before, I knew it at once.

I'd traveled to the other side of the planet to find one face among billions. I could do this because our brains give us a truly uncanny ability to remember faces, to identify one in a vast crowd. And this ability, and that child's face in particular, came to represent for me our vital capacity to use recognition and empathy to link ourselves together into larger communities. If I could just imagine the faces of the people in Kabul, down on the ground below me—if I could hold in my mind's eye, just for a moment, an image of what they might look like—maybe I could overcome my pernicious tendency to adjust and forget. Faces turn people into individuals, and by recognizing, remembering, and imagining faces, we can make bridges between our separate selves and turn individuals into communities.

As ingenuity gaps widen the gulfs of wealth and power among us, we need imagination, metaphor and empathy more than ever, to help us remember each other's essential humanity. I believe this will be the central challenge of the coming century—one that will shape everything else about who we are and what we become. Anatol Rapoport, a pioneering mathematical psychologist and one of the wisest people I have ever known, once told me: "The moral development of a civilization is measured by the breadth of its sense of community." Have we paid enough attention to the moral development of the global civilization we are creating today?

A sense of community, of shared humanity, isn't the only thing we need. If we're to maintain and improve our civilization in the next century, we also need to close, as best we can, those ingenuity gaps that debilitate people and societies. And here a final metaphor—the metaphor of flight—may point us in the right direction. The idea of flight wound its way through my entire quest to piece together the ingenuity puzzle. Sometimes—as with United Flight 232 or the troubles plaguing the U.S. air-traffic control system—it stood for the perils and unknown unknowns of modern technology. Other times, though, it stood for how technology often frees us from age-old constraints and allows us to seek new horizons. In the pop mythology of our modern civilization (and even in myths going all the way back to Icarus), the idea of flight is closely associated with the idea of freedom, and there are similar links between the ideas of flight, exploration, and discovery. In my own quest, flight gave me the freedom and opportunity to explore diverse places around the world—from Canary Wharf to Las Vegas—and it allowed me to find one face among billions.

But what can flight tell us about closing our ingenuity gaps? It turns out that we can learn some practical lessons from the experience of United 232. The captain of that ill-fated aircraft, Al Haynes, has since identified several factors that contributed to the relative success of the crash-landing, in particular luck, communications, preparation, and cooperation.[2] The people on the flight were lucky because it was daytime, the weather was good, and the accident occurred close to an airport. Good communication with the ground meant that the right personnel and equipment were ready when the plane touched down. And the people of Sioux City were well prepared because, amazingly, the city's airport, hospitals, fire departments, and other emergency teams had conducted a full drill for *exactly* that kind of accident only two years before. Perhaps the most critical factor of all, though, was cooperation, especially cooperation among members of the flight crew. Nearly a decade previously, United Airlines had started training cockpit crews to solve problems by sharing their expertise cooperatively, especially in emergencies, rather than by simply following the captain's commands. This training paid off brilliantly for United 232; in fact, Al Haynes believes that without it no one would have survived.

The factors that Al Haynes identified take on their greatest importance in times of crisis, when we have to supply ingenuity in response to sudden, nonlinear events, like the explosion of a plane's engine, a panic in financial markets, or a sharp, unfavorable change in climate. While we can't do much about luck in such circumstances (we can only hope that it generally works in our favor), we can do a lot about communications, preparation, and cooperation. For instance, we can ensure in advance that there are good communication links between the key people and groups who will need to talk to each other, and we can practice over and over again our responses to a wide range of possible emergencies. Most important, we can develop procedures for cooperative decision-making to make sure that people's experiential knowledge—the wisdom that comes from years of working with a complex system like a plane or a financial market—is available and used when it's needed most.

If we want to close the ingenuity gaps that we face in our fast-changing world, we need to recognize that each gap actually presents us with *two* distinct problems represented by the two "sides" of the gap: there's the problem of the rising requirement for ingenuity, and then there's the problem of supplying that ingenuity. Solutions to an ingenuity gap can involve either reducing the requirement for ingenuity or increasing its supply (or both). But for some reason we tend to think first—and sometimes almost exclusively—about increasing supply. It seems that we would rather look for after-the-fact solutions to the difficult problems we face than prevent our problems from becoming so difficult in the first place.

It's true that boosting ingenuity supply is often a sensible way to go. The metaphor of flight suggests we're very good at inventing things to free ourselves from constraints and to explore new possibilities for our lives. Whether it's a matter of meeting our energy demand by inventing new types of fuel, feeding a still rapidly growing world population by boosting grain yields, stabilizing the international financial system by making available more information on countries' finances, or stopping mass violence by setting up an international rapid-reaction force, we need to supply more and better ingenuity for more and better technologies and institutions.[3] This means that we should dramatically increase our funding for scientific research in critical areas—like energy and agriculture—in the hope we can invent new technologies. And it also means that we should reform existing international institutions (from the IMF to the UN) and build a range of new institutions (for example, to deal with climate change) to ensure global prosperity and peace. While a formal world government is probably not in the cards, at least not for a long time, we must accept that our *governance* of our global affairs has to become vastly more elaborate and sophisticated.[4]

But it's essential that we not forget about the other side of our ingenuity gaps—about our soaring requirement for ingenuity. Partly because of our larger populations, rising wealth per capita, and more powerful technologies, and partly because of our hypercompetitive economic and social systems, we seem to be doing more of everything, over larger areas, faster than ever before. It's as if we've got our collective foot slammed down on the world's accelerator pedal. We need to think creatively about how we might slow things down, how we might ease up a bit on that pedal. I'm convinced that if we don't—if we allow the complexity and turbulence of the systems we've created to go on increasing, unchecked—these systems will sometimes fail catastrophically. In other words, nonlinearities will, at some point, slow down and simplify things for us, whether we like it or not.

There are reasons for hope on this score: things are already happening that may slow our skyrocketing need for ingenuity. Birth rates are falling around the world, which in time will bring our population growth to an end; people are coming up with ingenious technologies for lowering our consumption of natural resources, which will lessen the burden we are imposing on the planet's environment; and there are some well-developed, albeit controversial, ideas for dampening the volatility of international capital flows.[5] But one fundamental change that could slow things down gets far too little attention: change in our values and in our perception of ourselves.

This can be most clearly seen in our consumption habits. What we value as wealth and as the "good life" has an enormous effect on our need for ingenuity. People in poor countries quite reasonably want more material things—things that those of us in rich countries think are essential and take for granted, like refrigerators, electricity, and good clothes. But are sports utility vehicles, five-bedroom houses, year-round air-conditioning, private summer cottages, and vacations in the Caribbean also essential elements of the good life? Do they really make us that much happier? Probably not, yet most of us in rich countries aspire to these things, and when we get them we greatly increase our environmental burden, especially, for instance, our output of carbon dioxide. A shift to less material values in rich societies would help reduce our overall need for ingenuity to manage our relationship with our environment.

More profoundly, we need to rethink our most basic perceptions of ourselves. Our seemingly limitless ingenuity has convinced many of us that we can have everything we want, that all things are within our grasp, and that we can separate ourselves from the essential foundations of life on the planet. But we really need to think less about what we want, and to remember instead our place in the broader scheme of things; to feel occasionally some awe before nature; and to reintroduce some real humility and prudence into our collective consciousness.

The great British geneticist and philosopher J. B. S. Haldane once wrote: "The universe is not only queerer than we suppose, but queerer than we *can* suppose."[6] He was right. But this is more than just a matter of fact: it's fundamentally an emotional, moral, and even spiritual matter, and it's in these terms that we can most clearly see the danger of our technocratic arrogance. Our modern approach to solving our problems tends to be rational and analytic—and thus starkly impoverished. I believe that reason by itself is not—cannot be—our ultimate salvation, and that we must instead call on our uniquely human capacity to integrate emotion and reason: to mobilize our moral sensibilities, create within ourselves a sense of the ineffable, and achieve a measured awareness of our place in the universe. These moral abilities are also innate human strengths, and if we can use them to root out some of our arrogance about our capacity to understand and control the complex systems around us, maybe we'll be more inclined—to paraphrase Mike Whitfield—to tread softly in their presence.

Just over nine hours later, the 747 touched down at Heathrow airport. I had a twelve-hour layover before my flight to Toronto, so after checking my bags I caught a cab into London to meet a friend in Lewisham, a borough across the Thames from the Isle of Dogs. It was early on a weekend morning, the streets were largely deserted, and the cabby was able to take me right through the heart of the city. Again I felt as if I had hyperlinked to an entirely different reality: from New Delhi with its congestion, heat, grime, and omnipresent poverty to the tidy, modern, wealthy, and weirdly empty streets of London.

After breakfast, I talked my friend into visiting Canary Wharf, since we could see Cesar Pelli's bold tower, capped with its pyramid, from her house. This time, though, I approached from a different direction: we took the Greenwich foot tunnel under the Thames into the Isle of Dogs and walked north through Millwall towards the tower. We passed the things I'd seen on my last visit—the restored loading cranes looking like praying mantises, the newspaper printing plant, and the redoubt of low-income housing surrounded on all sides by fences and walls. In the sun of a fresh, midsummer morning, though, everything looked far more benign than it had in the evening gloom many months before.

Soon, with Canary Wharf now in full view in front of us, we reached the edge of South Quay, a broad stretch of water that blocked our progress. This was where I had crossed that futuristic pedestrian bridge—the one constructed in a long horizontal spiral like a writhing snake. But this time the bridge wasn't there: it had been turned sideways on its pivot in the middle of the quay, so we couldn't cross. According to a local resident out for a morning stroll, the bridge's deck was very slippery when wet, and someone had recently been blown off it in a storm, so the bridge was closed till it could be made safer. Maybe, my friend remarked, a little less architectural finesse, and a little more practical engineering, would have made a better bridge.

Three kids, boys about ten years old or so—probably from the low-income houses nearby—were sitting on their battered bikes by the edge of the quay. They seemed to be waiting for the bridge to turn back so they could cross. We talked to them about the bridge for a couple of minutes, and they accepted that waiting any longer would be futile.

"Do you know," one of the boys asked, as they got ready to leave, "if there's a fountain over there?"

"Sure," my friend replied, "there's a fountain right in front of that big tower."

"Are there coins in it?"

"I don't know. Why?"

"Because we want to get some coins from the fountain!" And with that they laughed and rode off down the side of the quay, taking the long route to the tower. Now that was one of life's sharp edges! Three boys from a poor zone of London going to look for coins in the central fountain of a complex of buildings housing the immense forces of capitalism and worth hundreds of millions of dollars.

As the boys disappeared in the distance, we followed them on foot around the edge of the quay, and down the grand, Haussman-like avenue into the center of Canary Wharf. We were now in Cabot Square, in the middle of a bowl of huge buildings, with Pelli's tower soaring above us on one side and with five distinct types of architecture surrounding us on the others. One building recalled nineteenth-century Neoclassicism, another 1920s Modernism, and yet another the dreary utilitarianism of the 1960s. I looked at the tower. "The important buildings," I remembered Pelli had said, "are not in the scale of the body of man, but in the scale of his ideas. St. Paul's was like that, and I hope in its own way the tower will be as well."

On my previous visit to London I'd had dinner with an investment banker who worked in these buildings. He told me about an incident that had occurred two years before the IRA bombing on the other side of the writhing bridge. According to a security guard at the complex, a truck full of explosives had been discovered early one morning parked in this very square. The bomb's detonator had failed to go off. I later checked through back issues of London papers for any references to this event, but found none. Although I couldn't confirm that the story was true, it certainly didn't sound implausible. In this confined space, the damage would have been horrific. For a split second an image flashed through my mind—a boiling purple and orange fireball rising upwards, the buildings around us heaving from the force of the explosion, façades disintegrating and floors collapsing on each other, office workers' faces—faces again—shredded by shrapnel of concrete and glass.

There will be more attempts to attack the symbols of wealth and power in our rich societies—attacks by aggrieved people with newly acquired knowledge about the technologies of violence. Because our governments are acutely aware of this danger, very few will succeed. But as the head of the Central Bank of Sri Lanka told me, a terrorist only has to be successful once, while we've got to be alert all the time. And the potential costs of a successful attack could be much higher than we realize: an acquaintance of mine who has closely studied the risks of bio-terrorism argues that a single large-scale strike on a major Western city—say an attack in New York, Washington, London, or Paris that killed 50,000 people—could send urban property values plummeting in cities around the world, as people suddenly realized how vulnerable they are in dense urban cores.[7] An impossibly apocalyptic scenario, surely—until we remember that one such group, Aum Shinrikyo in Tokyo, tried to launch exactly this kind of attack.

Our intertwined global economic and financial systems are resilient enough to absorb a wide range of shocks, but a worldwide collapse of urban property values is almost certainly not one of them.

It was peaceful in Cabot Square—a couple of cabs idled quietly at a taxi stand and a family of tourists craned their necks to admire the buildings. The three boys, though, were nowhere to be seen. We strolled over to the fountain and the large circular pool that surrounded it and sat down on the carved low wall of black granite containing the pool. A shaft of sun reached us from high between the buildings. I looked down into the pool, past its rippled surface, and into its cool, dark depths.

There were no coins in the fountain.

NOTES

_____

PROLOGUE

1. Two potentially malicious interpretations of my argument must be put to rest at the outset. First, I am emphatically not arguing that there are innate differences in intelligence across human societies or ethnic groups. There is no credible empirical evidence to suggest that such differences exist. Second, I am not arguing that poor societies are poor because their inhabitants aren't intelligent or innovative. As I'll show in the following chapters, the principal obstacle to the supply of ingenuity, in poor countries as well as rich, is political opposition by powerful groups whose interests would be hurt by reform. In sum, my argument is about characteristics and constraints that are common to all human beings and all human societies.

CHAPTER ONE

1. Most of the technical information in the following pages is from "United Airlines Flight 232, McDonnell Douglas DC-10, Sioux Gateway Airport, Sioux City, Iowa, July 19, 1989," *National Transportation Safety Board (NTSB) Aircraft Accident Report AAR 90/06* (Washington, D.C.: National Transportation Safety Board, 1990); the cockpit conversation is from Stephan Corrie, "Cockpit Voice Recorder Group Chairman's Factual Report of Investigation" (Washington, D.C.: National Transportation Safety Board, 1990). Alfred Haynes, the captain of the flight, and Steven Predmore provided some interpretive details.
2. The right turns were unintentional and were caused by drag from damage to the plane's flight surfaces and skin. Turning right was also the only way the crew could correct the craft's heading.
3. The transcript of the cockpit conversation offers two possible interpretations of the first officer's exact words here. He may instead have exclaimed, "We're trying! We're trying! We're trying!"
4. Thanks are due to Jack Drake, Chief, Aviation Engineering Division, National

Transportation Safety Board of the United States, for data on the average RPM of a General Electric CF-6 engine on a DC-10.

5. *NTSB Aircraft Accident Report AAR 90/06*, 86–7.
6. Steven Predmore, "The Dynamics of Group Performance: A Multiple Case Study of Effective and Ineffective Flightcrew Performance," Ph.D. dissertation, University of Texas at Austin, 1992.
7. Ibid., 26.
8. Ibid., 40.
9. Interview with Steve Predmore, October 20, 1997.
10. "The Dynamics of Group Performance," 38.
11. Predmore interview, October 20, 1997.
12. "United Airlines DC-10," *NTSB Aircraft Accident Report*, 50.
13. The findings of this research are presented in Thomas Homer-Dixon, *Environment, Scarcity, and Violence* (Princeton: Princeton University Press, 1999).
14. Paul Romer, "Two Strategies for Economic Development: Using Ideas and Producing Ideas," World Bank, *Proceedings of the World Bank Annual Conference on Development Economics, 1992* (Washington, D.C.: World Bank, 1993).
15. The British philosopher Alfred North Whitehead once wrote: "Civilization advances by extending the number of important operations which we can perform without thinking about them." Quoted in F. A. Hayek, "The Use of Knowledge in Society," *The American Economic Review* 35, no. 4 (September 1945): 528.
16. Ingenuity requirement must be measured against some benchmark. In my work on environmental stress, I defined this benchmark as the amount of ingenuity needed to compensate for any aggregate social disutility caused by the environmental stress or, in other words, the minimum amount of ingenuity that a society needs to maintain its current aggregate level of satisfaction in spite of the stress. Without such a benchmark, our need for ingenuity is, essentially, infinite, because there are always problems—environmental or otherwise—that need to be solved. See Homer-Dixon, *Environment, Scarcity, and Violence*, 111.
17. Thomas Homer-Dixon, "The Ingenuity Gap: Can Poor Countries Adapt to Resource Scarcity?" *Population and Development Review* 21, no. 3 (1995): 587–612.
18. H. G. Wells, *Mind at the End of Its Tether* (New York: Didier, 1946), 34.
19. William McNeill, "Control and Catastrophe in Human Affairs," in *The Global Condition: Conquerors, Catastrophes, & Community* (Princeton: Princeton University Press, 1992), 136.
20. Jerome Glenn and Theodore Gordon, eds., *1997 State of the Future: Implications for Action Today* (Washington, D.C.: American Council for the United Nations University, 1997), 29.
21. The philosopher of science Nicolas Rescher has recently written an interesting treatment of the sources and implications of complexity whose arguments are in some respects similar to those I advance in this book. Unfortunately, much of Rescher's treatment is difficult to follow, and his arguments omit key literature on complex systems. He also fails, I believe, to provide an integrated set of conceptual tools that can help the reader better understand the modern world. See Nicholas Rescher, *Complexity: A Philosophical Overview* (New Brunswick, N.J.: Transaction, 1998).

22. Richard Cooper, *Environment and Resource Policies for the World Economy* (Washington, D.C.: Brookings Institution, 1994), 4.

23. See the analyses in Vaclav Smil, *Energy, Food, Environment: Realities, Myths, Options* (Oxford: Oxford University Press, 1987), 84; and Vaclav Smil, *General Energetics: Energy in the Biosphere and Civilization* (New York: John Wiley, 1991), 242–48. Richard Cooper might respond that ground-based solar collectors are not necessary: energy can be microwaved to Earth from satellite solar collectors orbiting the planet. While perhaps feasible, such a project would present enormous technical difficulties; at present, we cannot be certain that these difficulties are surmountable.

24. In a footnote, Cooper implies that brainpower is infinitely available over the long run. In economists' terms, its supply schedule is *perfectly elastic.*

25. Julian Simon, ed., *The State of Humanity* (Cambridge, Massachusetts: Blackwell, 1995), 7.

26. I was particularly influenced by the ideas of Simon, who was a professor of business administration at the University of Maryland at the time he died in 1998, as well as those of Jesse Ausubel of Rockefeller University. See, especially, Simon's *The Ultimate Resource II: People, Materials, and Environment* (Princeton, New Jersey: Princeton University Press, 1996). Three excellent examples of Ausubel's thinking are: "Resources and Environment in the 21st Century: Seeing past the Phantoms," *World Energy Council Journal* (July 1998): 8–16; "The Liberation of the Environment," *Daedalus* 125, no. 33 (Summer 1996):1–17; and "Does Climate Still Matter?" *Nature* 350, no. 6320 (25 April 1991): 649–52.

27. Food and Agriculture Organization, *The State of Food Insecurity in the World* (Rome: FAO, 1999), 10.

28. The political scientist Kal Holsti notes that people face "multiple realities" when considering grand issues like humanity's future; it's possible to build a thoroughly supported case for a great range of points of view. "My impression," he says, "is that many of the theoretical arguments . . . are really debates about optimism and pessimism, [about] our very general outlooks toward the world in which we live." K. J. Holsti, "The Horsemen of the Apocalypse: At the Gate, Detoured, or Retreating?" *International Studies Quarterly* 30, no. 4 (1986): 356.

29. James Gustave Speth, "The Plight of the Poor," *Foreign Affairs* 78, no. 3 (May/June 1999): 13–14. Speth notes that "individual consumption has dropped by about one percent annually in more than sixty [countries]."

30. The statistics in the previous two sentences are drawn from United Nations Development Programme, *Human Development Report 1998* (New York: Oxford University Press, 1998), 29–30.

31. Barbara Crossette, "In Numbers, the Heavy Now Match the Starved," *New York Times*, 18 January 2000, national edition, A10.

32. "Sharp Rise Found in Drug-Resistant Bacteria," *New York Times*, 25 August 1995, national edition, 8.

33. Robert Kates, B. L. Turner, and William Clark, "The Great Transformation," in B. L. Turner II et al., eds., *The Earth as Transformed by Human Action* (Cambridge: Cambridge University Press, 1990), 13.

34. World Meteorological Organization and United Nations Environment Programme, *Scientific Assessment of Ozone Depletion, 1998*, WMO Ozone Report, no. 44, (Geneva: WMO, 1998). The recent rapid decline in atmospheric concentrations of ozone-depleting chemicals has been largely the result of a decline in a single chemical, the cleaning agent trichloroethane. Concentrations of another powerful chemical, halon-1211, have remained constant for several years. See S. A. Montzka et al., "Present and Future Trends in the Atmospheric Burden of Ozone-Depleting Halogens," *Nature* 398, no. 6729 (22 April 1999): 690–94.

35. Ozone Secretariat, United Nations Environment Programme, "Environmental Effects of Ozone Depletion: 1998 Assessment, Executive Summary," *Journal of Photochemistry and Photobiology B: Biology* 46 (1998): 1–4.

36. Andrew Blaustein et al., "UV Repair and Resistance to Solar UV-B in Amphibian Eggs: A Link to Population Declines?" *Proceedings of the National Academy of Sciences, USA* 91, no. 5 (1994): 1791–95.

37. Andrew Blaustein and David Wake, "The Puzzle of Declining Amphibian Populations," *Scientific American* 272, no. 4 (April 1995): 657–66; Stephen Richards, Keith McDonald, and Ross Alford, "Declines in Populations of Australia's Endemic Tropical Rainforest Frogs," *Pacific Conservation Biology* 1 (1993): 66–77; Karen Lips, "Decline of a Tropical Montane Amphibian Fauna," *Conservation Biology* 12, no.1 (February 1998): 106–17; and Charles Drost and Garry Fellers, "Collapse of a Regional Frog Fauna in the Yosemite Area of the California Sierra Nevada, USA," *Conservation Biology* 10, no. 2 (April 1996): 414–25.

38. J. Alan Pounds, Michael Fogden, and John Campbell, "Biological Response to Climate Change on a Tropical Mountain," *Nature* 398, no. 6728 (15 April 1999): 611–15; and Lee Berger et al., "Chytridiomycosis Causes Amphibian Mortality Associated with Population Declines in the Rain Forests of Australia and Central America," *Proceedings of the National Academy of Sciences, USA* 95 (July 1998): 9031–36.

39. This estimate is derived from the *Global Biodiversity Assessment*, the state-of-the-art account of scientific understanding of biodiversity. Using species-area models based on island biogeography, R. Barbault and S. Sastrapradja conclude that "recent rates of deforestation . . . translate into a rate of extinction of about 0.25 percent per annum." The *Assessment* notes that this figure "should be interpreted as the fraction of species eventually going extinct according to the species-area relationship." See Barbault and Sastrapradja, "Generation, Maintenance and Loss of Biodiversity," section 4 in *Global Biodiversity Assessment*, ed. V. H. Heywood and R. T. Watson (Cambridge: Cambridge University Press, 1995), 198.

40. William Stevens, "One in Every 8 Plant Species Is Imperiled, a Survey Finds," *New York Times*, 9 April 1998, national edition, A1.

41. On coral bleaching, see Clive Wilkinson et al., "Ecological and Socioeconomic Impacts of 1998 Coral Mortality in the Indian Ocean: An ENSO Impact and a Warning of Future Change?" *Ambio* 28, no. 2 (March 1999): 188–96. The authors write that in 1998 "massive mortality occurred on the reefs of Sri Lanka, Maldives, India, Kenya, Tanzania, and Seychelles with mortalities of up to 90 percent in many shallow areas."

42. Captain Alfred Haynes, *United 232: Coping with the "One Chance-in-a-Billion" Loss of All Flight Controls,"* Flight Safety Foundation; available at www.natcavoice.org/av/avs/ual232.htm.

43. Jerry Schemmel, with Kevin Simpson, *Chosen to Live* (Littleton, Colorado: Victory Publishing, 1996), 56.

CHAPTER TWO

1. The name Hoe comes from Old English, and it means "projecting ridge of land or promontory." The word is also sometimes written Hough or Heugh.

2. For a history of the lighthouse, see Fred Madjalany, *The Red Rocks of Eddystone* (London: Longmans and Green, 1959).

3. I interviewed Mike Whitfield in September 1997; he retired as director of the MBA in June 1999.

4. Mike Whitfield, "Elementary Cycling," review of *Cycles of Life: Civilization and the Biosphere*, by Vaclav Smil (San Francisco: Freeman, 1997), in *Nature* 386 (6 March 1997): 35–36.

5. V. I. Vernadsky, "The Biosphere and the Noösphere," *American Scientist* 33 (January 1945): 1–12.

6. For a fuller discussion of emergence in complex systems, see Yaneer Bar-Yam, "Concepts: Emergence and Complexity," in *Dynamics of Complex Systems* (Reading, Massachusetts: Addison-Wesley, 1992), 9–14.

7. Whitfield noted that the thermostat metaphor really applies only to concentrations of greenhouse gases in the atmosphere.

8. United Nations Population Division, *World Population Prospects 1950-2050: The 1998 Revision* (New York: United Nations Population Division, Department of Economic and Social Affairs, 1998).

9. The Italian demographer Antonio Golini estimates the lower bound of fertility for large populations as 0.7 to 0.8 children per woman. See Antonio Golini, "How Low Can Fertility Be? An Empirical Exploration," *Population and Development Review* 24, no. 1 (1998): 59–73.

10. United Nations Population Division, *World Population Prospects*.

11. Robert Engelman, "Human Population Prospects: Implications for Ecological Security," *Environmental Change and Security Project: Report* 3 (1997): 47–54.

12. About one-third of the UN's recent reduction in its 2050 global population projection, from 9.4 billion in its 1996 estimate to 8.9 billion in its 1998 estimate, is due to increasing mortality rates in sub-Saharan Africa and parts of South Asia. Recent statistics on the effect of AIDS on mortality rates in poor countries, especially in Africa, are startling. In Botswana, life expectancy has dropped from 61 to 47 years, and is projected to drop to 38 between 2005 and 2010. Deaths from AIDS have depressed Zimbabwe's population growth rate from around 2.4 percent to 1.4 percent. United Nations Population Fund, *6 Billion: A Time for Choices, The State of World Population, 1999* (New York: UNFPA, 1999), 24.

13. See, for example, Ben Wattenberg, "The Population Explosion Is Over," *New York Times Magazine*, 23 November 1997, 60–63. See also Barbara Crossette, "How to Fix a Crowded World: Add People," *Sunday New York Times*, Week in Review, 2 November 1997, national edition, 1; Nicholas Eberstadt, "The Population Implosion," *Wall Street Journal*, 16 October 1997, A22; Max Singer, "The Population Surprise," *Atlantic Monthly* (August 1999): 22–25.

14. These challenges are nicely outlined in Peter Peterson, *Gray Dawn: How the Coming Age Wave Will Transform America—And the World* (New York: Times Books, 1999). See also Nicholas Eberstadt, "World Population Implosion?" *The Public Interest*, no. 129 (Fall 1997): 3–22. On the implications of low fertility for Europe, see Michael Specter, "Population Implosion Worries a Graying Europe," *New York Times*, 10 July 1998, national edition, A1.

15. John Bongaarts, "Population Policy Options in the Developing World," *Science* 263, no. 5148 (11 February 1994): 771–76.

16. Steven Holmes, "Global Crisis in Population Still Serious, Group Warns," *New York Times*, 31 December 1997, national edition, A7.

17. John Bongaarts and Rodolfo Bulatao, "Completing the Demographic Transition," *Population and Development Review* 25, no. 3 (September 1999): 515–29; Wolfgang Lutz, Warren Sanderson, and Sergei Scherbov, "Doubling of World Population Unlikely," *Nature* 387, No. 6635 (19 June 1997): 803–5.

18. See, for instance, Ester Boserup, *The Conditions of Agricultural Growth: The Economics of Agrarian Change under Population Pressure* (Chicago: Aldine, 1965); and Julian Simon, *The Ultimate Resource 2* (Princeton: Princeton University Press, 1996).

19. An early statement of this argument can be found in Ansley Coale and Edgar Hoover, *Population Growth and Economic Development in Low-income Countries: A Case Study of India's Prospects* (Princeton: Princeton University Press, 1959). The Coale and Hoover position was contentious among demographers and development economists, some of whom responded that there was no evidence that rapid population growth reduced domestic savings. Recent statistical research, however, has provided some support for the idea. See Allen Kelley and Robert Schmidt, *Population and Income Change: Recent Evidence*, World Bank Discussion Paper No. 249 (Washington, D.C.: World Bank, 1994). Most important, some analysts have concluded that lower fertility rates enabled East Asian countries to significantly boost domestic savings, capital investment and, consequently, economic growth from the 1970s into the 1990s. See Matthew Higgins and Jeffrey Williamson, "Age Structure Dynamics in Asia and Dependence on Foreign Capital," *Population and Development Review* 23 (1997): 261–93.

20. Although urban population growth has been lower than expected since 1980, it is still high. Between 1995 and 2030, the world's urban population will probably double, from 2.6 to 5.1 billion, at which point about 60 percent of the human population will live in cities. See Ellen Brennan, "Population, Urbanization, Environment, and Security: A Summary of the Issues," *Comparative Urban Studies: Occasional Paper Series*, no. 22 (Washington, D.C.: Woodrow Wilson International Center for Scholars, 1999). On urban population growth projections, see Martin Brockerhoff, "Urban Growth in Developing Countries: A Review of

Projections and Predictions," *Working Paper*, Policy Research Division, no. 131 (New York: Population Council, 1999).

21. Martin Brockerhoff and Ellen Brennan, "The Poverty of Cities in Developing Regions," *Population and Development Review* 24, no. 1 (1998): 75–114.

22. Thomas Homer-Dixon, *Environment, Scarcity, and Violence* (Princeton: Princeton University Press, 1999), 164–66.

23. This product formula was first introduced by Paul Ehrlich and John Holdren, "Impact of Population Growth," *Science* 171, no. 3977 (26 March 1971): 1212–17; for a revised version, see Paul Ehrlich and Anne Ehrlich, *The Population Explosion* (New York: Touchstone, 1990), 58–59; and for a discussion of this approach's weaknesses, see Thomas Homer-Dixon, "Environmental Scarcity," chapter 4, especially endnote 6 in *Environment, Scarcity, and Violence* (Princeton: Princeton University Press, 1999), 49–52, 194–95.

24. This estimate is based on the assumption that growth in Gross Domestic Product (GDP) per capita is roughly correlated with growth in per capita material consumption and waste production. Some might question this assumption, because in technologically more advanced economies in which information and services have become very important, economic growth shows evidence of decoupling from resource consumption. From the early 1970s to the mid-1980s, the *material intensity* of economic production (i.e., the quantity of materials or natural resources used to produce a dollar of GDP) in these economies declined quite rapidly. Since then, however, energy intensity, a major component of material intensity, has not declined as quickly, so there is reason to doubt that the decoupling will continue indefinitely. Moreover, the assumption of a close relationship between economic growth and material consumption is entirely reasonable for economies in the resource-intensive and "dirty" early and middle stages of industrialization. The majority of the world's economic growth in the twentieth century was of this kind, as will be a large fraction of the growth in developing countries in the first half of the twenty-first century.

Calculations like the one presented here must be treated with caution. Although common and useful, they both overestimate and underestimate human beings' actual environmental impact. They overestimate impact, because a certain proportion of the increased wealth produced during the period in question may be used for pollution control and other measures to protect the environment. They underestimate impact, because the effects of human activities on the environment are often cumulative. The incorporation in the calculation of *annual* growth in per capita GDP implies that environmental impacts from the production of that GDP occur entirely within the year the wealth is produced. In reality, however, the impacts may persist for years, decades or centuries afterwards.

For the calculation here, I used Angus Maddison's estimate of world per capita GDP in 1900 and 1989 ($1,263 and $5,197 in 1990 Geary Khamis dollars, respectively), extrapolated to 1999, to give a 1999 GDP per capita of $5,634. See "Table G-3. World and Regional Averages: GDP per Capita, 1820-1992," in Angus Maddison, *Monitoring the World Economy: 1820-1992* (Paris: OECD, 1995). On material intensity of economic production in industrial countries, see Albert

Adriannse et al., *Resource Flows: The Material Basis of Industrial Economies* (Washington, D.C.: World Resources Institute, 1997), 13–16; and Eric Larson, Marc Ross, and Robert Williams, "Beyond the Era of Materials," *Scientific American* 254, no. 6 (June 1986): 34–41. Jesse Ausubel argues that we can dramatically reduce our impact on the global environment through innovative technologies, resource substitution, and improvements in our efficiency of resource use. See Ausubel, "Resources and Environment in the 21st Century: Seeing Past the Phantoms," *World Energy Council Journal* (July 1998): 8–16.

25. Adriannse et al., *Resource Flows*, 23.

26. Ibid., p. 15. Each $100 (U.S.) of income generated in rich countries requires the use of an astonishing three hundred kilograms of natural materials.

27. If population increases between 2000 and 2050 by a factor of one and a third, and consumption per capita doubles, the environmental impact will be two and two-thirds times as great at the end of the fifty years.

28. Multiplying the sixteenfold increase during the twentieth century by the further two-and-two-thirds increase in the first fifty years of the twenty-first gives a forty-threefold increase in impact on the global environment from 1900 to 2050. Because I am using GDP per capita to measure the impact of individual humans on the environment, this increase also represents the estimated growth in the total world economy from 1900 to 2050.

29. Between 2000 and 2050, the growth rate of humanity's annual environmental impact will decrease, but its absolute growth—that is, its growth in real terms—will be far larger than ever before. This fact is usually overlooked by those who argue that the human threat to the environment is exaggerated and that we have already solved many of our environmental problems. One of the best recent examples of this perspective is Gregg Easterbrook, *A Moment on the Earth* (New York: Viking Penguin, 1995). Between 1900 and 2000, the growth rate of impact was about 2.75 percent per year, which produced the sixteenfold increase during that period. By 2050, the rate will probably drop to around 1.5 percent, largely because of slower human population growth. Yet, over the next fifty years the absolute growth in the total quantity of materials, energy, and waste flowing annually through the world's economy will approach twice the absolute growth of the entire preceding century. This seemingly paradoxical outcome has a simple explanation: although the growth rate of total impact is lower from 2000 to 2050 than from 1900 to 2000, this rate is nevertheless multiplying a much larger base figure of human impact. If we are concerned about the future of the world's environment, then the absolute growth of humanity's impact and its total magnitude are of more immediate interest than changes in its growth rate.

30. The statistics in the preceding paragraph are drawn from Peter Vitousek, Harold Mooney, Jane Lubchenco, and Jerry Melillo, "Human Domination of Earth's Ecosystems," *Science* 277, 25 July 1997, 494–95; B. L. Turner et al., eds., *The Earth As Transformed by Human Action: Global and Regional Changes in the Biosphere over the Past 300 Years* (Cambridge, U.K.: Cambridge University Press with Clark University, 1990), 6; and World Resources Institute et al., *World Resources: 1998-99* (New York: Oxford University Press, 1998), 195. In a famous

1986 article, Vitousek and his colleagues estimated that nearly 40 percent of the terrestrial energy fixed biologically by primary producers (mostly plants) and not used by them in respiration (called *net primary production*) is consumed, co-opted, or lost because of human activities. See Peter Vitousek, Paul Ehrlich, Anne Ehrlich, and Pamela Matson, "Human Appropriation of the Products of Photosynthesis," *BioScience* 36, no. 6 (June 1986): 368–73.

31. R. Jeffrey Smith, "U.S., Russian Paratroops Join in Central Asian Jump," *Washington Post*, 16 September 1997 A12.

32. Evidence derived from carbon isotope ratios measured in the baleen plates of Bowhead whales feeding in the Bering Sea suggests a 30 to 40 percent decline in the productivity of the entire North Pacific ecosystem over the last three decades, a decline in that may be caused by rising sea surface temperatures. D. M. Schell, "Declining Carrying Capacity in the Bering Sea: Isotopic Evidence from Whale Baleen," *Limnology and Oceanography* 45 (March 2000): 459–62.

33. A polished and often persuasive account of this incident from the perspective of the forest industry can be found in Gerry Burch et al., *The Working Forest of British Columbia* (Madeira Park, B.C.: Harbour Publishing, 1995), 62–68.

34. Michael Williams, "Forests," in Turner et al., eds., *The Earth As Transformed by Human Action*, 179–201. Closed forests are those in which the branches of the trees largely obscure the ground when viewed from above.

35. Ian Noble and Rodolfo Dirzo, "Forests as Human-Dominated Ecosystems," *Science* 277 (25 July 1997), 522–25.

36. Iddo Wernick, Paul Waggoner, and Jesse Ausubel, "Searching for Leverage to Conserve Forests: The Industrial Ecology of Wood Products in the United States," *Journal of Industrial Ecology* 1, no. 3 (1998): 125.

37. WRI, *World Resources 1996-97* (New York: Oxford University Press, 1996), 205.

38. Three countries alone—Brazil, Indonesia, and Malaysia—accounted for over half this loss. World Resources Institute (WRI), *World Resources 1994-95* (New York: Oxford University Press, 1994), 130–35.

39. Tom Gardner-Outlaw and Robert Engelman, *Forest Futures: Population, Consumption and Wood Resources* (Washington, D.C.: Population Action International, 1999), 26.

40. The term "greenhouse effect" is contentious among specialists, because although the glass in greenhouses does trap some infrared radiation, greenhouses produce most of their warming effect by suppressing air circulation that would otherwise take away heat. For an amusing discussion of the debate surrounding this term, see Craig Bohren, *Clouds in a Glass of Beer: Simple Experiments in Atmospheric Physics* (New York: John Wiley, 1987), 83–84.

41. The consensus on the likely magnitude, rate, and timing of human-induced greenhouse warming is summarized in the contributions of Working Groups I and II to the Second Assessment Report of the Intergovernmental Panel on Climate Change. See J. T. Houghton et al., eds, *Climate Change 1995—The Science of Climate Change*, contribution of Working Group I to the Second Assessment Report of the Intergovernmental Panel on Climate Change (IPCC) (Cambridge: Cambridge University Press, 1996); and Robert T. Watson,

Marufu C. Zinyowera, and Richard H. Moss, eds., *Climate Change 1995—Impacts, Adaptions and Mitigation of Climate Change: Scientific-Technical Analyses*, contribution of Working Group II to the Second Assessment Report of the Intergovernmental Panel on Climate Change (IPCC) (Cambridge: Cambridge University Press, 1996).

42. Houghton et al., eds, *Climate Change 1995—Science of Climate Change*, 6.

43. William Stevens, "Warmer, Wetter, Sicker: Linking Climate to Health," *The New York Times*, 10 August 1998, national edition, A1; and William Stevens, "Song of the Millennium: Cool Prelude and a Fiery Coda," *New York Times*, 9 March 1999, national edition, D5.

44. William Stevens, "Thinning Sea Ice Stokes Debate on Climate," *New York Times*, 17 November 1999, national edition, A17.

45. The scientists who analyzed the Vostok ice cores assessed past atmospheric carbon dioxide concentrations by directly measuring the carbon dioxide level in air that was trapped in bubbles in the ice cores. However, to estimate past temperatures, they used as a proxy indicator a ratio of oxygen isotopes in the trapped air, a ratio that varies with air temperature. Some specialists question whether this proxy indicator is accurate, because it can be affected by factors other than temperature.

46. The principal technical articles on the Vostok cores are: J. Jouzel et al., "Vostok Ice Core: A Continuous Isotope Temperature Record over the Last Climatic Cycle (160,000 years)," *Nature* 329 (1 October 1987): 403–8; J. M. Barnola et al., "Vostok Ice Core Provides 160,000-Year Record of Atmospheric CO_2," *Nature* 329 (1 October 1987): 408–14; and J. R. Petit et al., "Climate and Atmosphere History of the Past 420,000 Years from the Vostok Ice Core, Antarctica," *Nature* 399 (3 June 1999): 429–36. See also J. M. Barnola et al., "CO_2-Climate Relationship As Deduced from Vostok Ice Core: A Re-Examination Based on New Measurements and on a Re-Evaluation of the Air Dating, *Tellus* 43B (1991): 83–90.

47. This extraordinary increase will not be prevented by the prospective international treaty—based on the 1997 Kyoto protocol—that will probably govern greenhouse gas emissions. Even if major countries strictly adhere to the emission targets in the treaty, which is extremely unlikely, their compliance will only slow, not stabilize or reverse, the buildup of greenhouse gases. See William Stevens, "Despite Pact, Gases Will Keep Rising," *New York Times*, 12 December 1997, national edition, A10.

48. Jenny McElwain, "Past Carbon Dioxide Levels and Proxy Indicators," *The Globe*, Internet publication of the United Kingdom Global Environmental Research Office, no. 41 (February 1998), 11–13, available at http://www.nerc.ac.uk/ukgeroff/globe41.htm.

49. Much of the information in the following paragraphs is drawn from Vaclav Smil, "Global Population and the Nitrogen Cycle," *Scientific American*, 277, no. 1 (July 1997), 76–81. See also Smil, *Cycles of Life: Civilization and the Biosphere* (New York: Scientific American Library, 1997), 111–39.

50. William Stevens, "Too Much of a Good Thing Makes Benign Nitrogen a Triple Threat," *New York Times*, 10 December 1996, national edition, B8.

51. Vaclav Smil, correspondence with author, 17 September 1998.

52. Smil, correspondence with author, 24 September 1999.

53. Ibid., 81.

54. Ibid., 79.

55. Tim Beardsley "Death in the Deep," *Scientific American*, 277, no. 5 (November 1997), 17–20; Carol Kaesuk Yoon, "A 'Dead Zone' Grows in the Gulf of Mexico," *New York Times*, 20 January 1998, national edition, B11; and the Louisiana Universities Marine Consortium at http://www.lumcon.edu.

56. "Prospects for biotechnology to provide a significant breakthrough in yield in the next ten to fifteen years are limited; its major near-term contribution will be to provide greater resistance to pests and diseases as well as enhanced stability by reducing periodic decline in yields." Nural Islam, "Overview," chap. 1 in *Population and Food in the Early 21st Century: Meeting Future Food Demand of an Increasing Population*, ed. Nural Islam (Washington, D.C.: The International Food Policy Research Institute [IFPRI], 1995), 4.

57. For a survey, see "Nitrogen from Mountains to Fjords," *Ambio*, Special Issue 26, no. 5 (August 1997).

58. A more sanguine view is that of Charles Frink, Paul Waggoner, and Jesse Ausubel in "Nitrogen Fertilizer: Retrospect and Prospect," *Proceedings of the National Academy of Sciences, USA* 96 (February 1999): 1175–80. These authors suggest that the production and use of nitrogen fertilizer is beginning to level off. However, they appear to overemphasize the North American and European experience, while underestimating the likelihood of very rapid growth of fertilizer use in Asia and Africa.

59. For a full discussion of human cognitive adaptability and what it means for human adaptation to ecological change, see Robert Ornstein and Paul Ehrlich, *New World, New Mind: Moving toward Conscious Evolution* (New York: Touchstone, 1989).

60. Michael Manning and David Rejeski, "Sustainable Development and Risk: A Fit?" paper presented to conference on Comparative Risk and Priority Setting of Air Pollution Issues, Keystone, Colorado, June 7–11, 1993.

61. Edward O. Wilson, "Is Humanity Suicidal?" *BioSystems* 31 (1993): 242.

CHAPTER THREE

1. For a rich pictorial account of "the largest and most comprehensive system of docks the world has ever known," see Chris Ellmers and Alex Werner, *Dockland Life: A Pictorial History of London's Docks, 1860-1970* (London: Museum of London, 1991).

2. For a full and fascinating account, see Anthony Bianco, *The Reichmanns: Family, Faith, Fortune, and the Empire of Olympia & York* (Toronto: Random House Canada, 1997).

3. Ibid., 666.

4. Brian Edwards, *London Docklands: Urban Design in an Age of Deregulation* (Oxford: Butterworth Architecture, 1992).

5. Quoted in Bianco, *The Reichmanns*, 542.

6. David Harvey, *The Condition of Postmodernity: An Enquiry into the Origins of Cultural Change* (Cambridge, Massachusetts: Basil Blackwell, 1989), 9, 44, and 54.

7. Corporations in mature markets—such as those manufacturing common household items, from razors to batteries—work especially hard to increase product turnover rates. As Tom Vierhile of Marketing Intelligence Services says, "They have got to invent strategies to increase user rates. If you double the throwaway rate, you double sales." Quoted in Dana Canedy, "Where Nothing Lasts Forever," *New York Times*, 24 April 1998, national edition, C1.

8. In many of these parks, air pollution is actually worse than in urban areas, partly because they sit downwind from coal-fired power plants, and partly because many cities have aggressively pursued pollution abatement. See Matthew Wald, "An Ill Wind Blows at Vacation Sites," *New York Times*, 6 August 1999, national edition, A1.

9. Scientists now understand reasonably well the chemistry behind the formation of sulfate and nitrate haze, although the same cannot be said of the chemistry behind organic particles derived from compounds like evaporated solvents and paints. In clear skies, sulfur dioxide reacts with the hydroxyl radical (a molecule consisting of one hydrogen and one oxygen atom) to produce sulfuric acid; this compound then condenses on existing airborne particles to create sulfate haze. Such haze also arises from chemical reactions inside polluted clouds and fogs. In clear skies, nitrogen dioxide combines with the hydroxyl radical to form nitric acid, which then reacts with minute amounts of calcium or ammonia to form nitrate particles. Technical information on haze formation is available in Appendix A and B of National Research Council, Committee on Haze in National Parks and Wilderness Areas, *Protecting Visibility in National Parks and Wilderness Areas* (National Academy Press, 1993), 315–58; see also Figure 4.6 on 94.

10. Robert Charlson and Tom Wigley, "Sulfate Aerosol and Climate Change," *Scientific American* 270, no. 2 (February 1994): 48–57.

11. Personal communication with the author, 13 October 1998.

12. National Research Council, *Protecting Visibility*, 1. This report notes that natural visibility is less in the eastern than the western United States.

13. United States Environmental Protection Agency, Office of Air Quality Planning and Standards, chapter 1, "Executive Summary," and chapter 6, "Visibility Trends," in *National Air Quality and Emissions Trends, 1997*, (Washington, DC: 1997), http://www.epa.gov/oar/aqtrnd97/toc.html, 1, and 91–92.

14. Food and Agriculture Organization, *State of the World's Forests, 1999* (FAO: Rome, 1999), 3.

15. Annmarie Eldering et al., "Visibility Model Based on Satellite-Generated Landscape Data," *Environmental Science & Technology* 30, no. 2 (1996): 361–70.

16. William Nordhaus, "Do Real-Output and Real-Wage Measures Capture Reality? The History of Lighting Suggests Not," in *The Economics of New Goods*, Timothy Bresnahan and Robert Gordon, eds. (Chicago: University of Chicago Press, 1997), 29–66.

17. Nordhaus goes on: "The first recorded device, the Paleolithic oil lamp, was perhaps a tenfold improvement in efficiency over the open fire of Peking man,

which represents a 0.0004 percent per year improvement. Progression from the Paleolithic lamps to the Babylonian lamps represents an improvement rate of 0.01 percent per year; from Babylonian lamps to the candles of the early nineteenth century is an improvement at the more rapid rate of 0.04 percent per year. The Age of Invention showed a dramatic improvement in lighting efficiency, with an increase by a factor of nine hundred, representing a rate of 3.6 percent per year between 1800 and 1992." Ibid., 38.

18. Ibid., 33.

19. Ibid., 50. A lumen-hour is "the quantity of light corresponding to a flux of one lumen radiated for one hour," where a lumen is equal to "the flux emitted by a point source of intensity one candela (formerly, one candle) into a solid angle of one steradian." *Oxford English Dictionary*, 2d ed. (Oxford: Clarendon Press, 1989).

20. Brian Bowers provides a fascinating account in *Lengthening the Day: A History of Lighting Technology* (Oxford: Oxford University Press, 1998).

21. Stanley Coren, *Sleep Thieves: An Eye-Opening Exploration into the Science and Mysteries of Sleep* (New York: Free Press, 1996).

22. Jane Brody, "Facing up to the Realities of Sleep Deprivation," *New York Times*, 31 March 1998, national edition, B13.

23. For a discussion of how technology has changed the temporal rhythms of our behavior, see Leon Kreitzman, *The 24 Hour Society* (Profile, 1999), reviewed by Paolo Sassone-Corsi, *Nature* 401, no. 6756 (28 October 1999): 851.

24. On cities as loci of technological innovation, see "A Survey of Technology in the City," *Urban Age* 6, no. 2 (Autumn 1998): 9–21.

25. Lijbert Brussaard et al., "Biodiversity and Ecosystem Functioning in Soil," *Ambio* 26, no. 8 (1997): 563–70.

26. S. Ellis and A. Mellor, *Soils and Environment* (London: Routledge, 1995), especially chapter 2, "Soil Constituents and Properties," 9–56. See also John Reganold, Rober Papendick, and James Parr, "Sustainable Agriculture," *Scientific American*, 262, no. 6 (June 1990): 112–20.

27. Ellis and Mellor, *Soils and Environment*, 18–20.

28. Brussaard et al., "Biodiversity," 563.

29. And, in any case, notions of wilderness that depend on a strict distinction between the natural and human worlds are indefensible. William Cronon, "The Trouble with Wilderness; or, Going Back to the Wrong Nature," in *Uncommon Ground: Toward Reinventing Nature*, William Cronon, ed. (New York: W. W. Norton, 1995), 69–90, especially 88–89.

30. This is only one motive behind the rising interest in "wilderness" adventure; there are many others. The environmental historian William Cronon argues that wilderness is attractive as a source of the sacred and sublime and as a primitive frontier where people can test their mettle. Similarly, the journalist John Tierney contends that the male urge to find resources and mates through demonstrations of courage is behind the strange "glorification of exploration at a time when the entire planet has been mapped." And Edward Wilson has proposed that human beings have an "innately emotional affiliation" to other living organisms and the natural environment that might be satisfied by going to the

wilderness. See ibid.; John Tierney, "Explornography: The Call of the Pseudo-Wild," *New York Times Magazine*, 26 July 1998, 18–23; and Stephen Kellert and Edward Wilson, eds., *The Biophilia Hypothesis* (Washington, D.C.: Island Press, 1993).

31. I first came across the following night-sky exercise in Paul Churchland, *Scientific Realism and the Plasticity of Mind* (Cambridge, United Kingdom: Cambridge University Press, 1979), 30–34.

32. This analogy isn't quite correct, since the planets orbit at lower velocities the greater their distance from the sun, whereas if they were embedded in a fixed disc, their velocities would increase with distance.

33. For simplicity, I have left out of this illustration the fact that Earth is also rotating on its axis, a fact that makes visualization of our movement through space particularly hard. If you imagine looking down on the solar system from above Earth's North Pole, you will see Earth orbiting the sun counterclockwise and also turning counterclockwise on its axis. If we stand on Earth's equator, we are therefore moving feet-first around the sun at sunset and head-first at dawn.

34. "Our minds, perhaps, have been freed from the tyranny of a flat immobile Earth, but our *eyes* remain in bondage." Churchland, *Scientific Realism*, 30.

35. John Noble Wilford, "Hubble's Power Bolsters Count of Galaxies," *New York Times*, 8 January 1999, national edition, A15.

36. To arrive at this figure, I assumed two counts per second, a total of 5.25×10^{21} stars in the visible universe, and an age for the universe of thirteen billion years.

37. Giuliano Giuricin, "Galaxies, Local Supercluster: A Historical Perspective," in *The Astronomy and Astrophysics Encyclopedia*, ed. Stephen Maran (New York: Van Nostrand Reinhold, 1992), 256–58; and Timothy Ferris, *The Whole Shebang: A State-of-the-Universe(s) Report* (New York: Simon & Schuster, 1997), 150–52.

38. Shawn Carlson, "Unraveling the Secrets of Monarchs," *Scientific American* 277, no. 3 (September 1997): 90–91; Carol Kaesuk Yoon, "On the Trail of the Monarch, with the Aid of Chemistry," *New York Times*, 29 December 1998, national edition, D5.

39. Sandra Perez, Orley Taylor, and Rudolf Jander, "A Sun Compass in Monarch Butterflies," *Nature* 387, no. 6629 (1 May 1997): 29.

40. When I asked him to review these quotations for publication in late 1998, Bongaarts expressed greater doubt about the resilience of complex systems. "Given what we have seen with the Asian economic crisis in the last year, I'm not so sure anymore." However, he still believed that over the long run his original argument would prove correct.

CHAPTER FOUR

1. Although I believe that technology fundamentally shapes social behavior, I'm not suggesting that technology is an autonomous force that by itself drives the evolution of our societies. In this book I'm not, in other words, adopting a position of technological determinism. Technological change is always influenced

by social factors; moreover, it interacts with many other factors to produce its effects. A useful treatment of these issues is Merritt Roe Smith and Leo Marx, eds., *Does Technology Drive History? The Dilemma of Technological Determinism* (Cambridge, Mass.: MIT Press, 1995).

2. Quoted in David Shenk, *Data Smog: Surviving the Information Glut* (New York: HarperCollins, 1997), 56.

3. W. Brian Arthur, "On the Evolution of Complexity," in *Complexity: Metaphors, Models, and Reality*, eds. G. Cowan, D. Pines, and D. Meltzer, Santa Fe Institute Studies in the Sciences of Complexity, Proceedings, vol. 19 (Reading, Mass., 1994), 65–78.

4. The definition of "system" in this sentence is taken from Garnett Williams, *Chaos Theory Tamed* (Washington, D.C.: Joseph Henry Press, 1997), 3.

5. Brian Arthur, "On the Evolution of Complexity," 67.

6. What Brian Arthur calls the "genetic" material that is produced in this process can spread from one entity to another; thus microprocessors have been incorporated into everything from telephones to washing machines.

7. This idea is echoed in Stuart Kauffman, *At Home in the Universe: The Search for Laws of Self-Organization and Complexity* (New York: Oxford University Press, 1995), 296. He writes: "Persistent innovation in an economy may depend fundamentally on its supracritical character. New goods and services creates niches that call forth the innovations of further new goods and services."

8. Brian Arthur, "On the Evolution of Complexity," 71.

9. Ibid., 70–71.

10. Ibid., 73–76.

11. Isaac Newton: "Nature does nothing in vain, and more is in vain when less will serve; for Nature is pleased with simplicity, and affects not the pomp of superfluous causes." *Principia*, Book III. Cited in John Herman Randall, Jr., *The Making of the Modern Mind: A Survey of the Intellectual Background of the Present Age*, revised edition (Houghton Mifflin, 1940), 227.

12. Randall, *The Making of the Modern Mind*, 241. Randall provides a marvelously lucid and persuasive account of the intellectual revolutions discussed in the previous paragraph.

13. Robert Pirsig makes many points similar to those I make here in *Zen and the Art of Motorcycle Maintenance: An Inquiry into Values* (Toronto: Bantam Books, 1980).

14. A major reason for this steady increase in paperwork is Congress's continued passage of federal regulations requiring government agencies to collect information from the public. It is possible to argue, therefore, that the burden would be much higher without the constraint imposed by the Paperwork Reduction Act. See Michael Brostek, *Paperwork Reduction: Governmentwide Goals Unlikely to Be Met*, Testimony before the Committee on Small Business, U.S. Senate, GAO/T-GGD-97-114 (Washington, D.C.: General Accounting Office, 1997). The 1980 burden statistic has been adjusted upwards to reflect a later reassessment of the Treasury Department's paperwork burden. See Angela Antonelli, *Meeting on Curbing Regulatory Inflation: The U.S. Paperwork Reduction Act after Fifteen Years*, PUMA/REG(95)4 (Paris: Organization for Economic Co-operation and Development, 1995).

15. The classic discussion of tight coupling is Charles Perrow, *Normal Accidents: Living with High-Risk Technologies* (New York: Basic Books, 1984), especially 62–100.

16. Yaneer Bar-Yam provides this definition of resilience, or what he calls "robustness." Using principles of thermodynamics, he defines complexity and distinguishes between complex materials and complex organisms. See Bar-Yam, *Dynamics of Complex Systems* (Reading, Mass.: Addison-Wesley, 1992), 10–12, 58–61, and 91–95.

17. Paul Cilliers, *Complexity and Postmodernism: Understanding Complex Systems* (London: Routledge, 1998), 4. The boundaries of a complex system are usually defined by the purposes of people working within the system or observing it.

18. In the social sciences, the phenomenon I describe in this paragraph—the multiplication of components' effects within a system—is commonly referred to as *interactivity*. I have not used this term here, because, in common parlance, interactivity usually refers to no more than reciprocal causal links between things. "Synergy," unfortunately, is also not an entirely satisfactory term. In everyday use, synergy has a positive connotation; it implies that the combined actions of two or more things produces something better than they could produce by themselves. The way I use the word in this book, however, it can refer to either beneficial or harmful outcomes.

19. For a survey, see Chris Bright, "The Nemesis Effect," *World Watch* 12, no. 3 (May/June 1999): 12–23.

20. Joseph Tietge, et al. "NAAMP III: Deformed Frogs, Discussion of Findings Relative to Meeting Objectives," U.S. Environmental Protection Agency, Duluth, Minnesota, online paper at www.im.nbs.gov/naamp3/papers/6odf.html, 4.

21. Nonlinearity is closely related to some of the other features of complex systems discussed here. It is often a consequence of positive feedback, which tends to amplify small perturbations. And nonlinear systems are characterized by multiplicative (or what I have called "synergistic") relationships among their components or variables. A good introduction to the concept is Williams, *Chaos Theory Tamed*, 9–11.

22. On the nonlinear response of fisheries and other natural systems see Donald Ludwig, Ray Hilborn, and Carl Walters, "Uncertainty, Resource Exploitation, and Conservation: Lessons from History," *Science* 260, no. 5104 (2 April 1993): 17, 36; see also Nathan Keyfitz, "Population Growth Can Prevent the Development That Would Slow Population Growth," in *Preserving the Global Environment: The Challenge of Shared Leadership*, ed. Jessica Tuchman Mathews (New York: W. W. Norton & Co., 1991), 42–46.

23. J. C. Farman, B. G. Gardiner, and J. D. Shanklin, "Large Losses of Total Ozone in Antarctica Reveal Seasonal CLO_x/NO_x Interaction," *Nature* 315, no. 6016 (16 May 1985): 207–10.

24. See Schneider, *Global Warming: Are We Entering the Greenhouse Century?* (San Francisco: Sierra Club Books, 1989), 226.

25. See Owen Toon and Richard Turco, "Polar Stratospheric Clouds and Ozone Depletion," *Scientific American* 264, no. 6 (June 1991): 68–77; and Richard Stolarski, "The Antarctic Ozone Hole," *Scientific American* 258, no. 1 (January 1988): 30–38.

26. Seminal treatments of information theory are Claude Shannon and Warren Weaver, *The Mathematical Theory of Communication* (Urbana, Illinois: University of Illinois Press, 1949); and Elwyn Edwards, *Information Transmission: An Introductory Guide to the Application of the Theory of Information to the Human Sciences* (London: Chapman and Hall, 1964).

27. Williams provides a basic introduction to information theory and a similar illustration in *Chaos Theory Tamed*, 86–95.

28. Bar-Yam, *Dynamics of Complex Systems*, 703.

29. One approach is to relate the degree of complexity to the length of the computer program (or algorithm) that reproduces the behavior of the system. The computer program is assumed to be a string of information bits fed into a special type of universal computer called a Turing machine. The shorter or more compact the string, the lower the system's *algorithmic complexity*. (Technically, the "program" for the Turing machine consists of both the input string and a table of elementary operations that guide the machine's actions on the string.) Unfortunately, this measure can't always be relied upon because it tends to mistake randomness for complexity: reproducing a particular sequence of random behavior often requires an algorithm as detailed and complex as the behavior itself. This method of measuring complexity was first proposed by Gregory Chaitin, a mathematician at the Watson Research Center, and his colleagues. See George Chaitin, *Algorithmic Information Theory* (Cambridge: Cambridge University Press, 1987), 91–126. See also George Johnson, "Researchers on Complexity Ponder What It's All About," *New York Times*, 6 May 1997, national edition, B9.

30. Murray Gell-Mann, the Nobel Prize–winning physicist who discovered and named the quark and is a founder of the Santa Fe Institute, advocates taking the first of these approaches, which is to produce the most compact model that describes a system's behavior. This model, or set of rules (Gell-Mann calls it a *schema*), is analogous to the grammar of a language. The length of the schema is a gauge of the system's complexity. By this measure random behavior is not complex, because it can't be described by a grammar, and therefore the length of its schema is zero. The approach is useful, but has some important flaws. In particular, small differences in schemas seem to produce huge differences in the range and complexity of behavior of the systems they describe.

    The second approach, advocated by other Santa Fe researchers, doesn't assume elaborate foreknowledge of a given system's properties and behavior. Instead, it is based on an empirical assessment of the system's *self-dissimilarity*. Complex systems exhibit very different features or characteristics at different scales of analysis. The density and distribution of material in the human body, for instance, looks very different depending on whether one examines it at the micrometer or centimeter level, whereas the same is not true for noncomplex systems like gases or rock. By this measure, the greater the variation in density of matter, biological species, or information across scales of analysis, the greater the system's complexity. See David Wolpert and William Macready, "Self-Dissimilarity: An Empirical Measure of Complexity," working paper of the Santa Fe Institute, 97-12-087 (Santa Fe, New Mexico: Santa Fe Institute, 1997).

31. Experts in the field of information-based complexity have tackled this challenge. They define and measure the *computational complexity* of a scientific problem by reference to the mathematical procedure of integration in calculus: the complexity of the problem varies inversely with the amount of error one is prepared to accept in the integration's result, and it varies exponentially with the number of variables in the integration. In lay terms, the less error one wants in the answer to a scientific problem and the more variables in the problem itself, the greater the computational complexity. This computational burden rises very fast: calculating an integral with only three variables to eight-place accuracy (that is, to 0.00000001) would take today's most powerful computers millions of years. Alternatives are available, however. If mathematicians are willing to relax their error requirements and relinquish the guarantee that the error will fall within certain preestablished bounds, many scientific problems become computationally tractable. For a review, see Joseph Traub and Henryk Wozniakowski, "Breaking Intractability," *Scientific American* 270, no. 1 (January 1994), 102–7.

32. Ibid., 102.

33. Some folding is the result of the electrostatic charges of the protein's atoms: those with similar charges repel each other, while those with different charges attract each other. Other folding results from the differential tendencies of the various building blocks of proteins—amino acids—to be attracted to or repelled by water. Those that are repelled by water want to be on the inside of the protein bundle, as far away from the cell's water as possible, while those that are attracted to water want to stay on the outside. For a general discussion, see Bar-Yam, *Dynamics of Complex Systems*, 421–27.

34. George Johnson, "Designing Life: Proteins 1, Computer 0," *New York Times*, 25 March 1997, national edition, B9.

35. "The point, therefore, is not that 'complexity' is a problem entirely unique to our age. It is rather (1) that 'complexity' has now become a crucial and perhaps even unavoidable consideration in many of our most pressing questions about the world and (2) that to deal with 'complexity' seriously seems to present some extraordinary difficulties for our understanding" (Langdon Winner, "Complexity and the Limits of Human Understanding," in *Organized Social Complexity: Challenge to Politics and Policy*, ed. Todd La Porte [Princeton: Princeton University Press, 1975]: 40–76, especially 40–41, 49.)

36. Compared with people only two or three lifetimes ago, we all have so many things we can do, and our potential has been so expanded, that truly "fulfilling our potential" is now virtually impossible. Just in the information technology domain, for example, the computer consultant Charles Herzfeld contends that "we may soon have access to 15,000 television channels, a few hundred million books, and billions of pages of journals." One of the central questions we will face in coming years, he concludes, will be "how we cope with the enormous number of choices that will open to us in the digital world." Charles Herzfeld, "The Immaterial World," review of *Being Digital*, by Nicholas Negroponte, in *Scientific American* 273, no. 3 (September 1995): 214–15.

37. This idea is not new. In his discussion of the origins of the economic division of labor, the great sociologist Emile Durkheim, who dominated French social

thought from the late nineteenth to the early twentieth century, argued that the growth in human population, its increasing concentration in cities, and the rapid development of communication and transportation technologies raised the "dynamic density" of societies. "The division of labor develops," Durkheim wrote, "as there are more individuals sufficiently in contact to be able to act and react upon one another." See Emile Durkheim, *The Division of Labor in Society*, translated by George Simpson (New York: Free Press, 1968 [1933]), 257.

38. The statistics on Internet hosts are available from the Network Wizards web site at www.nw.com/zone/host-count-history.

39. Bank for International Settlements, *Triennial Central Bank Survey of Foreign Exchange and Derivatives Market Activity, 1998*, available at http://www.bis.org/publ/index.htm.

40. The figure on total world traffic volume is extrapolated from data in Andreas Schafer and David Victor, "The Past and Future of Global Mobility," *Scientific American* 277, no. 4 (October 1997): 61; that on world air traffic volume is drawn from Arnulf Grübler, *The Rise and Fall of Infrastructures: Dynamics of Evolution and Ecological Change in Transport* (Heidelberg: Physica-Verlag, 1989), 165.

41. Some historians even argue that the complexity of our societies tends to rise inexorably far beyond the point where it delivers benefits, eventually becoming so burdensome that it precipitates social and economic collapse. See, in particular, Joseph Tainter, *The Collapse of Complex Societies* (Cambridge: Cambridge University Press, 1988).

42. Bar-Yam, *Dynamics of Complex Systems*, 811. Bar-Yam calculates that the complexity of a human being is between 10^8 and 10^{12} bits of information. The complexity of modern human societies now far exceeds that threshold, in his judgment.

CHAPTER FIVE

1. Pierre-Simon de Laplace, "Recherches, 1°, sur l'intégration des équations différentielles aux différences finies, et sur leur usage dans la théorie des hasards. 2°, sur le principe de la gravitation universelle, et sur les inégalités séculaires des planètes qui en dépendent." *Mémoires de l'Académie royale des Sciences de Paris (Savants étrangers):* 37–232. As translated in James Crutchfield, J. Doyne Farmer, and Norman Packard, "Chaos," *Scientific American* 255, no. 6 (December 1986).

2. H. Poincaré, *Science et Methode, Bibliothèque Scientifique* (1908), English translation by F. Maitland (New York: Dover Publications, 1952).

3. Crutchfield, Farmer, and Packard, "Chaos," 46–57.

4. See also James Gleick, *Chaos: Making of a New Science* (New York: Viking, 1987); Garnett Williams provides a more technical treatment in *Chaos Theory Tamed* (Washington, D.C.: Joseph Henry Press, 1997).

5. Scientists can often identify key boundaries within which a chaotic system's variables and components must operate, which can allow them to make rough projections of the system's future states. Also, they can often predict changes in

macro-properties—like the temperature and pressure of a gas—that are averages of the behavior of all the components in the system.

6. Crutchfield, Farmer, and Packard, "Chaos," 48–49.

7. Edward Lorenz, "Deterministic Nonperiodic Flow," *Journal of the Atmospheric Sciences* 20 (1963): 130–41.

8. John Houghton, "The Bakerian Lecture, 1991: The Predictability of Weather and Climate," *Philosophical Transactions Royal Society of London*, A, vol. 337 (1991): 521–72. Recently, scientists have made exciting advances in prediction of seasonal and inter-annual variations in climate. In particular, they have identified apparently long-distance "teleconnections" between El Niño Southern Oscillation events in the South Pacific and changes in rainfall and temperature as far away as Africa. See Roger Stone, Graeme Hammer, and Torben Marcussen, "Prediction of Global Rainfall Probabilities Using Phases of the Southern Oscillation Index," *Nature* 384, no. 6606 (21 November 1996): 252–55; and Michael Glantz, *Currents of Change: El Niño's Impact on Climate and Society* (Cambridge: Cambridge University Press, 1996).

9. Houghton, "The Bakerian Lecture," 526–30, 566–67.

10. "Human beings are capable of learning and of purposefully organizing for the pursuit of collective goals. . . . Both individuals, and, more importantly, powerful corporate actors who have come to dominate in our highly organized modern societies intervene and try to control spontaneous processes if their anticipated outcome appears undesirable." Renate Mayntz, "Chaos in Society: Reflection on the Impact of Chaos Theory on Sociology," in *The Impact of Chaos on Science and Society*, eds. Celso Grebogi and James Yorke (Tokyo: United Nations University Press, 1997), 315.

11. The discussion of turbulence in this and the following paragraphs is largely based on Parviz Moin and John Kim, "Tackling Turbulence with Supercomputers," *Scientific American* 276, no. 1 (January 1997): 62–68.

12. Ibid., 62.

13. The velocity and pressure at one grid point are affected by the velocity and pressure at surrounding points an instant previously. So data from one round of Navier-Stokes calculations can be reentered into the equations to give estimates for each grid point at the next moment in time.

14. A doubling of the number of grid points increases the computational time required roughly tenfold.

15. Moin and Kim, "Tackling Turbulence with Supercomputers," 66.

16. Gregory Benford, "Climate Controls," *Reason* 29, no. 6 (1997): 24–30. For a popular discussion of geoengineering to prevent sudden climate change, see William Calvin, "The Great Climate Flip-flop," *Atlantic Monthly* 281 (January 1998): 47–64.

17. On the controversy surrounding such proposals, see Steve Nadis, "Fertilizing the Sea," *Scientific American* 278, no. 4 (April 1998): 33.

18. Benford, "Climate Controls."

19. Although related, prediction and management are distinct concerns. Predicting a complex system's behavior depends largely on the quality of our theoretical and empirical knowledge. But managing this behavior requires not only good

knowledge but also the logistical and technological capacity, as well as the will, to change the system's behavior, when that behavior is undesirable.

20. In 1976 the U.S. National Academy of Sciences issued a report calling for a major research effort in this direction. Sandra Blakeslee, "Hopes for Predicting Earthquakes, Once So Bright, Grow Dim," *New York Times*, 8 August 1995, national edition, B8.

21. Quoted in ibid.

22. V. I. Keilis-Borok, "The Concept of Chaos in the Problem of Earthquake Prediction," in *The Impact of Chaos on Science and Society*, eds. Celso Grebogi and James Yorke (Tokyo: United Nations University Press, 1997), 243–54, especially 245.

23. An earthquake-prone region, in fact, may reside on the cusp between an ordered and a chaotic regime, a situation that specialists refer to as "self-organized criticality." Ian Main, "Long Odds on Prediction," *Nature* 385, no. 6611 (2 January 1997): 19–20.

24. For a review of the latest expert opinion on this issue, see the Web debate sponsored by *Nature*, "Is the Reliable Prediction of Individual Earthquakes a Realistic Scientific Goal?" Ian Main, moderator, at http://helix.nature.com/debates/earthquake/equake_contents.html.

25. Quoted in Main, "Long Odds on Prediction," 20.

26. David Tilman and David Wedin, "Oscillations and Chaos in the Dynamics of Perennial Grass," *Nature* 353, no. 6345 (17 October 1991): 653–55; and Alan Hastings and Kevin Higgins, "Persistence in Spatially Structured Ecological Models," *Science* 263, no. 5150 (25 February 1994): 1133–36. Multiple equilibria and chaotic behavior in mathematical models of the growth of biological populations were first identified by Robert May in "Biological Populations with Nonoverlapping Generations: Stable Points, Stable Cycles, and Chaos," *Science* 186 (15 November 1974): 645–47.

27. William Stevens, "New Eye on Nature: The Real Constant Is Eternal Turmoil," *New York Times*, 31 July 1990, national edition, B5.

28. Carol Kaesuk Yoon, "Boom and Bust May Be the Norm in Nature, Study Suggests," *New York Times*, 15 March 1994, national edition, B7.

29. C. S. Holling, "New Science and New Investments for a Sustainable Biosphere," chapter 4 in *Investing in Natural Capital: The Ecological Economics Approach to Sustainability*, eds. AnnMari Jansson, Monica Hammer, Carl Folke, and Robert Costanza (Washington, D.C.: Island Press, 1994), p. 60.

30. C. S. Holling, "An Ecologist View of the Malthusian Conflict," in *Population, Economic Development, and the Environment*, ed. Kerstin Lindahl-Kiessling and Hans Landberg (Oxford: Oxford University Press, 1994), 84.

31. Ibid.

32. In a famous 1973 article, Holling distinguished between the concepts of ecosystem resilience and stability in ecosystems. While resilience determines "the persistence of relationships within a system" in the face of sharp and unexpected external pressures, stability, he argued, is "the ability of a system to return to an equilibrium state after a temporary disturbance." See C. S. Holling, "Resilience and Stability of Ecological Systems," *Annual Review of Ecology and Systematics* 4

(1973): 1–23. Ecologists have not universally adopted Holling's distinction or his conception of ecosystem resilience. See, for example, Stuart Pimm, "The Complexity and Stability of Ecosystems," *Nature* 307, no. 5949 (26 January 1984): 321–26.

33. Holling, "An Ecologist's View of the Malthusian Conflict," 88.

34. The relationship between ecosystem complexity and species diversity, on the one hand, and ecosystem stability and resilience, on the other, has been the focus of long debate among ecologists. Until the 1990s, mathematical models had convinced most ecologists that greater complexity produces instability. More recently, however, field research has shown that, in general, the greater the diversity of species in an ecosystem, the greater the system's productivity, stability, and resilience. More sophisticated, nonlinear mathematical models of ecosystem behavior have reinforced this conclusion: that complexity stabilizes ecosystems. On exemplary field research, see William Stevens's account of the work of University of Minnesota ecologist G. David Tilman in "Ecologist Measures Nature's Mosaic, One Plot at a Time," *New York Times*, 6 October 1998, national edition, B11; and on recent mathematical models, see Kevin McCann, Alan Hastings, and Gary Huxel, "Weak Trophic Interactions and the Balance of Nature," *Nature* 395, no. 6704 (22 October 1998): 794–98. See also S. Naeem et al., "Declining Biodiversity Can Alter the Performance of Ecosystems," *Nature* 368, no. 6473 (21 April 1994): 734–37; and D. Tilman et al., "Productivity and Sustainability Influenced by Biodiversity in Grassland Ecosystems," *Nature* 379, no. 6567 (22 February 1996): 718–20.

35. Holling asks: "Is the reserve and insurance that the resilience of nature has given us going to be the very attribute that blocks people's abilities to perceive and adapt to abrupt change on planetary scales?" Holling, "Ecologist View," 92.

36. Ibid., 93.

37. Holling, "New Science," 60.

38. Joel Cohen and David Tilman, "Biosphere 2 and Biodiversity: The Lessons So Far," *Science* 274 (15 November 1996): 1150–51.

39. William Broad, "Paradise Lost: Biosphere Retooled As Atmospheric Nightmare," *New York Times*, 19 November 1996, national edition, B5 and B8.

40. William Broad, "Too Rich a Soil: Scientists Find the Flaw That Undid the Biosphere," *New York Times*, 5 October 1993, national edition, B5.

41. Cohen and Tilman, "Biosphere 2," 1150.

42. Broad, "Too Rich a Soil," B8.

43. Cohen and Tilman, "Biosphere 2," 1151.

44. The possibilities for predictive modeling of these Earth systems are discussed in Hans-Peter Dürr, "Is Global Modeling Feasible?" in *Earth System Analysis: Integrating Science for Sustainability*, H.-J. Schellnhuber and V. Wenzel, eds. (Berlin: Springer-Verlag, 1998), 493–514.

45. Much of the information in the following paragraphs is taken from Wallace Broecker, "Will Our Ride into the Greenhouse Future Be a Smooth One?" *GSA Today* 7, no. 5 (May 1977): 1–6. Broecker's seminal article on nonlinearities in ocean current systems is "Unpleasant Surprises in the Greenhouse?," *Nature* 328, no. 6126 (9 July 1987): 123–26.

46. R. B. Alley et al., "Abrupt Increase in Greenland Snow Accumulation at the End of the Younger Dryas Event," *Nature* 362, no. 6420 (8 April 1993): 527–29. See also Jeffrey Severinghaus et al., "Timing of Abrupt Climate Change at the End of the Younger Dryas Interval from Thermally Fractionated Gases in Polar Ice," *Nature* 391 (8 January 1998): 141–46.

47. See, for example, Syukuro Manabe, Ronald Stouffer, and Michael Spelman, "Response of a Coupled Ocean-Atmosphere Model to Increasing Atmospheric Carbon Dioxide," *Ambio* 23, no. 1 (February 1994), 44–49; Stefan Rahmstorf, "Bifurcations of the Atlantic Thermohaline Circulation in Response to Changes in the Hydrological Cycle," *Nature* 378, no. 9 (9 November 1995), 145–49; Stefan Rahmstorf, "Risk of Sea-Change in the Atlantic," *Nature* 388 (28 August 1997), 825–26; T. F. Stocker and A. Schmittner, "Influence of CO_2 Emission Rates on the Stability of the Thermohaline Circulation," *Nature* 388, no. 6645 (28 August 1997): 862–65; and Richard Wood, "Changing Spatial Structure of the Thermohaline Circulation in Response to Atmospheric CO_2 Forcing in a Climate Model," *Nature* 399, as here no. 6736 (10 June 1999): 572–75.

48. Carsten Rühlemann et al., "Warming of the Tropical Atlantic Ocean and Slowdown of Thermohaline Circulation During the Last Deglaciation," *Nature* 402, no. 6761 (2 December 1999): 511–14.

49. Jodie Smith, Michael Risk, Henry Schwarcz, and Ted McConnaughey, "Rapid Climate Change in the North Atlantic During the Younger Dryas Recorded by Deep-sea Corals," *Nature* 386 (24 April 1997): 818–20; and Broecker, "Will Our Ride into the Greenhouse Future Be a Smooth One?" 2–4.

50. For a discussion of such carbon sequestration, see Howard Herzog, Baldur Eliasson, and Olav Kaarstad, "Capturing Greenhouse Gases," *Scientific American* 282, no. 2 (February 2000): 72–79.

51. Wallace Broecker, *How to Build a Habitable Planet* (Palisades, New York: Eldigio Press, 1985), 274–75.

52. Broecker, "Will Our Ride into the Greenhouse Future Be a Smooth One?," 6.

53. Quoted in Eugene Linden, "Antarctica: Warnings from the Ice," *Time*, April 14, 1997.

CHAPTER SIX

1. Quoted in Michael Rosen, "Crashing in '87: Power and Symbolism in the Dow," in *Organizational Symbolism*, Barry Turner, ed. (Berlin: Walter de Gruyter, 1990), 121.

2. Ibid., 126.

3. Quoted in James Stewart and Daniel Hertzberg, "Terrible Tuesday: How the Stock Market Almost Disintegrated a Day after the Crash," *Wall Street Journal*, 20 November 1987, 1.

4. Tim Metz, *Black Monday: The Catastrophe of October 18, 1987 . . . and Beyond* (New York: William Morrow, 1988), 139.

5. Metz, *Black Monday*, 176.

6. Ibid.

7. Stewart and Hertzberg, "Terrible Tuesday," 23.

8. Ibid.

9. Rosen, "Crashing in '87," 126.

10. Stewart and Hertzberg, "Terrible Tuesday," 23.

11. Metz, *Black Monday*, 218–19.

12. Stewart and Hertzberg, "Terrible Tuesday," 23.

13. See Rosen, "Crashing in '87," 127; and Metz, *Black Monday*, 210–51. Stewart and Hertzberg write: "Statistics supplied by the Board of Trade lend circumstantial support to the thesis that the index was driven upward by a small number of sophisticated traders." See "Terrible Tuesday," 23.

14. Quoted in Stewart and Hertzberg, "Terrible Tuesday," 23.

15. These positions are contrasted in Merton Miller, *Financial Innovations and Market Volatility* (Cambridge, Mass.: Blackwell, 1991), especially chapter 6, "The Crash of 1987: Bubble or Fundamental?" Miller argues that the chief cause of the crash was a change in perception of market fundamentals.

16. In this respect, the idea of path dependency is similar to the ecologists' idea of multiple equilibria in ecological systems, discussed in the last chapter.

17. Rosen, "Crashing in '87," 117.

18. Stanley Fischer, "Capital Account Liberalization and the Role of the IMF," paper presented at the IMF Seminar *Asia and the IMF*, Hong Kong, 19 September 1997, 1.

19. "Covering Asia with Cash," *New York Times*, 28 January 1998, national edition, C1.

20. Cesar Pelli, Charles Thorton, and Leonard Joseph, "The World's Tallest Buildings," *Scientific American* 277, no. 6 (December 1997): 92C-101.

21. Meredith Poor, letter to the editor, *Scientific American* 278, no. 4 (April 1998): 6.

22. The definitive treatment of the dynamics of financial crises is Charles Kindleberger, *Manias, Panics, and Crashes: A History of Financial Crises* (New York: John Wiley, 1996).

23. Cited in Jeffrey Sachs, "Power unto Itself," *Financial Times*, 11 December 1997, 11.

24. Robert Johnson, "What Asia's Financial Crisis Portends," *New York Times*, 29 December 1997, national edition, A19.

25. Quoted in Paul Lewis, "A Warning Light Largely Ignored in Thai Currency Crisis," *New York Times*, 1 August 1997, national edition, C1.

26. Paul Krugman argued at the time that the overriding objective of the IMF was to regain the confidence of international investors, even if it meant imposing measures contrary to those suggested by the country's economic fundamentals. See Paul Krugman, "The Confidence Game," *New Republic*, 5 October 1998, 23–25.

27. Quoted in Jeff Gerth and Richard Stevenson, "Poor Oversight Said to Imperil World Banking System," *New York Times*, 22 December 1997, national edition, A1.

28. John Heimann et al., *Global Institutions, National Supervision, and Systemic Risk* (Washington, D.C.: Group of Thirty, 1997), 8–9.

29. Ibid., 13.

30. Quoted in ibid.

31. Sachs, "Power unto Itself."

32. A good example of such opinion, although written later in 1998, is Charles Lane, "Super Markets," *New Republic*, 2 November 1998, 6.

33. Seth Mydans, "As Boom Fails, Malaysia Sends Migrants Home," *New York Times*, 9 April 1998, national edition, A1.

34. Nicholas Kristof, "To Some of Indonesia's Poor, Looting Gives Taste of Power," *New York Times*, 8 May 1998, national edition, A1.

35. The parallel between the behavior of foreign exchange markets and that of turbulent physical systems is strong. S. Ghashghaie and colleagues have shown that "there is an information cascade in [foreign exchange] market dynamics that corresponds to the energy cascade in hydrodynamic turbulence." See S. Ghashghaie et al., *Nature* 381, no. 6585 (27 June 1996): 767–70.

36. Quoted in Robert Hershey Jr., "Nintendo Capitalism: Zapping the Markets," *New York Times*, 28 May 1996, national edition, C1.

37. A superb treatment of recent decades' changes in international finance and the demands that these changes place on domestic and international financial institutions is Robert Solomon, *Money on the Move: The Revolution in International Finance since 1980* (Princeton: Princeton University Press, 1999).

38. Quoted in David Sanger, "After a Year, No Letup in Asia's Economic Crisis," *New York Times*, 6 July 1998, national edition, A1.

39. "Management Consultancy: The Advice Business," *Economist*, 22 March 1997, 66–68.

40. Quoted in Ibid.

41. Nicholas Kristof, "Fears of Sorcerers Spur Killings in Java," *New York Times*, 20 October 1998, national edition, A1.

42. Quoted in Thomas Friedman, "From Supercharged Financial Markets to Osama bin Laden, the Emerging Global Order Demands an Enforcer. That's America's New Burden," *New York Times Magazine*, 28 March 1999, 71.

43. Quoted in Alan Cowell, "Annan Fears Backlash over Global Crisis," *New York Times*, 1 February 1999, A10.

CHAPTER SEVEN

1. Most economic historians say that the first modern recession occurred in Europe following the Napoleonic Wars; the first in the United States may have been the panic of 1873. See Paul Krugman, "Seeking the Rule of the Waves," review of David Hackett Fischer, *The Great Wave: Price Revolutions and the Rhythm of History* (New York: Oxford University Press, 1996), in *Foreign Affairs* 76, no. 4 (1997): 136–41.

2. Steven Weber, "The End of the Business Cycle?" *Foreign Affairs* 76, no. 4 (1997): 65–82.

3. The ecologist Buzz Holling writes: "The success in controlling an ecological variable that normally fluctuated led to more spatially homogenized ecosystems over landscape scales. It led to systems more likely to flip into a persistent

degraded state, triggered by disturbances that previously could be absorbed." C. S. Holling, "New Science and New Investments for a Sustainable Biosphere," in AnnMari Jansson et al., eds., *Investing in Natural Capital: The Ecological Economics Approach to Sustainability* (Washington, D.C.: Island Press, 1994), 68. See also Donald Ludwig, Ray Hilborn, and Carl Walters, "Uncertainty, Resource Exploitation, and Conservation: Lessons from History," *Science* 260, no. 5104 (2 April 1993): 17; and James Scott, *Seeing Like a State: How Certain Schemes to Improve the Human Condition Have Failed* (New Haven, Connecticut: Yale University Press, 1998), 11–22.

4. Edward Tenner, *Why Things Bite Back: Technology and the Revenge of Unintended Consequences* (New York: Knopf, 1996), 273.

5. Vincent Perreten et al., "Antibiotic Resistance Spread in Food," *Nature* 389, no. 6653 (23 October 1997): 801–2.

6. On the coevolution of disease and humanity, see Randolph Nesse and George Williams, "Evolution and the Origins of Disease," *Scientific American* 279, no. 5 (November 1998): 86–93; and Christopher Wills, *Yellow Fever, Black Goddess: The Coevolution of People and Plagues* (Reading, Mass.: Addison-Wesley, 1996).

7. For a summary, see Stuart Levy, "The Challenge of Antibiotic Resistance," *Scientific American* 278, no. 3 (March 1998): 46–53. For a more detailed and technical treatment, see Polly Harrison and Joshua Lederberg, eds., *Antimicrobial Resistance: Issues and Options, Workshop Report*, Forum on Emerging Infections (Washington, D.C.: National Academy Press, 1998).

8. Gene Rochlin, *Trapped in the Net: The Unanticipated Consequences of Computerization* (Princeton, New Jersey: Princeton University Press, 1997), 86 and 88–99.

9. "Often," economic journalist Saul Hansell writes, "the senior managers of a company who are supposed to be doing the monitoring do not really understand the complicated new instruments and take a laissez-faire attitude toward the younger financial traders who have grown up on this sort of financial Nintendo." Saul Hansell, "For Rogue Traders, Yet Another Victim," *New York Times*, 28 February 1995; quoted in Rochlin, *Trapped in the Net*, 93.

10. Greenspan's remark came in a speech in Tokyo on Wednesday, October 14, 1992. Quoted in Steven Greenhouse, "Greenspan Sees Risks Globally," *New York Times*, 14 October 1992, national edition, C1.

11. Rochlin, *Trapped in the Net*, 99.

12. Tenner, *Why Things Bite Back*, 5–6.

13. Matthew Wald, "Autos' Converters Increase Warming As They Cut Smog," *New York Times*, 29 May 1998, national edition, A1.

14. Peter Lewis, "Mighty Fire Ants March Out of the South," *New York Times*, 24 July 1990, national edition, B5; see also Tenner, *Why Things Bite Back*, 110–13.

15. Nicholas Johnson, "Monitoring and Controlling Debris in Space," *Scientific American* 279, no. 2 (August 1998): 62–67.

16. Details of the *Ariane 5* explosion in this and the following paragraphs are taken from J. L. Lions, *Ariane 5: Flight 501 Failure*, Report by the Inquiry Board (Paris: European Space Agency, 1996), available at www.esrin.esa.it/tidc/Press/Press96/ariane5rep.html; and from James Gleick, "Little Bug, Big Bang," *New York Times Magazine*, 1 December 1996, 38–40.

17. Quoted in Gleick, "Little Bug," 40.
18. Peter de Jager, "Y2K: So Many Bugs . . . So Little Time," *Scientific American* 280, no. 1 (January 1999): 88.
19. Tenner, *Why Things Bite Back*, 269.
20. De Jager, "Y2K," 93.
21. Wayt Gibbs, "Software's Chronic Crisis," *Scientific American* 271, no. 3 (September 1994): 87.
22. On measuring software complexity, see Capers Jones, "Sizing Up Software," *Scientific American* 279, no. 6 (December 1998): 104–9.
23. Gibbs, "Software's Chronic Crisis," 89.
24. Kenneth Birman and Robbert Renesse, "Software for Reliable Networks," *Scientific American* 274, no. 5 (May 1996): 65.
25. John Markoff, "Network Problem Disrupts Internet," *New York Times*, 18 July 1997, national edition, A1.
26. Tim Golden, "Blackout a Caution Sign on Road to Deregulation," *New York Times*, 19 August 1996, national edition, A7.
27. See Birman and Renesse, "Software for Reliable Networks," for details.
28. Gary Stix, "Aging Airways," *Scientific American* 270, no. 5 (May 1994): 99.
29. Matthew Wald, "System Blackout Disrupts Flights Around Country," *New York Times*, 19 December 1997, national edition, A1.
30. Matthew Wald, "Ambitious Update of Air Navigation Becomes a Fiasco," *New York Times*, 29 January 1996, national edition, A1 and A11.
31. Quoted in Wald, "Ambitious Update," A11; Stix, "Aging Airways," 100.
32. Quoted in Matthew Wald, "Aviation Agency Delays Debut of Satellite Navigation System," *New York Times*, 6 January 1999, national edition, A19.
33. Quoted in Matthew Wald, "FAA Tackles Old Air Traffic Computers," *New York Times*, 13 January 1998, national edition, A12.
34. Stix, "Aging Airways," 96–97.
35. Todd LaPorte and Paula Consolini, "Working in Practice but Not in Theory: Theoretical Challenges of 'High-Reliability Organizations,'" *Journal of Public Administration Research and Theory*, vol. 1 (1991): 21.
36. Ibid., 32.
37. Rochlin, *Trapped in the Net*, 120.
38. Ibid., 109.
39. Ibid., 128.
40. Charles Perrow, "Negative Synergy," review of Brian Toft and Simon Reynolds, *Learning from Disasters: A Management Approach*, in *Nature* 370, no. 6491 (1994): 608.

CHAPTER EIGHT

1. For those who are interested, I explore these criteria, and a number of other technical matters, in more detail in the "Ingenuity Theory" section of this book's Web site, www.ingenuitygap.com.

2. Stuart Kauffman makes a very similar argument in *At Home in the Universe: The Search for Laws of Self-Organization and Complexity* (New York: Oxford University Press, 1995), 289–95.

3. Yaneer Bar-Yam, *Dynamics of Complex Systems* (Reading, Mass.: Addison-Wesley, 1992), 808.

4. Malcolm Carpenter, *Core Text of Neuroanatomy*, 4th ed. (Baltimore: Williams & Wilkins, 1991), 23.

5. Estimates of the total number of neurons in the brain vary widely. Jean-Pierre Changeux provides a reasonable guess of "at least 30 billion neurons" in the human cortex in *Neuronal Man: The Biology of Mind*, translated by Dr. Laurence Garey (New York: Pantheon Books, 1985), 51. Kandel and his colleagues give an estimate of 100 billion neurons for the brain as a whole, with 100 trillion synapses among them. See Eric R. Kandel, James H. Schwartz, and Thomas M. Jessell (eds.), *Principles of Neural Science*, 3d ed. (New York: Elsevier Science Publishing, 1991), 121.

6. Mark F. Bear, Barry W. Connors, and Michael A. Paradiso, *Neuroscience: Exploring the Brain* (Baltimore, Maryland: Williams & Wilkins, 1996), 24; Irwin B. Levitan and Leonard K. Kaczmarek, *The Neuron: Cell and Molecular Biology*, 2d ed. (New York: Oxford University Press, 1997), 45.

7. Harry J. Jerison, *Evolution of the Brain and Intelligence* (New York: Academic Press, 1973), 61–62. Jerison develops and uses a special statistic, called the *encephalization quotient*, to compare animals' relative brain sizes.

8. William Calvin, *How Brains Think: Evolving Intelligence, Then and Now* (New York: Basic Books, 1996), 12 and 117.

9. Ibid., 15; James Gould and Carol Grant Gould, *The Animal Mind* (New York: Scientific American Library, 1994), 68–70.

10. Rick Potts, *Humanity's Descent: The Consequences of Ecological Instability* (New York: Avon, 1997), 216.

11. Peter Wheeler, "The Evolution of Bipedality and the Loss of Functional Body Hair in Hominids," *Journal of Human Evolution* 13 (1984): 91–98; and Peter Wheeler, "The Influence of Bipedalism on the Energy and Water Budgets of Early Hominids, *Journal of Human Evolution*, 21 (1991): 107–36.

12. Leslie Aiello and Peter Wheeler, "The Expensive-Tissue Hypothesis: The Brain and the Digestive System in Human and Primate Evolution," *Current Anthropology* 36, no. 2 (1995): 199–221.

13. Richard Dawkins, *The Blind Watchmaker* (New York: Norton, 1987), 181.

14. Nicholas Humphrey, "The Social Function of Intellect," in *Growing Points in Ethology*, P. P. G. Bateson and R. A. Hinde, eds. (Cambridge: Cambridge University Press, 1976), 303–17; and Nicholas Humphrey, *The Inner Eye* (London: Faber and Faber, 1986).

15. Calvin, *How Brains Think*, 95–98.

16. Potts writes: "Dramatic alterations between cold and warm, steppe and forest, glacial and interglacial, occurred time and again in the late phases of humanity's descent, and when they happened, the change was measured on a scale from decades up to a few centuries. . . . Major biomes—savanna, forest, and desert— moved across the terrain in complex relays. Water and food—the key resources

of living organisms—appeared and disappeared over time." Potts, *Humanity's Descent*, 168.

17. Ibid., 159, 243–44.
18. Bar-Yam, *Dynamics of Complex Systems*, 808.
19. Potts, *Humanity's Descent*, 239; Calvin, *How Brains Think*, 55.
20. Potts, *Humanity's Descent*, 244.
21. John Noble, "Discovery Suggests Humans Are a Bit Neanderthal," *New York Times*, 25 April 1999, national edition, 1.
22. Steven Mithen, *The Prehistory of the Mind: A Search for the Origins of Art, Religion, and Science* (London: Thames & Hudson, 1996), 140–42.
23. Brian Hayden, "The Cultural Capacities of Neanderthals: A Review and Reevaluation," *Journal of Human Evolution* 24 (1993): 118.
24. Some researchers disagree with these assertions, and the degree of difference between Neanderthals and *Homo sapiens sapiens* is a matter of considerable scholarly dispute. For example, Brian Hayden argues for a contrary view (see note 23 above).
25. For another, and in some ways complementary, theory of the mind's development, see Merlin Donald, *Origins of the Modern Mind* (Cambridge, Mass.: Harvard University Press, 1991); and "Précis of 'Origins of the Modern Mind,'" *Behavioral and Brain Sciences* 13 (1993): 737–91, which includes detailed scholarly commentary on Donald's theory.
26. Two of the leading theorists in this area are Leda Cosmides and John Tooby. See Tooby and Cosmides, "The Psychological Foundations of Culture," in *The Adapted Mind: Evolutionary Psychology and the Generation of Culture*, eds. Jerome Barkow, Leda Cosmides, and John Tooby (New York: Oxford University Press, 1992), 19–136; and Cosmides and Tooby, "Origins of Domain Specificity: The Evolution of Functional Organization," in *Mapping the Mind: Domain Specificity in Cognition and Culture*, eds. Lawrence Hirschfeld and Susan Gelman (Cambridge: Cambridge University Press, 1994), 85–116.
27. A masterful discussion of the operation of the natural history intelligence in the modern human mind can be found in Scott Atran, *Cognitive Foundations of Natural History: Toward an Anthropology of Science* (Cambridge: Cambridge University Press, 1990); Leslie Brothers considers the evolution and modern form of our social intelligence in *Friday's Footprint: How Society Shapes the Human Mind* (New York: Oxford University Press, 1997).
28. Mithen, *The Prehistory of the Mind*, 55. For a general treatment of the archeological evidence on the sources of human creativity, see Steven Mithen, ed., *Creativity in Human Evolution and Prehistory* (London: Routledge, 1998).
29. Mithen, *The Prehistory of the Mind*, 71.
30. Sandra Blakeslee, "Recipe for a Brain: Cups of Genes and Dash of Experience; East and West, Neuroscientists Lock Horns," *New York Times*, 4 November 1997, national edition, B12.
31. Mithen, *The Prehistory of the Mind*, 209.
32. Ibid., 187.
33. Dan Sperber, "The Modularity of Thought and the Epidemiology of Representations," in *Mapping the Mind*, 39–67.

34. Mithen, *The Prehistory of the Mind*, 190–91, 209.

35. Ibid., 209–13

36. Ibid., 210.

37. Robert Boyd and Peter Richerson, "The Evolution of Ethnic Markers," *Cultural Anthropology* 2, no. 1 (1987): 67.

38. The principal statement of this theory is Robert Boyd and Peter Richerson, *Culture and the Evolutionary Process* (Chicago: University of Chicago Press, 1985). See also Joe Henrich and Robert Boyd, "The Evolution of Conformist Transmission and the Emergence of Between-Group Differences," *Evolution and Human Behavior* 19 (1998): 215–41; and Robert Boyd and Peter Richerson, "The Evolution of Norms: An Anthropological View," *Journal of Institutional and Theoretical Economics* 150/1 (1994): 72–87. For a good overview of several theories of cultural transmission, see William Durham, Robert Boyd, and Peter Richerson, "Models and Forces of Cultural Evolution," in *Human by Nature: Between Biology and the Social Sciences*, eds. Peter Weingart, Sandra Mitchell, Peter Richerson, and Sabine Maasen (Mahwah, New Jersey: Lawrence Erlbaum, 1997), 327–52.

39. This variety is sustained partly by copying errors and misinterpretations as cultural models are transmitted from one generation to the next.

40. Richard Dawkins, *The Selfish Gene* (Oxford: Oxford University Press, 1989 [1976]), 189–201.

41. Steven Pinker, *How the Mind Works* (New York: Norton, 1997), 209.

42. Potts, *Humanity's Descent*, 277.

43. Alvin Toffler, *Future Shock* (New York: Random House, 1970); David Shenk, *Data Smog: Surviving the Information Glut* (San Francisco: HarperEdge, 1997), 15. For an early, perceptive, and quantitative treatment of information overload, see Richard Meier, *A Communications Theory of Urban Growth* (Cambridge, Massachusetts: MIT Press, 196_), 132–36.

44. One of the most insightful treatments of this issue remains a 1975 article by the theorist of politics and technology Langdon Winner. "The inadequacy of modern thought when confronted with the massiveness and complexity of the technological society," Winner writes, "has led many important thinkers to conclude that the human intellect has now reached a dead end. Complexity may well be a brick wall, or part of such a wall, which the mind can neither penetrate nor leap over." See Langdon Winner, "Complexity and the Limits of Human Understanding," in *Organized Social Complexity: Challenge to Politics and Policy*, ed. Todd La Porte (Princeton: Princeton University Press, 1975): 43.

45. R. I. M. Dunbar, "Neocortex Size as a Constraint on Group Size in Primates," *Journal of Human Evolution* 20 (1992): 469–93.

46. These figures are averages calculated by Steven Mithen from Table 1 in Leslie Aiello and R. I. M. Dunbar, "Neocortex Size, Group Size, and the Evolution of Language," *Current Anthropology* 34, no. 2 (1993): 184–93.

47. On the increasing incidence of depression, see Daniel Goldman, "A Rising Cost of Modernity: Depression," *New York Times*, 8 December 1992, national edition, C1.

48. Bar-Yam, *Dynamics of Complex Systems*, 819.

49. Electricity travels along conventional wires at a substantial fraction of the speed of light, depending on the properties of the wires and their insulation. A reasonable average figure is 50 percent of the speed of light, or about 150 million meters per second.

50. C. D. Woody, *Memory, Learning, and Higher Function: A Cellular View* (New York: Springer-Verlag, 1982), 323–26. The information content of text is calculated on the basis of eight bits per letter and seven letters per word.

51. George Miller, "The Magical Number Seven, Plus or Minus Two: Some Limits on Our Capacity for Processing Information," *Psychological Review* 63, no. 2 (1956): 90.

52. Two surveys of the huge literature on this subject are Herbert Simon, "Invariants of Human Behavior," *Annual Review of Psychology* 41 (1990): 1–19; and B. A. Mellers, A. Schwartz, and A. D. J. Cooke, "Judgment and Decision Making," *Annual Review of Psychology* 49 (1998): 447–77. An earlier, seminal treatment is Richard Nisbett and Lee Ross, *Human Inference: Strategies and Shortcomings of Social Judgement* (Englewood Cliffs, New Jersey: Prentice-Hall, 1980).

53. Miller, "The Magical Number Seven," 88.

54. Donald Stuss and D. Frank Benson, *The Frontal Lobes* (New York: Raven Press, 1986), 1.

55. Etienne Koechlin et al., "The Role of the Anterior Prefrontal Cortex in Human Cognition," *Nature* 399, no. 6732 (13 May 1999): 148–51.

56. A. R. Luria, "The Frontal Lobes and the Regulation of Behavior," in *Psychophysiology of the Frontal Lobes*, eds. K. H. Pribram and A. R. Luria (New York: Academic Press, 1973), 15.

57. Donald Stuss, "Self, Awareness, and the Frontal Lobes: A Neuropsychological Perspective," in *The Self: Interdisciplinary Approaches*, eds. Jaine Strauss and George Goethals (New York: Springer-Verlag, 1991), 268.

58. Mark Wheeler, Donald Stuss, and Endel Tulving, "Toward a Theory of Episodic Memory: The Frontal Lobes and Autonoetic Consciousness," *Psychological Bulletin* 121, no. 3 (1997): 331–54.

59. Bruce McEwen, "Stress and Hippocampal Plasticity," *Annual Review of Neuroscience* 22 (1999): 105–22.

60. The hippocampus helps regulate the stress-induced release of the hormone ACTH from the brain's pituitary gland; ACTH, in turn, stimulates the adrenal glands on the kidneys to release the steroid hormone cortisol. Unfortunately, high levels of cortisol appear to disrupt the energy balance of neurons in the hippocampus, making them vulnerable to trauma. Over time, the degeneration of the hippocampus may produce a vicious cycle of chronically elevated cortisol levels in the bloodstream and yet more hippocampal neuron loss. Some of the best research on this subject has focused on baboons in the wild. See Robert Sapolsky, "Stress in the Wild," *Scientific American* 262, no. 1 (January 1990): 116–23. A popular account is Robert Sapolsky, *Why Zebras Don't Get Ulcers: A Guide to Stress, Stress-Related Diseases, and Coping* (New York: Freeman, 1994). For a survey of the state of research, see Bruce McEwen, "Stress and the Aging Hippocampus," *Frontiers in Neuroendocrinology* 20 (1999): 49–70.

61. Amy Arnsten, "The Biology of Being Frazzled," *Science* 280 (12 June 1998): 1711–12; and Amy Arnsten, "Development of the Cerebral Cortex: XIV. Stress

Impairs Prefrontal Cortical Function," *Development and Neurobiology* 38, no. 2 (1999): 220–22.

62. P. Shammi and D. T. Stuss, "Humor Appreciation: A Role of the Right Frontal Lobe," *Brain* 122 (April 1999): 657–66.

63. Donald Stuss et al. "Comparison of Older People and Patients with Frontal Lesions: Evidence from Word List Learning," *Psychology and Aging* 11, no. 3 (1996): 387–95.

64. Stuss and Benson, *The Frontal Lobes*, 195–97.

65. Robert Sternberg, "How Intelligent Is Intelligence Testing?" in *Scientific American Presents: Exploring Human Intelligence* 9, no. 4 (Winter 1998): 12–17; and Robert Sternberg and James Kaufman, "Human Abilities," *Annual Review of Psychology* 49 (1998): 479–502.

CHAPTER NINE

1. Ivan Amato, *Stuff: The Materials the World Is Made Of* (New York: Basic, 1997), 2.

2. For a useful survey, see Robert Barrow and Xavier Sala-i-Martin, *Economic Growth* (New York: McGraw Hill, 1995), 9–13. This book is one of the best comprehensive treatments of modern growth theory.

3. Adam Smith, *An Inquiry into the Nature and Causes of the Wealth of Nations* (New York: Penguin, 1982 [1776]), 115.

4. F. M. Scherer, *New Perspectives on Economic Growth and Technological Innovation* (Washington, D.C.: British–North American Committee, Brookings Institution Press, 1999), 22.

5. Robert Solow, "A Contribution to the Theory of Economic Growth," *Quarterly Journal of Economics* 70 (1956): 65–94; Robert Solow, "Technical Change and the Aggregate Production Function," *Review of Economics and Statistics* 39 (1957), 312–20. Also key to the development of neoclassical theories of economic growth was T. W. Swan, "Economic Growth and Capital Accumulation," *Economic Record* 32 (1956): 334–61. Neoclassical economics is a body of theory grounded in nineteenth-century marginal economics that emphasizes the relationship between factor prices and scarcity, the rational maximizing behavior of individuals in markets, the idea of a perfectly competitive economy in equilibrium, and the market's natural tendency towards full employment.

6. Capital accumulation, in turn, is a function of investment, which is determined by the savings rate.

7. Solow, "Technical Change and the Aggregate Production Function," 320.

8. Technology's role is revealed, in part, by *growth accounting*, an analytical exercise in which economists carefully measure the separate contributions of various factors of production to a country's economic growth. When growth accounting is applied to the economies of all the countries in the world for which we have decent data, it shows that increased inputs of labor and capital, conventionally defined, usually do not fully account for growth; they leave a residual portion that is best explained by technological change. For a survey of

growth accounting, see Angus Maddison, "Growth and Slowdown in Advanced Capitalist Economies," *Journal of Economic Literature* 25, no. 2 (June 1987): 649–98.

9. Paul Romer, "Idea Gaps and Object Gaps in Economic Development," *Journal of Monetary Economics* 32 (1993): 562.

10. Paul Romer, "Two Strategies for Economic Development: Using Ideas and Producing Ideas," World Bank, *Proceedings of the World Bank Annual Conference on Development Economics, 1992* (Washington, D.C.: World Bank, 1993), 64.

11. Paul Romer, "Ideas and Things," *150 Economist Years*, 11 September 1993, 72.

12. Paul Romer, "Beyond Classical and Keynesian Macroeconomic Policy," *Policy Options* 15, no. 6 (July/August 1994): 15–21.

13. For further details, see Richard Cornes and Todd Sandler, *The Theory of Externalities, Public Goods, and Club Goods* (Cambridge: Cambridge University Press, 1986).

14. Thomas Jefferson to Isaac McPherson, 1813, in Andrew Lipscomb and Albert Bergh, eds., *The Writings of Thomas Jefferson, Memorial Edition* (Washington, D.C.: Thomas Jefferson Memorial Association, 1903–5), vol. 13, 333.

15. Paul Romer, "Endogenous Technological Change," *Journal of Political Economy*, 98, no. 5, pt. 2 (1990): s74–s75.

16. Ibid., s75.

17. Romer, "Two Strategies," 71.

18. Romer's seminal statement of the ideas summarized in this paragraph is Paul Romer, "Increasing Returns and Long-Run Growth," *Journal of Political Economy*, 94, no. 5 (1986): 1008–13. Other key articles are Robert Lucas, "On the Mechanics of Economic Development," *Journal of Monetary Economics* 22 (1988): 3–42; and Elhanan Helpman, Endogenous Macroeconomic Growth Theory," *European Economic Review* 36 (1992): 237–67. There are some interesting similarities between Romer's idea of "spillover" and both Arthur's notion of spread of "genetic" material from one entity to another in coevolving systems (see this book's chapter "Complexities") and Dawkins's idea of the spread and evolution of memes within societies (as I discussed in the last chapter "Brains and Ingenuity").

19. Chidem Kurdas points out, however, that the mathematical restrictions implicit in Romer's modified neoclassical model (including the need to keep the functional form, production coefficients, and units of knowledge constant) allow him to "endogenize only a certain type of incremental improvement in technology." Sharp nonlinearities in technological development—like the shift from slide rules to computers—must remain exogenous. In general, New Growth theorists' treatment of the sources of technological change is rather impoverished, since it is only incidental to their primary theoretical goal of explaining economic growth. See Chidem Kurdas, *Theories of Technical Change and Investment: Riches and Rationality* (New York: St. Martin's, 1994), 72–75.

20. Jan Fagerberg, "Technology and International Differences in Growth Rates," *Journal of Economic Literature* 32 (September 1994): 1149.

21. Romer, "Endogenous Technical Change," S76; Barrow and Sala-i-Martin, *Economic Growth*, 11.

22. Wayt Gibbs, "Software's Chronic Crisis," *Scientific American* 271, no. 3 (September 1994): 95.

23. Joseph Schumpeter in *Capitalism, Socialism, and Democracy*, 2d ed., (New York: Harper & Brothers, 1947), 103–6.

24. See Romer, "Endogenous Technical Change," for a technical statement of this argument. An account of the evolution of thinking about endogenous growth is Paul Romer, "The Origins of Endogenous Growth," *Journal of Economic Perspectives* 8, no.1 (1994): 3–22. An excellent popular account of the process of creative destruction in the high-technology economy of Silicon Valley is Michael Lewis, "The Little Creepy Crawlers Who Will Eat You in the Night," *New York Times Magazine*, 1 March 1998, 40–81.

25. Alwyn Young, for example, has shown that the economic boom in East Asia during the 1980s and 1990s was mainly due to capital accumulation and the population's increased participation in the labor force, not to improvements in technology. Charles Jones produces data showing that rich countries' rising investments in research and development in recent decades have not coincided with rising rates of labor and capital productivity. But these rebuttals miss the mark. New Growth theorists don't deny that countries can achieve rapid economic growth over the short and the intermediate term by increasing their inputs of labor and capital, as Young shows, especially if their economies are underendowed with these factors of production or are using them inefficiently. Rather, they argue that sustained, long-run growth can't be achieved this way; it can only be achieved, they say, through technological innovation. And Jones's findings can be explained by the rising complexity of technology, which requires rising investments in research and development just to sustain a constant rate of innovation (a point I'll return to in the next chapter). See Alwyn Young, "The Tyranny of Numbers: Confronting the Statistical Realities of the East Asian Growth Experience," *Quarterly Journal of Economics* 110 (1995): 641–80; Paul Krugman makes a similar argument to Young's in "The Myth of Asia's Miracle," *Foreign Affairs* 43, no.6 (November/December 1994): 62–78. Charles Jones's well-known paper is "R&D-Based Models of Economic Growth," *Journal of Political Economy* 103, no. 4 (1995): 759–84. Philippe Aghion and Peter Howitt reply to Jones in *Endogenous Growth Theory* (Cambridge, Massachusetts: MIT, 1998), 417. Moreover, Jones's findings are not wholly supported by other research. See Rajeev Goel and Rati Ram, "Research and Development Expenditures and Economic Growth: A Cross-Country Study," *Economic Development and Cultural Change* 42, no. 2 (1994): 403–11. For an important early critique of New Growth theory, see Howard Pack, "Endogenous Growth Theory: Intellectual Appeal and Empirical Shortcomings," *Journal of Economic Perspectives* 8, no. 1 (1994): 55–72.

26. See, for example, Aghion and Howitt, *Endogenous Growth Theory*.

27. Romer, "Two Strategies," 9–10.

28. I discuss the issue of ingenuity quality further in the "Ingenuity Theory" section of this book's Web site, www.ingenuitygap.com.

29. On the paper bag, see Paul Krugman, "The Paper-Bag Revolution," *New York Times Magazine*, 28 September 1997, 52–53. Krugman writes: "What propelled

us to the world's highest standard of living was the relentless ingenuity with which our inventors and entrepreneurs applied [big] technologies to small things, things that made workers more productive or domestic chores easier."

30. The seminal treatments of tacit knowledge are Michael Polanyi, *Personal Knowledge: Towards a Post-Critical Philosophy* (New York: Harper Torchbooks, 1962); and Michael Polanyi, *The Tacit Dimension* (Garden City, New York: Doubleday Anchor, 1967).

31. Richard Nelson and Sidney Winter examine the role of tacit knowledge and organizational routine in economic production in *An Evolutionary Theory of Economic Change* (Cambridge, Massachusetts: Belknap, 1982), especially chapters 4 and 5, pp. 72–137.

32. In fact, anthropological evidence indicates that our capacity to teach skills and knowledge verbally is a relatively recent product of human evolution, first seen in the Upper Paleolithic period, some tens of thousands of years ago. See Steven Mithen, *The Prehistory of the Mind: A Search for the Origins of Art, Religion, and Science* (London: Thames and Hudson, 1996), 190–91. Before that time, hominids probably communicated most knowledge—regarding, for instance, how to make tools—by repeating, or miming, each other's physical movements. See Merlin Donald, "Precis of *Origins of the Modern Mind: Three Stages in the Evolution of Culture and Cognition,*" *Behavioral and Brain Sciences* 16 (1993): 737–91.

33. My distinction between technical ingenuity and social ingenuity is only a first step towards a satisfactory categorization of ingenuity. Within social ingenuity, for example, we can distinguish between "structural" ingenuity (used to create or reform institutions) and "policy" ingenuity (for actions pursued within an existing institutional framework). And for both technical and social ingenuity, we can make a temporal distinction between ingenuity applied to short-term problems or crises (such as that supplied to manage the Asian financial crisis) and ingenuity applied to long-term problems (such as climate change).

34. For arguments on how social institutions shape a society's capacity for technological development, see Alexander Gerschenkron, *Economic Backwardness in Historical Perspective* (Cambridge, Massachusetts: Belknap Press, 1962); Moses Abramovitz, "Catching Up, Forging Ahead, and Falling Behind," *Journal of Economic History* 46, no. 2 (June 1986), 386–406; and Björn Johnson, "Institutional Learning," in Bengt-Åke Lundvall, *National Systems of Innovation: Towards a Theory of Innovation and Interactive Learning* (London: Pinter, 1992), 23–44.

35. Paul Romer, "Idea Gaps and Object Gaps in Economic Development," *Journal of Monetary Economics* 32 (1993): 544.

36. On the timber shortage, see Sherry Olson, *The Depletion Myth: A History of Railroad Use of Timber* (Cambridge, Mass.: Harvard University Press, 1971).

37. David Pimentel et al., "Food Production and the Energy Crisis," *Science* 182, no. 4111 (2 November 1973): 443–49.

38. Julian Simon, *The Ultimate Resource* (Princeton, New Jersey: Princeton University Press, 1981), 345.

39. Ester Boserup, *The Conditions of Agricultural Growth: The Economics of Agrarian Change under Population Pressure* (Chicago: Aldine, 1965); Ester Boserup, *Economic and Demographic Relationships in Development*, essays selected and introduced by

T. Paul Schultz (Baltimore, Maryland: Johns Hopkins University Press, 1990). For similar findings, see also Mary Tiffen, Michael Mortimore, and Francis Gichuki, *More People, Less Erosion: Environmental Recovery in Kenya* (Chichester, United Kingdom: John Wiley, 1994).

40. A particularly interesting argument of the kind elaborated in this paragraph is *induced-innovation theory*. First proposed in the 1930s, this theory has recently been applied by the economists Yujiro Hayami and Vernon Ruttan to agriculture in the United States, Japan, and other countries. In successful economies, they argue, market prices signal the relative availability of factors of production, such as cropland and labor; these signals then bias technological change away from use of relatively scarce factors and towards use of relatively abundant factors. So if agricultural labor is scarce relative to cropland (as was the case in the United States during the growth of its agricultural economy), people will invent and deploy technologies, like mechanized plows and combines, that make labor highly productive. Seminal statements of induced innovation theory are J. R. Hicks, *The Theory of Wages* (London: Macmillan, 1932); and Yujiro Hayami and Vernon Ruttan, *Agricultural Development: An International Perspective* (Baltimore: Johns Hopkins University Press, 1971, 1985). For critiques, see Alan Olmstead and Paul Rhode, "Induced Innovation in American Agriculture: A Reconsideration," *Journal of Political Economy* 101, no. 1 (1993): 105, 110; and Richard Grabowski, "The Theory of Induced Institutional Innovation: A Critique," *World Development* 16, no. 3 (1988): 385–94.

41. "The notion of a growing number of people fighting over a fixed resource pie is Malthusian bosh. . . . Human ingenuity, energised by sensible policies, creates resources faster than people use them; people learn to substitute sand (in the form of microchips) for sweat, and fuel cells for petrol engines." "Sui Genocide," *The Economist*, 19 December 1998, 130–31.

42. H. E. Goeller and A. M. Weinberg, "The Age of Substitutability," *Science* 191, no. 4228 (20 February 1976): 683–89.

43. Harold Barnett and Chandler Morse, *Scarcity and Growth: The Economics of Natural Resource Availability* (Baltimore: Johns Hopkins Press for Resources for the Future, 1963), 11; for a more contemporary treatment, see V. Kerry Smith, ed., *Scarcity and Growth Reconsidered* (Baltimore: Johns Hopkins Press for Resources for the Future, 1979).

44. Barnett and Morse, *Scarcity and Growth*, 10.

45. New archaeological evidence suggests that overpopulation and cropland degradation helped topple Sumerian, Mayan, and Easter Island civilizations; and recent historical sociology shows that population growth was a major force behind civil strife in early modern Eurasian societies. See Daniel Hillel, *Out of the Earth: Civilization and the Life of the Soil* (New York: Free Press, 1991); Clive Pointing, *A Green History of the World: The Environment and the Collapse of Great Civilizations* (New York: Penguin, 1991); J. M. Diamond, "Ecological Collapses of Ancient Civilizations: The Golden Age that Never Was," *Bulletin*, The American Academy of Arts and Sciences, 47, no. 5 (1994): 37–59; and Jack Goldstone, *Revolution and Rebellion in the Early Modern World* (Berkeley: University of California Press, 1991).

46. For models of economic growth that embody this assumption, see Gary Hansen and Edward Prescott, "Malthus to Solow," NBER *Working Paper Series*, no. 6858 (Washington, D.C.: National Bureau of Economic Research, 1998); and Oded Galor and David Weil, "Population, Technology, and Growth: From the Malthusian Regime to the Demographic Transition," NBER *Working Paper Series*, no. 6811 (Washington, D.C.: National Bureau of Economic Research, 1998).

47. Theodore Panayotou, "Roundtable Discussion: Is Economic Growth Sustainable?" *Proceedings of the World Bank Annual Conference on Development Economics 1991* (Washington, D.C.: World Bank, 1992), 357.

48. Over the long run, though, the story may be less positive: careful analysis of data from several centuries suggests that prices do always trend downwards. In fact, rather than decreasing linearly, prices may follow a U-shaped curve—first dropping, then curving upward—and we may still be in the lower portion of the curve for many ores and minerals. See Margaret Slade, "Trends in Natural Resource Commodity Prices: An Analysis of the Time Domain," *Journal of Environmental Economics and Management* 9, no. 2 (1982): 122–37; and B. Moazzami and F. Anderson, "Modelling Natural Resource Scarcity Using the 'Error-Correction' Approach," *Canadian Journal of Economics* 27, no. 4 (1994): 801–12.

49. Uma Lele and Steven Stone, *Population Pressure, the Environment and Agricultural Intensification: Variations on the Boserup Hypothesis*, MADIA Discussion Paper 4 (Washington, D.C.: World Bank, 1989).

50. Per Pinstrup-Anderson, "Global Perspectives for Food Production and Consumption," *Tidsskrift for Land Okonomi* 4, no. 179 (1992): 167.

51. Economists would rightly add labor and physical and human capital to this mix of inputs.

52. On property rights, environmental protection and the conservation of natural resources, see R. A. Devlin and R. Q. Grafton, *Economic Rights and Environmental Wrongs: Property Rights for the Common Good* (Cheltenham, UK: Edward Elgar, 1998).

53. For a technical treatment, see David Stern, "Limits to Substitution and Irreversibility in Production and Consumption: A Neoclassical Analysis," *Ecological Economics* 21 (1997): 197–215.

54. Although there is a clear link between deforestation and flooding in small river basins, the relationship is not established for large rivers such as the Ganges, Yangtze, and Mississippi.

55. Robert Solow, "The Economics of Resources or the Resources of Economics," *American Economic Review* 64, no. 2 (1974): 11.

56. Jacob Schmookler, *Invention and Economic Growth* (Cambridge, Massachusetts: Harvard University Press, 1966), 199; see also F. M. Scherer, "Demand-Pull and Technological Innovation: Schmookler Revisited," *Journal of Industrial Economics* 30 (March 1982): 225–38. A number of scholars have produced marvelously detailed historical accounts of the factors that stimulate technological innovation and of how this innovation has produced the West's extraordinary wealth. See, in particular, Joel Mokyr, *The Lever of Riches: Technological Creativity and Economic Progress* (New York: Oxford University Press, 1990); and Nathan

Rosenberg and L. E. Birdzell, Jr., *How the West Grew Rich: The Economic Transformation of the Industrial World* (Basic Books, 1986).

57. See Arnold Pacey, *The Maze of Ingenuity: Ideas and Idealism in the Development of Technology* (Cambridge, Massachusetts: MIT Press, 1992).

58. Gene Grossman and Elhanan Helpman, *Innovation and Growth in the Global Economy* (Cambridge, Massachusetts: MIT, 1991), 335.

59. On the role of disequilibriums in economic growth, see Lester Thurow, *Building Wealth: The New Rules for Individuals, Companies, and Nations in a Knowledge-Based Economy* (New York: HarperCollins, 1999), 21–22 and 33–36.

60. The classic statement of the latter difficulty is F. A. Hayek, "The Use of Knowledge in Society," *The American Economic Review* 35, no. 4 (September 1945): 519–30.

61. Ibid., 527.

62. The role of the state in establishing the conditions for markets has long been noted; of particular importance is Karl Polanyi, *The Great Transformation* (Boston: Beacon Press, 1957), 139–140.

63. Peter Evans, "The State as Problem and Solution: Predation, Embedded Autonomy, and Structural Change," in *The Politics of Economic Adjustment: International Constraints, Distributive Conflicts, and the State*, eds. Stephan Haggard and Robert Kaufman (Princeton, New Jersey: Princeton University Press, 1992), 141 and 148.

64. Daniel Yergin and Joseph Stanislaw, *The Commanding Heights: The Battle Between Government and the Marketplace That Is Remaking the Modern World* (New York: Simon & Schuster, 1998), 11, 12–13.

65. For a comprehensive treatment, see World Bank, *World Development Report, 1997: The State in a Changing World* (Oxford: Oxford University Press, 1997). An interesting critique from the left of this report is Nicholas Hildyard, *The World Bank and the State: A Recipe for Change?* (Sturminster Newton, Dorset: Cornerhouse Public Outreach and Research Unit, 1997).

66. Because returns to capital will eventually diminish in rich countries, standard neoclassical growth theory suggests that investors will transfer capital to poor countries to reap higher returns.

67. Although some poor countries, especially in East Asia, have grown very fast, in general poor countries are not growing faster than rich ones, and as noted previously in this chapter, there is little evidence that growth rates and returns to capital in rich countries are leveling off. New Growth models help resolve this problem by showing how new ideas can offset diminishing returns to capital in rich countries; they also suggest how poor countries can grow faster—by investing in human capital and by importing economically productive ideas from rich countries. See Romer, "Two Strategies."

68. For an argument in support of conditional convergence, see Robert Barro, "Economic Growth and Convergence," chapter 1 in *Determinants of Economic Growth: A Cross-Country Empirical Study* (Cambridge, Mass.: MIT Press, 1997): 1–47. Moses Abramovitz similarly argues that the ability of developing countries to increase their growth rates is largely a function of their "social capability" to exploit new technologies. He writes that "a country's potential for rapid growth is strong

not when it is backward without qualification, but rather when it is technologically backward but socially advanced." Abramovitz, "Catching Up," 388.

69. Mancur Olson, "Big Bills Left on the Sidewalk: Why Some Nations are Rich, and Others Poor," *Journal of Economic Perspectives* 10, no. 2 (Spring 1996): 6.

CHAPTER TEN

1. Comparisons of the explosive power of black powder (a low explosive) and TNT (a high explosive) are difficult, because the two substances release their explosive energy in different ways. However, black powder has less than half TNT's available energy per unit mass.

2. Gerrard Holzmann and Björn Pehrson, "The First Data Networks," *Scientific American* 270, no. 1 (January 1994): 124–29.

3. "Record Time," *Scientific American* 274, no. 5 (May 1996): 18.

4. The figures on agricultural yields in this paragraph were calculated using information in B. H. Slicher van Bath, *The Agrarian History of Western Europe: A.D.. 500–1850,* trans. Olive Ordish (London: Edward Arnold, 1963), 280–82, 332; and David Grigg, *The Transformation of Agriculture in the West* (Oxford: Blackwell, 1992), 32–35.

5. W. Brian Arthur, "How Fast Is Technology Evolving?" *Scientific American* 276, no. 2 (February 1997): 105–7.

6. Arthur disagrees with this judgment. "I don't believe the evolution of technology in general is slower than the sequence in calculating machines. From what I see, the creating of new technologies, new techniques, and new products has speeded up in the last ten years. But again I'm not sure that 'speed' is well defined here." Correspondence with the author, 1 November 1999.

7. For a survey, see Kanu Ashar, *Magnetic Disk Drive Technology: Heads, Media, Channel, Interfaces, and Integration* (New York: IEEE Press, 1997); a popular account is Claire Tristram, "The Big, Bad Bit Stuffers of IBM," *Technology Review* 101, no. 4 (July/August 1998): 44–51.

8. Amy Salzhauer, "Plastic Batteries: All Charged Up and Waiting to Go," *Technology Review* 101, no. 4 (July/August 1998): 60–66.

9. Michael Riordan, "The Incredible Shrinking Transistor," *Technology Review* 100, no. 8 (November/December, 1997): 46–52.

10. An excellent survey of the state of current scientific knowledge on multiple sclerosis is John Noseworthy, "Progress in Determining the Causes and Treatment of Multiple Sclerosis," *Nature: Neurological Disorders*, supplement to *Nature* 399, no. 6738 (24 June 1999): A40–A47; see also Gina Kolata, "Study of Brains Alters the View of Path of M.S.," *New York Times*, 29 January 1998, national edition, A1.

11. Nathan Rosenberg, *Perspectives on Technology* (New York: M.E. Sharpe, 1976), 267–68.

12. Eli Noam, "Visions of the Media Age: Taming the Information Monster," in *Multimedia: A Revolutionary Challenge*, Third Annual Colloquium, June 16/17, 1995, Frankfurt am Main (Stuttgart: Schäffer-Poeschel, 1995), 20–21.

13. Echoing Buzz Holling, Winner suggests we need a new epistemology that can help us understand whole systems and the relationships among their components, not just the characteristics of the individual components themselves. Our current epistemology and scientific methods are thoroughly inadequate for this task: "It might be said that we now have obtained knowledge at the cost of understanding. We have knowledge in the sense that we possess detailed, highly reliable information about the parts of our physical and social universe. We lack understanding in the sense that we cannot combine the parts of this knowledge in ways which will make the complex wholes intelligible." Langdon Winner, "Complexity and the Limits of Human Understanding," in *Organized Social Complexity: Challenge to Politics and Policy*, ed. Todd La Porte (Princeton: Princeton University Press, 1975): 46.

14. These cognitive constraints are essentially quantitative—that is, they are constraints on the sheer quantity of information that our brains can process. But our brains may also face qualitative constraints. The evolutionary psychologists we encountered in the "Brains and Ingenuity" chapter argue that specialized intelligences—specifically what they call technical, natural history, social, and linguistic intelligences—evolved in the hominid mind to deal with practical problems of survival in the African environment. If these experts are right, then vestiges of these specialized intelligences may remain in our minds and may influence the quality of our cognition today; they may shape, in a sense, what the world looks and feels like to us. As the philosopher and cognitive anthropologist Scott Atran writes: "Children, tribal peoples, modern layfolk—even scientists in their non-working hours—readily partition the ordinary range of human experience according to cognitive domains that are pretty much the same across cultures." As well, because there is no specific "science" faculty in the brain, these specialized intelligences must be starting points for our scientific thoughts and practices, and they likely shape the character and direction of evolution of these things. In sum, despite our brain's versatility, cognitive fluidity, and capacity to improvise—and despite its ability to combine ideas and knowledge produced by its specialized intelligences—it may not be able to escape its evolutionary heritage, even when engaged in science. This difficulty is, I believe, most acute in the social sciences, which are still largely centered on ill-defined and scientifically dubious "folk" concepts of belief, desire, and action. See Scott Atran, *Cognitive Foundations of Natural History: Towards an Anthropology of Science*, (Cambridge, Cambridge University Press: 1993); and, on the folk-psychological foundations of the social sciences, see Patricia Churchland, *Neurophilosophy* (Cambridge, Mass.: MIT Press, 1985), 295–310.

15. Office of Technology Assessment, *Starpower: The US and the International Quest for Fusion Energy* (Washington, D.C.: OTA, 1987), cited in Vaclav Smil, *General Energetics: Energy in the Biosphere and Civilization* (New York: John Wiley, 1991), 283–84.

16. Malcolm Browne, "Quest for Fusion Power Is Slowed by Cutbacks," *New York Times*, 23 April 1996, national edition, B7 and B9.

17. Colin Macilwain, "Is Magnetic Fusion Heading for Ignition or Meltdown?" *Nature* 388, no. 6638 (10 July 1997): 115–18.

18. Like multiple sclerosis, cancer turns out to be caused by complex combinations of factors, including genetic predispositions, environmental toxins, and lifestyle decisions. In the United States, the death rate from cancer has recently shown a slight but significant decrease. Much of the decrease is probably attributable, not to new treatments, but to the disease's declining incidence in the U.S. population. Recent data show the first clear decrease since the 1930s in the overall incidence of cancer, a trend that encompasses significant decreases in the incidence of prostate, lung, and colon/rectal cancers. (Unfortunately, incidence is still rising for some important cancers, such as melanoma and non-Hodgkin's lymphoma.) Overall, the rate fell from 426 new diagnoses per 100,000 people in 1992 to 392 per 100,000 in 1995. For certain types of cancer, the cause of the decline is reasonably clear: lower smoking rates, for example, have reduced lung cancer rates, and better screening has probably been key to the favorable trend for prostate cancer. But for other types, such as colon/rectal cancer, no clear explanation is available. See Sheryl Gay Stolberg, "New Cancer Cases Decreasing in U.S. as Deaths Do, Too," *New York Times*, 13 March 1998, national edition, A1.

19. Derek de Solla Price, *Little Science, Big Science . . . and Beyond* (New York: Columbia University Press, 1986), 92–94.

20. Gene Grossman and Elhanan Helpman, *Innovation and Growth in the Global Economy* (Cambridge, Mass.: MIT, 1991).

21. Wayt Gibbs, "Lost Science in the Third World," *Scientific American* 273, no. 2 (August 1995): 92–99.

22. Shortages of human capital accentuate the problem of cognitive limits, because individual experts and decision-makers face a greater load of tasks. The statistics in this paragraph are derived from Robert Repetto, "Population, Resources, Environment: An Uncertain Future," *Population Bulletin* 42, no. 2 (July 1987): 37; United Nations Development Program, *Human Development Report, 1992* (New York: Oxford, 1992), 57; and "An Unwelcome Export Success," *Nature.* 366, no. 6456 (16 December 1993): 618.

23. William Broad, "Study Finds Public Science Is Pillar of Industry," *New York Times*, 13 May 1997, national edition, B7. On the problems with private funding of basic science, see Norbert Wiener, *Invention: The Care and Feeding of Ideas* (Cambridge, Mass.: MIT Press, 1993). Some would even argue that capitalism and innovation are antithetical. For example, according to the economic historian Nathan Rosenberg, the famed economist Joseph Schumpeter believed that "as capitalism expands the sphere to which rationality applies, it learns eventually how to supplant the entrepreneur, the human 'carrier' of innovation, with institutions that do away with the social leadership of the entrepreneur himself." As well, "the nature of the innovation process, the drastic departure from existing routines, is inherently one that cannot be reduced to mere calculation, although subsequent imitation of the innovation, once accomplished, can be so reduced." See Nathan Rosenberg, "Joseph Schumpeter: Radical Economist," in *Exploring the Black Box: Technology, Economics, and History* (Cambridge: Cambridge University Press, 1994), 55 and 53.

24. Robert Wright, "The Experiment That Failed: Why Soviet Science Collapsed," *New Republic* (28 October 1991): 20–25; and Sergei Kapitza, "Antiscience

Trends in the USSR," *Scientific American* 265, no. 2 (August 1991): 32–38.

25. As the effects of science and technology have penetrated every corner of our lives, often disruptively, they have raised fundamental questions about human worth and the meaning of our existence. Science is also increasingly incomprehensible to the layperson: its findings are now often remote from our common-sense, "folk" understandings of the world around us (understandings grounded in those vestigial, specialized intelligences we've inherited from our hominid ancestors), which makes it mysterious and threatening to some people. Finally, we now largely separate ourselves from the vagaries of our physical world, and we construct for ourselves multiple "virtual" realities (as discussed in the chapter "The Big I"). We are therefore less motivated to think that there is a single physical reality—a natural world outside and beyond ourselves—that requires scientific study. John Maddox discusses the first of these factors in "The Prevalent Distrust of Science," *Nature* 378, no. 6556 (30 November 1995): 435–37; while Thomas Nagle treats the second in "The Sleep of Reason," review of Alan Sokal and Jean Bricmont, *Fashionable Nonsense: Postmodern Philosophers' Abuse of Science* (New York: St. Martin's, 1998) in *The New Republic*, 12 October 1998, 32–38. A comprehensive critique of current anti-science attitudes is Paul Gross, Norman Levitt, and Martin Lewis, eds., *The Flight from Science and Reason* (New York: New York Academy of Sciences, 1996).

26. One of the best treatments of this issue is Kenneth Prewitt, "Scientific Illiteracy and Democratic Theory," *Daedalus* 112, no. 2 (Spring 1983): 49–64.

27. For a general discussion, see Everett Rogers, *The Diffusion of Innovation*, 3rd ed. (New York: Free Press, 1983).

28. The information in the following paragraphs is taken from Henry Petroski, *Invention by Design: How Engineers Get from Thought to Thing* (Cambridge, Massachusetts: Harvard University Press, 1996), 104–19.

29. John Horgan, *The End of Science: Facing the Limits of Knowledge in the Twilight of the Scientific Age* (Reading, Mass.: Addison-Wesley, 1996). For an extraordinarily subtle and thorough treatment of the limits of science, see John Barrow, *Impossibility: The Limits of Science and the Science of Limits* (Oxford: Oxford University Press, 1998).

30. James Gleick, "Days of Future Past," *New York Times Magazine*, 21 December 1997, 28.

31. Paul Wallich, "Remembrance of Future Past," review of HAL's Legacy: *2001's Computer as Dream and Reality*, ed. David Stork, forward by Arthur C. Clarke (Cambridge, Mass.: MIT Press, 1997), in *Scientific American* 276, no. 1 (January 1997): 114–15.

32. Gleick, "Days of Future Past."

33. Wallich, "Remembrance of Future Past," 114.

34. John Rennie, "The Uncertainties of Technological Innovation," *Scientific American* 273, no. 3 (September 1995): 57–58.

35. Herman Kahn and Anthony Wiener, "The Next Thirty-Three Years: A Framework for Speculation," in Daniel Bell and Stephen Graubard, eds., *Toward the Year 2000: Work in Progress* (Cambridge, Mass.: MIT Press, 1997 [1967]), 73–100.

36. David Jones, "In Retrospect," review of Herman Kahn and Anthony Wiener, *The Year 2000: A Framework for Speculation on the Next Thirty-Three Years* (Macmillan, 1967), in *Nature* 403, no. 6765 (6 January 2000): 20.

37. William Velander, Henryk Lubon, and William Drohan, "Transgenic Livestock as Drug Factories," *Scientific American* 276, no. 1 (January 1997): 70–74.

38. Laura van Dam, "The Gene Doctor Is In: Interview with Victor McKusick," *Technology Review* 100, no. 5 (July 1997): 47–52.

39. See, "Briefing: Xenotransplantation," *Nature* 391, No. 6665 (22 January 1998): 320–28; Sheryl Gay Stolberg, "Animals as Organ Donors? Not Until They're Germ-Free," *New York Times*, 3 February 1998, national edition, B9.

40. Gina Kolata, "Scientists Brace for Changes in Path of Human Evolution," *New York Times*, 21 March 1998, national edition, A1.

41. Robert Devlin et al., "Extraordinary Salmon Growth," *Nature* 371, no. 6494 (15 September 1994): 209–10.

42. Moore originally asserted, in 1964, that the doubling time was one year, but in the late 1970s the accepted figure became eighteen months.

43. David Patterson, "The Limits of Lithography," *Scientific American* 273, no. 3 (September 1995): 66.

44. Paul Packan, "Pushing the Limits," *Science* 285 (24 September 1999): 2079–81; D. A. Muller et al., "The Electronic Structure at the Atomic Scale of Ultrathin Gate Oxides, *Nature* 399, no. 6738 (24 June 1999): 758–61.

45. John Markhoff, "Intel Trashes an Axiom of the Computer Age," *International Herald Tribune*, 18 September 1997, 1.

46. David Patterson, "Microprocessors in 2020," *Scientific American* 273, no. 3 (September 1995): 67.

47. These devices are discussed in John Villasenor and William Mangione-Smith, "Configurable Computing," *Scientific American* 276, no. 6 (June 1997): 66–71.

48. For a brief survey, see Wayt Gibbs, "Programming with Primordial Ooze," *Scientific American* 275, no. 4 (October 1996): 48–50.

49. Douglas Lenat, "Artificial Intelligence," *Scientific American* 273, no. 3 (September 1995): 80–83.

50. Ivan Amato, *Stuff: The Materials the World Is Made of* (New York: Basic, 1997), 189 and 258.

51. Peter Atkins, "Limitless Horizons," *Nature* 370, no. 6485 (14 July 1994): 109–10.

52. John Ewen, "New Chemical Tools to Create Plastics," *Scientific American* 276, no. 5 (May 1997): 86–91.

53. Kaigham Gabriel, "Engineering Microscopic Machines," *Scientific American* 273, no. 3 (September 1995): 150–53.

54. MEMS technology should not be confused with nanotechnology, which, if it ever comes to pass, would operate at an even smaller scale. Boosters of nanotechnology argue that it will soon be possible to build self-replicating machines out of individually placed atoms and molecules. Controlled by computers, these machines could then conduct elaborate operations at the atomic level (such as destroying the genetic material of cancer cells within the human body) or construct, atom by atom, macro-scale objects for our use, such as food, furniture,

and household appliances. Critics raise numerous objections. In particular, they note, individual atoms are extremely difficult to manipulate and hold in place; moreover, it is not clear how energy and information would be delivered to atomic-level machines. For surveys, see Ralph Merkle, "It's a Small, Small, Small, Small World," *Technology Review* 100, no. 2 (February/March 1997): 25–32; and Gary Stix, "Trends in Nanotechnology: Waiting for Breakthroughs," *Scientific American* 274, no. 4 (April 1996): 94–99.

55. Malcolm Browne, "Micro-Machines Help Solve Intractable Problem of Turbulence," *New York Times*, 3 January 1995, national edition, B5.

56. John Markhoff, "Next Wave in High Tech: Tiny Motors and Sensors, *New York Times*, 27 January 1997, national edition, A1.

57. Henry Adams, from chapter 25, "The Dynamo and the Virgin," in *The Education of Henry Adams* (Boston: Houghton Mifflin: 1974), 380.

58. "History of the United States," *The New Encyclopædia Britannica*, 15th edition, vol. 18 (Chicago: Encyclopædia Britannica, 1982), 975.

59. The best account of the history of Harvard seals is Samuel Eliot Morison, "Harvard Seals and Arms," *The Harvard Graduates' Magazine* 42, no. 165 (September 1933): 1–15; see also Mason Hammond, "A Harvard Armory: Part I," *Harvard Library Bulletin* 29, nos. 3 and 4 (1981): 261, 263, 270–1.

60. Samuel Eliot Morison, *Three Centuries of Harvard, 1636-1936* (Cambridge, Mass.: Harvard University Press, 1965), 24–25.

61. Quoted in Morison, *Three Centuries of Harvard*, 279.

62. Quoted in Morison, "Harvard Seals and Arms," 11.

63. J. T. Morse Jr., *Life and Letters of Oliver Wendell Holmes*, vol. 1 (London: Sampson Low, Marston, 1896), 237.

CHAPTER ELEVEN

1. The letter's actual text read as follows: "I am certainly not an advocate for frequent and untried changes in laws and constitutions, I think moderate imperfections had better be borne with; because, when once known, we accommodate ourselves to them and find practical means of correcting their ill effects. But I know, also, that laws and institutions must go hand in hand with the progress of the human mind. As that becomes more developed, more enlightened, as new discoveries are made, new truths disclosed, and manners and opinions change with the change of circumstances, institutions must advance also, and keep pace with the times."

2. For discussions of these issues, see Mustapha Nabli and Jeffrey Nugent, "The New Institutional Economics and Its Applicability to Development," *World Development* 17, no. 9 (1989): 1333–47; and Chidem Kurdas, "Neo-institutionalism: Bounded Rationality," chapter 5 in *Theories of Technical Change and Investment: Riches and Rationality* (New York: St. Martin's, 1994), 85–121.

3. Michael Janofsky, "National Parks, Strained by Record Crowds, Face a Crisis," *New York Times*, 25 July 1999, national edition, section 1, 1.

4. See, for example, Inge Kaul, Isabelle Grunberg, and Marc Stern, eds., *Global Public Goods: International Cooperation in the 21st Century* (New York: Oxford University Press, 1999), 11. The editors of this exhaustive treatment of global institutional needs write that "today's turmoil reveals a serious underprovision of global public goods."

5. Valuable treatments of the challenges of institutional design in the modern international system include James Rosenau, *Along the Domestic-Foreign Frontier: Exploring Governance in a Turbulent World* (Cambridge: Cambridge University Press, 1997); and Vinod Aggarwal, *Institutional Designs for a Complex World: Bargaining, Linkages, and Nesting* (Ithaca, New York: Cornell University Press, 1998).

6. Leslie Gelb, "Smog of Peace," *Sunday New York Times*, 9 May 1993, national edition, section 4, p. 15.

7. An excellent summary of the issues is Oran Young, *Institutional Dimensions of Global Environmental Change: IDGEC Science Plan* (Bonn, Germany: International Human Dimensions Programme on Global Environmental Change, 1999).

8. The ecologist Buzz Holling emphasizes, in particular, these systems' differing scales in space and time. "The relevant biophysical processes operate over an enormous range of scales," he writes, "from soil process operating with time constants of days in meter-square patches, to ecosystem successional processes of decades to centuries covering tens to thousands of square kilometers, to biotic processes involved in the regulation and isolation of elements like carbon that have time lags of millennia and are global in their impact." C. S. Holling, "New Science and New Investments for a Sustainable Biosphere," in AnnMarie Jansson et al., *Investing in Natural Capital: The Ecological Economics Approach to Sustainability* (Washington, D.C.: Island Press, 1994), 63.

9. These arguments are well developed in Elinor Ostrom, "Designing Complexity to Govern Complexity," in *Property Rights and the Environment*, eds. Susan Hanna and Mohan Munasinghe (Washington, D.C.: Beijer International Institute of Ecological Economics and the World Bank, 1995), 33. Ostrom writes: "Since many biological processes occur at small, medium, and large scales, governance arrangements that cope with this level of complexity also need to be organized at multiple scales and linked effectively together."

10. These obstacles to successful negotiation are highlighted by Richard Cooper in "Toward a Real Global Warming Treaty," *Foreign Affairs* (March/April 1998): 66–79. An excellent primer on the Kyoto Protocol, the technical details surrounding it, and the state of current climate negotiations is available from the research institute Resources for the Future's Web site at http://www.weathervane.rff.org.

11. Research on past environmental treaties, especially fishery regimes, suggests that the political demands tend to be met first, while the technical, sustainability requirements are met later, if at all. See Charles Hall, "Institutional Solutions for Governing the Global Comments: Design Factors and Effectiveness," *The Journal of Environment & Development* 7, no. 2 (June 1998): 86–114.

12. David Victor and Eugene Skolnikoff report the results of a major research project studying this problem in "Translating Intent into Action: Implementing

Environmental Commitments," *Environment* 41, no. 2 (March 1999): 16–43.

13. Cooper, "Toward a Real Global Warming Treaty," 70–71.

14. Graciela Chichilnisky, *Development and Global Finance: The Case for an International Bank for Environmental Settlements*, Discussion Paper (New York: United Nations Development Programme, 1997), 15–16, and Appendix I.

15. Chichilnisky argues that the difficulties arise mainly because the right to use the atmosphere as a sink to absorb emissions is, essentially, the right to use a public good. In contrast to markets for private goods, the distribution of property and wealth in a market for public goods (a matter of *equity*) affects market *efficiency*. This difference, Chichilnisky contends, will require the international community to set up an International Bank for Environmental Settlements to facilitate trading of emissions rights. According to Inge Kaul, director of the Office of Development Studies of the United Nations Development Programme, this bank would "act as a clearing house for the global environmental market, matching parties in environmental trade, mediating borrowing and lending and ensuring the integrity of market transactions and their settlement." See ibid., vi.

16. Unlike the situation in Algonquin Park, though, the institutions and social relations we design to manage Earth's biosphere will require complex horizontal and vertical linkages—that is, linkages running both horizontally at single levels of social organization, like the village or the nation-state, and vertically across these levels, integrating, for example, the village, national, international, and biospheric levels. Such arrangements run the risk of being so large and cumbersome as to be unmanageable. On the problems of giant bureaucracies, see John Lewis, "Some Consequences of Giantism: The Case of India," *World Politics* 43, no. 3 (April 1991): 367–89. On the changing size of the human economy relative to Earth's biosphere, see Herman Daly and John Cobb, Jr., *For the Common Good: Redirecting the Economy Toward Community, the Environment and a Sustainable Future* (Boston: Beacon Press, 1989), 143–47.

17. The systems theorists Kenneth Watt and Paul Craig discuss the requirements facing an advanced society under severe resource constraints. "Such a society would be characterized by great efficiency in resource use, very diverse energy and materials sources and pathways through the system, a very large number of types of system components (i.e., occupations), and a rich variety of internal control mechanisms." See Kenneth Watt and Paul Craig, "System Stability Principles," *Systems Research* 3, no. 4 (1986): 197.

18. For an overview of research and data on land degradation, including a survey of regional "hot spots" and "bright spots," see Sara Scherr and Satya Yadav, *Land Degradation in the Developing World: Implications for Food, Agriculture, and the Environment to 2020*, IFPRI Food, Agriculture, and the Environment Discussion Paper 14 (Washington, D.C.: International Food Policy Research Institute, 1996).

19. D. Hawksworth and M. Kalin-Arroyo provide an experts' consensus estimate of 13.6 million species in total on the planet, of which some 1.75 million (or only about 13 percent) are known to science. See Hawksworth and Kalin-Arroyo, Magnitude and Distribution of Biodiversity," section 3 in *Global Biodiversity Assessment*, ed. V. H. Heywood and R. T. Watson (Cambridge:

Cambridge University Press, 1995), 111. The *Assessment* is the state-of-the-art account of scientific understanding of biodiversity.

20. Holling, "New Science," 62.

21. Peter Drucker, "The Age of Social Transformation," *Atlantic Monthly* (November 1994): 80.

22. Steve Lohr, "Hey! Computers Go Faster Than the Courts," *New York Times*, Week in Review, 26 April 1998, national edition, 3.

23. An excellent statement of the problem of complexity in the social sciences is F. A. Hayek, "The Theory of Complex Phenomena," chapter 2 in *Studies in Philosophy, Politics and Economics* (London: Routledge & Kegan Paul, 1967), 22–42. Hayek writes: "One of the chief results so far achieved by theoretical work in these fields seems to me to be the demonstration that here individual events regularly depend on so many concrete circumstances that we shall never in fact be in a position to ascertain them all; and that in consequence not only the ideal of prediction and control must largely remain beyond our reach, but also the hope remain illusory that we can discover by observation regular connections between the individual events."

24. I am more persuaded by arguments that stress a key distinction between the social and natural worlds: while things in the natural world are usually best categorized by their intrinsic properties (mass, density, molecular composition and the like), things in the social world are usually best categorized by their relational properties. Researchers studying political revolution, for example, will decide whether a particular violent event is an example of revolution, not by reference to the intrinsic physical characteristics of that event (such as the physical actions of the people involved), but by reference to how the event is understood by both actors and observers. They will examine, in other words, the *relationships* between the event and certain beliefs in the minds of the people involved in it. This difference raises serious questions about the possibility of causal generalizations in the social sciences. One of the best accounts of this difference between the natural and social worlds, an account that suggests the difference is not an insurmountable obstacle to causal generalization in the social sciences, is Jerry Fodor, "Introduction: Two Kinds of Reductionism," *The Language of Thought* (New York: Thomas Crowell, 1975), 1–25. See also Alan Wolfe, *The Human Difference: Animals, Computers, and the Necessity of Social Science* (Berkeley, California: University of California Press, 1993).

25. "[Neoclassical theory] addresses an artificial world where time is reversible, where individuals are self-contained, atomistic units, and where both extreme complexity and chronic problems of information and knowledge are excluded. The idea of rational, maximizing actors interacting and reaching an equilibrium is modeled precisely in these mechanistic terms." Geoffrey Hodgson, "The Reconstruction of Economics: Is There Still a Place for Neoclassical Theory?" *Journal of Economic Issues* 26, no. 3 (September 1992): 757.

26. The critical economists Robert Heilbroner and William Milberg write: "This inextricable entanglement of economics with capitalism appears to be the best guarded secret of the profession. . . . The failure of mainstream economics to recognize the insistent presence of this underlying social order, with its class

structure, its socially determined imperatives, its technologies and organizations, and its privileges and rights, derives from its preconceptual basis in a natural rather than a social construal of economic society." And later: "[The] universal grammar [of modern economics] does not communicate a message of any economic interest or significance, unless it applies to a society that possesses the institutional and cultural elements of capitalism: indeed, the very meaning of 'economic' would be unintelligible outside capitalism." Robert Heilbroner and William Milberg, *The Crisis of Vision in Modern Economic Thought* (Cambridge: Cambridge University Press, 1995), 111, 113.

27. Floyd Norris, "Decadelong Forecasts Are Usually Wrong," *New York Times*, 30 December 1998, national edition, A22.

28. Alan Greenspan, "Remarks by Chairman Alan Greenspan at the 15th Anniversary Conference of the Center for Economic Policy Research at Stanford University," delivered at Stanford, California, 5 September 1997, 4.

29. Ibid., 6.

30. Elinor Ostrom, "A Behavioral Approach to the Rational Choice Theory of Collective Action," Presidential Address, American Political Science Association, 1997, *American Political Science Review* 92, no. 1 (March 1998): 1–22.

31. For a devastating attack on the use of rational choice theory in political science, see Donald Green and Ian Shapiro, *Pathologies of Rational Choice Theory: A Critique of Applications in Political Science* (New Haven, Connecticut: Yale University Press, 1994).

32. Ostrom, "A Behavioral Approach," 1.

33. Rather than "democracy" and "autocracy," the task force used the terminology "more democratic states" and "less democratic states."

34. Daniel Esty et al., *Working Papers: State Failure Task Force Report* (McLean, Virginia: Science Applications International Corporation, 30 November 1995), 21.

35. Daniel Esty et al., *State Failure Task Force Report: Phase II Findings* (McLean, Virginia: Science Applications International Corporation, 31 July 1998).

36. Political scientist Daniel Deudney, one of the most thoughtful commentators on these issues, suggests that most social science theory since the beginning of the twentieth century has been "social-social" theory—that is, theory that posits social causes of social effects. He suggests we need to reintroduce nature into our explanations of social behavior and should try to develop sophisticated "nature-social" theory. See Daniel Deudney, "Bringing Nature Back In," in *Contested Grounds: Security and Conflict in the New Environmental Politics*, eds. Daniel Deudney and Richard Matthew (Albany, New York: State University of New York, 1999), 25–57. One of the best contemporary attempts to integrate social and ecological factors in an explanation of long-run social and economic development is E. L. Jones, *The European Miracle: Environments, Economies and Geopolitics in the History of Europe and Asia*, 2d ed. (Cambridge: Cambridge University Press, 1996).

37. Thomas Homer-Dixon, *Environment, Scarcity, and Violence* (Princeton, New Jersey: Princeton University Press, 1999).

38. The main problem facing the task force was the explosion of possibilities that occurs once researchers start creating interactive sets from even a small number

of explanatory variables. For instance, if a researcher is working with five possible explanatory variables and wants to explore the effects on violence of all possible interactive sets of variables drawn from these five (that is, all possible combinations of two, three, four, and five of these five variables), then the researcher has twenty-six possibilities to test. The State Failure Task Force identified seventy-five "high-priority" explanatory variables, which meant that the number of possible combinations of even two, three, and four variables was huge.

Researchers usually cope with this problem by using an overarching theory (in this case, of the causes of civil violence) to narrow down the range of possible interactive sets of variables. Many sets will simply not make any sense from a theoretical point of view. Early on in the Task Force's work, however, the team was told that it could not explicitly introduce theories of conflict into its work, because to do so might make its findings vulnerable to political attack in Congress.

39. Michael Janofsky, "After Malaise, a New Mood in Nation's Capital," *New York Times*, 11 November 1998, national edition, A1.

40. Joel Brinkley, "Information Superhighway Is Just Outside the Beltway," *New York Times*, 12 October 1999, national edition, A1.

41. Langdon Winner suggests these two responses—the application of centralized power to reduce complexity and the application of technology to understand complexity better—in his discussion of how large organizations try to manage complex environments. See Winner, "Complexity and the Limits of Human Understanding," in *Organized Social Complexity: Challenge to Politics and Policy*, ed. Todd La Porte (Princeton: Princeton University Press, 1975): 64–65. For a devastating critique of both approaches, see James Scott, *Seeing Like a State: How Certain Schemes to Improve the Human Condition Have Failed* (New Haven, Conn.: Yale University Press, 1998).

42. The classic statement of this decision-making approach, labeled "the method of successive limited comparisons," is Charles Lindblom, "The Science of 'Muddling Through,' *Public Administration Review* 19, no. 2 (1959): 79–88.

43. Careful readers will note that I have said two things about practical or experiential knowledge in this book. Efficiency improvements in our complex human-made systems often come at the expense of experiential knowledge (see the chapter "Unknown Unknowns"), which generally makes these systems less resilient in crisis. At the same time, though, our world is changing so fast that much experiential knowledge becomes obsolete quickly and may not, in the end, be of much value in helping our organizations and societies cope with their challenges.

44. Winner critiques both the "resilience through complexity" and "incrementalism" arguments in Langdon Winner "Complexity and the Limits of Human Understanding," 68–73.

45. Two concepts commonly used here are "homeostasis" and "homeorhesis." Biologists and ecologists use homeostasis to refer to the tendency of living systems to return to their equilibrium state even when displaced from that equilibrium by internal or external shock. For instance, the human body is a homeostatic system because it can respond to most illnesses and repair most injuries. Even if its vital signs, such as body temperature, heart rate, and blood pressure, are knocked

away from their normal values, the body can usually return them quickly to something approximating those values. But homeostatic systems can be pushed beyond their boundaries of initial equilibrium into an entirely new state. The human body can be so badly injured that it cannot recover; the result—the new equilibrium state—is death.

Homeorhesis is a similar but less common concept used by developmental biologists. It refers to the tendency of a developing organism—a human baby growing to adulthood, for example—to return to its normal trajectory of development even if that trajectory is temporarily perturbed, say by illness or inadequate food. The mechanisms of homeorhetic regulation in such systems don't take them back to an initial equilibrium (as is the case for homeostatic systems) but forward to some future point in the normal flow of development.

46. The nineteenth- and early-twentieth-century French sociologist Émile Durkheim explicitly viewed society as an organism, and the idea persisted up to the structural-functionalism of the American sociologist Talcott Parsons in the 1950s and 1960s. For a review of literature on the Gaia hypothesis, see Timothy Lenton, "Gaia and Natural Selection," *Nature* 394, no. 6692 (30 July 1998): 439–47.

47. An accessible, general statement of these theories is Stuart Kauffman, *At Home in the Universe: The Search for the Laws of Self-Organization and Complexity* (New York: Oxford University Press, 1995); a technical treatment of self-organization in biological systems is Stuart Kauffman, *The Origins of Order: Self-Organization and Selection in Evolution* (New York: Oxford University Press, 1993). In a famous article written over four decades ago, Warren Weaver distinguished between scientific problems of "simplicity," of "disorganized complexity," and of "organized complexity"; the latter problems involve what we would today call complex-adaptive systems. See Warren Weaver, "Science and Complexity," *American Scientist* (October 1948): 536–44.

48. Kauffman, "Conceptual Outline of Current Evolutionary Theory," *The Origins of Order*, 3–26.

49. The idea of a fitness landscape was first introduced by Sewall Wright in "The Roles of Mutation, Inbreeding, Crossbreeding and Selection in Evolution," *Proceedings of the Sixth International Congress on Genetics* 1 (1932): 356–66.

50. Kauffman, 252–67.

51. Wright, 363.

52. Robert Putnam with Robert Leonardi and Raffaela Nanetti, *Making Democracy Work: Civic Traditions in Modern Italy* (Princeton, New Jersey: Princeton University Press, 1993); Michael Woolcock, "Social Capital and Economic Development: Toward a Theoretical Synthesis and Policy Framework," *Theory and Society* 27 (1998): 151–208.

53. Rosenberg and Birdzell stress that this cultural attribute is both highly unusual and vitally important: "Growth is, of course, a form of change, and growth is impossible when change is not permitted. And *successful* change requires a large measure of freedom to experiment. A grant of that kind of freedom costs a society's rulers their feeling of control, as if they were conceding to others the power to determine the society's future. The great majority of societies, past

and present, have not allowed it. Nor have they escaped from poverty." Nathan Rosenberg and L. E. Birdzell, *How the West Grew Rich: The Economic Transformation of the Industrial World* (Basic Books, 1986), 34.

54. On the open-source revolution, see Chris DiBona, Sam Ockman, and Mark Stone, eds. *OpenSources: Voices from the Open Sources Revolution* (Sebastopol, California: O'Reilley, 1999); and Amy Harmon, "The Rebel Code," *New York Times Magazine*, 21 February 1999, 35–7.

55. W. Brian Arthur, "How Fast is Technology Evolving," *Scientific American* 276, no. 2 (February 1997): 105–7.

56. Institutions are grounded in culture, and culture generally changes very slowly. If both institutions and culture must change for a society to adapt to new circumstances, a society may not be able to migrate across its fitness landscape quickly enough to avoid disaster. On the difficulties of rapid and directed cultural change, see Harry Eckstein, "A Culturalist Theory of Political Change," *American Political Science Review* 82 (September 1988): 789–804.

57. Individuals and groups must often bear high costs to ask these questions and pursue answers that fall outside the range that the social and economic system defines as acceptable. Joshua Cohen and Joel Rogers brilliantly describe this kind of structural trap in American capitalist democracy. "The operation of capitalist democracy rewards and thereby encourages a narrow economic rationality oriented toward the satisfaction of short-term material interests. The satisfaction of such interests in turn provides a basis for consent to the continued operation of the system." See Cohen and Rogers, *On Democracy* (New York: Penguin, 1983), 146.

58. William McNeill, "Control and Catastrophe in Human Affairs," in *The Global Condition: Conquerors, Catastrophes, & Community* (Princeton: Princeton University Press, 1992), 136.

CHAPTER TWELVE

1. Robert Brustein, "The Las Vegas Show," *New Republic*, 4 & 11 January 1999, 27–29.

2. David Shenk, *Data Smog: Surviving the Information Glut* (San Francisco: HarperEdge, 1997), 31.

3. Sven Birkerts, an English professor at Bennington College, says "I never see a sentence with a semicolon in it anymore. People don't tend to read the kind of writing that has semicolons. We tend to read the prose of the age, and the prose of the age, influenced by the ethos of electronic communication, is almost overwhelmingly flat, punchy, and declarative." Amy Harmon, "Internet Changes Language for :-) & :-(" *New York Times*, 20 February 1999, national edition, A15.

4. Stanley Milgram, "The Experience of Living in the Cities," *Science* 167 (13 March 1970): 1461–68.

5. John Markoff, "A Newer, Lonelier Crowd Emerges in Internet Study," *New York Times*, 16 February 2000, national edition, A1.

6. The concept of social capital was first introduced by James Coleman in *Foundations of Social Theory* (Cambridge, Mass.: Belknap Press of Harvard University, 1999). See also Robert Putnam with Robert Leonardi and Raffaela Nanetti, *Making Democracy Work: Civic Traditions in Modern Italy* (Princeton, New Jersey: Princeton University Press, 1993); and Michael Woolcock, "Social Capital and Economic Development: Toward a Theoretical Synthesis and Policy Framework," *Theory and Society* 27 (1998): 151–208.

7. On the general issue of increased pace, see James Gleick, *Faster: The Acceleration of Just About Everything* (New York: Pantheon Books, 1999). On implications for our interpersonal relationships and family lives, see Robert Kegan, *In over Our Heads: The Mental Demands of Modern Life* (Cambridge, Mass.: Harvard University Press, 1994); and Arlie Russell Hochschild, *The Time Bind: When Work Becomes Home & Home Becomes Work* (New York: Metropolitan Books, 1997). For an enthusiastic statement of the case for acquiescence to the new reality in our personal and corporate economic strategies, see Stan Davis and Christopher Meyer, *Blur: The Speed of Change in the Connected Economy* (Reading, Mass.: Addison-Wesley, 1998).

8. Robert Sapolsky, *Why Zebras Don't Get Ulcers: A Guide to Stress, Stress-Related Diseases, and Coping* (New York: Freeman, 1994), 178–95.

9. Michael Marmot, "Social Inequalities in Mortality: The Social Environment in Class and Health," in Richard Wilkinson, ed., *Class and Health* (London: Tavistock Publications, 1986), 21–34; and Michael Marmot et al., "Health Inequalities among British Civil Servants: The Whitehall II Study," *Lancet* 337 (8 June 1991): 1387–93.

10. Michael Marmot and Tores Theorell, "Social Class and Cardiovascular Disease: The Contribution of Work," *International Journal of Health Services* 18, no.4 (1988): 659–74.

11. Amy Arnsten, "The Biology of Being Frazzled," *Science* 280 (12 June 1998): 1711–12; and Amy Arnsten, "Development of the Cerebral Cortex: XIV. Stress Impairs Prefrontal Cortical Function," *Development and Neurobiology* 38, no. 2 (1999): 220–22. The reaction of the frontal lobes to stress hormones may have had survival value in the wild: when the activity of the prefrontal cortex is inhibited, habitual responses controlled by posterior cortical and subcortical structures take charge of our behavior, and these responses may have been more successful in emergency situations.

12. David Shenk, *Data Smog*, 29.

13. To calculate the statistics in this paragraph, we counted the words in articles randomly selected from those published in 1979 and 1999. For *Time*, we used ten cover-stories from each of these two years; for *Scientific American*, we used ten standard research articles from each year; and for *The New York Times*, we used twenty op-ed articles that appeared from September through early December in each year.

14. Timothy Cook, *Governing with the News: The News Media as a Political Institution* (Chicago: University of Chicago Press, 1998), 101, 113.

15. Quoted in *USA Today*, 7 June 1995, and in Cook, *Governing with the News*, 114.

16. James Naughton, "This Just In! And This!" *New York Times*, 1 February 1998, section 4, national edition, 17.

17. Cook, *Governing with the News*, 121–22.

18. William Leiss: *The Domination of Nature* (New York: George Braziller, 1972), 21.

19. Quoted in Sean Wilentz, "Life, Liberty, and the Pursuit of Thomas Jefferson," *New Republic* (10 March 1997): 42.

20. Vannevar Bush, "As We May Think," *Atlantic Monthly* (July 1945): 108.

21. Jeffrey Young, "MIT Media Lab Plans New Effort for Children," *Chronicle of Higher Education* 44, no. 10 (31 October 1997): A39.

22. W. Brian Arthur, "How Fast Is Technology Evolving?" *Scientific American* 276, no. 2 (February 1997): 105–7.

23. Quoted in John Stackhouse, "Third World Begins Exploring the Internet," *Globe and Mail*, 29 June 1996, A1.

24. For general discussion, see P.J. Simmons, "Learning to Live with NGOs," *Foreign Policy* 112 (Fall 1998): 82–96.

25. David Halbfinger, "As Surveillance Cameras Peer, Some Wonder If They Also Pry," *New York Times*, 22 February 1998, national edition, 1; Carey Goldberg, "DNA Databanks Giving Police a Powerful Weapon, and Critics," *New York Times*, 19 February 1998, national edition, A1; Eric Scigliano, "The Tide of Prints," *Technology Review* 102, no. 1 (January/February 1999): 63–67.

26. Quoted in Barbara Crossette, "The Internet Changes Dictatorship's Rules," *New York Times*, 1 August 1999, section 4, national edition, 1–16. Speaking more generally of the information revolution, the foreign policy commentator Jessica Tuchman Mathews writes: "The new technologies encourage non-institutional, shifting networks over the fixed bureaucratic hierarchies that are the hallmark of the single-voiced sovereign state. They dissolve issues' and institutions' ties to a fixed place. And by greatly empowering individuals, they weaken the relative attachment to community, of which the preeminent one in modern society is the nation-state." Jessica Tuchman Mathews, "Power Shift," *Foreign Affairs* 76, no. 1 (January/February 1997): 66.

27. Niccolò Machiavelli, *The Prince and Selected Discourses: Machiavelli*, ed. and trans. Daniel Donno (New York: Bantam, 1971 [1513]), 27.

28. Drawing on the pioneering work of the economist Mancur Olson, commentators such as Jonathan Rauch and Robert Wright have described the debilitating activities of obstructionist subgroups in American politics. See Jonathan Rauch, *Demosclerosis: The Silent Killer of American Government* (New York: Times Books, 1995); Robert Wright, "Hyperdemocracy," *Time*, 23 January 1995, 41–46; and Mancur Olson, *The Rise and Decline of Nations: Economic Growth, Stagflation, and Social Rigidities* (New Haven, CT: Yale University Press, 1982).

29. Michael Wines, "Washington Really Is in Touch: We're the Problem," *New York Times*, 16 October 1994, section 4, 1E.

30. Hugh Heclo, "Hyperdemocracy," *Wilson Quarterly* 23, no. 1 (Winter 1999): 67.

31. Alison Mitchell, "A New Form of Lobbying Puts Public Face on Private Interest," *New York Times*, 30 September 1998, A1.

32. The accumulation of special interests, writes Olson, "increases the complexity of regulation, the role of government, and complexity of understandings." Olson, *Rise and Decline*, 73.

33. Mathews, *Power Shift*, 66.

34. Ronald Heifetz, *Leadership Without Easy Answers* (Cambridge, MA: Harvard University Press, 1994), 2.

35. This argument is developed in Robert Ornstein and Paul Ehrlich, *New World, New Mind: Moving Toward Conscious Evolution* (New York: Simon & Schuster, 1989).

36. Lionel Tiger, *Optimism: The Biology of Hope* (New York: Simon & Schuster, 1979).

37. On the role of goodwill, reciprocity, civic-mindedness, and trust in political and economic well-being, see Amitai Etzioni, *The Moral Dimension: Towards a New Economics* (New York: Free Press, 1988); Albert Hirschman, "Against Parsimony: Three Easy Ways of Complicating Some Categories of Economic Discourse," chap. 6 in *Rival Views of Market Society, and Other Recent Essays* (Cambridge: Harvard University Press, 1992), 153–57; Charles Sabel, "Studied Trust: Building New Forms of Cooperation in a Volatile Economy," in *Industrial Districts and Local Economic Regeneration*, ed. F. Pyke and W. Sengenberger (Geneva: International Institute for Labor Studies, 1992), 215–50; and Putnam, *Making Democracy Work*.

38. Dave Grossman, *On Killing: The Psychological Cost of Learning to Kill in War and Society* (Boston: Little, Brown, 1996), 315.

39. One of the most subtle treatments of this issue is Ronald Deibert, *Parchment, Printing, and Hypermedia: Communication in World Order Transformation* (New York: Columbia University, 1997), especially chapter 7, "Hypermedia and the Modern to Postmodern World Order Transformation: Changes to Social Epistemology," 177–201.

40. Frances Cairncross, *The Death of Distance: How the Communications Revolution Will Change Our Lives* (Boston, Mass: Harvard Business School, 1997).

41. James Gleick, *Faster*.

42. Steve Lohr, "The Great Mystery of Internet Profits," *New York Times*, 17 June 1996, national edition.

43. William Mitchell, *City of Bits: Space, Place, and the Infobahn* (Cambridge, Mass.: MIT Press, 1997), 30, 104–5, and 167.

44. Jeff Rothenberg, "Ensuring the Longevity of Digital Documents," *Scientific American* 272, no. 1 (January 1995): 42–47.

45. Laura Tangley, "Whoops, There Goes Another CD-ROM," *U.S. News & World Report*, 16 February 1998, 67–68.

46. Stephen Manes, "Time and Technology Threaten Digital Archives . . ." *New York Times*, 7 April 1998, national edition, B15. On strategies for dealing with these problems, see Klaus-Dieter Lehmann, "Making the Transitory Permanent: The Intellectual Heritage in a Digitized World of Knowledge," in Stephen Graubard and Paul LeClerc, eds., *Books, Bricks & Bytes: Libraries in the Twenty-first Century* (New Brunswick, N.J.: Transaction, 1998), 307–29.

47. Donald Stuss, "Self, Awareness, and the Frontal Lobes: A Neuropsychological Perspective," in *The Self: Interdisciplinary Approaches*, eds. Jaine Strauss and George Goethals (New York: Springer-Verlag, 1991), 255–78, especially 266 and 268.

48. Richard Easterlin, *Growth Triumphant: The Twenty-first Century in Historical Perspective* (Ann Arbor, Mich.: University of Michigan, 1996), 153–54.

49. A good example of the point of view described in this paragraph is John Tierney, "Our Oldest Computer, Upgraded," *New York Times Magazine*, 28 September 1997, 46–105.

50. Janny Scott, "Scholars Fear 'Star' System May Undercut Their Mission," *New York Times*, 20 December 1997, national edition, A13; Sylvia Nasar, "New Breed of College All-Star," *New York Times*, 8 April 1998, national edition, C1.

51. Robert Frank, "Talent and the Winner-Take-All Society," *American Prospect* (Spring 1994): 102. For a complete discussion of these and other forces that contribute to the winner-take-all economy, see Robert Frank and Philip Cook, *The Winner-Take-All Society: Why the Few at the Top Get So Much More Than the Rest of Us* (New York: Penguin, 1996).

52. Norm Leckie, "On Skill Requirements Trends in Canada, 1971–1991," research paper submitted to Human Resources Development Canada and the Canadian Policy Research Network (Ottawa: Human Resource Group, Ekos Research Associates, 1996).

53. For a general discussion of these issues, see Richard Freeman, *The New Inequality: Creating Solutions for Poor America* (Boston: Beacon Press, 1999).

54. Sheldon Danziger, memo to P. Llosa, *Fortune*, 5 January 1999; see also Sheldon Danziger and Peter Gottschalk, *America Unequal* (Cambridge, Mass.: Harvard University Press, 1995).

55. Lester Thurow, "Building Wealth," *Atlantic Monthly* (June 1999): 69; see also Lester Thurow, *Building Wealth: The New Rules for Individuals, Companies, and Nations in a Knowledge-Based Economy* (New York: HarperCollins, 1999).

56. For general discussion of the implications of these trends, see Mickey Kaus, *The End of Equality* (New York: Basic Books, 1995). A detailed empirical treatment of the complex relationship between cognitive ability and economic success is Kenneth Arrow, Samuel Bowles, and Steven Durlauf, eds., *Meritocracy and Economic Inequality* (Princeton, New Jersey: Princeton University Press, 2000).

57. For a detailed account of water availability and use in the Colorado River basin, see Harry Schwartz et al., "Water Quality and Flows," in B. L. Turner et al., eds., *The Earth as Transformed by Human Action: Global and Regional Changes in the Biosphere over the Past 300 Years* (Cambridge, U.K.: Cambridge University Press with Clark University, 1990), 256–70, especially 256–60.

58. Peter Gleick, *The World's Water, 1998-1999: The Biennial Report on Freshwater Resources* (Washington, D.C.: Island Press, 1998), 10–13.

59. Douglas Jehl, "Nile-in-Miniature Tests Its Parent's Bounty," *The New York Times*, 10 January 1997, A5, national edition; "Mighty Yellow River Becomes a 'Part-Time' Stream," *China News Digest*, 11 July 1996.

60. Linda Nash, "Water Quality and Health," in *Water in Crisis: A Guide to the World's Fresh Water Resources*, ed. Peter Gleick (New York: Oxford University Press, 1993), 26. See also Nicholas Kristof, "For Third World, Water Is Still a Deadly Drink," *New York Times*, 9 January 1997, national edition, A1.

61. Joseph Stevens, *Hoover Dam: An American Adventure* (Norman, Okla.: University of Oklahoma Press, 1988), 259.

62. Anthony Turton, "Water Scarcity and Social Adaptive Capacity," MEWREW,

Occasional Paper 9 (London: Water Issues Study Group, SOAS, University of London, March, 1999), endnote 23, p. 37.

63. Stevens, *Hoover Dam*, 196–97.

64. Ibid., 266.

65. I interviewed Brothers in November 1997. It is likely that the consequences of climate change have been more seriously considered since then.

66. Quoted from a report of a conference held in early March 1998, at the University of Texas at El Paso. See Mark Spalding, "Tilting the Balance: Climate Variability and Water Resource Management in the Southwest," *Journal of Environment & Development* 7, no. 3 (September 1998): 302–5.

CHAPTER THIRTEEN

1. The account in the previous paragraphs is based on reports in Colombo's newspapers at the time and interviews of witnesses by the author. Some details are in dispute. See A. S. Fernando, Elmo Leonard, and Hemasiri Kuruppu, "Bomb Rocks Fort: Bomb Rips Central Bank, Fires Spread to Ceylinco and Other Buildings," *Daily News* (Colombo), 1 February 1996, 1; Paneetha Ameresekere and Ranjith Premadasa, "Blast Was Preceded by Gunshots," *Daily News* (Colombo), 1 February 1996, 10; box and diagram by Wasantha Siriwardena, *Sunday Times* (Colombo), 4 February 1996, 1; "400 Kilo Bomb Used in Attack," (AFP), 5 February 1996; "Blast Kills 60 in Sri Lanka; 1,400 Injured," *New York Times*, 1 February 1996, national edition, A1.

2. "Wall Street Explosion Kills 30, Injures 300; Morgan Office Hit, Bomb Pieces Found; Toronto Fugitive Sent Warning Here," *New York Times*, 17 September 1920, 1; John Brooks, *Once in Golconda: A True Drama of Wall Street, 1920-1938* (New York: Harper & Row, 1969), 1–20.

3. An excellent and relatively unbiased account of the social and political tragedy of modern Sri Lanka, written from the point of view of a moderate Tamil, is S. J. Tambiah, *Sri Lanka: Ethnic Fratricide and the Dismantling of Democracy* (Chicago: University of Chicago Press, 1986).

4. A credible estimate of the war's cost is available in a report from the National Peace Council of Sri Lanka, *The Cost of War* (Colombo: National Peace Council, 1998).

5. Rohan Gunaratna, *International & Regional Security Implications of the Sri Lankan Tamil Insurgency* (St. Albans, UK: International Foundation of Sri Lankans, 1997), 44 and 28–29; Allan Thompson, "Tamils in Canada Cited in Bombing," *Toronto Star*, 9 June 1998, A6.

6. Gunaratna, *International & Regional Security Implications*, 42.

7. Rohan Gunaratna, *Sri Lanka's Ethnic Crisis & National Security* (Colombo: South Asian Network on Conflict Research, 1998), 85.

8. Gunaratna, *International & Regional Security Implications*, 4.

9. Detailed information on the relentless and exponential increase in weapon lethality over the centuries is available in Historical Evaluation and Research

Organization, *Historical Trends Related to Weapon Lethality*, a report prepared for the Advanced Tactics Project of the Combat Developments Command, Headquarters U.S. Army (Washington, D.C.: Historical Evaluation and Research Organization, 1964); Trevor Dupuy, *Numbers, Predictions and War: Using History to Evaluate Combat Factors and Predict the Outcome of Battles* (Indianapolis: Bobbs-Merrill, 1979), 8–10; and Trevor Dupuy, ed., "Firepower," in *International Military and Defense Encyclopedia*, vol. 2 (New York: Maxwell Macmillan, 1993), 944–45.

10. Michael Klare, "The Kalashnikov Age," *Bulletin of the Atomic Scientists*, 55, no. 1 (January/February 1999), 20.

11. Michael Klare, "The International Trade in Light Weapons: What Have We Learned?" in *Light Weapons and Civil Conflict: Controlling the Tools of Violence*, Jeffrey Boutwell and Michael Klare, eds. (Lanham, Maryland: Rowman & Littlefield, 1999), 18–19.

12. Until 1999, the distributor Loompanics Unlimited sold books on topics ranging from guerrilla warfare and torture techniques to home-made bombs and explosives through its Web site, www.loompanics.com. After U.S. senators Dianne Feinstein and Orrin Hatch sponsored legislation banning the publication or dissemination of information on bomb-making, Loompanics Unlimited and similar organizations stopped selling many of these books. But the Feinstein-Hatch law applies only to vendors who "intend" the information they're selling to be used for criminal purposes, so it has not restricted the sale of many of the same books on other Web sites, such as that of Amazon.com. See Jake Halpern, "Intentional Foul," *New Republic*, 10 April 2000, 14.

13. Quoted in Keith Schneider, "Hate Groups Use Tools of the Electronic Trade," *New York Times* 13 March 1995, national edition, A8.

14. Michel Marriott, "Rising Tide: Sites Born of Hate," *New York Times*, 18 March 1999, national edition, D1; Pam Belluck, "A White Supremacist Group Seeks a New Kind of Recruit," *New York Times*, 7 July 1999, national edition, A1.

15. Neal Stephenson, "Dreams & Nightmares of the Digital Age," *Time*, 3 February 1997, 47.

16. See the annual reports of the U.S. State Department titled *Patterns of Global Terrorism* available at www.state.gov/www/global/terrorism; see also Walter Enders and Todd Sandler, "Transnational Terrorism in the Post-Cold War

17. An early but still valuable assessment of the characteristics, health effects, and methods of use of chemical and biological weapons is World Health Organization, *Health Aspects of Chemical and Biological Weapons* (Geneva: WHO, 1970).

18. William Broad, "How Japan Germ Terror Alerted World," *New York Times*, 26 May 1998, national edition, A1.

19. Stephen Myers, "Federal Commission Predicts Increasing Threat of Terrorism," *New York Times*, 21 September 1999, national edition, A11. Recent literature by scholars and opinion leaders includes: Richard Betts, "The New Threat of Mass Destruction," *Foreign Affairs* 77, no. 1 (January/February 1998): 26–41; Ashton Carter, John Deutsch, and Philip Zelikow, "Catastrophic Terrorism," *Foreign Affairs* 77, no. 6 (November/December 1998): 80–94; Philip Heymann, *Terrorism and America: A Commonsense Strategy for a Democratic Society* (Cambridge,

MA: MIT Press, 1998); Bruce Hoffman, *Inside Terrorism* (New York: Columbia University Press, 1998); and Jessica Stern, *The Ultimate Terrorists* (Cambridge, MA: Harvard University Press, 1999). A more sensationalized treatment is Glenn Schweitzer and Carole Dorsch, *Superterrorism: Assassins, Mobsters, and Weapons of Mass Destruction* (New York: Plenum Trade, 1998).

20. Richard Falkenrath, Robert Newman, and Bradley Thayer, *America's Achilles' Heel: Nuclear, Biological, and Chemical Terrorism and Covert Attack* (Cambridge, MA: MIT Press, 1998), 171.

21. Quoted in "The New Terrorism," *Economist*, 15 August 1998, 17; see also Hoffman's book, *Inside Terrorism*, 197–205.

22. "The New Terrorism," 18.

23. Falkenrath, Newman, and Thayer, *America's Achilles' Heel*, 170.

24. Langdon Winner, "Complexity and the Limits of Human Understanding," in *Organized Social Complexity: Challenge to Politics and Policy*, ed. Todd La Porte (Princeton: Princeton University Press, 1975): 69–70.

25. President's Commission on Critical Infrastructure Protection, *Critical Foundations: Protecting America's Infrastructures* (Washington, D.C.: 1997), x.

26. Wendy Grossman, "Cyber View: Bringing Down the Internet," *Scientific American* 278, no. 5 (May 1998): 45.

27. Gene Rochlin, *Trapped in the Net: The Unanticipated Consequences of Computerization* (Princeton, NJ: Princeton University Press, 1997), 92 and 98.

28. Carol Marie Cropper, "Emergency Declared in Dallas As More People Die from Heat," *The New York Times*, 16 July 1998, national edition, A16.

29. Anupam Sheshank, "Lucknow Agog with Rumors of Calamity," *Times of India*, 6 June 1998, Patna edition, 5.

30. Praful Bidwai, "Regaining Nuclear Sanity: No Tests, No Bombs, Ever," *Times of India*, 6 June 1998, Patna edition, 8.

31. These figures, calculated by Shaukat Hassan, are adapted from data prepared by the Center for Monitoring the Indian Economy cited in Vinay Kantha, ed., *Bihar Economy* (Patna: Printaid Publishers, 1992), 3.

32. Three careful studies of events described in the previous two paragraphs are Sachchidanand Pandey, *Naxal Violence: A Socio-Political Study* (Delhi: Chanakya Publications, 1985); Nageshwar Prasad, *Rural Violence in India: A Case Study of Parasbigha and Pipra Violence in Bihar* (Allahabad: Vohra Publishers, 1985); and Amrik Singh Nimbran, *Poverty, Land and Violence: An Analytical Study of Naxalism in Bihar* (Patna: Layman's Publications, 1992).

33. On the extraordinary level of corruption surrounding flood-control works in Bihar, see Manish Tiwari, "Breach of Trust," *Down to Earth* 8, no. 13 (30 November 1999): 30–45.

34. Bindeshwar Pathak, *Rural Violence in Bihar* (New Delhi: Concept Publishing, 1993), 24.

35. For an account of the origins of the crisis in Bhojpur, see Kalyan Mukherjee and Rajendra Singh Yadav, *Bhojpur: Naxalism in the Planes of Bihar* (Delhi: Radha Krishna, 1980).

36. Dyke notes that the second law of thermodynamics "defines a space of possibilities for us, and does so rather tightly." See C. Dyke, "Cities as Dissipative Struc-

tures," in *Entropy, Information, and Evolution: New Perspectives on Physical and Biological Evolution*, ed. Bruce Weber, David Depew, and James Smith (Cambridge, Massachusetts: MIT Press, 1988), 355–68.

37. Harold Barnett and Chandler Morse, *Scarcity and Growth: The Economics of Natural Resource Availability* (Baltimore: Johns Hopkins Press for Resources for the Future, 1963), 10.

38. "Stripped of Funds, PU Finds It Hard to Print Certificates," *Times of India*, 6 June 1998, Patna edition, 3.

39. "Heat Wave Toll Crosses 2,300," *Times of India*, 6 June 1998, Patna edition, 12.

40. Two excellent reports from India's Center for Science and Environment that make this argument are "Special Report: Unmasking the Heat," *Down to Earth*, 15 July 1998, 30–3; and "Analysis: Hot as Hell!" *Down to Earth*, 15 July 1999, 27–31.

41. Julian Simon, *The Ultimate Resource* (Princeton, New Jersey: Princeton University Press, 1981).

42. A superb overview of the state of the literature on the relationship between population growth and economic prosperity is Geoffrey McNicoll, *Population and Poverty: A Review and Restatement*, Working Paper No. 105 (New York: Population Council, 1997).

43. See Fogel's Nobel address reprinted as Robert Fogel, "Economic Growth, Population Theory, and Physiology: The Bearing of Long-Term Processes on the Making of Economic Policy," *The American Economic Review* 84, no. 3 (June 1994): 387–8.

44. Richard Rosecrance, *The Rise of the Virtual State: Wealth and Power in the Coming Century* (New York: Basic Books, 1999).

45. On the roles of knowledge, human capital, and information infrastructure in economic development see World Bank, *World Development Report, 1998-99: Knowledge for Development* (Oxford: Oxford University Press, 1998); and Robin Mansell and Uta Wehn, eds., *Knowledge Societies: Information Technology for Sustainable Development*, prepared for the United Nations Commission on Science and Technology for Development (Oxford: Oxford University Press, 1998).

46. Celia Dugger, "India's High-Tech, and Sheepish, Capitalism," *New York Times*, 16 December 1999, national edition, A1.

47. Steven Mithen, *The Prehistory of the Mind: A Search for the Origins of Art, Religion, and Science* (London: Thames and Hudson, 1996), 192.

48. Elizabeth Gould, et al., "Proliferation of Granule Cell Precursors in the Dentate Gyrus of Adult Monkeys Is Diminished by Stress," *Proceedings of the National Academy of Sciences USA* 95 (March 1998): 3168–71.

49. Rick Potts, *Humanity's Descent: The Consequences of Ecological Instability* (New York: Avon, 1997), 206–7.

50. Carnegie Task Force on Meeting the Needs of Young Children, *Starting Points: Meeting the Needs of Our Youngest Children* (New York: Carnegie Corporation, 1994), 7–8.

51. Eitan Schwarz and Bruce Perry, "The Post-Traumatic Response in Children and Adolescents," *Psychiatric Clinics of North America* 17, no. 2 (June 1994): 311–26.

52. Daniela Kaufer et al., "Acute Stress Facilitates Long-Lasting Changes in Cholinergic Gene Expression," *Nature* 393, no. 6683 (28 May 1998): 373–77; Robin Karr-Morse and Meredith Wiley, *Ghosts from the Nursery: Tracing the Roots of Violence* (New York: Atlantic Monthly Press, 1997).

53. Richard Hellie, "Interpreting Violence in Late Muscovy from the Perspectives of Modern Neuroscience," paper presented at the 28th National Convention of the AAAS, Boston, 15 November 1996.

54. A seminal article on these effects is S. M. Grantham-McGregor, C. A. Powell, S. P. Walker, and J. H. Himes, "Nutritional Supplementation, Psychosocial Stimulation, and Mental Development of Stunted Children: The Jamaican Study," *Lancet* 338, no. 8758 (6 July 1991): 1–5.

55. An excellent overview is J. Larry Brown and Ernesto Pollitt, "Malnutrition, Poverty and Intellectual Development," *Scientific American* 274, no. 2 (February 1996): 38–43.

56. Patrick Tyler, "Lacking Iodine in Their Diets, Millions in China Are Retarded," *New York Times*, 4 June 1996, national edition, A1.

57. On the effects of pesticides, see Bernard Weiss, "Pesticides as a Source of Developmental Disabilities," *Mental Retardation and Developmental Disabilities Research Reviews* 3 (1997): 246–56. A comprehensive general treatment of neurotoxic agents and the brain is Committee on Neurotoxicology and Models for Assessing Risk of the National Research Council, *Environmental Neurotoxicology* (Washington, D.C.: National Academy Press, 1992). A more popular and somewhat sensational overview is Christopher Williams, *Terminus Brain: The Environmental Threats to Human Intelligence* (London: Cassell, 1997).

58. Peter Baghurst et al., "Environmental Exposure to Lead and Children's Intelligence at the Age of Seven Years: The Port Pirie Study," *New England Journal of Medicine* 327, no. 18 (29 October 1992): 1279–84.

59. The problem is acute and well-documented in Cairo, Egypt. See Douglas Jehl, "Under the Cairo, the Leaden Skies Can Kill," *New York Times*, 4 April 1997, national edition, A4.

60. At a later date, I explained to the girl's father, through intermediaries, that I wanted to use photographs of her and to tell her story in this book. He gave me permission to do so.

61. On "zones of silence," see Mansell and Wehn, *Knowledge Societies*, 196–97. Three useful discussions of the disparities between rich and poor countries in the exploitation of the benefits of communications revolution are Manuel Castelles, "The Rise of the Fourth World: Informational Capitalism, Poverty, and Social Exclusion," chapter 2 in *End of Millennium, Volume III: The Information Age: Economy, Society and Culture* (Malden, Massachusetts: Blackwell, 1998), 70–165; Jean-Jacques Salomon and André Lebeau, *Mirages of Development: Science and Technology for the Third World* (Boulder, Colorado: Lynne Reiner, 1993), especially Part 2, "The Information Revolution," 85–160; and United Nations Development Program, "New Technologies and the Global Race for Knowledge," Chapter 2 in *Human Development Report 1999* (New York: Oxford University Press, 1999), 57–75.

62. Krishna Guha, "Cyclone Hammers India's Busiest Port, But the Real Victims Are the Unknown Poor," *Financial Times*, 20/21 June 1998, 3.

EPILOGUE

1. According to the Boeing Commercial Airplane Group, Everett Site Communications office, of the six million parts in a 747, three million are fasteners, and about half of those are rivets. For the story of the 747 as an engineering marvel, see Henk Tennekes, *The Simple Science of Flight: From Insects to Jumbo Jets* (Cambridge, Mass.: MIT Press, 1997).

2. Captain Al Haynes discusses these factors in Al Haynes, "The Crash of United Flight 232," transcript of a presentation to NASA Ames Research Center, Dryden Flight Research Facility, Edwards, California, 1991.

3. On the needs in agricultural research, see Gordon Conway, "Food for All in the 21st Century," *Environment* 42, no. 1 (January/February 2000): 8–18.

4. For a broad discussion of ideas for reforming the United Nations, see Chadwick Alger, ed., *The Future of the United Nations System: Potential for the Twenty-First Century* (Tokyo: United Nations University, 1998).

5. Two books offering many excellent suggestions for increasing the efficiency of natural-resource use are Ernst von Weizäcker, Amory Lovins, and L. Hunter Lovins, *Factor Four: Doubling Wealth—Halving Resource Use* (London: Earthscan, 1997); and Paul Hawken, Amory Lovins, and L. Hunter Lovins, *Natural Capitalism: Creating the Next Industrial Revolution* (Boston: Little, Brown, 1999). A widely discussed but contentious idea for limiting the flow of "hot" capital in international financial markets is the Tobin tax. For a full account, see Mahbub ul Haq, Inge Kaul, and Isabelle Grunberg, *The Tobin Tax: Coping with Financial Volatility* (New York: Oxford University Press, 1996).

6. J. B. S. Haldane, *Possible Worlds and Other Essays* (London: Chatto and Windus, 1932), 286.

7. Robert Wright suggested this possibility to me.

ILLUSTRATION CREDITS

Page 13
Title: Flight Path of United Airlines Flight 232
Source: "United Airlines Flight 232, McDonnell Douglas DC-10-10, Sioux Gateway Airport, Sioux City, Iowa, July 19, 1989," *National Transportation Safety Board (NTSB) Aircraft Accident Report AAR 90/06* (Washington, D.C.: National Transportation Safety Board, 1990), 4.

Page 38
Title: The Little Girl in Patna
Photo Credit: Thomas Homer-Dixon

Page 44
Title: Smeaton's Tower
Photo Credit: David Nicholson

Page 50
Title: World Population Soared in the Twentieth Century
Sources: United Nations Population Division, *World Population Prospects 1950-2050: The 1998 Revision* (New York: United Nations Population Division, Department of Economic and Social Affairs, 1998); Judah Matras, *Population and Societies*, Table 1.2 "Estimates of World Population by Regions, A.D. 14 to 1971" (Englewood Cliffs, New Jersey: Prentice Hall, 1973), 21; U.S. Census Bureau, *Historical Estimates of World Population*, http://www.census.gov/ipc/www/worldhis.html.

Page 55
Title: Regional Fish Stocks Have Declined in Succession
Source: Adapted from *World Resources: 1998–99* (New York: Oxford University Press, 1998), 195.

Page 64
Title: Co$_2$ Concentrations and Temperature Have Varied in Lockstep
Sources: J.M. Barnola et al., "Vostok Ice Core Provides 160,000-Year Record of Atmospheric co$_2$," *Nature* 329 (1 October 1987): 408–14; and J.R. Petit et al., "Climate and Atmosphere History of the Past 420,000 Years from the Vostok Ice Core, Antarctica," *Nature* 399 (3 June 1999): 429–36.

Page 68
Title: Each Spring and Summer, a "Dead Zone" Appears off Louisiana
Source: Nancy Rabalais, Louisiana Universities Marine Consortium.

Page 75
Title: Canary Wharf
Photo Credit: Thomas Homer-Dixon

Page 85
Title: Milestones in the History of Lighting
Sources: William Nordhaus, "Do Real-Output and Real-Wage Measures Capture Reality? The History of Lighting Suggests Not," in Timothy Bresnahan and Robert Gordon, eds., *The Economics of New Goods* (Chicago: University of Chicago Press, 1997), 32.

Page 87
Title: Nighttime Lights of the USA and Europe
Source: National Oceanographic and Atmospheric Administration.

Page 117
Title: The Folded Hemoglobin Molecule Is Extraordinarily Complex
Source: Stephen Cammer and Alexander Tropsha, Laboratory for Molecular Modeling, School of Pharmacy, University of North Carolina.

Page 134
Title: Biosphere 2 Taught Us a Lesson about Managing Complex Ecosystems
Photo Credit: José Galves

Page 138
Title: The Atmosphere's Temperature Rose Abruptly at the End of the Younger Dryas Cold Event
Sources: K.M. Cuffey and G.D. Clow, "Temperature, Accumulation, and Ice Sheet Elevation in Central Greenland through the Last Deglacial Transition," *Journal of Geophysical Research* 102 (1997): 26383-96; K.M. Cuffey et al., "Large Arctic Temperature Change at the Wisconsin-Holocene Glacial Transition," *Science* 270 (1995): 455–58. Data provided by the National Snow and Ice Data Center, University of Colorado at Boulder, and the World Data Center-A for Paleoclimatology, National Geophysical Data Center, Boulder, Colorado. On the relationship between ice accumulation rates and temperature changes, see Jeffrey Severinghaus et al., "Timing of

Abrupt Climate Change at the End of the Younger Dryas Interval from Thermally Fractionated Gases in Polar Ice," *Nature* 391 (8 January 1998): 145.

Page 157
Title: Shanghai's Oriental Pearl TV Tower in 1995
Photo Credit: Thomas Homer-Dixon

Page 197
Title: Hominid Brain Volume Has Expanded in Two Bursts
Source: Adapted from data in Leslie Aiello and Robin Dunbar, "Neocortex Size, Group Size, and the Evolution of Language," *Current Anthropology* 34 (1993): 184–93.

Page 214
Title: The Left Cerebral Hemisphere
Source: William Calvin and George Ojemann, *Conversations with Neil's Brain: The Neural Nature of Thought and Language* (Cambridge, Massachusetts: Perseus, 1994).

Page 316
Title: The Luxor Hotel, Las Vegas
Photo Credit: Frank Reynolds

Page 319
Artist: Joel Pett, Lexington Herald-Leader

Page 341
Title: U.S. Income Disparity Has Increased in the Last Forty Years
Source: U.S. Census Bureau

Page 345–46
Title: Water Availability in 1995 and 2025
Source: Tom Gardner-Outlaw and Robert Engelman, *Sustaining Water, Easing Scarcity: A Second Update* (Washington, D.C.: Population Action International, 1997). Water availability in 2025 was estimated using the United Nations' medium population projections, obtained from United Nations Population Division, *World Population Prospects: The 1996 Revision, Demographic Indicators 1950-2050*, Diskettes 1-4 (New York: United Nations, 1996).

Page 389
Title: Komal Kumari
Photo Credit: Thomas Homer-Dixon

ACKNOWLEDGMENTS

IDEAS are rarely the product of one mind, and that is true of the ideas here. During the years I have been thinking about and writing this book, an astonishing number of people have given me support, information, and insights that have helped "the ingenuity gap" grow into the story told in these pages.

I wouldn't have started the project without the encouragement and inspiration of two people in particular. Bruce Westwood, who later became my literary agent, was the first to suggest that I write a book for a general audience. In those early days I wasn't keen on the idea, but now (with the project behind me!) I'm very glad he was so persistent. Since that time, Bruce has helped me understand the ins and outs of the publishing world, and he has invariably been there with a word of comfort when I wasn't sure I could continue.

Louise Dennys, my publisher and editor, has been a source of truly endless inspiration. I still don't understand how such professional skill, creative insight, and personal warmth can be combined in one person. No one has taught me more about writing or about the art of reaching a broad audience, and no one could have shown more patience as this project sometimes staggered through its middle stages. The writing of this book turned into a much longer and more arduous journey than I'd ever imagined it would be, and Louise was with me every step of the way.

Many others have helped me take a rough, unformed concept and transform it into something far more complete. Robin Bienenstock's ideas and influence are woven through nearly every chapter. Robin suggested I go to Canary Wharf; we traveled together to the Brooks Peninsula; and during a long conversation at the Jefferson Memorial she convinced me that the most important aspects of my argument were deeply moral and spiritual. Robin also listened to me read most of the book and gave me detailed advice that helped put life and excitement into my writing. Ian Graham, my oldest and one of my dearest friends, gave me intellectual guidance and moral support throughout the years of work. I drew on his expertise as a physicist and as one of the world's leading authorities on the World Wide Web, and during our countless hours discussing facets of my argument, he clarified technical issues for me more times than I can possibly remember. He also read large sections of the book and passed on specific comments regarding the implications of nonlinearity, complexity, and the vulnerabilities of information systems. And I'll always remember the fun we had exploring Las Vegas and Comdex together.

Accounts of my conversations with a number of people—including Mike Whitfield, Wally Broecker, John Bongaarts, Donald Stuss, and Kay Brothers—appear in these pages. Not only were these experts generous with their time in person, they also carefully reviewed the passages I wrote about our conversations. In addition, Steven Predmore, W. Brian Arthur, Buzz Holling, Rick Potts, Steven Mithen, and Paul Romer reviewed the sections of the manuscript that discuss their research. I'm tremendously indebted to each of these people for their time and thoughtful suggestions. Although none should be held responsible for how I represent their ideas, the story in this book is, in many respects, the story of their work.

Al Haynes, the captain of United 232, read my account of that ill-fated flight and enriched it with personal details that only he could provide. James Risbey, at Carnegie Mellon, reviewed the passages dealing with climate change and the climate treaty; Vaclav Smil, of the University of Manitoba, did the same for the passages on the global nitrogen flux. Glen Cass and Lara Hughes at Caltech helped me understand the phenomenon of atmospheric haze, while Dan Falk, a Canadian science writer, made sure that my description of the night sky and the planets was accurate. Marc Tessier-Lavigne, a neuroscientist at the University of California in San Francisco, helped me flesh out my description of biotechnology and its future. Tom Naylor, of McGill University, and Michael Klare, of Hampshire College, gave me detailed background information on the scourge of light weapons plaguing developing countries.

For their ideas and their help on various subjects, many thanks also to Ed Anderson, Bob Anglin, Angela Antonelli, Carl Benn, Alastair Cairns,

Dan Churniak, Joel Cohen, Ron Deibert, Jack Drake, Mark Engel, Wendy Feldman, Josh Foster, Barney Gilmore, Allen Hammond, Rod Knight, Doug Napier, Eli Noam, William Nordhaus, Anatol Rapoport, Don Razy, Sandro Rizoli, Peter Ross, David Shenk, Joe Speidel, David Victor, Patrick Watson, Edward O. Wilson, Robert Wright, and the members of the Committee on International Security Studies of the American Academy of Arts and Sciences. The William and Flora Hewlett Foundation provided financial support for writing this book.

In Toronto I was blessed with a wonderful group of researchers and support staff. Kimman Chan, Ashllie Claassen, Robbie Diamond, Michele Rizoli, and Jane Willms helped with research, while Jennifer Szalai and Sarah Bondy worked on the book's illustrations. Often they had to scour the world to find particular experts, key documents, or obscure bits of information. They never told me that I was crazy, but I'm sure they would have been justified if sometimes they had. Instead, as we worked together through each stage of the project, they gave me countless small and large ideas for improving the book, and our friendships grew. Outside the University of Toronto, a number of people helped us locate good illustrations, including Stephen Cammer, Bob Cleveland, Roger Doyle, José Galves, M. Imhoff, Joel Pett, Nancy Rabalais, Frank Reynolds, Alex Tropsha, and Jen Turner.

Finally, in South Asia, I had the assistance of many old and new friends. In Sri Lanka, D.L.O. Mendis spent days with me as I visited and interviewed numerous experts on the sad state of that country. D.L.O. also arranged my meeting with the Governor of the Central Bank of Sri Lanka, Amarananda Jayawardena, who was exceedingly generous with his time. In Patna, Meera Dutt and her family welcomed me once again into their home. K. Gopalakrishnan (or "Gopi," as he is universally known) rescued me from a chaotic Indian Airlines queue; and it was members of his staff, particularly Gopa Chatterjee and Vimla Menzies, who eventually helped me locate the little girl. Thanks so much to them all. And thanks especially to that little girl, Komal Kumari, who began the journey with me in spirit and finished it on the doorstep of her home.

INDEX